Remember the Rowan

Kirsten MacQuarrie

Ringwood Publishing
Glasgow

Copyright Kirsten MacQuarrie © 2024

The moral right of the author has been asserted

First published in Great Britain in 2024 by
Ringwood Publishing

0/1 314 Meadowside Quay Walk, Glasgow G11 6AY

www.ringwoodpublishing.com
mail@ringwoodpublishing.com

ISBN 978-1-917011-04-4

British Library Cataloguing-in-Publication Data
A catalogue record for this book is available
from the British Library

Printed and bound in the UK
by Lonsdale Direct Solutions

*In memory of Mij, in whose heart they met,
for Shep, the best boy since Jonnie,
and for Winnie, who is lovely, loved and love.*

'Kirsten MacQuarrie's deep research into the life of 20th century poet Kathleen Raine offers a brilliant reappraisal of a woman feted in life for her literary talent yet almost completely forgotten in Scotland today. Absolutely alive with emotion, this impressive first novel will help to ensure that Raine is remembered as the hugely talented and inspirational writer she was.'

Sara Sheridan, author of *The Fair Botanists*

Remember the Rowan

'I just did not understand how such love and hatred could coexist.'
Gavin Maxwell,
Raven Seek Thy Brother

'If hate were love, if love were hate
It could not make our tale untold.'
Kathleen Raine,
In Answer to a Letter asking me for Volumes of my Early Poems

Tambi with Kathleen and Gavin on the day they met, 1949

He has married me with a ring, a ring of bright water
Whose ripples travel from the heart of the sea,
He has married me with a ring of light, the glitter
Broadcast on the swift river.
He has married me with the sun's circle
Too dazzling to see, traced in summer sky.
He has crowned me with the wreath of white cloud
That gathers on the snowy summit of the mountain,
Ringed me round with the world-circling wind,
Bound me to the whirlwind's centre.
He has married me with the orbit of the moon
And with the boundless circle of the stars,
With the orbits that measure years, months, days and nights,
Set the tides flowing,
Command the winds to travel or be at rest.

At the ring's centre,
Spirit, or angel troubling the still pool,
Causality not in nature,
Finger's touch that summons at a point, a moment
Stars and planets, life and light
Or gathers cloud about an apex of cold,
Transcendent touch of love summons my world to being.

Kathleen Raine

Part One
1949

Chapter One

I open the door and see the stranger.

'Hello.' His eyes are hooded, lids falling heavy like both they and he have been brought low by life. A gaunt echo of elegance haunts his pale face, as if he has somehow broken through from a better, more classical time, and the shock of our modern-day inadequacies has come close to breaking him too.

'Hello,' I reply. I cannot tell what he thinks of me. I can scarcely say whether he sees me at all.

'Kathleen, meet Gavin!' Tambi springs out from behind the stranger's back, bounding up to my door with characteristically uncontained exuberance. My first publisher, as well as my first friend in London, M. J. T. Tambimuttu's eccentricities may be irritating to many. Who else goes out for milk and returns three days later, minus his shoes? But as the only person who believed in me from the start – believed, more fundamentally, in the poetry that makes up the woman I feel to be the real me – I am usually ready to indulge him. As it appears I must do again.

'Gavin's a portrait painter.' Tambi pushes forward the taller, thinner man until he has one foot resting on my threadbare excuse for a doormat. Like his face, his figure looks wretched, and I wonder fleetingly how a person can be so slim and still standing. 'He's going to paint you.' Gavin looks horrified at the thought. Alarmed too, as if this is his first time hearing about any such plan. Knowing Tambi and his whimsical ways, the prospect is very much possible. 'Come on, Kathie,' he play-whines, hopping theatrically from sole to sole. 'We're getting cold out here.'

'It's still August, Tambi.'

'Let us in, there's a good girl.'

'Tambi, it's not quite conv …' Am I the only writer who must ask her publisher not to disturb her while she's working? Heaven knows, I am often happy enough to encounter a distraction. But after last week's trip, I can feel new verses emerging: the hazy shapes of novel sentences tentatively finding their forms. Experienced enough in the art and agony

1

of composition to recognise it as a rare sensation, I must not squander it.

'But Gavin writes poetry too, don't you?' Tambi gives Gavin another enthusiastic nudge that almost knocks the man over entirely. 'Isn't it perfect?' All three of us are now clustered on the Paultons Square threshold, pressed together by the meagre limits of my four walls.

'Tambi, really I …'

'He also hunts sharks.'

'I … does he?' It would take a more generous hallway than mine to accommodate all this confusion. 'Is that true?'

'I'm afraid so,' Gavin answers. 'It was true, at any rate.' His voice sounds aristocratic. Far more than my own. And yet even in those few syllables, I hear the hint of an accent buried beneath the surface: a raw and gentle, almost tragic minor melody that beckons me back to some place I cannot remember forgetting. The familiarity should be unnerving in a man I do not know. But it serves only to deepen the sense, as intense as it is illogical, that a part of me already knows him.

'Why?' I ask. Why would anyone want or need to hunt a shark?

'Money,' Gavin says acerbically. 'That was the idea. If neither result nor reality.' The sarcasm seems to animate him. His eyes open momentarily, a spark of life alight as he checks how well his self-mockery has been received. Blue, I see clearly for the first time. His eyes are blue, cool and oceanic. Presumptuous as it might be, I feel inexplicable pride in myself at having coaxed even the weakest suggestion of interest; in having roused him, however briefly, from the depressive torpor in which he appears trapped. The feeling encourages me to push away the ghastly, ghoulish mental image of sharks run through with spears or – I dare not ask the technicalities – suffocated to slow and torturous deaths by thick-knotted fishing nets. *But it can't really be like that*, I tell myself while, at the impassioned behest of Tambi, Gavin takes a seat in my small living room. This man does not look capable of cruelty.

'Drink?' I offer with knee-jerk politeness. Poet or painter, I have never known a creative of my acquaintance to refuse.

'Whisky,' Tambi shouts. Gavin stays silent, but he looks less horrified than before. I retreat gladly into my tiny galley kitchen and scour my ill-stocked cupboards for a lonely, unimpressive bottle of Scotch tucked into a corner. Returning with three glasses, I permit Tambi to pour. Because his measures are more generous, of course. Not because I suddenly feel unsteady.

'To my two favourites.' Tambi salutes us, droplets spilling as his hand swings from Gavin to me and back again. Gavin nods, not quite smiling, and downs his drink in one. 'Better leave the bottle,' Tambi laughs. I do so, and Gavin pours his second himself.

After several minutes of stilted chit-chat – a little between Gavin and me, a lot with Tambi playing angel and devil's advocate to himself – it is suggested, and then commanded, that Gavin should take my photograph.

'To paint from,' Tambi asserts, unaware that behind him Gavin's ashen face has turned green. 'We're going to do an exhibition, aren't we? Famous faces of the fifties. And of course, I said to Gavin, "I know the woman for you, sir. The great Kathleen Raine, poetess and my personal friend." Meant to be, eh?'

Not quite. Every muscle in my face tightens at the thought of being photographed or painted. This plan might have appealed to me in my youth, before my children, when beauty brought me the attention I thought equated with respect. These days, I have a hatred of being captured. With all the preening and posing involved, most photographs only serve to remind me of the aspects of life that I most detest: its coarseness and materiality, the murky waters I want my work to transcend. No picture I can think of has ever depicted a true encounter of souls; a photograph has never successfully preserved the precise moment of spirit meeting spirit. Yet by the time I have composed my objections, the camera, produced from Tambi's rather than Gavin's bag, is already teetering on its spindle-legged tripod, the disinterested eye of its lens pointing towards me. Gavin bends behind it without saying a word. The click comes.

'Thank you,' he whispers in the same sad, melodic voice as before. A strange combination of notes, certainly, but they suit his appearance. Refinement veiled in sadness.

'Now the garden.' Tambi leaps from the sofa with energy most mortals would demonstrate only if electrified. 'Kathleen's pear tree is a beautiful specimen. You both love trees, don't you? So calming …' Without waiting for answers, Tambi takes to shepherding us out of the living room, driving us onward like an over-excited collie. My mind turns to Hardy's sheepdog, Young George – sharing a Christian name with my father makes the poor creature feel even less auspicious – who pushed the sheep in his charge over a cliff through sheer short-sighted enthusiasm. Nevertheless, soon we are indeed standing in front of the Paultons pear tree. Number 9 represents one of the rare strokes of luck I have had since

3

moving to London, and one for which I am grateful every day. The interior of the house is light and bright, if somewhat lacking in elegance and, I'm afraid to say, more tattered than when I moved in. But it is the outside, this small, sweet garden of solitude, I cherish most. Without a green space to retreat to, however modest, I cannot imagine being able to create.

'If only it were an apple tree,' Tambi chortles as he pushes us together with one hand on my right shoulder and the other on Gavin's left. 'Then the two of you would be like Adam and Eve. Still, a pair in front of the pear tree … Kathleen, you must write that down, it'd be delightful in a poem. If you two will stand like so …'

'No,' says Gavin. Quiet but firm. Even Tambi stops to listen. 'The camera has a timer. We'll take the three of us at once.' Tambi shrugs, smiles, and bounces over to my right, his head lolling a little towards my shoulder. He never could hold his whisky. I stare straight, impassive as I can, while Gavin walks away to set the timer before returning to my left side. His torso presses lightly against mine and the sensation takes me by surprise: one of strength, muscular and almost sculptural, despite his being so cadaverously thin. *Down but not out* is the idiom in my head while we wait for the camera shutter to snap in near silence (Tambi is singing softly). This stranger may have been beaten up by life, but he is not yet broken down by it. For a second or so, I sense Gavin's right arm reaching over my shoulder. The click comes. I look up. His fingers are wrapped around a trailing pear tree branch, floating in space barely an inch above my collar. His arm, although so near, was never around me after all.

*

'We should be heading off *shoon*.' Tambi slurs as his tongue stumbles beneath the weight of the afternoon's whisky. Two large glasses for him, one small one for me, and I believe I counted at least three for Gavin, who remarkably seems none the worse for it. Both men rise from their chairs: Gavin quick and quiet, Tambi slow and faintly shambolic, wobbling on the balls of his feet and studying me with intermittent, imprecise focus. 'I forgot to ask,' the letter 't' temporarily trips him up, 'how was *Norshumberland*?'

'Northumberland was beautiful, thank you, Tambi.'

'You were in Northumberland?' When I turn, Gavin's eyes are on me. The spark, that brief flicker I saw earlier, has become a true, blue

4

brightness.

'That's right,' I say. 'I grew up there during the Great War. In Bavington village, near Kielder.'

'So did I.'

'Really?'

'Well, partly.' He looks embarrassed, yet also excited, as if in receipt of an unexpected gift. Boyish, I realise. That is the best word. The broken man before me suddenly seems boyish. 'I spent holidays there ...'

'Tell the truth, Gavin,' Tambi pipes up, pointing a teasing, unsteady finger towards him. 'He owns Northumberland.' All three of us laugh, although I feel conscious of not yet getting the joke.

'No, that's not true,' Gavin demurs, although with a milder sort of negation than most would make against such a statement. It is as if Tambi is wrong but only in style, not substance. 'My late grandfather lived there.'

'Ha!' Tambi's merriment makes him reel backwards. For a moment, all three of us are occupied with keeping him upright. 'His grandfather was the Duke of Northumberland. Gavin Maxwell is heir to every blade of grass that grew beneath your little feet.' Gavin actually blushes at that, although he has no need on my account. I am not interested in inheritance. The most distracting thought in my head is how well he looks with colour in his cheeks.

'My brother is the heir. Not me. Hence the so-called commercial shark fishery.' A wry half-smile shot in my direction. I send my own back to complete it. Then I find that I must look away. My mind flits unbidden back to the childhood paths I have so recently retrodden; to the mythical, magical world in which my imagination and therefore my poetry has always been grounded. My own grandfather had no great lands, only a modest vegetable garden surrounded by wildflowers, flourishing irrepressibly around its borders and gathering in soil-stained gaps between the stones of the ageing walls. It was when reaching out to touch those flowers as a young evacuee, pressing my pudgy, juvenile fingertips to petals that quivered as if my touch had tickled, that I first felt like I understood something of the world. Understood my place within it.

Beyond that garden, I learned not very much later, was a wood into which I could escape whenever the pressures of conventionality bore down on me, finding shelter from society and all its petty, provincial norms within the embrace of those fairy-tale fir branches. Their thick bristles let little light in, but I cherished the shadows they created, because it seemed to me not darkness at all, only depth. A symbol of something that with a child's intuition I could neither articulate nor explain, but that I felt nonetheless my family, friends and neighbours had inexplicably chosen to abandon. A sense of connection to the wild world we ought never to have left; a willingness to sacrifice the hollow trinkets of greed so we might belong wholeheartedly in nature. Compared with Ilford, the town of brown brick boredom where my father worked and preached, in every sense, and where I was obliged to return after the war ended, those places of flower and forest felt like my true home. My personal Eden, long since lost. Had Gavin been there all along?

'Do you know the Kielder fir forest?' I ask him.

Gavin grins widely for the first time all afternoon. 'The Percy plantation. Ours from my mother's side.' The words could be smug, indeed, they ought to come across as an arrogant statement of superiority. But in truth, all I hear is sincerity. The desire, however tentative, to share something precious, preserved in lonely silence since childhood. Precisely the desire that I am feeling myself. 'I can't tell you how often I hid amongst those trees,' he confides. 'Trying to escape the rest of the world. Nature gives such shelter, don't you find?'

'I do,' I whisper. Gavin sighs, the sound soft and dreamlike, and I understand the memories carried within that single breath as if their message had come from within me. *He's back there. Returned to the place I always go back to.* 'I think I could have lain on that forest floor forever,' he adds. 'Delighting in the darkness, my eyes straining through the branches to try and see the stars ...'

'And the river? Do you remember the little bridge across the river?' Over thirty years have passed, but I can still feel how it was to be Kathie, a young girl standing on her tiptoes to peer over the side to the water, spellbound by the way her liquid reflection ripples and shimmers across the surface.

'Of course,' Gavin laughs. I realise how much I like the sound. 'I used to be scolded for hanging too far over the edge, trying so hard to keep sight of my reflection that I damn near fell in.' We are looking right at each other now. Old memories reflected in new eyes. 'Although, as I said,' he admits, 'I could only explore it properly during the holidays. For most of my childhood, I lived in ...'

'Scotland?' He nods. Finally, I can place the strange mingling of notes that makes up his accent. I can place what and who it reminds me of.

'My mother is Scottish,' I say. And she has always made it clear how much she wishes her parents had never left. She told me so when I was small, bounced on her knee as an infant and listening intently to the way her singsong voice shifted into a wistful lament for her homeland. When I grew older too, standing side by side at the highest point in the village as she pointed north and told me that there, 'right there, Kathie, is where you really come from'. Scotland had seemed to me a land of legend, a mythical realm where women with spirit and imagination belonged. And yet thrillingly, I could look upon it: the flowing indigo curves of the Cheviot hills a mere three miles from Great Bavington and the border, although it might as well have been three thousand to little Kathie. The first psalm I memorised at Sunday school was Number 121. *I will lift up mine eyes unto the hills, from whence cometh my help.* And I did, I tell Gavin. 'I spent hours looking to those hills.'

'Then you were looking to me,' he says.

I could not tell you when Tambi left. The next time I looked up, he had gone.

Chapter Two

Gavin leaves so he can return. He is taking me to dinner. Technically, I am taking him.

'You need fattening up,' I joke, and he laughs, heartily this time, as if the tension trapped within that wire-thin frame is finding release at last. It has been months since I dined out for pleasure and not as the reluctant, resentful accomplice in some scheme cooked up by Tambi to secure funding for *Poetry London*. I feel inexperienced, and far too old to be so. My temper threatens to flare as I struggle to decide on an outfit, then struggle with the self-contempt that comes from wasting time on such a trivial, clichéd concern.

'Women like you don't fall,' I remind my flushed and faintly flustered reflection. 'Not like this. And not this quick.' I hardly recognise myself, astonished if not appalled by a giddiness that bears no resemblance to my usually underwhelmed attitude to men, even allowing for a couple of regrettable past exceptions. Yet this does not feel like anything I've known before as romance. This feeling is closer to poetry.

Bordering on irascible, I resolve to stick with what I wore this afternoon. Can it really be that only a few hours have passed? A powder blue skirt suit – almost the same shade as Gavin's eyes, I think, before scolding myself again for girlish whimsy – and a loosely knotted silk scarf. Embroidered with a pattern of miniature florals and abstract dash stitches, it was a gift from my mother when my first collection was published.

'*Stone and Flower*, you see?' she had explained, proudly draping it over my hair to tie as a child might do in a chunky knot beneath my chin. A little literal, perhaps, and I pulled it down to my shoulders as soon as she left the room, but the effort she made to celebrate the milestone has never left me. It is not always so simple. Often my career and all that goes with it seems to bring my parents only sadness. On one hand, there is my father's stern disapproval of any life squandered on creative indulgence. To a teacher and lay preacher, I suspect I will always be good schoolmistress material gone bad. On the other, my mother faces the bittersweet prospect of her daughter doing her utmost to fulfil imaginative ambitions in a way that Jessie herself never had the opportunity to do.

'We didn't have your choices back then, Kathie,' she muses whenever an air of sadness descends. 'There was no chance of Cambridge for me.' I think my mother forgets that every choice I made came with a loss and not just a gain.

Now, surveying myself in the mirror with an almost acceptable level of satisfaction, I once again wriggle down the scarf my mother gave me to add a single-strand pearl necklace. My minor concession to festivity. *Not that he'll notice the difference*, I predict, moving to answer the door for a second time today to the man who no longer feels like a stranger.

'Hello, Kathleen.' Gavin's eyes flash straight to the pearls. 'You're making me long for the seashore.'

The restaurant is only a five-minute walk and, talking side by side as we go, I believe I could tackle ten times the distance without complaint. Nevertheless, when we arrive outside Sorbo's, I am struck by the sudden realisation that it must be a far less impressive establishment than the sort Gavin is used to. Authentically bohemian, with water stains on wood tabletops to prove it, Sorbo's opts to compress its clientele; waiters forced to lead hip first as they slip between parties of one, two or three, if the third is not put off by a pinched place setting. Every table is adorned with one candle, old wax droplets preserved mid-fall like fresco tears, and an empty wine bottle that holds a single flower stem, sinking as the evening goes on until only a parched cluster of petals remains.

'It's not Claridge's,' I apologise, giving a stab in the candlelight at the type of dining experience he will be accustomed to.

'I hate Claridge's,' Gavin replies. 'I should sooner die than spend another evening there.'

At first, I had thought that he too was dressed entirely the same as earlier. Yet stealing a glance across the table while he considers the menu – Italian, I am impressed to see, presents no problem for him – I notice one difference. A tie pin.

'My grandfather's.' Gavin catches my gaze and answers the question before I can ask it. 'It was his Order of the Garter pin.' He leans forward, face perilously close to the flame. Its flicker softens the fine lines of weariness that haunt the hollows of his cheeks, lending his complexion a luxurious pale gold glow. I reach into the warmth, tracing the pin's insignia with my index finger. The tip pricks me. I keep smiling. Pretending I

9

didn't feel the pain.

Service is slow here, I remember too late, before realising that tonight I do not mind in the least. While we wait for the food to arrive, Gavin reaches into the inner pocket of his jacket to produce a collection of photographs.

'I thought you might like to see these,' he says, passing the first fragile square over the tabletop. I take it from him carefully, my fingertips framing the corners as I stare down at a little boy, all rounded cheeks and tousled streaks of fair hair. His little hand a blur, the child waves cheerfully from the high stone side of a bridge. No, not a bridge. My bridge. Kielder bridge. Gavin offers me the next image. This time, the boy is captured leaning over the stone wall, just as he described for me earlier; too transfixed by whatever magic exists within the water below to pay attention to the camera and who is behind it. Thirty years later, that boy sits opposite me in silence. Looking at me, looking at him.

'I knew that I knew you,' I whisper. 'I mean, that through this place, a part of us had already met.'

Gavin nods. 'I know.'

I had telephoned my mother in the afternoon. A rare occurrence, it shames me to say. Why pick today? Perhaps some latent Presbyterian instinct inherited from our shared Scottish ancestors told me that I must temper the risks that come from unexpected joy with a return to dutiful, daughterly obligation. Whatever it was that compelled me, for once I spoke with Jessie at length, patiently enduring her melancholic might-have-been memories until our conversation flowed naturally to my recent trip.

'Did you ever encounter the Maxwell family?' I asked. Nonchalantly, I hoped, just as I hoped the incriminating high-pitched surge at the end of my sentence had not travelled down the line.

'The Maxwells ...' For a moment, I took my mother's hesitation to be uncertainty. Instead, it was only a pause, a beat of breath, while she slipped ever enthusiastically from the present back into the past. Jessie Raine, like her daughter, is dangerously prone to daydreaming. 'Lady Mary was exquisite,' she told me, voice distant as if communicating with me across the decades, rather than the distance of miles amongst other things that lies between us. 'So was her sister, Lady Victoria. The Percy girls, they were then. The village called them the Percy Princesses. As I recall, Mary went on to have sons.' My mother seemed to speak from

10

some liminal land, sitting on the threshold between then and now. A place from which I could not call her back, even if I wanted to. I found I didn't. 'I sat behind the girls in Kielder Kirk once,' she reminisced. 'They had beautiful coils of blonde hair. It looked like gold in the sunlight.'

'This sounds like the start of a Scots ballad,' I said, expecting her to contradict me. Father would. Silly little Kathie. Life isn't like a storybook.

'It was,' my mother sighed. 'That's exactly what they looked like. Just beautiful.'

I glance at the man sitting before me. 'Beautiful.'

'Sorry?'

'My mother says that your mother was beautiful.' Gavin smiles again, even broader than before.

'Still is. They must meet again. We'll arrange it; bring them together at my studio or your house in Paultons Square.'

'She would love that,' I say. *I would love that*, I think.

Our food arrives, the waiter adroitly weaving his way around coat-draped chairs to set down two generous plates with mismatched patterns. Gavin chose the fish.

'As if I haven't sickened myself enough with it,' he jokes, and I laugh, again pushing those poor spearheaded sharks from my consciousness. The first moment of silence between us falls as he attacks his meal, ravenous yet unmistakably aristocratic as he cuts, chops and consumes with elegant gusto. Far removed from the listless ghost of a man I met on my doorstep earlier, the ferocity of his hunger startles me into forgetting my own plate. Only pasta, nothing special. When it came time to order, I found my imaginative powers had been exhausted elsewhere. Regardless, Gavin eats his meal like a person recently recovered from illness, or recently released from prison. A starving man sated.

'This is the first time I've felt hungry in weeks,' he exclaims, mouth still slightly full. My eyes fall to the frail branches of his bony hands and wrists, blue veins exposed like the undersides of leaves by the fragile translucence of his skin. The smallest finger on his left hand bears a signet ring that swirls as he moves, too loose to fit in what should be its rightful position. He needs this nourishment, I realise. And I want to nourish him.

'Kielder hasn't changed much,' I remark, conscious of picking at my own food far more gracefully than I do with Tambi. 'Most villages are closer to towns now, but the fields and forest felt almost the same. I wanted to show my children before it's too late.' Dipping a toe in cold

11

water. Most men would flinch. Gavin does not.

'You're married?' he asks, still largely focused on his fish.

'Divorced.' I do not say twice. I am submerged to the knees already, or perhaps right up to my waist. I hope time enough lies ahead of us for me to dive into that particular tale.

Gavin glances up. 'That must be difficult. I'm sorry.'

'I'm not.' And I have never meant it more than in this moment. Doubt can so easily calcify within me, hardening my heart with shame, if not true regret, that often feels like it cannot dissolve. Showing my children the land where their mother grew up, and where she truly became herself, was easy. It was facing those whom I had left behind, breaking off with radical divergence from the paths laid out before them, that presented the real challenge. My wartime schoolfriends, all farmers' daughters, are now all farmers' wives, welcoming me into their warm kitchens where sheepdog puppies and freshly baked scones symbolised the life that might have been mine if I had wanted it. My best friend Sally had been a fresh-faced girl with a peaceful disposition. Something I always lacked. Decades on, she embraced me and my children before introducing her own little daughter. A sweet, smiling girl named Kathleen.

'I've thought of you often, Kathie,' Sally said. How could I fail to think of her and the life I would have led in her shoes? I have known since early adolescence that my soul's true north would be a road less travelled. The poet within me is certain the choices I've made, however painful, were necessary. But the mother?

'How old are your children?' Gavin asks. *Older than you'll expect*, I think optimistically.

'Anna is fifteen. James will soon turn thirteen.'

'And are they happy?'

'Yes,' I reply on instinct. 'I'd never rest if they were unhappy.' I touch the petals poking out from the neck of our table's wine bottle vase. A tired leaf, curling around the edges, comes away clean in my hand. I know my children are not unhappy. Helen would not lie to me about that. Entrusting them into the care of my closest, most capable friend – and the serenely spacious home she provides in Ullswater, many miles away from Blitz-blasted London, is a far more suitable one than my own – was not a choice but a necessity. In more ways than one. We needed money and I can make it here, at least as much as even a successful poet ever makes. Despite the distance between Paultons Square and Cockley Moor, we speak often and write almost incessantly; jokes and anecdotes flying through the post, the children's increasingly accomplished drawings and descriptions disgracing my own efforts at a well-illustrated correspondence. It is better this way. It has to be this way. Helen recalls, although Anna and James cannot, how precarious my survival became during the earlier days of motherhood. Trudging through the mire of postnatal mental sludge, I knew that if I could not continue to create, I would sink. The children needed me to swim. Will I be able to tell them the whole truth one day? I could not keep myself afloat without drifting a little way from you.

I tell Gavin, stretching our new connection as if to test its breaking point. It does not snap. He does not shy away. The blue of his eyes stills and softens as he listens, sea winds giving way to calm and leaving the ocean at rest.

'It takes courage to do things differently,' he observes. 'God knows, I've learned that the hard way. I admire your courage, Kathleen.' With difficulty, I break away from his gaze, feigning newfound fascination in the farfalle spoils left on my plate. My intention tonight, or so I told myself, was to hear him. Heal him. I do not want him to see me this close to tears.

'I fell gravely ill when I was not much older than they are.' Gavin takes a long sip from his glass before continuing. 'It started the day of my sixteenth birthday. I wasn't expected to make it.' He says the last part angrily, almost provocatively, and I feel uncertain where his outrage resides. With fate itself for taking him so close to the brink so young? Or with the people around him who apparently lacked faith in his ability to fight back? 'Henoch's,' he tells me. 'It's a haemorrhagic disease. Took numerous transfusions. I came close to bleeding away.'

'Your poor mother.' It is not what I mean, although it probably should be. *Poor you* is what I dare not say, just as I dare not reach for his hand. I settle for looking at it, noting with surprise the hint of a delicate mauve blood bruise.

'Is that from ...'

Gavin looks down. 'Ah, that. Funnily enough, no, just a birthmark, but you're in good company. When I was ill, Mother sent for the King's Physician, and he was convinced the two things were connected. Idiot of a man. Cost Mother fifty guineas to say there was no hope for me. I take comfort from the fact that I swore at him during the height of my fever. But no, this and the rest are just marks. Bloody blemishes. I always felt so ashamed of them.'

Slowly, Gavin pushes up his right sleeve, showing me small splashes of purple and violet that ripple up the inside of his forearm. In the candlelight, their colours warm, transfiguring to turn the same shade as my wine. Burgundy on silk; blots of red ink spilt on ivory paper. My eyes move in the direction of their flow and then against it, travelling from the seam of his jacket cuff to his newly exposed bare skin.

'You have nothing to be ashamed of.'

Gavin groans, stretching his arms as much as a tall man can do, given Sorbo's cramped quarters. The bruises slip back beneath his shirt sleeve, disappearing out of my sight.

'I spent long enough staring at them, and at the walls, during my convalescence. That was the real torture. Not permitted to leave bed for months, having to read on a book rest and ring for help each time I wanted to turn the page. Never mind being free to run, drive or shoot ...' His eyes dart left and right, waters churning anew with frustration at the memory of enforced inactivity. 'I suppose ever since there's been a restlessness within me. Have you travelled much?'

'Only a little,' I admit. 'Europe.' There are ties that come with motherhood, even for an unconventional kind of mother like me. My most meaningful journeys have been intellectual ones; the borders I care most about crossing are limits of a different, less tangible type. Still, I can never forget the freedom that comes with finding new land where one's soul can flourish. I can never forget the river and forest, nor those Scottish hills so near and yet so tantalisingly out of reach. 'I'd like to see more.'

Gavin beams at the encouragement. 'So would I. One simply can't live without the feeling of being able to flee it all if necessary. Although eventually, I suspect every man comes to want a home of his own.'

A waiter nears, about to interrupt. Gavin gives him a nod so subtle it is closer to a blink. The man is dismissed and I watch him walk away, smiling benignly as he goes. I am impressed, although I would rather not admit it, by the elite social powers of persuasion that come naturally to Gavin, even at his lowest ebb.

'After '44,' he tells me, tipping back the remaining contents of his glass, 'when I was invalided out of the army ...' Modesty stops him from adding that it was with the rank of Major. No matter. Tambi already told me, telephoning ten minutes before Gavin's second arrival to ask if there was any chance I had seen where he left his shoes. '... I used an

14

inheritance to set up the shark fishery at Soay. I wanted to prove that I could; to show I could create something on my own terms and succeed at it.' He stares with such intensity that for a beat or two, I have no response to offer.

'Of course,' is the best I can manage, and indeed, what else is there to say? Who could harbour doubt that the man before me ought to succeed at whatever he wishes to?

Gavin sighs. 'But now, this failure ... and it's not just financial.' He looks away, then back at me, as if beseeching me to understand something that cannot be put into words. And I will understand, I think, although I don't just yet. I will make myself understand. 'There was a failure of friendship. A shattering of trust. It's caused me great suffering. The portrait painting is a nice idea, but, after everything, I suspect I lack the gumption, not to mention the talent, to make it work.' He brings his thin fingers together, knuckles pressed tight as knots. The signet ring spins. 'Kathleen, do you think there's still hope for me?'

'I do.' I can hear my pulse surging as if a seashell is pressed to my ear. This is what I am here for. This is why he was brought to my door. I accepted long ago, or thought I did, that my personal Eden was lost to me, except for the pale imitation I strive to achieve in my poetry. Gavin's company is the closest I have come to rediscovering that paradise. This connection must count for something. I search for what succour I can give him; for what wisdom our two unknowingly interwoven lives have led me to appreciate.

'My Aunty Peggy, whom I lived with during the first war – we weren't as glamorous as your family, I'm sure, she was just a humble village schoolteacher in Bavington ...'

Gavin shakes his head and gives a small wave, the signet crest twisting to face me. Dismissing my dismissal, and I am glad of it.

'... Well, she lived in a manse house and each year without fail snowdrops would bloom at the feet of the beech trees.' Reluctant as I am to lose sight of the man before me, I close my eyes to conjure the ethereal magic of those flowers, delicate and dreamlike, their tiny heads bowed as if in prayer. 'There were hundreds, perhaps even thousands, or so it seemed to me as a child. The first time I saw them, it scarcely seemed possible to hope that such a miracle could happen twice, but eventually I learned to believe in their multitude. To have faith in the inexhaustible bounty that the natural world provides. I knew, and I still know, that there

15

could be no end to snowdrops. There is always new hope. Nature always gives back.'

Blue eyes meeting mine. His spirit meeting my spirit.

'Nature gives back.' Gavin murmurs my words like a mantra and, for a heartbeat, the trusting sweetness of repetition restores him once more to lost boyhood.

*

That night, a poem comes to me. I used to believe the best writing was about discipline, applying oneself to long hours of labour like the coalminers who attended Father's evening classes had to do during their working days. Chiselling the raw matter of words into elegant, well-controlled submission; chipping and polishing each letter with ruthless rigour until the detritus of wild instinct can be swept up and discarded. Yet growing older, I am starting to wonder if it is more often the opposite. I rest. I listen. Rising out of myself and becoming a woman – no, no longer a woman but a being – who is somehow both less and more than she was before. Dreaming while awake, or maybe awakening to a dream.

There is a tree. A rowan, I feel sure, flowing through its seasons in quick succession: white blossom metamorphosing before my mind's eye until red berries arise, glittering like rubies unfurled from ivory lace. It stands on a hill. I sense its height, the transcendence that comes with close proximity to great purpose, and what I think must be a blackbird nestled within the tree's embrace. A boy is asleep beneath it, his fair head resting on the roots. Something tells me that I must leave before he wakes.

When I come to myself again, already reaching for my pen, I wonder if what I saw was his dream or my own.

Chapter Three

'What time do you call this, Kathie? At least you look lovely.' I am the last to arrive for lunch. This unwelcome new vanity will be my undoing. Tambi gives me a vigorous wave from the far end of his long table, holding happy court amongst an eccentric assortment of acquaintances. As the people Tambi knows always do, they run the gamut from princes to paupers and back again. A few fellow poets – one knows them by the dark circles under their eyes – some publishing associates – whom will Tambi select this time to foot the bill? – and other unspecified patrons of the arts, identifiable from their relative lack of angst and the relatively well-ironed quality of their clothes. We are not at Sorbo's this time, which could never cope with such a large party, nor Tambi's insalubrious usual haunt, the Hog in the Pound, but an improbably illustrious Brook Street address that is apparently known as The Guards Club.

'That's Sir Aymer Maxwell. *His brother*,' Tambi stage whispers, having needlessly sprung from his seat to guide me along the table. 'It's thanks to him we've been let in here.' A bewhiskered, gold-braided Admiral Nelson on the wall behind us appears to sneer in objection to that fact. Turning from him, I steal a glance at Gavin's elder sibling – 'A friend of a friend of a friend,' Tambi tells me – who is too invested in conversation with an elegant female companion to notice me passing.

'1799 to be exact, although the land around Monreith has belonged to the Maxwells since 1482 ...'

'And you all share it?' the woman asks innocently. A violent snort of disdain, presumably echoed by Nelson if he could, disabuses her of such egalitarian notions.

'Hardly, although I'm sure the idea would appeal to my poor baby brother. Have you heard about all that's left of his latest *venture*?'

As Aymer sniggers, the glimpse I get of his profile makes me think of a fairground hall of mirrors in which one feature at a time is tweaked. Aunty Peggy snuck me into the travelling circus on one occasion and I remember it with the vividness that comes from childhood novelty.

17

It was most definitely without my father's knowledge: a central tenet of his beloved Methodism, over which we consistently clashed, is the fundamental mistrust of fun. Gavin's brother has the same fair aura of refinement that he does, but his features are thicker set. Jawbone squarer; shoulders broader. If we lived in the time of the Classics, as I often wish we still did, Aymer would be the mortal. Gavin the myth.

'Saved you a seat.' Tambi draws my attention back to the present day by pulling out an empty chair with a flourish. I tumble clumsily into the last vacant place.

'Hello,' says Gavin, seated on my left.

'Hello,' I say, as smoothly as I can, which is not very. 'Have we met before?'

Gavin laughs, loud and genuine. 'I'm starting to feel sure we have.'

'You're wearing your pin again,' I observe, pointing to his lapel. I think, deep down, I prick my finger deliberately this time. Perhaps I'm starting to find pleasure in the pain. Gavin already looks better, even healthier, than yesterday afternoon, and having eaten at least two full meals in two days cannot have failed to aid his recovery. I ask how he is feeling.

'More hopeful,' he confides, and a birdlike trill of hope sings within me too. He is coming to believe that portrait painting must fall by the wayside. 'The Academy will lose no sleep,' Gavin remarks with a wry glint of blue. 'But I feel the seeds of other ideas starting to take root.'

'I'm glad to hear it.'

'And I'm glad you're glad.'

'Kathleen, how could you sneak in past me without a word? What a ruthless heartbreaker you are.'

'Hello, Elias,' I offer in the direction of our interruption, trying to sound sincere. 'It's good to see you.' Canetti is one of the varied literary contacts to whom Tambi has extended today's invitation, and one-to-one I usually enjoy the intellectual challenge of his company. As writers, we stand on the same earth, but I am dedicated to looking up at the sky; aspiring beyond what is to what can be, a world of soulful dreams and spiritual rewards far richer than anything this mercenary plane offers us. Elias is more interested in what lies beneath and exposing that underbelly through his work; raking through psychological filth to find the base impulses stuck like grime under humanity's fingernails.

'Haven't you ever wanted to write from the point of view of a worm?'

he once asked me, only partly in jest. 'Just imagine it. So limited, so low.' When confronted with the grubby motives of either characters or real-life people, I see only profound tragedy; a failure to understand the full beauty of what the human spirit could be. Elias, by contrast, takes perverse delight in tackling the dirt. If I tried to tell him what Gavin and I have shared, retracing our steps back to our lost Eden together, I know he would never understand.

'Since when have you two been acquainted?' An eager, almost excessive curiosity burns bright in Canetti's expression as he studies me and Gavin side by side.

'Not long,' I reply, as simply as I can whilst not wishing to admit that it has been hours rather than days. Somehow it does not feel like it.

'It seems longer,' Gavin adds unprompted. Elias's eyes narrow.

'The Maxwell men have always belonged to the Scots Guards.' From the other end of the table, I hear Sir Aymer holding forth for his stylish friend. 'Most of the Maxwell men, that is.'

'And what did you do during the war?' These days, one question is deemed sufficient for taking the measure of a man. Like the rest of our sex, this young woman knows it. 'Did you see action?' Beneath Nelson's regalia-laden gaze, Aymer seems suddenly disinclined to answer her, preoccupied with the pressing issue of whether or not the wine is corked.

'And you, Gavin? Where were you until '45?' Elias's inquisitiveness, or something like it, once again overcomes him.

'Arisaig.' A new quality of silence falls over the conversation. Not awkward but awestruck. Hidden in the Highlands for their safety and ours, few knew about the clandestine Special Operations Executive while the fighting raged on. Only recently has their courage come to light. 'It was being up there that inspired me to take on Soay.'

Aymer attempts another snort, although in the circumstances this one fails to resonate. 'Inspiration, indeed. That's a rather romantic way to speak of the island that took everything but the shirt on your back, brother. In fact …' a gleeful flicker of sibling schadenfreude catches in the elder Maxwell's eye, no doubt delighted by the chance to deflect from his less dramatic war record while his date is still listening in. 'Why not tell the table what happened with your boat's alarm?'

'Ship, Aymer. The crew call it a ship's alarm.' As an only child, I cannot deny that a certain thrill comes from watching Gavin parry and thrust in this game of fraternal rivalry. He heaves a sigh as if equally unimpressed and unsurprised by his brother's nautical ignorance. 'I can't think anyone here is interested in my life aboard a shark fishing vessel.'

'I'm interested,' Elias counters immediately. His attention is fixed on Gavin's face as if anticipating a stumble. And I'm interested too, even if, for Gavin's sake, I do not say so. He needs none of my protection here, however, being more than capable of turning Aymer's apparent threat of embarrassment into a triumph.

'In my infinite wisdom,' Gavin begins, dryly self-deprecating, 'I had the alarm installed directly above my bunk. Our man on watch at the bridge – that's part of the ship, Aymer – might spot a shark's fin at any moment, you see. Day or night. We couldn't afford to waste time getting our harpoon gun in position.' *Don't think about the sharks*, I remind myself, the idea of vicious weaponry at risk of puncturing my pleasure in this story. *Think only of Gavin.* Soon enough, he is all I can think of.

'It had felt like the perfect plan,' he goes on with a smirk that feels specially intended for me. 'And my waking up with a shock seemed a small price to pay for a catch. Unfortunately, though, my race to reach the gun as fast as I could meant that I dashed up on deck before I was fully conscious. And did I mention that I prefer not to wear pyjamas?'

'I made sure to lay out overalls to pull on for subsequent nights,' he insists. 'But alas, it was too late to prevent the crew from seeing and, eh, christening my "harpoon".'

Bless Tambi for laughing so hard that he threatens to choke on his breadstick. Attending to him gives me a much-needed chance to hide my blushes if not my smiles.

'Bloody idiot.' Childishly churlish in the face of defeat, Aymer hurls both the insult and a bread roll at his brother. It appears that aristocrats are accustomed to getting away with a wildness in their table manners which peasants like me could never emulate. In a flash, Gavin catches the baked missile without even needing to turn. I guess sharp reflexes make sense in an SOE instructing marksman.

'But how?' I ask him, genuinely amused as much as wishing to extend the anecdote. 'How can you possibly sleep with nothing on?' The Bavington of my childhood was close enough to the border for me to gain some sense of what it must feel like in the bleak midst of a Scots winter. Thinking of my little blue bedroom in the manse will never fail to remind me of the misery that comes with simply having a body in winter. Wrapped up in woollens, a hot water bottle sandwiched between

20

each scratching layer, I can still sense the cruel chill that lingered just outside: those Jack Frost fingers I imagined clawing and grating against the windowpane like icy nails down the village school blackboard. How could Gavin form such a habit in Scotland of all places?

'I need my freedom,' he grins, breaking off a bit of bread to swallow. 'You know me.' My heart racing at his answer as much as the image, I smile back in blissful confidence that, yes, I do know him now.

When Gavin and I leave together, Elias notes it. Aymer remains intent on winning back his increasingly bored blonde acquaintance, opining over her while she picks at what remains of her sorbet, and Gavin himself is talking so animatedly to me that he does not seem to notice our sole observer. I feel self-conscious though, and therefore selfishly relieved when Tambi spills a flute of champagne down himself – panicked, no doubt, when presented with the bill – and we are able to slip out quietly in the midst of the ensuing uproar.

Gavin walks with me unhurriedly in the vague direction of Paultons Square. I lead him the long way around the park, following the loose route that enrings the pond as if I have not long since discovered its many, varied shortcuts. Indeed, on this first day of September, the burgeoning autumnal beauty of amber and gold is leaving me freshly dazzled. Parisian, it suddenly seems as we meander along an avenue of trees. Or perhaps it just feels as if we ourselves could be in Paris. A young squirrel darts across our path, so focused on foraging for winter supplies that it fails to notice us until too late. When it spots us, it freezes: tiny front paws suspended in shock while the creature balances on its haunches with fluffy balletic poise.

'Good afternoon,' Gavin greets it. The squirrel stares at him for far longer than I would have thought natural in a wild animal. Its head bobs as it double blinks, bending almost into a bow, before it remembers the instinctive wariness of man that one hopes its mother taught and scurries off, leaving us to our laughter. With no fellow humans nearby, our only remaining companions are the birds calling to one another from the branches. The last of summer's weary late-season leaves rustle above us as the treetop residents converse. Gavin tilts his head left and right to listen, concentration creasing his brow as if, with enough effort, he will be able to translate their meaning.

> '*The trees are in their autumn beauty,*
> *The woodland paths are dry,*

21

> Under the September twilight the water
> Mirrors a still sky.'

'That's beautiful,' he says. 'Is it yours?' If only.

'Yeats. *The Wild Swans at Coole*. It should be "October", but ...' I couldn't wait.

'I wrote a poem last night,' he tells me quietly when we walk on. 'Would you like to read it?' I can only ever imagine one answer to such a question.

'Please.'

Gavin reaches into the blazer pocket from which yesterday's photographs emerged. In his hand is a single sheet, folded neatly into quarters. In this glowing light, the paper appears fragile, and I know more than most how truly delicate this moment can be. After years of watching my creations be critically dissected, I appreciate the intense vulnerability involved in sharing new work. '*A shattering of trust,*' that's what Gavin spoke of last night. The hurt and betrayal of a nameless, shameful someone whose behaviour has brought him so close to collapse. I will not let Gavin shatter again. In the spirit of exchange, I search the coat pocket where my composition notebook lives.

'Here,' I offer. 'You can read what I wrote last night too.' The path ahead of us winds towards a wrought iron bench overlooking the pond, and we take our seats side by side. A sprinkling of dried leaves encircles our feet, covering our toes with flecks of russet and bronze. I kick them absent-mindedly to make more room; Gavin swirls them gently with his shoe until they settle in peaceful submission around his feet. Even before our swap can take place, another handful has drifted gracefully down to the ground. *Falling.* I say the word to myself, feeling the same sensation.

Gavin's writing is neat yet intense, flowing over the page in quick, angular strokes of red-brown ink. I read his creation; he reads mine.

'This is ...'

'I know ...'

A rowan. He has written of a rowan tree on a hill. And in its branches, a blackbird. Or rather, a black bird.

'I suppose I see it technically as an ouzel,' he says.

'A who sell?'

'An ouzel.' He spells it for me, but I am none the wiser. A relative of the common blackbird, Gavin informs me with the quiet confidence of a true outdoorsman. Almost indistinguishable, were it not for the ouzel male having a stripe of white across his breast. They are found in the spring in Scotland. 'They especially love rowan berries.'

Our poetic rhythms are not identical. His style is less confident than my own, and I find endearing beauty in that fact. There is no boy asleep beneath his tree; he sees it standing alone, which makes an exquisite sort of sense to me. But what both poems create, we share as one. We have been together. Seen together. Above parallels and beyond complements, this accidental telepathy speaks to me of more than our two worlds coming together. This is one world within two minds. One consciousness at work.

'You're a writer,' I tell him. Nothing gives greater nourishment than the truth. I see joy illuminate those blue eyes, the boy he once was alive again within the man.

'Meeting you,' Gavin says, 'is as if a goddess has turned her head and looked at me.' I would turn my head, but I am already looking at him. And I feel as close to a goddess as any woman could.

*

A second night spent sleepless. My mind is agitated; my soul unsettled. Perhaps Father's melancholic Methodists are right. Too much delight can be dangerous. I feel at sea, tossed on thunderous waves of emotion that refuse to give me rest, overwhelmed by the depths of a connection for which I never went looking, yet now feel I have spent my life searching for. The turmoil is intoxicating, sublime as a tempestuous Turner seascape, but even if goddesses can get by with no more than two hours of sleep in two days, a mortal woman like me cannot. I seek relief by turning back briefly into the shallows, flicking through my memories of the day like pages of a newfound favourite book.

'*I need my freedom. You know me.*' And I do.

I wear a stolen shirt to bed. Striped, faded, a little bit frayed. An accidental stowaway unreturned from when Charles gave back my few belongings. Why he made the mistake, I'm still unsure, because I never collected clothes, only books, as I sleepwalked through my life with him. Anyway, this shirt of his is the loosest, largest garment I have, its tails falling in cut-cotton arrows to comfortably cover my mid thighs. Staring down at the pale pinstripes, I lay my book on top of the bed. My real book, that is, from which I have failed to read a page tonight. I take a breath and slip my hand beneath the hem.

I press softly at first, with only my index finger, the same one knitting a

23

minuscule white scar from where I pricked it twice on the tie pin. With my other hand, I unfasten the buttons from above, brushing my palm across the swell of my already aching breasts. In moments, I am pushing inside myself, tilting my pelvis to meet each movement until my spine is arching in spasm. *Gavin's hands*, I tell myself. *Gavin's touch*. I imagine my lips playing leapfrog over his body, every scar on his arm – each beautiful blemish, the most perfect imperfections I've ever seen – celebrated and cherished beneath my kiss. Can he feel this? Can he feel me? With one world in two minds, I am somehow certain that he senses this too. In the same way I am certain that, when we do go to bed together, it will be unlike anything I've known before.

Chapter Four

I call Helen. I ask her about the children.

'Are they happy? Truly happy?' The question has been echoing in my ears, along with everything else I have heard Gavin say since we met. With the rest, I revel in our mental proximity, indulging in the intimacy that comes from hearing his voice in my head as I try to go about my day. But this question requires an answer. A more emphatic one than I gave.

'Kathleen, what a question. The children have everything they need.' I can picture Helen vividly as she does her best to soothe me: bright green eyes, light grey chignon, her appearance as well-kept and warm as the immaculate home into which she has welcomed several creative waifs and strays over the years. A rare patron of the arts who is prepared to put not just their money but their house where their mouth is, most of Helen's human 'finds' have lost their way whilst trying to reconcile their genius with reality. Although in my case, perhaps 'passion' is a better choice of word.

'James is forever off on adventures with his friends,' she reassures me. 'He's very popular. They go walking and climbing ...'

'Mountains?'

'Fells, Kathleen. Cockley Moor has fells. Remember?' I remember. It's not so long since I was there myself.

'And he's happy?'

'As any young man could be.' Walking. Climbing. It strikes me that James might enjoy Gavin teaching him to shoot. A rite of passage, maybe? His father will hardly show him such things. Momentarily, the idea pleases me, but then I think of my son shedding an innocent animal's blood, proudly holding up a pheasant carcass to be photographed. The only picture Gavin showed me that I did not wish to look at for long. No, not shooting. I shall think of something better.

'And Anna?' I ask. 'How is Anna?' A second's pause. A long time for a mother.

'She's well ...'

'But?'

I hear Helen compose herself before continuing, choosing her words with care. 'It's merely that some girls at school are starting to speak about *beaux*. It worries her.' It worries me too, although I have no right to such anxieties. I was a year younger than Anna is now when I was introduced to Roland, my father's former pupil and my short-lived – for obvious reasons – piano tutor. Proclaiming himself passionately in love, Roland had offered me a book of verse along with his youthful heart. I accepted the book, if not ultimately the boy, and the carnage that followed caused irreparable reputational damage to both romantic poetry and me in George Raine's fiercely moralistic eyes. I wonder what became of poor, pimpled Roland? I can only imagine how Gavin looked at eighteen.

And yet Anna herself still feels like a little girl to me, with her perfectly rounded cheeks and trusting doe brown eyes.

'Is she there? Can I speak to her?'

'They're playing a game together outside,' Helen says. 'I can call them in ...'

'No.' A game is good. 'Let them play.'

'You sound different,' my friend notes in the exacting tone she typically reserves for art appreciation. '*You* sound happy.' Helen misses nothing. That's why I trust her with the children.

'I am happy.' Childish it may be, but I enjoy the sound of the words said out loud; confirmation of this sudden new fact carried through the air and transmitted down the line. A truth told without fear or evasion. Isn't that what poetry ought always to be about? On my first visit to France, our sole exotic family holiday, I recall being shown a coastal cave where an earlier traveller had etched his emotions right onto the wall: '*Here I was happy.*' Since Bavington, since I lost sight of the snowdrops, I never dared to hope that I would write those words again myself.

'Ah.' Although a knowing nod cannot be fully communicated by telephone, Helen makes her best attempt. 'That sort of happy. May I ask his name?' She sets great store by name meanings. The library at Cockley Moor is a remarkable one – a fact that gives me further confidence in the children's presence there – and Helen has read almost everything by almost everyone, adding new knowledge daily to her vast intellectual archive and never letting a fact slip. 'Kathleen means "pure",' I remember her telling me from one particular onomastic tome, and I felt inexplicably heartened to hear it. My intentions in life are pure, even if the same cannot

26

always be said for the results.

'Gavin,' I tell her. 'His name is Gavin.' I enjoy saying that too. His name is the word I woke up to after I did, in the end, manage to sleep. My slumbering consciousness came to around the handsome contours of those letters, like I had lain back in the grass and spotted a cloud formation floating by in precisely the right shape.

'"White hawk",' Helen informs me instantly. 'Or sometimes "Godsend".'

'I'll tell him.' And I do. I cannot wait to. Walking together that very afternoon, once more opting to follow the long way around the park, Gavin laughs as I relay Helen's research, good humour relaxing the taut lines around his jaw and cheekbones. I realise again just how attached I have grown to the sound of his laughter.

'I think I'll stick with "white hawk",' he smiles. 'Reduce the risk of inevitable disappointment.' I disagree, of course, but decide I had better not say so. Continuing along our imprecise path, crisp strips of sunlight glide between the branches to illuminate pale gold highlights in his hair. 'White hawk' will do very well.

'What about your name?' he asks.

'Kathleen means "pure".' When I suggest it is too simple, Gavin shakes his head vehemently, causing the gold strands to glitter.

'It's perfect. After all, you purify things for me.' My heart delights at that, although my mind doubts how true it can be. In my own life, at least, I have a tendency to complicate everything.

'Jonnie!' Gavin shouts as a thick blur of black and white charges past us into the trees. 'That's a stick, not a squirrel, old boy. Honestly, call yourself hunting stock?' A solidly built springer spaniel, strong-pawed and powerful even if he is no longer a young pup, Jonnie was introduced to me today by Gavin with all the proud parental affection that I picture in myself when I imagine him meeting my children.

'Jondog's been with me through thick and thin, haven't you, boy?' Meeting me at our bench, as I already want to call it, Gavin had ruffled the crinkled curls on top of the canine's head, the dog in turn wriggling with pleasure undiminished by however many times they must have repeated the exchange. 'Couldn't have survived Soay without him at my side. He took quite unwell a couple of months ago, but touch wood' – there is plenty to hand, and like Gavin, I reached out to touch a nearby trunk – 'the worst seems to be behind us.'

27

'He certainly looks fighting fit.' As I spoke, Jonnie had come closer, investigating my outstretched hands before attempting to do the same with my pockets. His chunky black nose brushed inquisitively against my fingers; his woolly stump of a half-tail (a sad necessity, Gavin said, in gun dogs) giving out little lamb's shake quivers that I hoped denoted his approval.

'He does,' agreed Gavin, 'and he has good genetics in his corner. My family had his father before him, and his father's father before that.'

'His breeding's better than my own.' I had knelt to properly introduce myself to Jonnie, and Gavin looked down at me.

'No, Kathleen. You're unique. A species all of your own.'

While we walk, weaving our way with a deliberate lack of direction, Jonnie returns with well-mannered regularity to check on me. Like a gentlemanly escort – maybe that excellent pedigree manifesting beyond the Kennel Club's books – he appears at my side every few minutes, nuzzling my fingers before returning to the more thrilling business of deciphering cryptic cold-earth smells. It is to Gavin, though, that Jonnie devotes his greatest attention. No corner is conquered and no squirrel scent trail followed for long before the dog turns his large head in his master's direction, gaze fixed on Gavin's face in keen anticipation of his command. Joyfully uninhibited as the animal is – I sense that, if he could speak, his understanding of the natural world would astonish us – he cannot bear to let Gavin out of his sight.

I know the feeling, Jondog. I try to tell him so, silently communicating our shared secret through the medium of an ear scratch.

For his part, Gavin indulges Jonnie as one might do the beloved baby of a family. Gavin is in fact the youngest of the Maxwells and I the only child of the Raines, although I cannot think Debrett's is interested in the latter. Gavin lets the dog dive into the pond at will – 'Their coats have a waterproof layer,' he reassures me when I wince at the thought of the cold – and permits him to chase the park squirrels, despite, or most probably because of the fact that he has no prospect of catching them.

'It makes him think he's still young,' Gavin confides, whispering in a way that thrills me as if Jonnie might otherwise overhear our conspiracy. Ahead of us, a pile of leaves is sent flying by the dog, the movement making the treetop birds take momentary refuge in the skies. A flock weaves over our heads as one, a backlit swirl of feathered beauty binding an invisible thread above us both. Heeding what feels like a good omen,

28

I move closer to Gavin.

'Sparrows?' I wonder aloud.

'Starlings,' he corrects me.

As we reach the furthest end of the park – furthest, that is, from my home at Paultons Square – Jonnie starts returning to us more slowly, panting from his exertions each time he presents himself at Gavin's feet. His pink tongue lolls, moist with drops of drool, and yet his chocolate eyes stay trained on Gavin. A word from him and old Jonnie would run once more.

'Getting thirsty, aren't you, boy?' Gavin scratches the scruff of Jonnie's neck and the dog sits in weary relief. 'My studio isn't far from this part of the park. We had better take him back for a drink.' We. Not I. Words matter. Every writer knows.

'Yes,' I agree. 'We had better take him back.' I let Gavin lead me this time. As we near traffic, he slips a leash around Jonnie's neck, but from the dog's doting expression, I can tell there is no need for such precautions. Neither Jonnie nor I have any wish to leave Gavin's side.

His flat is smaller than I expected. It seems Gavin did not exaggerate the financial ramifications of his misadventures at Soay after all. The living room is comfortable enough, even if its spartan colour choices betray the eye of a man working without a woman's touch. Burnt orange, dark brown wood, and a small plain rug that exposes a border of chevron floorboards. On the back wall, a door opens up unexpectedly – and conveniently when it comes to animal care – onto a garage roof strewn with long grass. Clearly accustomed to the arrangement, Jonnie trundles immediately in that direction, seating himself in front of what must be 'his turf' to wait beside his empty water bowl. A neat sleeping gallery lies above us. My pulse quickens as I glimpse the corner of Gavin's bed.

This place is not what I imagined. It is far, far better. Only the day before yesterday, my mother had mentioned on the telephone, floatily imprecise as ever, that she remembered hearing people speak about the Maxwell family seat.

'Monreith? Or was it Moncreith?' I had visions of ivy tendrils creeping up castle walls and uniformed gardeners sculpting topiary hedges; of tapestries taller than our whole house at Ilford tumbling down to decorate elaborate spiral staircases. Terrifying suits of armour lurking in corners and glass-eyed stags' heads mounted on walls; that was the interior style I envisaged as apposite for dukedom. Perhaps in Scotland, it is. But here in London, Gavin lives not as a lord, but as a man.

'Make yourself at home,' he calls, heading for his tiny kitchen with Jonnie's water bowl in hand. As he passes, he stoops to give the dog another pat, murmuring nonsensical sweet nothings of affection that make my heart flutter. I take my chance to explore. Look but don't touch, isn't that the rule? Gavin's fireplace is topped with what I guess are authentic travel finds – a ship in a bottle, something that looks unnervingly like a shark's tooth – while lower down, half-complete canvases are propped against the skirting boards. I bend to study a painting. Gavin's fine, if tentative, brushwork hints at the unfinished faces of a society lady and her dog.

Bookcases, I am heartened to see, line three out of the four living room walls, and next I creep closer to read some of their spines. If there is a better way to judge a man than by his bookshelves, I've yet to learn of it. Very well-read, I realise with relief, as my gaze shifts from classical civilisations to natural history and, yes, my own poetry volumes. Here is *Stone and Flower* with the stylish illustrations that so impressed Mother. Uneconomical for Tambi, but he insists he has no regrets about inviting Barbara Hepworth to design them. Here too, is *Living in Time*, a more nuanced work, although less wholeheartedly embraced and, I'd say, less wholeheartedly understood in its critical reception. And finally, *The Pythoness*, published only months before Gavin and I met. Earlier in the year, I confess to having taken great pride in my third collection, daring to believe that my technical skills as a poet were sharper than ever when showcased in this volume. Yet in retrospect, some pieces read curiously unfinished, like something indefinable but integral was missing that I didn't know to look for at the time. Did Gavin truly own these books before we met? Do they live here on these shelves, staring out at him day after day? To my shame, I find that I hardly care. Wild-grown or planted, the flower of flattery blooms.

'Sorry, sorry, sorry,' Gavin sets down Jonnie's bowl, into which the dog immediately submerges his snout, and hurries over to the sofa to sweep up an armful of loose pages. 'These are mere scribbles.' I recognise the same intense scrawl as before, the ink even heavier here and with what looks like many words scored out. An isolated few of those that remain catch my eye as Gavin removes them. Sea. Storms. Crashing. Break. More poems? I'm encouraged. The emotions that have troubled him need to be expressed. And not just the troubling ones. I know how much I have written this week. More powerfully than ever, the words are pouring out of me.

'Drink?'

'If you're having one.' He is. Gavin disappears back into the kitchen. Glasses clink and a cupboard door clatters. While I wait, Jonnie joins me at my spot on the sofa. Satisfied and ready to sleep, he lets his large body drop so that he is sitting at my feet, his wet whiskered chin sinking into my lap. He looks up at me with endearing drowsiness, like a child too tired to slumber, and his hangdog brown eyes droop: heavily lidded, faintly bloodshot. I stroke his crown soothingly, soft fingers rippling through his hair, the way I once did when coaxing Anna and James to sleep post-bedtime stories.

'John Maxwell, you're a disgrace.' Gavin is joking, of course, but I see Jonnie turn to check before giving his master a woolly stub-tail wag. I believe his worst fear in the world is to displease him. 'If you're tired, old boy, then it's time for your basket. Don't just sit there drooling over Kathleen's beautiful dress.'

'Really, I don't mind.' I don't mind at all, especially now I know he has noticed my dress. Jonnie, however, seems grateful for permission to retire from active duty. Taking a final pat from us both, he enters his blanket-lined basket, padding circles until, satisfied by some magnetic alignment undetectable to us, he lies down to sleep.

'Apologies, madam, for my friend's shameless hounding.' Gavin offers me a mock bow, his neat nod from the neck still somehow convincingly courtly. 'I guess he finds you irresistible.'

'I'm used to it.' That was true, once upon a time. I learned at Cambridge there is nothing like being aloof to attract attention. Years later, after overindulging at one of Tambi's shambolic soirees, a former classmate told me of a club that he and some of the other young men had formed, keeping score on how many times each of them saw me walk past on my way to the library that week.

'The beautiful bluestocking' was the *nom du jeu* with which they had apparently crowned me, as I learned to my acute embarrassment and Tambi's acute delight.

'You're a muse as well as a poet. What man could ask for more?' I will tell Gavin that story at a later date. Right now, I don't want his thoughts of me to be linked with other men.

'To us,' I offer as a toast when Gavin passes me my glass.

31

'To us,' he echoes obediently, although it appears that he has already taken a sip from his own. I cannot blame him for being a little distracted. I feel the same. 'And to the rowan.'

'Our rowan.' Emboldened and exhilarated as if my intact drink has infused my blood by osmosis, I move near enough for our thighs to brush.

'Kathleen ...'

'Yes, Gavin?' Beside me, he is struggling to settle; his long limbs crossing and re-crossing like book pages agitated by a breeze. Soon, Gavin is standing, then moving towards the window and pressing both his forehead and his glass against the pane. The light is failing outside, the autumn sunset losing its golden heat to shadows, and it adds to the strange feeling of furtiveness that suddenly fills the room as he looks left and right along the street. Fearful, it seems to me, that we will be seen or overheard. *He's nervous*, I realise with a frisson of delight. How sweet. As discreetly as I can, I let my eyes flick up to what I can see of his bedroom. It's been so long since I've been kissed.

'There's a certain way I can't love you,' Gavin says. 'Do you understand?' *'Tread softly because you tread on my dreams.'* I read more poetry for pleasure these days, as well as writing more myself.

'I understand,' I say, although of course I don't. All I know is that he is in pain, distress cutting across the elegant planes of his face like it did when I first opened my door to him, what feels like another lifetime ago. A strange, pleading sort of vulnerability has taken over Gavin's expression, some hidden hurt only a hair-trigger away from defensiveness. His eyes are fixed on me. Troubled seas, seeking safe harbour.

'I find myself feeling ... one can't help these things, you know?' Abruptly, he turns his back. Gavin taps his whisky glass against the window, as if the words he can't say are to be coaxed in from the cold.

'I know,' I tell him, although I don't. Not yet.

'It's not a choice, not at all, and I've done everything I can to ... we can't control what we feel, can we?'

'No.' I can answer honestly this time. Gavin returns to sit on the other side of the sofa and starts hurriedly searching his pockets. My thoughts turn rather ludicrously to Roland's fumbled proposal in my parents' living room. He could not yet afford a ring, he said, but would I accept *The Romantic Poets*? Gavin produces a silver cigarette case. He offers me one. I decline. Technically, I believe it is considered ungentlemanly to light up regardless, but Gavin's anxiety seems such that he no longer has

32

any choice.

'It's in my nature to be more of a man's man.' The repetition strikes my ear. The poet in me hears him more clearly than the woman. 'A man's man, sexually.' *Tread softly because you tread on my dreams.* I am surprised. Shocked at my surprise. I thought we were too closely linked for him to surprise me. I take a drink.

'I understand,' I say. And I try to. I have known or at least heard of this in men before. I am not so very naive. What sort of poet would I be otherwise? My extended circle is rumoured to encompass a spectrum of unspoken preferences. It has never concerned me before. It has never been Gavin before.

'Can I have a cigarette after all?' When he opens the case for me, I grip the paper hard, clenching the cigarette I take between my fingertips to prevent Gavin from seeing that my hands have started to shake. On instinct, he leans in to light it for me. *This is as close as we will get tonight*, I think, hit by a wave of nausea and nicotine. From the floor, Jonnie seems to sense that something is amiss with that acuity of animal intuition no human could ever hope to match. Even through his haze of sleep, the tension between us is transmitted through the air to him. He curls his body tight inside his basket and his ears begin to twitch.

'Kathleen?' Gavin is staring at me with all the desperation of a drowning man. I want to help him. He needs me to help him. Isn't that why I'm here? Some cosmic, uncalled-for connection that is so much more powerful than either of us alone? I force myself to focus not on where he treads, not on what of me has fallen beneath his feet, but on what he has chosen to place in my hands. His faith. His trust. Quite literally, his freedom. The wrong words spoken to the wrong person would mean prison for him. Prison and utter, irredeemable disgrace. The dukedom is not so very distant from this flat, after all. Someone like him, from such a family as his, and with his war record; newspapers are sold on the sordid tales of those prosecutions, men humiliated on the stand and shamed in the streets for things they have done or even just felt in private. Imprisonment is the usual sentence. Chemical castration the alternative. I take another, longer drink. The shaking does not stop.

Gavin may not want me the way I want him to. Not the way I want him. But he trusts me enough to let me hold his freedom in my hands. And isn't trust the most important part of love?

'I have fought it.' The hoarse anguish in his voice affirms he is telling

33

me the truth. The hollows of his cheeks no amount of physical nourishment can fill; the indigo shadows I've noticed settling under his eyes at the end of each day when he grows tired. Outward scars of an internal war. A constant battle waged against what one feels. I look at Gavin's face in the lowering autumn light. God knows, I could not win it either.

'A failure of friendship.' The phrase, like so many of his words, has not left me. He spoke of suffering a 'shattering of trust': the true tragedy of Soay, plummeting him to depths far more dangerous than its disastrous financial implications. Broken in spirit. Almost a broken man.

Gavin sighs. 'Yes. Raef. He's gone up to Cambridge now. Very bright.'

At first, I imagine he means intelligence, but to my horror, Gavin visibly brightens when finally able to speak Raef's name. My sickness worsens. A swirling tide of smoke and whisky floods my throat. I recognise the warm glow from within that comes when you glimpse a certain person, even if only for a moment in your mind's eye. I see it in the mirror every time I prepare to meet Gavin.

'You were ...'

'He meant a lot to me.' *That means nothing,* I tell myself.

'You were ...'

'Friends. Close friends. And we trusted each other, or so I thought. Thought the best of one another.' He downs what remains of his drink with one swallow. 'Maybe I was foolish, believing that even the deepest friendship could last with a young man like him. A boy who still has his whole life ahead of him.'

Gavin is thirty-five. I worked it out after our first dinner together. Six years younger than me. Raef, it appears, is even younger.

'But in his company, it felt like I could get back a little of what I lost when I was that age, do you see?'

A girl I knew at Girton College was obsessed with Freudian analysis. Homosexuality, she claimed, stems from an emotional injury early in life. 'Developmental arrest,' I believe was the phrase she used. I was relatively uninterested at the time and wish I'd paid closer attention, being more concerned just then with fending off my heterosexual followers. Now, my thoughts turn to the marks on Gavin's arm, the hint of one subtly visible between his cuff and pulse point. The marks I've dreamed of pressing my lips against every night since we met. I remember asking Gavin about them at dinner, leading to the story of an adolescent boy's brush with death and a torturous, protracted convalescence that forced him back into

34

the helplessness of childhood. Arrested, one might say, at the very point when a developing young man would most fervently wish to break free.

'I think I do see.'

'Raef cut off contact with me when he went up to Cambridge.' Gavin's voice grows strained, speaking almost through gritted teeth. Re-enduring the sting of an injury that is not yet fully healed. 'Out in the world, he understood the way I am. Understood what people would think of him, if they ever found out about me.'

It is wrong. The way he is. It goes against nature; it violates the perfectly balanced beauty of the natural world in whose shared love we have found each other. Doesn't it? A shrill voice starts screaming in my ear, howling barely articulate insults about sin and physical perversion. Cruel and uncompassionate, the words feel oddly familiar. Are they from one of the many sermons my father required his dutiful daughter to sit through? I of all people have no right to claim late-in-the-day piety. How often in my life have I tried and failed to find conventional faith? In time, I've come to accept the paradox of my poetic temperament: a religious person without belief, or in truth, a person who believes, yet cannot abide by, the petty rules of religion. In my girlhood at Great Bavington, struck by the overwhelming power of nature all around me – a world so exquisite that its Creator surely did not make mistakes – I'd ascend our cherished Bab Crag overlooking the surrounding fields, respectfully clutching my Bible until I realised that each day I returned with it still unopened. Now, a provincial echo with a puritan streak wants to throw that book back at me. It shrieks that Gavin ought not to feel this way. He cannot. I tell myself it is the voice of my father's Ilford, of narrow minds in bowler hats, of all my creative hopes being blocked up by brick walls. The voice I have spent my life as a poet trying to silence.

'I don't care,' I say to Gavin. 'What we have goes beyond all that. It's spiritual.' I will not accept the muddied mire of ordinary life dragging me down. Not again. Not when I want so desperately for both my work and myself to transcend it. I have already suffered too grievously in the fallout from that conflict, my own internal battle between being a woman on earth and a poet whose hopes live in the skies. And I was not the sole one to suffer. My children's faces flicker before me, open and pure as the flowers that first made me want to write. I refuse to let the connection that Gavin and I share be sullied by the parochial low horizons of my father's folk, or the vulgar fetishisation of filth that Canetti and his cohort adore. What are practicalities and technicalities, analyses and diagnoses, compared with love? And what is love if not the miraculous, mystical meeting of spirit with spirit? We can rise above it all. I want to. And I must. If not, won't I lose him altogether?

'It doesn't matter to me,' I tell him. 'It's not what's most important.' I push away the memory of my nightshirt hem riding up, crumpling and tossing it under my mental bed.

'Are you sure?' Gavin asks. I see in him what I saw the first time I opened my door. A man who needs what I can give him. A man whose soul's journey is entwined with my own.

'I'm sure.' He presses his palm to my cheek, the touch even more tender than I'd dreamed of. This is not what I dreamed. But I know how it is to make sacrifices. The return to Eden requires it. Gavin makes his sacrifice every day, being the way that he is, and so will I.

'Of course, no man is an island,' he tells me, relief flooding his features. 'And every man needs a woman in his life.' *I am yours*, I think. I cannot be mistaken in this. I feel enough has been said for one night, though, so I simply watch Gavin while the light fades.

Chapter Five

Poetry pours from me. Tambi is delighted. Elias, I suspect, is jealous. I send snippets to the children several times a week – versified quips written just to amuse them, dashed off in less time than it used to take me to decide on a single word – and then the rest of my day is devoted happily to composition, new lines about new ideas flowing from mind to pen like water through the roots of a rowan tree. Sleep comes secondary; food and drink are fleeting thoughts. As autumn falls to winter and the bare branches stretch as if seeking to embrace the crisp pale sky, I feel I could raise up my own arms in thankful worship, filled with gratitude for this miraculous return to the psychic soil from which my work flourishes. *Northumbrian Sequence* is the title I give my new pieces. The poem Gavin was first to read becomes number five.

He, too, is writing. Not unexpectedly, portrait painting has been abandoned and the half-finished woman with her lapdog haunts his flat as the sole visual reminder of a brief, less-than-illustrious career. 'Her husband announced they were divorcing before I could complete it,' Gavin tells me, failing and not really trying to hide a smirk at his former client's aristocratic absurdity. 'He said that since she wouldn't be getting any money, neither would I.' It is the stories of Soay that energise him now, re-enacting the drama for me until I insist he writes it down. His talent is for prose, I realise quickly, much more than for poetry. Gavin can spin a sentence on a sixpence, twisting between comedy and tragedy as adroitly as a gambler flips a coin, and his words have the rare authenticity of a real-life adventurer. Seductively compelling, he makes the perils of the sea seem exhilarating; every danger his crew faced is given a sheen of dark, witty glitter. Putting aside my sympathy for the poor sharks – the island needed the industry, Gavin reassures me, and besides, basking shark brains are too small to feel real pain – I surrender to the power of his storytelling, laughing aloud at his scorn for the superstitious fishermen who feared bumping into a woman before boarding their boats, lest she taint their luck at sea. One Soay local swore to his dying day that a female's passing words on the shore had brought about his ruin.

'He had moored the boat in such a way that when the tide went back it was lifted by a rock below the keel and capsized – but he was not likely to remember his inefficiencies when he had so desirable a scapegoat as the witch-woman to bear them into legend.'

Gavin telephones me at all hours of the day and night to read aloud what he has written, outlining his manuscript chapter by chapter and absorbing my suggestions with a reverence that bolsters my poet's pride. Midday or midnight, I am always happy to answer him, and soon my heart swells to hear the harsh ring that once seemed so grating and disruptive. Whenever he needs me, I halt my writing to tend to his. As soon as I return, I have so much to say that the ink runs out before I do.

On reflection, I decide that things are made more perfect, not less, by the sexual sacrifice I am making. That we are making together. I would never have married again anyway, I remind myself, and a 'poetess', as Gavin delights in calling me, requires her freedom every bit as much as an adventurer. Haven't I already learned that lesson the hard way? We are lucky to have found each other, if luck had anything to do with it. Me, discovering a man who wants neither to possess nor control me; he, finding a woman who will forgo sexual love for something so very much greater.

Like mine, Gavin's rowan poem is soon to be published. After I re-read it for the umpteenth time, struck on each occasion by the power of our shared poetic vision, I had begged him to let me send it to a trusted friend for her opinion. That my friend is Janet Adam Smith, Literary Editor of the *New Statesman*, was something I decided to keep secret until I heard back from Janet herself. As it turned out, Janet sprung the surprise before I had the chance, writing directly to Gavin on the same day I placed his poem in her hands.

'Kathleen tells me that you insist you are an amateur; I can only say that, as a hardened reader and chooser of poetry, I haven't for a long time met a poem that I was so sure I liked straight away, and so sure I would like in six months' time. It will be our pleasure to publish it.' Gavin glowed all weekend. In my joy at having played a part in making him happy, so did I. A small Buddha statue lives on my mantelpiece, an inexpensive market find I was inspired to purchase after reading a book on Eastern philosophies, and it had become my habit to write down wishes, tucking them behind his chubby ceramic ear. Now what I write is for Gavin, his name inked on every scrap of paper. Wishing for his success. His prosperity. His happiness.

'He says I've saved him from the abyss,' I tell Tambi in the *Poetry London* office. The term 'office' is a loose one: Tambi's bed lies flush against one wall of the sub-basement premises – 'worth it for Fitzrovia' – and its wooden frame is supported in one corner by a pile of books and papers in lieu of a leg. Elias arrives before I leave, intent on discussing promotional plans for his latest work, and we hover awkwardly while Tambi searches for his missing manuscript. It turns up eventually, its extraction leaving the bedframe even more unstable than before.

'I fear that, for you, Gavin is the abyss.' Canetti asserts himself calmly, a cold statement of would-be sagacity, and it takes me a moment to gather the right response.

'You listen too much to fear, Elias. Too little to love.' The shadow cast by his words begins to lift as soon as I trot up the basement steps, returning to the brightness of the outside world. Trotting quickly because I am, as it happens, on my way to meet Gavin.

From our bench, and it truly feels like our bench these days, we watch the swans that have suddenly, exquisitely, settled into the park. Elegantly synchronised, they drift serenely around the pond circuit, occasionally ruffling their wings to create a dazzling snow-white spectacle. When spring comes, I will hope for cygnets.

'What do they call a group of swans?' I wonder aloud.

'A bevy,' Gavin tells me. 'Or a ballet.' Perfect.

> *'Unwearied still, lover by lover,*
> *They paddle in the cold*
> *Companionable streams or climb the air;*
> *Their hearts have not grown old.'*

Yeats again. I murmur the words but, when I turn to Gavin, I am shocked to see his eyes have filled with tears.

'I'm so sorry,' he says.

'Don't be,' I reply, taking his hand. I have within me the strength he needs, and I am glad to give it.

He still talks of Raef now and then, whenever a mood of melancholia descends. Despite my best efforts, the floodgates occasionally open, locks lifted by an especially emotive piece of music or a rediscovered memento of Soay. In his despondency, Gavin grows desperate to confide in me more about him, along with another young man he knew and wanted – I will not say loved – when he was only Raef's age himself. We sit together on his sofa, Jonnie snoring contentedly in his basket beside our feet, and I steel myself to offer Gavin all the reserves of patience and empathy from which I can draw. Sometimes in profile and sometimes looking at me – I let my eyes flick to the painted woman and her dog if it becomes too much to bear – I watch his fine features change with his feelings: soft sadness, hard resolve and, just when I start to think I can withstand it no longer, heartfelt gratitude that I am here to listen. I imagined him once at eighteen and I can still imagine him now, but these days I do not see simply a handsome golden boy determined to build back his strength. I see confusion. Conflict. Torment. If I'd been there then, how different might things have turned out? Yet while Raef remains in Gavin's mind, I endure it as best I can, helping him to remember today so that tomorrow he will be able to forget. My gut contorts and cramps when he speaks at length about their friendship, but even this agony seems somehow to befit my role as Gavin's helpmeet, a quaintly biblical term I know my father would love. Although how much else he would love of this arrangement is debatable.

'Raef's at Cambridge now, isn't he? I had my own troubles there.' I raise the subject for distraction, to create a break in the conversation before the seizing pains in my stomach –really a little higher, nearer my heart – become too severe to ignore. God knows I would not mention it otherwise. Gavin is not the only one whose past contains a disastrous chapter or two. Still, in the spirit of emotional solidarity, I decide to tell him more about Hugh. It transpires, however, that Elias has already alluded to the unflattering circumstances of my first marriage. If such a nasty, brutish and short endeavour deserves to be called a marriage at all.

It sounds preposterous and, indeed, it is preposterous, that I should have considered marrying a man I neither loved nor particularly liked. More inconceivable still that I actually went ahead with it. I had arrived at the end of my degree with no prospect of a career in sight. Natural Science was my foolhardy subject selection; a more practical choice than poetry, I had supposed, when still too young to realise the cataclysmic futility that comes from pretending to be what one is not. That Christmas, a college friend introduced me to Virginia Woolf, whom we had heard speak on the importance of having a room of one's own, but she dismissed me without mercy as a Hogarth Press prospect for, in her eyes, 'being the size of a robin and having the mind of a snowball'. My parents, of course, saw the path before me with devastating clarity. A return to Ilford and a return to Methodism, inheriting my father's weekday role as a schoolteacher and consigning every poem I dreamed of writing to dust. As a woman, I would naturally be expected to sweep up the dust afterwards.

I could not go back. I would not go back. And so, when a chance came to stay on at Cambridge, I was willing to take it at any price. Even if that price turned out to be myself. For all his faults – and standing before him in my sweet, unsullied white lace, I was too innocent to imagine what they would be – Hugh Sykes Davies was established enough at the age of twenty to be able to offer me a home. A room almost of one's own. Why did Hugh want to marry me? I tell Gavin now about the Cambridge Club of my admirers. It does not hurt to remind him how much I have been wanted by other men. With Hugh, it was a marriage not of minds but of exchange, even transaction, in a way that does no credit to my dignity as a woman. Or as a poet. The wedding itself was a pathetic non-affair, attended by almost no one. If I had thought matters through, I should have refused to attend it myself. When Charles entered our lives three soulless years later, a once aspiring poet now dedicated to Communism – 'Come with me,' he said, 'and I will give you a cause to live for' – I saw in him my escape from Hugh. Then the children came before I could conceive of who, or what, should be my escape from Charles.

The chaos those choices created made me a failure in the eyes of my parents, yet I know in my soul that my mistake was not in leaving. It was in marrying them at all. Anna and James were still small when, slogging through the lonely peat bog of housewifery that had managed to sink me, I allowed myself to be seduced by another man. Charles showed rather less interest in the drama than I had expected. With good reason, it turned out, having already impregnated a mistress of his own. Alastair, he who briefly became my lover, was a notorious lothario in our circle; a Don Juan resolutely uninterested in my mind when there were softer, less challenging parts of me to explore. Familiar to him, I'm sure, from the many, many women who'd gone before me. I think my plan, such as it was, involved diminishing my value until it was no longer worth locking my gilt-coated cage. It occurred to me too late that a woman might free herself. Still, if anyone had asked me then, I suspect I would have said that I loved him. Them. Any of them. It's what one says, isn't it? It feels funny to tell Gavin of all people, although he listens with great

41

compassion. *I thought I loved before you.* I have the sense of confiding in the sun that I once confused it with a matchstick flame.

*

'I feel like the Queen is coming to tea.'

Gavin laughs, without contradicting me. The warmer weather has blossomed and we have arranged for our mothers to meet, working together to straighten out Gavin's small yet seldom tidy living space. Jonnie seems to share my anxiety, forced with great reluctance into Gavin's bath this morning and scrubbed until the off-white patches of his coat came up gleaming. Crinkled ears half-dried and drooping, he stares out from his basket with forlorn *et tu, Brute?* eyes. 'We're in the same boat, boy,' I try to reassure him, plumping Gavin's cushions before checking my reflection in the shining silverware.

Given the effort involved in polishing up both it and me, it feels fortuitous that our mothers are meeting in Gavin's home rather than mine. What would Lady Mary Maxwell make of Paultons Square? Even Gavin's studio seems too humble to accommodate almost-royalty. I do not exaggerate; confirming Jessie's memories, Gavin told me that his mother's maiden name was Percy, the same branch of the gentry whose ancestor had an affair with Anne Boleyn.

'Never fear, poets are the real aristocrats,' he says, and I very much want to believe him. 'Besides, you already have the pride.' Is that an insult? I feel piqued, along with, well, yes, a little pride. 'Oh, you understand what I mean.' Gavin flicks a tea towel in my direction, making me smile again despite myself. 'You know the place you ought to have in the world and won't accept anything less. We need visionaries, people like you with the courage to write the truth and the talent to make it resonate. Why shouldn't you be proud of yourself? I am.' For once, the poet and woman in me are united as I stand on tiptoe to kiss Gavin's cheek. The doorbell rings.

'My boy.' Lady Mary seems to glide rather than walk as she enters his flat. Tall and slim, just like her youngest son, whom she is already holding in an intense, almost suffocating embrace. Her famed hair is now closer to white than blonde, threaded with silver, not gold, and piled high in a style more suited to the turn of the century than its midpoint. She appears in no hurry to let Gavin go – a little peeved, I watch her kiss him twice on the same cheek that I did once moments ago – and thus

42

I have a lengthy opportunity to study the woman before me. Mother is right. Lady Mary must have been a great beauty. Her large round eyes are attractively heavy-lidded, with high cheekbones adding elegant polish to a countenance that already feels familiar to me through Gavin's. He has her nose too, I notice, although if one were being ungenerous, the aquiline profile suits a man better, being technically a handsome feature rather than a pretty one. Combined with those serene, watchful eyes, it lends Lady Mary a curiously avian quality. As she finally breaks from Gavin to face me, I think that she, and not her son, is the real 'white hawk'.

'Good afternoon, dear.' She takes my outstretched hand in both of hers, cool and slender fingertips interlocking around what now feels like my pudgy, embarrassingly pedestrian palm. I resist the bizarre impulse to curtsey.

'It's such a pleasure to meet you.'

Lady Mary smiles, then gives a subtle nod, at which signal Gavin instinctively springs forward to show her into his studio living room. Once seated, I offer her some cake at the same moment she instructs Gavin to pour tea for me. A few territorial seconds tick by in silence as we try to work out which woman is hosting the other.

'That must be my mother.' Liberated by the doorbell, I jump to my feet and rush to give poor Jessie a more enthusiastic reception than I suspect she has ever received from me before. Dressed in her plain navy Sunday best, Mother arrives to take a quiet part in our afternoon tea proceedings, following the conversation with wide, near disbelieving eyes. For once, her daydreams and reality are flowing into one, as she listens transfixed to Lady Mary deliver an abbreviated version of Maxwell family history.

'My husband, Sir Aymer, fell in the first war when Gavin was just three months old.' Mary's hand climbs Gavin's arm to rest against his cheek. 'What would I have done without my brave little soldier?'

He never knew his father. Is that why he is the way he is? Or does it stem from the fact that his mother is half in love with him herself? It would not take eyes as attentive as mine to notice that Mary tries to touch her son whenever he comes within range, although I ought not judge another woman for that understandable impulse. As our polite chit-chat progresses, I constantly catch sight of those cold fingertips sliding towards Gavin's arm, hand or wrist, and even once – showcasing impressive flexibility for a more mature lady – reaching right across the sofa until her palm settles on his thigh. Gavin has told me how his teenage illness terrified his mother, and perhaps a part of her has never recovered from her cherished boy coming so close to slipping through her fingers. In her shoes, I suspect I would also wish to keep a tight grip on him. As for Gavin, such a dutiful son and so sensitive to her feelings – could his body have forbidden him the love of other women to please her? I wish I knew the married name of my Cambridge Freudian friend, so I might write to her seeking answers to the many new questions I have.

Regardless, with the attention of all three women on him, Gavin's charm shines brighter than ever. Skilfully commanding our conversation as a conductor does an orchestra, he compliments and flatters each of us in turn, the effect all the more masterful for being achieved with such a light touch. His natural charisma can be dialled up to dazzling with imperceptible effort, and neither Mary, Jessie nor I is robust enough to resist his showmanship.

'Mother, you're outrageous, how can you tell such a tale? I'm quite sure I never kept gosling chicks in my bedroom.'

'Now Mrs Raine, you must have another slice of cake, please, do it for me.'

'Kathleen, just see the way Jondog's looking at you. The old boy's infatuated.' Laughing, we revel in the way he plays us, piano keys looking up adoringly at hands that use us at their will. Why resist the manipulation? He's the one who makes the music.

The hours of the afternoon slip leisurely towards dinner time, and as the porthole clock on Gavin's mantelpiece – a fitting memento from Soay – strikes six, he escorts our mothers to their respective taxis. Jessie, eyes bright and almost feverish from having spent the best part of her day in a fairy-tale, is going to stay with my Aunty Peggy, who has long since left the manse where my beloved, abundant snowdrops grew, and now resides in a southern retirement home. Lady Mary is visiting her eldest son Aymer before returning to Monreith.

'You'll see it soon for yourself,' Gavin whispers to me as he sees his mother out the door.

'Yes. I do hope we shall meet again.' Mary clasps my hand surprisingly tight in those frail, pale fingers. I smile at her, then widen the grin for Gavin, although I would prefer to have him know that his family seat has never interested me. The real him, I am sure, is right here, amongst his books and his writings, his discoveries and his dog.

Alone in the studio, I exhale with relief at a day's successful entertaining before kneeling on the floor to pat Jonnie. Having spent the past few hours in a similar state of excitement, animated to tail-wagging frenzy by all the extra attention, he is also ready to relax. I start stroking the dog's well-groomed coat, tickling his hairy stomach as he rolls onto his back with pleasure.

'Such a handsome boy,' I praise. 'Just like your master.' When I glance up, Gavin is standing in the doorway. Listening and looking delighted.

'You did well with Mother,' he remarks, bending down beside us. 'Truth be told, I'm surprised she took to you as much as she did.'

'Why?' My fingers find a residual tug in Jonnie's coat. I try to tease it out gently. The dog squirms.

Gavin groans. 'Jealousy, you know. She prefers meeting my male friends to female ones. Not used to women like you, that's for sure.' I take the comment as a compliment, certain that he means it so.

Chapter Six

The following morning, I go with Gavin to a publisher. Not Tambi this time but a more established player on London's literary scene, whose office windows let in daylight and whose authors' names ring a distant bell to the average person on the street. Rupert was encouraging about my work the first time we met but judged it 'too esoteric for today's readers, sadly'. I wanted to disagree, made more difficult by the fact that he was almost certainly right, and so we parted amicably, although in my opinion he still owes me a favour. Today, armed with Janet's esteemed recommendation, it is time to collect.

'Cursed things. Where are they?' On our way in, Gavin suffers a panic at having misplaced his cigarettes. I have yet to see him manage a minor moment of stress without them. As he rifles through his pockets, he passes his manuscript to me. *Harpoon at a Venture*. I trace the handwritten title, its words inscribed with such neat, carefully controlled intensity that the letters feel raised like braille. There is magic within these pages. Magic, too, in my wishes for him. He will succeed, and I'll be beside him when he does.

'I think I'm ready,' Gavin mutters, cigarette case safely located.

'I never doubted it.' He holds open the door for me to walk through first.

Rupert's office is comfortable, like Tambi's, and professional, unlike Tambi's. There are bookcases in place of the *Poetry London* bed and, conversely, furniture legs in place of the *Poetry London* books. Offering us each a firm, fast handshake, Rupert gestures towards our seats and I take the chair further from him, hurriedly passing the manuscript back to Gavin.

'At Cambridge with Kathleen, were you Gavin?'

'Oxford, actually.'

'Excellent.' We agreed beforehand not to mention that Gavin took his degree in Estate Management. Or that he only scraped a Third.

'So foolish,' he had lamented this morning, slaving over his fair copy pages while I knelt on the floor of his flat, encircled by loose sheets needing set in some semblance of order. 'No inclination or interest in studying. I was only happy when off in the hills with Jonnie's father, and I took every opportunity I could to do just that.'

'Most people would have failed outright,' I had observed. Gavin turned to flash me a deliciously conspiratorial twinkle.

'Well ...' he leaned towards me, affecting a whisper as though the 'loose lips sink ships' war mentality still applied. My pulse felt like rapid fire. 'At the end of our second year, three friends and I did sneak into our tutor's house to snatch a peek at the exam papers in advance.'

'Snatch? Sneak?' Shock, albeit of a humorous sort, stopped me in my tracks. 'Do you mean to tell me, Gavin Maxwell, that you burgled a house to cheat in your exam?'

'Naughty, wasn't I?' Good God, his smile when he's been up to something. He could confess to having stolen the crown jewels and I wouldn't care, beyond working out a way to go on the run with him. 'And a damn lot of effort we put into pulling it off. Having keys cut, finding torches and masks: an entire reconnaissance mission.'

'If you'd put that much effort into your studies, you wouldn't have needed to cheat.' The prim young scholar I once was obliged me to voice something in favour of academic standards.

'An excellent point, beautiful bluestocking.' Alas, one look at Gavin's face and my earnest inner girl grew as giddy as the rest of me.

In Rupert's office, our friendly preamble continues for a minute longer, before he asks to see the book itself.

'Let's have a gander.' Rupert holds the manuscript loosely in his right hand, pulling down his spectacles with his left and seeming to skim over the first few lines. He gives it back to Gavin. My heart plummets, then soars. 'Read it to me.' Rupert reclines into a plush, port-coloured leather chair worth more than Tambi's entire enterprise. 'I want to hear the first chapter.'

Gavin takes a breath. 'This story begins in 1940,' he reads. Here in 1950 we listen, soon spellbound. Familiar as I am with the waves and swells of his narrative, Gavin's voice pulls me once again into the adventure, dragging me into his old world deeper than ever before. We sail past the end of chapter one but if Rupert has no objections, and I can tell from his knowing smile that he does not, then neither do I. The scenes of Soay's tragedies and triumphs feel so vivid that I could be standing on

47

the deck myself: I see Gavin astride his harpoon gun, wrestling to subdue the monster that lurks in the depths below. This is a Moby Dick for the modern age, a ferocious battle of wills between man and elements he cannot control. Gavin torments himself with memories of his defeat, but in Rupert's face I see that, this time, he will be victorious.

'I've drawn illustrations, too,' Gavin adds almost shyly when the reading finishes. He passes over his hand-drawn harpoon designs, along with a page of tiny inked sharks.

'Excellent,' Rupert repeats. 'Leave them behind with the manuscript, will you, dear boy? There are a few other people whom I should like to take a look.' We walk out smiling calmly, maintaining all the composure we can, but as soon as we reach the street, Gavin and I break into laughter, dizzy with shared joy as we burst back into the sunshine. At home, I tuck a tiny prayer behind the Buddha, just to be sure.

*

'Why am I nervous? What sort of mother feels nervous before she sees her own children?' I berate myself aloud while wrestling with an unruly camp bed sheet.

'A mother who cares.' I pause to try and absorb some of the serenity that comes from Gavin's kind blue gaze. I need it. The summer holidays have arrived and my children are arriving with them. Now it is the turn of Paultons Square to suffer the undignified upheaval of a hectic, belated spring cleaning as I hurry to air all the spare linens I have, wrangling the haphazard smattering of books and reviews scattered around the house. Tambi has been promoting my new pieces almost as rapidly as I can commit them to paper, and the critical response has been unprecedently encouraging.

'Kathleen Raine's poems are like drops of water: clear, self-contained, and sometimes iridescent,' read *The Observer* review by Vita Sackville-West. Not bad for the 'mind of a snowball' her beloved Virginia icily dismissed. Now, however, in panicked preparation that befits a head of fluffy white foolishness, I push my own titles into the shadows of my shelves, pulling forward those that Anna and James enjoy. At least, they did enjoy, last time they were here.

Helen travels down with the children by train and I sense her studying Gavin while Anna, James and I embrace. Watching them over the top of James's tousled, untamed head – how can I have missed this messy mop of hair so much? – I recognise Helen's expression as Gavin takes her hand and kisses her cheek. Discerning and exacting, it is the same view she brings to appraising a new artistic acquisition. If public decency did not deny her the pleasure, I feel sure Helen would produce her magnifying glass to check Gavin's finish for flaws. Still, reunited with my little ones – not so little anymore – nothing can temper my happiness, and I do not doubt Gavin has it in him to deliver on even Helen Sutherland's scrutinising standards.

'Very noble.' My friend offers her verdict as we walk arm-in-arm along the platform; Anna on my other side and James, already smitten, bouncing beside Gavin to offer assistance as he carries their bags. 'Like a Norman effigy. Or perhaps a *fleur-de-lys*.' Half-sword, half-flower. Wholly appropriate, although I shall not tell Gavin so.

'Was it a pleasant journey?' I turn to Anna and her beautiful brown doe eyes. My daughter's cheeks are not as rounded as the last time we saw each other; the delicate angles of her face refining further into adulthood with each passing month. She's taller too, I note with unwarranted shock. I had grown accustomed to looking down at her and her little brother, but now I suspect only the squat block heels of my shoes stand between us being the same height.

'Fine, thank you,' she responds politely. Shame surges, a bitter hit of nausea singeing my throat, as I realise how stilted Anna and I are with one another. In the early years of living apart, physical separation seemed like a technicality. Mother and daughter, woman and child. When a bond is so profound, surely no distance can alter the connection? Except I see today that alter it must, when the most important part changes. Matures. Outgrows. We cannot stay woman and child because Anna herself is no longer a child. She is becoming a woman. Day by day, hour by hour. With or without me.

'He has a dog!' James yelps with glee from the front of our pack as Gavin untethers Jonnie from the station railings. Earlier he had exchanged strong words with the railway manager who refused to permit Jonnie into the platform waiting room. Evidently one may occasionally come across the exception that proves the rule: a person – a 'bloody jobsworth', according to Gavin – immune to the power of this soon-to-be published author's considerable charms. Reunited with his master and showered with kisses by the children, Jonnie's excitement compels him to unleash a volley of loud, harsh barks, bouncing off the station walls and gratifyingly causing far greater irritation to other passengers than his silent presence at Gavin's heel ever would have. Undeterred, the children fuss Jonnie like a long-lost friend, Anna tickling the crinkled tips of his ears and beaming as he shakes before coming back for more. A glimpse, if only that, of the girl I used to know. Our five becomes six with the jolly addition of Jonnie, and we take our leave of the station to begin making our way back home. My home, I should say. Their home is elsewhere now.

'First thing tomorrow, we'll visit the library.' Back at Paultons, Anna proves too grown-up for even the newest of her old books, and I make an anxious promise to acquire reading material more to her taste.

'Maybe,' is all she murmurs in response. With a tinge of terror, I realise that I have misplaced my maternal instinct to be able to tell what my daughter is thinking.

Shouts of wild merriment, punctuated by woofs no less jubilant, call our attention to the garden window. Together, we crowd the pane to watch James and Gavin play some exuberantly rowdy game of their own invention that seems to involve man and boy chasing each other around the pear tree. Young in outlook, if no longer in joints, Jonnie has assumed the role of self-appointed referee. He sits under the tree's branches, heart-shaped foliage flowing over his crown, and cheerfully issues vocal objections at what appear to be regular rule infractions. While we watch, James cocks his fingers to shoot at Gavin, who drops dead theatrically and tumbles onto the grass. Jonnie, overjoyed, starts licking his face. *Blood sport without bloodshed*, I think, pleased by the neatness of my solution to the problem.

Chapter Seven

'I've taken a house in the Highlands,' Gavin tells me. 'More of a cottage really. Right on the coast.' We are watching the cygnets. They have grown during summer and autumn, their ungainly grey feathers preparing to shed and turn pure, brilliant white just in time for the first snow. My own offspring are long since safely settled back at school: James hated to leave, the threat of departing tears thankfully averted by a kind and well-timed 'keep your chin up' from the Major, whereas I fear Anna was glad to go and found myself equally afraid to ask her either way. Alongside my ever-frequent letters to them, my correspondence includes messages to Gavin whenever we are apart. Amongst other things, I relay to him the activities of these birds and their colourful park companions. We exchange postcards and telegrams with no need for salutations, only frank observations of avian behaviour – he enjoys the facts, I prefer the symbolism – so that we can continue to see the world through each other's eyes. I scribble notes to him and he sends more back to me about plump tail feathers, eye-catching breasts and ever-expanding wingspans. Somewhere out there, I like to imagine a postmistress tutting at a filthily euphemistic lovers' code that for us is entirely literal.

'They say the place is mine if I can keep it up,' he continues. 'Standing empty, not one stick of furniture, and the nearest neighbours, if one can call them so, must be two miles inland.' It seems a man can be an island after all. A coastline collection of islands, each unique and unexplored, awaiting him a stone's throw from the threshold of a humble, white-washed cottage where ocean waves chap his front door and a free-flowing burn to the back weaves and ripples around his feet.

'And a waterfall,' Gavin says, eyes shining as if he can see its glistening torrents before him. In fact, I believe he can. I can almost see them myself. Certainly, I sense something of this wild place's power to do him good. An unusual stillness comes over Gavin as he describes its landscape, a rare serenity that lets me trust his troubled soul is finally finding peace.

'Does it have a name?'

Gavin smiles. 'Sandaig.'

'Jonnie will love it there.' I watch an adolescent cygnet stretch its wings and, in surprise, be borne up to the skies in virgin flight.

'So will you,' Gavin says. So will I. *This is true intimacy*, I think. More than intercourse could be. The world we share is more meaningful without the downward drag of bodily distractions; my feelings for Gavin are stronger, not weaker, for residing in the poetic rather than the physical realm. This, surely, is how one soul ought always to love another. An appropriately watery quotation flows into my mind:

My bounty is as boundless as the sea,
My love as deep;
The more I give to thee, the more I have,
For both are infinite.

Precisely one month later, I wait for Gavin by my Paultons Square window. Perched on the arm of a living room chair, my packed bag sitting expectantly in the hall, I try to affect an aura of impassive observation, akin to the lazy cats that one sees lounging on sofa backs elsewhere along the street. And yet the nonchalant effect is lost every time I stare at each vehicle that passes, checking its driver is not the one I want. I do not know what Gavin's car looks like and feel girlishly afraid that I might miss it. Miss him. He is on his way to Sandaig – with as yet no electricity or even running water, there is always work to be done – and I am catching a lift as far as the border to visit Winifred. How wonderful that I know someone who lives *en route*, I observed as soon as I had found out what his route was going to be.

Sincerely, Winifred is a friend I feel very fortunate to have, even if geographical distance dictates that we most frequently communicate through letters and telephone calls, and she is also one of the finest artists I know. Her fluid, vibrant paintings embody a hopefulness that I have never seen equalled on canvas, a deceptive delicacy in her windowsill still-lifes – expressive but never naive – that would see a male painter feted for his conceptual boldness (in my experience, Cubists tend to be rather one-dimensional people). Like myself, Winifred also knows about surviving as a divorced woman, after her husband and fellow artist Ben left her for Barbara Hepworth and incidentally added a rather awkward backstory to *Stone and Flower*. I confronted him about it here in London, or at least, I thought I did, noting that he had been fortunate indeed to have had not one, but two talented women in his life.

'You're right,' Ben nodded. 'You're absolutely right. From Winifred I learned a great deal about colour, and from Barbara I've learned a great deal about form.'

Agitated anew at the memory, I unfold this morning's newspaper for distraction, only to discard it in an instant. *Alan Turing Dead* cries its lurid bold headline. *Gross Indecency Suicide*. I plant it face down on the floor, thankful for the new prayer-poem that I have placed behind my Buddha.

> *Let him be safe in sleep*
> *As leaves folded together*
> *As young birds under wings*
> *As the unopened flower ...*
> *Let him be healed in sleep*
> *In the quiet waters of the night ...*
> *Where the troubled spirit grows wise*
> *And the heart is comforted.*

Let the woman in this man's life keep him safe.

While Winifred paints up north, I will write. My poems continue to flourish, *Spell of Sleep*, *Spell of Safekeeping* and others, yet this new abundance of inspiration is also coaxing me to consider poetry as a form in greater depth than ever before. William Blake in particular commands my analytical attention because I see in his work the visionary power of a man – no, not a man, a soul – who surrendered to the skies in the way I have always wished to do, prophetic and courageous as he transcended earthly concerns. The more I read, the more I want to read, following what feels like a golden thread from Blake to his intellectual descendants. Samuel Taylor Coleridge, Wordsworth's wilder and freer contemporary. William Butler Yeats, who was, I believe, Blake's modern-day inheritor. For the first time in years, I dare to dream that my poetry may one day reach the rich, verdant heights required to thrive as a single leaf on that tree. If so, I feel certain it is Gavin I have to thank.

In the distance, an engine growls. The sound intensifies second by second, fearsome and predatory as it stalks towards Paultons Square. Birds that had dwelt happily in the winter branches while more sedate vehicles passed now hurriedly disperse, seeking refuge in flight as an unseen menace approaches. In a moment, thunder turns to lightning; a harsh screech resounds as the car apparently attempts a corner skid. I stare in disbelief as a monstrously large red Bentley careens towards my door. Loose stone chips fly like sea spray and a wave of minor convulsive movements occurs across the Square as my neighbours' curtains twitch.

'Ready?' Waving wildly at me, Gavin shouts over the engine's roar. 'Isn't she a beauty?' No other response audible, I nod. Naively, I believed I had seen every side to him by now, over one year – and what a year – since we met. Sweet boyish soul and debonair charmer, the sensitive poet-painter and the dashing aristocrat. But the man behind this wheel is the war hero in action, the famed Scots Guard Major with fair hair swept back in eager, full-blooded readiness for adventure. Hurrying to the passenger door he has opened for me – the car's imposing bulk is such that I deem it best to let Gavin decide where my bag should go – I find Jonnie, who makes room by wriggling as best he can into the gap between the footwell and my knees. The dog greets me with gentlemanly aplomb, a wet nose pressed to my hand in a manoeuvre I now recognise as his canine approximation of a kiss, but then he curls himself back into a tight, unrelenting ball. Head down, tail tucked, Jonnie acts like he is bracing himself. I soon understand why.

'Isn't this glorious?' Gavin yells. At least, that's what I think he yells, coursing through the countryside at well over a hundred miles an hour. The vehicle's growl turns to a primal hunting howl as we tear strips off the rural roads, England reduced to a passing flurry of shapes that puts me in mind of not Winifred's flowers but the ruthlessly abstract Futurists – all jagged angles and cut-metal chaos – whose unsettling exhibitions I used to see back at Cambridge. The car has no roof, or if it does, Gavin deems it superfluous to our requirements, so I hold onto the sides, speed shocking the breath out of me while my companion beams behind the wheel.

'You know,' I shout in an effort to be heard over the engine, 'Winifred wrote me the strangest letter a few months before I met you.' I had been flicking back through our correspondence when I found them, obscure lines from early '49 that now feel extraordinarily prescient. 'She said she'd dreamed that a wild wind was coming for me from over the hills.' The Cheviot hills, I understand now, although I didn't know so at the time. '"Something is in store for you, Kathleen," Winifred wrote. And it was.'

Gavin grins. 'Women's intuition. Sometimes I think you're all witches.' I keep my eyes fixed on him as he drives, knowing I am the one bewitched.

His signet ring fits now, and I catch a quick glint of gold as Gavin's hand spins on the steering wheel. Carefree and exhilarated, perhaps I can understand a little of what this fierce momentum must be giving him. Something about the speed seems to let Gavin forget himself, troubles and anxieties trailing behind for a few borrowed moments of outrun. The mirror image, maybe, of the stillness he discovers at Sandaig. There, in primeval peace and quiet, I believe he does not lose but finds himself.

Now and then, Gavin whips his head to survey the darkening sky ahead of us, brooding over the horizon and bearing a heavy burden of grey.

'Snow in the forecast. I wonder if we'll get there before it hits?'

'I'm too busy wondering whether we'll get there alive.' If I have to die, I suppose I'd rather it was in his arms.

'Ha. You know I'd never let that happen. You're not saving my life just to leave it. Here, take the wheel.' I take it, laughing while screaming, as Gavin drops to scan the car floor for his perennially misplaced lighter.

We do not beat the weather. Incredulous though I am that any element, natural or manmade, could possibly move faster than Gavin with his foot down, the flecks become flakes and the breeze becomes a cruel, chilled wind, until we are forced to take shelter for the night in a village somewhere close to the border. As I step a little shakily from the car, Jonnie rushes ahead of me, relieved to put his paws on terra firma, even if that solid ground is swiftly disappearing beneath a powdered coating of snow. Having wrestled a worryingly flimsy canvas hood into position over his luxurious leather seats, Gavin stands before the Bentley with his hands thrust into his pockets, a lock of blond tumbling over one eye as he surveys with disdain tyres already embedded by more than an inch. I see the thwarted frustrations of Soay etched on his face, Gavin's eternal disappointment that sheer willpower cannot move mountains, oceans or snowdrifts. No man could have done more to try. Indeed, our ransom to speed has already been paid with what little we had to offer: one scarf torn from my head ('oh no') and one cigarette packet whipped out of his hands ('cursed bloody things').

'We'll have to find somewhere to stay,' Gavin admits, scanning around us to where stone homes encircle a village green cloaked with white. When he turns back to me, I am surprised to see he is smiling. 'Do you know where we are, Kathleen?'

I shake my head. I have seen no landmarks clearly since the blur of Paultons passed by. Gavin beckons me closer and puts his hands on my shoulders, spinning me gently until I face the direction of the snow-dusted fields.

'Look familiar?' I rise onto my tiptoes, the top of my head beneath Gavin's chin. Through the shimmering haze of snowflakes, bricks so dainty at this scale they could belong in a doll's house, is Kielder Bridge. Our bridge. I turn to Gavin, still held loosely in his arms. 'We'll go there tomorrow,' he tells me. My spirits lift, rising to fit the warm, hopeful shape of his words. Tomorrow, we will return to our Eden together.

The village in which we are stranded has one small inn across the green. We trudge inside as a trio, the sudden surge of heat from the fireplace prickling my numb frozen flesh back to life. No patrons have lingered, deterred from staying longer by the storm, and only a few swaying footprints in the snow provide evidence they were ever here. A woman remains behind the bar, frowning as she washes the last glasses. She wrings out her dishcloth with a firm, almost scolding hand, as if it recently caused her offence and will not get away with such cheek a second time.

'Our sincere apologies for the late hour, madam, but we're in need of a room for the night. Do you permit dogs in your establishment?' From the sign pinned to the wall behind her, no. From the look in her eye when met with Gavin's charisma at full strength, perhaps.

'Well-behaved ones,' is the concession she offers him.

'Oh, he's very well-behaved,' I say, my hand pressing lightly on Gavin's back. We snigger. The woman frowns.

'Major and Mrs Jonnie Madge.' Gavin produces a swirling faux signature when invited to write in the guestbook and I giggle again, to the owner's obvious displeasure. I've not known him use my married name before. Despite the cold, I am not wearing gloves – I rarely do, finding them an immense irritation when one wants to write as frequently as I do – and I feel the woman's gaze fall to my left hand, noting with disapproval the absence of a wedding ring. Still, a booking has been made and money has changed hands, so she gives the room's key to Gavin, indulging in a pointed sigh and one last look of condemnation towards me. Whatever scandal she thinks we are running from, or perhaps towards, it is clearly my fault for corrupting him. As Gavin bends to gather our bags and Jonnie's leash, I catch sight of my reflection, rippled and distorted across a row of empty glasses. My flushed cheeks are ruddy; my scarfless hair windswept and knotted. I suspect the proprietor will spend tonight wondering, her mind reeling, what would make such a handsome man choose an unglamorous scruff for his mistress.

The room we receive is quaint, with a dressing table and twin beds set, surely no accident, a couple of feet apart, upon which lie chenille coverlets embroidered with snowdrops, violets and roses. The sole window peeks from behind weighty floral curtains. I pull them wide to find a pane filled with glistening silver flakes. Gavin drops our bags beside the door and soon he lets himself drop too, falling backwards onto the nearer bed's blankets with a timber crash that sends its sewn flowers flying into the air.

'I'm exhausted,' he adds needlessly, eyes already shut. Gavin stretches out his arms, bridging the gap between the beds easily if he wished, then folds his hands neatly behind his head. I glimpse a fleeting glimmer of mauvish purple from the birthmark on his right wrist. Can he really fall asleep so quickly? I decide not to ask, preferring to simply take the opportunity to observe him closely. As if I don't devote enough time already to the activity. Yet it is not usually like this. Gavin is not usually so visible and yet so unaware of my gaze. He is not usually in bed either. Stepping over Jonnie, who has found his own spot to sleep on the floor beside his master, I sit on the opposite bed. From here, I can study the subtle sweep of Gavin's nose, elegant enough to have been carved from marble. I dwell on the fine, fair stubble that is starting to shadow his top lip and jawline. Untidy on any other man. Not so, never so, on him. I start to notice the way his ears stick out a little at the top; right more than left, its cartilage tip curving almost imperceptibly away from his hair. Boyish, I think, not for the first time. There is something so boyish about the man I love.

'What sort of room has nothing to read?' Not asleep then. Gavin stretches again and Jonnie follows suit, a wave of gentle movement flowing from the man to his dog and back again. Slowly, Gavin draws himself up to sit with his back resting against the headboard, opening his eyes to survey our twee surroundings. I realise he is right. Nothing to read in sight.

'I have this.' Dipping into my coat pocket, I tentatively produce my notebook. Gavin has seen it before, of course. He has read from it before. But how many pages have I filled since our rowan tree day; how many embryonic pieces of poetry has he inspired me to birth? With its scratched binding and furled, dog-eared pages – well-used and well-loved – this book feels more like a diary to me now. The words within it are raw and

57

unvarnished, just like the nearby fir trees under which we sheltered as children. I mix poetic verse with simple statements, swirls of imagery rippling into my recollections of real-life scenes. Often, things don't feel wholly true until I see them written down.

'Are you sure?' Blue eyes bright. Fixed on me. And a smile, with no trace of weariness left. 'Am I in it?'

My smile back is broad. 'What do you think?' I hand him my notebook and, however humble the words may prove to be, he receives it with the respect and reverence that I feel the gesture deserves. This is the closest I can get, the closest Gavin will let me get, to giving him my heart. I feel exposed, yet willingly so, and I surrender to the sensation. Creeping over Jonnie, now restored to slumber and twitching deep in dream, I return to the windowpane. Snowflakes are forming filigree patterns on the glass, invisible movements of the air revealed through the ephemeral artistry of ice. Bavington is in the distance. I can't see it, but I know. I feel it. I think back to France, although the vibrant sunshine of its coastline seems many miles away, and I wish with childish desperation to write on the frosted window as I might have done as a girl. *Here I was happy.*

'How could you?'

Chapter Eight

Until I turn, I believe Gavin is speaking to Jonnie. Reprimanding him for some rare transgression, perhaps of the unsavoury sort that canines relish committing in unfamiliar premises. It must be bad, I think. I have never heard Gavin so disgusted. I spin to face him, keen to appease his sudden anger and plead poor Jondog's case. Keeping the peace, isn't that what the woman of a family is meant to do? But when I see Gavin, I realise it isn't Jonnie who has horrified him. It is me.

'How could you write this?' Fury flashes in his eyes, lightning striking a cool blue sea. Gavin holds out my notebook at an open double page, angled away from his body as if in revulsion.

'Write what?' The confusion is not contrived. I have written so many lines, poured so much of my soul into those pages, how can I know what has upset him? Writers are primed for insecurity, as Gavin himself should now know. Embarrassment throbs through me, a painful heat pounding into my cheeks. Does he find it clichéd? Derivative? He praises my old poems often; the copies in his bookshelves turned out to be genuine purchases. Have my new works-in-progress disappointed him into distaste?

'This.' Gavin thrusts the notebook at me. I rush to catch it as one would do an infant about to fall. Vision quivering, my eyes already threatening to fill with tears, I strain to read the page in question.

'Oh. That.'

'Yes, that.' Gavin leans forward on the bed, pointing to the words whilst avoiding actually having to touch them. '"He told me why he could not love me with erotic desire, yet in the very telling there was love. He was, he said, homosexual."' A poetic moment, I have come to believe, albeit one I chose not to turn into proper poetry. What happened next felt more important; the visionary world we have come to inhabit together was the one that warranted transforming into verse. It strikes me, through the cloud of dismay that has descended, I have never heard Gavin read aloud something I've written before. I have imagined it, the perfect fusion of media and method, the natural, nostalgic beauty I strive to capture in words already there so effortlessly within his lyrical voice. But this is not what I imagined. He recoils from both the book and me.

'It's outrageous.' A strange choice of word, the poet in me thinks. The woman in me is too distressed to think anything. It is certainly genuine though, for Gavin truly does look outraged. Ears pulsing pink, nostrils flaring in fury. '*I have fought it.*' His tortured words from my first visit to his flat resound in my head with solemn resonance; today's anger blurring into last year's anguish. Perhaps no military man likes being reminded of the one battle he never won.

'Imagine if someone found it.'

'Found it?'

'Found it, stole it ...' Gavin tries to stand but discovers Jonnie still asleep on the floor where he would otherwise put his feet down. Forced into retreat, he hovers on the edge of the bed. Unsettled, unnerved and – how well I understand his inner workings – deeply grieving the loss of his cigarettes.

'Who would possibly want to steal my notebook?' Kathleen the poet speaks first. After years of fighting to persuade people to read what I write, until recently to very little avail, it feels ludicrous to conceive of first draft theft. But Gavin is clearly convinced by the scenario. Without proper space to move or better express his agitation, he resorts to viciously twisting the signet ring on his finger. The gold flashes at me, hard and accusatory.

'Anyone, Kathleen. Anyone who wanted to use it against me. Against my family, anyone out for money. God knows, with that written down you could ...'

'I would never.' He knows that. He must know that. We are alive in each other's minds, sharing one consciousness between two souls. He must know that I would sooner die than hurt him. It would be like hurting myself. No, worse. I watch Gavin's fair features darken. This is worse.

'Others would,' he counters ominously. I forget that, even in Eden, we came from two contrasting social worlds. The ne'er-do-wells of my people were the pickpockets and public drunks; petty crimes committed by petty people. But Gavin grew up in a land, quite literally, his land, where inheritance is not just genetic but monetary and meaningful, where even the criminals are of a different class. Fraudsters. Blackmailers. This is not theoretical; this pulse-racing rage, underwritten with anxiety, is no hypothetical prospect for him. I know Gavin well enough to tell that he is no longer imagining.

'The first boy …' The first boy he met, the first boy he wanted. Back when he was Raef's age. I start to feel queasy. I always do when I remember Raef. Gavin, too, looks nauseous. He bends his long legs up on the bed, elbows on knees and head resting in cupped hands.

'If you love me as you say you do, Kathleen, you will destroy that.'

'If?' If I love him? He is not averse to emotional blackmail. That single word offends me almost as much as my own word choice offended him. How can Gavin look me in the eye and say it? How can he let doubts and suspicions take root here, of all places, just a few short miles from where our souls' shared journey began and where the seeds of my poetry were planted? 'You want me to destroy my whole notebook?'

'Only the mentions of me.' As if it were that simple. As if the essence of him is not woven through every word I have written since we met. Each letter I craft takes its shape from Gavin in some description. A 'I' for his straight spine and lithe torso. Commas for the delicate curves inside his ears. An 'M' for the subtle bow crest of his top lip. Gavin shrugs, shoulders rippling through the wave of a 'W'. 'The rest doesn't concern me. You can keep it, if you like.'

'Can I, indeed?' Words matter. Every writer knows. Perhaps before he said that, we could have compromised. Agreed certain confidences require no repetition; in contrast to the habits of our beloved birds, some things are best communicated in code. I could have reassured him. Comforted him. Not now. There are two quick tempers in this room tonight. I tell myself I am a poet, infuriated and insulted by his unjust reception of my work. Not a woman, hurt and humiliated by his rejection of my heart.

'Nobody tells me what to write.'

'I will tell you not to write about me.' Icy eyes, storm-ravaged seas. *Let the tempest come*, I think. He might as well try to tell me that I must not write in English. Until I abandon the alphabet altogether, a part of me will always be writing about him. Gavin should understand that. I am, after all, the writer between us. At least, I was the writer first.

'No man will stop me writing,' I hear myself hiss, over-emphasising a point that my rational mind knows I have little legitimacy to make. The beauty of Gavin – at least, one facet of his complex beauty – is that he is not like other men. He does not treat me as an object to be exploited; when he looks at me, he does not see new land on the horizon, ripe to be

61

conquered, plundered and despoiled. He is not like other men. It's why I'm willing to make the sacrifice I do. Still, he looks stung by the suggestion, the rage burning across his face briefly doused by vulnerability.

'You know I didn't mean it like that.'

'No one tells me not to write. No one.' I start shouting without really meaning to, wrestling with the confines I have spent my life trying to resist. They are smothering me. Choking me. I am a horse bucking against heavy harness; a shark struggling with ropes knotted around her jaws to make her suffocate. 'I won't let you. I won't.' I am no longer raising my voice at Gavin, or not only at him. I am screaming at my father, at Hugh, Charles and Alastair, at my mother and the ghosts of her long-lost hopes that have haunted me all my life. At every pompous, port-guzzling editor who told me no, Miss Raine, the real world will never be the way you dream it should be.

We've woken Jonnie. Woozily, he starts to bark. With a sweetness that touches my heart, enraged and engorged with anger as it is, I see confusion cross the dog's face when he realises we are quarrelling. He looks at Gavin, then looks at me, his brown eyes turning to two pools of pleading sadness as he implores his battling humans to make peace. Then, reluctantly, Jonnie reorients his barking to place me in the firing line. A harsh, raw rumbling sound rises from him, not far from a growl. I know Jonnie loves me too in his way, but his loyalty is absolute. He has been with Gavin through war. He will not side against him if it comes to a fight between us.

'Major Madge? Is something wrong?' The inn owner is outside, tapping with rapid, reprimanding knocks. I wonder how long her ear has been pressed to the door.

'Come now, Kathleen.' Gavin offers his hands, opening his palms as if beckoning me onto the bed. How desperately have I dreamed of him doing precisely that? But this is no dream. This is a nightmare. 'Try to keep calm, won't you?' He speaks with the low, soothing pitch that men save for subduing wild animals and hysterical women. Gavin has certainly tamed enough of the former. He once told me with joy how his childhood pets included an owl, a jackdaw and even a heron. This man can, quite literally, charm the birds from the trees.

'Don't tell me to keep calm!' It seems we can fall into certain clichés of the sexes, albeit not those I would wish. Jonnie's barking grows so loud that the snowflake window starts to shake.

Another hard-knuckled rattle. 'Major Madge, I must insist.'

'Think of it from my perspective,' Gavin exhorts me, straining to be heard above the dog. 'Think of me, Kathleen.'

'Think of you?' Does he not know that all my waking thoughts and most of my dreaming ones are of him?

'MAJOR MADGE.'

'If I couldn't write what I feel,' I tell him, 'my life would be like a prison.' It used to be.

Gavin regards me coldly. 'And I don't intend to risk real prison, should you lose your book of scribbles.'

I tear open the door. Standing so close to the threshold, the inn owner wobbles.

'Mrs Madge.'

'I am not Mrs Madge.' Not anymore. A glint of vindication, self-righteous satisfaction, momentarily makes her dull eyes bright. I push past her, stumbling down the steep staircase and leaving her appeasement in Gavin's highly capable hands. He'll have no problem winning her over, I'm sure. Jonnie's barking has ceased, and the abrupt silence sets my ears ringing. My notebook remains clenched in my hand, still open at the offending page.

Darkness has fallen fully as I stride out into the snow. The landscape glows, otherworldly mounds of white looming at me through ghoulish shadows. I have no coat and only flimsy shoes fit for London. My stockings dampen, cool moisture creeping up my calves as I struggle to move my feet. I feel my thin blouse billowing in the iced night air, chills seeping through the inadequate fabric until my flesh erupts in goose pimples. Having fought through a foot of snow to reach the far end of the village green, I turn back to see that the inn owner – her own room kept warm enough for the windows to stay clear – has already returned to her post. I knew Gavin would deal with her sort quickly. The woman spots me and stares, without moving to offer help. I suspect she thinks whores do not deserve it. What would she say if she knew the Major does not even want me for his whore?

I start to run, as much as anyone can through these packed, powdered flakes. Is he following? I cross a field before I check, lest Gavin think it is easy giving me chase. I turn to peer through the sinister, supernatural gloom. The only footprints are my own. This land is rugged, coarse and less well kept than the green; rogue stalks stick out from the snowdrift, their tiny frostbitten flowers frozen in mid-air. Framed by jagged ice silhouettes, their sharp edges pierce and ladder my nylons. Even a pinprick of pain is no longer pleasurable. Narrow trees line the horizon, their spindling bare limbs extended like talons ready to swipe and claw as if attempting to pull down the moon.

'Why can't he trust me? Why can't he have faith in me?' I shout the words, beseeching the night air to answer. All I receive in reply is a brief haze of breath, faint fog hovering momentarily in front of my eyes before it evaporates into the dark. *Why can't he want me?* Even alone, I dare not speak that one aloud.

Labouring towards the trees, I hear water: rushing, tumbling and occasionally dragging as if caught on a strange sticking point. I batter through the criss-crossed branches, forcing the snow to part with vicious kicks from my sodden soles. I have reached the river. And the bridge. Ice has cast its paralysing spell over the water and whole blocks of it are set adrift. Translucent bergs of brightness, floating eerily through the black, are becoming jammed on the bridge's underside; cold water cascading over their gloss-slickened tops until the pressure causes them to crack.

Shoes slipping, the rough brick barrier digging into my palms, I make it to the centre. This is where he and I stood as children. Alone together. I bend over the side, tipping far enough for it to feel frightening. The churning, swirling waters are in shadow. I cannot see my reflection. My notebook is still in my hands and I raise it to rest on the edge, peering to make out the open page that Gavin could not bring himself to touch. Snowflakes have stained it, speckled droplets causing the ink to run. Soon, my tears join them. The words that cut through us, perhaps only one word, become blurred and smudged. Meaningless.

I bend my head to the bricks, dishevelled hair snagging on the rougher stones. I should throw myself in. Surrender to the grappling weed tendrils; let them drag me down into the cold depths of muddied filth and grim, soiled nothingness. The violent notion surges through me, fast-flowing and foolish. There is one thing a mother must never do. Even a mother like me knows that. Feeling my way, numb fingers struggling to find my notebook's sewn spine and well-worn fragile leaves, I work to tear out the page that has torn Gavin and me apart. Crushing it within my shaking fist, I raise it over the side and let it fall. Light though it is, I fancy I hear it tumble into the water or, more likely, it is the sound of another iced slab about to break. For a few moments, my pulse pounds in my eardrums, grip tightening around what remains of my book and fingernails sinking into its tattered leather binds. With a scream, the howl half-exertion and half-grief, I hurl the rest into the river.

I return to the inn soaked and shivering, so pathetically bedraggled that even the owner has no heart to throw me out. With a fresh towel in her arms and the curl of a sneer on her lips, she shows me to a single room – really a cupboard with a bed wedged in – that is across the hall from Gavin. Teasing out wet tangles of hair and wondering whether I will be colder with my drenched blouse on or off, I do not expect to be able to sleep. Gingerly, I lay back on the hard mattress, head throbbing, body aching. As I close my eyes, I realise my lashes have frozen solid. Still, the chilled exhaustion works to numb my racing brain, and eventually I drift off into a fitful, frightening dream. I am at Sandaig. I have never seen it, of course, except through Gavin's eyes, but as always, that feels like enough. The cottage is a distant white speck nestling on the coast like a shoreline bird. The clear burn flows in a ring around the landscape until its path marries the waves, carried off into the wild embrace of the ocean. But there are wooden railings around the house, high spear-tipped struts guarding the perimeter. Whichever direction I take, whatever angle I attempt, I cannot get in.

Morning brings about a thaw. The roads clear; the temperature mild enough for trains and buses to run. I journey to Winifred's alone.

Chapter Nine

'Post,' Winifred calls. 'There's one for you.' Contemplating her latest windowsill painting, an experience more than equal in pleasure to looking out of her garden window itself, I set down what remains of my breakfast cup of tea. Still tepid, I feel reluctant to relinquish it, just as I am cautious about removing the chunky woollen cardigan I did, eventually, get the chance to unpack. I never want to feel cold again. Even so, a fresh chill runs through me when I recognise Gavin's handwriting. Intense and richly calligraphic, brown not black ink as if forwarded from another era. The smudged corner postmark is stamped from Mallaig, the final port town he passes before retreating into the wild West Highlands. I wonder if the serenity of Sandaig has worked its magic once more.

'Forgive me for my cowardice,' he writes inside. 'I do not have your courage.' Persuasive strokes of his pen sink into the heavy-weight ivory paper, the voice so clear and unmistakably his that I feel he could be here, whispering each word. 'Love, Gavin.'

'It's from him, isn't it?' Nothing escapes an artist's eye.

'It is.' I have told Winifred we quarrelled, but not why. If I could go into detail, we would not have quarrelled in the first place. 'He asks me to forgive him.'

Winifred raises an eyebrow like she has spotted a blot on her canvas. 'And will you?'

'I already have.' White-hot rage can only burn for so long, and raking through the raw embers, I am starting to glimpse again that bright glimmer of gold: the link between our souls that is surely strong enough to survive all earthly misunderstandings. Miles apart and unable to share what we see and feel, the past three weeks have not felt like a typical lovers' tiff or even an emotional fracture between family members. Brother and sister, husband and wife: no relationship between two people feels right for describing us anymore. Gavin is within me, not without. In conflict, I am not separated from him so much as severed from some vital part of myself. Not to reconcile, not to try to understand him, would be like

66

abandoning an aspect of my own spirit to darkness. Two branches of one rowan. That is the simplest way I can describe who we are now.

I am new to this, I remind myself, and I cannot always appreciate how hard it must be for him. Being the way that he is. The daily fears he has to combat; the constant threat of shame against which he has to defend himself. And Gavin – his name reappears so readily in my mind as a source of joy, its letters glinting in the winter sun of Winifred's garden and gathering in the loose swirl of our tea leaves – Gavin is equally inexperienced when it comes to being a real writer. Yes, his *Harpoon* publication day is imminent and Rupert delights in his new golden boy, but he is still a relative novice to the life of literary devotion I lead. He cannot yet comprehend the depth of my impulse to depict what I love in words. In truth, the soulful necessity of it. Next time, I'll express it and myself better. I'll make it easier for Gavin to grasp.

'Forgive me too …' Borrowing paper from Winifred, I write back immediately, spoiling the first attempt in my haste to set it all down. Hurrying to the village pillar box to beat the lunchtime collection – Winifred tells me that service is prompt here and I don't want to take any chances – I feel relief that I am not obliged to reply with a lie. *Forgive me?* Whether I felt it or not, it is increasingly hard to imagine refusing Gavin anything. As it is, I feel only hopeful again. Happy again. Warm. Winter won't last forever.

By the time I return to London, our winged messengers are airborne once more, migrating birds turned to telegrams that carry through the air our mutual affection and shared optimism for spring. Back in the city, the cruelness of Kielder's cold seems remote, more like a splintered fragment from my horrid wooden fence nightmare. Here, there is always heat to be had, however unglamorous the source: coal fires and scratching scarves, boiling pipes and thick street smog. What remains of the pain, I turn into poetry, beginning a new notebook and telling myself that I would not have wanted to return to the old one anyway. I keep the new book on my person and my references to Gavin opaque. If privately I regret the loss of my work, the latent dregs of a Methodist conscience remind me to hold my temper in better check next time. Act in haste, repent at leisure. I wish I could be sure this is the last time I will have to learn that lesson.

Fortuitously, or maybe miraculously, Tambi manages to locate copies of my entire *Northumbrian Sequence*, although when it transpires that they sit atop a teetering pile of his unpaid bills, I suspect a part of him wishes he had not. Nevertheless, we formulate plans for a new full collection, rooting the sequence that began with the shared rowan tree vision at its heart. *The Year One* will be the title. Life really is beginning again.

'So, it's a yes? Say it's a yes, Kathie.' Before Gavin and I left on our ill-fated trip, I had told Tambi of my ideas about William Blake, and with typical enthusiasm he proceeded to tell just about everyone else. I return to London to find him wafting a British Council invitation, asking me to write the Blake pamphlet for their new *Writers and their Work* series. Academia. Not quite my intended path, but still in sight of my true direction. Writing poetry and writing about poetry are not so far removed from one another. Are they? Besides, I feel excited to share the new knowledge, or rather the new wisdom, that I have discovered. There are subtle, significant threads of thought that I can see woven through Blake's work, pulling together philosophy, art and religion, as well as his own intensely spiritual vision. My findings are purified, I decide, by being a poet first and foremost. It soon becomes apparent that I have more than enough material for a pamphlet. In fact, I am coming to think there will be enough to turn into a book. Not before Gavin's though. His book comes first.

The *Harpoon* launch – how nice to be reunited, we say, so we can laugh at weak puns like that – is taking place in a swish two-storey bookshop only yards from Rupert's office. The centre of London and the literary establishment, or so it seems as the great and the good of publishing start fishing for invites, flooding Gavin with requests for review copies and sending letters of congratulations cascading through his studio letterbox. Friends gather around as the anticipation builds, new acquaintances following on from old like rapidly expanding ripples. I must admit I didn't realise he was so popular, although it should not surprise me when I know his character and charms like I do. Reading name after name inside the cards of his well-wishers, some recognised but many not, I feel grateful that what we share goes deeper than these fair-weather associations.

'Imagine this many people interested in shark fishing,' Gavin exclaims, carrying in the latest thick wad of correspondence from the morning post. Rising on slightly stiff back legs, Jonnie does his best to assist his master, conveying one envelope after another via his impeccably soft if somewhat salivary muzzle. Make-believing the letters are mallards, I wonder? A few reach Gavin's hands wetter than their senders intended, but not one envelope is crushed by the gentle folds of Jonnie's mouth.

'It's not the fishing they're interested in,' I correct Gavin. 'It's you.' He beams at me, joyful and genuine, and I feel myself warmed, caught up in the stream of bright light that is simply radiating from him. His pleasure is magnetic, a sparkling energy that pulls me towards him as powerfully as ever before, and by the time I leave his flat on the evening before the 'big day', I am vicariously charged by proximity to a literal literary dream coming true. Gavin has no need of my Buddha's ear these days. I write a wish for him, even so.

An hour before the party – Rupert calls it an opening, although I am more used to book openings involving creased spines than champagne – I meet Gavin outside the bookshop to watch the window display taking shape. Improbably, perhaps from their smaller sister premises near the Thames, the staff have acquired a rowing boat. Although nothing like the Sea Leopard aboard which Gavin and his crew actually worked, it takes pride of place in the shop window, stuffed with sufficient copies of his book to undoubtedly sink if ever put to sea.

'Goodness.'

'Goodness,' Gavin agrees. Entering the shop, he reaches into his overcoat and produces a brown paper parcel wrapped with string. 'Wait until you see what I found,' he whispers, tugging to hurriedly untie the bow. 'It was in that little antique bookshop near Paultons. You know the one?' I do. Gavin opens his hands to reveal a small volume. Its red leather binding has turned burgundy with time's passage, gold leaf pages as thin and translucent as those of a family Bible handed down through generations. Gavin flicks past the cover page and I stare in surprise. What had appeared merely unusual turns out to be entirely unique. An authentic tribute to Victorian botany, this is no printed book but rather a personal journal, the painstakingly handwritten descriptions of an anonymous seaside enthusiast set out beside every specimen discussed. Genuine seaweed samples have been affixed to its pages with astonishing attention to detail; twisted curls of deep red and fragile fronds of dark green perfectly preserved by the leaves onto which they were pressed far back in the previous century.

'It's incredible,' I tell Gavin, stroking a softly crinkled piece of kelp with one light, tentative finger.

'It is.' With a grin, he rips out the seaweed cleanly. Moves to the next page. And the next. Calling for string and the bookshop manager's assistance, Gavin starts pinning samples around the display window frame, letting the pieces hang until they ripple around his book. 'So lucky I found it in time, don't you think?' Unable to speak, I simply nod. Standing motionless, somehow holding out this irreplaceable little book for him while he works, I feel the remnants of what was a smile pulling taut across my cheekbones.

*

The night itself is a triumph. Guests assemble until the space becomes standing room only, Gavin reading a vivid passage from *Harpoon* just as he once did for Rupert and me. Just as we were, his audience is entranced. By the end of the evening, Gavin jokes with me that his hand is cramping from having signed so many copies. It turns out there are some problems of literary life that even I have never come across before.

We relive his success in his studio the next day. Sniggering together, we gossip briefly about Elias being so strangely quiet. With nothing negative to say, I suspect he found himself in the unexpected position of having nothing to say at all. My personal highlight, however, was when a British Council member called me into an encouragingly intense conversation about my work, asking in-depth questions on Blake and wondering aloud whether I had given thought to a longer piece? After the man left in search of champagne, I had cast my gaze across a room crowded with both friends and strangers, unable to see Gavin but sure something of his presence would inevitably draw my eye. A small upright piano had made an unlikely appearance and some wit was taking it upon himself to give a turn of 'Mac the Knife'.

> *Oh the shark has pretty teeth, dear,*
> *And he shows them pearly white ...*

I spotted Gavin soon after at the centre of a circle composed of loudly loquacious new acquaintances. Fair hair princely amongst the blacks and browns; his posture poised and refined compared with their hunched or sloping shoulders. By coincidence, or perhaps our strange telepathy, Gavin turned towards me in that instant. Raising his glass, he gave me a wink and a wide smile.

'"So, what's next?"' I tease him now, mimicking the many members of the literary elite who put that question to him last night. '"Not intending to stay with Rupert for your second book, are you?" They were circling you like sharks.'

'Actually, sharks don't circle when they hunt,' Gavin tells me. 'They tend to attack from below.'

'Then what shall we call those people?' I persist. 'Limpets?' Far be it from me to discard a good nautical metaphor prematurely. 'They certainly want to stick to your success.'

That same broad smile as before. 'I only need you to stick with me.'

Jonnie has been snoring contentedly at our ankles while we speak, choosing to forgo the plush comfort of his basket in favour of staying as close as possible to Gavin. Now the dog gives a snort, back leg muscles spasming in quick succession, and he half awakens from his slumber with a low, rumbling moan. Instinctively, I bend to stroke him, hoping that the touch of a comforting hand will coax him back into his dreams.

'Whose are these?' A pair of women's gloves has fallen beneath the sofa. Not mine, needless to say. They feel expensive as I pick them up, slim tapering fingers crafted from luxurious cream leather.

Gavin seems uninterested. 'I suppose they must be Clement's.'

'Clement Glock?' There must be more than one woman in London with that first name, although it often doesn't feel like it. An incessant hum of gossip surrounds this particular queen bee, which even I, resentful of any interruption by the anodyne drones of the social swarm, have been unable to ignore. Clement Glock is stylish. Striking. Androgynous in an attractive way, with hair cropped to show off her bone structure and suiting her occasional forays into paint-splattered men's slacks whenever creating a new stage set. She works – she doesn't have to, naturally, but she wants to – at the Royal Opera House; a beautiful building of tall pillars and glass domes, every bit as elegantly imposing as Clement herself. She is married and renowned, or rather notorious, for her glamorous affairs. And wasn't she once a dancer? I imagine gazelle-like legs easily extending over a ballet barre and feel like a squat Shetland pony by comparison. 'When was she here?' Eliminate the impossible. That's what Sherlock Holmes advises. Relationships with women, at least relationships of the sort that Clement has with her men, are impossible for Gavin. I ought to know.

'A few days ago.'

'Alone?' An irrational wave of envy washes over me, so visceral that my intellect is momentarily submerged. Their meeting must have been innocent – although I doubt that word is often used to describe Clement – and yet I feel a possessive, animalistic outrage at the thought of her pretty pointe shoes or worse, her faux bohemian bare soles, setting foot in this flat.

'She came with Aymer. Didn't I mention?'

'No.' Let the wave flow through and away from me. Act in haste, repent at leisure. Remember? Gavin has nothing to hide from me. He would hide nothing from me. Didn't I fight through storm and snow, didn't I almost freeze to death, in my desperation to win his trust? I swing my legs to the side of the sofa so as not to reawaken Jonnie. 'Anyway, I have to go. I'm sorry.' At home, I can gather my emotions out of sight, or if I fail, chastise myself in peace for letting my imagination run wild. Pathetically, I do not want Gavin to see my complexion in this unflattering shade of green.

'Why? What's wrong?' He looks concerned, notes a selfish sliver of my mind. 'Kathleen, what is it?'

'Women's troubles.' I blurt it out stupidly, the only excuse I can think of in time that is certain of doing the trick. And it does. Gavin looks suitably aghast. His cheeks pale, then faintly flush, and he asks me nothing more.

Soon, great social buzz surrounds the fact that Clement has indeed been having an affair with Aymer. Shocking even for her, she has separated from her husband. She and Aymer elope to Paris – abscond may be a better word – and on their return to England they announce their engagement. The gloves can be forgotten, I realise with relief, the threat they represent dropped just as easily as they were by the woman herself. Gavin stuffs the pair into a little-used bureau drawer, in case Clement returns to collect them. I make surreptitious checks when I can. She never comes back to his flat.

Chapter Ten

'Lock?'

'Loch.'

'Lochuh?'

'No, loch. Roll your tongue.' Gavin swivels to show me his tongue tucked behind his bottom teeth. I shriek as the Bentley swerves.

'Look out.'

'No, loch out! Try it again.' A comical severity takes over his face, brows furrowed by the same strictness that I imagine in the schoolmasters who so petrified him at boarding school. The threat of being beaten with a cricket bat will do that to a boy. I hope that, unlike mine, those tutors weren't simultaneously trying to stifle their laughter.

'Locchr,' is my next attempt. Gavin shakes his head in mock dismay.

'And you, the daughter of a Scotswoman. Mrs Raine would be ashamed.' As if she isn't already ashamed of me. Two divorces will do that to a girl. But I refuse to think of such things today. I will think instead of the tree-trimmed ribbon of road that is rapidly unravelling before us. I will taste the salt-heavy hint of seashore coasting in from only a couple of miles away. I will listen to the woodwind notes of the wild birds, beckoning us through the forest they and their families call home. I will think of this journey and the man taking me on it.

'Mother asked especially for you to join us at Monreith.' Gavin's right hand is outstretched, catching the full force of the breeze as the Bentley powers past the ancient trees sheltering his family estate from the outside world. Sheltering it, I suppose, from prying peasant eyes like mine.

'Did she really?' I find it difficult to imagine the regal Lady Mary making such a request. In truth, it feels hard to conceive of anything, beyond her obvious adoration of Gavin, hiding behind that unfailingly serene half-smile.

'Of course.' Gavin turns to me again and the car twists with the camber. 'When have I ever lied to you? I suspect she couldn't stand it after I said you'd never attended a Burns supper.' 25th January 1953. The anniversary of Robert Burns' birth. Also Virginia Woolf's, according to today's newspaper, although I am certainly not going to think about her. Dutiful son that he is, Gavin arrived back in his homeland several days earlier, while I took the train up from London alone, willing the admittedly striking scenery to pass quickly so I might hasten towards the moment when he would collect me from Newton Stewart station. The ride gave me a rare opportunity to let Blake take a figurative back seat, allowing the undulating amethyst hills and bristling emerald forests to unearth what I hope will become poetic treasures of my own. The train's momentum lulled me into new rhythms, its hisses and clicks punctuating each line as my mind roamed through the unpeopled landscape just beyond my carriage window, transfiguring that fleeting view into forms that could be permanently preserved on the page. Draft down, I added a tiny dedication beneath the title. *'For G.M.'* Although I won't show it to Gavin until it is ready this time. A discomfiting twinge of sadness had hit me when the train swept past the surrounding lands of Kielder, its slumbering hills still dusted with snow-like feathers left after a pillow fight. Nostalgia is how I chose to reframe the feeling. Tender, bittersweet fondness for a place that now belongs firmly in the past. It is why our return went awry, I've come to realise, why as adults we could not successfully retrace our steps to our childhood spiritual sanctuary. We ought never to have tried. Except through poetry, perhaps.

'Would you like anything, Miss?' A young boy pushing a confectionary cart had interrupted my musings with a light knock on the carriage door. The 'Miss' alone was enough to make me smile. It is almost exclusively 'Madam' these days.

'I have everything I need, thank you.' And I did, as soon as I saw, or rather heard, the Bentley's predatory purr awaiting me at the station.

'I'd thought you would send a chauffeur,' I told Gavin, feeling exceedingly glad he had not.

'Oh, Mother got rid of him as soon as I learned to drive,' he laughed, before frowning at the impending irritation of a tractor up ahead of us. It did not stay ahead for long. 'She said she'd never need anyone else but me.' Now, as my personal chauffeur – and who can blame Lady Mary for seeing no need for another? – speeds us towards Monreith, I continue trying and failing to roll my Scots 'r's. Eyes to the skies, I call mentally upon my Celtic ancestors for their assistance. A few fat droplets of rain are their pointedly dour response.

74

'So, what happens at a Burns supper?' I ask Gavin, tugging my scarf until it covers my hair more thoroughly. Windswept does not work for me, another lesson I learned from the snowstorm, and with an inferior pedigree weighing me down, I have no wish to give his mother an extra reason to think me uncouth. 'Will there be bagpipes?'

'Och no.' That voice, a melodic mingling of country house and countryside, dips into broad Scots with surprising ease. The sole goal is to make me laugh, and as in almost everything else Gavin does, he succeeds. 'My brother Eustace isn't allowed to play his pipes anymore,' he tells me after reverting to his typical accent. 'Banned for life. There will be an Address to the Haggis though.' Those last words catch my interest just in time, before I succumb to pondering the mystery of Eustace Maxwell, whom I have yet to meet, and his strictly prohibited pipes.

'How does one address a haggis? What exactly is a haggis, for that matter?' Some sort of meat, I recall, without remembering which one. I should have telephoned my mother before I left, cramming what local knowledge I could from her ephemeral memories of youth.

'Ah, the haggis.' Gavin's eyes gleam, blue glittering in mischief. 'A funny wee creature. It's rare to spot one during the daytime, although naturally they've been bred on the estate for centuries.'

'Naturally.' The gleam becomes a glint.

We seem to be travelling along a private road now. Perhaps we always were. The path weaves, tall evergreen firs tightening on either side until only slivers of winter sun can squeeze through their bristled branches. Gavin slows – slow for him, that is, which is still too fast for any other driver unless either their engine or their person had caught fire – and one final spin of the steering wheel sets us on course for the approach to the house.

Circles. Monreith is composed of circles, great Georgian rings of blond sandstone spreading out towards the onlooker in a dazzling display of affluence. Sandaig, too, is a place of spheres. Voice lilting in his joy, Gavin speaks often of the way that the burn ripples around the cottage there. And yet this house, this mansion, has none of that natural peacefulness. These circles are closed; cut from stone, not flowing with water. They do not blend or unite. They define inside from out. Coils of ivy creep up the entrance pillars, curving over the façade and framing its long rows of imposing windows. The shade they cast makes the house seem secretive and almost suspicious. Not a place into which a stranger would dare to wander without invitation.

'Last night, I dreamt I went to Monreith again.'

'Hm?'

'Never mind.' A few more raindrops bounce off my headscarf. Travelling closer, my attention is drawn to a flagpole erected on Monreith's roof, Scots Lion Rampant billowing red and yellow in the breeze. In London, the only flag one sees regularly is that of Buckingham Palace. It is flown, if my memory for trivia still serves, to tell the public that Her Majesty is in residence.

'Is your mother at home?'

'Should be,' Gavin nods. 'Can't think where else she'd be, without me to drive her. I should say, this land – and the loch' – while he speaks, I practice silently, and in my head I deliver the word perfectly – 'has belonged to the Maxwells since 1482.' I remember Aymer sharing the same fact with a beautiful Clement-like blonde during our first meeting. Now, Gavin's hand sweeps over our heads in a gesture that I understand is meant to encompass the whole estate. As far as the eye can see. Quite a bit further, in fact. I wonder what my ancestors were doing in 1482? I suspect I'll never know, because they almost certainly could not write. Probably some had the plague.

'Although,' Gavin goes on, 'this house wasn't the original. That was Myrton Castle, our ancient seat. Quite a travesty when they pulled it down to use as the bones for this place. Seeking a more "genteel residence",' he adds somewhat scornfully. 'The castle ruins are still there in the forest.'

'Did you have hundreds of servants growing up?' I decide to pursue the only angle from which my ancestors might theoretically have crossed paths with his.

Gavin looks shocked. 'Heavens, no. Only nine.'

'Nine?'

He starts counting with the fingers of both hands. Instinctively, I reach over to take the wheel.

'Let's see … Butler. Cook. Chauffeur, till I was seventeen. Nurse. Nursery maid. Housemaid. Under housemaid. Pantry boy and kitchen maid. And a governess. Wait, that's ten. Wave!'

Before I know it, I am waving at an elderly man in an oversized tweed suit. The long double barrel of a shotgun rests against his shoulder – is there no upper age limit beyond which men are stopped from wielding such weapons? – and he stands to rigid attention as soon as he spots our approaching car.

'That's Hannam, the gamekeeper.'

'Eleven.'

'Eleven what?'

'Eleven servants, Gavin.' I keep my voice lowered as we screech to a stop next to the old gentleman, although locked in his militaristic drill stance – Dad's army, at the least – Hannam shows no sign of hearing.

'Ah, but a gamekeeper's different. Han-nam!' Gavin bellows, enunciating each syllable as one might do for an aged relative, 'this is my friend, Kath-leen. I told you about her ear-li-er, remember? She wants to hear about the haggis you've caught for tonight.'

The earthy black furrows that line Hannam's face sprout into sudden merriment.

'Master Gavin, dinnae ye tease tha poor lassie.' He guffaws heartily, a wheeze lingering on each exhale, before turning to me with his watery eyes twinkling. 'Why, haggis isna onything mair than a sheep's offal. Her heart, her liver an her lungs.'

'Sounds delicious,' I say hoarsely. Hannam continues to chortle. When we drive on towards the house, waving goodbye as we go, I worry that he will respond likewise and risk losing his precarious balance or, Heaven forbid, detonating his shotgun. Instead, the aged gentleman presses a hand to the peak of his cap, tugging where a forelock should be to give a subtle salute to Gavin.

At the house, the circles continue. Trotting up shallow sandstone steps, Gavin heaves open the oak doors. It is a job I would have guessed should fall to a servant, but if so, Gavin lacks the patience to wait for them. Wood panels part to reveal an astonishing large rounded atrium.

'Mother?' As if magicked by the word, Lady Mary appears with one hand lightly gracing the balustrade. The staircase loops from one floor to the next, and as she descends to our level, I realise that the portrait on the first landing is her own. When she moves, subject and object are set in direct, disorientating alignment. The double image gives me the curious sensation of having drunk too much, whilst knowing myself to be stone sober and ironically in need of Dutch courage.

'Kathleen.' Cool hands extended. Kisses almost but not quite touching my cheeks. 'I particularly hoped you'd be able to join us.' I sense Gavin smirking in my peripheral vision, the cheeky trace of a told-you-so smile on his face. His mother embraces him before I get the chance to enjoy it properly, squeezing with an intensity that would suggest a year's, and not only an hour's, absence from her company. Thus excused, or more accurately excluded, I take the opportunity to look around. I have the distinct feeling of everything being above me. Guns again, wall-mounted with brass brackets; white porcelain busts on high columns that look like Plato but may be Percys. Ornate ceiling cornices and branched chandeliers; a towering statue of an eagle, its outstretched wing feathers tipped with gold. The Maxwell family emblem, according to my own 'white hawk'.

'Fidelitas is free.' When I refocus, Gavin's mother is looking at me expectantly, anticipating a reply that I have no idea how to give.

'I'm sorry?'

'Your bedroom,' Gavin elucidates. 'They're all named.'

'Or Concordia, if you'd prefer?' Lady Mary adds, and I panic in the belief that my hesitation came across as dissatisfaction.

'Fidelitas will be lovely, I'm sure,' I garble. 'Thank you.' My mind scrambles to piece together the cracked mosaic of my girlhood Latin. Father was adamant all future schoolmistresses should have it. *Fidelitas.* Faithfulness. I suppose I am nothing if not faithful to Gavin.

Lady Mary tilts her head in the direction of the staircase, the move so understated that one could not be certain of having seen it, yet somehow definite enough that her meaning is not mistaken. 'Show her, Gavin.'

'Yes, Mother.'

'Where's Jonnie?' I ask when we are tackling the second flight of spiral stairs. Every window we pass reveals yet more winter greenery and Gavin seems strangely incomplete in a rural setting without an animal sidekick at his heels.

'Sandaig,' he says. 'He's so settled up there, it seemed unfair at his age to bring him back for a short time. Mary MacLeod, the roadmender's wife, is wonderful with animals, and she's fallen utterly in love with Jondog too. She'll take good care of him until I return.' He halts us in front of a white wooden door. 'Fidelitas' is engraved onto a ceramic plate above the frame.

'Home sweet home.' Gavin strides inside, ignoring various examples of intricately carved furniture – a large wardrobe, two deep chests, and a lavish four-poster bed – in favour of the view. 'I'm glad Mother gave you this one,' he remarks, hands pressing into the windowsill as if straining to break through the glass. 'Even if it is the smallest.' Smallest? 'From here, you can almost see Elrig.' Gavin points towards the forest, his fingertip leaving a minuscule smudge. I hope a maid will not be scolded for it. 'Seven miles or so from here, straight through those trees. That's where I was born, the house I truly loved growing up.' I feel faintly alarmed at how Gavin speaks of having a favourite among his childhood homes in the way that I might describe having one among my books. Still, the worry pales in comparison with my interest in hearing about his childhood. It is not usually a topic on which he enjoys elaborating.

'I don't think I was ever happier than then. Before school, before … everything.' Gavin leans forward, forehead pressing into the pane. 'Playing barefoot in the bracken, breaking free beyond the gardens to discover a natural world so untamed. So untouched. So free.' Sadness seeps into his tone like the draught I can feel from the sash window. 'Adulthood can be a prison, don't you think?' Prison. He has mentioned that word before. My thoughts drift back to the Buddha sitting on my mantelpiece, to the wishes through which I hope always to keep Gavin safe. Personally, I prefer being an adult to a child, or perhaps, the relative freedom I have now compared with being dependent on either my parents or my husbands, but as Gavin turns, I nod in agreement. I hate the thought of him feeling alone.

'I wrote a poem on the train,' I tell him.

'I'd expect nothing less.' Blue eyes bright. 'I bet it's wonderful.'

'It's for you,' I say. 'For you, not about you.' A rather clever compromise, if I do say so myself. Gavin grins and I feel my heart flip.

'Thank you,' he says. 'Although I'm sure I don't deserve it.' Before I can disagree – which I do, of course – he has withdrawn to the bedroom doorway. 'I had better give you a few minutes to settle in. See you downstairs?' I nod again and watch him go.

Alone, I move back to the window, focusing on the clustered forest branches as if, with enough persuasion, they might part and reveal the House of Elrig to me. Needless to say, they stay literally unmoved. I can, however, see the edge of the lake – the loch – and my eyes flow from the still, silvery expanse of water in the distance to the well-tended gardens of Monreith below. Looking down on the terrace, I stare for several seconds to process a sight that scarcely seems possible. I blink twice. It stays put. What would appear on the ground as unremarkable garden growth is an entire sentence written in short-cut hedge. 'The days of man are but as grass.' Psalm 102. Thank you, Father. The days aren't grass if you own this place, I think, rising to the balls of my feet to try and make my forehead fit where Gavin's was. Taking root here, his family have made themselves immortal.

Back down the spiral staircase, I meet more Maxwells. Eustace, the ebullient middle brother who is banned from the bagpipes, shakes my hand in an aggressively enthusiastic welcome that only stops when he can no longer resist the impulse to punch Gavin hard on the upper arm. Then there is Christian, the sole sister of the family. Quiet and almost translucently fair, I like her immediately, despite or perhaps because of the fact that she feels like she has one foot in another, intangible world. An artist, Gavin has told me, as well as a secret Communist. Secret from Lady Mary, at any rate. Aymer, too, is here; the sibling most like Gavin and with whom he seems to share many of the same notes, albeit played in different keys. They call Aymer 'Max' here to distinguish him from his late father, so in a funny way he feels like a new person too.

'Four children in four years,' Gavin murmurs as we move from the family group. 'Imagine how many of us there would be if father had lived.' One of him is more than enough for me.

Clement has also come to Monreith, as Aymer's guest, and is every bit as intimidatingly elegant in person as I'd feared. I lack even the consolation of telling myself that she is frivolous or foolish: in the shadow of the Opera House, Mrs Glock has creative clout of her own in a far more performative way than me. Physically, she seems angled where I am soft, refined where I am coarse, and I am dwarfed when she draws nearer to shake my hand.

'Pleasure,' she observes, in a tone that suggests anything but. Fresh from a tour of the gardens, her hand is gloved again. Navy this time, but the same smooth leather as before. I watch intently as Gavin greets her, hawk-like myself. He is civil and charming, but no more so than with any other woman. Any other than me. The woman in his life.

There is another couple too, a pair of family friends.

'Edward and Lavinia Renton,' Gavin tells me as we watch them chat cheerfully with his mother across the room: a man with unmistakable military bearing and a delicate blonde who looks to be in her late twenties at most. 'Ted and I were in the Special Forces together. He's trying to cut it as a conductor now.' I find myself more interested in the wife than the husband. Lavinia reminds me of the storybook princesses Anna used to adore, despite my best efforts to distract her from feminised tropes. Yet this young woman is not a two-dimensional drawing but exceptionally pretty flesh and blood, from her dainty nose and kind eyes to a self-possessed style of carriage that a plebeian person like me could never emulate. From afar, I watch the trio talk and laugh together, Edward wrapping his arm around his wife's slender waist.

'All for show,' Gavin mutters. 'Everyone knows they're on the rocks. Ted's rather a complex character.'

'Imagine that,' I reply, although I don't think Gavin hears the irony.

Chapter Eleven

After a silent stream of servants has delivered platters of circle-cut sandwiches for tea – apparently, no 'afternoon' prefix is necessary for those who call even a casual evening meal their 'supper' – the men go out walking. Or is it stalking? I can't deny that I am struggling to take it all in. The moment they leave, Lavinia politely excuses herself to retire upstairs with a headache. I don't ask where Clement chooses to go. I don't want to know.

'Come with me, my dear.' Lady Mary lays her cold fingertips on my wrist. 'There are things I should like you to see.' I walk with her down the hallway – no, not *the* hallway, *a* hallway – and any bearings I had are rapidly lost to disorientation. I resolve to use artwork as landmarks, but their interchangeable subjects soon prove as useless as Hansel and Gretel's breadcrumbs. A black flat-coat retriever with a dead duck in its jaws. A square-headed springer spaniel – Jonnie's grandfather? – carrying the corpse of another bird whose species I cannot determine, although I am sure Gavin could tell me. Various portraits of Imperial officers flanked by passive, blank-faced manservants. 'Natives,' I take it, whose expressions were not thought worth filling in.

Two maids appear, their arms full of pristine folded linens. Didn't Gavin say there was only one?

'M'lady,' they murmur in unison as they curtsey to Mary, so skilfully synchronised that my own knees knock together instinctively. Maybe an echo of my peasant ancestry is alive within my bone marrow.

Mary pauses us at an alcove, within which sits a single photograph. 'My Aymer,' she whispers, her softened gaze resting on the serious, stiff-upper-lip gentleman inside the frame. A handlebar moustache tops off his military uniform, the silk sash running from shoulder to hip broken only by the glittering discs of his many medals. Static and seemingly unyielding as he looks in this photograph, I find that I can imagine the late Sir Aymer Maxwell in motion, if only because of the cacophony it would create. Regalia chiming as buttons struck against battle decorations; silver

82

spurs clinking in time with each heel-led marching step. I lean in as close as I dare to search for Gavin's features in the father he never knew. I find few. The ears, perhaps. A furious focus glimpsed when Gavin suspects that the fates have conspired against him, like the Bentley's tyres sunk into snow. Yet his eyes are inherited from his mother. Just like his nose, his fair hair, and the narrow elegance of his profile.

'After it happened,' Mary's sights stay fixed on Sir Aymer but I nod sympathetically nonetheless, 'I could never have coped without him.' She seems well aware that she need not specify Gavin's name. Perhaps the sole thing we have in common is how often our thoughts turn to the same man. 'No love is stronger than a mother's for her son,' Mary muses.

'Or her daughter,' I add. Advocating for Anna as well as for Christian. Mary turns to me, icily intrigued. Like Gavin's, her eyes are ocean blue, but Arctic rather than Atlantic.

'That's right,' she murmurs. 'You have two children by your former marriage.'

We move into what feels like a portrait gallery: a long arch-ceilinged hallway with paintings peering down at me from either side. Too heavy to hang unsupported, many are suspended from gold chain harnesses that glint like cobwebs illuminated by the sun. Not that I have seen any real webs haunting Monreith's thoroughly dusted hallways. Mary guides me along this great row of Gavin's ancestors; generations of aristocrats going back in time from top hats and breeches to brocade doublets and concertina ruffs. I even spot a codpiece or two. From pose alone, it is clear their owners did not wish them to be easy to miss. Mary pauses in front of a Victorian wedding day scene, the lace-bedecked bride demurely taking the hand of her groom who wears an elaborate white silk waistcoat. The next picture must be of their crest, its harsh red and black design less heraldic than jingoistic.

'Our families have always married well. It makes all the difference in life when one finds an equal.'

'A marriage of true minds?' Mary's smile stays put, although the muscles around it tighten and twinge. At the end of the passageway, an architectural mirror image of the alcove where the late Sir Aymer's photograph resides, I can see another golden eagle. Rather, an eagle made from gold. Enormous wings outstretched, it sits above a large gilt-lettered etching of the Maxwell family motto. *'Reviresco.'* I shall rise again. It had sounded spiritual when Gavin first mentioned it, a rousing

83

call to resilience that I felt could only do him good to remember. But here, in this familial hall of fame, the message seems oddly strategic. A modus operandi for accumulating greater status and riches. Generation by generation, marriage by marriage. The Maxwells rising again, further out of sight and reach.

'It took time for me to feel at home here,' Mary confides, letting her fingers dance over the dips and ridges of the eagle's expansive wing feathers. I'd never dare to touch them myself. It would be like shaking hands with a National Gallery statue. 'In the beginning, I desperately missed Northumberland. That's Percy country, of course. Your grandfather was a schoolmaster there, I believe?' With ladylike poise, she lets the comment float, suspended in the air between us without the second half we both know should complete it. My grandfather was a schoolmaster. Gavin's was a duke. 'But in time,' Mary glides her hand down to stroke the bird's hooked beak, 'I fell in love with this part of the world. Just as I had done with Aymer. And Gavin ...' her fingertips hover at the sharp tip '... this is where he was born to belong.'

Eyes still on the eagle, my thoughts turn bizarrely to Gavin's Oxford University burglary. I picture him and his student friends creeping along dark corridors in search of exam papers, making sure to wear gloves so their touch would leave no prints. An audacious plan pulled off to perfection. Just like his mother's. She has left no fingerprints on me this afternoon, no tell-tale trace of poison in her words that speaks of anything other than a warm welcome if I repeated them to a third party. '*I particularly hoped you'd be able to join us. There are things I should like you to see.*' And indeed, what better way to make me see than by bringing me here in person? What more stylish solution could Mary have found than deigning to show me Monreith in all its historic glory? She wishes me to see it for myself, so I will understand why I should never come here again. I do not fit in this world. I cannot. And if her beloved boy thinks differently, if he tells me inside his modest London flat that poets are the real aristocrats ... Mother knows best.

I turn abruptly to go, although I have no idea where to.

'Wouldn't you like to see the library?' Those cool, light fingers somehow steer me once again. Another corner, another door, and we are inside the largest room yet. 'The finest private library in Scotland.' I don't doubt it. As my gaze falls from the vaulted ceiling, I try to take in row upon row of leather-bound volumes, bookcases climbing to triple my height with sliding rail ladders to reach the titles at the highest altitude. I draw nearer despite myself, the poetess fighting with the woman in me so that I might stay to explore these embossed spines. The glint of gold leaf pages is just visible inside many bindings, the lettering on some so ancient that each over-elaborate 's' reads at first glance like an 'f'. Exceedingly rare, I'm sure. My early work may well end up rare too, although I suspect not for the same reasons.

Even so, it troubles me to think of any book being worth more closed than opened.

'Gavin tells me that you wish to dedicate poems to him.'

'Yes,' I say, trying not to make it sound like an admission. How does she know that? This day is beginning to blur; the strain of trying and failing to blend in causing my memories to fragment. Perhaps walls really do have ears. Even those made from thick sandstone. Mary smiles again, a move that does not quite reach her pale eyes.

'Such a clever girl.' I am hardly a girl, any more than her son is a boy, but it would be discourteous to labour a point that comes so close to a compliment. 'Such a *very* kind thought. But to put a dedication in print, well, we'd hate for anyone to get the wrong idea, wouldn't we?' Arctic waters icing over. 'Some people can be so … vulgar.' The last word leaves Mary's lips and sinks through the air, its burden landing square on my shoulders. I want to wrestle against the weight, fighting the shame of Ilford and the menial, lower-middle class aspirations with which Mary wishes to silence me. It would be easier to resist if I had never felt ashamed of them myself.

But no one tells me not to write. Daughter of a duke or otherwise. Haven't I already trodden this painful terrain with her son? With no little reluctance, I accept that Gavin interprets my writing about him, or at least, about certain aspects of him, as a betrayal of trust, an uncomfortable intimacy that verges too close to an indiscretion. But a dedication is different. And didn't Gavin thank me for the idea this afternoon? If he objected – and really, how could he object to such a small, symbolic gesture – then I'm sure he would have told me himself. He is hardly the sort of man to let his mother do his dirty work. Still, panic surges through me at the thought of us again being at cross purposes.

The library books around me fade as the Kielder snowstorm swirls through my memory, that hauntingly cold, dark night whose ghost I have yet to fully exorcise. Cold, dark and lonely. Focused on my past and not my present, Mary has no inkling of what I sacrifice, willingly and uncomplainingly, in my love for Gavin. Four children in four years? She should do. She should understand. Not that I dare raise such a subject. A divorced woman with two children cannot afford to appear vulgar.

Before I make any reply – and what reply can I honestly make, without betraying either myself or the man whom Mary and I both adore – one of the maids returns with another bobbing curtsey. It transpires that she is now acting as an emissary from Cook – with no definite article, I imagine a capital letter – who seeks Mary's approval for a minor change to tonight's menu. I embrace the opportunity to excuse myself from her presence, escaping under the cover of this domestic drama in microcosm with the pretence of not taking up more of her valuable time. Alone, I work my clumsy way back through Monreith's labyrinth of corridors, retracing our path with more than a few missteps. At one point, a breathy singsong voice starts echoing, and I spot the second, younger servant girl. She really is a girl: the same age as Anna, if that. Unaware of my presence, she swings a fluffy bundle of white towels from side to side while she walks, playacting a babe in arms or perhaps a young man's embrace as they dance.

'Excuse me?'

The girl startles. Whomever the towels represented has their face squashed against her apron. 'I'm sorry, ma'am.' Her deep curtsey deepens my embarrassment.

'Can you please point out the way downstairs?' Humiliating as my enquiry is, the girl blinks sweetly, relief flooding her round face at having apparently averted a scolding. It makes her look even younger. Drilled in obedience, she takes my words more literally than I meant them, pointing to a door at the distant end of the hall.

'Through there, ma'am, and to the right.' The girl's eyes flit in the same direction, following a mental map of what is clearly a complicated route. 'Then it's right, left, and right again.'

'Thank you.' Should I give her a coin? Monreith is not a hotel, of course. I decide to simply offer a smile, but the girl's training seems to tell her that she must avoid eye contact as she retreats. Alone again, I follow the path she pointed out and spot yet another alcove eagle, this one accompanied by a vase of ice-white, tall-stem lilies. Mary's favourites, I presume. The flowers make me recall with guilt, or more truthfully, with shame, the way I treated my own mother when I returned home from my first term at university. She had made our little house spotless, every surface gleaming in bright anticipation of a daughter's happy homecoming, but in the arrogance of newfound intellectual betterment, I saw it all through the grimy film of provincialism. A small spray of mimosa was sitting on our dining room table, held inside a mass-produced blue and white jug of the sort that imitates Chinese porcelain. Newly purchased for the occasion, I realise in retrospect.

'Aren't they beautiful?' my mother had asked.

'No,' said my student self. I think now that murders must have been committed with less cruelty. Young Kathleen thought herself too good for those simple stems; set so far above my mother's waste land of furniture polish and cheap blooms that even a brief kindness was beneath me. More honestly, I feared the condescension would risk me toppling back down into it with her. I was not a mother myself then. I could not yet comprehend how much my behaviour must have hurt. But in that moment more than twenty years ago, I wonder if I did not somehow sow the seeds of my fate today. Facing judgement at the threshold of a foreign world to which love has brought me. Facing it and being found wanting.

Thanks to the young maid's guidance, I eventually make it back to the spiral staircase that leads to Monreith's entrance. With a grunt of effort – the wood is heavier than Gavin made it look – I push open the doors. Fresh air flows over me, the breeze bracing yet welcome as I hurry away from the house. The cleansing scent of fir trees mingles with moist earth as I move in the direction of the forest. I breathe deep, letting the wind fill my lungs and displace the cloying, claustrophobic stuffiness of indoors. How remarkable that a mansion should feel more constricting than Paultons Square. I suppose the size of rooms matters less than who is in them. Genteel flecks of gravel crunch beneath my feet as I walk, a soft rolling scuttle like falling hailstones. Mine are surely not the first footsteps to have fled from Monreith House, escaping its prison of privilege and seeking solace, even sanctuary, in the natural world nearby.

'Kathleen! Kathleen!' Gavin's voice, urgent and anxious, calls from the trees. I spin frantically, trying to determine its direction; not confident that it is more than a hallucination of my troubled, tired mind, but ready to follow its lead even so. 'Kathleen!' I start running, committing myself to charge at the section of forest where, still unseen, I guess that Gavin must be. All indignation at his mother's words and whatever he may or may not have said to provoke them evaporates into a childlike sense of purpose. If he needs me, I will come. What and why can wait. I am almost at the frontline of firs when he emerges, crashing through the branches and setting the needles aquiver about twenty yards from where I am.

'Kathleen! Thank God.' Once close enough, I see there is something cradled in Gavin's hands. Something fragile. Something breathing. 'I found him in the forest.' Gavin gently opens his palms and I look down at the creature inside. A baby bird, barely a fledgling, with tufted new feathers poking out of its crown and a handful of wrinkled, light grey bare patches on its neck where further plumage is still waiting to sprout. For its size – its torso fits Gavin's outstretched hands to perfection – the wings look relatively well-developed, but its belly betrays the soft, downy texture of an infant until recently accustomed to life inside a nest. The creature blinks, eyelids bobbing drowsily. Staring without seeing me.

'What …' is it? I suppose that is my first question. *What can I do?* is the next.

'A squab,' Gavin informs me, turning the bird on its side to check for injuries with such tenderness that it does not object, beyond opening and closing its mouth a few times in juvenile reflex. 'A baby wood pigeon,' he adds, when it must be clear from my face that I have no idea what squab means. 'I suspect that he –' not it, he, 'was caught and dropped. There are birds of prey in the forest, of course.' Of course. 'Not hurt, from what I can see. But he's badly stunned by the fall.' I stare down at the bizarre apparition in Gavin's hands. Its long, half-naked neck and bulbous unfocused eyes seem prehistoric in their strangeness, framed by half-grown plumes that point bolt upright with sticky, serrated edges. Ugly to an uninterested observer. But I am interested. In fact, I find its primordial oddness rather endearing. Gavin holds out his hands to me, fingers curved protectively around the little bird's body. 'I thought you could …' his eyes dart towards the trees as if afraid his brothers will overhear. 'Wish for him.'

From deep within the foliage, audible but invisible, comes the heavy rustling of branches. I imagine stalks being swept apart with sticks. There are snaps too, the curt sound of cut stems being decimated underfoot.

'Gavin? Where the bloody hell are you, old boy?' In a different season, or at a different time, this tiny, disoriented creature would have already been despatched, just as soon as he or she – two can play this anthropomorphising game – was spotted by their boys' own adventuring party. Gavin himself probably killed a number of its ancestors during the shooting parties of his late teens. It feels like another life to him now, he has told me more than once, confessional and contrite during our many late-night telephone calls. It might as well have been another man. The man he was before we met, I like to think, although I do not like to think of him killing at all. It is one of the quirks or perhaps the hypocrisies of this upper-class universe that I simply cannot understand: why the most ardent of animal lovers are unperturbed at making annual sport of their slaughter. And yet we all feel shame re-reading certain chapters from our past. *I could also be cruel at that age*, I remind myself, thoughts returning to my mother's mimosa.

I take the bird from him. It feels warm. A good sign. I feel its heart racing and wrap my fingers around it, lightly stroking the sprawled spread of plumage that lies dishevelled across its stomach. Its breathing is shallow. Rapid. A frantic flitter of oxygen, in and out and in. Eyes open yet seeing nothing, the tiny beak begins to twitch. It lets out a mew, exposing a sliver of pale pink tongue. Wishing for a mother's sustenance.

'Shh.' I rest my thumbs on the tiny bird's breast. 'You're safe, little one.' Raising it up, I start whispering words; less interested in meanings than sounds that feel like they can comfort. I coo each syllable in a singsong trill, murmuring the sentences that happen to be freshest in my mind. The lines of the poem I wrote on the train.

'Look,' Gavin gasps as the bird flaps its wings. A frenzied whirl of chaos springs from my hands as the bird tumbles from my grasp, landing with merciful softness on the grass. Gavin and I both bend to look at it. The bird stares back. It can definitely see us now. Eye to eye to eye, we remain, until with a second feathery skirmish the squab finds itself airborne. It hovers like a mirage between us, shock comically obvious across its little dinosaur face. The bird's spindle-thin legs coil tight beneath its body and its newly emboldened wings move so fast that they are vibrating rather than beating. In a final flourish of fluffy disarray, it shoots into the trees. Laughing, we watch it go.

'Well, that was good timing,' I declare, my fingertips still tingling from the sensation of warm feathers. 'He must only have been dazed.'

Gavin shakes his head vehemently. 'I knew you were magic.' Darkness is falling, the long shadow cast by the house sinking into the greyish depths of a winter's evening, but I can tell that his eyes are shining. Does he truly believe I have such powers? Swept up in the vicariously uplifting euphoria of a young bird's first flight, his conviction is almost enough to convince me too. Yet it would hardly be true to say I get everything in life I wish for.

'Did you ask your mother to tell me not to ...' Gavin's focus remains on the forest, peering through the deepening gloom after our avian friend, and I find myself unable to finish the sentence I have started. I decide I don't need to. A man who feels so much for a little creature like that would take no part in Mary's cold-hearted schemes. Gavin does not share her low opinions of me and the background I am unable to alter. He, of all people, is wise enough not to judge for the things we cannot change. When my poetic dedications are published, they will be precious to him, because my work is precious to him. And what we share through our writing – because now we even share the act of writing itself – is a spiritual world set high above his mother's suffocating social judgements; an imaginative space in which we are liberated from the material concerns of all those long-faced, long-forgotten ancestors whose standards oppress him as much as me. It is no habitat for gold eagles on plinths, but real-life fledglings with ruffled feathers. And if Mary cannot appreciate the humble beauty of the latter, well, I am sorry for her. It feels good to turn the tables on which one of us should pity the other.

Monreith House is still in sight, dwarfing the dark horizon with its imposing stone circles. Yet it feels more distant now. Turning my back to the building, I choose to follow Gavin's gaze, searching the shadowy branches to try and see where our bird has flown.

Chapter Twelve

Reacquainting myself with Fidelitas when nightfall forces us to return indoors, I check my reflection. Face flushed. Hair shambolic. Heaven help me, will Gavin never see me looking groomed? Not that it would make a difference to our situation. That is not how these things work. I don't think. Once as satisfied as I can be with my appearance, I reach beneath my silk-encased pillow to draw out my notebook from its hiding place. Leafing past the pages on Blake, I arrive at my train poem and read over the lines with what is, for me, a relatively high level of authorial satisfaction. These words have power. Nature knew it. And now Gavin knows it too. I am still reading when I hear a light, well-mannered knock at my door.

'Come in,' I call, confident it is him without being able to say why.

'Dinner's in thirty minutes.' Gavin smiles, his blond head ducking around the door frame. He shifts his weight from one foot to the other, the sound of his shoes oddly heavy. I spot a hint of tartan.

'Let me see.'

Grimacing, Gavin takes one thick-soled step sideways. 'What do you think?' I think it's not often that I'm speechless. A black epauletted jacket hangs casually from his fingertips, its brilliant buttons complementing the subtle glint of his signet ring. Above it, he wears a white dress shirt tucked into a thick belt, its oblong silver buckle sitting high on his slender waist, and from a whip-thin strand of leather around his hips hangs his ... sporran? Is that the word? For once, the woman in me is successfully silencing the poet. Gavin's kilt falls in inch-wide pleats from thigh height to just above his knees. Mossy greens with warm yellows, the wool threads seem interwoven with the promise of spring shades soon to come. Their plaid pattern is intricate, more so than I appreciated south of the border before seeing such a garment for myself, and some strands even appear to change their colours halfway, mid tones elevated to emerald and amber as part of the fabric's rich, mesmeric flow. Evidently, my eyesight has never been sharper than at this moment, and I feel grateful for it.

Amongst other things.

Gavin wears wool socks that match the texture of his kilt checks, knitted in cream with strange green garters, while the laces of his heavy dress shoes play a complicated cat's cradle game up his slim shins. Resisting their pull, one sock has slid, exposing a hint of taut calf muscle and a dusting of fine, fair hairs. His tie, slotted under a collar with the top button surreptitiously unfastened, is held in place by his grandfather's pin. I recall the first time I saw it, our first evening together, after I had told Gavin of a girlhood spent staring longingly towards the Cheviot hills. In all my fevered adolescent imaginings, I never dreamed that this was what lay beyond them.

'Is it awful?' Gavin looks at me looking at him. 'We wore kilts every day as youngsters. I forget how odd it must seem to an Englishwoman.' Not this Englishwoman. Transfixed, I watch him open his sporran and produce both lighter and cigarette case. Is that thing made from real fur? I disapprove, officially. Unofficially, I would very much like to touch it.

'You're the most handsome man I've ever seen.' Was that vulgar? Too late. The words flow from me, easy as breathing. And they make Gavin happy, I can tell, although with a nonchalant drag on his cigarette he tries to feign disinterest. Shoes leaden on the floorboards, he steps over the bedroom threshold to check himself in my mirror. When he draws close, my heart beats as fast as the bird's. Perched on the bed's edge, I see myself in the middle distance behind his reflection, the blurred aura of my dark hair casting a shadow around his light.

'It'll fade with age,' he sighs, drawing hard until his cigarette tip glows red hot. In the exhalation of smoke that follows, my image disappears.

'Not the beauty of your soul,' I insist. Gavin turns to me with an appreciative grin.

'And what will you wear?'

*

'This is a lovely surprise, Kathleen.' Lavinia answers my knock at once, evidently recovered from her headache and just as beautiful as before. Only her ever-so-slightly bloodshot eyes betray a hint of anything having been amiss. 'Please, do come in.' After a tactical survey of my options – thoughts panicked and erratic, I would never cut it as a wartime Major – I have selected this young woman as the best or possibly the only person whom I can feasibly take into my confidence. No sign of Edward, I'm

92

relieved to discover as Lavinia beckons me into her bedroom. And for the first time since my arrival, Fidelitas really does seem small. This room is opulent where mine is merely refined; sumptuous and luxurious compared with only spacious. The four-poster bed is trimmed in a rich *Toile de Jouy*, its sweeping curtains complementing the plush, over-stuffed upholstery of a full-sized sofa beside the window. The latter is largely obscured by the dresses that have been tossed over it: a dazzling, multicoloured medley of what I assume are the latest fashions. Shoes, too, are scattered across the floor for consideration, and Lavinia trots over the discarded obstacles with an easy dressage-like elegance.

'I'm so sorry to disturb you.' Cheeks pulsing with heat, a few poorly tamed strands of hair breaking free to fuzz around my face, I confess to Lavinia that I have forgotten to pack my dress for dinner. It feels less humiliating than the truth: that I was wearing the newest, most expensive item in my wardrobe when Gavin innocently looked right through it and asked what I planned to change into. 'I feel like such a fool,' I burble truthfully, fingers worrying at its seams as if to unpick the stitches would be the same as retracing my steps. It cost me a lot to end up worthless.

'Not at all.' Lavinia's kind eyes widen. 'I can't tell you how many times something similar has happened to me.' She sounds convincing, despite looking so perfectly pulled together that it is doubtful she has ever made a mistake in her young life. Unless 'complex character' Edward counts. 'Why, once I arrived at the palace to find I had the most hideous ladder in my stocking. Just as well Mummy always carries a spare pair in her handbag.'

'The palace?' I am briefly distracted from my wardrobe woes by considering how aristocratic one has to be for 'Buckingham' to become redundant.

Lavinia nods, entirely in earnest. 'Daddy is private secretary to Her Majesty. While we were growing up –' does she mean her siblings, I wonder, or herself and the new Queen Elizabeth? '– he served her father, King George.' With friends like these, no wonder Lady Mary thinks me a peasant.

'I really am glad you're here,' Lavinia insists. 'You can help me decide.' Focused as I am on my own predicament, it is only now that I notice she is still in her dressing gown. Silk, naturally, and cinched until only a svelte whisper of the lace slip underneath is visible. I suppose her hair is also technically unfinished, the lower half not yet pinned and falling to her shoulders in glossy rose-gold ringlets. What would look messy on me is a chic innovation on her. If she wore the style in public tonight, half of London would adopt it tomorrow.

Lavinia takes my hand and draws me towards the dress-draped sofa. 'Choose any one you like.'

'I …' Lifting an intricately embellished lace sleeve at random, I examine without knowing what I am looking for. What is the collective noun for a group of dresses? A haberdashery? Haberdressery? Running a cautious hand over the next garment in line, I realise that Lavinia's selection is not comprised of dresses at all, but gowns. Floor length and many with trains, they are fit for balls and not just dinners or, worse, the dreaded lower-middle class 'tea'. It never occurred to me that, for Gavin, going home would involve a more elaborate dress code than going out.

Lavinia reaches over me to pluck a swathe of crimson silk from the pile. 'Perhaps this Hartnell?' She holds it out for my approval, the gown sinking between her outstretched arms like a swooning damsel in distress. It has a full skirt, a sweetheart neckline, and a trail of tiny appliqué flowers blooming diagonally over the bodice.

'I couldn't.'

'Nonsense. Here, try it.' Excitedly, Lavinia holds it up to my torso and lets go. I grab it before it falls, some deeply suppressed feminine instinct telling me that a design like this should not have its dignity degraded by being allowed to hit the floor. 'Don't worry, I won't look.' Doll hands pressed theatrically over her eyes, Lavinia spins to face the other way, and I have no choice but to wriggle out of my cursed tea dress and negotiate the inner workings of what I suspect is called *haute couture*. Well, no choice except the increasingly appealing idea of hurling myself out the bedroom window.

'Ready,' I mutter eventually.

Lavinia turns. 'It's perfect. Really, it suits you so much better than me.' I cannot decide what is more likely: that such a sweet-looking young woman is the world's most convincing liar, or else she means what she says and truly is this unstintingly generous. Moving slowly if not serenely as befits the gown, I let myself be manoeuvred towards the mirror, stumbling as I struggle to negotiate the long hem and discarded heels on the floor. Lavinia is right. It does look good. My tree bark brown hair becomes chestnut rich beside the crimson silk; the translucent pallor of my library lover's skin is turned porcelain by the jewel tones of the embellishment.

94

She has a talent for coordination. In these pressing social circumstances, my own gifts seem embarrassingly esoteric in comparison.

'What a pity about the hem,' Lavinia murmurs, placing her hands on my hips to pull up three inches or so of trailing material. 'But we can sort that.' The gown is not too tight – thank God, or perhaps the Buddha, for small mercies – but it is indeed far too long for me. I look down at my diminutive lower half, thinking of Clement and her willowy limbs roaming elsewhere in the house. The high that had accompanied my uncharacteristic foray into glamour is quick to wear off.

Lavinia steps over the scattered shoes to tug on a hanging cord that matches the four-poster's fringe trimming. The action recalls the emergency pull on a train, but if it brings a screeching halt to business below stairs, the disruption remains hidden from us.

'A maid will tailor it for you,' Lavinia smiles. 'Call it a temporary quick fix.'

'I can't let you do that …' A distant trill of recognition tells me that it is sacrilegious to perform the ad hoc surgery she proposes on a Hartnell gown.

'Kathleen, you worry too much.' As Lavinia bats away my concern, my eye is caught by the glint of a large diamond on her finger. 'I have others.' That much is true. Satisfied with her plan, she returns to the dress-strewn sofa and, with all the unselfconscious sorority spirit of a girl in front of her best friend, she lets her dressing gown drop. What on earth goes on at those boarding schools? I avert my eyes regardless, facing the mirror and focusing on how to adjust the faintly gaping fabric across my bust. That, too, is smaller than Lavinia's. A swishing waterfall sound soon suggests that she is ready, and I turn to find her robed in an astonishing architectural gown of deep blue. Beneath its fitted bodice, the full skirt is cut to sweep back like the waves of an outgoing tide. Cinematic, one might call it. Cinderella, Anna would say.

Another knock on the door, and the maid appears. Number two. Anna's age. The towels she carried have been deposited out of sight, yet as soon as Lavinia tells her of our predicament, the girl produces an improbably well-stocked sewing kit from her apron pocket. She sets to work with silent skill, crouched and revolving around my feet to quickly reduce the gown's train to a more modest, less model-like length.

'Next, your hair …' Lavinia reaches out to touch my face. I jump, the gown moves, and the maid issues a muted squeak from pricking her

95

finger. Undeterred, Lavinia draws a soft, sweeping side parting above the arc of my left eyebrow. Much as I hate to admit it, it does frame my face in a flattering way. 'Perfect,' Lavinia declares.

'Ready, ma'am.' The young maid rises shyly and all three of us look down to admire her handiwork. Her stitches are delicate, baby's breath wisps of thread that will preserve the gown's new hemline for a few hours without causing permanent disfigurement. If I'm lucky, their magic may take me to midnight.

'Very well done indeed, Rosie,' Lavinia rewards the girl, before giving her a nod as subtly communicative as that which Gavin once gave our waiter at Sorbo's. Fluent in the upper class's unspoken language despite her tender years, Rosie knows to take her leave. After she goes, I experiment with a few tentative steps around the bedroom to try out my new silhouette, while Lavinia moves to the jewellery box on her dressing table.

'Do you have children?' she asks, holding out a sapphire necklace for me to fasten onto her.

'Yes. Anna and James,' I say while closing the clasp. Their names sound strange in these lavish surroundings. Pure, like doves put in with peacocks.

'I have two little boys.' Lavinia turns to face me, her pretty features illuminated by pride. 'Children are the best thing about marriage, aren't they? But of course, you're not –' her hand to her mouth, she looks aghast at the indiscretion. 'I'm sorry.'

'Don't be.' Unsure of how much she knows about me, or rather how much Lady Mary has told her, it is hard to know whether Lavinia is sorry that I was married, or sorry that now I'm not. Maybe a bit of both.

'You know, Edward speaks very highly of Gavin.' Characteristically stylish, she recovers with reference to my favourite subject. 'Of how daring he was during the war.'

'I can imagine.' I often do. Suddenly reticent, even though we are alone, Lavinia lowers her voice to a confiding whisper. She stands to come closer; our layered skirts rustle.

'How old is he?' she asks. 'Early thirties?'

'Nearer forty than thirty now,' I admit. 'Not that he looks it.'

Lavinia seems thrilled on my behalf. 'A girlfriend of mine says that certain bachelors often change around forty. It happened to Edward, the Prince of Wales. They mature and then they … rediscover a man's rightful nature.' Biting her lip, her cheeks flush from her own boldness. As, to my shame, do mine. For all she claimed to know, my Freudian friend never mentioned that. Lavinia and I start to giggle, the sound bubbling up between us like schoolgirls, and I let our shared laughter distract me from indulging in the hope that she might be right.

Chapter Thirteen

Downstairs at dinner, having triumphantly negotiated the spiral staircase without wrecking the maid's conscientious hem work, I discover that eating haggis and pretending to enjoy it is another sacrifice I must make in the name of love. As if seeing Gavin in his kilt does not make the first one hard enough. Still, I take solace from the fact that I am almost a match for him in my beautiful, borrowed finery. As I descend the stairs, appliqué flowers set aquiver by my movements and skirt layers blooming around me like crimson petals, I see Gavin's fair brows rise in surprise.

'Look at you,' he exclaims as he kisses me, once on either cheek.

'Look at me,' I laugh, although I fear it comes out like an instruction. And I regret the twirl in retrospect. Gavin cannot look at me easily now, sandwiched as I am between Eustace and Aymer at the far end of the dining table. Dealing out our places, Mary has shuffled the party like playing cards and kept the ace for herself, pointedly guiding Gavin to sit at the place on her right.

'No, Kathleen, my dear,' she had cautioned when I moved towards his other side. 'Your place is down there.' This Hartnell gown is many things, but warm is not one of them, and the exposed hairs on my forearm prickled when Mary laid her cold fingers over it. A light touch heavily imbued with meaning, with which I went, or rather was sent, to a vacant chair at the other end of the room. Aymer and Eustace stood to let me sit between them, a polite performance of gentility made less convincing by their bashful, faintly resentful expressions. I had the distinct impression of having interrupted the punchline of a joke not intended for female ears.

Keeping my eyes on the head of the table, I watched as Mary invited Lavinia to take the seat on Gavin's right side and felt relief, of sorts. Better her than Clement. The latter is opposite me on the other side of Aymer. Apparently, certain guests are permitted to stay with the family member who invited them. Edward and Christian complete the group gathered around this glossy mahogany table. 'Dining' seems too parochial a descriptor for it; perhaps 'banqueting' is better. Christian stares trancelike into the flame of a nearby candlestick, content to roam solo through the rolling landscapes of her imagination. Edward scowls, sinking sullenly into the wallow of an ill-disguised sulk, and I wonder what ails him. Is his wife too sweet for his taste?

Their chairs face the windows, high arched panes that stretch from gleaming floorboards to corniced ceiling to frame Monreith's elaborate ornamental gardens. During daylight, at least; night descends early in wintery Scotland. At my end, however, the view at all hours is blighted by a mounted stag's head. Grotesquely immense, he protrudes at a two-foot distance from the wall, and I wriggle in discomfort within the theoretical sightline of his vacant, glassy-eyed stare. The dried shards of his ancient antlers sprawl out at an appallingly wide range. Crucifix-shaped, I think, as Aymer delivers the *Selkirk Grace*. Seeking a less gory object on which to fix my gaze, I look down to see tiny multiples of myself reflected in the prismatic crystal panels of my empty glass. Kaleidoscopic fragments twist and contort in the flickering candlelight: dark hair, pale face, red gown. Aymer concludes and Eustace reaches over to fill my glass for me. The reflection of my crimson dress blurs into a swirl of wine.

A plate soon appears, presented as if by sleight of hand with such speed that I missed the person who delivered it. Yet there is no mistaking its contents. The infamous haggis. Would that which we call mince by any other name be as revolting? Pale slivers of gristle worm their way through the earthen-coloured churns of meat. As I stare aghast, the soily mound of flesh starts to crumble and collapse before my eyes. The unappetising question of how I will manage to consume it takes on a double sense when I notice the fiendish puzzle of cutlery around my place; more silver pieces at one setting than I suspect exist in the entirety of Tambi's office-flat. Like the middle-class interloper I am, I know only one gold-plated rule for certain: that I should use the cutlery in what feels like reverse order, working from the outside in. I would like to confirm it by following the example set by Gavin's brothers, but neither Eustace nor Aymer is hindered by dining table decorum. They treat the invisible rule book with the casual disdain of those born to rewrite it, dog-earing the pages of established etiquette and sullying them with sticky fingers. Aymer stabs at his meat as if not quite satisfied it is as dead as it might be. Eustace prefers to stick his fork straight down into his haggis like a haystack whenever holding forth with an opinion so vehement that it requires the dexterity of both hands to be communicated. '*Her heart, her liver an her lungs.*'

Nothing will be left of this sacrificial lamb when the Maxwell brothers have finished with her.

But not all three brothers. Not Gavin. A minute or so after the rest of us have been served, a secondary commotion catches my eye at the other end of the table. Gavin receives a different dish, his modest plate not heaped to excess like his brothers' and showing no sign of our mulchy brown mounds. Eustace, having retrieved his pitchfork after a passionate interlude about salmon fishing, notices me looking.

'It's Gavin's ulcers,' he informs me mid-chew. 'Du-o-den-al.' The syllables are separated by swallows. 'Mother insists that certain foods make them worse.' I've not known ulcers to bother Gavin at home. At his studio, I mean. In the London that we share. Try as I might – and I confess, I stopped trying hours ago – I will never be able to think of this place as his real home. I cannot read his expression down here, but I assume a certain level of stress from how frequently his slim wrist reaches for the wine bottle. Weirdly, unlimited alcohol is deemed permissible by Mary and the medical powers that be.

'Slow down,' I try to communicate telepathically, to no discernible avail. It doesn't always work in the Bentley either. At a loss for what else to do, I take a sip myself to force down a socially acceptable amount of haggis.

I would forget the food and focus on the people, but the conversation around me is even more befuddling than the cutlery. Childhood nicknames abound, without explanation for familial latecomers like me, until it seems like there are twice as many people in attendance as I can physically count. Eustace is not infrequently Doody to his siblings. Aymer is also answering to Max. Kiss, I gradually realise, is Christian, and that leaves … Maxwell Minimus? It's what they called Gavin at school, I deduce. The youngest brother. A strange memory stirs from Gavin's months as a portrait painter. Sharing the same blond aristocratic bearing but wearing it in different ways, it seems to me that he and his siblings might be one subject rendered in multiple media. Eustace in vibrant, clashing acrylics; Aymer in classic history painting oils; Gavin sensitive and luminous in watercolour; and Christian an ethereal pencil sketch of a woman. Use too much pressure and she is liable to be rubbed out altogether.

Eustace will not waste away anytime soon. Bloated by his Herculean efforts to demolish his haggis, he lolls beside me as close to prostrate as his high-backed chair will allow. Soon, he is stretching his arms above his head, giving a groan of overindulgence before folding them across the brow of a visibly swollen stomach. From this stuffed, capsized sort of posture, he takes notice of me for the first time since his food arrived.

'You write poems?'

'That's right,' I say. 'And I'm also researching William Bla ...'

'Jolly good,' chimes in Aymer, apparently under the impression that we have never met before. His head remains angled towards Clement, who is herself intent on eliciting a response from the conversationally challenged Edward.

'Ah, but I love poetry.' Unexpected enthusiasm for my vocation lights up Eustace's sweat-glossed brow. He sits up again; I hear his stomach gurgle in protest. 'I've even been known to dabble myself.'

'Is that so?' High time I had a pleasant surprise today.

Eustace nods with the vigour of a puppet on strings. 'Met a fine filly once on a hunt, and she had the most glorious ...'

'Eustace.'

'Sorry, Mother.' No need to wonder why this man is not permitted to play the bagpipes. He is loud enough without them.

'How's the cottage, Gavin?' I hear Lavinia ask at the other end of the table. For the second time tonight, I feel thankful for her presence.

'*Cottage*,' Aymer echoes sardonically, not facing my way but unmistakably rolling his eyes. His tone makes Gavin's hideaway sounds like an ailment. Psoriasis, perhaps, or what Eustace calls a du-o-den-al ulcer.

'Your rustic retreat wouldn't suit Margo, that's for sure.' That comment, too, comes from Eustace. 'Did you know that Gavin once escorted Princess Margaret?' The brother on my left nudges me mid-sip. A rogue droplet of red wine saturates the bright white tablecloth.

'It was twice,' Aymer corrects him.

'No, we're both wrong, Max Maximus, it was three times that he squired her.' The thwarted poet in Eustace warms to his theme. 'Alas, he never had the chance to take her for a ride.'

'Eustace.'

'Sorry, Mother.'

'Gavin's hardly Prince Charming,' Aymer mutters to Clement. I am struck by how sick one can feel when having consumed so little food.

'Yes, rotten luck, Minimus.' Eustace rallies quickly after his mother's reproach. 'But maybe Her Highness isn't an animal lover.' Finally, I think, a subject I can contribute to. Flowering under layers of silk and chiffon petals, my heart swells to recall the delight that Gavin takes in Jonnie. I ache to speak of the joy he finds in cherishing the birds that reside both here and at home. Yet before I can, Eustace bumps my elbow again. I am quick enough this time to set down my glass, but my place still wobbles. 'Did Gavin ever tell you about his so-called compassionate leave?'

'Eustace …' This time Gavin interjects, in the half-hearted tone of one who knows the effort futile before he begins. And he is right. Eustace starts sniggering so hard that he is briefly incapacitated, but soon his wish to regale the company is such that it overtakes private hilarity. 'Mother telegrammed to tell Gavin that his beloved flock of flamingos had flown out to sea. All presumed dead.' His bottom lip protrudes in faux solemnity. 'Minimus was so distraught, he asked his commanding officer for compassionate leave. Slap bang in the middle of the war.' Eustace slaps his hand down on his thigh as if otherwise I might not grasp the image. 'I daren't tell you what his Captain called him.'

'Eustace.'

'Mother, I didn't actually say the word.' Laughter at his little brother's expense once again overcomes him, and I am left with a story that presents my war hero in an unexpected shade of pink. Straining to see past Eustace's convulsing shoulders, I look to Gavin, whose complexion is closer to pale green than flamingo. Love flushes through me, a painful tenderness powered by a throbbing pulse of anger at the way this thoughtless, cruel world dares to judge him for showing sensitivity that most men, most people, could never comprehend. I clear my throat to say so, pushing past the residual awkwardness – and really, how much more can I disgrace myself today? – but Aymer gets there first with a strange single word.

'Gavotte.' In an instant, both he and Eustace have collapsed into reinvigorated guffaws.

'Gavotte!' Eustace waves his white napkin in delight. It is certainly not in surrender. 'I'd forgotten about her.' He turns to me with newfound urgency, anxious that I must understand every last detail of the new tale. 'She was a stupid old ewe that fell into the river. Gavin dragged her out. We named her after him, the only creature on earth more accident-prone than him.'

'I don't think you're accident-prone.' I say it too loudly, my voice hoarse and clumsy from tonight's uncharacteristic lack of use. Yet I am determined that Gavin will hear me. Yes, he is apt to make misjudgements

102

when sheer enthusiasm overtakes him, as I believe it did towards the end of Soay. But I have also seen him twist the Bentley clean around corners that would give a professional racing driver pause. I have viewed his hand-drawn illustrations, intense crosshatched linework to represent the scenes of his stories without an ink dot out of place. I have read, and had read to me, passages written in the early stage that any other writer would consider first draft, but which glide from Gavin's pen in exquisite, often unimprovable prose. That he is passion-prone, I will accept. But accident-prone? Never.

'Then you don't know the real him,' Aymer retorts. To me, without looking at me. Eustace has likewise lost interest, complaining that it is taking too long with the pudding. In silence, I try to swallow one last forkful of haggis, gag softly, and give up. A vague flicker of movement from the other end of the table tells me that Gavin is refilling his glass.

*

After dinner, Lady Mary retires to bed. The men rise and so do I, until I realise my mistake and try to disguise it with a feeble scuffing of my chair legs against the floorboards. My eyes feel strained, neck muscles knotted and tense. It seems Lavinia's headache is contagious. As the last to leave the room, I linger in front of the mounted stag's head, drawing close enough to make out the shadows of our tabletop detritus in his unseeing marble eyes. Checking behind me to confirm that I am alone, I reach out to touch. Wire hairs bristle beneath my fingertips, the rigidity of death in every stiff follicle. His nose is dry and crusted, the skin around it paper thin. The strong sinews of his long neck ought to flex with fine-honed muscles, but of course, this magnificent beast will never move again.

I find the others gathered in a lounge room closer to what one might expect in a hotel than a home. It runs as long as a minor town promenade and I fantasise briefly about what it must look like during the day: one room able to accommodate two weather systems simultaneously, the sun rising in the east while the distant west slumbers on in darkness. Our party has largely relocated to amply stuffed armchairs and sofas, conveniently situated beside a well-stocked drinks cabinet. A gramophone's proud brass horn sticks out from a nearby side table, mushrooming upwards from its glossy box stand. Aymer beckons to the young maid standing silently in the doorway. From either osmosis or prior instruction, Rosie produces the record he wishes to play.

103

A lively, fast-tempo rendition of *The Banks O'Doon* crackles through the room, the nasal drone of an accordion and a rapid scraping of strings soon accompanied by laughter, shouts – mostly from Eustace – and the inharmonious physical jumble of several people rising to dance, full stomachs forgotten.

> *Ye banks and braes o' bonnie Doon,*
> *How can ye bloom sae fresh and fair?*

Astonished, I watch an impromptu ceilidh spring to life: hands clapping, feet stomping and ladies spinning amidst the chaos of what looks to my outsider's eyes like some sort of collective cultural seizure. Settled on a plump, port-red leather sofa, and I suspect a little well-lubricated by his almost entirely liquid dinner, Gavin starts to sing along.

> *How can ye chant, ye little birds,*
> *And I sae weary, fu' o' care ...*

Another shock. He is tone-deaf. Gavin's voice, so mellifluous and elegant in speech, with such an impeccable ear for prose, falls to a low, off-key drawl that flatly submerges the original tune. It seems improbable, indeed, impossible if I was not being forced to hear it for myself, that such an unattractive sound could come from this beautiful person. My man of light, the man of my dreams, has a singing voice like a sea lion. Awful as it may be, I want to laugh, not at him, exactly, but at the relief that comes from being audibly reminded of my Godsend's mortality.

Couples whirl about us, swept up in flailing trails of tartan and taffeta, and I reach for Gavin's hand. To stop him singing as much as anything.

'Teach me the dances.'

He groans, a vast improvement in sound. 'I'm too tired, Kathleen.'

'Please.' I give a comedic pull of persuasion, tugging on his arm until he slides towards the edge of the couch. 'I won't know what I'm doing without you.'

Gavin sighs, but smiles. 'Then you'd better hold onto me.' My hand in his, he flings me into the heart of the merriment, crossing our wrists so that we spin, toes together, in time with the music. The momentum grows so fast I feel I'd take off into orbit if Gavin ever let go, but his grip is so strong that I have no fear whatsoever he will. Where this wild tune takes us, we are going together. Soon, a new movement takes hold of the dancing pairs and one couple after another is sent skipping down the rows: stripping the willow, I suppose, the only ceilidh dance I can recall my mother ever mentioning. My favourite, though, is when Gavin wraps his arm around my waist. We travel together around a furniture-dodging circuit, the coarse fabric of his kilt jacket scratching my bare skin. The relentless friction ought to be unpleasant, but my God, I don't want it to stop. Gavin's sporran digs into my dress; a vulgar thought, I have no doubt, but I am too happy to care. I can feel my hem disintegrating, fluttering unevenly around my ankles, yet while repairing damage to this dress would cost more than my annual income in a fallow poetry year, I'd give every penny I'll ever earn if it meant Gavin and I could keep going. Our bodies are pressed together, faces close enough to kiss, and we laugh as we twirl, the whole room spinning until he becomes all I can see.

As the evening draws on, Eustace and Christian drift off to play an eccentric chess-based drinking game, their opinions diverging on which part is the greater priority. More dramatic is the angry squabble that breaks out between Clement and Aymer; its subject is unclear, although I believe Edward's name is mentioned. Demonstrating a strong if unsubtle sense of theatricality, Clement takes off for the nearest hotel in Aymer's Bentley, which is blue rather than red but equally as monstrous as Gavin's. Her beau, if that is what Aymer remains, is left standing on Monreith's sandstone steps to howl his frustrations at the sickle moon.

'I want it back! No, not her, the car!'

Edward and Lavinia sit at either end of the same sofa in pensive, uncomfortable silence. Only Gavin and I are still smiling, slouched in happy exhaustion after the dance. *Ours would be the happiest marriage here*, I think, *if it were one.*

Alone in Fidelitas later and finding it difficult to sleep, I look out of the window towards Elrig. The cold night has grown too clouded for stars, a gauze layer of mist slung over the land so that I cannot see further than the hazed outline of the dark forest. But I know it is there. The place Gavin truly loved. A childhood dreamscape of nature and freedom, of fledgling hopes and unlimited imagination that his boyish heart has carried with him into adulthood. *Monreith doesn't matter*, I tell myself. *It is only his Ilford.*

Chapter Fourteen

Despite the short hours of winter sunlight, we make good time on our return journey south. I doubt that travelling the entire length of Great Britain would challenge Gavin once he got behind his Bentley wheel, and he certainly takes England in his high-rev, tyre-screech stride. Having long since abandoned all attempts to read road signs while he drives – the blur makes me queasy and my bearings are never improved – it is with surprise that I realise he is, unprecedentedly, slowing down to point out a weather-worn signpost ahead.

'We should say hello,' Gavin suggests, as if there is only one house in the town. In his world, there usually is. Perhaps in Gavin's head I belong to the Raine family's House of Ilford. I fail to articulate an objection in time, having too many to choose from when I think of the small-minded, closed-hearted town that seems to embody in rough red brick the very antithesis of my poetic spirit. At my father's firm behest and my mother's passive acquiescence, I was plucked from the snowdrop-dappled Northumbrian fields when the Great War was over and returned to this uninspiring town. Heaven help me, my young self would have thought it worth continuing the fight if only to stay away longer. 'The slumberous mass,' that is what Blake called the soulless, sluggish mundanity of a life without vision, and ever since I left I have feared this place's dull power to drag me back down into the void. Street after street of humdrum monotony awaits Gavin and I, lurking to expose my lowly social beginnings and justify Lady Mary's belief that I will never be good enough for the former escort of a princess. If there is one thought stranger than me being at Monreith, it is Gavin in Ilford.

And yet my power of speech seems to separate from my mind as I obediently spell out the route to my parents' house. It does not take me long to do so; this town is diminutive in every sense of the word. It occurs to me, fleetingly and farcically, that I might lead Gavin on a wild goose chase, but I soon decide against it. Can I really pull off pretending I have forgotten my own way home? Showing myself up as barely scraping middle class is one thing. As insane is quite another. Still, the incongruity is acute as I watch Gavin make his way towards my parents' modest front door, waiting patiently inside the confines of a clipped privet hedge low enough for his head and shoulders to stick out above it. West View. Where the sun never rises. Father has added a few potted plants since my last visit, neat soil still bound by the memory of the cubic shapes in which he purchased the original seedlings. His lawn, too, is a perfect square. 'The days of man are but as grass'? Cut shorter every year, living here.

Somehow, though, the excruciating shame I expected to feel on my unplanned return turns out to be more of a twinge than a torment. I dreaded seeing this place through Gavin's eyes, fearing the consequences of having him witness first-hand how many rungs of the class ladder I am below him. But standing beside him, Ilford does not seem ugly anymore. Unambitious, perhaps. Unenlightened. Yet no worse. Gavin has all the material reasons in the world to scorn or dismiss my humble origins, his Bentley dominating our little street like a thoroughbred stabled with mules. But he does not do so. He does not judge me. The grin he wears while we wait for my parents feels genuine, its warmth undiminished by our cold concrete cul-de-sac surrounds. For so long, in our writing and elsewhere in our increasingly interwoven lives, the dynamic has been one of Gavin learning from me. I realise now that I have failed to appreciate just how much I can learn from him.

'Yes?' My father answers the bell warily, spectacles low on his nose as he peeks around a sliver of opened door. Confronted with his only child on the step, his shock is such that, for a beat, I think he barely recognises me. Could I be a cold caller? Trying to hock her surplus poetry supplies? Once invited inside with an ambivalence that I guess a prodigal daughter deserves, we meet my mother in the living room, roused from her daydreams by the real-life thrill of seeing Gavin again. While his back is turned, or rather bent to remove his shoes, she gives me a look that suggests I owed her the courtesy of an advanced warning about his visit.

'I'm sorry,' I mouth. Spinelessly, I hope that the apologetic energy may count towards the re-remembered mimosa incident too.

Blinking fast and breathing faster, Jessie rises to the occasion to pull together an impromptu afternoon tea for us; distinguished here from both the constant cups of PG Tips consumed throughout the day and my parents' unvarying clockwork dinnertime of ten minutes past six. When the teapot and strainer appear, I am mortified to see that my mother has dressed the former in its bright knitted cosy. Even more so when she brings out an enamel cake-stand that has for decades leaned Pisa-like to the right. Gavin eats eagerly anyway, as if he has recently been starved. I suppose he has. He compliments my mother's squint cherry bakewells with no less enthusiasm than if they came from Harrods' patisserie. In response, Jessie's eyes glisten with rare delight; life's excitement for once equalling or even exceeding her dreams.

'Ah yes, *Turdus merula* ...' Gavin converses at length with my father about birds, eliciting from him a detailed knowledge of natural history that I never realised George Raine had. Father in turn speaks passionately of scripture. I cringe inwardly, but Gavin is undaunted. Indeed, he speaks on the subject with thoughtful, well-read wisdom, contemplating his answers with care and demonstrating a familiarity with the Word that I never guessed he possessed. Lady Mary is pious in her way, Percys and Maxwells united decades ago in a strict and exclusive branch of upper-class religion that might explain their rejection of family planning. But who knew Gavin was interested? I express my surprise while my mother is in the kitchen making yet another pot of tea and my father is upstairs scanning his bookshelves for a prized volume he especially wishes to show Gavin. *Animal Iconography of the Bible*, I believe.

'I've given it a lot of thought,' Gavin tells me, stirring his teaspoon and watching the liquid swirl into a vortex. 'I believe God is love, in fact, I think that's all there could ever be to God.' The tea stills; Gavin continues to stare. 'But I can't believe in these rules and what they do to people. The suffering they cause.' I reach out to touch his hand. His fingers are warm from the cup.

My father, who has historically objected on principle to any inkling of romance in his daughter's life – I'm sure he too still thinks occasionally of luckless, lovelorn Roland – seems oddly at peace with Gavin's presence. Bemused as I watch them together, swapping humorous anecdotes about flight and serious verses about duty, I wonder if Father senses, without conscious understanding, that I have stumbled upon a relationship truly one of a Platonic ideal. He always cared for the Classics. Something we share, I suppose, or would do if not for his pride and my fall. Today, an even less likely pair lean over the book together, my father's balding head almost touching Gavin's blond hair. Thick bottle glass spectacles and oceanic blue eyes flick left and right in synchronicity as they follow the flow of words.

108

'This is fascinating, Mr Raine.'

'Call me George, Gavin.'

'Yes, George.' Perhaps this weekend was not about Gavin going home, but me. Finding peace in the very place where I waged a one-woman war for so long. All I know for sure is some change has occurred between us, even more so than that miraculously taking place between my parents and me. A subtle, subtly profound shift between the giver and the gift.

*

Back in London, I am writing my Blake book when the telephone rings. Work has wholeheartedly absorbed my attention, sitting desk-bound for hours as the milky pale sky sank beneath the weight of a smog-shrouded sunset, itself eventually submerged by an unambiguous flat black. Several shrill rings are necessary before my focus breaks from Blake's imaginative realm, returning with disappointment to the untidy, book-barricaded room around me. Rising stiff-limbed and resentful of the intrusion, an old, bobbled cardigan wrapped around my shoulders – no need to worry about my appearance when I'm alone – I pick up the receiver. Static hisses down the line. I hear no words at first. And yet somehow, from the peculiar pattern of his breathing, I can still tell it is Gavin.

'J-Jonnie's ... d-dead.' His voice rasps, faltering between sobs. 'He d-died in ... M-Mary's arms.' Shocked and horror-stricken, I learn that Mrs MacLeod had telegrammed Gavin this afternoon to relay the vet's sombre prognosis for his best friend, still under her care at Sandaig. Gavin thought Jonnie's cancer defeated. We all did, I realise desolately, recalling the day he introduced me to the dog and we both touched wood to reinforce his respite from ill-health. Yet tragically, the remission turns out to have been only a temporary reprieve. In his master's absence, illness's slow, unseen march through Jonnie's dignified and distinguished body had become a vicious final assault, attacking his ageing system on multiple fronts. For the dog's welfare, Mary told Gavin kindly but clearly, the vet said the end must come soon.

'I c-couldn't face it.' Wretched and drowning in his despair, Gavin gasps for air. 'I knew w-what had to be done, and I ... c-couldn't face travelling to be with him. I couldn't do it, n-not after everything I've already lost.'

'What else have you lost, Gavin?' I ask as gently as I can, but he is sobbing too hard to answer me. Another unspoken request for understanding that I will commit to in the name of trust. I'm sure the details will be revealed when he is ready.

'I'm a c-coward. Coward. Coward. Coward.' The telephone judders, thick blows resounding down the line until I must jerk my ear away; painful, blunt thumps like Gavin is striking the receiver against his temple. 'It s-should've been me,' he cries, no longer trying to hold back the tide of his hysterical grief. 'It should be me lying dead. Not him, not Jonnie, always so pure and good and innocent.'

'Please,' I repeat myself too, my free arm reaching into the empty air of my living room in my desperation to comfort him. 'Please … please don't.'

'Come.' Gavin sniffs, then speaks with sudden lucidity. 'Come over now. I need you, Kathleen, or else I don't know what I'll do.'

I run through the park. There is no time to wait for a taxi. During daylight hours, these trees appear friendly, branches extending like arms outstretched for an embrace, but now they contort into sinister silhouettes; lean limbs curled like grappling fingers that are trying to claw me back into the black. No human with a warm bed waiting for them remains out in the open this late. Lost souls seek their slumber on the park's cold iron benches, ineffectually protected by threadbare, hole-ridden blankets. From nearby bushes, women of the night eye me with worldly disdain, one giving a perfunctory head turn as I pass to check there is no police officer on my tail. Her customer, otherwise engaged, does not notice me at all.

When at last I reach the road that leads to Gavin's studio, there are a few streetlamps to light my way. Their glare shows up the Thames in the distance, a rolling dark mass dotted with intermittent reflected glints. Road and pavement blur into an indistinct greyish bilge whenever I step beyond the streetlights' narrow beams. I cannot see the flat clearly, but my mind often travels this way in the darkness. Now, my body is merely following its lead.

Gavin opens his door before I reach it. He has been waiting for me. No lights are on inside and the nearest one from the street casts harsh, haunting shadows over his face. Drawing near, I see that his bottom lip is bitten, shimmering with a suspended single teardrop of blood. His blue eyes are rimmed red, angry welts digging into their corners where he has rubbed his tears away. His fair eyelashes are askew, clumped by moisture and violent scrubbing to give him the startled look of a new-born animal.

110

'Kathleen.' A fat tear falls down his thin face. Gavin puts out his arms for me as I hurry towards him and he half-collapses onto my shoulders. I stumble, ankle twisting in a way that will hurt later, but I remain standing. *Let me bear it*, I want to say, although the moment feels too overwhelming for words. Much as I love them, I love him more. I want to carry this weight for him. *Your pain won't break me*, I try to communicate through the silence, my speechless lips pressing against Gavin's ear. *For better and for worse, I am beside you.*

'Will you stay with me?' Gavin pulls back slightly to look me in the eye. His pupils shine wet, irises grey rather than blue when caught in the brass orange glare of the streetlamp.

'I will.' An indefinite question with a definite answer. How long does not matter. He can have the rest of my life if he likes.

Gavin sniffs, wiping the back of his hand across his face like a boy. 'To sleep?'

'Sleep?' I am still supporting his weight. My shoulders are starting to ache.

'Yes.'

'Yes.' I follow him upstairs. The sleeping gallery is in shadow, bed unmade and blankets scattered wildly. Gavin switches on the only lamp, sitting on a tiny bedside table for reading. My heart surges within my chest at the sight as if straining to be closer to his. The lamp gives out a mellow filtered glow, diminishing with distance across this small space. Its plain shade has been knocked sometime earlier and now sits at an awkward angle: the light strongest at his side, weakest on my own. Breathing laboured as if wearied by the fight to suppress yet more sobs, Gavin starts to unbutton his shirt. I sit on the edge of his bed, sheets rumpled and creased underneath me. There is a mirror propped against one wall. In the reflection, I see him undress.

Gavin lets his shirt fall, bare shoulders rippling with the movement. His back twists, a lithe mixture of muscle and bone, and when he turns, I watch the taut sinews of his torso flow like the cragged curves of those longed-for Scottish hills. I see the five exposed birthmarks on his forearm, ink blots written indelibly onto his skin. He begins undoing his belt; I close my eyes and let my dress slide to the floor.

Gavin climbs into bed. I follow. I tuck the top blanket over him, over us, because I fear he will get cold, but Gavin does not seem to notice it. He rolls towards me, his face resting against my neck; I feel fresh tears stipple my skin like warm raindrops. I stroke his back and shoulder blades, my fingers coasting over his bare flesh. Our thighs are touching. I could cry too, as much for myself as for poor Jonnie.

'He never knew.' Gavin's voice is soft, mouth muffled by my hair. 'He didn't know he was going to die.'

'It's better that way.' I continue to hold him, my lips poised at his temple in an unborn kiss.

'No,' Gavin insists. 'I'd want to know.'

'Why? What would you do?'

'I'd send for you.'

I cradle him, whispering sounds more than words as my touch flows to his ruffled blond crown and back again, fingers lingering over the little gold coils that lie in wisps at the nape of his neck. Gavin's cheek slips down until it is resting on my breast. He does not remove it. My own tears start to fall. We stay this way, folded together like the pages of a book, until eventually I sense his breathing change. Steadier. Softer. Peaceful. I feel his body soften as his mind slips into a dream, and with my lips not an inch away from his ear, I tell him all that I would never dare say if he was awake. Much later in the night – I am still not able to shut my eyes – Gavin stirs and murmurs something, the sentence pillowy and indistinct.

'Hmm?' I ask.

'What we have will last all our lives,' he says. Then there is silence as he falls back into sleep. My arm remains wrapped around him, softly draped across his bare chest. His ribs feel firm beneath my palm, billowing down and up on the rhythmic tide of his breath.

When I am first to wake, unaware that I ever slept, I watch the gentle stream of sunlight from downstairs drift across Gavin's face. Still dreaming, his fair eyelashes are flickering and a tight muscle within his cheek gives a twitch. While I watch him, there is only one clear thought in my mind, persistent and anchored in certainty as the porthole clock soon to strike a new hour below us. As long as I live, I will never share a bed with another man again.

Chapter Fifteen

'The Ma'dan,' Gavin tells me, excitement spilling from the strange shape of the new word. 'That's what the Marsh Arabs are called by those in the know.' He is going to Iraq. Travelling as far from his grief as he can get. Not just to Baghdad like the occasional British tourist, but to the country's most remote and enigmatic marsh territories. He plans to immerse himself in the culture, becoming acquainted with a rare, precarious way of life that may soon be lost for good if the plague of anodyne Western uniformity continues its nullifying spread across the globe. While it lasts, Gavin wants to explore one of the few places left untouched. Undiscovered. Unwritten. His next book is waiting for him there, he insists, prospective pages flickering on a distant, exotic horizon. It's a feeling I am familiar with. That and the impulse to flee when sadness becomes too much to bear.

With good fortune, plus I hope a little help from my wishes, Gavin has even found a travel companion to accompany him or, technically, for Gavin himself to accompany. An explorer of renown and experience, Wilfred Thesiger wishes to write his own book about their journey, travelling deeper into terrain to which he is already no stranger. Serious and handsome in a severe, militaristic style, I meet him in the studio when he comes to advise Gavin on what to pack. More accurately, on what to unpack, with an entire extra suitcase of books, fresh shirts and complex, newly purchased camera equipment falling foul of the more experienced man's edict to 'travel light'. He may be many things, and increasingly he is everything to me, yet even I cannot in good conscience describe Gavin as a methodically-minded man. Thesiger, meanwhile, feels oddly Victorian in dress with a stiff white city collar and an ivory-handled umbrella, the fine bones of a gentleman still apparent beneath an explorer's coarsened, desert-parched skin. Stiff upper-lip, I realise: a man made in the same mould as Gavin's never-known father. Watching them bicker about how many volumes of poetry Gavin will have time to read in the Middle East – 'None,' insists Thesiger, *The Year One* unceremoniously hurled onto the leave-at-home pile and my pride not far behind it – I confess that I doubt their ability to rub along without irritation.

'Does your wife miss you when you travel?' I ask him, attempting to defuse Gavin's heated explanation, already dismissed once by Wilfred, of why he simply must pack *Arabian Nights*.

'He doesn't have one,' mutters Gavin, abandoning literature to search instead for his lighter.

'It's in your blazer pocket,' I remind him. His scowl softens into a smile when I am proved right.

'More importantly, have you been practising like I told you, Maxwell?'

'Practising what?' I ask Thesiger.

He sinks to the floor, lanky limbs bending with improbable flexibility. 'Sitting crossed-legged.' His wrists rest on knobbled knees, thin legs in turn pressing deep into Gavin's floorboards. 'An essential skill with the Ma'dan. You sit this way to travel by canoe during the day, then do the same in the evenings to socialise in the marshmen's huts.'

'Course I've practised.' Gavin scoffs, although I notice that his eyes have widened. As Wilfred continues his ruthless scrutiny of the luggage, I watch Gavin surreptitiously crossing his shins, trying and failing to lower himself to the ground. A foot or so above his goal, he winces, then feigns distraction with the mechanics of his recently rediscovered lighter. Waving the pair off for the airport in their suitcase-stuffed shared taxi – Thesiger issuing yet more instructions to Gavin as they go – I wish I felt more confident that this friendship will last the distance. But what I wish more than anything, as my mantelpiece Buddha will attest, is for this journey to help Gavin find whatever he is searching for.

While he's gone, I have my own journey to make. My own adventure to witness and put into words. Gavin has given me the key to Sandaig, its cool metal warming inside my palm as I take my seat on the Caledonian sleeper. Tiny Saltires and Union Flags have been embroidered into the white cotton headrests. I take a seat facing front and watch the Scots symbol opposite wave in welcome, the beckoning folds of its coverlet ruffled by the breeze from a nearby open window.

As the train trundles north, I work steadily on Blake and about Blake. Writing about writing about writing. An application is also discreetly tucked into my manuscript binding. This work has gone so well, initiating me into the hidden rites of such a dazzling intellectual dynasty, that I have hopes of developing my research further if I am able. A Girton

114

College Research Fellowship in Arts; a return to my alma mater with greater wisdom and less angst than the first time. I need no longer feel torn between my father's sharp-eyed spiritual scrutiny behind me and Hugh's lascivious gaze up ahead. If the College Board and fate combine to facilitate my return, I will not squander the opportunity out of misplaced loyalty to a man.

Anna, amazingly, is also preparing her undergraduate application.

'We could be there together,' I had exclaimed when she told me about the coincidence. Well, Helen told me first, before calling Anna over to the telephone. She sounded slightly less enthused than I was about the prospect of mother-daughter attendance.

'If we both get in.' A stark yet truthful assessment, which in itself bodes well for her. Admissions panels like logical thinking. Indeed, I have the utmost confidence in Anna's application, if somewhat less in my own. What I do know for sure is that I cannot be a weight on her young shoulders if we come to attend Girton together. I must not bear down upon Anna with the vicarious, bitterly oppressive burden that Jessie's unrealised hopes and dreams became for me. Idiosyncratic and admittedly imperfect as my approach to motherhood has been, I take comfort from the certainty that my daughter has witnessed a woman fight for her own liberation, and I want nothing less – rather, a great deal more – for her. Above all else, she must feel free. Including and perhaps especially of me. Even 'good' mothers can so easily stifle. Windswept lands of southern Scotland still fresh in my mind, I think of Gavin and Lady Mary, re-imagining the prickling sensation of his mother's fingertips against my skin. I close the carriage window, suddenly feeling a chill.

Only when night falls and we rattle over the unseen border do I permit myself to abandon academia and let Scotland rekindle the flame of my poetry. It burns bright through the darkness, Gavin's vivid descriptions of Sandaig penetrating my internal vision until I lose consciousness as if from sheer pleasure. My notebook lies open beside me on the berth bed while I sleep, screeds of newfound imagery spilling out over previously untouched pages. When I wake, I work on until mid-morning when we reach Mallaig: the literal end of the road and the track. Luggage in hand, I slip away from the crowd pouring from the train and wander towards the less bustling edge of the cobble-stoned harbour. The sun is low over the Isle of Skye, shining pale through satin ribbons of cloud that twist and unfurl above the ocean. At this end, the little town sinks to sea level, the cobbles beyond my feet glossed and smoothed by the lapping caresses of the sea.

'Miss Raine?' I turn to lock eyes with a man about Gavin's age. He seems shy, serious and sharp-featured, but with a warm island lilt to his voice that is instantly endearing.

'Bruce?' The Sea Leopard's skipper. A key character in *Harpoon*. Bruce charters vessels himself now, Gavin has told me, along with serving as coxswain – have I remembered that word correctly? – of the Mallaig lifeboat. The man nods; the peak of his captain's hat bobs.

'How did you know me?'

Bruce breaks his sober expression – not dour but not far off it – with a small smile. 'Frae his letter. Nae one describes like the Major.' How true.

Together we set sail, or maybe heave to. However many times I must have read Gavin's book, from conception to delivery and at every stage in between, I could never comprehend quite what the latter term meant. Anyway, we end up at sea, which is certainly a feat I could not have accomplished alone. Only Gavin could choose a home that, while technically on the British mainland, is so remote and inaccessible that to go by boat is quicker than road for the uninitiated. And yet what had looked on land like a calm ocean expanse feels like a churning maelstrom out here. High waves slap the boat's sides, spray disintegrating into mist upon impact; fine droplets flying over and above us before being absorbed back into the atmosphere as if rain is falling in reverse. We hit a broad swell, the watery hillock rising from the depths to block our path, and the boat pitches sideways. My suitcase slides from port to stern, or stern to starboard. Too bilious to think straight, I give up on the terminology. It was never the seafaring of *Harpoon* that interested me.

'Fine day fer it,' Bruce observes. 'Didna expect the goin tae be this guid.' My stomach plummets, acid burning the back of my throat as the boat floor rises and falls with the whipped-up, white-tipped waves. My captain seems content to sail on in silence and I am relieved to escape further conversation, focusing most of my attention on retaining an ill-advisedly hearty train breakfast.

Deciding to look up, not down, I see that gulls have congregated along the cliffs. White specks with wings, their feathers glint against the dove grey stones, the birds emitting harsh squawks as they take to the air and loop the ocean in casual circuits of effortless elegance. One swoops over our heads, the airborne motion as finely polished as the boat's rough course

116

is choppy. The bird dives, strong wings pressed to its torso to create a sleek line of entry into the water, before re-emerging after a moment with a haunting victory cry. Its sharp beak gapes to expose a scarlet interior, claws wrapped around a murky grey-green undersea discovery that may be a fish or simply seaweed.

'Tha's Tormor.' Bruce recalls my attention by taking one hand off his wheel to point. Clenching the unnervingly low rail that stands between me and the ocean floor, I stare across the open sea to an odd cliffside cabin. As our boat coasts in its direction, I make out a corrugated iron roof, camouflaged to almost military standard by the steep slope behind. This place looks more like an eagle's eyrie than a human home. Edged by sheer slices of indigo rock, it sits halfway up a mound layered with mossy grasses, the hillside drenched in saturated tones of deep charcoal grey and damp, dark green. Sea and sky are its vertical bookends, the incorrigible current below looking like the frenzied, broken mirror image of the cool grey-blue veil above. Bruce's boat closes in as much as the tide will allow.

'Tormor's hame tae the MacLeod family.' I cannot see anyone in the house's vicinity, but thanks to Gavin I already have a remarkably strong sense of how to imagine Mary MacLeod. Level-headed yet kind-hearted. A fellow mother and animal lover, who comforted Jonnie as he drew his final breath. Gavin clearly respects and trusts her, which feels like enough authentication to me.

'Sandaig's aboot a mile an a half frae there.' Both hands back on his wheel, Bruce gestures with the peaked brim of his cap.

'Then I'll walk the rest.' My seasickness is, slowly, beginning to subside, but I find myself keen to travel the last leg of my journey on foot. It is how Gavin does it. With the MacLeods' permission, he parks his car on the unseen single track that winds down the rugged hillside, the end of the road just on the other side of Tormor. The terrain beyond is tough, he has warned me, a treacherous non-path of peat bogs and jagged outcrops before a sharp final descent to Sandaig by the sea, but he loved hiking it with Jonnie. Perhaps one day, he will do so with me. 'I'll walk the rest,' I repeat. 'You've done more than enough for me already.'

Bruce's brow wrinkles, a deep crease of concern visible under his hat. Moral codes mean a lot to folk up here. The strict spiritual inheritance of the Kirk, perhaps, or simply the natural sense of kinship that comes to a small community whose members must rely on one another to survive

117

at the brink of the habitable world. I see Bruce's mind cogitate as the boat wheel judders right and left. What is more in keeping with Highland gallantry: to let a woman have her way or see her safely to the door despite her protests?

'I'm starting to feel queasy.' I add what I hope will be the clincher, even if it is an understatement five minutes overdue.

'Breathe through yer nose,' Bruce advises me. 'This'll no tak lang.' He harbours us – parks us? – on a shingled strip whose loose stones crackle under our weight. Limbs accustomed to the boat's momentum, even if my mind is not, I stumble over the side and land heavily on the pebbles. Some are slick with kelp, glittering like starlets as they peek out behind oily curtains of seaweed. Others remain coarse, freshly fallen from high on the cliff and not yet baptised by the cleansing touch of the waves.

'I'll stay wi ye.' Bruce's boots crunch behind me as I follow his advice and inhale heavily through my nose. The extra air surges through me, restorative and soothing, if somewhat tainted by the strong taste of fish.

'No need,' I insist. 'I feel better already. What do I owe you?'

Worried furrows reappear on Bruce's face. 'The Major taks care o everything. But are ye sure yer alricht?'

'Sure,' I say. Without nausea to accompany it, my racing pulse is turning to excitement. I am close. Just over a mile from Gavin's paradise. I want to walk the way he does, travelling in his wake to see this corner of the world through his eyes.

Bruce gives me a reluctant nod, his hand pressed to his cap as if in polite deference to what he believes is a bad idea. Climbing back into the boat, he heaves to (I think), causing the seaweed-covered shingles to pop and crunch. Pulling away, Bruce gives me the wide sweeping wave of one experienced in sending distress signals.

'Ye've nae phone at Sandaig,' he shouts, 'but Mary'll get word tae me if ye need it.' I wave back as he recedes, voice drowned out by an ocean soundscape of shrieking gulls and rolling waves. 'Yer a brave woman.'

I wait until the boat shrinks to a dot on the horizon, then turn to start clambering up the slope. The suitcase – impractical for uphill, I realise too late – is a cumbersome weight that I must swap from side to side with irritating frequency, and all the while my new walking boots rub my heels with each grating step. Spotting a false summit ahead, I speed up, ignoring the thuds of suitcase corner against thigh until I can briefly set down my burden for readjustment. Pausing for breath, I survey the landscape. Like a pointillist painting, hazy from afar yet dotted with lively details, thousands of tiny flower faces peer up at me from the turf; resilient little blooms undaunted by life in such a tempestuously exposed habitat. Many are no bigger than forget-me-nots, their delicate filigree petals laying low enough not to ruffle in the wind. I reach out to touch one, feeling its short stem quiver like an infant tickled for the first time. Blake wrote of such flowers.

To see a World in a Grain of Sand
And a Heaven in a Wild Flower
Hold Infinity in the palm of your hand
And Eternity in an hour.

Slipping on an extra pair of socks for comfort, I pioneer an idiosyncratic technique of carrying the suitcase squarely with both arms in front of me. Peering past the case's bulk, I can see Tormor on my left, its green door and camouflaged façade blending in with the murky earthen shades all around. Up close, the house looks more spacious than I had realised, angled side-on as if confiding in the hillside. A set of washing poles is planted deep into the small space between the wall and steep land to the back. A garden, I suppose, although the term seems rather redundant out here.

Thigh muscles burning – in London I too often exercise my mind at the expense of the rest of me – I peer past my hefty suitcase and see with delight that I am approaching the peak. I also see that I am no longer alone. Two children are looking down on me, the sun behind them serving to illuminate their matching, motionless silhouettes. Two little boys. Two wee boys, as they are in Scotland. They must be Mary's twins, whom Gavin has mentioned, specifically the various trials they put their mother through in their relentless pursuit of mischief. As I draw level, they stare with curious elfin expressions, small features impish enough to make me fancy that they have sprung straight up with the hillside flowers.

'Hello,' I say. 'How do you do? I'm on my way to stay at Sandaig.' At the shock of this unanticipated revelation, perhaps coupled with that of my English accent, one boy's mouth drops open in astonishment. His brother, who may be an eighth of an inch taller, shoots me a scowl. His disapproval reminds me of an over-zealous blackout warden I had the misfortune to meet during the war. Although I suspect these boys were not even born back in 1939.

'Did the Major say ye coud?' The brother-in-charge demands of me. His slack-jawed associate turns his gaze from me to his sibling and back again.

'Aye, he did.' I take the chance to practice my Scots, although once again the accent falls flat. 'Gavin's my friend,' I elaborate in my normal voice. The 'big' brother continues to stare, scepticism tussling with intrigue. Twin Two, however, is instantly overcome by jealousy.

'We've bin fishing wi him,' he blurts out. His long, fawn-like eyelashes flutter in indignation. 'Have *you* ever bin fishing wi the Major?'

'Can't say that I have,' I admit. The twins turn to each other, relieved.

'Once, we dinnae even need tae go oot tae git the fish,' the slightly taller one adds mysteriously. 'The fish came tae *us*.'

'That was lucky,' I say. The boy shakes his head with an elder stateman's sagacity, like one who has seen more of life's triumphs and tragedies than I can possibly imagine. His brother, missing the start of this new movement, begins his own head shake a split second too late. Their movements jar on an irregular left-right, right-left rhythm for several moments before they synchronise.

'It wisna luck.' A born storyteller, Twin One pauses for proper build-up. Everyone tells a good tale up here, Gavin says; another way in which their remarkable collective spirit manifests within a landscape that is itself seldom short on drama. 'It wer a *killer*.'

'A killer?'

Both boys nod, in perfect alignment this time. 'The biggest killer whale ye've ever seen.' Twin Two picks up the narrative with the confidence of one well-rehearsed in its telling. He holds his arms out wide so I may gain some sense of how large the killer really was. I decide not to burst his bubble by pointing out that, having never encountered a whale in my life, even a shrimp-sized tiddler would technically count as the biggest. The boy stands arms aloft but clearly feels that even this extreme stretch does not do his story justice. He nudges his brother, who obliges him by lending a hand on his other side.

'The killer came tae Sandaig,' he says, 'and it were so big tha it sent the dolphins swimmin, who sent the big fish swimmin, who made the wee fish get fearty and swim right intae the bay.'

'There were a million.'

'A bazillion.'

'A gazillion trillion pillion squillion!' The boys start jumping, giggling

120

as they go, as if no human body could hope to contain such excitement while staying either stationary or silent.

'That does sound like a lot of fish.'

Twin One looks at me as if I still don't know the half of it. 'An they were glittery.' By way of another demonstration, his brother holds up ten stubby fingers to wiggle at me. I don't believe he is aware that his eyebrows are wiggling with them. 'The Major said tae tak as many buckets as we cuid carry o them.' The boys' giggles return. 'We ate til we were sick.'

'Tell me, is your mother in?' The last thing I want is to think again about vomit.

'Housekeepin on the mainland,' the twins answer in unison. We are still officially on the mainland, but their way of speaking seems appropriate. A true island surrounded by water on all sides could feel no more distant from the rest of Britain than Tormor and its timeless, isolated coast. I knew that Gavin 'escaped' to Sandaig, but until I came to this part of the world myself, I didn't realise quite how far from ordinary life he was retreating.

'Mum'll be back fae tea,' Twin Two tells me. Tea. The word does not sound so bad in his lyrical accent.

'Then please tell her I said hello.' I lift my suitcase. 'Will you be able to remember my name?'

'Well, tha depends on whit it is,' says Twin One, very sensibly.

'Kathleen Raine.'

'Tha's a sad name,' says his brother. The little fingertips he used to mime glittering fish are recast to play falling raindrops.

Chapter Sixteen

I hear Sandaig before I see it. The bracing crash of the waves; the playful, teasing trickle of the burn; and the whisper of the unseen waterfall that rises to a roar as I approach. My route from Tormor draws me down, not up as one might expect to travel in the direction of paradise, and the early spring marsh ground feels unsteady beneath my feet as I sink into its squelching grasp. I pull, wrenching my mud-soaked calves back to the surface with a pop, and my virginal walking boots re-emerge caked in thick, oozing sludge. I feel both pairs of socks becoming sodden and chilled. The sea's own footprint on the earth can be sensed with every step, water coursing through the muddy veins of this moistened soil and flooding the land with its lifeblood. There are more wildflowers, plucky indigo and ivory petals sticking their heads audaciously through the peat, just as the sun finds occasional breaks in the mist of pale grey cloud through which to shine at full strength.

Taking sound rather than sight as my guide, I stride across the bogland, suitcase swinging. I have no landmarks to follow except for the dappling of flora and an intuitive, gut-felt sense of being right that has usually served me well in life, with a few quite spectacular exceptions. I start to wonder if I have wandered off course. Then, in the distance, I spot a bridge. I hurry towards it, running as fast as my load will let me, and all at once, the mysterious burbling of the burn translates into a gushing, galvanising call of encouragement. Reaching a higher point, I realise that the water was always at my side, guiding me by its voice alone as I wove and twisted my way to the world's edge. This bridge has stone piers but wooden struts, well-worn by wind and rain if not human footfall. I pause at its centre, poised between old world and new, while the burn tumbles and cavorts in bubbles of ecstasy beneath me. I can see the house. Gavin's house. Ringed and illuminated by this brilliant stream of water, glimmering bright white as the sun alights on the waves.

Without knowing why, or at least driven by reasoning that I cannot put into words, I let the burn draw me to the house in a circular approach.

Like Tormor, it faces side-on and not straight. Putting its shoulder to the wind, I realise now, while the sea swells and lashes only a stone's throw away from the threshold. The horizon is framed by the Cuillins, the Isle of Skye mountain range of which Gavin sometimes speaks dreamily, and I can make out a delicate dusting of snow still lying atop its angular peaks. Except the cottage itself, the only human-made construct is a small automatic lighthouse, mounted on the largest island within Sandaig bay. Its flash is faint in the daylight, a starshine-subtle glint more welcome than warning. Even so, I move closer with caution, my free hand reaching tentatively towards the nearest white-washed cottage wall as if the building were a wild animal, as shy as it is mysterious and instinctively averse to sudden movements. Slowly, my fingers touch. Uneven stonework ripples under my palm.

'Hello.' My words to the twins linger in my mind. 'I'm a friend.'

Sandaig's door is double-panelled, each side having a small glass square to let the light in. Gavin told me that he had painted them recently in this uplifting shade of sky blue, but unremitting sea wind exposure has already stripped off some of the finish. Beside the right panel, Gavin has planted a rose, its three delicate red flowers still tightly wound in bud. Droplets of ocean spray cling to their fragile leaves. Soon, I think, spotting a growing stick tied optimistically to the plant's short stem. Soon it will grow and soon we will be together. I reach into my notebook pocket where the key has been waiting since London. Gentle and reverential, I open the door.

The walls are pitch-pine panelled. The ceiling is laced with antique, black-eyed beams. Setting down my suitcase, I walk inside with my eyes still adjusting; the pale sky and sun above the shimmering waves outside creating the sharpest possible contrast with this dark-varnished retreat. Gavin had warned me that provisions would be primitive, and it seems he made no exaggeration. Without electricity, the only indoor light sources are candles, dotted about the room in various states of melted dissolution, and an oil lamp propped beside a corduroy covered sofa that Gavin made himself using swept-ashore fish crates.

'Everything one needs washes in with the tide, given time.' How right he was. A pearl of wisdom to live by, understood only by those well-acquainted with the ways of the ocean. The tide will bring you what you need. It has brought me here, after all.

The fireplace is unlit, of course, yet well-stocked with driftwood.

Above it, the mantelpiece displays an array of fan-shaped scallop shells; above them, a tightly pressed row of Gavin's most treasured books. I scan their spines. *Brideshead Revisited. Death in Venice.* And me. I trace the letters of my name on each poetry collection, fingers flowing from 'K' to 'a', the swirl of a second letter that Gavin and I share. When at last I lower my eyes, I notice that the stone chimneypiece itself is engraved.

NON FATUUM HUC PERSECUTUS IGNEM

Think, Kathleen, I command, brushing the cobwebs from my teenage Latin tutorage. '*It is no will o' the wisp that I have followed here.*' I close my eyes and am struck by a sense of Gavin's presence so powerful that a part of me expects to see him when I reopen them: whisky glass in one hand, cinder-tipped cigarette in the other. I know precisely whom I have followed here.

There is a tiny Primus stove in the corner on a salt-scratched, copper-bound barrel stamped with a whaling company logo. One pan and one fork are on the stovetop; clean yet poised, they are angled for action as if the visceral 'Gavinish' energy with which this room is imbued is so strong that his echo may soon become hungry. Having eaten well on the train and come close to losing it all on the boat, the growl of hunger within my stomach is still a timid one. I decide to continue my exploration elsewhere first, stepping over the boxed-up supplies that constitute the rest of this 'kitchen corner'. Tins and long-life cartons mostly. Perhaps Mary's twins can teach me to catch my future suppers.

Two-up and two-down is the cottage layout, but so far, the tides have not deemed it prudent to wash up furniture for more than half the rooms. Passing the unfurnished ground floor box space that is intended to become some sort of kitchen-parlour-dining room or, knowing Gavin, a library-study-parlour-dining room, I head to the staircase. It is steep, formed from rickety wood risers that creak and grimace with my footsteps. And yet I know it is more robust than it looks, from an anecdote of Gavin's that will surely pass into Highland legend.

'Guess who I met on the stairs at Sandaig,' he had challenged me in London not long after first taking up the cottage. 'I should say, guess who I met wedged halfway up them.'

Any conventional suggestions I might have made, perhaps members of the MacLeod family, had to be abandoned after that comment. 'Who?'

'You mean what,' Gavin laughed, and soon I was laughing too as he recounted hearing deep bellows of distress while still a quarter of a mile away. A heavily pregnant cow, having somehow negotiated her bulky body through the front door – how she opened it will forever remain a mystery – had been inspired by her triumph to tackle the cottage's stairs. Halfway up, however, her expectant belly got the better of her and, aghast, Gavin returned to find her stuck, barred by a potent mix of terror and physical logistics from moving down or, Heaven forbid, up.

'Instinct did equip her with a solution of sorts,' he remarked wryly. 'Although whether it came from fear,' he fished for my curiosity, 'or from an intelligent desire to reduce her body weight, I'll never know.'

I took the bait immediately. 'What was it?'

Gavin gave a snort. 'Defecating down the stairs.' My giggles had turned to guffaws, tears streaming as Gavin treated me to a foul-mouthed re-enactment of his futile efforts to restore order, until, at last, kicking out viciously at him for his troubles, the cow succeeded in sending herself hurtling back down to ground level.

'Her calf was fine, thank God,' Gavin concluded after pausing to produce a handkerchief, monogrammed G.M., for me to wipe my eyes. 'Born a fortnight later, the wide-eyed, wobbly-legged picture of perfect health. I worried for it.' I loved him for that.

Remarkably, the Sandaig stairs now show no trace of their past trauma. How Gavin – and Mary MacLeod, I expect – managed to get them clean is beyond me, but despite bending down for a tentative close inspection, I can see and smell only polished, well-worn wood. I continue to Sandaig's first floor, my journey thankfully less eventful than that of the bovine intruder. Just like downstairs, one of the rooms remains empty; a sparse spare bedroom without any furniture to speak of. I walk to its window, the cold damp lintel depressing slightly beneath my touch. Outside though, the dappled clouds of mist have parted, letting this whole stretch of coastline bathe in the afternoon sun's cool luminosity. At the ocean's edges, tapering mounds of silver-veined rocks rise from the water to frame the waves, complementing the view beyond the sill like the double mount of one of Winifred's paintings. What this room lacks in comfort is immaterial compared with the scene of raw, uncultivated beauty that nature itself has created.

I move next door. Habitable this time or, at least, a room recently inhabited by Gavin. I find another oil lamp sitting on an upturned lobster creel. As in his studio, Gavin has placed it beside his bed for reading late at night. I think of my own volumes, waiting downstairs with the fan-shaped shells, and a warm wave of happiness rushes into my heart. Gavin has flowed through every word I have written since we met, my lifeblood and love intermingling as they are channelled through ink in the same way that Gavin's vital spirit can somehow fill these rooms even when he himself is three thousand miles away. Yes, I researched the distance. It matters little. Thirty thousand or even three-hundred thousand miles could not sever the golden thread woven between our souls.

His bed is small, closer in width to a childish single size than a full adult double. I suppose it would be a struggle to get anything larger up that narrow staircase, as the bovine mother-to-be found out to her cost. I sit on the mattress, smoothing over the fuzzy wool wisps of one of the three blankets laid out on top. Essential, I suspect, if my memories of rural winters still apply. The material turns static beneath my touch; I raise my hand and the fibres follow, broken fragments floating up like flower stems reaching for the sun. My gaze moves towards the window, glimpsing the same exquisitely rugged coastline as next door, just a few feet further to the left. This time, a writing table is also nestled neatly beneath the sill. I rise to admire its perfect fit, my hand skimming the wood plank surface until I realise that this, like the downstairs sofa, is a unique homemade construction. From nautical detritus turned in by the tide, Gavin has managed to concoct a totally functional desk. Deeply impressed, I see that there is even a drawer of sorts; a crooked inlet dug into the wave-scarred wood, complete with a bottle cork in place of a handle. My imagination is inspired, invigorated by the thought of my Blake manuscript finding its home away from home here. Gavin's handiwork and mine, united in one place. I want nothing more than to race downstairs and retrieve my notes, yet curiosity compels me to open that little drawer first. I give a gentle tug on the cork. A shallow compartment appears, with a note and a seashell inside.

Found me. I knew you'd never be able to resist a writing desk. Welcome to my Avilion.
    Love, Gavin.

The island-valley of Avilion. That's Tennyson, I recall, rolling the smooth pale grey shell in my hand. Its exterior is a silvery gloss, freckles buried under the porcelain glaze as if it spent too long in the sun some centuries or even millennia ago. The shape is similar to that of a conch, no longer than my open palm, and two ridged lines ripple along its underside, giving the sweet, if rather surreal, impression of a teeth-exposing smile. I fold my fingers around it. Avilion ... In the poem, Avilion was King Arthur's mythical retreat at the end of his life, an imagined paradise where his soul would live on in sanctuary from suffering.

"It lies deep-meadow'd, happy, fair with orchard lawns and bowery hollows crown'd with summer sea, Where I will heal me of my grievous wound." But Gavin's wounds are not grievous. He is not yet at the end, and neither is his note. Sensing the faint imprint of further ink overleaf, I turn the sheet over.

Ps. Did you see the rowan tree?

I go to the window. The cowrie shell is still clutched in my hand, its cold tide-polished curves growing warm within my fist. I stare out at the landscape, my free hand straining as I press it into the sill, my forehead bearing against the glass pane just as Gavin's once did at Monreith. Within moments, I am rushing back down the stairs, tumbling over a missed bottom step with all the clumsy, ungainly urgency of that poor pregnant cow. Opening the door, the full force of the western sea winds strikes me, but soon their power is at my back, pushing me on as I sweep round to the side of the house. Pebbles washed in with the tide roll and crunch beneath my feet. The ocean air adds a buoyancy that propels my flailing limbs forward. But when I see it, I halt. Logically, I know it must always have stood here. I was simply too distracted on arrival to notice it before. Yet this tree feels new-born. Newly grown. A miraculous, mythical lifeform arising fresh from the earth, sun-charged seawater flowing through its roots as if my reading Gavin's words was a spell to make it manifest. In front of me, our shared dream is a reality, flourishing within an auspicious, horseshoe-shaped twist of the burn that ripples around Sandaig. A rowan tree. His rowan tree.

Its bark is flecked with silver and gold, narrow rings in precious metal shades interlocking along its length. In shape, it shows the influence of its environment every bit as much as the cowrie shell, trunk coaxed into subtle waves by the unrelenting sea gales and asymmetric lay of waterlogged land below. Narrow ovals of emerald crisscross as if to shelter the nascent nubs of blossom that will, in time, metamorphose once more into ruby berries-to-be. Froths of the former are already emerging, delicate petalcups outlined in ivory like the foam cuffs on the Atlantic

127

waves washing up a few feet away. I dip beneath the nearest branch and feel its feather-light foliage brush my face. Exposed whorls of new growth snag on loose strands of my hair, but the sensation is not one of capture. Rather reclamation.

I rest against the wood, leaning my spine into the tree's gnarled vertebrae, and stare up at the slivers of cool blue sky beyond its leaves. From this angle, those embryonic blossom buds seem ripe with curiosity, peering down at me from swaddles capped with white as soft-spun and frilly as lace. I thought when Gavin and I met and saw through one another's eyes that our shared rowan was pure transcendence: the fruit of an imaginary realm, at home more in Blake's world than our own. But here at Sandaig, I can touch it. See it. Sense it. The earthly embodiment of what we have found together, growing in the place that Gavin's soul calls home. I reach up, cowrie in one hand while my other entwines with the branches. There is nowhere I would rather be than here and now.

Chapter Seventeen

I stay for several minutes, my eyes closed as if in prayer inside the rowan's embrace. With sound as my sole guide, I grow able to distinguish the whispering rustle of trailing branches from the rhythmic swirl of the waves, and both from the playful, glockenspiel twinkle of accompaniment that ripples out from the surrounding burn. Another noise is also audible in the distance: the fierce, full-bodied gush of the waterfall. 'The soul of Sandaig.' That's what Gavin calls the fall.

Wriggling out gently from the rowan's enveloping grip, I trust the burn to show the path I should follow. Its stone-laid bed starts to widen as I walk upwards and I extend a hand as if in greeting, letting the cool water course over my skin. It feels just like Gavin told me it would. Even the sunlit portions are chilled, as if some unseasonal source of snow lies perpetually preserved beneath the soil.

Clambering further up the embankment, I notice the trees that have sprouted on either side of the burn. Not rowans, of which 'ours' seems to be the only one, these tall specimens bear strange chartreuse pinecones; whole handfuls growing amongst their vibrant green leaves with wavy, almost shredded edges. Alders? I remember Gavin mentioning the species on one of the first occasions that I had cause to picture this place through his eyes. 'A sure sign of water nearby.' Whatever they are, the new trees narrow together as my self-devised route progresses, and my eyes dart to catch rogue flickers of movement from just beyond their clustered branches. Rabbits? Deer? I soften my footsteps on the peat mulch and am rewarded by a few brave pairs of extra eyes following my steps. As Coleridge, Wordsworth's wild-hearted companion always said, one is never alone in nature.

Clovers cover the ground as I approach the waterfall, their dainty leaves demurely overlaid until it looks like the flowers are hand in hand. Lucky, I think, inhaling their fresh honeyed scent and trying not to crush their delicate forms underfoot. Birds are whistling nearby, a sweet and pure song that ends with an upward trill. A linnet's call? I follow on foot to where it beckons me from the treetops. My path takes one last turn, alder boughs arching as if to cover my eyes before a surprise.

Where to look first? I had expected one torrential cascade but find myself faced with a multitude, like seeing the inner workings of a mind trying to hold a thousand fast-flowing ideas at once. The waterfall rockface streams with interconnected pathways, from fragile trickles that have no more gusto than a leaking London tap to a succession of sheer drop descents stretching many feet wide, pouring from the hillside with a forceful vigour that could knock a person off their feet. The bordering rocks have stark angles, stones jutting through fern frond curls to send the watery rapids askew. Their jagged shapes make me think of glaciers, yet the colours are those of warmth: forest brown, fawn and bronze. The water's momentum is such that it hits each new level hard, bubbles streaming upon impact while creamy foam collects in the whirlpool chaos of its wake. Awe-inspiringly intricate, this network seems to me a triumph of natural engineering that man could never hope to match: breathtaking in its complex power and transformative in sheer beauty. If any part of me should return when I am dead, Gavin says, it will be here. I believe him.

*

I walk along the ocean's edge on my way home. To Gavin's home, I mean. Despite its severely limited modern conveniences, the thought of his unassuming cottage is already invested with a rich familiarity that makes me wish to call it home too. Perhaps it is the intensity of Gavin's descriptions, or else the psychic magic we share, but I have the inescapable sense of having returned to a cherished place that a part of me has simply failed to remember. '*Anamnesis*', Plato called it. An 'unforgetting'. Only hard, earthbound logic reminds me that I cannot have been here before.

Heading back to the house, I realise that the tide is making a return journey too, steel-blue waves lashing the turf as water floods over the coastal rocks. Laughing, I scramble to escape its clutches, dashing light-footed across the sand like a young girl rushing to avoid a reprimand after staying out too late. My walking boots are now not only christened, but coated with sea sludge, letting in water at an alarming rate of knots through obscure breathing holes punched in their toes. Cheerfully capitulating to the inevitable, I remove them to tie their sodden laces together, squashing two pairs of wet socks and my fatally shredded stockings inside the toes before swinging the damp bundle over my shoulder.

I carry on unshod, the icy current stinging the bare flesh of my ankles and calves as waves continue to pour over me, yet the pain feels oddly exhilarating. Thrilling as much as chilling, like the time I fell into a Great Bavington water trough. It had iced over, and my eight-year-old self felt inspired to try and walk on water, compelled by a spirited impulsivity that life has tried to freeze out of me ever since. Not today, though. Sometimes I stand still, as if asking for more, and the ocean obliges me with enthusiastic immediacy. There are Blake paintings that show almost precisely this scene: women of the ocean with veils of waves and froth ripples flowing from their hair and skirts until one becomes unsure of where one lifeform ends and the other begins. Nymphs and mortals alike dance along the shorelines of his paintings and poetry, their joy undiminished and perhaps even enhanced by its transitory nature. I think back to my ceilidh steps with Gavin and start kicking up foam with my bare feet, smiling as sea-spray droplets are born aloft on the ocean wind.

Only when the enchanting, mauve-tinged skyline sinks to indigo-black do I accept that my playtime is over. The sand turns charcoal coloured in the shadows, clumping around my exposed wet toes the way that snow once did around dear Jonnie's hangdog ears. With most of my clothing drenched and feeling suddenly desperate for warmth, I head straight for the living room fireplace as soon as I reach Gavin's cottage, stopping only to briefly brush my hand across the tender rosebuds at his door.

Gavin's has plenty of matchboxes – say what one will about smokers, their paraphernalia often comes in handy – and I set to work lighting the fire. Greedy for heat, I strike three matches in quick succession, tossing each onto the driftwood pyre that awaits me in the grate. Sparks fly. Accustomed to dull, slow-smouldering lumps of dirty London coal, I dart back as the shards splinter and crackle, glowing a luminous amber before they break apart in explosive spasms. Rolling the damp hem of my skirt, I sit with my bare feet together, toes pointed as I hold my soles as close to the open flames as I dare. A welcome, pleasurable warmth creeps through me, thawing my body from its extremities to its core and melting the piercing Atlantic ice inside my veins. Letting the heat take hold, I stare into the fire as the driftwood erupts into miniature fireworks. Red-gold flickers rise from each flash, new flames caressing one another like a couple making love.

Reluctant to relinquish the only warm spot in the house, I decide to bring my work here: writing furiously, fiercely, desperately, as the fire continues to burn, each fresh flare illuminating my words until the intense surging heat almost singes the back of my hand. Gavin finds equilibrium in this place, a serene tranquillity with which to heal his wounds, yet the very spot that brings stillness to his soul is setting my own alight. I turn what I can of it into words, letting my pen take the lead, and I do not dwell on the fact he is not with me. His essence is embedded into the pitch-pine panels and gold inscription; he is there in every water drop that cascades from the falls or rises to nourish the roots of his rowan tree. In purely physical terms, I am alone, but emotionally and spiritually, the realms that matter most to me, I feel only belonging. Knowing Sandaig exists and Gavin has admitted me into this sanctuary, I cannot see how I shall ever feel lonely again.

When at last I rise, rain is falling. I stand up and step back, almost instantly losing my cloud of hard-earned heat as I carry Gavin's little oil lamp to the darkened window. One might be tempted to call it a spring shower, yet there is nothing genteel about this deluge. Ocean winds screech and shriek as they sweep up loose stones and turf, whipping them over the coastline before dragging them back out to sea. Sheets of rain strike the pane with shuddering horizontal force, battering the glass with such ferocity that I duck on instinct as one would do if thrown a punch. Sandaig is a liminal spot, its landscape more closely aligned with sea and sky than earth, and when the ceiling beams begin to quake, the overriding sensation I have is of being inside the heavens as they open. My thoughts travel to Gavin halfway across the world, struggling through the dry, dusty heat of Iraq or perhaps a freezing black foreign night. On top of his mantelpiece bookshelf sits a small gold-encased compass, scratched and weathered enough to be a survivor from Soay, war or both. I seek south-east for Iraq and reorient myself to face the Sandaig stairs, taking private delight in making my body's alignment match that of my heart.

'Gavin?' My voice is hoarse from the fireplace heat and not speaking since I left the twins hours ago. 'Gavin.' No one can hear me, naturally, although a part of my heart cannot help but wonder whether he does.

The storm continues to stir up chaos along the coastline, rattling Sandaig's roof until upstairs I can hear loose slates chattering like teeth. Doubtful that even three bed blankets will create a sufficient barricade, I curse myself for neglecting to bring more woollen wear. But then my eye is caught by another lobster creel, pushed into the bedroom's corner to store Gavin's cold weather odds and ends. Within Sandaig's magical laws of serendipity, surely innocent curiosity is permissible?

A few sweaters in, I find one that I recognise. The image of this jumper has stayed with me since Gavin's *Harpoon* bookplates as an unforgettable component of his seafaring wardrobe. Dotted with distinctive checks of cream and brown – not quite a natty harlequin print, but nearer to it than the basic navy sailing gear worn by his colleagues – this thick, heavy knit was designed for Scottish spring-times just like the one currently raging about me. Its wool feels weighty in my grasp, a halo of friction fuzz rising along the inside of the sleeves and – a girlish wave of delight flows through me – below the waist where Gavin must have tucked it repeatedly into his belt. I can see him in it now, crisp full-colour mental pictures springing from the book's black and white photographic plates. Gavin standing on the bridge with his crew, the indigo inclines of a Hebridean island receding into the distance; Gavin reloading his harpoon gun with skilful nonchalance, cigarette dangling rakishly from his lips. Although I know I am alone, I scan around me automatically. Who knows what Highland ghosts have drawn close, lips pursed and brows knitted, able to read and disapprove of my most dissolute inner thoughts? Satisfied I am unseen, I slip on Gavin's sweater. The high neck scratches against my skin and the cuffs sink well below my fingertips so I must roll them three times to free my hands. But I am happy. The words could be embroidered right in with the pattern. *Here I was happy.* I no longer feel cold at all.

Like this, I climb into bed. Into Gavin's bed. I let my body sink into the mattress's embrace, pulling the blankets over me and burrowing inside the fabric cavern they create. I press my cheek into Gavin's pillow, feathery and silken compared with the coarse wool covers on top. My head is resting where his has lain, and I think of his thoughts. I wish to dream his dreams. Our minds are in accord, our spirits forever in tune; three thousand miles means nothing to the symphonic harmony of spheres within which all that we are to each other resounds. Twice now, Gavin and I have shared a bed, both occasions as innocent and chaste as fresh sand spread high on this deserted shore, untainted by human footprints and unmoved by the fearsome passion of the waves. In body, yes, I ache for him, but in spirit I choose to rise above the gnawing, animalistic hunger of a woman for the transcendent, no less fervent desires of a poet. It gives me pleasure, deeply felt intellectual satisfaction, to see us soar together in my mind's eye, relieved of life's weight and united in a new world. Or perhaps the oldest world there has ever been. A land of soulfulness: shore, sea and sky.

With my eyes shut and my body sheltered by the blankets, I can still sense the momentary shock when a streak of lightning jolts the blackened ocean. Even the storm here seems sent by the Gods, electrifying the landscape with violent bolts hurled down from the clouds as if for divine amusement. The low thunder moan that echoes a second or two later is loud enough to channel through the protective layers I have amassed, its impact vibrating into my bones until my whole skeleton is shaking. Too excited to be fearful, I wrap my arms around myself, the movement pressing Gavin's jumper firmer against my skin. Exertion and exhilaration, plus the rapid changes in temperature, have combined to dizzying effect. In the strange, hallucinatory haze that submerges me, I feel my hands could be his.

*

When I wake, the rain has stopped. The hour is still early and it seems more like last night's starlight has spread; Sandaig's scenery is now lit by the pale, ethereal translucence of a rising sun felt more than seen, yawning just over the ocean's horizon in anticipation of morning. From Gavin's window, I can discern flecks of white sea foam that mirror the cotton-wool clouds. Faint strips of azure, lilac and coral decorate the distance as if, with the sun's re-emergence, these underwater tones have also chosen to rise to the surface. A thin band of gold is all that separates ocean from skyline. If I watched for another few minutes, I feel sure I would see the world turn.

I go downstairs, careful footed this time because I am unable to fight the illogical conviction that this fragile early morning atmosphere may shatter if spooked with rough handling. Ignoring my socks and soaked walking boots, I continue outside barefoot, Gavin's jumper pulled over my slip to complete an outfit of such shambolic eccentricity that it could only ever fit in hermetic territory like here. I greet the rosebuds as I go, their little petals glistening with rainwater drops that fall to the ground under my touch. The few clouds above us appear feathered, scoring the pale blue sky with wisps like the miniature marks on my cowrie shell. At the ocean's edge, the tide now flows tranquil over the shingles and newly revealed rockpools. When I reach them, I kneel before carefully rolling up Gavin's sleeves. With a deep breath and a wince, I plunge my arms into the ocean.

134

The sharp sting of cold makes me gasp as the iced water hits, splashes seeking out the hem of my slip and plastering it to my thighs. My forearms glisten beneath the waterline, hands nebulous and indistinct until they no longer feel like parts of my own body. I accept the idea gladly, eager to go beyond the confines of my limited physical form – the thin veil of flesh, as Blake calls it – to be reborn within this water, cleansing myself of past woes and letting them float off on the restorative tide. My arms sink, the ocean lapping over my skin as I dodge teasing tendrils of seaweed and sift through silt millennia of mud. This world is where the cowrie came from; Gavin's gift to me, a tide-kissed shell that speaks the language of the depths. I intend to return the favour, to find my own treasure to give him, another token of eternity that will be a worthy symbol of my love. Fine billows of buried sand stir beneath my fingertips, underwater clouds of dust and debris clearing to reveal gemstone shades glinting up at me from the seabed. White and purple coral drift past in easy union with the gentle current and I bend until my face is barely an inch from the quivering surface.

'You.' My fingers alight on a spiral shell. Not the biggest or most ostentatious, but a small, perfectly formed pearlescent discovery in the shape of a cathedral spire. Reverentially, I raise it to the light. Still glistening, its unbroken skelter reads like a twisted scroll of symbolic lettering, hieroglyphic characters that tell of a time long before Gavin and I were born. A time when Sandaig shore was not the edge of the world, but its centre. 'Hold infinity in the palm of your hand and eternity in an hour.' Blake's words. My heart. Gavin's gift.

When I rise, my slip is clinging to me, but I ignore the sensation of damp silk gripping my contours to pause for a beat on the shoreline. Listening to the sound of the silence. Filling it in my imagination with the soft crunch of shells beneath Gavin's feet.

'Soon,' I promise myself, turning to face south-east. 'One day soon.' At this angle, my eye is drawn to the rowan, resilient and deep-rooted enough to have survived last night's storm unscathed. In fact, I fancy a few more nubs have sprung up since yesterday, prospective rubies and garnets glittering in anticipation beneath their blossoming surrounds like jewelled rings worn inside white lace gloves. As I watch, a bird settles within the rowan's branches. A black bird.

'Are you an ouzel?' I ask it. Nestled within the tree's boughs, I cannot see if the bird has a ring over its breast. Breaking off a bud, now destined never to ripen, it stares bright-eyed and unafraid. Then it flies away.

135

Chapter Eighteen

I set my spiral shell for Gavin on his windowsill. A good place for a collection, I decide, feeling the avian impulse to forage for more treasures and trinkets with which to decorate our nest. The sight of the unused stove also reminds me and my stomach that I have not eaten for almost twenty-four hours and my gut grumbles, starving muscles spasming in indignation until yesterday's nausea threatens a deeply unwelcome resurgence. I set to work and am in the midst of a heated discussion with the Primus stove – or rather, an unheated discussion, which is the crux of the problem – when through the window, I see Mary MacLeod approaching. We have not yet met in person, but Gavin's Sandaig stories and the vivid mental images they conjure mean I have no trouble recognising the only other woman within a five-mile radius. Impressed, I watch Mary traverse the tricky peat bog terrain with the confidence of one well-versed in its pitfalls.

'Thought I'd check how you're settling in.' Her voice carries the same softly melodic lilt as that of her young sons, but her pronunciation is more polished. Will adulthood buff the rough edges off her boys? Somehow I hope not. 'I'm Mary.'

'I know. I mean, I'm Kathleen.' In place of my inadequate walking boots, Mary wears knee-high wellingtons with trousers, and as I beckon her inside, she slips them off to tuck sensibly behind the door. Her trouser hems are held by thick knitted socks, and I add a pair to my mental list of items I will need next time I come to Sandaig. I expect it will grow longer before this day is done.

'The wee ones said they'd met you yesterday.' Pulling down her hairscarf, knotted more securely than I have ever managed to achieve, Mary turns to me with a healthy blush of exertion blooming over her cheeks. Her strong brows and naturally tight auburn curls, threaded here and there with strands of steel, are saved from severity by an impish vital spark in her cat-shaped green eyes. They, too, remind me of her sons. 'Apologies for the pair of them.'

'Whatever do you mean?'

Mary frowns, although the hint of a smile stays on her lips. 'Only that they're a handful. Make that two handfuls. Why, sometimes it's like trying to tame a wild animal. Mother to mother, you know how tough it can all become, don't you?'

'I do.' I like Mary already.

'Mine are mischievous wee sprites, and they're very, very curious about strangers. We don't see many here.'

'What are their names?' It occurs too late that knowing will not help me differentiate between Twin One and Twin Two until we meet again.

'Willie and Jim,' Mary tells me. 'Roddy is their big brother.' Three handfuls. Plus, a home halfway up a mountainside. Gavin's admiration for Mary is clearly not misplaced.

'Well, they're charming boys,' I insist. Mary stares sceptically as if she suspects a case of mistaken identity. 'I have a son myself,' I add, lest she deem me deluded as to the realities of children's temperaments. 'James. And a daughter, Anna.'

'Oh, a daughter.' Mary's smile expands to a warm beam of delight. 'How lucky you are.' I am lucky. I know it. So why were there times when my emotions lagged behind that knowledge? The happiness in Mary's face, the proverbial pride and joy she cannot disguise however naughty her offspring are, makes me recall sweet-hearted Lavinia at Monreith telling me about her boys. Motherhood seems so simple for most women. So straightforward. This candid start to our conversation aside, I never sense a trace of shame or inadequacy in other mothers; still less the humiliating exposure of awkwardness or, God forgive me, ambivalence. Not that I have ever felt ambivalent about the children themselves. Rather, about myself, and my ability to provide what they seemed to demand of me from screaming, colic-seized infancy onwards. Anna's wails in her first months will stay with me until my last: agonised shrieks of an internal torment I could never soothe, her tiny face turning puce with rage and leaving me pale and trembling. 'When we are born we cry that we are come to this great stage of fools.' *King Lear*. I fear I was always better equipped to be a poetess than a parent.

Oh, I excelled at the make-believe, in more ways than one. Whenever Anna and James needed a playmate to accompany them through the happy fields of their ripening imaginations, I was as playful and whimsical a companion as any child could wish for. In our wartime Lake District sanctuary before Helen's house, Anna, James and I stayed as a

137

trio in what had been Martindale vicarage, devouring bramble jam and diligently building up a homemade nature reserve on the landing. How many caterpillars must we have acquired on our fell walks, carried home in plump young palms and coaxed to crystallise into butterflies that we later set free on the lakeside? How many times did we glimpse fish darting through the beck that flowed along the bottom of our small, overgrown garden, each bright flash of scales as elusive as the poetry I sensed, without evidence, lay waiting just below my own surface? Yet even then, in the darkest recesses of my heart, the fear never left me. That I could only pretend to be the mother society expected. That my vision as a poet was irreconcilable with my responsibilities as a woman. Shadowed by the ever-encroaching threat of poverty on our horizon, my days were stifled by the lonely, relentless and profoundly unpoetic rhythms of domestic drudgery. Wash, mend, weep, repeat. I wrote little. I felt even less. As months slipped into years and my marriage – at least, the meagre material sustenance that marriage had represented – slipped further from me, I truthfully thought I might die from the depression. Once, I very nearly did. What would have become of my children if I had succeeded?

In the end, the best compromise I could come up with was to provide for Anna and James while protecting them from my personal insufficiencies. Isn't that what a 'good mother' does? Place danger out of reach of little hands? Even if that danger exists within herself. It is what I told myself I was doing when the war ended and I left for London without them. I doubted myself then too, on that grey-shrouded autumn day, my legs bound with the stiff rigidity of a corpse as I forced myself to walk away from Cockley Moor. I remember turning, cold bones creaking from tension, and giving a falsely chipper wave from the foot of the hill on which Helen's home stands. If I descended far enough before looking back, I had told myself, I would be able to resist the impulse to return. I think now I should not have tried to resist. Seeing Anna and James with their little hands clasped in Helen's, their distant young faces round and uncertain as the dots of two question marks, I had felt my heart fracture. After so long praying to feel something, anything, perhaps it served me right to be hit with more pain than I had thought a human body could hold. And yet I kept waving. Kept walking. Without my poetry, without giving it my all to become who my soul told me I must be, my broken heart would stop beating altogether. The biggest choice of my life, the choice I know I will always be judged for, did not feel like a choice at all.

I wonder, and wish I was brave enough to ask, do mothers like Mary also feel forever caught between the devil and the bright, bitter sea?

'Kathleen?' Mary's voice brings me back to the present. Embarrassed, I realise that I am indeed looking out to the sea: not bitter yet undeniably bright, shimmering in the mid-morning light as the sun sails higher over Sandaig. At least she does not look offended by my lapse in concentration. A little concerned, perhaps.

'I'm sorry. I was miles away.' *I am now*, I remind myself. I am light-years away from all that I have known before, miles away from past pain and past mistakes.

Mary nods. Perhaps this landscape provokes reflection and rumination in many an awestruck newcomer. It is as if, Gavin once told me with perfect solemnity, the veil between this world and the next grows gossamer-thin in this spot. Something about the translucency of the ocean colours or the ephemerality of the light. Having seen both for myself, the notion is hard to argue with.

'How are you finding it all? Gavin asked me to make sure you felt at home.' My mood lifts, elevated as always by the mere mention of him. Although after last night's transcendence, physical as well as spiritual sustenance would not go amiss.

'Wonderfully well, thank you. Except I can't seem to get the stove to ...' I gesture pathetically in the direction of the unlit Primus.

'Ah, that old trickster. Let's take a look.' Stepping forward, Mary stoops to confront the recalcitrant stovetop. 'You haven't filled the spirit cup.'

'The what?' A spirit cup sounds like something Blake would drink from, awaiting an inspiring visitation from one of the angels only he could see. The reality turns out to be more prosaic, a little black metal dish that sits beneath the head of the stove burner. Plucking a bottle of methylated spirits from the assorted stove-side debris, Mary lets a small amount trickle before reaching for Gavin's matchbox. 'Mind never to fill it all the way, or it'll splash out and set the place alight. Now, you just vent it and pump it.'

'Excuse me?'

'Vent it ...' From near the Primus's base, Mary twists a tiny valve I had failed to notice. 'And pump it ...' She withdraws an odd-looking lever with what looks like a doorknob on the end. Vigorous pulling and pushing ensues until a tentative flame creeps up the neck of the stove.

139

'Give it a minute to take hold. What are you making?'

I shrug, the jumper's high wool neck rough against my bare skin. 'Whatever Gavin has left for me.'

'He's happy here, isn't he?'

I nod. The wool scratches. I tug at Gavin's rolled-up sleeves, unfurling them to find flakes of silt and dried sand from my earlier seashore adventure.

'He can be himself here,' Mary adds. The quiet implication that Gavin cannot be himself elsewhere echoes unacknowledged between us. In conversation as in poetry, it is often words unsaid that speak the loudest. The bones of a friendship seem to already exist between her and I, yet suddenly they feel too brittle to support more than awkwardness. Perhaps Mary thinks me misguided. Naive. Don't I understand what Gavin cannot give? Yes, I understand, and I do not care. Or perhaps I care but cannot stop. One does not turn back the tide. Practical and capable though she is, Mary surely knows how it feels to recognise something as a fact within one's mind but find the heart unwilling to cooperate. Her family's precious, precarious way of life, raising children in communion with the ocean, shore and sky, seems unlikely to survive indefinitely in this soulless modern era. Yet they stay on at Tormor, even so. It is no will o' the wisp that they have followed here.

'Can I post letters nearby?' I coax Mary towards a change of subject, leading us away from riskily intimate terrain that I am certain Gavin would not wish covered in his absence. Increasingly, I turn away from such matters in my own mind too. The mere idea of him desiring anyone else, however long ago and however wrought with confusion he must have been, makes my gut twist and my pulse staccato. Even my ravenous appetite is briefly diminished. Besides, fresh from last night's compositions, I do indeed want to turn my sense of Sandaig into words for my loved ones: for Anna and James, Helen and Winifred, even Tambi, who may send a package with more Blake-related research books, if I ask politely and promise to repay postage. And for Gavin, naturally, even if I have only the Consulate-General address and cannot fathom how my correspondence will reach him while he explores the remote nomadic marsh territories.

'Yes, there's a Land Rover that takes the Tormor Road once a day after the mail boat docks. J.D. and the other men all take a turn driving it.' John Donald, Mary's husband, is another never-seen figure whose image is already formed in my imagination, thanks to Gavin and his evocative descriptions. Wiry and erudite, I know Mr MacLeod is an autodidact whose grasp of literature, history and politics can put the Oxford-educated Major Maxwell to shame. According to Gavin, that is; I suspect he exaggerates for dramatic effect. 'I'll send one of the boys to collect your letters later,' Mary offers. 'Is an hour long enough?'

'More than.' Time ticks by differently here. '*Eternity in an hour.*' I sometimes feel Blake was envisaging a place like Sandaig, a century before Gavin or I were born. I look down at my wristwatch to find that water submersion has caused it to stop. I tap it, then shake, and the second hand swings in an inebriated, liquid-logged stupor before collapsing where gravity commands. Eternity it is.

'You have an incredible home,' I compliment Mary as we move to the Sandaig doorway, miming the steep Tormor ascent with the side of my hand.

Pride once again glows in her face. 'Thank you. Not many can say they live on Ben Sgriol.' *Ben.* What the Scots call their mountains. Gaelic, I believe, a language in which both the adults and children I have met here will be fluent. How I wish I could say the same, already enchanted by the fluid lyricism that seems to stream through every syllable of that ancient tongue. Maybe I am not too old to learn a little? 'I think Sandaig is the more beautiful spot, though,' Mary suggests politely. 'The waterfall and the burn.'

'And the rowan,' I add. 'The rowan is a very special tree for us.' Mary's eyes dart to Gavin's jumper. I wriggle, self-conscious and flushed as the stove flame grows stronger.

'Special,' she repeats softly. 'Yes, rowans are meaningful indeed in Scots culture. Guardians of goodness. The tree of life, some call it. You'll find no man around here willing to chop down a healthy rowan. Most folk won't even crush a berry from its branches. It's the lifeblood of the tree, they say, and it mustn't be spilt for self-serving ends. If you misuse a rowan's power, you may live to regret it.'

'I can believe it.' And I do. What a wise heritage these Highlanders lay claim to, their long centuries of tradition commemorating what Gavin and I found, without searching, when we first saw the world together. Two branches of one rowan; soulmates drawing strength from each other's roots. It seems only right that to abuse such precious power should rebound upon the perpetrator.

'It's quite common for Highland cottages to have a rowan outside,' Mary tells me. 'The tree is believed to preserve blessings given to those who dwell in the home.' Together on the Sandaig threshold, we stand in sight of our subject. A beam of pale sunlight enrings the tree; the silver strips of the rowan's bark glint. 'Curses too, legend has it, if anyone was wicked enough to cast one.'

Chapter Nineteen

I discover that days here do not pass so much as drift, bobbing from dawn to dusk with the rhythmic rise and fall of the tides. I wake early, then go down to meet the sun still hovering on the ocean horizon, warming the water in broad brushstrokes of light until the whole scene gleams coral, amber and rowan berry scarlet. Sometimes I bathe in Gavin's waterfall, curling my bare toes around a rock ledge and bracing myself before I lean back into the torrent, emerging breathless from its stream as my skin tingles then burns from the freezing cold. A pleasurable pain, or perhaps a painful pleasure. So much of what I experience these days is a peculiar blend of both.

When my morning writing is done, sculpting and refining the raw inspiration that tends to strike first thing and last, I make a habit of collecting more shoreline shells, uncovering treasures from the depths that feel as if the world's jewellery box has been upturned underwater. There are ombre scallops large and coquettish enough to serve as ladies' fans; a tortoiseshell ruffle-trimmed trumpet conch that, childlike, I press to my ear, listening to the watery sway of my pulse while the real sea performs symphonic heartbeat swells just beyond. I find powder-blue periwinkles, daintier than my littlest fingernail, their fossil shells furled tight like the waterfall ferns and bent over as if locked in perpetual sleep. Razor shells too, marbled slivers of hard cartilage, and shimmering pearl mussels, their cool shell casements deep black on one side and lustrous cream-white on the other. These ocean fragments feel like pieces of a poem, each unique ridge and ripple telling a story that I cannot read yet feel I understand. Day after day, I brush the sand from another treasure, setting it on Gavin's windowsill to wait for his return.

In view of his rowan, I tend to the red roses growing around his sky-blue cottage door.

Till a' the seas gang dry, my dear,
And the rocks melt wi' the sun;

I will love thee still, my dear,
While the sands o' life shall run.

Whisper-singing Burns' words, I turn to face south-east. A flock of geese sails above me in V formation, silver wings beating in haste to make their Icelandic homecoming. Where most boys fantasise about being soldiers, or even explorers like he turned out to be, Gavin's childhood dream at Elrig, odd as it was, involved being the first man to own a goose from every species on earth.

'It takes all sorts,' I had teased when he told me.

'Exactly.' Old enthusiasm sparked anew in those blue eyes. 'There are all sorts of geese out there.' According to Gavin, Sandaig's wintering visitors are known as greylags: handsome silver birds whose migration augurs the return of spring and, I hope, his own return home with it.

The best part of a fortnight passes before I next sense manmade commotion on the wooden bridge. Both twins are attending me, chattering happily – in Gaelic, I think – as they approach Sandaig. They swing a large postage box between them, the envelopes perched on top tossed violently with the momentum.

'Hello, Willie. Hello, Jim.' Relieving the boys of their burdens, I try to disguise the fact that I still do not know which is which.

'Hello, Miss Raine!' They reply in unison as if I am their teacher calling out a class register. Do they go to school or are they taught at home? Where is the nearest school, come to that? Regardless, the boys express excitement when their uninvited investigations of the cottage lead them to discover my growing shell collection. After obtaining solemnly sworn promises that they will handle them with care and subtly withdrawing the precious cowrie and spiral to be on the safe side, I agree to let them touch and not just look. Young guests thus distracted, I read my return correspondence.

Gavin, understandably, is yet to write. My letter is probably still waiting for him at the Consulate-General, and the anticipation of surprising him with it feels good enough for now. Then my words will do their work, as the best poems ought always do: empowering one pair of eyes to see the sights of another and narrowing the physical distance between us until many thousands of miles become meaningless. The elegant reeds and rushes of the Iraqi marshes will transform into the sheltering alders of Sandaig; the lush teal waters in which Gavin paddles will reflect the glimmering bright burn that encircles his spiritual home. Before I arrived here, a tiny part of me had wondered why he wanted me at Sandaig in his absence, but now I know. I am here to turn his world into poetry.

Tambi, generous as ever, has enclosed all the books I asked for and more. Shelley, Wordsworth, and Coleridge ... By now, I have familiarised myself with Blake's oeuvre, so far as any follower can familiarise themselves with the visionary, vibrantly illustrated universe in which his imagination reigned. My next move, I have decided, is to not just read what he wrote, but what he read. Earlier writers on Blake present him as an idiosyncratic genius, but I am coming to feel only half that traditional description is true. His allusions may be obscure to us in this ill-informed modern world, but the ideas he explores are not without foundation. He studied widely, with sharp critical scrutiny, and I want to deepen my understanding of his message by reading each text he mentions, however tangentially.

'Don't work too hard, I never do!' Tambi has scribbled onto a piece of newspaper shoved inside the box. Only when I turn it over do I realise this is no ordinary news cutting.

'Arts Council Poetry Prize nominees announced,' reads the clipping, followed by a shortlist on which Tambi has vigorously circled the last name. 'Miss Kathleen Raine – *The Year One*.' I press the flimsy print fragment to my heart, the shock pounding in my chest quickly turning to deep gratitude. There would be no *The Year One* without *Northumbrian Sequence*. And there would be no *Northumbrian Sequence* without Gavin.

Trying to calm myself by moving slowly on to the rest of my letters, I see that Helen has enclosed all three replies from Ullswater. Her own outlines possible origin tales for the two shells I described, drawing on the great library of Cockley Moor to assist her enquiries.

'The cowrie is auspicious,' she notes. 'From what I have read, a long-standing symbol of good fortune. In fact, the Chinese character for money is based on it. Your GM has riches in store.' While it is difficult for me to imagine how such a prophecy might manifest, knowing first-hand how little writers typically make, I do not doubt the truth in Helen's prediction. From his refined Roman nose to his fair crown and regal bearing, Gavin seems positively made for money. The spiral shell that I claimed as my own to give him – as much as any of these tokens borrowed from the ocean's bounty can be said to belong to people – also enjoys an equally positive, if less lucrative, iconography. The shell is a whelk, Helen tells me, and its spire symbolises eternity, the coils believed in some cultures to embody a soul's ascension 'up the spiral staircase to heaven'. I wrap my fingers around it along with my prize nomination.

His scrawl almost as untidy as Tambi's, James's letter is short and cheery, jotted down in what I suspect was a rare moment snatched between schoolwork and sports. I try to sublimate my wounded pride with the happy knowledge that he continues to thrive in Helen's care. He would love to come to Sandaig – 'will Gavin be *their*?' he asks, making the editor in me cringe – and will do so just as soon as his holidays arrive. Of course, he still has his studies. What sort of mother forgets her own child's school schedule? Not Mary and Lavinia, I'm sure. My own escapist spirit is such that I forgot the rest of the world is still turning.

Anna's letter is also short. Crisp. Grammatically faultless. She thanks me for writing and says that Sandaig sounds like a lovely place. Her preliminary examinations went well and her teachers predict that, if she maintains her strong performance, she has a good chance of getting into Girton.

'I believe I will be happy there,' she writes, sounding so much older than her years. My sins seem to stare back at me, writ large in ink. Yet in this remarkable new world of blessings and possibilities, a truly magical land where time itself can stand still, surely it is never too late to retrace one's steps? Or to take new ones. In new company, if necessary. Perhaps having the right man by your side makes motherhood less overwhelming. Less solitary, certainly. I think back to London and picture Gavin and James playing together in the Paultons Square garden; Anna and I watching their juvenile hijinks whilst sharing snorts of laughter. For some time, an idea has been prodding me, nudging me not to ignore it despite the pain that comes from considering pleasures which can apparently never be. What would life be like if Gavin and I had a child?

'Ye leuk sad, Miss Raine,' observes Twin One. Three shells are balanced precariously on his crown, little turrets sticking up through his hair like an improvised mermaid tiara. Twin Two is in the process of adding the fourth and largest yet, his tongue sticking out from intense concentration at the improbable feat of engineering they are attempting. I think back to his twinkly little fingers falling through the air like raindrops.

'I'm fine, thank you boys. Please be careful with those shells.'

At least Winifred has accepted my invitation. She writes back eagerly, the artist in her as enticed by my evocation of Sandaig's early morning colours as a musician might be to hear of new notes in a register previously unknown to human ears. Practical arrangements are made, with help from Mary, and one week later, I stand on the shoreline to watch Bruce's boat rise and fall as the waves guide him and his passenger towards Sandaig. When she sees me, Winifred waves enthusiastically, grinning as she leans over the low front rail. Her sea legs must be sturdier than mine. Bruce docks – heaves to? – on a tide-slicked mass of shingles, and Winifred springs from the boat laden with her easel and paint box. She hurries to hug me, wellingtoned feet – my recommendation – popping and crunching over scattered coils of kelp.

'Thank you for having me,' she exclaims, smile and eyes equally wide as she takes in her first glimpse of the scenery. Even as we embrace, I feel her focus shifting towards the painterly midground of indigo rocks and white-tipped waves, yet I am not offended. Far from it. Like me, Winifred will always be an artist before a woman. Like me, I think she wishes life did not so often force her to choose between the two.

'It's my pleasure,' I say, and it is. My pleasure, too, to bask in the proprietorial, chatelaine-like quality with which her visit is investing me. I feel confident and self-assured as I stand in front of the cottage door, thrilled to see Gavin's faith in me reflected back through Winifred's eyes. The proud, slightly smug sensation reminds me of certain newlywed women I have known, insufferably keen to show off their marital homes. Perhaps I deserve my turn now; I don't remember feeling it when I was actually married.

'Will you come in for a cup of tea, Bruce?' Quietly well-mannered as ever, Bruce has removed his cap and now stands sheepishly to one side while Winifred and I reunite. Gaze to the ground, his fingers clenched around his hat brim, he looks mortified by what must be to him an effusively feminine welcome.

'Thank ye, but I cannae, Miss Raine.' Bruce nods to Winifred and me before replacing his cap and dipping the brim once more for good measure. 'It's ma turn fae the Land Rover the day.' We watch his boat go, shrinking to the size of a tiny cork cast onto the ocean, before I welcome Winifred inside. In my letter, I had warned her about the primitive facilities, but as we step across the Sandaig threshold – like always, I brush a soft hand over the growing roses – Winifred appears admirably unfazed. My friend has inner reserves of steel. Divorced women must, I know. Introducing the cottage room by room, I pause for a moment at every windowsill, allowing Winifred to reflect on whether this one or the next will be best for painting from. There is only one bed, of course, but I have already planned for my sleeping on the sofa.

'You can't, Kathleen. Didn't you say it's made from fish boxes?' The homespun charm of Gavin's handmade furniture is something of an acquired taste.

'It's surprisingly comfortable,' I insist. Not compared with a mattress, true, but much better than the rough shingled coast or the chilled waterfall ledge. Life here involves sanding down my material standards, weathering away my pretensions and leaving only what is essential to survival. I think I like it.

'But Kathleen ...' Winifred looks worried.

'Honestly, I'm happy.' Knowing too well my stubborn resolve, Winifred reluctantly accepts our sleeping arrangements and sets down her rucksack – another recommendation of mine – on the bedroom floor.

'I can certainly see why Gavin felt drawn here ... and he's renting it to you?' The pecuniary tone startles me.

'N-no,' I stammer. 'No, he's ...' I reach for the right word and return empty-handed. Gavin is loaning it to me? Again, the language feels wrong, financial terminology tainting what should be beautiful and pure. I'm taking care of it for him? Still, the sentence retains a transactional quality I deeply dislike. 'We are sharing it,' I settle on. And we are. More or less. Gavin pays no real rent, only a nominal pound per annum to take it off the owner's hands. Money does not matter here. Not compared with cowries and spiral shells.

'I see.' Winifred looks sombre. 'So you'll stay here together?'

'Yes.' I assume so. Why wouldn't we? Her questions drag me down to earth with a thud and it feels impossible to explain in this clumsy, flightless state of mind that I sometimes forget Gavin is not already here. Still, I suppose I should accustom myself to dealing with what people on the outside may think when looking in on our ... arrangement? Agreement? No everyday word seems worthy. 'Nothing improper, you understand.'

'I understand,' Winifred says, although I doubt she does. 'Just be careful, Kathleen. Won't you?'

'Careful of what?' Her seriousness makes me want to laugh. So weighed down with worldly cares and considerations, while my soulmate and I inhabit the skies. 'Strong tides?' Winifred smiles, although her eyes still betray apprehension. We stay stuck in our stalemate for several moments more, until eventually Winifred turns to the window.

'My goodness, the light here is really something.' On that, we agree. The sun is approaching its midday peak, soaring high above the glowing white light of the ocean horizon and letting its vibrant orange rays pour over the bay. Another few seconds and every aspect of this scene will shift, alive and attuned as it is to the breath of the natural world. Ephemeral yet timeless. A transitional beat in which almost all is where it should be. 'It gives one a glimpse through,' Winifred murmurs. *Through what?* I should ask. But I already know.

Winifred does not delay in setting up her easel, while I likewise ready myself with my notebook and pen. The bedroom windowsill, I'm sure, will feature in many compositions to come, but today my friend decides to begin outside: taking her place in a landscape ringed by colours that I know she will capture with her characteristic light-touch brilliance. Together we dig tiny holes to embed Winifred's easel struts in the sand, deploying my suitcase – finally, a good use for it – as an additional support for her palette. At a non-distracting distance, I sit on a rock with my notebook, stretching out until my ankles drape over the rowan's roots. In my peripheral vision, I feel Winifred's brush flowing across her canvas as she illustrates the pale sea and clouds of sun-warmed cotton. Her rhythm matches the soft scratch of my pen, itself in tune with the compelling lull of the waves.

'We're true earth goddesses now, aren't we?' she remarks, and I laugh, realising that the sandy soil has crept beneath my fingertips while I scribble.

'I hope you're missing me out.' I bend back on my rock as if trying to wriggle out of a photograph's frame.

'You're in all of it, Kathleen,' Winifred replies, without raising her eyes from her canvas. 'All of us are in all of this.'

Night falls at what I guess is around five, a shockingly quick descent into shadows that forces us to beat our retreat indoors. In the living room, I light the fire and stove, and while we wait for our food to cook – fish, kindly donated for the occasion of Winifred's first night by the MacLeods – we confide in one another about the creative hopes that this landscape inspires.

'These poems feel like the ones I am meant to write,' I say, voice lowered as if the fates might otherwise overhear and, out of capricious cruelty, decide to separate me from my muse. My daimon, as I think of it: not demonic but ferociously insistent, an inner voice of conscience mixed with inspiration that I ignore at my peril. I cannot describe it so for everyone, of course, most folk would never understand and tend to fear what they cannot comprehend. It takes a fellow imaginative spirit – like Winifred, like Gavin – to appreciate the idea that what we create is not taken from the world but given.

'Then you've been brought here for a reason,' Winifred observes, and I nod. We need say nothing more.

When it becomes time for bed, she takes herself upstairs, albeit reluctantly, and I settle myself on the sofa to watch the last of the fireplace flames die out. Cocooned within my covers, Gavin's jumper is again pulled snug around me. The fireplace embers throb and occasionally sizzle, the valiant spark of a fight still in them as they resist capitulation to the dark. The cindery last light they provide, closer to candle than electricity, is just enough for me to read the chimneypiece inscription.

'I would follow you anywhere, Gavin,' I whisper into the night air, turning to face south-east as the final flames slip away.

Chapter Twenty

'I have a surprise.' The sound of his voice as he beckons me into his flat is like a song calling me home. Melodic, sometimes a little melancholic, although certainly not today, and laced with a lingering tartan thread of Scots that feels even more precious now I associate its brackeny texture with Sandaig. Can it really be three months since I heard it? Heard him? Gavin's hair is longer, having spent so long beyond the reach of barbershop scissors, and his fair locks fall from forehead to cheekbone in a dashing, dishevelled sweep. Accentuating the elegant angles of his fine-boned face, the effect makes him look even leaner than usual, recalling our earliest days when he was whip-thin, weary and lost. But Gavin is no longer lost. He is home. Or here in London, at least.

'Oh, Gavin.' I want to run into his arms, finally held within the embrace I have imagined falling asleep inside every night and waking up to every morning. But Gavin is gone before I get the chance. Eyes tired yet somehow still shining, that animated bright blue straining past a spider's web of bloodshot vessels, he gestures frantically for me to follow him inside, in search of the surprise that clearly cannot wait. Bizarrely, we seem to be heading for the bathroom. Trailing after him, I realise that Gavin's frame, like his face, is thinner than when he left, draped in an informal jumble of Iraqi and English garments that includes an embroidered scarf in place of a tie and linkless cuffs billowing about his wrists. And while playing 'spot the difference', didn't I also notice something oh-so-slightly off about his nose?

'I broke it in the marshes,' Gavin admits when curiosity overcomes my manners.

'Broke it, but … how?'

He turns to give me a ghoulish smile, crossing his eyes until they are angled at a subtle dent on the bridge of his nose. 'A gun backfired in my face. The canoe boys thought it was hilarious. God, Kathleen, you should've been there.'

'I'm rather glad I wasn't.' Still smiling, Gavin brushes a few stray

151

strands of hair from his face. Like me, he seems somewhat unaccustomed to the longer length. A blond whorl rifles through his thin fingertips, coming to rest in a ruffled half curl above his ear.

'There's someone I'd like you to meet.' Gavin's grin widens as he reaches for the bathroom doorknob. Despite the purplish shadows rimming his eyes, the warmth of his expression ripples through me; I picture Sandaig's fast-travelling burn ringing eternally around his Highland house, brilliant and glittering when caught in bright sun. Doing my best to ignore the sudden thrill of physical proximity as we are pressed together by the room's modest proportions, I resolve to focus on my spiritual joy at us being reunited, but I am brought back down to earth by the realisation that my feet are wet. Not damp, but sodden. Soaked through. Water seeps up my stockings, chilling my soles and sloshing over my toes with every step I attempt. The whole floor is submerged, black and white tiles swimming beneath puddles that are rapidly expanding into one lake-like liquid mass. At first, I assume the bath must be overflowing. Then I realise that something, someone, is making it overflow.

'Kathleen, meet Mij.' Breathless with excitement, Gavin points into the bath. I lean over, feet squelching, to watch the water being churned into a whirlpool by the wild, frenetic rotations of a chocolate blur beneath the surface. Overlooking Gavin's bath is a mirror, itself now heavily streaked with rogue droplets, and the double image multiplies the swirling chaos before me until I can barely see where the watery vortex ends and its splash-stained reflection begins. 'I said "Mij"!' At the sound of Gavin's voice, louder and firmer this time, the blur stills. All is quiet. Then with a heaving splash that sends yet more liquid cascading from tub to floor, the underwater creature springs up in a reverse dive, planting two leathery paws on the porcelain rim and staring up at me with quizzical, button-sized brown eyes.

Its head and body are covered in a strange watertight fur, clumped in misdirected brush bristles that leave its scalp crowned by dragonish spikes. Its clawed fingers – four, I believe, or maybe five – are webbed and wrinkled; its paws are almost but not quite like little hands, clumsy and seemingly indexterous as a human's in ill-fitting gloves. Close in size, if not shape, to a small dog, the animal watches me with a dark glossy gaze, pupils glinting under the ceiling light like shingles on Sandaig shore. I bend down. Its silky white whiskers are glistening with water droplets.

'I've told him all about you.' Gavin is almost burbling with boyish delight. 'Haven't I, Mij?' The third repetition of his name – and what a weird name it is – seems too much for Mij's odd little body to bear. Glancing up at Gavin, then back down to me, he opens his crescent moon mouth to expose two rows of razor-sharp teeth. The effect might be menacing, but the expression reads almost comically clear as one of unadulterated joy. With a final exuberant swell of bathwater, Mij launches himself out of the tub and lands heavily in my arms.

'Ha!' he exclaims while I struggle to support his weight; a breathy, excited sort of sound that flows from him as an exhale of mirth and mischief.

'He likes you.' Gavin beams while Mij and I sink simultaneously into the lagoon that has become his bathroom floor. The animal is heavier than I expected, or might have expected, had I more than a split-second to prepare for his violently enthusiastic friendship, yet the burden is eased by the fact that its distribution is seldom static for long. Mij pours over me, spilling and tumbling through my outstretched arms before bubbling up to face height as if he wishes nothing more than to whisper his secrets in my ear. 'Isn't he incredible?'

'He's …' A moist, juicy blackberry of a nose starts nuzzling my own, 'an otter?'

'A very special otter.' Disregarding the wet, Gavin kneels beside us both. Mij gives a squeak of renewed pleasure and shoots in one fluid motion from my arms into his. 'He was caught in the marshes. No one's been able to tell me for sure what sub-species he is. You're unique, aren't you, my boy?' In reply, Mij flips onto his back, exposing a waterslick sliver of pale underside coat. A look of intense paternal pride on his face, Gavin cradles him, gently rocking the otter back and forth while it chitters with satisfaction. 'I'll need to spend a day researching him at the Zoological Society, but I can't leave him alone just yet. Last night I was on the sofa, sleeping – if you can call it sleeping – with Mij's lead tethered to the wooden leg beneath me.' Still looking at Mij, Gavin's fair eyelashes give a quivering triple blink, the battle between exhaustion and pure adrenaline being waged in his face. 'You won't believe what I went through to bring him back into Britain.'

Otter still in his embrace, Gavin recounts the tale of their nightmarish, never-ending journey featuring all the requisite elements of a heroic battle against the odds in the form of blood, sweat and tears (all human). In accordance with flight regulations, Mij had been confined inside a wood

153

box, but Gavin's zinc-lined innovation was already splintered, gnawed and near-shattered by the time their taxi reached the airport. Further drama ensued when Mij managed to liberate himself from his bespoke prison mid-air.

'A rat! A rat!' Gavin mimics his panic-stricken fellow passengers, accompanied by squeaks of emphasis from Mij. All had seemed lost until a serene, supremely elegant air stewardess took control. She calmly advised Gavin to remain in his seat while Mij, showing admirable loyalty to a human he had only known for a matter of weeks, soon returned of his own volition to his grateful master's company.

'That stewardess was a goddess,' Gavin recalls, with a wistful fondness I could do without. Mij indulges me with what I think is a chirrup of sympathy. 'At least we're home now, eh, boy? Home for now, until I take him up to Sandaig.' Gavin turns to me, his otter in his arms. 'I loved your poems.'

'My poems ...' Those words I conceived between Gavin's rowan tree and his waterfall. They made it halfway across the world. Made it to the man for whom I wrote them. My heart aches to imagine Gavin reading my creations alone in an exotic foreign land. 'I've never seen anywhere as beautiful as Sandaig.' I have more to say: indeed, I will never run out of things to say about the place that both he and I now love. But before I can, Mij begins wriggling like a giant tadpole, inspired by my voice to leap back into my arms with another jovial 'Ha'.

'Bring him through to the living room,' Gavin suggests. 'Although I suppose we had better try to dry him off first.' He passes me a hand towel.

'Thank you,' I reply on instinct, although one towel feels about as functional as a snow shovel at the foot of an avalanche. 'Will he mind being dried?' *Will he bite me if I try?* This convivial animal seems suspiciously tame for a wild-born creature. And if there is one defining characteristic of Mij I have observed in the past three minutes, it is being at his happiest when wet.

'Oh, he just thinks it's all a game, don't you, my boy?' Gavin wraps the towel loosely around Mij's torso, inspiring the otter to unleash a full body shimmer that sends yet more droplets soaring. On the plus side, I am no longer aware of my feet being wet, primarily because no part of me is still dry. I am baptised a third time as Gavin rubs over his restless companion, focusing on Mij's improbably elongated middle portion and paws. Mid-ablution, Mij turns to face me, overspilling with squeals of delight as his coat turns increasingly static. I see that his ears are like tiny tunnels carved into his skull, symmetrical concave structures lined with furry brown fuzz. How both canals are not full of water, I cannot fathom. Yet another miracle of nature.

As promised by his new master, Mij treats being towel-dried like a hilarious game, the unspoken yet unmistakable objective being to transfer as much water as possible from his lithe, wriggling body to our own. If medals could be won at this aquatic sport of his invention, Mij would be a gold medal champion. Succeeding only in soaking ourselves further, Gavin and I are soon submerged by laughter as the otter clambers over us both, rising like a tidal wave to place his little paws on my shoulders. Cheeky curiosity written into every inch of him, Mij runs his odd leathery fingers through my hair, loosening my bun and trying to twist the freed strands around his claws. Thwarted by an anatomically frustrating lack of opposable thumbs, he reverts to oral fixation, sucking on my hair before moving up to nibble my earlobe.

'Ouch!' My squeak only encourages him, inspiring the urge to restore balance by 'piercing' my other ear too.

'Sorry. It's an affectionate nip, I think. He's done it to both my lobes.' Gavin leans over to show me. My pulse quickens, although only Mij seems to sense it. I study the small puncture scars on Gavin's skin, yet more perfect imperfections, then look away before I blurt out something embarrassing like the desire to kiss them better that is suddenly surging through me. Bored by our human distractions or perhaps bothered by the inexplicable increase in my heart rate, Mij chooses this moment to slip from my lap, waving his little limbs as he slides like a child at play. He lands, blissfully contented, in one of the many puddles around our feet.

'I surrender. Mij, you win.' Sighing theatrically, Gavin opens the bathroom door and the otter scampers over the threshold, his graceless lolloping gait half-concertina, half-caterpillar. In the living room, the fire is lit, albeit barricaded safely behind a cast iron folding screen, and Mij shows no interest in investigating it when there are well-stocked bookcases and a high-backed couch to ascend. As Gavin readjusts his furniture in an effort to circumvent the most precarious climbing routes, I kneel beside his fireplace and borrow its heat to dry my dress. The flesh of my nearer thigh soon starts to tingle and ache from warmth, and while Gavin removes his valuables from the mantelpiece, I turn to toast my other side. Stretched out along the sofa back, Mij watches my movements with intrigue before curiosity once again gets the better of him. With a wild flying leap, he streams straight into my lap.

'Oh.' I manage to brace, better equipped second time around for an oncoming assault of otterly affection, but the momentum gathered by Mij's long airborne body is still nearly enough to upend us both. Once secure in my arms again, he covers my face with squelching wet kisses. In time, the otter settles down for what I think – I hope – is a nap, curling into a chocolate croissant curve and burying his nose into the crevice behind my knee. As with all young creatures, the sweet innocence of sleep makes one forget and forgive all transgressions. I watch Mij's velvety ribcage rise and fall, whiskers like spun silk billowing with every breath. He is adorable. Magical. Irresistible.

'May I be his godmother?' I ask Gavin.

'I think you already are,' he smiles. In my lap, the otter burbles in his slumber. 'But enough about him and me. What else did you think of Sandaig?' Finally, my words can flow. This is the moment I have been waiting for. I stroke Mij's fur as I relay my tales of the paradise that Gavin has shared with me, the warmth emanating from the fire restoring the little animal's natural lustre until his plush coat gleams with luxurious shine. Not until I am recounting Winifred's arrival does Mij begin to stir, stretching before he pads off to where I assume his food and water are located. Gavin himself is wholly drawn into my descriptions of the place he loves more than any other, his soft smile aglow as together we envisage another world. A better world. A world that two souls – and perhaps now three – can inhabit.

'I saw a blackbird in the rowan.' The words would sound puerile to anyone else, but I trust that Gavin will grasp their poetry. 'I couldn't tell whether or not it was an ouzel.' Gavin moves to reply, perhaps to share some ornithological identification tip or, as I'd prefer, another glowing opinion about my work. But before he can speak, there is a crash.

'What the devil ...?' From the sleeping gallery, a bud vase falls, shattering onto the chevron floorboards and sending slices of china ricocheting across the room. 'Mij!' Confident as a tightrope walker and cocksure as a ringmaster, Gavin's otter is gleefully edging his way along the sleeping gallery partition. Upstairs, the waist-height wall beside the bed must have seemed like an excellent hiding spot, so ostensibly inconspicuous that Gavin unfortunately selected it as the place to stash his valuables. Now, as Mij makes his merry way along the gallery's

156

length, the swinging momentum of his powerful foot-long tail is sending one item after another tumbling down over our heads. The porthole clock topples, caught by Gavin a second before it strikes the floor. The Soay shark's tooth fairs less luckily, hurtling to ground level at missile speed and ending up embedded in the long-suffering, splintered chevrons.

'Mij!' With a jubilant squeal, the otter lets himself fall. Gavin's angry eyes widen in disbelief, then dismay, and it is with desperate relief that he catches the animal in his arms. 'What a bad boy you are, Mij.' Infractions forgotten, the otter chitters cheerfully in his adoptive father's tight embrace. 'I'm afraid we're a pair of bad boys, aren't we?'

'Don't say that,' I object. 'You're not bad, are you, Mij?'

As afternoon gives way to evening, I learn that Mij's full name – his Sunday name, as my father would say – is Mijbil, after an Arab sheikh with whom Gavin and Wilfred stayed. I also realise that Mij is much more than a mere flight of fancy; far from the whimsical, attention-grabbing additions that prowl and prance through Harrods' exotic pet hall. Gavin has fallen in love with him. God knows, it is a state I should recognise. He dotes on Mij, delighting in his every move, and in the rare moments when we are not speaking directly about him, Gavin's attentive, affectionate eyes seek him out like a magnet drawn to its opposite pole.

'There was an otter cub before him,' he confides as Mij swirls around our ankles in pursuit of an elusive marble. 'Chahala. Astonishing little thing. I used to carry her about in the neck of my pullover. The Arabs even started calling her my "daughter". But she died before I could bring her home. Poisoned by the digitalis they use to kill their fish. I didn't know …' Tears swim in Gavin's eyes, a sorrowful translucent gloss glazing over the cool blue. 'It was all my fault.'

'No,' I whisper. My own tears threaten to stream as I reach for the hand I have waited three months to hold. Gavin's fingers feel bony beneath my touch. When I look down, his fair skin is tanned and roughened from his adventures. Slowly, our thumbs and forefingers interlock. 'It's not easy trying to care for a wild creature. You did everything you could.'

Gavin sniffs. 'I sobbed and sobbed after it happened. Big baby tears pouring down my face. Wilfred says I ought to be locked up, feeling so strongly about an animal I'd only known for a week.'

'Wilfred's wrong.'

Gavin blinks, clouds clearing from spring skies. 'Oh, but he's very clever about that part of the world. He showed me … well, he showed me things that I could hardly believe possible.' Conviction helps him to compose himself. 'Kathleen, the way we live in this country is not the only way to live.'

'"The world that you inhabit has not yet been created."'

A glimmer of a smile. 'That's from your poem.' He does not phrase it as a question. Gavin already knows my Sandaig poems by heart.

Mij starts scrabbling furiously at our feet, his marble lodged fast beneath the sofa. I kneel to retrieve it, a supplicatory position that the velvet-coated creature takes full advantage of by nibbling again at my exposed earlobe.

'You're making a good start with this one,' I tell Gavin when I rise, blinking back a wave of dizziness. 'Living differently.' Mij is reunited with his missing toy to only brief elation, the object's enticing appeal lost as soon as he has it back in his grasp. I've known men who were much the same. For the moment, Mij is more interested in having humans to play with, and Gavin and I take turns in letting him surge over us like a breaking wave. The otter whistles with glee as his webbed toes prod our bodies, and when at last he drops into another deep sleep we stare down at him like dazed new parents. Wearily euphoric; blissfully exhausted. 'Is it silly to say that I already love this otter?'

Gavin shakes his head. '"Never was anything in this world loved too much."'

'Thomas Traherne?' Another important influence on Blake.

Gavin nods. '"Never was anything in this world loved too much, but many things have been loved in a false way, and all in too short a measure."' A new sound bubbles up from Mij, a faint 'Ha' reaching us from the distant shores of his sleep. I fancy that, for a moment, all three of us are dreaming of the sea.

Chapter Twenty-One

'Unpolished rice?'
'Tick.'
'Cod-liver oil?'
'Tick.'
'His favourite blanket?'
'Tick.'
'His squeaky rubber chocolate éclair?'
'Gavin, we've been through the list three times. Mij has everything he'll need at Sandaig.' All eyes in Euston are on us as Gavin, Mij and I make our way along the platform. My cheeks pink, unused to such intense attention, yet a part of me also basks in the warmth flushing through me as I sail past the staring crowds with this fine, fair gentleman by my side. Gavin attracts notice at the best of times and the addition of a mystery four-legged friend turns subtle head swivels into undisguised gawps. Mij himself streaks proudly ahead as far as his custom-made leash and harness will allow, little paws pattering out a quick, excited rhythm as we make our way to the Caledonian Sleeper.

Only he and I are travelling today; Gavin has business in the city. His new agent, Peter Janson-Smith, cannot wait to read the first chapters of his Iraqi adventure, and Gavin will be happy to oblige just as soon as he has them written.

'Well, they're *written*,' he insists, tapping his temple to indicate where those precious words are stored away. 'They're just not *written* written.' Writing or *writing*, I have no such commitments to hold me back. With an academic hat on, or rather an academic pen in hand, my Fellowship application is still under consideration by the Girton Board of Electors. Creatively, too, recent years have provoked such an outpouring of poetry from me that Tambi decrees it high time I publish a volume of collected works.

'As an Arts Council prize winner, you're not a junior poet anymore.'

'Do you mean I'm not young anymore, Tambi?' Having just clinked

159

our glasses to toast my recent success, Tambi had pretended he was too busy imbibing to hear me.

'In you get, good boy.' Gavin helps Mij and me into our compartment, handing me the dog ticket he has taken to using when travelling *avec loutre*. 'Elysian Poodle,' reads the breed. I take the 'poodle' leash from Gavin and Mij promptly starts leading me, investigating every corner of our compact berth with his indefatigable nose and paws. An early favourite find is the tiny wash basin. Through that mystical animal intuition we humans can only dream of, Mij is apparently able to tell that this basin has held water before and may be persuaded to do so again. He sinks into it, cramming his long body into a crescent before rotating to lie on his back in a determined effort to twist the tap.

'It's just luck,' Gavin insists as we watch Mij's paws paddle furiously against the metal. 'A triumph of operant conditioning. Half the time it works, the other half he tightens it further.' Unable to resist, I tickle the exposed underside of Mij's pale belly. A few droplets fall from the spout as my hand skims it and the otter wriggles with delight to feel water seeping into his fur.

'I'll be up at Sandaig in a week.' Gavin reaches across me to give an affectionate scratch of Mij's crown. 'Then Mary says you can sleep at hers if you want to stay on.'

Not at ours? 'Not at yours?' The otter pauses mid-scuffle with the stiff metal tap, seeming to sense the sudden tension. 'But why?' Gavin feigns focus on unpacking the rest of Mij's belongings. 'Why can't I sleep at Sandaig when you're there?' I hear a shrill, scolding tone taking over my voice, that unattractive pseudo-wifely nag I hate to catch myself using. But am I not entitled to indignation? I thought we shared everything now. Paultons Square and the studio. The cottage. The otter. And we've shared a bed before. Not that we have spoken about it since. In the months that have passed since that strange grief-stricken night of innocent intimacy, it has come to seem more dream than reality, even though the memory of Gavin's bare skin against my own, his hot tears sinking into my breast, still feels like one of the realest things I have known. I carry its essence like a hidden locket clasped to my heart, yet since his return it seems Gavin needs it to stay locked away. In the cruel, cold light of day, he does not want to remember himself as a fragile child in need of comfort. He is a man who needs no comfort, nor anything else it seems, in his bed.

'Why?' I ask a third time, struggling to steady my voice so it stays closer to curious than cross. 'We've spent the night together before.' Metallic thuds echo through the carriage as Mij recommences smacking his paws against the tap.

Gavin groans. 'Kathleen, please ...'

'Please what?' My cheeks heat, but not from pride this time. I feel my temper threatening to surge; one wrong word and I will boil over.

'That time was different.'

'How so?'

'Just different, Kathleen. Special.' A beautiful word to describe us. I should be delighted to hear Gavin use it. But right now, it sounds far from delightful.

'You mean it was a one-off?'

'Not necessarily. But on that night, I wante ...'

'You wanted me with you, and now you want to be alone?' What I want does not seem to figure, although that is probably for the best. There could be no easy return to friendship if I said aloud all that I want and do not get from Gavin.

While Mij persists in his plumbing labours, Gavin winces as if the memory of his old vulnerability is quite literally paining him. Or perhaps it is me causing him pain.

'Don't put words into my mouth.'

'Then speak them yourself. Why can't I sleep at Sandaig with you?'

'Because it's my ... Mij!' There is a clatter. A clash. A deeply frustrated 'Ha'. Mij's exertions in the sink have sent the soap dish scattering through the compartment, skimming the floor like a spun pebble before juddering to a halt at my feet. I reach for it, but Gavin gets there first, bending with an elegant swoop to save me the bother. I suppose graceful manners are ingrained when one comes from a place like Monreith. Propriety can never be seen to slip. 'It wouldn't be right for us to stay overnight together,' he says quietly as he hands the dish to me.

'Right for who? I mean, for whom?' My schoolgirl error rattles me further. But, really, for whom would it not be right if I were to sleep at Sandaig with Gavin? The MacLeod family, a mile and a half away, or the gulls and greylag geese that fly overhead? Does Gavin fear disapproval from the windswept heather or twisting burn; the tall sheltering alders or the wise, intricate waterfall?

'It wouldn't be right,' he repeats. 'I'm sorry. I don't make the rules.' His people do. His aristocratic ancestors quite literally made the rules by

161

which life in this country is governed. And Gavin is more aware than most of the risks in falling foul of them. 'Besides,' he adds as Mij redoubles his scuffling, sticking his heart-shaped nose as far as he can up the faucet, 'you're familiar with Sandaig now. It's a place that suits solitude. You'll get much more work done while it's just you and Mij. If we stayed there together, I'd only hold you back.'

'That's not true,' I insist, although I suspect it is.

'Yes, it is.' Sometimes it really feels as if he can read my mind. 'In many ways, I think we're alike. We both need our ...' Space opens up in the sentence when Gavin fails to complete it. Inside the basin, Mij issues a mew that echoes out from the tap into which he has wedged his snout. 'Of course, only one of us is a prize-winning poetess.' I smile in response, forgetting my annoyance until too late. 'And you're the only person I trust to be at Sandaig when I'm not. You understand that, don't you, Kathleen?'

Trust. It is not easy for Gavin. Not with humans anyway. I watch him kneel beside Mij, murmuring nonsensical sounds of affection to which the creature replies in enthusiastic kind. It is rare indeed for Gavin to feel as safe with a member of our species as he does in the company of animals. Ever since his lonely boarding school days and those protracted months of teenage convalescence, he has turned to the natural world for solace and escape; an Avilion from the wounds inflicted on him by our cruel human equivalent. In an animal's faithful, deeply dependent eyes, he is a hero, and they cannot betray or humiliate him by spilling the secrets – really, the sole secret – upon which the life he has built for himself depends. To trust a fellow person must be a terrifying prospect in comparison.

I think of the nascent roses growing around Sandaig's door and the Burns tune I sing for them. 'So fair art thou, my bonny lad, so deep in love am I.' And yet even I, so deep in love, do not always get it right. Only a week ago, I remarked to Gavin that one evening during my first visit I had drawn down *Death in Venice* from his cottage bookshelf. It was a novella I had heard of without yet reading for myself: the tale of a gentleman writer transfixed by, and soon obsessed with, a strikingly beautiful adolescent boy. The book was old, perhaps even a first edition, its spine worn and creased while the binding glue disintegrated into clumps. Those yellowing pages resisted even a gentle pull as I attempted to open chapter one, threatening to tear the print entirely if I was dogged enough to persist. Well-read, without doubt. Smudged thumbprints appeared in several places I could see, furtive shadows lurking over the opening passages made in what looked like graphite or charcoal. Maybe the marks of an artist's fingers.

'That book's filthy.' It had felt like a throwaway comment, tossed out while I was rolling a marble for Mij. But when I turned to Gavin, he looked horrified. Shocked. Shamed. 'I mean, it's damp,' I blurted out, scrambling to repair the damage. 'Quite a few of the books are the same.' Whether that was true or not, I could not recall. My fleeting glance at *Venice* had put me off exploring other unfamiliar titles on his shelf.

'It's very old.' Beneath the lingering trace of his Middle Eastern tan, Gavin's face had turned pale.

'Yes.'

He looked down at his slim hands. No smudges or paint daubs; not an artist's fingers anymore. 'I haven't touched it in years.' We had averted our eyes from each other and turned in unspoken unison to Mij, squirming happily across the studio's chevron floorboards with his marble clasped to his chest.

Now, I see the taut lines of Gavin's face soften once more as he watches Mij contort his long body inside the sink. The otter's leathery paws are protruding, tail spilling out over the basin side and swinging smooth as a clock pendulum. Gavin beams, illuminated by fatherly pride, before he looks back at me.

'I understand,' I say. And I do. I understand that Gavin trusts me as much as he is able to, even if some troublesome mental mix of propriety and privacy means he cannot accept us sleeping together at Sandaig. Pride aside, perhaps it is enough that he has shared his sanctuary at all. 'But why this here and now only when I loved I knew.' Another line from my Sandaig poems. And there are more to write, I know it. Maybe time apart from Gavin in body, if never in spirit is what I need to release them from my psyche. If necessary, I will turn the pain into poetry.

'HA!' Unleashing a euphoric exhale, Mij rejoices as water streams over him, having at last overpowered human plumbing and twisted the tap to full gushing strength.

'Mij, no!' Gavin and I leap as one, our hands plunging into the sink and coming up cupped full of water but entirely empty of otter. While we scramble, Mij uses Gavin's lowered shoulder as a springboard, managing to attain the dizzying height of the parcel shelf and – momentarily lacking a better outlet for his energies – fixing his attention on the enticing emergency cord. Edging towards it with all the stealth in his bizarre

163

little body, his leather-gloved front paws reach for the irresistible red string. I wince, braced for inevitable catastrophe in the form of a shrill alarm or horrid jolt, whilst thanking God for the far from small mercy that our train is not actually in motion. Yet soon all I hear are chuckles, human and lutrine. Tentatively, I reopen my eyes to find Mij half-hanging from the parcel shelf, chortling breathily while Gavin ruffles the otter's approximation of armpits.

'The tickling trick.' Gavin laughs as a fresh wave of merriment bubbles up from the dangling animal. 'For when all else fails.' Softly snorting, Mij peels himself from the shelf to yet again land in his master's arms. Gavin cradles the animal for a moment before passing him to me.

When the penultimate whistle sounds and Gavin is obliged to step from our carriage, he stands on the platform waiting to wave us off. From my carriage vantage point, I notice several members of both sexes glancing in his direction and, smiling from vicarious flattery, I gently raise Mij's right paw, wiggling it before the window so that he too may wave adieu.

'Take good care of our boy,' Gavin calls as we pull away. My heart sings, louder than the warning whistle.

Chapter Twenty-Two

'Mij. MIJ!' Two hooded crows startle and take flight from the alders. Mij knows his name, and I know he knows it, but that is seldom enough to recall him to my side once the wild, elemental energy of Sandaig's waterfall has bewitched him. Somewhere between anxiety and awe, I watch as the otter coasts over the twists and turns of the fall's rapids, his round brown head barely visible as he courses through its streams at a speed even the strongest human swimmer could never emulate. Gavin was not wrong when he guessed that Sandaig would provide an ideal habitat. I had not even dared to let Mij glimpse the open ocean while we travelled over on Bruce's boat, apologetically locking my animal companion away in his basket with his harness still attached for double security.

'He's a character,' Bruce had observed as he helped me on board, laden down by my small clutch of belongings and Mij's vastly more complex travelling paraphernalia. The carrier door was closed, but warbling cries of lutrine longing made it clear that he could already smell the sea.

'Do you mean Mij or the Major?'

Bruce merely smiled, sinking his hat brim down into a small salute. 'Guid luck to ye, Miss Raine.'

At Mij's first sight of the ocean at Sandaig, I had felt his body tense. Locked in shock. Spine rigid, right down to the tip of his tail; neat tunnel ears swivelled forward as his black button eyes stared straight ahead. Not one whisker twitched. Was he afraid? I did not have to wonder for long. The tide breached, waves scattering across the shingles, and as if heeding an urgent call of instinct that only he could hear, Mij leapt, stocky limbs turned to springs as he hurled headfirst into the sea. In fierce, furious ecstasy, he dive-bombed the waves, his whole body absorbed by bright crests of foam while I flailed far behind. Travel basket discarded, his harness leash, that lone residual token of domesticity, was whipped away through my frantic, grappling fingertips.

'Mij. MIJ!' In the water, Mij knows no fear, which is ironic because waiting for him on the shore, waterfall ledge or burn side, I am in a near-constant state of terror for his safety. Yet no matter how enthusiastic his explorations while he plays – and these remarkable displays of aquatic agility are indeed 'play' to him – he always returns eventually. Showering me with droplets in an ebullient attempt to dry himself; clambering over my torso as if to confide all the wonders he has witnessed beneath the waves. This landscape is enchanting enough on the surface, and the growing cottage shell collection gives me a tantalising glimpse of what its underwater riches must look like. A submerged Eden of multicoloured anemones, urchins and starfish perhaps, their floating fingers tickling Mij as he dives down into an alternate watery universe? To his credit, the otter tries to take me with him on his journeys, tugging my skirt hem with paws and jaws until I end up half-submerged myself. Only the obvious inadequacies of my land-dwelling human body prevent us from going further together. I fancy that Mij sometimes pities me, glancing back forlornly to where I wait on the shingles, before the cry of his heritage grows too loud to resist and, with a splash and a flourish, he is gone.

If the waterfall is the soul of Sandaig, then Mij is that same element made corporeal. At all hours of the day, and night if I would permit him, he flows through its deep pools and over its cascades with such symphonic unity of passion and purpose that he appears less like an animal in water and more the spirit of water itself, transfigured to take momentary possession of his long, fluid form. He comes alive in this landscape and it in turn never seems more alive than when he is powering through it like a tidal wave. The perfect fit makes me wonder what the world might be like if humankind were content to take its true place. Living within nature; letting nature live within ourselves.

Sandaig's fierce beauty likewise encourages fresh words to flow from my pen, as if channelling the same power that is absorbing my companion. Clinging to inspiration can feel like trying to tame a wild animal – one learns with experience that it can only be coaxed, never trapped – and seeing Mij flourish in his natural element seems to give my soul permission to do the same. Notebook in hand, I take up the grass-covered ledge at the waterfall's side, an unexpected sun trap in which I am happy to be caught. I write as Mij swims, returning to me now and then in convivial curiosity until the pages of my new poems become speckled with water droplets.

Perhaps my Blake work should be on hold until I learn the outcome of my Fellowship contention, yet the strategy of retracing the great poet's steps to uncover his sources has also proved an inspiring one. New and intricate intellectual connections are forming before my eyes, linking unexpected sources together like ganglia, nerves and sinews that will revitalise Blake's prophetic work for the next generation. Take Thomas Taylor, a writer whose very un-vogueishness in his own time appeals to a perversely unfashionable part in me. Blake read his Greek translations, that much is clear, and I sense their influence woven throughout his work. A perennial favourite of mine is his retelling of Cupid and Psyche. A fair-haired deity, his overbearing mother and a long-suffering, lovestruck mortal woman. What a tale. Come to think of it, I consider a little bitterly, I suspect that Lady Mary has expressed her own opinion about the properness, or lack thereof, of me staying at Sandaig with Gavin. In the myth, Cupid defies his mother's orders and falls in love with Psyche anyway: spiriting the girl away to make her mistress of his enchanted home, where she feels the presence of her beloved even though he is hidden from her sight.

'"Well nigh at the fall of the river was a princely edifice, wrought and builded not by the art or hand of man, but by the mighty power of God … it glittered and shone and gave out light such as it had been the sun."'

I recite for Mij, fancying that he enjoys the story. We are alone together, bearing silent shared witness to what can only be described as wonder, and I come to realise that I feel greater accord with this animal than with many humans I have known. We both need the same things to survive. Sandaig. Freedom. Gavin.

'You love him too, don't you?' I ask Mij as he shimmies up my body for a soppy, in every sense, post-waterfall embrace. Nose dripping as he presses it to my cheek, he chitters softly into my ear as a reply.

Having come prepared this time, I plant the foundations of a tiny herb garden around the cottage door, optimistically trusting that the warmer months will give it time to take root despite Gavin warning me not to stake my hopes on a Highland summer being hot or dry.

'Not for longer than three or four days,' he had remarked acerbically back in London, 'to say nothing of their being consecutive'.

Undeterred, I sprinkle my seeds and tend to his roses, their chiffon petals now as full-bodied and expansive as the sweeping skirt of my Hartnell ceilidh gown. I also start gathering up the elfin wildflowers that have been blown loose to land amongst the kelp-strewn pebbles, pressing them flat inside my books before using their crisp, delicate foliage to enliven Gavin's plain furniture with pattern. I experiment with attaching scrapbook fragments of dried flora to the metal casing of his oil lamp, and at night, the flame sends flickering shadow flowers dancing joyfully around the room. I do not linger on the thought that Gavin should be here to see it. He will be. And in a way, he already is. I am living in his house, collecting his shells, bathing in his waterfall and watching his greylag geese soar through the sky. These are his waves upon his ocean; his sun is binding me inside an eternal ring of light.

The only human souls I encounter are the twins, delivering a single letter with their characteristic double-strength enthusiasm. Squashed to fit an ill-suited square envelope, I recognise the blotted scrawl of Tambi's slapdash style with surprise and a heart full of fondness. Nine times out of ten, he fails to write timely replies to the letters he receives, so it seems nothing short of miraculous that he has sent unsolicited correspondence.

'Dear, dear K,' Tambi begins, the line slanting drastically down to the right in ink-smudged disarray that is a perfect match for its author. *'The Collected Poems of Kathleen Raine* is going ahead. Do we i.e. you wish a dedication? Write it below and return post haste. Your obedient servant, Meary James Thurairajah Tambimuttu.' I wonder how great literary agents like Rupert and Peter write to their authors? Most likely, secretaries do it on their behalf. Still, I reply immediately. These words, above all others, are not difficult to find.

> *Dear T,*
> *Dedication to read as follows please:*
> *'To Gavin Maxwell, with whom I share paradise.'*
> *Yours, Kathleen Jessie Raine.*

Let Lady Mary say her worst. Gavin's mother may control Monreith, and by some complex, would-be Oedipal way even manage to have a say in the bedroom arrangements up here, but no one tells me what to write. And if she wishes to object, well, she will have to admit that she has read my collection, won't she? The thought of anyone reading it is thrilling. My own collected works – works so far, I should say – is an honour I have hardly dared dream of, and I can think of no one more deserving than Gavin for the dedication. I have never been the sort of poetess whose work thrives on agony or angst, as productive as those states prove for other writers. I need peace, a gold string tying me to something greater, and a

168

meaningful purpose to call my own. With Gavin, I find it all. Literally and spiritually, he is my messenger from home.

Rhythmic as the tide, my imagination returns to Psyche, and to Taylor's Platonic descriptions of when she first came to her magical marital abode. Her love could only visit her under the cover of darkness, Cupid's presence strictly conditional upon his going unseen. Trust your heart, not your eyes, was the edict, yet lovestruck Psyche disobeyed as I suppose women with spirit are always apt to do in stories. Her attempt to expose her love to the light against his wishes led to her losing him altogether, forced to enact a painful penance until, after many long years of agony, the Gods pitied poor Psyche enough to let her rejoin her lost beloved in the ethereal world of souls. I write in sympathy for her suffering, sitting by the fireside every evening after at last cajoling Mij back indoors. Whenever I err, scrunching my spoiled paper into a ball, he proves ecstatically excited to retrieve it, nosing through my discarded notes as if he believes some may still be worth a second glance. A natural editor, I fancy, until he starts trying to eat the scraps.

At night, we sleep together in Gavin's bed. Mij's preferred spot is in the hollow behind my knees, but he will occasionally creep up to curl over my lower stomach in the spot where my pregnancies grew. I expect I'd be too old to conceive now. I am unlikely to ever find out. Still, I have this water baby, don't I? And his father will join us soon. Close to slumber, the otter nuzzles my skin with his silver thread whiskers and a sound starts coming from him that I have never heard before: a plaintive, poignant cry that strikes my ear with the fluid, flute-like rise and fall of Gavin's first otter. Chahala. Cha-ha-la. Cha-ha-la. Named partly for a nearby river and partly for this distinctive lutrine call, Gavin has told me of how that tiny cub also made the noise in her sleep. Subconsciously crying for her mother, he suspected. I lower myself a little further down the mattress, curling my body around Mij's. His crying ceases. Before long, I too am slipping, drifting into sleep myself, and my last conscious thought is the hazy hope I will dream of Gavin.

Instead, I am underwater, wading through an opaque, never-ending black as I struggle to keep up with Mij. Diving deeper, he surges away from me, his strong tail striking against a few murky, floating objects that I recognise as the broken pieces of my seashell collection. I call out, begging Mij to slow, but my mouth only fills with water as I watch our otter swim away. Kicking out, I find that coiling tendrils of undersea weeds have ensnared my ankles and wrists; a silent swirl of bubbles engulfs me as I try and fail to scream. When I wake, it is with a jolt: limbs tangled up in the bedclothes and face half-smothered by loose covers. At least that explains why I could not breathe.

*

Revelling in unanticipated rays of Highland sun strong enough to warm the sand and whiten the waves, Mij and I spend our morning at play on the ocean's edge. Me, dipping cautiously into the rockpools in search of yet more shells; he, barrelling into the surf like a frenzied, fur-pelted torpedo. I am laughing aloud at Mij's exuberance when suddenly the otter freezes, foam washing over his motionless paws and his glossy coat glinting as he turns to face the direction of Tormor. Mij's blackberry nose twitches, silken whiskers aquiver, and his head cocks to tune into some far-off sound still inaudible to me. With a squeak and a whistle of delight, Mij takes off, charging across the uneven lay of the land with all the awkward ungainliness of water forced to flow uphill. His long body creases with every stride, paws striking out a lolloping double-time canter. Running myself, I raise a hand to my brow to try and glimpse whatever it is that Mij has seen. What, or rather who, the otter loves even more than water.

The sun is behind Gavin, his approaching form backlit so that for a few moments he appears composed of slender shadows that shimmer in a high-contrast haze while he walks. He follows the burn's weaving route downhill from where I expect he has just left his Bentley, and slowly the details of his appearance start to sharpen for me. The plaid pleats of his kilt swing with every step, yellow-green threads mingling with the sun-glazed turf. His white collar is unbuttoned with shirt sleeves rolled up to his elbows, the fabric thin enough to reveal the rippling movements of his slim, muscular torso underneath. Ahead of me, Mij has devised a clever way to unite his two passions, shooting headfirst into Sandaig's burn so that he may more quickly reach his master. The otter swims hard to cover in seconds a distance that would take most land mammals several minutes, leaping out of the burn at Gavin's feet with ebullient chirrups of joy. Whilst still yards away, I hear Gavin greet his companion with deeply affectionate murmurings, scooping him up for an emotional reunion embrace. He comes towards me with the otter in his arms, kilt swaying softly with each long stride. Summer's vibrant shades seem to float and almost orbit us both, giving the landscape the peculiar impression of a

170

photographic plate not yet fully developed. Ringed sunbeams of red and green are following Gavin's footsteps; I lower my hand and watch the wild scene before me burst into glittering dashes of light with him and Mij at their centre.

'Fàilte,' I say. Welcome. The twins have been teaching me a few phrases of Gaelic.

Gavin smiles, surprised. 'Tapadh leat,' he replies. Thank you. Then he laughs, a sound I would love in any language. 'That's all I know.'

'Me too.' Giggling, I go to embrace him, and Mij squirms with excitement, pouring from Gavin's arms so he lands paws first on coastal ground that is half long grass, half shingle. From there, he starts mischievously circling my ankles, his body once again tumbling through the dysrhythmic caterpillar wriggles that an excited otter is obliged to employ on land. I dare not move.

'I had better come to you.' Gavin takes a step towards me with both hands outstretched for my own. He kisses my cheeks, interlocking our fingers, and it is here we remain while Mij flows from one to the other, our shared laughter rippling through the air as the otter's sunlit form shines like bright water.

Emitting a whistling wheeze on each exhale, Mij weaves a swirling figure of eight that invisibly binds Gavin and me together. The pattern feels almost mathematical in its precision; dividing Mij's devotion equally between the two humans he knows and loves. He is not like Jonnie, I realise as he rotates around my calves, squeaking loudly and occasionally smacking my foot with his tail. Wonderful as the dog was, a pure soul the epitome of both fierce loyalty and earnest sweetness, there was never any doubt that he belonged to Gavin. No amount of ear scratches or treats could have supplanted his master in his heart, and I would never have wished it otherwise. Yet with Mij, things are different. He loves me. Trusts me. I see it in the boisterously demonstrative welcome I receive after briefly leaving the room, those button-bright eyes softening into the joy of safe, familial affection as soon as he sees me return. He listens for my voice, searches for my face, and if Mij is technically Gavin's, then the animal does not know it. Neither does the cottage, I think with pleasure, giving a glance back to Sandaig. Home is not where we live, but where we love.

'Remember when I mentioned researching his sub-species?' Gavin asks me after we have finally persuaded Mij to walk on or rather, to swim

171

on, following the vague direction of his humans' landbound path while periodically darting off to circumnavigate the small islands of Sandaig's coast. 'I've spent the week looking into it.' The fact that Gavin was meant to spend the week writing his opening chapters is one I quickly decide to bypass. 'Kathleen, you simply won't believe what I've found out.' Gavin's eyes glow with pure pleasure, a cloudless summer sky blue. 'The Zoological Society says they've never encountered a live specimen of his sort before. And yet Wilfred and I had brought back from the marshes an otter skin that's unmistakably the same type as Mij. I took it with me to the British Museum, to the Natural History Department, and they showed me all the sub-species that are currently known to man. Not one of them is quite like Mij.' I catch a glimpse in Gavin's expression of the earnest child he once was, that fine-boned fair-haired twenties boy who spent summers at Elrig crouched alone over his nature collections. 'They're going to name him after me.' Pride burns bright in his face, his tone growing hushed in reverence. '*Lutrogale perspicillata maxwelli.* Maxwell's otter.

'The only downside is that old Thesiger is annoyed.' Gavin sniggers. 'Furious about it, to be blunt.' Like a comic actor pulling on a prosthetic, he somehow manages to twist his face into a wickedly accurate impression of Wilfred's lurcher-like profile. The Scots tinge to Gavin's aristocratic accent is shed, emulating instead the received pronunciation of the English explorer. 'He says it should've been him; he's the one who asked the Ma'dan to look out for an otter cub for me. If it wasn't for him, he says, I wouldn't have Mij in the first place.'

'Forget Thesiger,' I advise, as I might do for James if he had quarrelled with a classmate. Gavin nods, kneeling to let Mij burrow back into his open arms. Exhausted from the exertions of such an enthusiastic welcome, the otter happily flips onto his back, letting his strong tail turn soft and flop over his master's forearm.

Gavin cradles him. 'He's the only being to take my name.' I say nothing, but reach out until I can touch them both.

Gavin deposits his rucksack in the cottage and we share some refreshment – a cup of tea for me, showing off my newfound skill in operating the Primus stove, and a glass of watered-down whisky for him – as I point out my decorative improvements.

'Very pretty,' he notes of the oil lamp, stretching across it for a match with which to light his latest cigarette. 'Before it's time to turn it on, shall we make the most of this Scottish summer?' Heading outside again, Mij in tow, I clock the ominous implication that this sunny day may constitute the season in its entirety. 'The light is like a well-kept secret up here.'

'Do you ever think Sandaig itself looks secretive?'

'Hm?'

'The cottage. I think it has a secretive face.'

'Face?' Gavin raises a rakish eyebrow, but I can tell he understands. We see what the other sees. That is how it has always worked with us.

'Yes,' I insist. 'It looks as if it holds some exquisite secret.' An unexpected comparison comes, which I welcome as any open-minded poet should do. 'It's like a young woman's face during her first pregnancy.' Silence. Embarrassment surges through me seconds too late to bite back my words. I do not speak or even think about pregnancy often. I certainly don't mention it to Gavin. What is it about this visit that keeps calling my mind back there?

'You're right,' murmurs Gavin eventually. 'I never saw it before, but you're right. I imagine that pregnancy is a quite perfect description for it. Some exquisite secret.' What first pregnancy should be, although it is not always so. Not for all women. Awkward and flushed, I scrabble in search of a change of subject from one that I foolishly raised.

Fortunately, sharing the discovery of Mij's species – technically, his discovery of it – appears to have filled Gavin with energy, and Mij himself is likewise ready to return to the wilds after enjoying a brief, envy-inspiring doze with his head resting in Gavin's lap. As we leave the cottage surrounds, I see the sun has lowered into its mellow early evening position, rich beams of ore extending over the bay to set the seawater sparkling with flecks of white light.

'As children, we invented a word for when the sea looked like this,' Gavin tells me. 'Shinkly.'

'I'll never think of it otherwise,' I promise. 'It's perfect.' This is perfect. Our eccentric little trinity walks in a westerly direction like three pilgrims in thrall to the sunset. 'Better this way than north,' Gavin cautions. 'If Mij swam free up there, he might end up too close to the village.' Glenelg, or the Big Smoke, as I have heard him factitiously refer to the cluster of homes six miles or so to the north of Sandaig. Not all here are as welcoming as the MacLeods. Evidently there exists a handful of cold, conservative locals disinclined to warm to a glamorous lowland Major when he shows up in his racing car with a pet otter at his side. I suppose small minds and low horizons can crop up anywhere, although I cannot help thinking they would feel more at home in Ilford.

We reorient away from their inhospitable ilk and continue walking where the sun beckons us, Mij alternately weaving between our legs and delving into whatever water source he can find. There is no sign of our fellow humans here, friendly or otherwise. And yet as we continue to stride over the terrain, wellingtons squelching and sinking into the peat, the land slowly shifts from tide-marked sea tangles into something more agrarian, if still rugged and uncultivated. I spot a small, dilapidated croft tucked into a hillside, its off-white walls flaking and cracked. Where a door should be, there is merely a slab, held in place by a half-rotten wooden strut to prevent what I assume are animal squatters.

'No one's lived here for some time, have they?' If inhabited, this rundown little house would be Sandaig's nearest neighbour. And yet Gavin appears disinterested, keeping his focus on Mij.

'I think the landowner rents it occasionally,' he replies without looking at it or me. Drawing nearer the croft – a single room, I see now, with cobwebbed windows and damp streaks seeping from an unsound roof – I struggle to see why anyone would want to stay, however short-term, in such conditions. But Gavin already seems bored with the subject, so I scramble to follow where he and Mij have walked on.

A roughly delineated field appears up ahead, home to a small herd of shaggy-pelted Highland cattle. A generation down, perhaps, from the unfortunate female who came close to delivering her baby on the Sandaig staircase. The cattle are predominantly orange, except for a few brownish-black and one especially attractive coat of pale gold. In spite of his loud, yodelling protests and violent squirms against restraint, Mij is instantly scooped up by Gavin so he can refasten the lead to his harness. At last, a practical use for it in the Highlands beyond identifying Mij as a pet to any theoretical passers-by. Thus secured, we continue on our way. The cattle stare at us, passively intrigued, from behind the thick fringes that hang over their eyes like curtains swamping small windowpanes. Their hooves are wedged into the still-marshy bog ground; some even seem to be in the process of cooling their feet by standing in mud. Whatever their coat colours, all have ivory horns pushing through their shaggy hair, curling up and out from their foreheads.

'Females,' Gavin informs me. 'The horns on males stick out straight without curving skywards. But look, here's a little lad.' With delight, I watch an infant calf totter out from around his blonde mother's body, nascent horns no more than tiny cream nubs nestled beside his floppy ears. Gangling limbs keen yet uncoordinated as he stumbles to claim his milk, he tucks himself under his mother to suckle, while on their left, a brown-black calf appears from behind its own parent. A girl, I decide as soon as I catch sight of her Anna-ish dark eyes.

We sit on the grass at a respectful distance, watching the tousle-haired infants suckle hungrily – painfully, the woman in me thinks – but neither mother betrays any sense of discomfort. They look blandly in our direction, staring without seeing as they feed their children, and we in turn sit transfixed, reverent with awe at their silent, subtle tribute to the power of natural instinct. Even Mij, motionless for once, stares open-mouthed in astonishment.

'It really is a wonderful achievement,' I whisper to Gavin, 'having an animal named after you. *Maxwelli* …' The Latinisation of his surname gives it a twist, and I enjoy the novelty of playing with a word that has dominated my brain for so long. 'It makes you sound wise.'

'I don't have wisdom, but I do have understanding,' Gavin murmurs. His eyes are on the cattle; his hands are still holding Mij.

We stay in place as the sunset throbs through its deeper shades, the day's golden glow turning to bronze, copper, then rust. Blinking hard as if in an effort to process all the sights this world has to offer, the inquisitive girl starts making her coltish way over to us, followed a few seconds later by the boy who, apparently too excited to walk straight, gives a series of sweet little kicks.

'Be careful,' I warn Gavin, instinctively pulling Mij back despite his muscular efforts to resist me. Motherhood may have been a struggle but I can recall that ferocious first hit of love, the animalistic sense of protective parenthood that could arouse even the gentlest soul to violence if she believed her little one was in danger. And yet the bovine mothers remain calm, watching their babies investigate their audience without any demonstrable upset. Perhaps Gavin and I are too innocuous to be threatening, or else it is simply clear that we would be no match for their cloven-hoofed bulk should they choose to use it against us. We take turns, one holding the otter's harness while the other shuffles forward to greet the youngsters, gently stroking their sides. Our fingers follow the delicate, crinkled grooves that still ripple over their necks and flanks as if barely dry from natal waters. Palm outstretched, feeling the warm breath of juvenile nostrils drifting over my skin, I stare mesmerised at the little girl's fluttering, feather-soft eyelashes. Half blink, half breeze. Her plush velvet lips graze my fingertips until, finding nothing of interest in my hand, she bends her head to the grass and begins to sniff. One tiny yellow flower in particular seems to pique her youthful interest.

'That's a buttercup,' I tell her, smiling to see how the flower's soft gold glow casts a pinprick of light under her dark chin. I remember playing a similar game with my schoolfriends in Northumberland. Do you like butter? Let's ask the flowers! I turn to Gavin, eager to share this bliss with him.

'As a child, did you ever play ...' But his eyes have filled with tears. 'Gavin, whatever's the matter?'

'They're going to suffer,' he whispers. His voice is hoarse, his knuckles white from clenching Mij's harness in an effort not to break down. 'There's so much suffering ahead of them. That's what life is, isn't it? Suffering.' Gavin uses the hand which so recently stroked the little calves to wipe a stream of tears from his cheek. 'I feel such guilt, Kathleen. Coaxing them into the world, with all its hatred and cruelty and wickedness. It's as if my touch has sullied them.' Guilt? I only feel lost. Gavin and I share one mind and one love, even one otter, but I cannot begin to understand what has brought about this melancholy. Rising to be nearer him, I move too fast, causing the calves to startle and their mothers to eye me disapprovingly from the other side of the field. The scene before us remains the same, lush summer abundance domed by an expansive evening sky, yet Gavin's mood has flipped from white to black. It frightens me to hear him speak so. Surely he knows that his touch could never sully anyone? In my dreams, for what it is worth, his touch has never sullied me.

'Mij isn't suffering,' I try to console him. Gavin sniffing, we both turn to the otter. Having grudgingly conceded that he will not get the chance to smell the calves at close quarters, Mij has taken to occupying himself by rolling around the long grass. Harness lead tangled beneath him, his short limbs flail mischievously, exposing the white flecks on his belly to the sun-infused air. 'See? He's blissfully happy.' As am I. Or was. Now I feel, not scared exactly, but unsure what to do for the best. It might help if I understood why Gavin's mood changed so rapidly. Latent weariness from the long journey perhaps, or some unspoken struggle with the chapters he was meant to complete? Maybe in a strange way, the low is connected to the high. Has Gavin's pride at the naming of Mij's sub-species, and his own symbolic acceptance into the naturalist canon, reminded him of the parts of himself that can never be accepted? That perennial sadness he will never uproot; the hidden shadow side he can never dare expose to the light. I feel the urgent desire to comfort him, without quite knowing how. Last time Gavin was this low, we spent the night together.

Eyes still watering, Gavin watches Mij roll and scuffle, a pebble clutched between his paws like precious treasure held tight to his torso as he rocks. Gavin reaches out to stroke his stomach, making Mij writhe with delight.

'I love him because we're the same,' he tells me. 'Kindred spirits. Strangers in a foreign land. Not literally in my case, of course, and yet … Mij is different to a human being.'

'He is.' Well-acquainted as I now am with otter spraint, the green-grey excrement Mij loves to leave as a mark of his travels, I can hardly dispute the point.

'Oh, I know he can be wild.' Mij rolls once more with merry, tail-waving abandon. 'But he's fair. Free from duplicity. If I'm kind to him, he's kind to me, and he doesn't see me as … he doesn't judge.'

'Not every human judges.' Haven't I accepted Gavin as he is, falling in love with his flaws along with his fair beauty? I do not condemn him for what he cannot change. For the damage done long ago to make him the way that he is.

Gavin says nothing. I wait, but he stays silent. We let Mij squirm through the grass a few more times before, as one, we rise to our feet. The cattle have wandered to the far end of the field, and Mij is willing enough to come away on the solemn promise of a fresh fish dinner back home. The sunlight is in its final throws, dying embers of vibrant rose and violet flames visible only across the skyline. By the time we reach Sandaig, night has fallen.

Chapter Twenty-Three

When the Paultons telephone rings, I know it is Gavin before I answer. Our psychic synchronicity feels stronger than ever these days, and I set down my pen in anticipation of hearing his voice before I even pick up the receiver. A congratulations card sits on my desk, intended for Anna after she received her own good news about her studies. Together at Girton, I hope we may regain some of the closeness I have let slip through my fingers. My little girl is a young woman now, just as James is very nearly a young man, and God willing, the struggles that went before will be washed away on the outgoing waves of their sparkling futures. In my future? I see Gavin, Mij and the sun over Sandaig's burn.

'Kathleen? Can you come now?' The phone line sounds strange. Harsh bird cries echo in the background, chaotic shrieks and shrill squawks turned tinny by the poor connection.

'Gavin, where on earth are you?' A screech of the sort one might expect from a rainforest canopy is followed by a chorus of lively chattering.

'London Zoo,' Gavin replies matter-of-factly, as if faintly surprised I had to ask. Perhaps he too has absolute trust in our magical mental connection. 'The Director let me borrow his office extension.' Of course he did. 'But can you come to the zoo? Now?'

'I ...' An explosive elephantine trumpeting provokes a succession of squeals and a renewed spate of wing flapping. A few muffled human voices follow.

'Listen, Kathleen, I have to go,' Gavin adds hurriedly. 'Meet me at the aquarium.' The line cuts off. An especially grating animal call, like a loud hoot interbred with a cackle, lingers in my ears as I put down the telephone.

'It'll be closed at this hour, love,' my taxi driver cautions me, but at my insistence he gives a squat-shouldered shrug and puts his foot down. London's streets pass by in a grey blur, dappled with welcome hints of occasional green, and as the vehicle approaches the zoo, I see its inelegant exterior bulging out in bulky curves and skylights; the unnatural architectural cross between rhinoceros and armadillo. Paying my suddenly sanguine driver with a note of over-generous denomination, I trot up the concrete steps and peer through the locked railings.

'Kathleen!' Gavin races towards me from the other side, a frazzled heavy-set zookeeper on his tail. 'Come in, come in. Quickly now.' Unable to suppress his excitement, Gavin flaps his hands in frustration while the zookeeper slowly opens the gates. First, he must locate the right key on a preposterously loaded ring, by which time Gavin is hopping from foot to foot in ineffectual agitation. 'Yes,' he announces as the padlock pops, his slim arm shooting through to take hold of my wrist and half-drag me inside. 'This way to the aquarium.' My hand sliding into his, I try to keep up as we run in his chosen direction.

Arriving at the blond sandstone outbuilding that houses the zoo's aquatic residents, I realise a third person, not counting the zookeeper still stumbling in Gavin's wake, is also here after hours. A serious chap with an artfully dishevelled appearance, he clutches some sort of portfolio and wears a shoulder satchel of drawing materials, almost as well-stocked as the one Winifred brought with her to Sandaig.

'He's going to do the sketches,' Gavin informs me.

'Sketches of what?' Before I can have my answer, the puffing, red-faced keeper interrupts us, initiating another lengthy jingled search for the aquarium door key. At last, we spill inside, Gavin the natural leader of the pack as he continues to pull me forwards.

'This way.' He bundles us down two flights of stairs before halting in front of the underwater viewing tank. As soon as he catches up, the nameless artist silently commandeers a bench behind me, setting out his materials before, sketchbook open at a blank page, he turns expectantly towards the water. The tank is immense, a spectacle in itself despite being presently empty of inhabitants. An enormous window made from what one hopes is reinforced glass scrolls out in a subtle curve, at least twelvefeet in height by perhaps double that in length. The setup would provide ample space for large crowds of the theoretical viewing public to glimpse all that goes on beneath the surface.

'Gavin, what are we doing here?' With a *shh* finger pressed to his lips, Gavin points to the top of the tank. White light is shimmering at its heights, soft ripples highlighting the fluid forms of a world beyond the water we cannot see from down here in the depths.

'Just watch.' Over my head, Gavin gives the zookeeper a nod. The gentleman retreats, with relief, I suspect, and several moments pass in near silence, save for the mellifluous trickle of freshly piped water and muted scratching as the artist sharpens his pencil.

A commotion occurs. I hear distant voices; a latch-like click. In shock and sheer amazement, I see Mij – my Mij, our Mij – diving straight into the water, his streamlined brown body the embodiment of underwater elegance as he immerses himself in his natural element.

'I can't believe it.' For the first time ever in our acquaintance, I am not interested in looking at Gavin, so compelling is Mij's display of watery virtuosity. With effortless skill and an expression of effervescent joy, the otter twists and spins through the tank; his lean, lithe form flowing in loops while strong strokes of his tail leave a glistening train of parted water. Behind me, I hear what sounds like the sharp staccato mark-making of the artist at work, but I cannot break my gaze to turn and confirm it. Mij is powering through the water with hypnotic God-given grace, every inch of his small body shining as he swims free at what feels like the speed of light.

'They told me I could hire the tank to watch him,' Gavin says, his voice rendered hoarse by raw emotion. Without taking his eyes off Mij, he tips his head to gesture at the man behind us. 'Michael's here because I wanted drawings to commemorate it. Remember it always, you see? For ten shillings a minute hire, I should do.' Gavin permits himself a snigger, but from its huskiness I can tell he is very close to tears.

'This is …' Words may be my own element, but in articulating this mercurial beauty, I am unequal to the task. We watch our otter with all the pride of parents seeing their child take its first steps, yet this infant shows no clumsiness or stumbles, only an innate smooth strength that seeps and pours through the tank with the dazzling, mesmerising drama of liquidated gold.

While we stare, utterly spellbound, at Mij's nature-endowed white magic, a secondary disruption near the surface catches the animal's attention. Showcasing an aquatic adroitness that no human swimmer or vessel could mimic, he stops mid-spin and, angelically crowned by an ephemeral halo of bubbles, turns his tiny head towards the ceiling. A darting glint of scales, a scattering of new ripples, and three unfortunate goldfish are added for his amusement. A renewed spark of energy visibly surges through the otter, channelled from long spine to tail as he spots his unfortunate prey. The poor fish dart like em dashes unleashed from a scathing editor's pencil, but in mere moments, Mij is performing exuberant underwater acrobatics with an ex-goldfish under either arm and a third clamped between his teeth. From this position, he tilts his head in our direction: a coincidence, I accept, yet one that makes the otter seem knowing, even expectant, of his audience's astonishment and awe. Indeed, although the design of the tank is surely such that he can neither see nor hear us, it feels unnatural not to applaud.

As Mij continues his liquid pirouettes, at one with the water despite never staying still for a drop-in-the-ocean instant, I realise that in my fifth decade of life, I have never witnessed such sacred unity between a living creature and its world. Mij is ecstatic, quite literally buoyant, and his pleasure infuses the water he swims in until the happiness contained inside that tiny otter's heart seems to fill the entire room. Tears flood my eyes and my vision blurs, Mij's body briefly becoming hazy. In the shift, I see the reflection of Gavin and I as we stand watching our otter through the glass. Forgotten in all the excitement, my hand remains in his.

'Have you ever seen anything so beautiful?' Gavin asks.

'No,' I admit.

With the eddying swirls of Mij's celebratory cartwheels still visible in the background, I focus on the two of us: the fair shimmer of Gavin's blond hair complementing the darker shadows of my own. 'Into my dark I have drawn down his light,' I wrote in *Northumbrian Sequence*. Perhaps I should have written that it is he who has drawn me up.

Back at Paultons, after another telephone call from Gavin has confirmed that the now exhausted Mij is sleeping soundly at the foot of his master's bed, I return to my book-buried desk in a daze. Mindlessly, I sift through the academic detritus that has washed up on this wooden shore, returning books to their rightful homes until another day's research begins. I realise only after I shuffle the piles that one is Gavin's. What is *Harpoon* doing here? I do not recall taking it out again so recently and wonder vaguely whether Gavin himself put it there. He has a key now, of course. All that I have is his, even if he chooses not to take it. I pick up my copy with the tenderness that precious firstborn progeny deserves. When I turn to the opening page, there is an inscription I have never seen before.

'We met at last in the heart of an otter.'

*

London looks different, as if the shift within me is manifesting without;

seeds of my happiness carried off on the wind as I walk and pollinating all I can see with growing optimism. I start to notice pretty-petalled weeds peeking through pavement cracks and irrepressible tree roots ready to burst through the concrete, branches breaching the wrought-iron barricades wrapped protectively around their saplings' bark hearts. When Gavin next comes to Paultons with Mij, we head for the garden where our wild creature loves to ripple around my own flourishing pear tree, his humans squinting up at the dun brick façade whose future increasingly occupies my mind.

If successful, my Girton Fellowship comes with rooms, and I imagine finding it more convenient to split my time between them and Paultons than to remain here permanently. Either way, Anna will have her own room in her college and hopefully one larger than mine in first year, which I hear has since been reconverted back into a stationery cupboard. James, too, is on the move: preparing for National Service before fulfilling his own academic ambitions.

'Why architecture?' I had asked, as encouragingly as I could. His father's political inclinations evidently held little appeal, but I had wondered whether James might opt to follow in Gavin's still-idolised footsteps. Not that cheating his way through exams and amassing more absences than attendances is the sort of example I'd like my son to follow.

'It's my dream,' James said. A wave of sorrow surged through me for not having known it before. 'I want to build homes for people.'

'Better to make them than break them.' I heard Anna mutter the aside as she walked past the telephone before being scolded for it by Helen. Pain and shame sat heavily on my chest that night like an incriminating scarlet letter, until I resolved to put the remark down to the understandable stress of transition. Life is not always easy for sensitive young women like Anna. I of all people should know.

While we watch Mij weave brown silk spirals around the pear tree, I discuss the matter with Gavin. Not the children, but the rooms, and what to do next.

'I could never sell the place,' I insist. Impractical poetess I may be, but even I know better than to surrender a property in London. Helen – who else? – is the person I have to thank for it. When I moved to the city in '45, without either a publisher or even a permanent place to rest my head, Helen encouraged me to introduce myself to an eccentric, elderly artist acquaintance of hers who was also living alone. At first, I rented a single room from Constance – affectionately nicknamed Cooie by all those who knew her well – but soon I was helping to care for her too during the long dark nights through which her kind, ageing heart began to fail. I did not resent the responsibility. Evenings of broken sleep and the dark circle days that followed them felt like oddly appropriate penance for all that I had left behind in the Lakes.

When Cooie died, the lease for Number 9 became my own in an act of profound posthumous generosity I am sure I did not deserve. On occasion, the Paultons doorbell still tinkles of its own accord, just as Cooie's gentle little bell for my assistance used to do during her lifetime. It makes me wonder whether she is watching. I hope I have not disappointed her.

'Of course you mustn't sell,' Gavin concurs. Staring up at the house, his eyes narrow into sharp, discerning slits as if suddenly seeing more than simple brickwork and cream cement. 'What's that window up there? Can't say I've noticed it before.'

'It's an attic,' I tell him. 'But it can't be used. No flooring.' The only negative of inheriting a house, if one dares to express anything so close to ingratitude, is that the day-to-day budget often fails to live up to the gift's magnitude. Not that I would have any idea of how to go about having an attic floored, even if I could have afforded it after the war ended.

'Ah, but that's easily solved.' Gavin speaks with the carefree confidence of a person not used to doing so much as having things done. 'And while they're at it,' he continues, 'couldn't you open up the basement?'

'I … I suppose.' Truthfully, I have no clue, and I wonder whether Gavin does either. Although he continues sizing up the exterior with an expression of worldly-wise building experience – indeed, all that is missing is a stub pencil behind his ear – Gavin is about as pragmatically minded as me, with far more grandiose ambitions. As we speak, his last big idea continues to spin around the pear tree, Mij's webbed paws wearing a strange-gaited groove into the summer grass. His rotations soon churn up a hitherto unseen pebble from the lawn and he squeals in excitement at the discovery.

'With an attic and a basement, you could fit two small apartments into the one house.' Gavin turns to me, ocean blue eyes gleaming. 'Two people living in one house.'

It takes me a moment to process what he is saying. I am more concerned at first by the thought that, with a few feasible adaptations, Paultons might have accommodated Anna and James all along. That rather upsetting notion distracts me, until I am distracted again by the look on Gavin's face. Does he mean what I think he means?

'Mij likes this garden,' I say neutrally. As if in confirmation, Mij rolls onto his back and starts writhing with the stone clutched to his belly.

'He loves it.' The sun is out, Gavin's blond hair vacillating between dashing glints of white and gold. I look back at my house. Could it really become ours?

'If I took ...' Feeling my way around the concept with tentative, almost disbelieving caution, I raise my eyes in the direction of a theoretical attic floor that did not exist until a few seconds ago. 'Upstairs. And you two took downstairs?' The idea seems perfectly bizarre, yet also bizarre in its perfection. At times, I think there must be an animal residing somewhere inside Gavin's brain. And I believe I know what species. Like our high-spirited water baby, his singular imaginative intellect seems to relish wriggling past the confines of human convention.

'I'd rent it from you,' he states firmly. *You wouldn't have to*, I want to reply. '*With all my worldly goods I thee endow.*' And I don't pay Gavin anything towards Sandaig. I hold back, however, for fear that to speak further along financial lines would only embarrass him.

'We'd be sleeping under the same roof,' I observe instead, trying to curtail a girlish trill that seems to have snuck into my voice. Gavin smiles, then frowns with faux solemnity.

'But we must ask Mij first.' In an expansive theatrical flourish, he bends his long limbs down towards the otter, presenting himself before Mij like a waiter offering his options. 'Would Sir care for a garden with a pear tree?' Apparently already in on the joke, Mij rises onto his compact yet muscular hind legs to chitter mischievously.

'What does he say?' I hope that I can guess, but I defer to the man who was Mij's first translator. Gavin scoops up the creature into his arms, cradling him joyfully as they both make their way to me.

'Yes please, Fairy Godmother.'

Within weeks, we start moving Gavin in and me up. Boxes block up the narrow hallway and threaten to spill out onto the street, forcing anyone who comes or goes to negotiate a convoluted cardboard fortress that grows more impenetrable by the day. Books make up the vast majority, whichever direction the box is travelling in. A running gag concerns stowaway copies of our work: I strain and grunt to carry one inordinately heavy bundle of kitchen implements, only to discover no fewer than ten

Harpoons at a Venture on top of my tea towel-wrapped cutlery. I get my own back, of course, although I confess to feeling somewhat outmatched by the Major. Tambi's spendthrift publishing practices and my own esoteric poetic tastes mean there is rarely an excess of my collections lying around for practical jokes.

During tea breaks – tea for me, a watered-down whisky for Gavin if he decides he has exerted himself – we sit on the floor with our sandwiches and biscuits, sifting through each other's nearest belongings for alternate amusement and mockery. Having Mij around means that opening any box at random becomes a relatively high stakes game. More than once, I absent-mindedly lift a cardboard flap to find a furry chocolate face topped off by a bewhiskered blackberry nose.

'What are these?' I ask Gavin as I investigate a box. It proves otterless but crammed with yellowing papers, each bearing water stains and tatters suggestive of Soay or even earlier memories.

'Old nonsense,' he mutters, taking the bundle from my hands. 'Letters and the like. I should pitch out the lot. Ah, but look at this one.' With a sardonic grin, Gavin holds out one fragile typewritten sample. 'Good God, I'd forgotten I ever wrote this.'

'"Mr Gavin Maxwell, aged twenty-three,"' I begin, '"educated Stowe and Hertford College, Oxford, is seeking a post". Any post in particular?'

'Anyone who would have me.'

'"… a fair and careful shot … an excellent and careful driver." Really? Careful driver?' Gavin shrugs as my eyes search for the Bentley stationed outside, two wheels high on the kerb. '"He is willing to be useful in any way."'

'Well, I was.' Grown-up Gavin laughs before knocking back the last of his whisky. 'Still am, in fact.'

'Then you're hired,' I say. 'Now carry that box of books upstairs for me.'

Chapter Twenty-Four

I sit alone at the waterfall ledge with my notebook in my hand, staring into the silver torrents that tumble over their slick rock peaks while I listen for Mij's paws. Despite Gavin's warning that summer may last for only a matter of hours here, Sandaig and its surroundings are aglow with seasonal warmth, and our otter's domesticity likewise appears to be approaching boiling point. Roaming widely wherever I walk, he leaves no stone unturned either on shore or underwater, flowing with wild, wilful delight between the two territories of his domain. Still, even with many miles of west coast at his disposal, I know Mij will not resist the fall's call for long. That lion's roar of rushing water is as majestically magnetic to animal ears as it is to human ones.

Only two-thirds of our trinity have travelled to Sandaig together. P.J.S, as Gavin has somewhat impertinently taken to calling Mr Janson-Smith, was overjoyed by his opening chapter.

'So good, my dear boy, one only wishes there were more,' read the telegram I glimpsed. Original deadline receding like a speck in the Bentley's rear-view mirror, Gavin has been obliged to remain in London throughout the past week, completing his subsequent chapters with that fine Roman nose to the grindstone while I whisked a certain furry distraction off to Scotland.

Here, the dry summer weather has let the long grass on either side of me flourish and I sit on a bed of soft strands, flowery tendrils rising as if to tickle my fingertips whenever I bend to write. Fighting the water's flow, darting glimmers of light denote tiny elvers in the stream; dainty eel-like fish wrestling valiantly with gravity in their death-defying quest to reach the waterfall's top level. Leaning over, I scoop a handful of the wriggling, gloss-grey creatures and deposit them on the next plateau up.

Perhaps one or two of their squirming multitudes, in total numbering hundreds of thousands, if not millions of miniature fish, will attain their goal. For the rest, exhaustion at the effort or consumption by a water-dwelling predator or maybe even Mij himself is the best they can look forward to. And yet that sliver of hope, a margin as narrow as their own svelte, slippery forms, is enough to sustain each creature in its endeavour. 'Destiny is not decided by a roll of the dice.' I remember saying so to Alastair during the war, after telling him that I was moving to London to write. My so-called lover replied, with characteristic disdain, that the odds of success were against me. But that man belongs to another lifetime; the bogged-down bottom wading pool of my waterfall. I am above it all now.

Above me, indeed, the ethereal wings of pale green dragonflies shimmer in the air. Their bodies are long and fine, aquatic in type despite being technically airborne, and I fancy these few flickering creatures might be the lucky elvers who managed to ascend, or else the happy reincarnations of lost fish souls gone to heaven. A butterfly, too, is dancing on the wind that sweeps in a gentle circle around this sheltered spot. Its vibrant wings quiver before coming to rest on a stone, around which one of the smallest streams trickles to rippling notes like harp strings.

Blake depicts Psyche with butterfly wings. For him, she was a soul in transcendence; more than a woman, an elemental representation of imagination and true love. Letting my left hand trail and feeling delicate drops of spray kiss my face, I watch the water cascade over my bare third finger. It leads straight to the heart, according to mythology. And in truth, I can already feel the waterfall's complex power penetrating my skin, the water's flow crafting a band across my finger until it almost appears that I am wearing a ring. My other hand reaches for my notebook, withdrawing an envelope that I furtively preserved once my ever-enthusiastic postboys Willie and Jim were no longer looking.

'Have ye seen whit they've called ye, Miss Raine?' the boys had giggled. 'Juist wait till ye tell the Major, Miss.' The letter itself contained the best possible news from the Board of Electors, confirming that full fellowship has been granted – application and references highly persuasive, they said – and I should begin the further research required for my Blake book at my earliest possible convenience. Forwarded by an unknown person from Paultons to Sandaig. C/O Mrs Maxwell.

I always told myself marriage did not matter. More than that, it was not something I wanted. Not now. Not again. A poetess must be free; didn't I discover that uncomfortable, incontrovertible truth way back in my painful romantic past? Over time, it has strengthened my spirit to reclaim the power men typically take from women when they wed. I have no desire to answer to an unimaginative Neanderthal who will never understand what I write. I do not wish to have my working hours curtailed by pressure to put food on the table during the day, only to serve as a glorified bed warmer at night. I love my freedom. I need it. And with that freedom, it turns out, I choose to stay by Gavin's side forever. Here at Sandaig, I feel like Psyche, living in my love's house, and we have no need of the menial trappings that too often define mortal life. Not when every inch of this exquisite natural world seems symbolic of our spiritual union.

He made his vow in inviting me here. Summoning me to share his sanctuary and his animal soulmate. Gavin has not married me in church with stained-glass saints looking down in judgement and me wearing shop-bought jewellery that will soon become tarnished. He has not married me on paper, inking out scribbled signatures as if I am a woman to acquire on hire purchase and he a man too busy to read the fine print. He has married me with all of this: a marriage of minds and souls, conceived in the beating heart of nature where we share one consciousness and one calling. One otter, most importantly of all. Instead of white lace, we have rowan blossom. Instead of pungent florist bouquets, we have a flourishing carpet of wildflowers. Instead of a ring, we have our burn, weaving around the cottage and glittering in the pale gold sun. I have not taken a bridegroom, but as I sit here by his waterfall, I pledge to take a man. This man of light whose dazzling spirit brightens my heart.

*

The next morning starts strangely. I rise wearing only my slip, Gavin's jumper lying abandoned on the bedclothes after the wool proved far too warm, before padding down with Mij to the water's white-frothed edge. The heat is already here, more so than the dim, sultry light, and despite the gentle glittering of the waves, the scene seems unnaturally motionless. Undaunted, Mij plunges straight into the ocean, flowing from the shallows towards its heart like a lightning-quick skimmed stone. Much like his master, he has an explorer's insatiable urge for adventure. In the wrong mood or having worn the straps for too long, the otter now even takes to fussing at his harness with his paws, digging those razor-edged teeth into the leather until it grows pockmarked from silent vexation. *He is growing up*, I remind myself. It is only natural he should wish to swim freely. Mij is not a pet, after all. Not just a pet.

Today, I simply laugh to witness the otter's watery pleasure but the sound fades into silence, absorbed by the oddly dense hot air. This morning's colours are unlike anything I have seen on this coastline before. Our shore is shadowed by thick clouds of pewter cotton, outlined with glinting grey threads as if an inside-out greatcoat hangs suspended above the sea. *This day would play in a minor key*, I think: a weird thought to accompany the weird shades that surround me. Unnerving, although still exquisite in their way, these weighed-down tones anticipate the advance of a summer storm, although I have learned one can never predict weather with confidence amidst such wild, volatile elements. Leaving Mij to play, I return inside for my notebook. I have begun dating each entry as one might for a conventional diary, should I ever need to retrace my compositional steps. I turn to today's blank page. Saturday 14th July 1956. One day before Gavin's forty-second birthday.

As the sun rises and our theoretical thermometer with it, my animal companion and I attempt to cool ourselves off in the rockpools left dotted over the coast by the outgoing tide's retreat. Mij amuses himself with feats of aquatic aerobic exercise, leaping madly from point to point, his webbed toes squelching every time he lands on a slick new rock. Not once does he miss his footing, but occasionally the otter slides into the water for the sheer joy of the sensation before scrambling back up the nearest incline to begin the cycle all over again. Barefoot beside him, I occupy myself by sifting through the underwater sand for yet another shell to add to my collection. I am more discerning now, a connoisseur of cowries and clamshells, but when I stumble upon a remarkable blue-hued scallop in the same shade as Gavin's eyes, I know that the ocean has bestowed the best possible birthday present to accompany my own. *The Ring*. Part two of *The Marriage of Psyche*. Begun beside his waterfall.

I set Gavin's scallop shell on the windowsill with the rest of my treasured discoveries, poem carefully folded within its cradling centre. Then I replenish my wildflower decorations and add a fresh posy on top of Gavin's latest furniture acquisition: an antique curiosity cabinet with row upon row of time-worn wood drawers into which his travel artefacts can be slotted. Outside, the roses are in full bloom, satin petals open and inviting as they beckon me to recross the fragrant threshold. I brush one with light fingertips, as has always been my custom, but an under-developed petal breaks off: the bottom layer of a flower that has struggled to receive sufficient sunlight. Cupped in my palm, I am disappointed to see the paper-thin sliver is not pink but pale brown.

Mij hears Gavin first, but only just. His watery horseplay halts, tiny tunnel ears twitching as if in response to some mysterious radio signal, before he rotates his little round head until he is facing the direction of Tormor. I know our animal well enough to trust in the superiority of his senses, but within moments I can also hear it for myself: the soft, rustling rhythm of feet hastening over the drying-out bogland. Gavin's hurrying, I think happily, rising from the edge of a rockpool at the far side of the house. The double-time rush of his steps mingles with the waterfall's murmur, and for a beat or two, my heat-dulled head cannot comprehend how he is managing to walk at such a pace. I move closer to Mij, following his gaze up the hill. Only then do I realise what we heard was not just Gavin's footsteps. There is someone else here with him.

Gavin has not noticed me yet. He is too busy talking to the man. His fair head is turned from me as he relays to his companion something that looks like it could be a joke. I say man, but this stranger appears not much more than a boy. Even at a distance, I can make out an athletic, almost Achillean build and a glamorous hint of youthful bronzed skin. Twenties, not thirties. Certainly not forties like us. The young man's hair is slightly darker than Gavin's and his shoulders a little broader, but both men share a refined, militaristic bearing as they stride cheerfully in tandem across the peat. If I didn't know better, I'd say he could be Gavin's brother. A significantly younger brother, whom I know he does not have. Closer to a son? But no father looks at his son like that.

While I watch, Gavin cracks another joke and his companion laughs heartily, his thick head of hair swinging in time with his guffaws. It is in this way he spots me, catching sight and exchanging a brief word of query with Gavin before raising his hand to wave casually. My own fingers rise in response, an unconscious reflex making my muscles disconnect from my will, waving back at this unknown man just as if I am pleased to see him. He and Gavin continue to walk side by side, winding their way down the hill with Gavin pointing out the pitfalls to yet more shared laughter. Up close, the resemblance is still remarkable. Only in dress, and age, are they distinct. The younger man wears canvas clothes in camouflaged explorer shades, his untucked shirt and loose fit trousers eminently suitable for an outdoors holiday. Gavin is wearing his kilt again.

'Hello, Kathleen,' he says when, at last, he notices me. 'Still here?' He steps forward to kiss my cheek, so abrupt and fleeting that I only kiss air in return. Then he turns to his companion again. 'She's not staying.' Back at me. 'Are you, Kathleen?'

'I …' The right words will not come in time. Confused, scrabbling rather than swimming, I blink stupidly as I look from Gavin to the stranger.

'How do you do?' asks the new man, extending a large palm in my direction. 'I'm Gavin.' I wonder quite sincerely whether I have been struck down with heatstroke. How many times a day does that name resound through my head? Without thinking, without any conscious effort on my part, I find that I am shaking this new Gavin's hand. His grip is firm, fine-boned yet full of confidence. Before he lets go, my fingers glance the cool metal side of his signet ring. 'Same name. Funny, isn't it?' The man smiles broadly, having clocked what must be the obvious confusion in my face. 'I'm Gavin Young.' Of course you are. God himself could not have named you better. As it always does in times of distress, my mind starts rifling unbidden through literary memories, searching for a line that may bring clarity. I think of Tennyson, albeit not the poem that Gavin – my Gavin – left for me in his homemade desk drawer. This one spoke of a 'golden youth', precisely what this new gentleman looks like. Golden and youthful. I am neither.

'Well, now.' Gavin not-so-young is growing impatient, shuffling from shoe to shoe as if we are outside the aquarium again and he cannot wait for the excitement to come. 'Are you ready for Mary's, Kathleen? Here, let me help you with your things.' Although I hardly know how it happens, I end up inside the cottage with both men. Gavin Young hovers close to the doorway while the real Gavin, the right Gavin, starts gathering my stray books and papers, amassing small piles so I may more quickly pack them away. I watch him, unable to move as if I am locked inside a nightmare. I believe I am. Gavin actually hums to himself as he pulls together my belongings, coming back down the stairs with my rucksack almost filled. The lifeless wool sleeve of his Soay sweater droops from the bag's drawstring top, bundled inside with such haste that Gavin failed to realise the garment is not mine but his.

'Has Mij behaved himself?' he asks me pleasantly, without stopping to wait for an answer. 'You know, Gavin was there in Iraq on the day I first found him.'

I turn to Gavin Young just in time to see him nod. 'I enter the Consulate-General to find a wriggling sack on the floor, with a long-haired, scruffy shape of a man sitting beside it.' He cocks his thumb teasingly in my Gavin's direction and both men share a laugh. My stomach seizes into a gnarly spasm reminiscent of early labour.

"'Please excuse me,'" the new Gavin mimics the old one, "'and stand clear a second. There's something very interesting in this bag and it's coming out.'" The two men erupt into renewed laughter, blue eyes and brown seeking out each other above their smiles. I grip the back of Gavin's flotsam-made sofa like a life raft.

'Can you imagine it?' He glances over, too fleeting to realise that I would sooner die than imagine anything more. 'We first meet halfway across the world, and then this week we bump into each other in London. "You simply must see Sandaig, my old friend," I said.'

I fail to see how an old friend can be as young as this man. But in truth, all I see now is the look on Gavin's face. It illuminates him, like an inner glow of gold: this electric, exhilarated frisson that is intangible and yet cannot be concealed any more than a beam of pure, strong sunlight. I know him too well. I know every inch of his countenance just like those of my children. Better, I think, gut contorting into a tight twist of shame. However much I want to look away, to clamp my eyes shut or claw them right out of my skull, I am transfixed by the light shining bright in Gavin's expression: an eager energy pulsing through him every time he turns towards this man. With the total, desperate desolation of one who has looked for years without truly seeing, I realise it has never been there in all the times Gavin turned to me.

'I don't suppose there's any food? And perhaps somewhere I can wash up?' Gavin Young addresses his query to me, well-mannered yet somehow putting me in mind of the complex social arrangements at Monreith. Another bolt of shock strikes. Good God, he thinks me a housekeeper. Is that what Gavin has told him? *Don't be stupid, Kathleen*, I chastise, although 'stupid' seems the only term I dare use for myself now. *Gavin hasn't told him anything. Gavin hasn't mentioned you at all.*

'We use the burn.' I reply to this young stranger with the flat sullenness of a genuine servant. Does this man understand that I live without proper sanitation for Gavin? That I wash amidst the ice and launder our bedding by hand, all out of my love for him? When Eve first recognised her nakedness before being cast out of Eden, she could not have felt more shame than I do in this moment. Unable to bear it, I turn away: facing the window and spreading my trembling hands over the sill as if to shelter my shell collection from this stranger's inquisitive gaze. 'I found this for you.' Fingertips quivering, I offer the scallop shell to Gavin. It looks different to how I imagined it would in his hands. No longer manna fallen from heaven or a timeless treasure gifted up to us by the depths. Its crinkled ridges tell no great secrets; its fan-shaped curves bear no cryptic markings of mystical meaning. It is cracked. Old. Worthless.

'It's lovely,' Gavin says kindly, as one might on receiving a birthday gift from a maiden aunt. And yet he turns over the shell, studying its form for a few seconds, and in those brief precious heartbeats, I pray that I am mistaken, that this is all just some fever dream akin to William Blake's delusionary discourses with the ghost of a flea. All is as it has been. Here, I am happy. Just Gavin, Mij and me.

Gavin sets down the shell with the rest. My poem stays folded inside. He picks up my rucksack and carries it towards the door.

'Well, look who it is.' Gavin Young's vigorous voice calls out as Mij lollops over the threshold. The man kneels, encouraging the otter into his arms. 'It's been a while since we met, Mijbil.' *Don't touch him*, I want to say and almost spit at him, bubbling with all the envious vitriol I remember from my children's squabbles when small. Bitter and brittle, the unspoken warning sits burning a hole in my tongue. *Don't you touch what's mine.*

'I think he remembers you,' my Gavin remarks. And indeed, Mij seems happy to accept the new man's affectionate attention. He wriggles into the tickle flowing down his long spine, permitting Gavin Young to stroke him behind his ears. But as the man rises, apparently with a view to carrying the animal indoors, Mij slips effortlessly out of his grasp and scuttles loyally across the flagstones to me. Touching my heart, even as it breaks, this wild, sweet-souled creature delves into my outstretched arms, wrapping himself into rings as a playful response to my touch. I bow my head, burying my face in his fur, and I feel the familiar, faithful comfort of his silken whiskers against my cheek. *Don't let the tears come*, I tell myself, but the advice is useless, like most I have given myself over the years. I press my face into Mij's velveteen coat and its tiny tufts moisten like grass stems laced with dew. When I raise my head again, I see his fur glistening before my eyes grow blurrier still.

A dragging sound on my left suggests Gavin has fastened my rucksack drawstrings. 'I'll walk with you over to Tormor, if you like,' he suggests. The quicker to get me gone.

'How can you do this to me?' I am still crouching on the ground, but the words finally come loud and clear. They echo out from the cottage threshold, vulgar and uncouth as if they are the true intruders. When I stand, I see Gavin Young averting his eyes, feigning intense newfound interest in the mantelpiece bookshelf. Gavin Maxwell is looking at me.

'I'm not doing anything to you, Kathleen.' On the surface, he seems puzzled. His brow is creased, expression confused and almost concerned. But there is anger too, I can tell. Lurking in the depths of those oceanic eyes. If there is one thing Gavin will not tolerate, it is humiliation in front of others. He takes a step closer. My heart gives an instinctive flutter. 'I'll telephone you back in London,' he whispers. Gavin's hand moves to my arm, fingertips brushing my bare skin as gently as when he cupped the scallop shell. Yet somehow, I find myself manoeuvred through the sky-blue doors, caught in unsought motion until I stand on the grass-strewn shingles in front of our house. Is it our house, still?

'Take your hand off me,' I snap when we are outside, wrenching my shoulder away in a painful, awkward twist. Heaven knows, I never imagined myself saying those words to Gavin. I never imagined any of this. Around us, the day's heat has depleted into a sunken haze of humidity, the landscape more like a photographic negative with bulky shadows piped in steel grey.

'Whatever's got into you, Kathleen?' The volume of Gavin's voice can return to normal now he has closed the door. Ordinarily it is a sound that touches my soul, the mellifluous Scots-tinged elegance of his speech imbued with myths and natural magic. Coming home. That is what his voice always meant to me. But all at once, I no longer know where my home is. 'We agreed you'd sleep at Mary's when I came up here,' Gavin reminds me. His speech is slow and measured, like that of a schoolteacher endeavouring to keep patience with a fool who has forgotten her homework.

'There's only one bed.' I state the sentence like a mantra, as much to myself as to Gavin. There is only one bed. That is the reason I am meant to sleep at Mary's. That is why with Winifred I took the sofa, drifting off to sleep in front of the fireplace inscription and dwelling on the miraculous twists of fate that had brought me to this place. No will o' the wisp, but the inexorable current of destiny. That is the reason. Isn't it?

'We'll work something out,' Gavin says softly. 'I know the number of beds in my house.' His house. Not ours. Sandaig was never, ever ours. Sickness swirls through me, singeing my throat and churning violent swells inside my stomach.

'You said you wouldn't.' Did he? Or did I say it on his behalf? I think of my first time in his flat, Gavin's handsome features framed by the fading light. The first time he told me about being the way he is. 'Every man needs a woman in his life,' he said. And he has had me, whenever and however he wished, so what else can this man possibly need? My mind flickers back to our sole night together in London: Gavin distraught after dear Jonnie's death and my chaste embrace the only thing in the world that could comfort him. I see myself back then as if looking down from above. Gazing over Gavin's dreaming form as the sun rose, innocently transfixed by the twitching of his fair eyelashes. I had promised the next morning I'd never share a bed with another man. It never occurred to me that Gavin would.

Another surge of nausea hits, so ferocious it seems to cleave me in two; parting some Red Sea inside me composed of blood rather than water. I was wrong earlier, as I have been wrong about so many things. Broken-hearted is too prosaic. Unpoetic in the extreme. It is my soul that is breaking, my spirit cracking up and fracturing right down to its core. 'Things fall apart; the centre cannot hold,' wrote Yeats. Now, I am centreless. Cavernous. All that held me together is gone. Didn't I recite a Yeats poem for Gavin the first time we walked together through the park? Swans and sorrow; flight and freedom. How happy I was. How little I understood.

'You said you feared going to jail.' Finally, a hard fact. Something set in concrete that neither of us can deny. The brutal bluntness of my words forces a real reaction from Gavin at last. I watch his face tighten and twinge, muscles taut from repressed pain. When he speaks again, it is with cold, upper-class formality.

'I'm at liberty to live as I see fit at the edge of the world. This is my house, after all.' His house. Not mine. Never mine. Psyche lost her place in the home of her beloved because she could not resist holding him up to the stark, unforgiving daylight; so desperate in her desire to possess him entirely that she exposed what he needed to keep hidden. Cupid hated her for it. Her love had wanted to dwell in the darkness. Now, I understand why.

'Everything alright out here?' With a rust-hinged creak that makes us both jump, the wood panels swing open to show Gavin Young in the doorway with Mij weaving rapidly around his ankles. 'I think this little fellow is missing you.' Strong legs astride as our otter flows around them, his lean, muscular arms folded loosely over his chest, Young looks every inch the dashing explorer. My stomach heaves and I swallow hard. In this tempestuous, tricksy lowering light, he might be Gavin's ghost of adventures past. That handsome youth who became *Harpoon*'s protagonist, charming all who crossed his path yet heeding only his quest for elusive glory. Is this what arouses Gavin's interest? A man who might be himself, before suffering and shame and so many different kinds of loss? Is this what touches the parts of him that I, with my worthless, lovelorn womanhood, have never been able to reach?

Stopping mid-spiral as he rotates around Gavin Young's boots, Mij spots us on the shoreline. He shoots over like a little harpoon himself.

'HA.' Mij binds a single ring of otter footprints in the sand around Gavin and me, tiny scallop-shaped imprints that the next tide will wash away. Satisfied, he then pours himself headfirst into the waiting, windswept ocean. The threat of a storm to come is no concern to a creature like Mij, eternally at one with even the wildest elements. If only I had his courage.

'Are you sure you're alright?' Young asks us again. He is clearly a practical chap. A problem solver. Like another young man I might mention, 'willing to be useful in any way'. If his poor host at Sandaig is having a domestic with his domestic, something must be done to assist. He turns to my Gavin. If 'my Gavin' is who he still is. 'Shall I fetch Raef?'

Raef?

'If he's up, he could be here soon.'

Raef. A tidal wave of sickness breaks over me. My throat burns. My eyes sting. He means Raef from the Soay venture. Raef of Gavin's broken heart. Raef of his very-nearly nervous breakdown. Raef, the boy who had just left school when Gavin and I met.

Young is watching me, worried. Simple housekeeper that I am, perhaps he fears I still do not understand. Out of highborn courtesy, he tries to elaborate: one slow, torturous sentence at a time as if I am one of his noble natives paddling a canoe for him through the marshes.

'Raef rented a cottage near here last summer. For his holiday?' *'You don't know much, do you?'* his tone seems to suggest. On that, we agree. Young raises a tanned arm to gesture. 'He said it's on the other side of the bay.' He points, this young man actually points, as if I am unfamiliar with the coastline and may benefit from more detailed directions. He points to a spot just beyond Sandaig. Just beyond Heaven. Just out of my sight.

'Wait inside for me, will you, Gavin?' Gavin Maxwell's eyes are on me at last. Still blue; still beautiful. He knows me better than anyone else on this earth, although suddenly I feel I do not know him at all. Adroit social operator that he is, Gavin understands the urgency of getting his guest away from what will come next.

Young nods and makes to disappear behind the blue doors.

'Wait,' I command. 'Take the otter.' I walk to the water's edge, movements as rigid and unnatural as Dr Frankenstein's creature finding its feet. The wind's strength is building to such a furious, Lear-like pitch that I doubt whether Mij will even hear me call his name. And yet mercifully, miraculously, I have no need to. As soon as the tide starts pouring over my boots, Mij swims towards me: ebullient and buoyant as ever. I scoop him up, chattering my teeth to try and reassure him in his language, even though I cannot stop my hands from trembling. Forcing my leaden feet to beat a retreat over the shore, I carry him to the Sandaig door. 'It's not safe for him out here,' I tell the stranger in our midst. 'There's a storm on the way.' Young nods once more and moves inside with Mij in his arms.

My Gavin stays with me. No, not my Gavin. He is not my Gavin anymore. The brooding sea winds have started whipping the water into weapon-sharp spikes, and from behind a swirl of sand and spray, his form appears to shimmer. The details of his handsome face disintegrate briefly with each new gust, every feature I have adored blown apart into meaningless atoms. *Wait for me.* How often I have waited for him. It turns out others were waiting too.

Raef. That thoughtless, faceless young man whose damage I have healed; that wicked man-child who shattered Gavin's spirit into shards I laboured for years, *years*, to piece back together. How dare that boy come here, desecrating and defiling the paradise we have found? Fingering our shells, soaking himself in our waterfall, resting his empty head on our pillow and watching the berries of our rowan tree blossom? In my mind's eye, I follow the direction in which Young pointed, realising he can only mean the tiny, tattered croft that Gavin and I once stumbled upon. I recall struggling to think who would want to rent such a rundown, ramshackle space, as uncomfortable as camping were it not for a roof to provide basic cover … but that's it, I understand suddenly, betrayed heart seizing and starting to weep within my chest. It was only ever meant as a cover.

When did Raef lose his inhibitions? His mortal fear of being smeared, tarred with the same brush of shame that has coloured so much of Gavin's life. When did he let go of the misgivings that made him cut off contact

197

in the first place, causing Gavin so much pain and leaving a broken man on my doorstep? Perhaps it was this place. Perhaps it enchanted him too. The inspiring, mesmerising magic of Sandaig: so secluded and seemingly liberated from society at large. Perhaps Raef felt free here. He and God alone knows how many others.

'Gavin, I ...' He will not marry me with a ring. He will not marry me at all. Even if my poetry could flow again, fresh inspiration springing from the dry, cracked-bed deltas that suddenly fissure my fertile imagination, what words known to man, or more importantly to woman, could do this agony justice? I have no lover. I have not wanted one since we met. I have ached through my nights alone, every cell in my body crying out in pulsing, thwarted protest even after I swore that my mind was reconciled to the way he is. I have lived untouched. Unwanted. I chose to sacrifice it all for our love. Gavin's nature has cut the sex out of me; not, after all, out of him. Like a lone warrior who hallucinated a loyal comrade at her side, I have fought alone against the grime-ridden mire of everyday life; a fatalistic, one-woman crusade against all that I decided was wrong with the world. The unspiritual. The inelegant. The unpoetic, profane urges of old-fashioned flesh and blood that I told myself I was wiser, cleverer, better to rise above. Every second of the struggle felt worth it to be with him.

Where were these boys, these young men with stars in their eyes and lust between their legs, when I held Gavin as he sobbed? Where were they when he discovered his power to write, receiving with gratitude the gift of his soul's true calling and making a success of it with me by his side? Where were they when Mij swam, elevating and uniting our spirits as together we bore witness to the sheer wonder of nature? Raef was not even born when Gavin and I shared our childhoods in Northumberland, alone and yet somehow still together, as I have always believed we were born to be. *'Tread softly because you tread on my dreams.'* I can feel mine crushed beneath the soles of their young, carefree feet. What does he even do with them? To them, I should say. I could never call it making love. I remember now, although I wish fervently that I did not, drawing down my encyclopaedia earlier in our acquaintance to read about others who had felt Gavin's desires. Ancient Greece appeared prominent, those adventurous classical days with codes of conduct so different to our own. Are those brief moments of physical pleasure really worth risking his liberty? Would my touch, my thighs, my mouth have been so very different? I would have let him do worse. I would have let him do anything. He could have degraded me however he wished. I would have called it transcendence.

And yet I suppose Gavin might ask me the same question. Would another's touch have been so different? *Yes*, my heart cries, beating through anguished death spasms as if it knows these are the final few seconds of my life in which it will be whole. Since the day we met, I have wanted no man's touch but his. And now he uses that touch to sweep me away. One flick of that fine-boned wrist and I am dismissed. The Heaven I thought I had created here, garlanded with Platonic love and my dried-out, spinsterish wildflowers, is brushed away for a better offer. My sacrifice made meaningless. His own, never made at all. Fracturing under the weight of misery, my mind conjures a vivid image by William Blake. He wrote of man's intense unhappiness when friendless, divorced from the other living creatures of the world and left 'a little grovelling root outside of himself'. But I cannot grovel. I refuse to. I am a mother and a poet. I will fight.

'Grown up has he, Raef? Gotten over his squeamishness? Wish I could say the same.' Hurt flashes across Gavin's face, a wounding for which he was unprepared. Good. We can both cause pain. Both say things we do not mean. Didn't he whisper to me late at night as we lay together in his bed, stripped of clothes and defences, that what we have would last for the rest of our lives? The memory of that raw, naked vulnerability is more than my body can bear. I feel like an animal, cornered and threatened; terror transmuting into rage as my last faint hope to stay alive. Claws out. Teeth bared. Anger is all I can stand to feel.

'Keep your voice down,' Gavin instructs me, sharp gaze darting left and right to confirm our isolation. He has no need. He knows we are alone in this wild landscape. Except for the man inside Sandaig, of course. The man he invited here.

'Why, Gavin?' I goad as the nastiness in me gathers pace. 'Aren't we at the edge of the world? Aren't we at *your* house?' I am starting to shout, my trembling index finger jutting towards Gavin's chest like a talon with which I might run him through and spill out his entrails onto our shoreline. His shoreline. I am too old to be an ocean nymph, only a wretched, loveless harridan, and as my behaviour descends into hissing fury, Gavin's merely rises to newfound dignity. They play to win, these aristocrats.

'This is beneath you, Kathleen.' But he is wrong. There is nothing beneath me now. I am sinking into the unfeeling black of a bottomless, unchartered ocean. I am drowning in a sea of my own salted tears. 'We've worked out our misunderstanding.' For one mad moment, I believe Gavin means him and me. He might be a fortune teller, resurrected from the funfair I attended with Aunty Peggy, who wrapped her fingers around a glittering crystal ball to promise me that *yes, little Kathie, you will one day find your prince*. But Gavin doesn't mean me. This is not our happy ending. 'Raef is a good friend to me these days,' he says. 'We began corresponding again, after he heard about *Harpoon* being published.' *A likely story*, the bitch dog in my brain starts to snarl. I suppose there is nothing like fame and fortune to teach a young man who is in his best interest. But I do not fully believe it, much as I wish to. No one on earth would need to pretend they had fallen in love with Gavin.

'We don't even see each other often.' I can hardly tell whether he is trying to comfort me, or just complaining. My bearings are lost and scattered, his mind a foreign, hostile territory whose landmarks I no longer recognise. 'Not since Raef's degree finished and he went back to Eton teaching. We write mostly.'

'Mostly.' Scorn drips from the word and I hear myself scoff, a harsh, mocking callousness I never knew I possessed. I cannot shake the illogical idea that my hurt will lessen if I can hurt Gavin in return. Bitterness oozes from me, poison lingering in my mouth like the taste of tainted rowan berries. I think it is because our connection remains, invisible and unwanted yet still hovering in the air between us, like the toxic dust that gathered in London's grey-shrouded skies long after the last bombs had fallen. I can see the world through Gavin's eyes, and now I see him with Raef, Young and the rest. Together with them in ways that have consumed my imagination for years, picturing lips and fingertips dwelling on each exquisite inch of his skin even as I endured all those lonely nights alone. How perverse that it can horrify me to picture the same things I have dreamed of. Happening to someone else, it is my nightmare.

I see Gavin harden in response to my hostility, spine rigid and shoulders square-set. He is well-drilled in defence against an assault of enemy fire. Yet even now, my heart shattering into fragments of sea glass right in front of him, his thoughts stay spilt between me and that boy. 'Raef's friendship comforts me.' Good God, have I not comforted him enough? Gavin is staring at me now and I catch a strange hint in his face of what looks like genuine confusion. Eyes wide and questioning, despite the defiantly raised chin and neck tendons tense enough to snap like twigs. Skilled, stylish wordsmith though he is – and only today do I fully appreciate just how seductive his words have been – there is something that Gavin, too, cannot articulate. Something he feels I ought to understand, and he seems puzzled, almost saddened, as to why I am unable to. It is as if I have disappointed him too. But what on earth did he expect? That I would be happy to be his ally? Complicit in his crimes? Technically, that is the correct term for what he has done with these men. Although the only victim I see anywhere in this tragic, sorry tale is myself. I doubt the Law Lords who condemned that which dare not speak its name were concerned by the thought of my broken heart.

'Have there been others?'

Gavin gives no answer, which I take as an answer in itself. 'You've brought friends here too,' he says eventually. 'You've shared Sandaig with other people.' The words might sound defensive or even petulant, but in truth, I hear only weariness seeping into his tone. The relentless sea winds around us have risen to rattle the thick charcoal clouds. An ugly bulbous one erupts over the horizon, sending a smattering of droplets to strike the ocean surface even while the land where we stand stays dry. *Not for long*, I think blackly. *We can't hold off the storm much longer.*

'I brought Winifred.' I throw my retort back at Gavin, angered anew at the sacrilege of hearing the name of our paradise dragged down into this dirt. 'She came here to paint. I didn't bring her to …' Words desert me once more. The poet and the woman cede to the animal raging inside me. But this is no natural creature: this infuriated, foaming-mouthed beast is deformed, cloven-hoofed and black-horned. It is brutish. Savage. Demonic. 'You disgust me.'

I disgust myself even as I say it, but it achieves what I only realise in retrospect was my intention. I see it strike Gavin's face, my show of revulsion hitting him with all the bloodied, brutal viciousness of a wildcat's swiped claw. One word, once again, and just like in Kielder, we are severed from one another. His cheeks flush as if I have slapped him. A violent low blow, hard and fast enough to leave us both reeling. In the silence that follows, I watch him summoning up his strength. Tall and upright, injured yet undeniably courageous. I admire him for it, I realise in shock: deep, abiding affection rippling like drops of fresh water within the blood-stained bilge of my hatred. Heaven help me, a part of me still loves him. As long as I live, a part of me will love him. But I did not speak of love, did I? Only disgust.

'If that's true,' Gavin says, 'it's even more reason for you to leave.'

I lash out, a howl of anguish born aloft on the air at the thought of being cast out of our Eden. My limbs slash towards him and I see shock flit across Gavin's face before, with military-perfected precision, those famous reflexes kick in. He seizes my wrists, a tight grip holding me away from his torso so I flail like a rag doll tossed to the wind. With all the physical strength I possess, even with the waterfall's weight of fury coursing through my veins, I cannot overpower him. The throb of nascent bruising is pushing through my skin; my pulse beats with impotent fury against the pressure of his firm fingertips. His physical power startles me, even as I writhe and resist. I remember the first day we met, opening my door to a stranger who looked too fragile to stand without support. Gavin needed strength from me back then.

I kick out, walking boots swinging wildly like those of a woman breathing her last on the gallows. Inevitably missing my target, which I believe through my vague mist of rage was Gavin's shins, I sink, collapsing tattered and dishevelled into a heap at his feet. Only then does he let go. Dropping me as one unwanted. Snatching my wrists back, I turn from him, my palms pressing painfully into the coarse shingled grass. My gut growls and I retch. Choke. Splutter. A distant, coolly calculating part of my brain tells me that Gavin will think I am sickened by the thought of the physical act, and with a womanly instinct for manipulation – the only asset I have that he and his dashing young companions lack – I am grateful for the extra hurt it will cause him. My true disgust, though, is with myself. With the crazed, childish delusion I have indulged in. With the shame, overwhelming and inescapable, that is all I have left to show for it.

Through a stream of tears that fall of their own accord, I look up to see Gavin standing above me in his kilt. The gold and green threads zigzag; his thin shirt is spotted with rain and sweat. His sleeves are rolled up and I can see those beloved birthmarks clearly. I feel a wrench inside me as if my own skin were burning, smouldering into rotten flesh or sliced into ribbons. My stomach gives a second heave and like a dog I am forced to lower my head back to the grass. Bile dribbles from my lips, a glob of lurid yellow spit sinking into the shoreline. I cough, stomach spasming, but there is nothing left inside me. I have given all I ever had to Gavin.

'I love you.' I fight through the acrid taste of vomit to cry out like these will be the last words I ever speak. 'I've loved you in spite of everything you are.'

Gavin's lip curls. There is an animal, too, inside the aristocrat. 'A noble sacrifice, I'm sure,' he sneers.

'May God forgive you,' I mutter, my head dropping back towards the earth. The rain is falling hard now, spattering the ground until the soil jumps and freckling my face with dirty droplets that leave me sullied with sea brine and mud. I cannot tell whether or not Gavin has heard me. Perhaps his thoughts remain down here in the dirt; perhaps he thinks I am talking purely about the sex. Truly, although it devastates me more than all the rest, I don't believe he realises what he has done to me. Once, I thought us soulmates: two spirits entwined for all time. Now I know we are oceans apart.

'May God forgive you,' I shriek into the storm.

'He will,' Gavin says.

*

Night falls around me as I remain motionless, midway between home – no, neither the place nor the man I love were ever truly my home – and Tormor, having set out in search of refuge yet found myself unwilling to impose on that innocent family's sanctuary and, less altruistically, to expose my shame to them. Only standing in fading sight of the ocean feels right: my mind is storm-blasted, a jettisoned shambles of torn sails and splinters no longer seaworthy. It is impossible to imagine poetry rising from the wreckage. The storm worsens and soon I am barely standing at all, imperious sea winds forcing my back to bend into a low, obsequious bow. Fighting for a single step in the darkness, I stumble and slip on the hillside; cries carried off without a chance of being heard by fellow humans. When I fall, I land heavily, mud-slicked and self-pitying. A hot, horrible twinge of pain near my ribs reminds me of my age. As if Gavin Young had not already done so.

Headfirst in horizontal rain, I start making my long, laborious way downhill. Again and again, I reach out for help that does not exist, grappling fingers searching the black only to return empty. Eventually, after an undignified on-all-fours slog, I sense the squelching soil start to level. Beyond, perhaps a mile along the burn side, is Sandaig. The sloshing ground seems to delight in the downpour, already imbued with the fluid energy of the ocean, and it adapts to this elemental deluge just as naturally as Mij would if given the chance. The thought of our otter, the precious waterbaby who will forever bear Gavin's name, is like an arrow to my heart; the weapon lodged in my breast and letting my life's blood slip out from beneath my rain-soaked pyjama shirt. I no longer wear Charles's, having realised I wanted no trace of any other man on my body. If only Gavin had felt the same.

I stride madly across the waterlogged fields, soil pooling in craters where the driest patches of land have been too slow to absorb the storm. Several times, my feet plummet into ankle-twisting sinkholes, and I think of the unseen wildflowers being crushed beneath my feet. From all the characters and images rattling without context through my brain, I pluck out ill-fated, fair Ophelia: picturing myself floating in morbid serenity along the Sandaig burn, the flowers I used to cherish forming my funeral bower. Or perhaps, flicking forward in literary time, I am that other Cathy, haunting the moors with cries for her Heathcliff to let her into the warmth again. But my love has already turned me away. Sandaig's doors are barred and bolted. I am cast out of our garden alone.

Not totally alone, an eerily calm voice hisses from the disturbed depths of my mind. *Gavin has used other people too.* None quite like me, it must be said, for no one else has had their heart sacrificed so bloodily or mercilessly upon the altar of his mercurial affection. But we have all had our parts to play in making his dreams come true. Me, Mary, Tambi, and even his mother. He makes each of us only a single volume on his bookshelf; no one person more than a neatly labelled drawer in his curiosity cabinet. How many must give their all for one man to glimpse happiness? And we were happy to do it. An oxymoronic truism: we were his willing slaves. My function was to support his soul … no, no, that creepily pragmatic voice slithers into my ear again. *Not exclusively his soul.* My letters to Janet Adam Smith loom towards me through the darkened landscape, compelling my friend not to miss the chance of featuring a brilliant new author on the up. I see Gavin and me in Rupert's luxurious office, all firm handshakes and book jacket smiles as Gavin was introduced – as I introduced him – to the promising professional future now his present. Whatever the cost, I gave myself gladly to satisfy Gavin's desires. We all did. All do. Even Raef, Young and the rest, I expect.

'Come now, Kathleen. I need you, Kathleen.' What feels like years of my life have been spent in half-slumber beside my telephone, anticipating

Gavin's iconic post-midnight calls. I remember needing to close my eyes on the other end of the line, too tired to keep them open yet unwilling to set down the receiver and miss that melodic soul's song of a voice. Now, bereft and sleepless, I wonder about the nights I rested soundly. Dreaming of Gavin, while for once undisturbed by him. Who else was he calling? Only now can I start to guess.

Stumbling towards sea level, I start to hear the waterfall's rush, overflowing and gushing above the violent howl of sea winds. The intricate network of falls sounds invigorated by the drama of this downpour, thriving in chaos just like the man to whom it belongs. In the dark, I am able to discern only the vaguest, most menacing shadows, and when I reach the stone-pier bridge over the burn, my hipbone collides with its wooden struts. I let out a yelp, fresh tears flooding my eyes to mingle with raindrops and salt spray, but the sound is no more meaningful or resonant than a single leaf's fall from a mighty oak. In pain, I pause to assess what little I can see. To my right, the darkened ocean is tossed and churned, an aggressive stippling of surface rain revealed only by brief snatches of moonlight. To the left, Gavin's white cottage walls glow through the gloom, ghoulishly illuminated like the snow on Kielder Bridge.

Like a woman, or perhaps a poet, possessed, I charge in the direction of the sinister, shadowy waves. Closer than I had realised in the darkness, the next surge of the sea's squalling current hits me hard: a sudden cold blow coursing over my legs and chilling my bones while I let out a breathy half-scream. The summer sun is long gone and only the iciness of night remains. As the tide briefly recedes, my meagre clothing clings to me before billowing out wildly on either side when the waves return with a vengeance. They drag me forward until the water is waist-height, choppy and chaotic, and my feet stumble on uneven sand so that everything below heart level is submerged. Faint at first, I start to hear the sea's seductive siren call as if one of my precious windowsill shells were pressed to my ear. It would be quick. Easy. Just let go, unburden myself to the elements, and allow the current to pull me under. Then all of it – the humiliation, the wasted years, the love that springs from the very fountain of my soul yet is still not sweet or pure enough to make Gavin return it with his own – will be washed away. Perhaps feeling nothing ever again is a price worth paying to be rid of this pain.

The children, Kathie. Think of the children. Their names needle in my brain, wrestling with the waves so that even through the darkness I can glimpse the bright, light memory of Anna's doe eyes and James's sweet, ever-excitable grin. An undeserved angel on my shoulder, hovering just above the rapidly rising waterline, whispers that my children need me, whatever mistakes I have made. *No woman is perfect*, she insists. *Anna and James deserve their mother.* At that thought, a devil speaks up on my other side, stirring the iced seawater until it seizes like a cold iron collar around my neck. *Haven't I told you before, Kathie?* His cruel voice prods me, jolts me, harpoons me with what feels like my most shameful truth. *They'd both be better off without you.*

Gavin. The thought of him suddenly floods me: his elegant voice, his fair, handsome face, the ripples of laughter that sounded like my life was finally being played in tune. My heart contorts, then cracks, and full-blooded anger surges into the chasm left by what he has done to me. The spark of fury spreads to my limbs, catching alight as it ricochets from core to extremities, and I push back, inspired at long last to struggle against the storm-strong current doing its utmost to drag me beneath the waves. My arms paddle, frantically fighting for my life; my legs kick out in panicked desperation until I make it back within my depth. That man will not leave my children without a mother. Gavin will not gain the romantic, rakish notoriety of having taken me away from them. He has already taken more than enough.

I stumble to the shore, so warmed through with rage I barely feel the seawater dripping from my clothes or the rain-dashed wind whipping my wet hair into my face. I have lost my boots somewhere in the sea and realise with odd, disembodied surprise that my bare soles are bleeding over the shingles. Psyche roamed the earth until her feet were cut to raw strips, searching and suffering for the beloved who had cast her aside. That man of light whose transcendent touch of love summoned her world to being. I walk on, ignoring the pain as I am borne back ceaselessly to Sandaig. There might be a magnet in my centre, or else I am being pulled by the boundless circle of the stars I have so often looked out upon from the bedroom Gavin and I shared. A soulless woman drawn to the side of her soulmate, but it is no longer love that drives my bloodied, broken feet. If I am to live, I must feel something. I resolve to make it anger rather than sorrow as I stride in barefoot fury across Gavin's beach.

Dizziness combines with each ferocious gust to make me wobble as if inebriated. How I wish I were. My real-life steps merge with those I cannot help but retrace in my mind: my once-precious memories slipping

206

through my fingers and stripping my skin as they go, like the ropes lost to the ocean by Gavin and his Sea Leopard crew. I think of us watching Mij rejoice in the water. Our naked limbs entwined as we slept in his bed. Dear dead Jonnie running through the autumn leaves while we watched the swans and spoke of Yeats. In days gone by, I would turn to poetry for solace, but Gavin has succeeded in even taking that away from me. For what poem have I produced since the day we met that was not in some way written out of love for him? My notebook compositions, both drowned and resurrected; our letters and the pending collection with a dedication to him that is no doubt already in print. Gavin inhabits every syllable, flowing through each stroke of ink; embodying the vision with which I was foolish enough to entrust him. Can I keep writing without him? Will my words be forever tainted by the love he did not want? Vengeful, vicious outrage throbs through me. Time might let me forgive the wounds I have suffered at his hands as a woman. But never as a poet. I keep walking.

The lights are out at the cottage. Gavin and his guest must be asleep. How many nights have I lain awake thinking of him, willing our spirits to unite in a way our earthbound bodies never could? He has not once lost sleep over me. I look to the moon, or what I can see of it through the smirry storm clouds, and some vague intuition tells me that it is well past midnight. 15th July. Gavin's birthday. I ought to wish him happy returns. I march my bare feet up to the sky-blue door whose colour I cannot see through the shadows, feeling sick at the thought of thumping my fists to demand re-entry, then sicker still when I realise that I have already lost my nerve. Adrift, I stare through the darkness at ugly lumpen shapes representing the roses I have nurtured on Gavin's behalf, cultivated with all the tenderness I was never permitted to show him. But roses have thorns too. I reach through the gloom to the closest flower. Gritting my teeth, I clench my fist tight around it. Ragged dead-end splinter stems puncture the soft flesh of my palm; rogue thorns jut into my skin as the pretty rose petals are crushed.

O Rose, thou art sick:
The invisible worm,
That flies in the night
In the howling storm,

Has found out thy bed

Of crimson joy;
And his dark secret love
Does thy life destroy.

Spirit willing but flesh weak, I bear the pain only a second or two before I am forced to spring back, wrenching my hand away at an angle that turns the tear into a gash. One thorny nub remains embedded, obliging me to pluck at it in the dark with pinched thumb and forefinger until, at last, I am free, if likely scarred. The elemental gale still raging over the ocean takes another vicious swipe at me, frenzied winds spinning me until I face the rowan tree.

The most precious, painful memory of all. Gavin and I still little more than strangers yet sharing one vision between soulmates. Or so I told myself. Now powering through the storm, I raise my head to look at the real thing. The Sandaig rowan's branches are convulsing in the wind as if overtaken by their own tears, leaf clusters shuddering and shaking like they are inconsolably bereft. The steel grey bark glints silver when caught in the intermittent moonlight, shining bright for the briefest of moments before cloudcast brings back the black. At this time of year, blossom is ceding to berries; its final ivory offcuts lie like Miss Havisham's mottled old wedding veil, clumps of soiled and sullied lace decaying into unloved barren filth. Legs unsteady, I square up with the misplaced bravado of a drunkard, inspired to confront the tree as if it were Gavin himself. Awaiting me at an altar to which I know now we will never arrive.

'I loved you.' Soaked through with rain and tears, I implore those trembling branches to understand. 'I loved you.' Quieter, too quiet to be heard above the storm. 'I love you.' It is just as well the tree cannot speak. There is no response on earth I could bear to hear.

I stay staring at it, remembering that tarnished silver trunk so recently draped in galling lace finery, and I start to think of how often trees and tragedy go together. Seeking sanctuary in literature once more, my muddled and muddied mind draws me in the direction of Thomas Hardy and his mythical Wessex. Farmer Boldwood would have lived a long, happy life were it not for the Valentine's card that Bathsheba sent him in thoughtless jest. Why seek him out to reject him, scorned in such a way that her actions paved the road to his madness? Hardy would have understood my outrage, as well as my sorrow. The timeless agony of she whose true love has proved false. How did he put it? "When a strong woman recklessly throws away her strength, she is worse than a weak woman who has never had any strength to throw away."

I feel the last of my strength deserting me as I remember those words. Any power I had is draining down into the rowan's roots, fearful that I will be left forever empty of both passion and poetry. In this shattered shell of a body, I cannot physically bear to cry any longer, so I let the rain do the work for me: freshwater tears sliding down my cheeks, weeping and seeping away to the soil on which I thought Gavin and I had built our home. I feel desperate, close to drowning on dry land, and my raw, ragged fingernails start to scratch at that precious tree's trunk. Reaching through the last remnants of blossom, I take hold of the tight, unripe kernels that should become next season's ruby berries, treasured jewels of the kingdom from which I am banished. A handful come to rest in my palm and I crush them, squeezing out bitter juices into a hand already bleeding. I wince as the tart sting of their essence flows into my open flesh.

I must return. I must get back. Back to when Gavin and I were as one; sharing vision, soul and spirit as two branches of our tree. If we cannot be together in Heaven, I want him here with me in Hell. My blood-soaked hand is on the rowan's bark when I speak.

'Let Gavin suffer, in this place, as I am suffering now.'

Part Two
1956

Chapter Twenty-Five

Work. I will work rather than rest. I will think, so I do not need to feel. When your own life is not worth living, set to work to improve the lot of others: that was the overarching lesson my father's Methodists drilled into me during dreary years of interminable Sunday sermons. I hated it at the time, my back and buttocks growing numb from a cold church pew while my mind likewise turned vacant and unfeeling, alienated by a pessimistic, puritan stoicism that held no space for hope or poetry. But now, I believe their creed may very well save my life. I have neither hope nor poetry left.

I return to London by train, curled up sorrowfully in my seat, keeping my aching head down and my swollen eyes averted from fellow passengers. My hand is clumsily bandaged inside a handkerchief, my feet so raw and tender I am forced to limp, but if the mostly male travellers inside my carriage notice, they give no sign. Whatever walks of life otherwise divide them, all agree that an injured woman is none of their business. Reaching the city, I hurry upstairs to my half of Paultons – because my home, like my heart, is now cleaved irreparably in two – and gather together only the most perfunctory luggage to take with me to my Girton rooms. I fill a suitcase with clothes and an unloved handbag is requisitioned to be a satchel, stuffed with books and pens until it obstinately refuses to close. I bring it even so. Better that than my Sandaig rucksack.

The college is different to how I remember it, or perhaps it is me who is different. Twenty-five years older, if not wiser, than the first time I set foot here. On arrival, I am led by a rosy-cheeked young woman under the tower to Cloister Court, past the terrace of dainty, red-gabled gingerbread houses where Anna and the other new students will soon be ensconced. What they call the Elephant Ears doors give a low oak groan upon opening. The sound, more than the sight, beckons me back through the years to my student days. I barely noticed my surroundings as an undergraduate, caught up in the minute social dramas that then seemed monumental. Yet today, I am struck by the soft, cultivated quiet of Girton's inner sanctum. This courtyard feels contemplative. Cloistered. An intellectual retreat with the spiritual serenity of a convent, pointedly set apart from the main university thoroughfare to dissuade marauding male undergraduates. With limited success, as I recall.

After the storms that have savaged me inside and out, I appreciate the tranquillity of these genteel formal gardens. I am glad of the small, well-tended orchard beneath whose branches a few early girls are studying. I discovered only a couple of weeks ago that Sandaig has apple and plum trees, sprinkled at random along the route from the bridge to the waterfall. They were easily missed, dotted amongst the towering alders and growing produce so quirkily misshapen it seemed too otherworldly to be edible. The fruit of another world, where I no longer belong.

'Can I do anything else for you, Dr Raine?' My sweet, spherically-faced escort hovers earnestly at my side when we come to my apartment. I should correct her, returning a doctorate I do not deserve, but something in the girl's gleamingly youthful eyes holds me back. Perhaps I will earn the honour through my Blake research. Better Dr than Mrs.

'No, thank you, except ... remind me of your name again?' My contract includes a handful of teaching hours and I feel I should take any chance I can to familiarise myself with the students.

The young woman colours, the rest of her face flushing to match her pink cheeks. 'I'm Sally, Dr Raine.' Sally. I think of my girlhood counterpart back at Great Bavington, my companion in those happy fields of flowers and sunshine long before I knew of the darkness that awaited me. Perhaps this new Sally will be a friend to Anna when she arrives, guiding my daughter down a wiser path than her foolish mother followed.

'And are you happy here, Sally?'

Peony pink deepens to fuchsia. 'Very.' Sally's wide, white-toothed Cheshire Cat grin makes me smile a little too, until her youthful enthusiasm reminds me of myself pre-graduation – pre-everything – and even that brief flicker of joy is extinguished. I let the girl go, her neat brogues clipping out a quick, self-conscious patter along the corridor.

Work, I remind myself as I twist the doorknob of the room that is now my own. Work, then work harder still if necessary. Ignoring a tender twinge where my palm has not quite healed, I open the door, silent and solemn as one taking the veil or entering a cell. Perhaps both. There is a small study stocked with bookcases. A narrow annex with a single bed. And a bathroom, as minuscule as I have seen, with a tiny oblong tub from which one could touch the walls on either side. A spinster's quarters. A room of one's own for a woman who reads rather than lives. For the first time in my life, I am making a reliable living from poetry. Pity it is not my own. The walls here are dark, boarded with mahogany but not pitch-panelled pine, thank God. Setting down my mismatched baggage, I sit at my new desk. It is polished, well-crafted and glossy, and I stare at the smooth, featureless surface to try and stop myself thinking of another. A handcrafted writing desk in the West Highlands with a cork for a stopper and a shell nestled inside its drawer.

'Work.' I say it aloud this time, unconcerned with whether anyone passing in the hallway overhears me. Surely as a Fellowed bluestocking – I have dropped the beautiful – I may talk to myself while I go about my business? And I do have business to attend to. I reach across the desk for the telephone, my fingers flicking the dial around to a number I know by heart. I have to ring him, to make contact by phone and not by face, because I cannot let him see me in this condition. With strangers, I can keep my swollen hand hidden, walking gingerly on the scraped-raw soles of my feet. But he would tell in an instant. We have never hidden things from each other.

'Tambi?' My friend's decommissioned payphone, whimsically installed as a joke gesture at curbing call times, bristles with static. I picture Tambi tangled up in the crinkled cord, receiver squashed between his ear and scrunched shoulder. He will be letter writing simultaneously or perhaps even proofreading (good luck to that author).

'Kathleen.' Words tumble from him, enthusiastically verbose as ever. 'Where on earth have you been, my precious poetess? I sent a letter to Sandaig, but …'

'Is the dedication printed?'

'What's that now?' A flurried ruffle of papers resounds down the line as if a manuscript has been knocked over. Tambi's voice fades, muttering a few mild expletives in the background before his attention returns to me.

'The dedication in my collected poems,' I persist. 'Is it printed yet?' The rustling stops. 'Tell me the truth, Tambi. Please.' Tambi is silent. After years of joking with each other, we both know when it is time to be serious.

'It's almost ready, but … what would you rather it said, Kathleen?' His voice grows steady and solemn. A considerable departure from usual. The

215

line crackles and hisses, emitting pips that in its former life would warn I had run out of credit.

'Are the proofs already set?' I ask. 'Am I too late?' The deep familiarity of our friendship, a decade in the making, tells me this is no time to be evasive. 'Can we afford to make a change?'

'Let me worry about the cost,' Tambi says firmly. 'That's how it's always worked with us. I take care of the money and you take care of the words.' No doubt. No question. *I don't deserve him*, I think, staring across at the wood panels opposite until they blur into a mournful dark brown.

'Then write this down, please.' Borrowing what I can of Tambi's confidence, I force myself to sound more decisive than I feel. My fingers ache from being clenched tight around the telephone. I move to change hands before remembering the other is still bandaged.

'To Gavin Maxwell,' I begin. My voice falters, suddenly breathless. I pretend the poor line is at fault. 'With whom I share the recollection of ... "an Iland salt and bare, The haunt of Seales and Orcs, and Seamews clang."'

I hear the scratching of Tambi's nib. 'Is that all?'

'That's all.' Silence. A few wisps of white noise try to fill it.

'It's *Paradise Lost*, isn't it?' I nod, momentarily forgetting that I am only on the telephone.

'Yes,' I manage eventually, voice faint and frail. '*Paradise Lost*.'

*

Each day when I wake, ignoring the vivid summer sunlight that seeks to stream through my sole small window, I thank God for William Blake. How odd that a man whom I will never meet, a great poet born a hundred and fifty years before this minor one, can sustain and console me with his eternal imaginative vision, his words speaking to me from a depth of understanding no contemporary has ever attained. Well, perhaps one. But unlike him, Blake cannot hurt me, nor reject what little it is I have to offer him. My intellectual devotion, that is, dedicating my waking hours to the belief that what he had to say still matters.

My research gathers pace, aided by hours hunched over the leather-bound books of the college library. One lukewarm pleasure of late summer is that, when the dim stacks start to loom too depressingly even for me, I need not abandon my work altogether. Instead, I take it outside: claiming my spot on the grass with overhanging orchard boughs to shade my pages. Girton's grounds are designed for reflection, with flourishing borders framing the lawns and pretty paving stones to entice walkers off onto efflorescent secret passageways. My only distraction is when a resident cat draws near in search of an affectionate head scratch. There are plenty with both scholars and students permitted to keep pets, and soon several members of our feline sorority learn to greet me when I take up my spot beneath the trees. I smile to feel their prickled-fur spines rubbing in welcome along my shins, comforted by their dainty heart-shaped faces and low, loud purrs when nestled into my lap while I read. Above all, I try not to compare the cats' company unfavourably with that of an otter.

My few human friends here are those who did not know my life at Sandaig well, or else are compassionate enough never to mention it when we are together. I write to Winifred as always, although the letter proves uncharacteristically laborious to compose, ashamed as I am of my blindness when forced to face what her sharp artist's eyes saw all along. Closer to college, there is also Gay Taylor, a passionate amateur astrologer I first encountered in Helen's orbit, who makes for an unexpected and eccentric addition to my diminutive social circle. We reconnect in Cambridge by accident, although Gay insists it was fate, and she undertakes various valiant attempts to raise my spirits, regaling me with outlandish tales from her own romantic misadventures.

'I sometimes have to send my lovers away, so I can really *think* about them,' Gay confesses over a cup of tea in my rooms, the prelude to her reading the leaves for me. I nod, feeling like I understand. It is difficult to see clearly when a man of light shines straight in your eyes. Inspired by Gay's boldness, I agree to give her my birthdate along with Gavin's so that she can draw up what she loftily calls our 'star charts'. Our lives are linked, she tells me solemnly, yet more in sorrow than in joy. 'Star-crossed lovers' indeed. Once, I would never have believed her.

Edwin and Willa Muir, fellow writers for whom I have always had the utmost respect, are a couple I have known since my marriage to Charles. I kept the friends, if not the husband, and feel grateful as I come to realise only now the full extent of the wisdom they can impart to me, if I will accept it. Edwin is a gentle Scots poet who hails from Orkney and when I read his work I feel that for once I am not alone in my quest to unite poetry with what makes life meaningful. He too rejects the material and mercenary, focusing on a more spiritually sustaining world for which he remains hopeful. Edwin's wife Willa strides out beside him on every step

217

of their intellectual way, translating texts with distinction and writing her own feminist treaties that strengthen rather than weaken their bond. Although wife and husband are sensitive enough to my plight not to flaunt their marital bliss, in their company I am moved to witness two halves of a whole. Willa and Edwin are together in every endeavour, as much as Gavin and I are now worlds apart.

Finally, completing the small ring of sustaining connections around me, there is Thetis. An intense, imaginative young opera singer turned artist, her kind companionship comes to bring me as much joy as I can feel in this dull, emotionally deadened state. Her sister Carmen is a scholar here, but as the first weeks of my Fellowship merge into a month, it is the other girl I get to know better. I say girl, although Thetis is around Lavinia Renton's age – my mind still readily returns to Monreith and all that took me there, much as I wish it would not – but she is serious rather than glamorous, her soulful eyes half-hidden behind thick-rimmed spectacles and her long black hair piled up in a style that, since our first meeting, has looked uncannily like my own. If it did not risk embarrassing us both, I would try to persuade her that there are far more fashionable examples to follow.

Named inventively after the shape-shifting sea goddess and mother of Achilles, Thetis is adamant that she herself will never marry. 'I want my work and my freedom. I want what you have.' Her dark mane shakes vehemently, glasses bouncing on the bridge of her nose, every time she repeats the proclamation. Appreciating its august origins, sometimes her name also makes me think of Thel, one of Blake's most intriguing and compelling creations: a soul unmoved by the promise of sensual pleasures on earth who did not wish to 'descend' to mortality at all. A secret, selfish part of me hopes Thetis will stick to her resolution. With Willa as the exception that proves the rule, it is a rare woman whose life is improved by a male mate. Up close, Thetis's art is astonishing, ephemeral yet richly dynamic, and I cannot deny that it soothes my troubled soul to watch her work whenever she brings a sample to Girton, rhythmically stippling each cloth corner with the colourful dots that form her pattern.

'What's this technique called?' I ask her on one such afternoon, grateful to feel even a glimmer of interest in anything that is not my own woe.

'Batik.' Thetis smiles without raising her gaze from the piece. 'It's Indonesian.' The reminder that a world exists beyond London, and even beyond Sandaig, is a welcome one. From what had looked like abstraction, I can discern the shape of a phoenix starting to rise, its fiery plumage luminous and magnificent as it soars in triumphant resurrection from ashes.

'Can I touch?' I whisper.

Thetis nods, smiling wider. 'You can.' One delicate, reverent finger resting on the phoenix's heart, I beg it to impart a little of that warm strength to me. Thetis watches my movements, suspending her own for a moment. 'Kathleen, he really didn't deserve you ...' Dark eyes meet mine. Break away. We fall to silence and Thetis hurriedly resumes her work.

More than anything, academia is teaching me how much I do not know. Within weeks, I am appointed as a Director of Studies: a rather pompous title for what amounts to being in charge of a small group of girls. Every time I look out at the young women in my charge, wide-eyed and eagerly awaiting any pearls of wisdom I care to bestow, I feel self-conscious and shamefaced by all I have failed to understand in my life. How can I teach when I still have so many things to learn? My inadequacies gnaw and grate at me each night when I return to my small room alone. My inability to practice what I preached; my failure to uphold the vision of a spiritual life to which I claimed I was devoted. What Gavin and I had was meant to be a Platonic love: a profound soulful connection that transcended primitive impulses. But was I not, in truth, the first one to drag us down?

Lying in my perfunctory single bed, or in the tiny porcelain tub while tepid, soap-scudded bathwater swirls around me, my body revisits those memories even though my mind tries to bar the way. Night after night aching for Gavin's touch, throbbing for him with an animalistic appetite; awakening after a broken night's sleep to the sound of a moan I must have unknowingly begun in my slumber. I was not dwelling then on our shared consciousness, nor on our eternally linked spiritual journeys. Only his eyes of ocean blue and the fair sweep of hair waving across his forehead. Only the sensation of his bare skin pressing against my own. 'She that is without sin among you, let her cast the first stone,' the Methodists command. As weeks go by without him, I have fewer and fewer stones that I feel justified in casting at Gavin.

Sometimes I can taste my words of cruelty and bitterness towards him, my mouth unclean as if the vomit of that awful night still lingers, raw and rank, inside my throat. Disgust. Revulsion. Did I have the right to lay such accusations at his feet? Gavin lied to me. At least, he let me lie to myself. Yet as I reconsider our great battle with the perspective that comes from retreat, my conscience prods me to remember that I was not entirely innocent of falsehood. Didn't Gavin tell me about the way he is during our very first days together? It is hardly his fault if it was already too late. One cannot choose to fall in or out of love. Certainly not a love like this. Looking back from the vantage point of my scholarly spinster's cell, I see that Gavin was honest about his feelings when I was not brave enough to be. I was unable to admit my emotions were not the grandiose, floral garlanded verses of a lyrical poetess, but instead the earthbound, body and soul desires of a woman who was desperate for him. A woman who is desperate for him.

Staring out late at night at the wood panels that now surround me like a poor woman's Kielder Forest, I think if Gavin is a hypocrite then so must I be, for there is nothing he shared with any of those young men that I would not have sold my soul for him to share with me. In that incontrovertible knowledge, I see my betrayal of what we built together, every bit as much as his. The notion that somewhere, somehow, my failure brought about our Fall feels depressingly familiar, like an ineradicable shadow that has trailed me throughout my life. I have certainly let down my parents, not to mention both my husbands; indeed, the fact there are two says it all on that particular, painful subject. And the children. Time and time again, I have failed my children. Lacking from their earliest days some sweet nectar sent by the Gods to the good mothers of this world, then inadvertently stinging them in my attempts to protect them from that deficiency. As the summer sun depletes daily, the world around me drifting ever closer to autumn, I stay seated in the Girton orchard until dusk and stare numbly up at the trees, clouds of foliage blurring into the evening sky. Pear. Apple. Rowan. Eve sinned first, the Methodists say, and only then did Adam follow her lead.

'What do you think?' Having telephoned to tell me that my collection is ready, Tambi looks on anxiously as I raise a copy from one of several boxes just delivered to his *Poetry London* basement. The volume looks neat, wrapped in a dust jacket of exercise jotter buff brown: plain except for a small, stamped filigree border running top and bottom but not sides. I suspect the cost of reprinting had to be reclaimed elsewhere in the process, and this paper bag cover is the result. My collection looks simple – too simple, I fear, to attract the attention of booksellers – yet it feels oddly right, its spartan style correct in a way that nothing else has been since Sandaig. My name is outlined in fine black letters, silhouetted but not filled in. Empty, I think, staring down at the 'K' and 'a'. Kathleen Raine is empty.

'It's perfect,' I tell Tambi. It is not, but the right words do not come to me the way they used to. 'Thank you.' Unable to turn to the dedication I demanded, I open the volume at random:

> *Because I love*
> *The sun pours out its rays of living gold*
> *Pours out its gold and silver on the sea.*
>
> *Because I love*
> *The summer air quivers with a thousand wings,*
> *Myriads of jewelled eyes burn in the light.*
>
> *Because I love*
> *The iridescent shells upon the sand*
> *Take forms as fine and intricate as thought ...*

I cannot read on. But one day, perhaps, it will be worth the pain of remembering.

Later, I walk through the park near Paultons with my collected poems under my arm. Masochism, what do the Methodists say about that? I think I can guess, although a subconscious strain is surely embedded within the perverse pride they take in self-denial. Autumn's arrival is unambiguous now, the precise moment at which the balance of the seasons tipped unnoticed by me until too late. The trees that still have their leaves are brown, like my book, while those with bare branches form thin outlines against the sky, uncannily similar to the flat lettering of my name. Shuffling as if decades rather than years have passed, I stand by what I came to call 'our' bench. Fallen leaves cluster around my feet, a few flecks of sullied ore glinting through the mulch. Alone, I swirl my toes, trying to restore these shrivelled, sad little corpses to motion, but the effect emphasises death rather than life. Their crisp, thin curls lie dormant, uninspired by my attempt at reanimation and continuing to decay before my eyes.

I decide to return via Paultons Square. Do I decide? Or do my heavy, slow-healing feet choose to pace out a path of their own accord? Only when I notice the intricate black iron railings and sprawling hedges that I once encountered daily do I recognise the route I have taken. It will be dark soon, the autumnal sun already ebbing away, and I will need to take a taxi back: an unnecessary extravagance I can ill afford. *Unjustifiable,* I reprimand myself, and yet I continue along what is still, technically, my road. The Bentley is absent, but parked in its place outside Number 9 is a car even more ostentatious: cherry red with an outlandishly tunnelled bonnet that looks like the vehicular equivalent of a large, angry aardvark. 'Grand Prix Maserati' reads a gold-embossed logo. We all cope with distress differently. *Turn back,* I think to myself, even as I keep going.

Hovering on the King's Road corner, I hear them before I see them. Mij's chirruping mixed with excited squeaks. He might be the Sandaig burn itself, burbling and trickling through a strange musical stave as he plays in the Paultons Square garden. There is a beat, a happy 'Ha' that travels through the air to touch my heart, before Gavin's voice: gentle and lyrical as he converses with his otter. Out of sight, I lay my hand on the wall and wait.

Mij must smell me, or otherwise sense my presence, for all at once he abandons his hijinks to seemingly pour himself in my direction. Hearing his paws scrabble against brick, I mirror what I imagine to be the same posture on my side, rising to my toes as I strain in vain to see him. To see them.

'Mij, my boy,' Gavin calls, 'what is it?'

'It's me. Kathleen.'

A pause, silent save for lutrine squeals of joy. 'Come in.'

Hurrying through what was once my own hallway, I arrive in time to watch Mij's lengthy spine concertina as he lollops across the grass, the small paws I have adored since he first set foot in England charging over the lawn until he flows into my arms. Mij squirms in smooth, liquid-like delight while I hold him, pressing his frame to my chest as if reunited with a missing piece of my heart. His squished blackberry nose nuzzles my cheeks and I cannot help but smile to feel the ticklish touch of his whiskers. My stockinged knees dig into the dirt; my new collection is tucked protectively under one elbow. I rise with the otter in my arms before I turn to face Gavin.

'Hello.'

'Hello.'

Struggling in awkward silence for a beat or two, I study the tiny changes that have taken place in his face, intimate tweaks visible only to me. Gavin looks older, his eyes heavy-lidded and almost veiled

222

with tiredness, fragile creases crisscrossing beneath the line of his pale gold lower lashes. Ounces he did not have to spare have been shaved off his thoroughbred physique, turning what was a lean frame into one unnervingly stick thin. He seems weary. Weighted. Gavin looks like he has suffered.

'I'm …' sorry is the word I cannot say.

'Me too,' Gavin replies. In this, I think, we understand each other still. A residual spark from the embers of shared consciousness I had thought entirely extinguished.

Tumbling from my grasp, Mij performs a circus-style prat fall onto the grass before planting himself between our feet and wriggling blissfully on his back. Gavin and I laugh, unable to resist Mij's joy as we look down at the animal we love. No matter what was lost along the way, there remains some strange, unbreakable bond between us in every beat of this otter's heart. God help me, I share two human children with Charles Madge, and still I could not find it in myself to reconcile with him.

'Is that your collection?' Gavin gestures to the book under my arm. I hand it to him, leaning over the otter who continues to cheerfully squeak and squirm. Gavin opens the volume gently. Almost warily. His tired eyes widen when he reads the dedication.

'*Paradise Lost.*' Not a question. He knows the answer. '*Paradise Lost*,' Gavin murmurs a second time, voice drifting as if his mind has been beckoned back to Sandaig's deserted shore. He nods, then goes to hand the book back.

'Keep it,' I say. 'It's yours.' Never a truer word spoken.

'Thank you.' Gavin tucks my collection beneath his left arm, within touching distance of his heart.

Mij rolls between us, exposing his pale-haired belly, tail twisting with pleasure at having us fleetingly reunited. Pushing away the memory of when last I saw our otter, rejecting the image of blood staining the rowan's bark, I focus instead on the Paultons pear tree. The dull, dusky shades of this overcast late afternoon have been elevated by one final burst of sunlight, illuminating the thick branches to highlight vibrant amber tones in their leaves. They feel rich and rare, deep golds of yellow and rose, and all at once, a day that had seemed mundane is made precious again. Colour, I realise, taking in the dazzling interplay of copper, terracotta and the shade Gavin taught me to call Naples yellow. The world has colour in it once more. Gavin, too, seems struck by the sudden shift. He reaches out to touch the foliage of a bountiful, leaf-heavy branch before turning back to look up at the house we still officially share.

'Would you like me to leave?' he asks.

Honesty. We ought always to have been honest with one another. 'No,' I say, while at our feet, Mij tumbles and flows from one human who loves him to another. 'Don't go.'

Chapter Twenty-Six

I redecorate my Girton rooms, despite now splitting my time between them and the Square. Viewed through less depressed eyes, I see the need to enliven my staid academic study, and I take small yet significant pleasure in adding a flower vase to my windowsill, along with a painting by Winifred that depicts almost precisely the same scene in oils. 'A glimpse through,' that is what she called the effect of Sandaig, and finally I can glimpse through the clouds of melancholy that have overshadowed me: a glimmer of possibility on the horizon like the snow-capped Cuillins I used to gaze at across the sea. A fresh fluency imbues my Blake lectures and eventually I grow bold enough to resume writing too. My poetry feels fragile at first, delicate and ephemeral, but all the more precious for that. I delight in watching my pen move over the page: crisscrossing good words with better ones, improving each line in turn with a whisper of the linguistic deftness I had feared totally silenced. I might be riding a bicycle, wobbling a little but learning to regain my long-lost balance, or conversing in a rusty first-tongue language I love yet rarely get the chance to speak. Evocative imagery takes root; single phrases blossom into themes. I write in the upstairs Paultons apartment with Gavin and Mij one floor down. *I have learned my lesson*, I inwardly insist; I have suffered Psyche's roaming, raw-soled punishment for failing to stick to my side of our spiritual bargain. I shall not fail it, nor us, again.

Amidst this welcome renaissance of wordpower and wordplay – and I do feel playful, for the first time in many weeks – I resolve not to write of marriage, earthly or otherwise. Certainly no rings. Gavin is neither my husband nor my lover, and perhaps that is not altogether a bad thing, for both titles now seem too ordinary to encapsulate a connection I feel belongs with Blake in his Heaven. Captured, if it can be caught at all, in poetry more readily than prose. Do we always understand each other? No more than any person understands every enigmatic, ultimately unknowable aspect of themselves. As Psyche had to accept of Cupid, he does what he must in the dark. Yet distilling it down to its essence, as all poetry should do, Gavin is a part of me I am glad to no longer be parted from.

'I read the rest of your collection,' he tells me, sitting an otter's length away on the high-backed sofa he brought with him from the studio. Sincerity illuminates his fair features, softening the lines around his eyes until he looks no older than in the first weeks after we met. 'No one could capture Sandaig more vividly than you.'

'You could.' I stroke Mij's plush pale belly while the otter waves from side to side, at play with this week's marble of choice clasped to the odd waterproof fluff of his chest. 'You should.' In our early days, before denial and secrecy submerged us, I always saw it as my role to encourage Gavin's writing. Didn't he once call me a goddess because of it? Today, he says nothing more for the moment, only reaching over with light, thoughtful fingers to pet Mij.

Perhaps I should feel hostile to the thought of Sandaig shore. The house, certainly, takes on a dark complexity in my imagination that never existed before the storm broke between us. With effortful yet necessary deliberateness, I draw my mind away from the bed we once shared, cheeks hot from mortification mixed with other emotions that have no place in my spiritually centred new life. In my perfunctory Girton tub or – what bliss to be back – the bathroom I am accustomed to at Paultons, it embarrasses me to recall the primitive ritual of washing myself in an ice-cold waterfall. And I still feel sick, despite fighting to swallow down the biliousness, whenever I picture Gavin Young standing by the sky-blue cottage door, Mij rippling around his feet.

Yet the thought of the landscape transcends it all. It is stronger. Steadfast. Grounded and resilient. With the perspective of hindsight as well as physical distance, I recall hard-lined black rocks jutting out from the translucent ocean; jagged thorns hooked along the lengths of those delicate red rose stems. Brittle glints of grey bark lurking beneath the rowan's white blossom. Both eternal and eternally changing, all life is there on Sandaig's monumental contrasting coastline, as in Shakespeare's sonnets or Blake's oeuvre. Its sublimity is surely too profound to be affected by anything mere mortals say or do. We inhabit it, yes, but only as a sand grain takes its place upon the strand or a blade of grass occupies the steep, seaward slope of Ben Sgriol. Our lives, the pain and the pleasure, are drops in the ocean. The thought feels like something to hold on to, in the spirit of letting go.

'I had a letter from James yesterday.' From the sofa in his half of the house, Gavin's comment recalls my attention to London. 'You must be very proud of your son.'

'I am.' Busy with his National Service, James never had the chance to hear about our schism, even if I had deemed it appropriate fare for correspondence between a mother and son. Regardless, the boy is too preoccupied these days to write more than once a month, and whenever he does get a letter to me, it gives my heart an anxious pang, seeing his childlike scribble on an envelope stamped with a military base seal. He always asks after Gavin and clearly also sends letters of his own, adding details of his training or the trickier aspects of barrack life that it takes a fellow serviceman to understand.

'I wish I was a parent,' Gavin reflects, his eyes on Mij. 'I should dearly love to be a father.' I, too, train my gaze onto the otter, afraid that to look into Gavin's face would risk spilling the tears that still occasionally surge inside me. 'At least I've got this boy.' He tousles the ruff of strange soft-tipped fur spikes around Mij's neck. 'I love him like a son, you know.'

'I know.' Marble abandoned, Mij rolls onto all fours and clambers up Gavin's torso.

If James was unaware, Anna appears not to care whether I am resident at the college or Paultons. In truth, we do not speak as often as I had hoped when she first applied to be a student. Naturally, she is carving out her own niche at Girton, and my colleagues report that she is successful and well-liked by her classmates. But whatever route she and her new friends take through the Elephant Ears doors, it does not pass my room. Perhaps it is just as well I do not live there permanently anymore. Nonetheless, with two desks in two houses dedicated to the endeavour, my Blake book is gathering pace, and, no doubt bullied by the sheer force of Tambi's enthusiasm, the British Council has approached me to produce another pamphlet for *Writers and their Work*. Samuel Taylor Coleridge is my subject this time, that untameable spirit who roamed the north with Wordsworth at his side until the pressure of its own wild genius caused his mind to implode into madness. Of course, opium did not help matters. However inspirational the cragged fells and daffodil-dappled shorelines of the Lake District are, their picturesque beauty could not keep Coleridge on the path that should have been his poetic destiny. As Gavin and I both know, even the most distant retreat is not necessarily a peaceful place.

Whenever I am back at Paultons, the chill of winter whistling through the tail-end of the autumn air, I find myself drawn into the old pear tree's presence. It is leafless now, the sparsity revealing an intricate network of charcoal nubs and knotted branches that go hidden in verdant spring and summer. Pressing my hand tenderly to its bare, vulnerable bark, I let my thoughts drift to the Sandaig rowan and pray it will absolve me of my sin. I didn't mean it. Not really. Most of my life has involved labouring in vain to have my words resonate within the world, the overriding message relayed back to me again and again that what I say scarcely matters. Surely one sentence, a single line uttered as a desperate heart's cry before being swept away into the storm, is no different from all the rest?

It is at Paultons I next see Tambi, meeting him to toast the start of 1957.

'I'm tired, Kathie,' he moans, his feathered mop of black hair – like mine, now flecked with grey – dusting the tabletop as his head flops into his hands.

'I'm not surprised,' I retort a little unsympathetically. The irresistible enticement of Tambi's two favourite pastimes, drinking and revelry, being made mandatory for one night of the year inevitably proves too much for him, exacerbated if the Hog in the Pound is within stumbling distance. In over ten years of friendship, I have yet to see him make it to midnight fully conscious on New Year's Eve, or what Gavin charmingly calls Hogmanay. 'Drink your tea.' I push the sweetened cup I have prepared towards his tousled locks. At Tambi's insistence, there is also a small glass of whisky – 'hair of the otter', as Gavin jokes – and I take the opportunity of his eyes being elsewhere to water it down. 'You need a good sleep, Tambi.'

'No ...' Tambi's moan turns to a groan as he raises his bloodshot eyes. 'It's not only that. I'm tired of London.' He gives a gaping yawn for emphasis. 'I'm exhausted with it. So unimaginative. So fearful.' Tambi may be many things, but afraid is never one of them. To him, there could be no greater failing than cowardice, in either an individual or a populace. 'The English wrap their feelings up in cellophane. They're all scared, Kathleen, terrified of work that doesn't fit in their ...' Brain fog of alcoholic fumes too thick to continue, Tambi resorts to miming the shape of a small box with the unsteady flats of his hands.

'Maybe it's just me.' The reviews of my collection, or rather the lack thereof, cannot have helped Tambi's despondent mood. Gratifyingly, those published were complimentary.

228

'A meditative, intimate, feminine poet with a real gift,' wrote Cyril Connolly. The feminine comment intrigued me, and I must say, I don't dislike it.

'Her poetry is pure as from a well-spring, and has a natural beauty undecorated and undefaced by influence.' That was dear, ever-generous Edwin, no doubt with Willa whispering in his ear. And yet I sense my work is falling far outside the rigid boundaries of stark, straight-lined modernist fashions. Most of my contemporaries reject myths and imagination in favour of nihilistic 'realism', more absorbed by the minutiae of their own punctuation than the noble poetic heritage left to us by Blake, Yeats and the rest. I cannot, I will not follow suit, but the punishment for creative transgression is served cold, not hot, by the critics. 'There is only one thing worse than being talked about,' as Oscar Wilde put perfectly, 'and that is not being talked about.' A man who would have understood Gavin's difficulties far better than I have been able to.

'I want to go somewhere they're not afraid of poetry that means something.' Tambi smacks his palm on the table to make his point, setting both beverages aquiver. 'Somewhere open, not smoky and staid and scared like London. I am going ...' a dramatic pause, allowing another gulp of whisky ... 'to America.' The announcement hovers in the air until, with a soft thud, Tambi passes out completely. Lifting those shambolically scattered locks to check the cause is nothing more sinister than sleep, of which his snores reassure me, I reach over my friend's slumped, slumbering form to pick up the untouched cup of cooling tea. *He'll forget*, I tell myself as I take a sip. That is if being too drunk to remember in the first place can be called forgetting. Either way, I need not worry now about what I would do without him.

A month or so ago and I would have been tempted to go with Tambi, should his fantasy voyage become a reality. But if Girton is not my spiritual home, it is my professional one, and it has been a touching surprise to realise I am getting to know and love the girls. When I watch them drift into my lecture room, giggling as they glide with the unconscious elegance of young swans who still believe themselves to be cygnets, I am struck by the responsibility of helping to guide their first flights into the world. Their peaches and cream complexions glow, eyes ever-bright with curiosity – certainly, I have never felt more matronly or middle-aged myself – but the beauty of Girton's girls goes further than skin deep.

'Why?' They question incessantly, as indeed I encourage them to do.

'Why did Blake depict Thel with anemones and not another flower?' A detail spotted by young Sally, to whom my answer is that I believe the womb-like petals represent the world of 'generation' Thel did not wish to become part of.

'What did Mary Wollstonecraft mean when she wrote about free love?' A more robust query from one of Sally's classmates, which made for a lively lecture hour. As the term goes on, I realise that I am tasked with the challenge, unsought yet accepted, of not just telling but showing these young women that the world is theirs for the taking. They need not heed the manipulative advice of housekeeping journals; they should not be concerned by those who claim to know a woman's place. They can listen instead to Coleridge. Yeats. Blake. They can grasp the golden string, if they refuse to take no for an answer.

*

'Where would I be without you?'

'Iraq, perhaps. Or back on a shark-fishing boat.' Easter approaches, my first scholarly holiday, and a trip to Sandaig beckons again, accompanied by one of the males in my life.

'Seriously, Kathleen,' Gavin insists, leaning forward within the taxi transporting Mij and me to Euston, 'this is good of you. Thanks for taking him off my hands while I write.'

What are friends for? Reluctant to articulate the right reply in time, I focus on Mij. Intrigued as ever by travel, the otter is occupying himself on the taxi seat between us, rolling Gavin's fountain pen to and fro across his chest as if investing it with the heartfelt essence soon to be expressed in his master's new book. Gavin follows my gaze and we stare down at him together, amused by his amusement. Around us, central London sinks into evening shadows only to be almost immediately reborn: a fluorescent phoenix rising from the ashes as the vibrant theatre fronts and cinemas of city nightlife come alive to illuminate the gloom.

'Just look at the lights reflected in his coat.' Gavin gestures to the lustrous sheen of Mij's velvet fur. The otter's pelt gleams like poured chocolate whenever he moves, pooling at his centre before he rises up to bubble over us both. Gleeful, he proffers his fountain pen trophy to one human after the other. The dancing, dazzling lights that stream through the taxi window are making his coat ripple with glitter; we pull up at traffic lights and watch Mij's silhouette flow through red and amber into

230

green. For one shimmering, miraculous moment, I might be in 1949, not 1957, with autumn leaves around my feet and a life no more complicated than that of an ordinary woman falling in love with an extraordinary man.

'*Otter Nonsense,*' Gavin teases the animal – I hope – as Mij squirms. While his serious Iraqi travel text remains in the works, it is the life story of our unique companion that enlivens his imagination now. Gavin means to write a comic tribute to this mischievous creature: the perfect testament to Mij's cheeky character and the myriad of ways in which he has enriched our lives. Well, Gavin's life. I have asked him not to include me.

He lives for Mij, I have realised since our reunion, with what should not have come as a surprise. No children. No wife. A family who would never accept him if they knew who he truly is. What was it Gavin told me through tears on that summer's day with the calves? 'I love him so much because we're the same.' He trusts Mij, treasures him, and has reconstructed his life to revolve in a ring around this remarkable little being. This unique creature has become Gavin's whole world. Entrusted again into my care.

He kisses us both before we go. Once each on either cheek, Mij burbling in reply. From our carriage window, I raise the otter's paw as our self-styled tradition dictates and we wave cheerfully through the glass. Gavin waves back at us from the platform. Then he is gone.

Chapter Twenty-Seven

This cottage used to remind me of pregnancy. Now, it feels more like my body post-childbirth. Unchanged to others; irrevocably altered to me. I twist the key in Sandaig's stiff lock, the loop of Mij's harness leash swirling around my wrist as he wriggles with excitement. The war-torn roses at the door have resurrected as three wary, tight-wound buds, the petals I crushed last summer long since blown away. Is it my imagination or do the new blooms recoil as I pass? Beside their stems, fine flakes of paintwork are chipping off around a mildewed windowpane that has gone too long without warmth. Indoors, the fireplace grate also lies lifeless, weighed down by two winters' worth of charred driftwood remains. Lacking the bright, flickering flames to animate it, even the chimneypiece inscription looks dull and dirty.

Pulled further into the living room by Mij, I catch sight of myself in an old mirror Gavin found while beachcombing that is heavily scratched but miraculously not broken. *A good omen*, I thought at the time. Something in its image drags me back, quite unwillingly, to seeing my reflection for the first time after Anna's delivery. A naive new mother, I recall struggling to stand as I negotiated the throbbing, intimate pulp pressed between my trembling legs. The swell of a pregnancy just over still haunted my pale, strangely pliable midriff; nipples cracked, my breasts throbbed angrily at me while I studied them, as if even this snatched moment of solitude was a betrayal of the infant asleep in her cradle a few feet away. My old self had been sacrificed and slaughtered, blood spilt on another's altar when my gory innards tumbled out along with the baby to whom, I was told, the rest of my life must be devoted. But I would heal, the midwife had reassured Charles with knowing confidence. I was still Kathleen. Still the same woman. More battered and bruised than before, naturally. But the battle itself? Once the scars had knitted, only I would remember the difference.

Gavin's house feels that way now. The site of a bloody conflict both sides have chosen to consign to history, our battlefield left fallow until

232

little remains but wildflowers and the memories of those who fought for their lives in it. Breathing deep in an unsuccessful effort to steady myself, I take a hesitant step towards the shell collection still on the windowsill. I lift the cowrie that Gavin gave me and pocket it for safekeeping. 'The world that you inhabit has not yet been created.' These glittering examples of ocean floor stardust once inhabited a purer, more perfect world than our own, a universe in which only the essence of our souls was in existence. And soul to soul is how I must love Gavin. Rising above what went before. The alternative, if I can call it that, is not having him in my life at all. Turning away, I see that the wildflowers I used to decorate the lamp have decayed into shrivelled paper-thin slivers as translucent as the glass behind them. I peel them from it, petalled wisps disintegrating in my hands. Crumpled like poem drafts no longer needed, I toss them into the cold grate.

Mij, characteristically, is unaffected by my reservations. He quickly sets out reacclimatising himself to what is, depending on how one chooses to divide Paultons Square, his second or third home. His paws press against the stone chimneypiece, sniffing inquisitively as if re-reading its words for himself. '*It is no will o' the wisp that I have followed here.*'

'I suppose I've followed you here this time.' Mij chirrups what I take to be his approval. I set our bags down, keen to settle my raw nerves with a warming cup of fireside tea, but the otter remains restless and seems intent on returning outside. I indulge him as always, pulling my wellingtons back on after extracting the excited animal tail-first from one boot, and rebutton my coat to brave the sea air once again. 'You lead, I'll follow, Mij.'

The otter's happiness at being in the Highlands channels through every cell of his supple long body, and while he and I walk along the coastline – in truth, I walk while Mij dives, spins and swims – I look out to the distant Cuillins of Skye, capped with a delicate dusting of white that blends into the clouds and cold sunlight. Glinting trails of snowfall have sunken into the carved-out grooves of the mountainsides, their motionless ivory rivers whiter still when framed by rugged grey. It may be Eastertime, but spring has not yet spread this far north, and Sandaig remains ringed with icy water and snow-brushed hills even as the pluckier primroses dare to peek out from the frost-hardened bogland. The chill brings stillness, a cool serenity muffling the shoreline and the ticking clock hands of life with it, until the precise time, and even year, become indeterminate. Mij could be a wild creature born and bred here rather than three thousand miles distant. I might be my old self the first time I set foot in Sandaig, or even the ephemeral visionary version of me who roamed and relished this land long before I had seen it for real. Gavin's words were all that I required for it to come alive in my imagination. His new book will do the same for countless others, I am sure.

Mij's magnetic enthusiasm for exploration draws us ever onwards, enringing the coast until eventually we return to the rowan tree. Its roots protrude through the winter soil; its exposed branches are thin, curved and contorted almost indecently without enough foliage to protect its modesty. I feel awkward to face the tree, as shamefaced and inarticulate as I was when first reunited with Gavin beside the Paultons pear. And the rowan looks like it too has been through the wars. Like it has suffered. Tucked away at the edge of sea level with only the softest inkling of spring in the air, the tree's ivory blossom is still in bud, tiny, closed cups of lace that match the snow laying low over Skye. Its cool-hued bark has been torn into strips by the winter winds, broken into silver pieces.

'Forgive me.' I reach out to trace that trunk, trying to communicate regret from heart to fingertips. 'Please, forgive me.' A fresh breeze courses in across the coast, ruffling my hair and rippling my coat hem. The rowan remains unmoved.

'Ha.' A hearty splash and squeal of joy remind me that Mij has a low tolerance for human reflection, remorseful or otherwise. Gladly turning away from the tree, I hurry to where he is wrestling playfully with the pull of the tide, his slick brown body cutting through the white cuffed waves with perfect timing, delving into their depths before they break into foam fragments over the kelp-slicked stretch of sand. On land, I accompany his course as best I can, scrabbling clumsily in his wake like a nanny or butler in thrall to a changeable, charismatic young master. I imagine Gavin was just so at Monreith. Not wearing his leash, I nonetheless follow Mij's lead, and as he compels me to charge up to the waterfall, the otter's joy at being back in the land he loves is contagious. More sheltered than most spots along this shore, the fall is already decorated with the quiet insignia of spring. Fern fronds are beginning to curl around its rock-lined rims, and if there are no butterflies or dragonflies yet, the verdant emerald shades suggest that their emergence is not far away. Water streams over the fall beds, its bubbles and burbles mixing with Mij's bright chirrups as in one boneless, mercurial movement, he flows straight into the swell of the current. Listening silently, their liquid music starts to soothe my own spirit. I can feel hints of my old happiness, if I am careful about where I look.

I write to Gavin in the evening, seated comfortably in front of his fireplace. Mij coils up in my lap, ostensibly content, although I sense from his wriggles that it would take only the smallest encouragement for him to spring into action yet again. In his own idiosyncratic way, I believe the otter has matured since last year: an adult, more than a yearling or juvenile, and wilder than before if such a thing is possible. His formerly lithe muscles are suddenly strong; his torso is more solid, if equally streamlined. Any quaint notions of him being a domestic pet are swept away as easily as the sand outside bearing his distinctive five-clawed imprints.

This room feels warmer than when we arrived in every sense. Enlivened by firelight, the wood panelling is cosy rather than imposing; above the flames, the chimneypiece's Latin lettering is once more illuminated in gold. The dry heat from disintegrating driftwood forms a comforting cloud, engulfing me in its embrace just as Gavin's Soay jumper used to do. I still have the garment but choose not to wear it anymore. The heat is too much for Mij, though. Unsurprisingly, I feel him start to fidget. Pen poised mid-word, my page begins to shake as the otter decides to dig for victory, burrowing into the tiny space between my crossed calves in an apparent effort to tunnel himself outside or perhaps to Australia, given the vigour with which he applies himself. Fearing damage done to his delicate pads, I scoop him up around his long middle until he is raised off Sandaig's flagstone floor, holding the indignantly airborne otter in one hand while I complete my written thought with the other.

'Hmm.' Mij makes his frustration known by emitting a hum, an expression of annoyance that seems to mimic either a broken generator or Gavin's off-key singing. His wordless retort strikes a note of adolescent resentment that, in either animal or human form, necessitates no translation.

'I'll tell your father,' I half-threaten, half-tease. 'Just wait until Major Maxwell hears about this.'

'HA.'

Affecting my own sigh of resignation, I rise to reach inside Mij's basket. At once, his black eyes grow wide and glossy. Terrapin shell time. Gavin brought this unremarkable artefact back with him from Iraq and, realising by chance how much it piques Mij's interest, he has devised a new amusement to rival 'the tickling trick'. I knot the shell inside a towel, Mij watching intently like the sole, astonished audience member of a magic show. Pulling to check the ties are as taut as I can make them, with exaggerated slowness I set it down upon the floor. At once, Mij pounces, worrying the fabric with all his might to liberate the shell from its terrycloth prison. With his extensive experience at sea, Gavin knows of knots complex enough to keep the otter occupied for up to ten minutes. Alone, I suspect I have two or three at the most. In that knowledge, I exploit Mij's distraction to hurriedly conclude my letter, doing my best to ignore the rhythmic, towel-muffled clack of terrapin shell smacking against flagstone.

'About his harness ...' Seeing afresh how Mij's adventurous spirit knows no bounds, I write to tell Gavin I am worried. Snagging branches. Tangled water weeds. Is having him wear it up here really worth the risk? What would happen if it caught somewhere on one of Mij's increasingly far-flung solo adventures, dragging him into danger or, Heaven forbid, trapping him beneath the tide for longer than even he can hold his breath. Transported back once again to the difficult days of early motherhood, I feel my anxiety mounting; the futile instinct to eliminate every threat that was so hard to tolerate I came to prefer feeling nothing at all. But this is one problem we can mitigate. One danger I can protect Mij from. To keep him safe, we must set him free, isn't that the ironic crux of the matter? Not unlike what my heart has had to do in order to keep Gavin in my life.

'Ha HA!' Mij exhales in righteous triumph as the terrapin shell clatters from its towelling bind. Two and a half minutes. A new personal best. Cheered by the distraction of his achievement, I reach over to reclaim the shell and towel, preparing them for round two of his favourite game. And yet another capricious change of mood has taken over Mij. Instead of waiting for further play, he dives into my arms. I hold the otter to me, his dark brown velvet brushing my pale skin as he pours himself in and out of my grasp. Beside the fire, Mij's unencumbered form flows like liquid, his fur transfigured into an elegant reflection of the flames as they spark, flicker and fade.

Chapter Twenty-Eight

'Wait!' Mij and I rose early today, for different reasons neither of us keen to linger long inside the house, and half-stupefied with tiredness, I have opened the door before pulling on my second wellington. The otter shoots from Sandaig straight into the sea and I am forced to hop sock-shod across the shingles. 'Wait, Mij, wait!'

What precisely I mean to tell him if he does halt, I cannot say. Don't be long? Don't go too far? Slip your harness if you can? Heeding my increased urgency, Mij momentarily turns to bob in time with the swaying waves. His head protrudes through the foam as he gives one of the mischievous grins that only Gavin and I know an otter is capable of. Then he is gone, carried off in blissful communion with the wild tide as it sweeps and swirls around the small, scattered islands of Sandaig bay. His vague direction is towards Tormor and I snatch up my letter to Gavin before leaving the cottage in the hope that the MacLeods may be willing to post it today. Hurrying uphill, I follow in Mij's wake, just like the water that streams in frothy ribbons behind his tail.

'Hello, you two.' Mary looks unchanged since last summer, her curls swept up into a scarf and a housework pinny layered over her jumper. Still in the doorway, I fight the instinct to take off my coat uninvited, purely to prove, as if she asked, that I am not wearing Gavin's sweater. Mij, meanwhile, flows merrily around Mary's ankles, pressing his leathery webbed paws to her calves as if to plead with her to pick him up. When she obliges, the sea-sleeked otter gives a squeak of delight. Exploiting his new elevation to human height, Mij peers past the rogue ringlets tumbling from Mary's headscarf, staring into the Tormor croft as if in search of something, or someone, in particular.

'The boys aren't here,' Mary informs him. 'I'm sorry, son.' Never one to let disappointment win, Mij flips over in Mary's arms until he can sink headfirst into her enticingly large apron pocket, the tip of his tail waving wildly in the air. 'He's still a character,' Mary laughs, dodging from side-to-side as the furry brown point tickles her chin.

'I wonder if you might post this for me? If it isn't too much trouble.'

'No trouble at all, Kathleen.' With Mary's vivid green eyes on me, I search for new signs of old pity.

'How ...'

'... are you?' Resisting the silence, we ask the same question simultaneously. Both laugh. Both fall quiet.

'Tell the boys I say hello,' I add eventually. 'I mean, we say hello.'

'I will,' Mary replies. 'And tell Gavin ...' the thought fades unfinished, her gaze sinking to the name on my envelope. I am glad when Mij, diving from Mary's arms back to the floor, charges off in fresh pursuit of the rippling burn. Apologising as I go, I leave her house to follow where he leads.

The morning's routine is one that we come to repeat throughout the week. Mij streams ahead of me, his elongated spine flowing fast with the waves, burn or waterfall, the liquid wanderlust of an animal in his prime leaving me scrabbling, slipping and more often than not tripping far behind. Given time, some mystical magnetic pull invariably draws him, and therefore me, to the fall's gushing summit. I sit on the ledge, ignoring the chill rising up from the moss, while Mij plays in the twisting rapids for hours at a time. Gavin has given me permission to leave the otter, so long as Mij knows the land and we are not approaching sunset. Yet I find it impossible to walk away from such a small, solitary creature, even one who becomes a literal force of nature when set loose amongst these cascading spirals of water. The anxiety I feel for his welfare is almost unbearable, but perhaps it could never be otherwise. I am the closest thing to a mother Mij has.

Pebbles, pinecones, a single stick plucked from the mud: the most mundane objects can take the otter's fancy, his attention flitting from one tiny natural treasure to another during our lengthy rambles together. On one such occasion, rolling waves of panic break over me when I cannot see him anywhere. I push past the tall fern fronds that line the waterfall's edge, stumbling through the slender alder trees and over their roots lying knotted underfoot. Finally, I spot Mij drifting downstream, dozing in carefree contentment with a blackened clutch of last year's rowan berries pressed to his chest.

It is the day before Good Friday when the twins bring me Gavin's reply. For once, Mij has chosen to play within sight of Sandaig, so I am seated with my notebook on one of the smoother rocks near the house as the two boys approach. I am being honoured by a double act to deliver a single envelope. Although, tossed from one boy to the other, their rowdy back-and-forth game leaves me doubtful that the letter will reach me in one piece.

'Hello, Willie. Hello, Jim.' After all this time, I am still unsure who's who.

'Hello, Miss Raine,' the twins reply in unison. 'We've a letter fae ye.' A dispute occurs, centred on who will be the one to hand me the envelope. Not torn, I am pleasantly surprised to see, if bearing a number of incriminating peaty thumbprints. For several seconds, each young man holds fast to his corner, until Twin One wins out and pointedly passes me my correspondence. To my shock, he then begins to blush. His brother, as taken aback as I am, promptly flushes puce in solidarity.

'Thank you.' The sudden vicarious embarrassment is such that it is all I can do to stop heat sweeping over my own cheeks. Have the nine months since my last visit turned the impish children of whom I have grown so fond into a pair of bashful young bachelors? Twin Two, I see, is now the taller by an inch, and when they shrug, the height difference sets their physical rhythms ever-so-slightly out of sync. Still ruddy-cheeked, their elbows bump awkwardly, a disjointed bony wave flowing from one boy to the other. 'Mij is up there,' I tell them, using the letter to point along the bay.

'I telt ye he'd be back,' Twin One gleefully reminds his brother. Smiles spring back onto the boys' faces, wiping away the raw unease of early adolescence, at least for now. I watch them rush along the coast, sand churned into spray as they gallop towards their four-legged friend. They seem to race each other for the final straight, auburn hair bouncing as a few friendly shoves are thrown out on either side. Some things never change.

I turn to Gavin's letter.

'The design of Mij's harness has occupied my imagination for some months,' he begins, abrupt enough for my eyes to flick up, checking this letter is indeed meant for me and not some animal tack manufacturer or the Zoological Society itself. 'It does not impede his movement nor irritate him unduly and has the additional plus of proclaiming his domesticity to would-be human aggressors.' Gavin continues in the same vein for much of the page, his tone as starkly functional as it is unexpectedly defensive. Certainly, he offers none of the comfort that I realise now

239

I had been hoping for. No 'I understand, Kathleen.' Not even a 'thank you, Kathleen.' Locked at cross purposes, we seem condemned to cross words; I might be an impudent harpoon designer who has objected to Gavin's draughtsmanship or a lackadaisical printing house employee to whom Peter must speak sternly. Sinking in dejection back down onto my rock overlooking the ocean, Gavin's words strike me more like a lawyer's reprimand than a letter sent friend-to-friend. Having survived two divorces, I know their latent, between-the-lines hostility better than I would wish.

'During my last visit to Sandaig,' he continues, 'Mij went missing for several hours and returned home with his old harness burst.' *You see.* I shake the letter in frustration as I want to shake the man who wrote it. *Don't you realise the danger he's in?* And why on earth didn't Gavin tell me that had happened? Bad temper building, I read on. 'It was then that I ordered this particular one to be made, after consulting with experts on animals in captivity both at home and abroad. The perfected version, I would venture to say, of all my earlier efforts.' That patronising pomposity alone is enough to send anger surging through me. Gavin chooses the most infuriating times to play the part of a conventional male. And anyway, Mij is not in captivity. Isn't that the point? I cast my eyes over this coastline of limitless natural splendour, drifting up to where, Mary's boys still in his thrall, Mij plays merrily amidst the lashing waves. His freedom is what makes it worth it, all the early rises and aching muscles that even an open fire's fierce heat cannot fully ease. My composition notebook holds twice as many first as last lines these days, yet I am prepared to temporarily sacrifice my soul's destiny to bear witness to this incredible creature fulfilling his. More than our network of flourishing falls or the unforgettable, full-spectrum sunsets, it is Mij's untamed spirit that embodies the true beauty of this place. Surely to keep an otter here and not let it roam free would be worse than not having one at all?

'You must understand, Kathleen,' Gavin implores, no, instructs me from London. 'It is I who knows Mij best. I'll be with you both in a few days. Love, G.'

'You are not my husband.' I address the letter aloud, thin sheet squeezed so tight between my knuckles that they blanche as my fingers turn numb. 'You are not my husband, Gavin Maxwell.' A grey-waistcoated hooded crow, pecking lazily at pebbles on the other side of the shore, glances up when I raise my voice. I turn away from it – him, I feel sure – to face

240

Sandaig's secretive sash windows, refusing to let my gaze dwell on the silver-white rowan's reflection.

Gavin made it abundantly clear last year that he does not want me as his wife. And I accepted it. Didn't I? I accept the way Gavin is, irrespective of what it has cost me, and the faint glint of a silver lining on that dark cloud is my single woman's prerogative to make decisions as I see fit. If Gavin declines to be my husband in the eyes of the world, he has no right to play the imposing, imperious part of a spouse in private. Poetesses, like otters, do not respond well to restraint.

The tide is incoming, frothed waves coasting within feet of the cottage door. I step back to kick childishly at the speckled sand and water pours into my wellingtons, dousing my toes in ice-cold discomfort. Gavin's coolly impersonal tone likewise resurges, replaying in my head like one of his flat, repetitive tunes. Bruised ego aside, why address me like a stranger he wants to impress? Why does Gavin write as if the world were looking over our shoulders, as if I might one day expose his mistakes for others to judge? *I am not one of them,* I ache to say as the chill creeps up my calves. *I am not a person you need fear, not another one of that faceless, frightening crowd whose attentions you resent almost as much as you covet. I'm not a stranger, I'm not a threat. I'm your ... I'm your Kathleen.*

And Mij is mine too. As much as he has ever been Gavin's. He knows our otter best, does he? The crushed letter scrunches further inside my fist. Who wakes with Mij and sleeps with him? Who stirs the sickly, claggy concoction that is his unpolished rice and raw egg breakfast before smoothing fresh sand over his spraint? Who amuses him for long hours at a stretch before rocking him to sleep like a babe in front of the fire, leaving Gavin free to devote his days to the writing that was my great purpose first?

Feeling more alone than before I wrote and judging it wise to leave a few days' grace – really, a few days to quell my temper – before I send Gavin my reply, I am forced to improvise my own strategy for coping with Mij's relentless energy. Counter-intuitively, I resolve to walk him further: my theory being that yet more vigorous exercise may lessen his impulse to stray. It is an approach I can remember deploying, as it were, against my own children after we evacuated to the Lake District. Entirely alone, until I met Helen, with two youngsters of whom the older was not yet six, the long days of watching and waiting yawned before us in the beginning.

241

Not infrequently, they ended with all three of us in tears. Anna and James were overwhelmed by their father's absence and underwhelmed with me in comparison. Having read to them until I was hoarse and crawled over the floor in play until my stockings were torn and my knees bleeding, I verged close to despair each time I looked at the clock – barely noon – and realised the children still needed amusement. With no new toys, even if I could have afforded them, the Lakes offered only one alternative. But what an exquisite one it was.

'Rise and shine!' I would tickle Anna and James under their little chins, cajoling them out of bed with a singsong voice that sounded much brighter than I felt so early in the morning. Time would be spent gently slotting their tiny limbs into jumper sleeves and trouser legs until, at long last, we were ready to walk. Small fingers linked with my own, our trio waved good morning to the placid, slate grey Herdwick sheep, continuing to stride over Place Fell until we reached a plateau just in time to see the sunrise. Sitting together at our child-sized summit, I would unpack the squashed jam sandwiches that I presumptuously called our picnic while we three watched the sun sweep over Ullswater, awakening the lake with broad brushstrokes of daffodil-yellow light. All I could hear was birdsong, accompanied by the soft murmur of the children's chewing, and at that high, private altitude, it finally felt like I could breathe. I wonder if Anna remembers those days? I must ask her at Girton. But first …

'Off we go, Mijbil.' I rouse the shocked otter the following morning in the manner of a much-detested school games mistress. Laid bare where I have thrown back the bedclothes, he blinks at me in momentary astonishment. Yet by the time we are outside, fresh air has flushed through Mij's system to revitalise him thoroughly and make my plan backfire badly. Marooned in unfit midlife my body may be, my mind is nonetheless determined not to give in: I stomp and slosh across the wide-spanning peat bog, ignoring the growing suspicion that I am exhausting myself more than Mij. I sense that we are arriving at a more arable stretch of land when my wellingtons start sinking less frequently into the ground, while Mij, having happily splashed through terrain that waters down all distinctions between ocean and dry land, is reluctantly forced to adapt his gait from a rippling swim to an odd rocking canter. We press on, traipsing over the remnants of old coastal farmland that has surrendered itself back into the wild. We are rounding the coast, reaching a southernly point just out of sight of Sandaig, when I spot a cottage. A sole room, ramshackle

242

cottage with rain-streaked walls and an uneven, weed-covered roof. Raef's cottage. At least, the cottage Raef claimed to stay in. Claimed to sleep in.

Bile burns in my throat before I can resist it. Knees sinking, I buckle to the grass, palms pressed to the dirt as my body is brought low by the visceral memory I try every day to make my mind forget. My stomach seizes, gut spasming around its early morning emptiness; my pulse thunders in my ears and turns to a fierce, throbbing beat behind my eyes. With a sweet squeak of alarm, Mij rushes across the overgrown field, nuzzling my face in concern while his soft whiskers tickle my cheeks. *Bless his heart*, I think hazily, digging my nails into the soil and steeling my core against the choking urge to dry heave. Bless that precious, playful heart of an otter in which Gavin and I met.

'We'll go north tomorrow,' I tell the animal as soon as I can speak again. My voice is hoarse, crackling from acid, yet surprisingly firm and forceful. Whether Mij understands English or not, my tone is decisive enough to make him listen.

Our return to Sandaig therefore comes much quicker than I had planned. The exertion has made no discernible difference to Mij's wild streak: indeed, the only real change to be observed is that I am wearier than I was before. In heart even more than in body. When Mij does briefly settle for a doze on the fish crate sofa, I dutifully pick up my poetry notebook yet struggle to keep hold of the elusive, quicksilver glint of inspiration that once rippled through my work here. It darts overleaf and out of sight, leaving me and my pen to wade through clotted pools of wasted ink.

Within hours, the rested otter is agitating for me to take him out yet again. Head pounding from the strain of staring at the same page for too long, I am already on a short fuse when I call him over to fasten his harness. My fingers are tired, thick and ineffectual, and the procedure is hardly helped by Mij's energetic resistance. From having been happy in my arms, he writhes in protest when I produce the leather straps, swelling up and spilling out of his restraints like a liquid Houdini. Attempting to secure the fastenings for a third time, I succeed only in pinching my skin.

'Cursed thing.' My anger is not at Mij, of course, but expressed near enough for him to be unsettled by it. I reach out, trying to communicate through touch that if I am cross, it is not with him. In truth, the root cause of today's disturbance is something I can barely bring myself to admit, even if Mij could comprehend the explanation. His harness is still in my hands as I stretch, and Mij remains resolute on avoidance. Each time I reach, he dodges me with swift, sinewy ease, that fluid form eluding my every effort and leaving me sprawled across Sandaig's floor.

'Come now, Mij,' I plead, breathing deep to draw on my last reserves of patience. 'Don't be difficult.' The otter starts humming at me: a dull, somewhat sinister warning drone that transports my mind back to air raid days. 'Mij.' I caution him as firmly as I can, sidestepping the hint of unsteadiness that has crept into my voice. I thought I knew all his sounds by now. 'That's enough.' The hum becomes louder. Tenser by the minute, I dig my fingernails into the leather straps still clenched within my fist. In this moment, I might be any other mother in the world, battening down the hatches for a battle of wills as a perfect storm of physical exhaustion and emotional weariness sweeps over us both. Perhaps it would be easier if my actions and emotions were not misaligned; if I was not cajoling Mij into doing something that in my heart I would rather he did not have to do. 'Gavin says it's for your own good.' Harness in one hand, I reach for Mij's paw with the other, meaning to guide it through the strap opening as I used to dress Anna and James. But Mij bucks and rears against me, round head rolling back and long spine concertinaing in utter determination to break free. Struggling and slipping on the flagstones, I might as well be trying to trap a silk scarf in a snare for all the undignified impossibility of keeping hold of this mercurial creature.

'Hold still, Mij. Let me look after you.' Tears blur my vision, having inadvertently blurted out the words I would say to Gavin if I dared. *Let me look after you. Hold still and let me love you.*

In a coincidence born from the chaos, the harness straps meet around Mij's middle. For one beat, I breathe a sigh of relief. In the next, Mij screams as if scalded and swings round at me, jagged teeth bared. I spring back, wrenching my hands away as together we tumble onto the stone floor. Mij darts for one corner of the room and I retreat to another; pushing back, my spine meets with a hard sofa leg and I lean against it to catch my breath. The atmosphere feels thick from the near miss, our little room smouldering as if overcome with cordite after a shot. The small space echoes with the gnash of Mij's jaws.

I raise my right hand shakily in front of my face, while from the other side of the living room, Mij watches with wide, wary eyes. The tears that had threatened now fall in earnest over my cheeks. I blink a few times, dazed and dizzy, before studying my skin. On the back of my hand, a red welt is rising: an angry ridge bearing the ragged razor imprint of where Mij's teeth must have grazed it. Not a near miss after all. A raw scrape edged with white flakes, it might be the map of a miniature mountain range drawn in relief inside one of Gavin's books; a fault line of cragged peaks crafted from flesh. It swells as I stare, one staccato line starting to dominate, tooth-shaped snags running along its edge just like the underside of my cowrie shell. On impulse, I squeeze the highest point with the thumb and forefinger of my opposite hand. A single globe of blood springs from the summit, gleaming against my pale skin. One perfectly round droplet of rowan-berry red. I brush it flat with my fingertips, leaving a crimson smear.

Startled, I sense that Mij has returned to my side, nuzzling me with his muzzle and whimpering pitifully in what can only be instant remorse. How well I know that feeling. His blackberry nose twitches when he notices the blood streak, and he begins rubbing his plush little cheek against my skin, whiskers dusting the wound so delicately that I have no need nor desire to pull away.

'It's alright,' I whisper while he mews mournfully. I dip my head until our dark brown crowns are touching. 'It'll be alright.' What else does anyone ever want to hear from their mother? 'We've all done things we regret,' I tell Mij truthfully. Our eyes meet in what feels like shared, silent understanding. The wretched harness is still trailing him, looped around his back paw and dragging wherever he moves. Gently, so gently, I help him step from it. Then I bury it deep inside a lobster creel, bundled out of sight beneath the fireplace lettering.

Chapter Twenty-Nine

The next morning, we walk to forget. The weather is fine, still crisp yet warmed through with a subtle hint of spring light, and the coming season seems to hide on the other side of the horizon, readying itself to reappear like the sun finally drifting out from behind thick, winterish clouds. Determined to embrace the optimism in the air, I abandon my wellingtons on the strand before we walk north, paddling barefoot in the shallowest waves while Mij's unadorned form flows through the glittering ripples. The rich chocolate of his fur looks glossed and sleek from the water he adores, and I feel awestruck as ever to witness him at one with the ocean. Before leaving the house's vicinity, he charges one last time towards the burn, plunging into the sway of its current with audible bubbles of joy. I stand to watch the otter swim an elegant arc around Sandaig, pouring himself into the ring of bright water that binds us both to Gavin's home.

The sun is high, spring winds dancing over the sea, and as Mij immerses himself he is almost spotlit, glistening from the caresses of pale gold ocean crests as they stream and pour over his coat. Amidst the shells and sea-garden anemones below the surface, a cluster of yellow flowers floats past us: rogue calf field buttercups, perhaps, or even narcissi risen against the odds from an overboarded bag of seeds. I reach for them, sleeves growing sodden from the effort, but the winds pick up, current springing to life like a ceilidh band striking up-tempo, and the little blooms drift away. Squinting against the brightness, I see Mij's tiny face glow with elemental delight as he bobs cheekily up and down with the waves, lit up by that mischievous grin Gavin and I love. With a flick of his tail, he dips. Dives. Disappears.

'Mij.' Laughing, I call his name, addressing the direction of the ripples he has left. 'Mij.' A strong gust sweeps the shore, ruffling my headscarf and carrying off the tail end of my laughter.

'Mij.' I try my telling-off tone this time, or at least a mimicry of it. A mother's voice, one might say, although I do my best to retain a playful tinge. 'Mij.' The fun quickly wears thin. I check my watch, repaired

246

since its last dip, and try to calculate how long the average otter can stay underwater. Old waves are washed away by the new.

'Mij.' I sound scolding now, impatience taking root as my worry grows. I am staring at the correct spot, eyes affixed to where Mij last emerged. Why do I have the feeling that he is nowhere near anymore? 'Mij!' I half-scream it, a grating gull's cry that scratches my throat. Stepping forward unthinkingly, I find myself ankle deep.

'Mij. Mij!' Pushing past the hoarseness, I shout his name again and again, scanning the coastline and begging its blank expanse to part and reveal his watery hiding place. Always a strange word, Mij's name loses all meaning in repetition, and yet suddenly it is all that means anything to me. A fierce blast of sea air tears across this fine strip of sand, ripping the scarf from my hair and tossing it onto the water. I am too focused on the horizon to care.

'Mij. Mij. Mij!' Splashing and struggling, I run into the waves, water encircling my waist as my coat and skirt spread out in unwieldy jellyfish billows. 'Mij!' The fearsome swells come close to rocking me off my feet; my arms paddle, flailing ineffectually against the tide as I wobble on uneven layers of submerged sand. Desperate, I keep calling, shrill urgency taking hold of my voice as gathering winds threaten to drown me out. 'Mij, Mij, Mij!'

Mij is missing.

I rush back for my boots, cursing my foolishness at having discarded them in the first place. Propelled by the shaky, uncertain logic of rapidly rising panic, I decide to charge first in the direction of the waterfall, hoping against hope that its whirlpool magic has enchanted Mij once more and I will arrive to find him safe on our ledge, chittering contentedly after having beaten me to our sanctuary. Running at the most furious pelt I can muster, I follow the burn's twisting route, pushing past the flourishing fern fronds that have seemingly sprung up tall overnight. Their leaf tips arch across the waterfall path, forming interlocked feather-light chains that I must break before continuing. Delicate swarms of dragonflies are disturbed as I shove through the foliage, and hurrying past I sense from the corner of my eye a series of tiny wings set aflicker, shimmering glints of vitality that dart and flit towards the alders' sheltering shadows.

'Mij. Mij!' I stand alone on the rock ledge and call out in every direction, straining to make myself heard above the gushing cascade. Droplets bounce and foam flecks tumble; my head spins to glimpse one

247

fleeting red-herring movement after another. A fallen branch, coursing downstream as fast as Mij delights in doing; a slick riverbed stone that looks, for a heart-lifting moment, to be the same shape as an otter's round brown head. One by one, my hopes are dashed on the waterfall rocks. I am alone. Wherever Mij is, he cannot or will not heed my cries. *Thank Heavens*, I repeat to myself like a mantra, *he isn't wearing his harness.*

'Mij. Mij. MIJ!'

Soon, the sole option left seems to be taking my search up rather than down. From watching Mij play, I suspect there are mysterious, folkloric areas of the falls that he can reach while I cannot: truly wild territory beyond the ungainly limits of human agility where the animal kingdom can bathe in peace. Fixing my eyes on the fall summit, I start to climb, attempting to scale the rock face with what little strength and skill I possess. After each tentative movement, I call Mij's name again. My fingers seize onto the few jagged protrusions I can find but rogue streams of water strike right angles against the stone walls, spurting into my face and forcing me to close my eyes. From below, I hear a squeak. My stomach flips and my pulse stalls as fresh hope rises higher than my fears. It turns out to be the sole of one of my cumbersome wellingtons, slippery and stupid without proper purchase on the rocks. I would have been better off barefoot after all, I realise, crying out for Mij and feeling more animal than human myself.

A few feet above the ledge, I stretch too far and lose my footing. Screaming in shock, the sound still vaguely shaped around the peculiar contours of Mij's name, I slide back down to where the thriving ferns are waiting to fortuitously break my fall, although my knees collide with the rockface and I feel a gash open up on one shin. With no time for self-pity, I scramble to my feet straight away, praying the accidental shriek has travelled far enough to reach Mij's ears. Several more minutes pass without a sign. Feeling a sticky trail of blood beginning to ooze over my calf, I think back to last night and Mij's ability to sniff out my injury. I bend to tear my ripped stocking further, exposing my skinned shin to the air.

'MIJ!'

Giving up on the waterfall, I resort to retracing our daily route along the ocean front, spinning as I call in an effort to exploit the changeable direction of the coastal winds. The sweet springtime sun has been engulfed by pale grey clouds and the sea has likewise lost its serenity, churned up into choppy metallic peaks that bar the horizon like castle wall spikes. I besiege them with screams and shouts, challenging the indifferent ocean to reveal the secrets it once shared so freely with me. I know from what Gavin and I saw in the aquarium – that dazzling, miraculous moment when we witnessed Mij's innate underwater beauty – that the otter might easily have dived to depths I can scarcely fathom. Indeed, he could have swum many miles along the coast, in either direction, in the time I have spent so far in my search. If only there was a boat, bemoans a childish part of my brain, although I would have little idea what to do if there were. Sandaig is hardly Battersea Park pond, decorated with pretty pleasure boats for a gentle afternoon's rowing, and I am not Bruce Watt, equipped with none of his calmness or level-headed competence even if I had been to sea. But Gavin has. Gavin would know what to do. The thought of him travels through me as a chill, the iced burn water that never warms channelled directly into my veins. My recent anger is swept away, engulfed by a breaking wave of guilt.

'Mij. Mij. MIJ!' *Come back for Gavin's sake*, I plead from my heart and not just my lips, staking faith in the odd yet undeniably profound connection that this animal and I share. I am standing on the stone-pier bridge, the perfect vantage point from which to scan both the sea and Sandaig itself. Yet I cannot see Mij. *Come back for Gavin, if not for me.* His words back at Paultons seem to swirl windswept around this scene, orbiting me like the ring of unconditional love within which he holds the sole creature who bears his name. *It's you and not I who makes his life worth living, Mij. Please. Come back for him.*

Approaching Sandaig, I sprint as if in a race with myself, praying that my pounding heart will find comfort in the sight of Mij curled up on the fish crate sofa. I fling open the blue doors, clattering inside and searching one downstairs room and then the other. Nothing. No tell-tale wet paw prints waiting on the floor; no incriminating untidy scene of dishevelled blankets or ripped-up papers to suggest an inquisitive otter's influence.

'Mij! Mij, are you here?' I am vaguely aware that I am still shouting, without conscious effort anymore. The noise alone would surely draw Mij out if he were anywhere in this house. Even so, I keep calling for him as I hurry upstairs, the wooden doors of both rooms banging open explosively as I slam them to hasten my search. I dive into cupboards and empty clothing creels in the weak hope that Mij is playing hide and seek. I rip the blankets and sheets from the bed we share, abandoning them in a crumpled tangle when the exposed mattress reveals no otter. I place my hand briefly on its bare centre, just to be sure. Stone cold. He has not been back. When I swallow, my throat stings from screaming. Yet the silence sounds worse than continuing to call Mij's name.

Possessed by a ferocious animal spirit of my own, I press on with upturning boxes and scattering linens, leaving our little household's belongings strewn and spilt across the room in a shambolic, monkey house mess that only Mij himself could better. A burglary or a bombsite, that is what Gavin says a place looks like after an otter has had his way with it. Sandaig fares no better under my hands, but my frenzied search proves fruitless. Having rifled through my rucksack – didn't he hide in here once before? – I am momentarily detained by the sight of Gavin's sweater, tossed thoughtlessly across the narrow bed frame in the midst of my ransacking. I stare at it, transfixed by the thick-knit patterned sleeves that have warmed me in so many ways, and suddenly I can see Mij in his master's arms, here or at Paultons, cradled with an affection that could melt the hardest, ice-cold heart into tenderness. My own heart feels far from frozen. A part of me wishes it were.

Looking down, I realise that my own clothes are almost dried, albeit crinkled and creased just like the first time Mij flowed over me, springing out from the studio's small bathtub and changing three lives in one waterlogged instant. *There will be more firsts to come*, I tell myself as I stagger downstairs. *More milestones lie ahead of us all.* I focus on imagining them as I scan the ground floor for a second time. Much of my life, and certainly the best part of my poetry, has been devoted to intangible realms of imagination, and I resolve to summon up that visionary power now to push aside the terror threatening to swamp me. Clenching the cottage bannister until my nails dig into the wood, I believe I can see, really see, Mij's ecstatic reunion with Gavin tomorrow: a happy pair taking equal delight in each other as they stream into an embrace on the shore. I picture Mij's irrepressible movements, bubbling blissfully up and down within the total safety of Gavin's arms. I imagine Gavin's laughter, that gentle, silvery trickle of joy – the first part of him, I believe, that I ever fell in love with – drifting towards me on the springtime sea air. I see myself, engulfed in relief, retelling today's drama without excuses or omissions. *Yes, I will tell him*, I pledge to whatever capricious, hard-to-please Highland spirits may be listening. I have promised to be honest with Gavin and I shall not, I cannot, fail in that commitment again. Let

250

him rage against me, let his anger at almost-disaster cause him to bar me from the place I love once more. I no longer care what I have to endure, so long as I can place Mij back in his father's arms.

My violent second sacking of the living room is almost complete, pitch pine-panelled walls looking on in lofty disdain as I leave not an inch of the space undisturbed. I grab one last, little-used lobster creel and shake out its contents onto the flagstones. Mij's harness falls, those hated leather straps snaking towards me over the floor.

'At least he's not wearing it.' Savouring the hint of relief that short sentence offers, I repeat it aloud as if its words were an incantation. At least Mij is not lost while wearing this accursed contraption. I step over the straps and return outside, forcing my failing voice back into action as I bawl Mij's name out to sea. The tide has turned, half a day slipping away while I was preoccupied with panic, and now the waves appear to taunt me, rushing forward only to retreat until it feels like I am pursuing them too.

The light is beginning to fail, the distant Cuillins blurring into a deep damson horizon, and the gulls soaring overhead look no more than shadowy specks tossed to the air. The pale grey ocean is now nearer to steel, its details lost as the sun sets into a murky, amorphous mass from which I cannot pick out the rocks, let alone a small otter's dark head. The gloaming, that's what Gavin calls this ethereal, transitory time of the day. I will not let Mij get lost in the gloaming. But what else can I possibly do?

Trudging through the twilight up to Tormor, I realise too late that I ought to have turned to the MacLeods earlier. Mary and her boys were born on this land, while John Donald's long working days must mean he knows it like the back of his labour-lined hand. They may be able to suggest a corner of the shoreline I have forgotten to comb; some secluded spot I overlooked that could attract a young otter swimming free. Although none of them understand Mij the way that Gavin and I do. *The way his parents do*, I want to say, even though the thought is a harpoon to my heart.

Well-concealed at the best of times, with its corrugated green roof nestled halfway up the mossy slope like a seabird's camouflaged eerie, Tormor seems more mysterious than ever in these conditions. Ben Sgriol's immense, crag-topped bulk casts darkness downhill like a tumbling landslide of shadows, and if I were less well-acquainted with the route or less anxious to complete it quickly, I suspect I might miss the house altogether. What can Mij see where he is? I have no doubt that his night senses are infinitely superior to my own. I keep shouting his name as I walk, encouraged by the echo to hope that my call will reach him, wherever he is. 'Mij. Mij. MIJ!'

Tormor's door bangs open to show a standing figure in silhouette, clutching a slim, narrow object that is pointed in my direction.

'Who's thare? Show yersel.' I stare in disbelieving horror at the shotgun angled to my chest.

'It's Kathleen, Kathleen Raine, I ...' I hold up my hands like a genuine criminal, feeling them tremble as the man who must be John Donald shifts his weight, letting light leak from inside.

'Aye, richt enough.' Tortuously slowly, he lowers his weapon. 'The Major described ye well,' he observes. In circumstances less fraught, I would pause to wonder what Gavin goes around saying to people about me when I am not there.

'Mij is missing.' The words stick in my hoarsened, scream-shattered throat. It is the first time I have had to speak this awful new reality aloud.

'Missing?' Mary appears behind her husband, grasping what turns out to be a torch. I flinch nonetheless, raw nerves rattled by the shotgun still held low in John Donald's hands.

'Mij and I went swimming earlier,' I start to ramble, 'well, he went swimming in the ocean while I watched, and then he ... he's gone.'

'I'll help you search,' Mary announces, torch beam bouncing as she steps from the door. 'What direction were you heading when he disappeared?'

'North,' I tell her immediately.

Caught in a flare from the torchlight as Mary moves, I watch her and John Donald exchange a cryptic look. 'Towards Glenelg village?' she asks me softly.

'Yes.' Another ambiguous glance. 'At least he's not wearing his harness,' I blurt out, determined the MacLeods will appreciate the silver lining that has sustained me so far through this storm. 'I've been terrified it would snag and trap him somewhere.' Mary nods once, giving a solemn look back at John Donald.

'There's those o us tha like animals fair enough,' he tells me, 'sae lang as they stay in their richtful place. Unner man's heel.' After gesturing unnervingly to that very spot with his shotgun, he returns inside to their boys.

252

'Let's check the north side of the slope,' Mary suggests, beckoning me with her torch beam to follow around the right of the croft. Together, we start combing what we can of the cliffs, she and I both calling Mij's name. Soon, the moon emerges to watch over us from behind a covering of steel wool clouds, its pure luminescence even more watery and translucent when set against the harsh, searching yellow of torchlight. Mary swings the beam side to side, scanning for hints of animal movement in the grass. I am put in mind of London's air defences during the Blitz, although remembering those nights of intense inner-city terror – visiting only, thank goodness, with Anna and James safe many miles away in the Lakes – is hardly an idea to bring comfort.

As the moon recedes behind the clouds, I feel my own energy flicker and fade. After so many hours searching without food or rest, my body is weakening, heaviness sinking into my limbs even while my mind remains agitated. The earthly realm lets me down yet again. An indistinct yet vaguely square shadow up ahead tells me that Mary and I have looped around the hillside, making it back to Tormor without a sighting of Mij. Despair to match the darkness suddenly overwhelms me and I stumble on the incline.

'Go home, Kathleen.' Mary turns, feeling me falter.

'I can't.'

'Go home,' she insists. 'You're no use to him in this state. You must get some sleep. And try to remember that Mij is a wild animal, with a wild animal's instincts. He knows how to take care of himself.' *Not anymore*, I think helplessly, while my limbs shake and spasm from the exhaustion I can no longer keep at bay. Mij has not been wholly wild since the moment a man three thousand miles away shoved him into a sack, knotting it tight against his squirms and dropping the bundle at Gavin's feet on the Iraqi Consulate-General's floor. Not since he flew home first class with elegant air stewardesses attending to him; not since he bathed in a white porcelain tub on a street overlooking the Thames. Alone in the dark, more than a year since he last saw the marshes, does he know how to survive?

When I make it back to Sandaig, guided by the narrow beam that does little to stop me tripping into peat bog pitfalls, I go to close the door behind me before thinking better of it. What if Mij makes his way home during the night only to meet a door bolted against him? What if – I struggle to stifle a hoarse, scratching sob – he thinks I have already given up on him? Removing my wellingtons, I jam them lengthways against the lintel to hold it ajar, unconcerned with the cold midnight air coursing through the cottage if I can increase the chance of Mij coming back before sunrise. Whipping my tired limbs into action for one last time tonight, I conduct another search of the house: calling for the otter until the crackling remnants of my lost voice finally desert me, then clapping my hands in sad mimicry of the applause he likes to receive upon unwrapping his terrapin shell. Still nothing. He is not here. He has never been here.

Afraid that I will faint if I do not consume something soon, I make a cup of tea at the fireside, spilling clumsy droplets of boiling water over my fingers because I cannot stop them from trembling. *I should sit down,* my body groans, overused middle-aged bones aching for a break from this tension. But to rest would be to accept that today's search is truly over, and so I must stand, cup clasped in unsteady hands as I train my eyes on the open door. Several times, the cruel coastal winds send a broken branch or piece of whipped-up seaweed rolling across the shore. The shadowy glimpse of uncertain movement jolts my heart back into brief, futile hopefulness, sparked up then dampened down like a temperamental sports car Gavin would try and fail to jump-start.

You have to sleep, a faraway voice beseeches me. Is it my mother's? Or the angel who saved me from the waves? I shake my head at her, whoever she is.

'I can't.' My words resound through the empty house before being swept off with the night air.

You must, Kathleen. You need sleep. I need Mij. Without him, I cannot contemplate going to bed; indulge myself in snug safety beneath the blankets, rest my head on Gavin's pillow while Mij sleeps … where exactly? Where in this pitch-black, unfeeling universe is he curled up tonight? The world I can see through the opened door is one of swirling sea spray, still chilled by the lingering cast of winter. The cloud cover is too opaque to reveal a glint of the stars. Wherever he is out there, this house is Mij's home, his holt – the technical term for an otter dwelling, Gavin says – and whatever he has to suffer tonight, I resolve to endure it with him. '*Chahala, Chahala, Cha-ha-la,*' I imagine him calling like Gavin's first, ill-fated otter: the haunting minor melody of an animal overwhelmed by fear. *Mother. Mother. Mother.*

Stiffly, my limbs having already seized up when offered the faintest suggestion of the rest they crave, I pad upstairs to the bedroom I earlier left in disarray. Plucking the bulkiest blanket from the jumbled pile on the floor, I drag it down behind me until I am back in the cottage doorway. I push my boots aside, manoeuvring myself until my body becomes a doorstop, then I delve into the blanket's shelter and let its woollen swathes envelop my head and shoulders. Eyelids drooping from sudden warmth, I sense my mind starting to roam of its own accord, returning, as it so often does, to Gavin's side. I picture him in London, in the bedroom that used to be mine, sleeping in peaceful ignorance of the trust I have inadvertently betrayed. Of the faith in which I have failed him.

'Come back, Mij.' I keep on murmuring for our otter even as unconsciousness overtakes me. 'Come back for him.' I fight the drowsiness as it descends, submerged beneath a dark, dead weight more like anaesthesia than conventional rest. My legs twitch hard as I slip away, uncomfortable jerking spasms that to my disconsolate mind feel more like small seizures. Perhaps a part of me is still out there walking. Still searching for Mij until dawn.

Chapter Thirty

'Mij?' I wake midway through already saying his name. 'Mij?' The coastline is calmer, glowing faint as the morning sun strains past gauzy layers of pale grey clouds, so near to the sea that the effect is more like a low-lying mist. The ocean gleams silver, without even a hint of blue. From these monochromatic tones, I might think I was looking at a photograph, were it not for – my exhausted eyes must be hallucinating – unseasonal glints of rowan berry red.

Rising stiffly, my feet tangled as I step from my blanket, I search each cottage room in turn. No otter footprints. No nibbled furnishings, or at least no new ones. No patch of warmth on the sofa or bed where I might have just missed Mij.

'Come back,' I whisper croakily, reaching for the cold remnants of last night's tea to soothe my fiery throat. 'Please, Mij. Come back to us.'

Within minutes, I am outside, eyes narrowed against the strange luminosity as I scan the coastline yet again. How long has he been absent? Not quite twenty-four hours? As I look over the ocean and along the kelp-scattered strand, I feel my happy memories of Mij in this landscape being forced to make room for new ones: torturously vivid images of screams and tears being swept up with the wind, staring out to a world of rugged, bracing beauty that lacks nothing except the small otter I seek. Unbearable as it is to admit, Sandaig no longer feels like the place where Mij is. It is starting to feel like the place where he is not.

Gavin arrives today. In the name of all that is holy – in the name of William Blake, I might say – how can I face him having lost the one he loves most? *I won't need to*, I resolve, *because I will find Mij today. I must.* I resume my search of Sandaig bay as if seconds not hours have passed since last time. Scrambling over flinty slivers of exposed rock before the next tide magics them away; staring into their pockmarked craters and pools, unsatisfied for once with finding only beautiful shells glinting back at me. Awaiting and almost anticipating my attention, the cowries and clams gleam and sparkle beneath the clear surface. How can water so peaceful and pellucid, transparent enough for me to see the grit-sand bases of the rockpools, still hold so much mystery? How can it readily reveal objects lost to the depths for centuries, yet refuse to offer a hint as to where Mij has gone? With wisdom carved into every intricate coil and crinkle, I wonder whether these tiny shell emissaries of the ocean would tell me, if only they could speak.

'Miss Raine, Miss Raine!' I spin to see the twins hurtling downhill, red locks flailing as they speed almost as fast as Mij can surge through the burn, if not half so smooth or elegant. Twin Two has longer legs than his brother these days, but commanding the unruly new assets is apparently proving tricky. Arms windmilling in his haste to reach me, I watch his frantic feet strike the ground, spinning like the pedals of a bicycle veering dangerously out of control, until Twin One – smaller, stockier and determined not to be left behind – seizes onto his brother's sweater and the pair rebalance each other.

'He's bin seen,' Twin One yells when they are still feet away. 'Mij's bin seen!'

'What? Where?' Weariness forgotten, I find that I am running myself, hurrying uphill to meet the boys beside the bridge. 'Tell me.' Hoarseness exacerbated by sudden exertion, I cough, choking until I bend with both palms pressing into my knees. The twins, sweetly, want to wait for me to stop spluttering, but I wave my hand to make them go on.

'Our Da's bin asking ilka body on the road.' Twin Two begins the story, bright-eyed and exhilarated, 'An a man says he seen Mij cross his land yesterday. He were near his hens, the man said, an he were aboot tae shoot him ...'

'What?' A fresh fit of coughing overtakes me, during which time Twin One picks up the tale.

'Bit then he realised tha Mij wisna interested in his hens at all. He walked richt past them.' *He would do*, I think, hope suddenly surging through me as if a tide inside my heart has turned. Gavin always said that the Ma'dan would not tolerate a pet who preyed upon one of their few food sources. Since cubhood, Mij has been trained to show no interest in poultry.

The boys respond to my obvious relief with beaming smiles. 'I ken then tha it were the tame otter,' Twin Two says, impersonating the anonymous and exceptionally sensible bystander. 'I kent it must be the Major's otter.'

The Major. So many folk up here still give Gavin his title, even though

257

the war was won more than a decade ago. The plaid-clad traditions of Highland culture are hard-wearing. Respect. Duty. Deference. I wonder what they call me, if anything? Presumably I warrant no title of my own, the woman – even more of an outsider than Gavin – who for years has followed behind like a devoted, lovestruck shadow. The woman who lost Gavin's namesake, the little creature he loves more than any other in this world. But Mij is not lost anymore. He has been seen. He can be found.

'Did the man say anything more?' The twins nod in unison, shared delight sufficient to let their bodies' rhythms briefly re-synchronise.

'He said tha Mij were headin south, last time he saw him.' Matching impish grins, cheeky and cheerful as the day we met. 'He were coming hame.'

'Home.' Too happy to hesitate, I pull both boys into a hug. They squeeze me back, laughter muffled by our embrace and teenage embarrassment cast aside in favour of pure joy. One boy starts bouncing, physically unable to contain his excitement, and soon his brother does likewise until all three of us are at it: a human spinning top of shared cheer springing over the grass. Relief flows through my frame, tingling sparks animating all that was tired and depleted from my fingertips down to my toes. My aching heart is elevated, almost singing within my chest. 'Thank you for telling me,' I say to the twins when, head spinning, I eventually break away. 'You'd best go back to your mother. I'll be fine here alone, I'll ...' Happiness rather than hoarseness stops me from speaking this time. 'I'll wait for Mij to come home.'

I walk with the boys uphill before breaking off to take my place at the spot where I believe I have the greatest chance of seeing Mij as he returns. This part of the hillside gives me the best view of Sandaig bay and I fix my gaze on where Mij seems most likely to appear, irrespective of whether he chooses to walk or more likely swim home. If he were another animal, a land-dwelling species like a dog, then I would set out to try and meet him somewhere between here and Glenelg, but with ocean, burn and waterfall, I know that Mij may opt for any number of watery routes home and I am mortally afraid of missing him. The unnamed man saw him heading south yesterday? By now he must be very close at hand. In fact, I am almost surprised that Mij has not made it back already.

At first, hands clenched in front of me, I stand and stare resolutely to the north. The minutes tick by, although I refuse to look at my watch, and eventually I permit myself to sit, arms wrapped around my knees in a posture of childlike, Christmas Eve anticipation. Again, my eyes pick out minute movements of wind-dishevelled flotsam on the shoreline, but I am no longer left despondent by each false alarm because I know, I can feel, that the search is finally over. To occupy myself while I wait, I daydream of Gavin's imminent arrival: the pleasure of seeing him sharpened by having sailed so close to disaster without, in the end, hitting the rocks. I picture Mij in his arms, otter and owner together, chitters and laughter interlaced in the air as we three share our joy at a bond unbroken.

I do not hear Mary behind me until she calls my name. But when I turn, one look at her pale, haunted face, and I know what she has to tell me.

*

'He swears the otter he killed was a wild one.' Mary repeats herself as if I asked her to. In truth, I cannot ask anything. I cannot speak. My head is bowed over her kitchen table, staring without seeing at the crosshatched scores and whorls of the wood grain while we wait – still, we wait – for further news. My palms compress my face from both sides, fingers spread slightly so I will still be able to hear the telephone ring. It lurks within the shadowy corners of my vision: an insistent, inescapable presence even when my eyes are averted. I feel as afraid of that phone now as I have come to be of the rowan tree.

'Kathleen, did you hear me? I said he swears it was a wild one.' I have no reply for Mary, my words blasted away by shock. In other circumstances, I might compliment her on the warmth, in every sense, of Tormor's kitchen, vaguely aware that I have never been inside it before. Given this reason, I wish I still hadn't. 'Angus insists it was an old, wild otter walking south on the Glenelg road.' A third time, repeating her own repetition, apparently unaware that the words have already infiltrated my bloodstream, oozing into my brain and poisoning my thoughts. 'And I asked him how he knew. He said …' I raise my head in time to see Mary halt, her mouth open: half from the unfinished thought and half, I think, from her own mortification. She looks aghast, appalled and consumed with guilt like a courtroom witness whose testimony has convicted the very person she wished to defend.

'What did he say Mary?' She chooses not to face me when she answers.

'He … he said he knew because the otter wasn't wearing anything. No collar, he said. No harness. Not like a pet.' A pet. People often use

259

that word for Mij. It feels foreign to me, inaccurate and even absurd, like calling Anna a china doll or James an action figurine. Mij is not a toy for mere amusement; he is far from an expendable fur stole that Gavin and I take pleasure in petting. He is our kindred spirit. Our cherished companion. Mij is the Sandaig burn embodied by a living being; my source of joy and Gavin's soulmate, he is our ... he is so much more than a pet.

Mary moves to the other end of the table, needlessly sweeping a cloth towards herself, hand cupped just beneath the rim to catch crumbs that I do not believe really exist. I suppose distress presents itself in different ways. I can only imagine finding relief from anxiety in housework. 'I told him then that the Major's otter hadn't been wearing his harness when he went missing.' A rogue blemish on the table, invisible to me, consumes Mary's attention. She scrubs and scratches at the mark: preferable, perhaps, to looking directly at me. I do not blame her. I would not look at me either. I try to follow suit, fixing my eyes on the pristine yet well-loved wood tabletop. But all I can see is Sandaig's flagstone floor and Mij's discarded harness lying empty.

'But no, Angus kept insisting it must've been a wild otter he killed because the coat was so poor: mangy and scabbed, obviously old. Not worth keeping, he told me. He said he threw the body into the ocean.'

'How did he kill it?'

'Kathleen.' I look up again to see Mary grimace, face flinching at the thought of whatever it is she would rather not tell me.

'How did he kill the otter, Mary?'

Mary takes a breath, knuckles white as she clenches the cloth. 'A pickaxe to the skull.'

Ice in my brain. A shard of iron splitting my crown. My own head cramps, sinews squeezing like twisted tendrils of choking ivy while the thumping pain of pulsing blood hammers me from the top down. For several seconds, I can barely see Mary at all through a ghoulish, gruesome aura of vomit yellow.

'Why?' My voice crackles, a fading fire that no one can stop going out. What little belief I had left in human goodness swept away on an outgoing tide. 'Why would a man do that?'

Mary speaks softly, her voice pure as an elegiac Gaelic lament. 'I suppose some folk consider them vermin.' On the last word, she sinks to a whisper, but the spiky, nasty angles of its letters still wound me. It strikes my ears as a slur, offensive and ugly as any I have heard against myself. Try surprising a proud man with the news that you are leaving him; your coarse vocabulary will be enriched. Just like those words, the 'b's, 'f's and even 'c's whose linguistic infamy is such that one letter is enough to speak the unspeakable, the very existence of the insult seems to degrade both sides. A shadow over Mij for the unjust aspersion he suffers; a shadow, too, over mankind for the violence of its ignorance.

'Some might also want to sell the pelt.' The thought of Mij separate from his skin makes me dig my nails into my hands until the tips split.

'But he ...' I can barely say it, and yet I must. 'He threw the body away. This ...' I lift one hand to wave, the other flushing warm with relief from the pressure. 'This Angus. He threw the body away because the fur was mangy.' From the extinguished embers of hopelessness, an infinitesimal spark of light. I cup it with trembling fingertips, blowing frantically to transform it into a flame. 'He said it was scabby, didn't he?'

Mary nods. 'Dirty and thin, even hairless in places. He said it had to be an old otter because of it.'

Fast pulse throbbing, I think back to the taxi journey I so recently shared with Gavin: London's lights glinting and glittering across Mij's plush velvet sweep of gloss brown. Red, amber, green. All illuminated in his rich, rippling fur. He is not old. He is vibrant and dynamic, fluid in form and sheer, dazzling perfection in spirit. A young, fit otter in the veritable prime of his natural life.

'Then it can't have been Mij, it just can't have been. His coat was ...' I gasp at my own mistake. 'His coat *is* perfect.' The accused's testimony turned prosecution evidence. Hung out to dry, or simply hung, by my own blundering words. The vomit-coloured aura is inside me; I swallow hard to prevent it spewing out.

'J.D. will try to learn more,' Mary insists. Afraid to hope, afraid to not, I resume my silent vigil staring down at her tabletop. In time, I grow vaguely aware of Mary's soft bustling movements in my peripheral vision, no doubt getting on with the minor kitchen tasks to which I am, yet again, a major interruption. This sense of paralysis, of my utter helplessness while routine business carries on around me, is a strong reminder of the time I was in hospital. God knows that memory only resurfaces in times of acute distress. Unless it is only in times of distress that I lower my guard against its resurgence. *But come now, Kathleen*, the wise yet weakening inner voice tries to advise. *It won't help Mij if you think about that now.*

261

The kitchen door creaks open and I startle, having hazily believed Mary and I were alone in the house. Roddy, as this young man must be, looks like an elongated version of his little brothers. I see in him a hint of their sweet expressions and a thatch of the same tousled auburn, but his teenaged jawline is squarer and more mature than their pointed elfin chins. Equally surprised by my presence, his face turns the florid hot pink that only an uncomfortable redhead can attain.

'Missraine.' My name tumbles from his lips as a single word, landing somewhere between 'mistake' and 'refrain'.

The telephone rings. I jump, and Roddy springs back from fright like I transmitted an electric shock. Not looking at either of us, Mary moves to answer. I watch her take a long, steadying breath before she picks up the receiver. The indistinct metallic timbre of a voice at the other end of the line bristles through the kitchen. Desperate as I am, I cannot distinguish the individual words. All I can tell is that the speaker is a man, but not, I think, John Donald. For what feels like an age, I am forced to endure his crackling, code-like fragments of static interspersed with Mary's muted replies. She cups her hand around the mouthpiece, murmuring what sounds from intonation alone like one question and then another.

Mary turns, her ivory skin ever paler than before.

'He wants to talk to you.' Legs weak, I walk to the receiver.

'Ye should know the truth,' the man says. I don't catch his name. I don't think he gives it. 'If Big Angus didna know it were the Major's otter when he killed it, then he did after I told him. "Ye're a bloody fool," I said, "if ye think that's a wild otter, or that a wild animal would wait in the road for ye tae get the pick frae yer lorry and kill it." It trusted humans, that beast, and that's the sorry truth of it. Well, Angus panicked then, and threw the body intae the water. But it's no right tae let ye think that yer pet is still out there. No, not a decent action in a man at all. No when the animal's dead.

'Word's got tae Mallaig,' he adds before ringing off. 'The Major already knows.'

262

Chapter Thirty-One

Bruce brings Gavin home by boat, a dark speck emerging from the mist as the vessel drifts slowly towards Sandaig. The wind has dropped, unruly waves dull and strangely subdued as if the ocean itself is in mourning for the watery spirit who made this landscape complete. Watching the small boat's progress as it glides across the eerily calm steel sea, I tighten my grip on the cool, crag-faced rock upon which I sit, struggling to force down even a single shallow breath. My fingertips dig into the pitted stone, worrying its jagged indents until the feeling reminds me too much of Mij's teeth to continue. There are scars on my hands, silver threads crisscrossed from occasions when his rambunctious playtimes turned too raucous for my thin human skin. Those marks will never leave me. And I would give up all I have for Mij to be here, making more.

Gavin's boat continues to coast nearer, the mist behind it thick enough to block out all traces of the snow-capped Cuillins beyond. He has not come from Skye but the north, first taking his car to Glenelg, according to what John Donald told me. The latter's call to Tormor came a matter of minutes after I had spoken with the nameless man: a well-intentioned if belated effort to forewarn me of what I was about to hear.

'The Major wants tae speak wi Angus himsel,' John Donald had advised me solemnly, tone heavy with the menacing hint of a 'man-to-man' challenge that sounded nothing like the Gavin I know. 'Then Bruce will bring him doun the coast.' Although technically we inhabit the same coastline, the route to Glenelg village is so convoluted by road that the journey back to Sandaig is significantly shorter by sea. Where will Gavin leave the Maserati? In truth, I do not care. I doubt he does now either. Pressing my palms hard against my rock face, I permit its gravelly ridges to scape and scratch my skin, willing the needling sting to replace my emotional pain with a physical one.

When still searching for Mij – and who could ever have believed I would think back almost fondly to those hours when a sliver of hope endured? – I had thought my efforts to visualise his safe return would help

263

it manifest into reality. Through sheer force of will, I hoped to coax his wild spirit home; tapping into the mystical power embedded within this place and channelling the profound cosmic connections inherent in a spot where the sea meets shore and sky. But as I watch Gavin's boat come in, I realise that my agitated, over-active imagination has only succeeded in creating a new form of mental torture, because I can see two versions of the same scene playing out before me: one sunlit and celebratory, the other shrouded in sorrowful grey. In many ways, the fantasy version feels realer than reality. I should be returning Mij to Gavin. I should be watching him smile. I should be sharing in his affection for the otter in whose heart we met, offering Mij back to the man who adores him and, embodied by that remarkable animal, as much of my love as Gavin can accept.

'*Lutrogale perspicillata maxwelli.*' I murmur Mij's Latin label to myself, letting the strange syllables fade into the sea air. Gavin always said that our otter would be the only creature to bear his name. Like a bitter civil war or virulent outbreak of pestilence, I have ravaged his sole hope of a dynasty, decimating his greatest achievement and breaking apart the only lineage he cares about. What of Monreith's cut-grass proverbs and majestic gold-clad eagles? Mij was the legacy that mattered to Gavin. My eyes stay trained on Bruce's vessel as it slides through the lacklustre waves, prow cutting smoothly through ethereal clouds of condensation. Remarkable just how slowly a boat can move. It looks weirdly similar to a death ship of literary legend, just like in the Tennyson poem that Gavin quoted long ago. Departing his earthly Avilion with impassioned prayers to arrive at the real thing, King Arthur's body was carried off on a weak, woeful current, drifting away on a ship that soon evaporated into the mist. The poem left his ultimate fate uncertain. I will know mine imminently. What will Gavin do? Scream at me, strike me or send me away for eternity? *I deserve it all,* I tell myself as my moment of judgement sails nearer. I deserve to be burnt by his vitriolic fury; chilled by contemptuous, ice-cold disdain. It will be recompense for the grievous wound that my mistakes have inflicted on him. And whatever words Gavin sees fit to unleash, they can be no worse than those I have already said to myself.

By the time the boat crunches onto the Sandaig shingles, the grey water and overcast clouds have blurred to create a wall of shadow. The vessel's weight sends shivers across the stones and I think of all the delicate shells trapped and broken beneath its heavy hull: innocent paragons of ocean beauty that, in one instant of manmade intervention, are shattered and

264

lost forever. The boat's motion stills, the crunching ceases, yet Bruce remains on board. Standing with one hand still on his wheel, he meets my eye, spine straight and rigidly formal. Without a word, Bruce respectfully removes his cap.

Gavin steps over the side, the anaemic sun straining through the fog to lie low on the water behind him. It outlines his silhouette, a darkened form ringed with pale gold. His shoulders are sagging, back hunched as if to unfurl fully would be more than his despondent body could bare. Limbs as long and thin as his own ink lettering, Gavin walks away from the pallid brightness and into the shadowlands where I sit. *'Into my dark I have drawn down his light.'* Words written back when I thanked the universe each night that we had been blessed enough to meet one another.

He spots me waiting on the rocks and speeds up. I rise, trembling slightly, and feel the sand shift beneath my feet. Gavin strides towards me with sudden purpose, his expression illegible in this dim, sombre light. Fear, futile and pathetic, flows through me as he approaches, determination driving his every movement as he powers his way across the shore. I deserve this, I tell myself sternly, preventing unchecked cowardice from taking control. I deserve Gavin's hate for my mistake.

'Kathleen.' He holds out his hands for mine. 'Oh, Kathleen,' he whispers hoarsely as our fingertips touch. 'You made his last days happy ones.' Shock hits me, a fresh lightning bolt when I had believed no more could strike, and I stumble, the uneven tide-swept sand once more giving way under my boots. Gavin's grip on me tightens instinctively, his forearms taut and sinewy as he lends me the strength to keep standing. Without him, I am sure I would fall. 'Oh, Kathleen,' he murmurs again. His arms enfold me until my bloodless face is buried into his chest.

He forgives me. God in Heaven, he forgives me. After all that I have held against him – my petty resentments and mottled, dark green jealousy; my unjustified slur of disgust (which he knows about) and momentary, accursed cry for vengeance (which he does not) – Gavin can still find forgiveness for me within the unchartered depths of his heart. My cheek presses against the static wool of his sweater, one side of my face growing warm while the other stays exposed to the sea air. Standing together, our arms entwined on the shore, I sense Gavin drawing on reserves of unguessed empathy to support me, in every sense of the word. Even with my many years of poetry, all those long, solemn hours of intellectual contemplation, I doubt that I could possess the same mental strength.

'I'm sorry. I'm so, so sorry.' The words spill out from me in a ragged-breath shudder, coursing along a lengthy exhale I did not realise I held until it left my lungs. Around Gavin's back, my fingers seize onto his jumper until I suspect the clench is hurting us both: my tight grip beseeching those wispy wire fibres to absorb some of my sorrow and regret. 'I'm so sorry.' Tears start and refuse to stop, my sobs punctuating words already smothered by Gavin's sweater until I am sure they would be utterly incomprehensible to anyone but him. 'I'm – so – so– so– rry.' The flat, faintly salted taste of weeping seeps into my mouth, fallen teardrops sliding from my cheeks to land on my quivering bottom lip. Mij would lick them away. He hated to see me cry. The memory turns the hastening trickle into a full-blown waterfall torrent.

'Shh.' My crown is tucked under Gavin's chin. His arms are folded around my shoulders. *This is the closest we have been in years,* my aching heart reminds me. *The first time in many months he has not shied away from my touch.* It shames me for such a thought to occur, to admit even a fleeting glimmer of pleasure at our now rare physical proximity, when all the while our little otter is still out there, his broken body drifting down through the murky depths until he comes to rest alone on the cold, shadowy seabed. I unleash a fresh howl into the comfort of Gavin's sweater, bereft at the thought of all that we have lost. The tears keep tumbling; I gasp and almost choke, like a greedy child who has stuffed herself swollen with berries and has no one but herself to blame for the pain.

'Shh, Kathleen. Please don't cry.' Gavin whispers the words with great gentleness, yet his voice sounds strained from the effort. Attuned to him as I am, my ear only an inch away from his lips, I can hear the subtle undertone of a different type of distress. A note of growing caution creeping into his speech. I raise my face to see his, agonisingly aware that I must look like a tear-streaked fright. A private struggle is there in Gavin's eyes, his inner conflict not quite hidden behind those heavy lids just the same way that churned-up waves cannot be smoothed by the reflection of peaceful skies. Few men of my acquaintance could endure a woman's sobs, or indeed any open displays of raw, unrestrained emotion. Tambi, as ever, is the notable exception. I have long suspected that our one tearstained night together is something Gavin has resolved never to dwell on, even though for me the memory is forever embedded into my soul. Aristocrats do not weep. And if they do – if their tears occasionally fall, as for all humans they must, and salted droplets of their sadness

266

stipple the skin of the one person whom they trust enough to comfort them – then they must never speak of the indiscretion. *I doubt one would catch Lady Mary crying*, I think mournfully as wracking sobs begin to shake me and my inflamed nostrils start to stream.

Yet try as I might, my sobbing will not stop: the floodgates open and the dam breached beyond repair.

'That's enough now, Kathleen. Please.' Gavin's rebuke gives way to a plea, his own pale blue eyes glazing over with clouded moisture. Only for so long can he be strong for the both of us. I give a sniff, loud and unladylike, and pull back until I face away from him, intending to spare Gavin the sight of further tears, while also sparing myself the shame of having failed him once again. Wiping my nose surreptitiously on my cardigan sleeve, the sort of childish move for which I frequently scolded poor James, I glance up by chance to the right side of the cottage. The rowan. Through my tear-stained gaze, its bark shimmers as a mass of dark silver pieces. *Judas*, say the glittering fragments. Judas, the double-crosser. Judas with his kiss of death, who regretted his betrayal too late.

Deliberately, desperately, I face the other direction. It appears that Bruce has already retreated, his quiet dignity once more speaking for itself as he leaves Gavin and me to our private grief. His boat is at sea, receding into the dusk-shrouded mist until, were it not for Gavin's presence beside me, I might believe that I had only imagined the vessel here. I watch its slow reverse progress over the ocean, trying to make my breathing fit the soothing rhythm of its smooth movements. I inhale, a stuttering drag that rattles grotesquely within my sore, raw-rimmed nostrils, then on the exhale I exercise all the control I have left not to once more dissolve into tears. My nails curl into the plump flesh of my palms; I bite my lip, still wet from earlier weeping. This discipline does not come naturally. I am clearly not meant to be an aristocrat.

Gavin and I sit on the rocks overlooking the sea. I am unsure who guides who: our hands are still linked, if only just, my smallest fingertip hooked onto Gavin's as we decide in silent agreement to watch what we can of the shadowed waves. The tide is coming in, this moment of stillness cannot last, and yet for now we remain side by side, motionless in our sorrow as off-white cuffs of foam sweep ever closer to Sandaig. We both know what we should see. The splash of a fearless, headfirst dive as an exuberant otter immerses himself in his element. We are both looking for a little brown head, cherubic in its charming cheekiness, that will never bob up to the surface again. My tears have almost ceased flowing, but my breathing remains erratic. An airy splutter escapes my lips before I can help it. The sound comes cruelly close to a 'Ha'.

Looking out to sea, Gavin keeps my hand in his. His thumb runs soft, mindless circles over my skin, stroking the back of my hand in tiny spirals again and again. He seems unaware of what he is doing and I do not point it out. He would stop. Instead, I close my eyes, hoping that further tears cannot fall while my dry, stinging lids are squeezed shut. My mind drifts beyond the pink-tinged veil of darkness that descends to recall Gavin's own tears – yet more weeping we never speak of – after we stumbled upon the new-born calves. Didn't he say that he feared his touch had sullied them? Yet it is my hands that are unclean. Corrupted. Bloodied. My touch killed Mij, after all. Maybe I did not wield the weapon; I was not the one to shatter that sweet, trusting skull with the lethal point of a dirty pickaxe. But I know in my soul I am responsible. Gavin gave the creature he loves most in this world into my care for safekeeping. In return, I cannot even give him back a corpse over which we may grieve.

Gavin raises our interlocked fingers to light himself a cigarette. I feel the gentle pull of my forearm and hear the ringing metal click of his lighter, but I only turn my head when I smell it: that acrid, bitter tinge, polluting the pure sea air yet somehow never clinging to Gavin's skin and clothes the way it does with lesser men. He offers me a drag. Unusually, I accept. I draw too much, strong smoke backing up and choking my hoarsened, scream-sore throat. I cough pathetically, a dirty grey ring hovering in the atmosphere between us. It disintegrates into nothingness.

'You went north?' Gavin asks. I nod, unable to speak. 'He wasn't wearing his harness?' I can hardly move my head at all. I give a weak squeeze of Gavin's fingers instead. He replies with a sigh, gentle and sorrowful. A thin cloud of smoke dissipates with it. Our hands stay clasped together. I wonder what Adam said to Eve when they sat thus with their heads bowed, outside the walls of the garden meant to be their paradise. What words could ever express the loss she had caused them, the binding fate that her grave error had brought crashing down on them both? Perhaps language is too much for such moments. Too much and not enough.

'Is there anything to drink?' Gavin asks abruptly.

'I … I think so.' I spring up, dropping his hand to hurry back inside the cottage. I feel desperate to perform this small, pathetic service for him, successfully delivering the oblivion I know he desires. But in the living room, I have to halt. This is the first time I have stood here since knowing for sure the worst is true. That Mij, our Mij, is never coming back. Struck afresh by a wave of grief, I reel, rocked on the swollen balls of my feet as if a vicious blow has struck my stomach. My palms turn clammy, tingling with the sick, yellow energy of distress; my legs falter, barely able to support my weight as they turn to jellied tendrils of kelp. I take a couple of clumsy, coltish steps to touch Mij's little blanket, the fabric still dappled with short brown hairs. I turn to look at his basket, the compartment in shadow, so that if I scrunch my eyes to blur my vision and force my heart to withstand the torture, I can almost pretend his face may peek out at any moment. Beside the basket lies his coveted squeaky éclair, his well-worn knotted towel and his beloved terrapin shell. Toys he will never play with. Happiness he will never know. Love he will never again feel from us, even though I know both Gavin and I will love Mij until we draw our own dying breaths.

I return outside with two glasses, my own already short by a sip. Gavin reaches out for his, not troubling to study what I have handed him. He tosses it back, swallowing his double measure in one. Only then does he pause to look into the now empty glass, his fair brow darkening with scorn as if the drink, too, has disappointed him.

'Are you coming back to London?' I do not sound like myself. Too tentative and frail. My voice trembles with the twee, unattractive fragility of an invalid's, made weaker still by changing my mind on the wording halfway through. *Are you coming home?* That is what I wanted to say. Sandaig used to be home. It does not feel so anymore.

Gavin shakes his head, still looking into his drained glass. 'To Canna,' he says. 'John invited me to stay with him and Margaret after they heard what happened …' For few telephones and an infamously erratic postal service, word travels fast in this part of the world. 'You could come too, if you wanted?' Ever the gentleman, Gavin makes a valiant attempt at pretending he would like me to accompany him. At least, I think he must be pretending.

'No.' It sounds starker than I intended. 'I couldn't.' The Lorne Campbells are good people, from what I hear. John is the kind-hearted scholarly Laird of their little isle – Gavin has not lost his knack for attracting friends in high places, even in the remotest reaches of the Highlands – while Margaret, his wife, is reputed to possess for real that mystical second sight power upon which centres many a Scots myth. At any other time, I should very much like to meet them, delighting in exploring their verdant island of legendary beauty and climbing the famed Compass Hill with Gavin at my side. Our steps might match the thick beat of wild rabbits thumping their feet in the bracken; we could return to Canna House in the evening for wine and intellectual conviviality. At any other time than this. Now, though, I must be alone. Or I must be like this. It is a strange quirk of what we have become that Gavin's company no longer counts as being with somebody else.

'I can't return to Paultons,' he counters quietly. 'Not yet. I just ...' at a loss for words and lacking the enthusiasm to search for them, Gavin gestures loosely with his glass to the cottage behind us. He might be toasting it, I think, with a vague superstitious recollection that it is bad luck to do so with an empty vessel. But can worse luck befall us now? My heart's cry at the rowan stacked the odds long ago.

'I just can't,' is all Gavin eventually manages to say, more to himself than to me. With an earthy groan as if the past few minutes have aged him years, he rises, glass rim pinched as he walks away to face the dull, drab excuse for a sunset. The strange light effect of earlier now seems to be occurring in reverse, the last of the tepid brightness clinging to the outline of his slender form while charcoal shadows close in. I watch Gavin step towards the water's edge, waves coasting over his boots as he stares out to the ocean. From the faded vestiges of our mental connection, I am certain that I know what he is thinking. *Where?* He wonders where Mij is. I do too, each time I look at that dark, endless expanse.

Exhaustion and desolation are shifting sands inside me, tussling for supremacy just as Gavin once told me the undertow and cresting waves are apt to do. As the light falls, his form shrinks and swells before my tired eyes, creating the unnerving illusion that the distance of ten or fifteen feet between us is utterly unbreachable. Is this how it will be between us now? Divided not only by distance, but by his noble clemency set against my eradicable stain of shame? Aristotle, I think, was the one who said we can forgive those who hurt us far easier than those whom we hurt. In the company of the former, he observed, we see ourselves in a good light; in the latter, we never can, and it makes their presence almost impossible to bear. Will this be my true punishment, reminded every time I look at the man I have loved for so long that he is suffering because of me? Me, the woman who wanted only to do him good, having done myself and even,

God forgive me, my children grave wrongs in my desperate, futile quest to make him happy? Gavin has given me his forgiveness with poignant gentleness and grace, at a time when I did not expect him to have the strength. Now I wonder whether I am strong enough to accept it.

The sun is vanquished, the mist victorious, and the shoreline horizon is shrouded in hazy black. Yet Gavin does not move. He continues to stare into the rapidly encroaching shadows, even as the tide seeps past his toes and starts to flow in cold, foaming swirls around his heels. *He has already left here*, I realise bleakly, as the world around us descends into darkness. And in the storm-ravaged, closed-up cowrie shell of my heart, I fear that I have not lost one wild soulmate, but two.

Chapter Thirty-Two

'No wee friend today, Madam?' an excruciatingly friendly ticket inspector enquires on the Mallaig platform. Clutching Mij's little dog ticket, a space still unstamped for the return journey he will never make, I shake my head, silently keeping it down. The man will think me rude until someone tells him the truth. Would that Big Angus – the cretinous nickname only makes Mij feel smaller – was decent enough to be truthful too.

Before we parted on the Sandaig strand, Gavin had muttered dark, unsettling threats about what he ought to have done to that man. The coastline was wholly black by then, his mood, abetted by another swiftly despatched double whisky, more than a match for it.

'With my bare hands ...' he had growled into the gloom, words sinking into shadowy incoherence. 'Or strike him down with ... without warning ... like Mij.' Unable to see for sure, I heard a watery thickness weighing down Gavin's tone. A frantic scrubbing movement, sensed more than seen in the dark, suggested that he was rubbing his eyes. 'He should've ... he should've had one chance to use his teeth against his killer. Don't you think, Kathleen?'

'I do.' Imagining Mij's razor-rimmed jaws sinking into that man's flesh gave me a rare glimpse of comfort, until I remembered that it was mere fantasy. Mij trusted people. Even strangers. We never thought to teach him not to.

Oafish and obstinate, Big Angus is sticking to his story. The thought of Gavin having gone alone to confront Mij's killer somehow makes him feel more fragile to me than ever: a broken-hearted boy pretender no match for the brutish lout who has so thoughtlessly decimated his world.

'I was furtive when I approached,' Gavin told me, his voice hoarse with horror. 'In case Mij's pelt was hanging outside.' The idea had made my blood run colder than the burn. And yet there was no trace of our otter, indoors or out, and Angus himself was too scared or stupid – most likely both – to admit the truth. In vain, Gavin had tried to make him understand how much additional pain his unsustainable falsehood was causing him.

Causing us.

'He were very old and skinny,' was all that Angus would repeat, bulbous features so blatantly betraying the lie to add insult to literal injury.

'Murderer,' Gavin had snarled afterwards on the shoreline, clenching his empty whisky glass so hard I feared it would shatter in his hand. 'Bloody murderer.' A murder indeed, if not a crime in the eyes of the world. An animal has no legal rights, no worth save what one can prove of its financial value. Will people ever understand how much our otter meant to us? Recalling Gavin's words makes me think now of the human murders one reads of in newspapers, grim headlines revelling in the salacious horror of a killer unwilling to disclose where a body is hidden. Without Mij's remains, we cannot convince ourselves he is at rest; we cannot come together, even if it were the last time that Gavin and I ever did come together, to mourn the cherished memory of the creature we wholeheartedly adored. 'He threw the body in the ocean.' Mij's ocean. The idea that our boy will dwell forever in the element he loved should feel more of a comfort than this.

Now tonight, sleepless on the Caledonian sleeper, I strain through the black to see what I imagine to be the ugly, thick-set features of Angus's leering face. How heavy is a pickaxe? I have never held one. Yet ten pounds or ten tonnes, I know that with this rage inside me, I could do it. I could raise my weapon high above that brainless, brawny head, shrieking with the unleashed fury of a madwoman – worse, a grieving mother – as I drove the metal point down into the grisly fat of his flesh. His skull would splinter, dense as wood; the few fragments of brain power in Big Angus's possession splattering red onto his whitewashed cottage walls. He might not die straight away. Maybe he would crawl towards me, vision blinded by streaming blood, his hands, those hateful meaty stubs that put an end to Mij's life, waving for help before I crushed them beneath my boots. Yes, I would make the agony last for Angus. Unlike what he did for Mij. I would not let him depart this earth with one sharp blow of oblivion. And when, finally, it was over, I would stagger back home to Sandaig, bloodied and triumphant. Do you love me now, Gavin?

'Madam? Are you quite well? We've arrived in London.'

Blinking groggily, I strain through a slowly lifting sleep fugue to stare at the young woman hovering over me in my berth. Her dark eyes are wide with concern; her neat brown bob is held back by a girlish tortoiseshell clip. The rosy apples of her cheeks are ripe with youth. She cannot be,

273

although my blurry vision and desperate heart tell me that she is. '*Anna?*'

'Alice, Madam.' I blink repeatedly. The young woman steps back in embarrassment. Her trolley cart of teacups jingles.

'I'm sorry.' Although I have made worse mistakes in my life. 'I'm … I'm fine. Thank you.' Relieved, the girl smiles sweetly before taking her leave, crockery clinking softly as she goes. With a grimace and a groan, I untwist my neck from the knotted, awkward angle at which I must unexpectedly have slept. My left hand feels numb, unusable until I look down to find Mij's 'dog' ticket crinkled inside my fist. I lay it on my knees to refold as neatly as I can, slotting it into the breast pocket of my coat so that, when dressed, I will be carrying it beside my heart. Then I reach for my bag. For Mij's belongings too. Soon, I step from the train alone.

*

It is a month before Gavin returns to Paultons. I realise when he does that a secret, unspoken part of me had feared he never would. From the upstairs flat, I hear the Maserati engine – even its monstrous screech seems subdued these days – and hurry to the window like I used to do, back when this whole house was mine and Gavin's roaring, high-rev visits were the only thing to rouse the quiet street into fresh life. From above, he appears to be shuffling, making his way to our shared door with movements stilted and unnaturally slow. The distance is short, only a few feet from the kerb, but at one point, Gavin pauses, resting a thin, steadying hand on the black iron railings that guard the terrace. I see his narrow fingers clench the metal struts as if borrowing from their firmness to stay upright. His breathing looks laboured, the effort emotional rather than physical. I understand. Perhaps I am the only other person who can.

As if hearing my thoughts, Gavin glances up. Our eyes meet. He lifts his hand from the railings and gives me a small, muted wave. I return it with my own, handprint squeaking when I press it to the glass. I look down at him looking up at me, and suddenly my tears flow again: fat droplets surging over my raw, stinging rims and beginning to stream over my face until I am forced to turn away.

'I'm so sorry. I'm so, so sorry.' I murmur the mantra around which this awful new life of mine seems to revolve. Gavin can no longer see me, let alone hear me, but even after the sound of our front door softly closing, I find myself rooted to the spot. A thwarted nurturing instinct pulses painfully in my breast, intuitive and no less acute than in our early days when a beautiful, broken boy appeared in that very doorway in need of the sustenance it seemed only I could give. But now I am the cause, not the consolation of Gavin's suffering. His help cannot come from me. Can it? Locked into an inescapable cycle of cowardice, I repeatedly cross the room only to retreat, tapping out an odd rhythm of ambivalent footsteps that will surely puzzle him from below.

'I didn't think you were coming,' Gavin observes flatly when I finally make it down to his half, having shakily composed myself with a series of cold-water splashes to the face. With a lacklustre head tilt, he invites me into the room that used to be mine. Gavin already has a glass in his hand; another nod tells me to take my own.

'Writing,' I say. An excuse, fictive or otherwise, we have both used often enough with others. Crossing the room, I pour myself a water, holding back on the whisky with which Gavin has mixed his equivalent. 'What was Canna like?'

'It must be the greenest island I've ever seen in the Highlands,' he observes. 'Lush. Leafy. And one can count the humans on a hand. It might almost be a land out of a fairy-tale.' The faintest glimmer of his old enthusiasm becomes visible in Gavin's expression, momentarily reconjuring the magic of that part of the world he loves. Occasionally, for the sparky vagaries of our electrifying mental connection were never truly under my control, I can still see things through his eyes. For a heartbeat or two, I am no longer trapped in London; I am on that verdant, naturally vibrant little island with Gavin at my side.

'I think Compass Hill would appeal to you, Kathleen,' he goes on. The admirable effort to remain upbeat touches my shattered heart. 'You can see tiny dents in the turf where it's been nibbled short by the wild rabbits.'

'Why is it called Compass Hill?' I try to follow Gavin's lead, keeping the tone of our conversation light and curious, yet I fear my attempt at Canna chitchat falls flat. Still, ever the gentleman, Gavin sustains our stilted momentum.

'Well, it's made of tuff – no, not turf, *tuff* – a type of rock composed of volcanic ash.' I nod along numbly. What is one more detail of this life that I will never understand? 'It's called Compass Hill because of the iron content. The level is so high that it distorts the compasses of passing ships, pointing them to the hill instead of true north.' Mimicking a magnetised needle, Gavin swings his index finger from my direction to his. 'And of course ...' A more elaborate explanation of geological intricacies ensues, my brain too broken down by misery to follow. Talk of compasses makes me think of the scratched implement still resting on Gavin's Sandaig bookshelf; of me reorienting myself so I could childishly face where I believed he was. And as for north itself? Now, north points to danger. Disaster. The direction I went with Mij, only to return alone.

'Kathleen?'

'I'm sorry.' When I came downstairs, I had the sense to secrete a handkerchief up my sleeve: one of Gavin's, given and not returned after his cow-on-the-stairs Sandaig story made me weep with laughter long ago. I bury my nose in it, permitting myself what I hope is a discreet blow. Compressing the cotton between my knuckles with pressure hard enough to stop hypothetical bleeding, I grit my teeth against another breakdown. 'Keep going. Please, Gavin.'

Eider ducks. It transpires he was talking about eider ducks. 'Striking plumage,' he informs me, and I nod again. Why not? 'Although there are fewer breeding pairs in Britain these days. Did you know it's the fastest flier of its kind in Britain?' I did not. Gavin sighs, oddly wistful, as if willing his imagination to be carried off on those powerful wings. 'Perhaps I should start a colony of them.'

'On Canna?' My fingers worry at a small hole in the worn-out handkerchief fabric. Without Mij, without the animal who made his world there complete, will Gavin want to leave Sandaig?

'No …' he replies pensively. 'Not Canna. I haven't come up with the right place yet.' The unnerving sensation I had on Sandaig shore ripples through me once again. Gavin is still only feet from me at the other end of my – of his – living room, but suddenly he might be many miles away. A passing cloud too high to reach, cirrocumulus wisps scattered like white cotton fragments across our slate-grey London skies. A distant star beyond my sphere, orbiting intangible seas of time and space into which my lowly spirit cannot penetrate. Like a child escaping into fantasy, Gavin seems to find solace in revisiting the high-flying dreams of his youth: rebecoming the golden boy of Monreith who believed that all would be well in the world if he could only own a goose from each species within it. Strangest of all? I believe him too. If one day, Gavin chooses to turn the spotlight of his brilliance on creating an eider duck colony, there is no doubt in my mind that he will achieve it.

'The water's remarkably clear around Canna harbour,' he tells me thoughtfully. 'Almost like Sandaig …' As if caught on a receding tide, his words drift into silence. Neither of us can think of that water without our souls crying out for Mij.

'What's water but the generated soul?' asked Yeats, whose *Wild Swans at Coole* once moved Gavin's heart so profoundly. Moved it towards me, or so I thought at the time. I recall falling for him as the autumn leaves fell from the trees, warm glints of amber and gold mingling momentarily in the air before settling in a swirl about our feet. But Mij is not in motion now. There is no life force where his kinetic vitality once was. Opaque navy shadows are once again nestling beneath Gavin's blue eyes; his attenuated limbs look ready to snap like spindling winter branches. His gaunt cheekbones have their own shadows and the weight has fallen from his lissom frame, as it always does in times of trouble. Half the man, in every sense, he was before losing our waterbaby.

I lost a baby once before. *Words matter, Kathleen, and so does the truth.* I chose to lose what would have become a baby. It happened while I was with Hugh, still a girl when we wed until the short, sharp shock of what they euphemistically call 'womanhood' shattered my innocence: deflowering and destroying the embryonic hopes I nurtured for a simple scholarly life as a poetess. I thought Hugh believed in my work. I trusted him when he said that was why he wanted to marry me. I reminded myself of it prior to our pathetic excuse for a wedding service: Hugh had read what I had to say and glimpsed something within my words that made it worth helping his fortuneless friend to stay on at Cambridge. Poor, gullible little Kathie. What he really wanted from me had nothing to do with poetry. At least, not my kind of poetry. Legally, I learned too late, a wife has no right to refuse her husband.

Only a girl, then, but the woman in me knew what must be done, whatever the cost and whatever the risk. Gavin is not the only one of us who has broken the law. I travelled alone, as so many women must have done before me, to the place a few of my more worldly collegemates had spoken of in hushed tones. I never felt lonelier, then unable to guess at the sheer number of us who must have trodden the same path in unsought sisterhood. Traipsing up and down those unfamiliar, unclean pavements, maintaining the wide-eyed pretence of looking for nothing in particular; staring blindly out of fogged-up train carriage windows, their grimy opacity offering no view of our once bright futures. I doubted myself all the way. Never that the decision was wrong – on that point, I was sure – but whether it was folly to be taking the risk. Yet how could I attempt it at home? Novels had only taught me so much. A hot bath and large gin were impossible with Hugh prowling outside the door, knocking as the mood took him to be let in and exercise his 'right to watch his wife' while she bathed. A knitting needle? I dared to dip into a run-down haberdashery after checking what little was left in my purse, the brassy shop bell ringing out my shame to the street beyond. Picking up a single '14', I stared at its sharp tip until my eyeballs quivered. A jolly sales assistant approached.

'My word, you must be working in a fine gauge. They snap so easily, don't they?' I knew the feeling.

The address to which I had no choice left but to go was hidden between the pages of the book I had brought with me. Stupid Kathie. This was no hairdresser's waiting room. Indeed, it turned out to be no obvious room at all: I had to enter from a side street, climbing a steep, unlit staircase up from an insalubrious doorway whose smells and stains combined with my hormonally heightened senses to make me retch. Reaching the right number, I knocked. Waited. Several long minutes passed, with me fighting the impulse to run. Where to? Then a man let me in. I am not tempted to call him a doctor. I am certain that he wasn't one. The fewer people who knew the better, he said, once the door had shut behind me. It meant there was no one to hold my hand.

I returned by train, tearful and trembling as I slipped into my seat, arms folded tight across my already spasming abdomen. The sooner I left, the man said, the safer it was, but inside it felt like something was not going but still coming. The dark rumble of storm clouds was brewing below my navel, earthy discomfort turned hellish and pitch black. Appropriate when I was, according to all that George Raine had ever taught me, destined irredeemably for Hell. The train groaned as we pulled away from the terminal and I felt the same grinding ache from within. Some intricate system of tracks laid out inside me was being wrenched from my innards in a twist, the pressure gathering pace as an unseen tonne weight was transported, trundling rapidly downhill in a blur of hot steam and sharp-edged steel.

At the next stop, I took refuge in the station tearoom. Hands shaking, I splashed water on my ashen face in the lavatory, but I was too afraid to enter a cubicle and check what had or had yet to happen. Walking out, I managed only a step or two before fainting. My weak legs buckled; my skinny arms flailed. I brought the nearest table down with me in a violent crash of shattering china that sounded so strangely distant to my ears it might have been a mild commotion on the opposite platform. The hazy, discordant clatter of broken teacups and jingled cutlery dimmed into insignificance as, barely conscious on the floor, I sensed a pulsing outpour of blood between my legs. All women grow familiar with that warm sticky flow, but this was a torrent compared with a trickle. 'Every Female is a golden loom,' I later learned from William Blake. Back then, all I knew was that I was unravelling: furling out and fading away into tattered ribbons of blood.

'Help! Somebody, help!' Were those my cries or someone else's? I couldn't tell. A kind stranger came from behind to elevate my shoulders, offering me sips of water that I failed to swallow. Looking down, I saw a pool of dark crimson blooming rapidly across my skirt. Reaching feebly towards it, I caught the yellow glint of my wedding ring. Much as I had come to detest it, that thin band of gold was going to save me one last time.

'Poor young wife,' declared the voice of the invisible stranger at my back before I plunged into unconsciousness. 'Must be a miscarriage.' From time to time, I still think of her: the mysterious woman whose face I never had the chance to see. Likely she had no idea what I had done and would have been horrified if she realised. Or maybe, just maybe, she understood in an instant. Offering a decoy that I doubt I deserved.

The nursing home knew. As soon as they examined me. Whatever ugly cuts had been made on the inside could not be disguised by pretty words on the surface. No one spoke to me about the matter directly, of course. The cold tea and absence of painkillers more than communicated how they felt. That was the time I was in hospital. A time that, until Mij died, I had promised myself I would never think of again. I wrote to Charles, not Hugh, from my hard-mattress hospital bed. Begging a boy I barely knew for rescue. And to his credit, Charles rose to the call of those shakily pencilled little notes, taking me away from what I no longer had it in me to withstand. Soon after, too soon, I found out that I was expecting Anna, and I knew with unwavering conviction that I could not go through such a thing again.

Gavin is the sole person on earth I have told about the abortion. Not that I was seeking a confessional: whatever else he thinks of me now, it could hardly be enhanced by such an admission. But that time at Sandaig, so briefly yet memorably together, when I remarked on how the house wore its secretiveness, something in his beautiful face, or perhaps the beauty of the place itself, made me confide that my first child was not my first pregnancy.

'I'm outside of God's grace forever,' I had muttered at the end, wrapping my arms around my stomach as if that acute girlhood pain was still real.

'No,' said Gavin. Quiet but emphatic. 'God is Love, Kathleen. I'll always believe that.' I wish he would listen to himself more often. That night at Sandaig, alone together, Gavin had shared something with me in return. Something an adult did to him at a farm just outside Elrig, when he was only a boy and had accidentally explored too far. He was six. Five or six, he said. It was unspeakable, yet he did speak of it to me.

'I push it down, but it resurges.' He made it sound like a recurring illness. I think for him, it is. 'It shatters me when it does.' Perhaps I should have known then we are both too broken to ever make each other whole.

Now, I refocus on the Paultons living room to find Gavin cradling his head in his hands. There is no sound, but his shoulders shudder softly, meek ripples shimmying across the bones of his back until they quiver through his shirt like rose petals shaken by a downpour. I rise, unsure even as I begin to move whether I should cross the room to comfort him or leave to let him mourn in peace. Before I can decide, Gavin reaches out.

'Stay.' Slim fingers encircle my wrist. 'Stay with me tonight, Kathleen. Like you did after Jonnie.'

'No.' The word jars. It sounds stark and unpractised, the plucked string of an instrument left too long out of tune. I realise how seldom I say it to Gavin. He looks up at me, the vulnerability of raw surprise visible within his watery blue eyes. Then he remembers himself. His defences rise; a psychic drawbridge lowers. Our gaze breaks and in silence, the movement almost casual were it not for the choked sniff that accompanies it, Gavin lets go of my wrist. My skin tingles from the absence as if not yet ready to lose his touch. *Why say no?* it demands of me, and indeed, an unquiet part of my mind is asking it too. How can I refuse him after all the hurt I have caused? Why not give Gavin the one thing he asks me for; why strike another pickaxe into the heart I still love with all of my own? 'I can't bear it,' I whisper truthfully. Stoic though I try to be, and stubborn as I know I am (Gavin surely knows it too), I fear further pain will destroy me beyond salvation. And when I think of our night together, it is the pain that I remember. 'I'm sorry,' I murmur to Gavin, my own tears muffling the words. I go back upstairs alone.

Chapter Thirty-Three

We live in the same house yet I hardly see him. More than a single floor divides us now. Our shared grief has splintered in two what might have been our final bond, becoming the reason why, it seems, we must inevitably break apart. My reaction when Gavin first arrived back at Paultons was a warning: to see him is to weep, often hard and uncontrollably, and he in turn appears repulsed by the wild indignity of my distress. 'Vulgar,' I suspect Lady Mary would call it. My crass, ill-disciplined peasant ancestry betraying me once again. Perversely, knowing how much Gavin hates it when I cry makes the task of stemming the flow nigh on impossible. Fat, glossy bubbles spill from my nostrils each time I look into his face, tacky liquid streaming until I taste the sharp, salted tinge of my tears. I cannot control the outbursts any more than Gavin can control his revulsion at them.

'Enough now Kathleen,' he always says after a while. 'That's enough.' Can't he see it will never be enough? I could cry the ocean dry and it would not bring back Mij. Gavin understands that deep down. I know he does. He doesn't realise I can hear him downstairs when he himself cries alone in the dark.

Our half-lives at Paultons limp on, in tandem if not together. The reason for sharing this house in the first place was so we could share Mij along with it. Without our otter at its heart, the entire terrace feels askew. Arrhythmic. The building might be resting at a slant, sinking into subsidence or tipped by the pressure of old, decaying roots that are choking it from the foundations up. I never look at the pear tree now. Gavin can chop it down for all I care. I see only absence within its presence: Mij no longer rippling over its roots and Gavin's arm not quite around me on the first occasion we met.

It is six weeks after Mij's death when I realise I have not menstruated. Valiantly misguided, my body tries to trick itself into believing the past is still present, moving through the phantom motions of monthly discomfort like water swelling and malingering headaches. The same sinister anxiety

281

as always returns to haunt me through the long, lonely nights. *Why bother?* I want to ask it. *What's left to worry about?* But the storm never breaks. The blood never flows. My riverbed is dry, inner deltas cracked and turned to dust. I am waning without waxing; a phase is passed and no other will begin. Who knows whether the cause is age or distress, or some complex interaction of the two? All I am certain of, if I ever dared to hope otherwise, is that Gavin and I will never have a child. Yet in a way, we did have one, didn't we? Our spiritual child, the otter in whose heart we met, Mij's miraculous little body imbued with all the glittering vitality of the waterfall and the wise, eternal energy of Sandaig's shells. He was our treasured animal offspring. And he died because of my mistakes.

My friend Gay telephones and, in a less melancholic mood, I might appreciate the irony of a psychic ringing up unexpectedly. I take the chance to call again on her astrological wisdom. She tries to comfort me with assurances that Mij's soul is at peace.

'I believe you,' I reply. It is my soul in torment.

'I see a journey across an ocean for you,' Gay offers unprompted. But I cannot bear to think of the ocean, so I simply thank her and hang up.

Whenever I do see Gavin, steeling myself before I go downstairs so as not to snivel excessively, he is writing. My own words obstinately refuse to emerge, recalcitrant and uncooperative when I try to force them out onto the page. Yet each time I go through Gavin's flat, I catch sight of him scribbling avidly: fountain pen in his right hand, cigarette in his left. I do not know what he is working on. He does not say, and soon I find I am afraid to ask. Not *Otter Nonsense* surely? There is no playful happy ending to Mij's story now. On the rare occasions we do speak at length, Gavin brings up the odd, amorphous idea of a trip to Sicily. Could that be what his new book is about? Whenever the subject is raised, he tells me about a great-great-great aunt who ran off to get married on the island, a strange story with straggling ends that never tie up neatly. It is not the whole truth. That much I can tell. The mystery makes me wonder who really did put the notion to travel there in his head.

Irrespective of subject, when not writing, Gavin paces the floorboards hard. From above, I hear his agitated footsteps as he roams from room to room, seemingly in restless search of something that can never be found. At odd hours, that nervily unsettled energy carries him right out of Paultons and into the impersonal throng of the city. The front door slams and I resist the urge to watch him walk away, pointedly averting my thoughts from where or to whom he may be going. *Write*, I instruct myself fiercely every time I hear him leave. At best, a few underwhelming lines of verse that I cannot in good conscience call proper poetry stutter out onto my page. Once, I was attuned to the subtle timbre of words, hearing pricked to pick out their wind-soft whispers confiding in me how they wished their stories to be told. Now, my ears are preoccupied with listening for Gavin's return.

*

'Harrods.' An answer at last, and not just to where he's been. Where *she's* from. 'Kathleen – Kiko.' Blue eyes sparkling again and almost feverishly bright, Gavin beckons me downstairs to my – I mean, his – living room, introducing the creature he proudly calls his 'new arrival'. Dangling upside-down from the curtain pole, the animal's lurid orange eyes look out unblinking from an impassive, pale fur face. 'Incredible, isn't she?' Gavin takes a step nearer. Kiko's pumpkin irises swivel suspiciously. 'A ring-tailed lemur, right here in London!' The creature's dexterous grey paws, embedded with sharp black claws, allow her to cling suspended from the pelmet despite her not insignificant size. Her head is pure white except for eye sockets rimmed in panda-style black and a dark pointed nose: nostrils flared, apparently by design, in a way that appears perpetually angered. 'It turns out they have an exotic pet hall. Can you believe it?'

I cannot. 'How much was she?' Expensive as anything else in Harrods, I shouldn't wonder. Gavin mumbles a figure, deliberately disguised by a low tone and muffled lip movements. 'Sorry?'

Even his second reply is *sotto voce*. 'Seventy-five.'

'Pounds?' The fact I have not yet seen a penny of Gavin's rent for the downstairs flat, never asked for by me yet still loudly promised by him, flits into my mind before I can stop it. As does the knowledge that, at the exceedingly generous rate I had mentally calculated, Seventy-five pounds would cover three months.

In the end, however, Kiko and very nearly Gavin lasts only three more days. Alerted by an almighty crash that shakes our shared house, I return downstairs to follow a grisly trail of port-coloured footprints to my – his – bathroom. I find Gavin trouserless, sitting on the bath's rim with his belt squeezed tourniquet-tight around a blood-soaked upper thigh. Smoking a cigarette, naturally. Several aspects of the scene might have, in other circumstances, sprung straight from the pages of my unwritten fantasies.

It has been years since I saw Gavin in only his briefs. Yet even for me, the splashes of arterial red streaked over his skin are unerotic in the extreme. Nor have I escaped the bloody disaster myself, I realise too late, looking down to find my thin-stockinged toes dipped in a squelching pool of my beloved's life force. At the sight, my shaky legs finally give way. I cling to the sink and inhale through my nose to suppress a retch. Calmly, Gavin stretches over to offer me his cigarette.

'Kiko's moved out,' he announces as I take a slow, steadying drag. 'Bloody Harrods.'

The vicious acquisition is donated to London Zoo whilst remaining officially under Gavin's ownership. Why he would wish to stay tied to a creature that hurt him so badly, I am sure I will never understand. In the lemur's stead, having evidently opted for exchange rather than refund, he brings home a bush baby, the most peculiar bug-eyed being I have ever encountered. This new addition has the face of a bat-mouse hybrid, with flapping translucent ears far larger than the tiny skull from which they protrude. A squirrel in colour; a rat in size. *Just what London needs more of*, I think uncharitably as the miniature monkey scurries up my sleeve, back hunched like a Grimm fairy-tale gremlin. Unromantically, her hobby proves to be what Gavin coyly calls 'solitary and embarrassing', grinding herself against his smallest sofa cushion.

'There must be something wrong with her,' he declares in dismay, more flustered than I have seen him in quite some time after having prized the poor thing off the soft furnishings. 'Surely it isn't natural for females to feel such urges?' I do not answer.

Grudgingly, Gavin comes to accept Mij's exceptionality and that, as a rule, London is not conducive to the keeping of wild creatures. Yet rather than abandon the idea of such companionship or settle for something appropriately prosaic like a cat, he decides the solution to his ongoing angst will be found in feathers, not fur. Gavin duly appears with a baker's dozen of tropical birds and starts turning the long, narrow living room of the downstairs flat into an improvised aviary. I am invited down again to watch them at airborne play, silvery singsong voices filling the air like little bells as they dart from bookshelf perch to perch with fluttering glints of jewel-tone plumage. When all thirteen are in motion, some so dainty and trinket-sized they float like dropped leaves or down escaped from a pillow, it feels hard to conceive of each being a distinct creature in its own right. These birds belong *en masse*, a collective consciousness compelled into flight just like the elvers in their glittering multitudes were moved to scale the towering heights of the Sandaig waterfall. Truly, no one could be trying harder than Gavin to recapture the magic of our old paradise.

He has the living room repapered in black, then adds spotlights – a distractingly heavy-hammer business for me in the flat above – so the birds' vibrant shades will be illuminated more vividly. Gavin hangs fruit for them on sticks affixed to his highest pieces of furniture, jutting out at odd angles to form aesthetically pleasing perches. As dusk sets, his feathered friends are at their most animated and, when invited, I sit with him to watch their shimmering shades catch the artificial light.

'Have you ever seen such a spectacle?' Gavin asks me urgently, as if trying to convince himself. Our chairs are in shadow, the dark wallpaper impractical for writing or even reading. Perhaps after working at such furious intensity, Gavin likes being forced to take a break. The slackening muscles of my own dominant hand cramp at the thought, a touched-nerve twitch of insecurity as if subconsciously clutching an invisible pen. Still, the birds are exquisitely pretty, their bright carnival colours sparkling like hints of treasure hidden deep inside a dark storybook cave. We can look, but rarely touch, which I suppose is the case for most precious things in life. And yet watching them, or more precisely, watching Gavin watching them, drags my mood as low and close to melancholy as this inadequate lighting is to darkness. It was never this much effort before. *I have seen a spectacle,* I want to remind Gavin, *and it was effortless*; a triumph of truth and unconscious beauty each time Mij entered the water and swam with the fluid, elemental virtuosity of his birthright. That spiritual simplicity cannot be resurrected with shop-bought birds and decorative tricks.

It would be cruel to say so, but this expensive stage set feels as tragically unconvincing as the last scene of *Death in Venice*. I did eventually read the book, having recklessly decided late last summer I had nothing left to lose. How little I knew. Shortly before his demise, the tortured protagonist paints his face in garish pancake makeup: a pitiful, futile attempt to recapture the promise of his youth. That scene, agonising and elegiac, is what these birds really remind me of. Well, that and Oscar Wilde, who I have read decorated his ceiling with a pattern of peacock feathers. Reputed to bring bad luck, according to certain beliefs. I suspect poor Oscar believed it too, in the end.

Chapter Thirty-Four

'Fine,' I inform my reflection, speaking aloud in an effort to believe it. 'You look fine.' Gaze fixed on my face in the mirror, I cup my hands beneath my chin and pull, contemplating with something close to dismay where my jawline used to sit. Moving up, I drag the tissue-thin skin around my eyes towards my ears, elevating my brows from where they have sunken slightly over the sockets. I try to blink. My eyelids half-flutter impotently. I let go and watch my middle-aged face fall back into place. 'Fine,' I repeat a little louder, as if my ageing reflection is also hard of hearing.

I have had little time for my mirrored self of late, too overwhelmed by grief and guilt to heed my appearance or, indeed, to want to look myself in the eye. Anyway, what sort of poetess allows herself to be distracted by the vagaries of shallow vanity? Too late, I realise that the weight of sadness bearing down on me during these last few wretched months has taken a heavy physical toll. The relentless stream of tears has carved stinging grooves in the corners of my puffy eyes; a few ugly, clumpish gaps have been left where my war-torn eyelashes admitted defeat and broke away. Would lipstick improve things? I try a swipe from an old, little-used tube, but the unpractised application is too heavy. Disappointed, I watch the berry red shade seep into tiny, dry cracks on my long-unattended lips. I blot twice, then reach for my handkerchief to remove it altogether. It seems unbecoming to look like I am trying to be kissed.

'What happened to the beautiful bluestocking?' I ask the wan woman peering back at me. My clothes do little to enhance me either. Full skirts are the fashion, according to what I see at Girton, yet mine have stayed straight. Plain. Pencil-cut and frumpy, falling to an awkward length around my lower calves that befits an academic, born-again spinster. The jacket on top does have a smockish, swinging aspect to it, cut in a vaguely artistic style that Winifred would pull off with aplomb and pretty Thetis would turn heads in, should she wish to. But I fear I do neither. My figure has slumped. Not fat exactly, for I have had no appetite since what happened to Mij, but nonetheless succumbing to an unattractive laxity of posture, defeatism and resignation built right into my tired bones. My body has carried the habit of unhappiness for so long, I can scarcely recall how to hold it another way.

I am not the only one getting older, of course. But why does Gavin wear his age so much more attractively than I do? When he is low, the tender fine lines of his careworn face appear only to ask for comfort. When he is serious, his heavy lids seem thoughtful and sage, yet never severe. And when he flashes the occasional smile or lets escape a note or two of that melodic, lilting laugh … I cannot imagine Gavin ever growing old in my eyes.

It is thanks to him that I am in this position, dragged out of my increasingly hermetic existence and forced to cobble together a look fit for company. We are dining tonight at The Buttery, the lauded and glamorous restaurant of the Berkeley Hotel where, needless to say, I have never been before. It was something of a surprise when Gavin selected it, no less than the fact he had invited me at all.

'It'll do us both good to get out,' he insisted, the defensively emphatic tone offering no opportunity for dissent. In truth, I suspect this dinner was booked as a treat to himself, an occasion to look forward to after enduring a day in the literal bosom of his mother's stifling embrace. Gavin's trip to Monreith is also my fault, or at least the result of my request. Finally, the rent for the downstairs flat is being paid, yet, rather surreally, the transactions appear to involve neither Gavin nor myself. When the cheques began to arrive, they were signed not with his intense inky signature but Lady Mary's thin, quill-like swirl. Reluctant to rock the Sea Leopard, I chose not to concern myself with why an author in his forties still requires his mother to pay his rent. What did concern me, however, was that the cheques were not made out to Miss Kathleen Raine. They came to Mr James Madge.

'Why would she send them to my son rather than me?' I had demanded of Gavin, out of my depth yet again with the illogical intricacies of upper-class etiquette.

'I suppose it's how she thinks things should be done.' He accompanied the lacklustre explanation with a shrug, keeping his eyes on the living room birds as if the whole matter had very little to do with him. But how exactly does Lady Mary think things should be done? Leaving delicate, feminine flowers to wither away in affected helplessness while their closest male relatives deal with everything on their behalf except, it seems, actually paying for themselves? Yet I could hardly think that Mary, of all people, disapproved of women taking control. The problem seemed more likely to be me and her barely disguised desire to cut me out of Gavin's business. Indeed, I suspect she would cut me out of his life altogether, if she could only find a knife sharp enough.

'But it's ridiculous.' Feeling increasingly petulant, I had kept up my complaints while Gavin did his level best to ignore me, pointedly preferring to watch his birds swoop and soar. 'Gavin!'

'I'll speak to Mother about it soon.' He groaned heavily, stretching his arms in the hope that a bird might alight on his fingertips.

'When?' I said it too harshly, the grating tone nearer to a nag than I intended. A bird that had come close flitted away without landing.

Gavin frowned. 'I said soon.' We fell into silence, save for the unpleasant sound of my shrill voice revolving around my head. Enjoying none of the perks associated with being a wife, I fall victim to a surprisingly high number of the perils.

Today, true to his word, Gavin has been speaking to his mother. And after a long afternoon of her oppressive and cloying affections, plus an accelerated drive home that would take a lesser mortal two days to complete, he will have earned his lavish dinner, along with however many whiskies he wishes to wash it down with. *He is right*, I think as I take a step back from studying my reflection, noting sadly how the distance improves it. *It will be good for us both to get out.* My mental picture of us striding down the Square side by side, toasting one another's health in the rippling glow of restaurant candlelight, evokes memories of pleasure long repressed yet not forgotten. Something deep within me stirs, like a familiar song played for an amnesiac or perhaps the gentle stippling of raindrops on parched desert ground. I move to my dressing table. Well, to my writing table, which has an old jewellery box tucked in the far corner. Reaching inside, I pick out the pearl necklace I wore to Sorbo's when Gavin and I first dined together. The cool, creamy pearls roll between my fingertips. I close my eyes and see those sky-blue eyes from years ago, darting to where this strand sat serenely across my collarbones. I fasten it. For the first time tonight, I smile at myself in the mirror. Checking the clock, I realise without surprise that Gavin is late. How Lady Mary hates to let go once she has dug in her claws. I perch on the edge of my bed to wait. To remember.

From his footsteps alone, I can tell he is drunk. The front door slams, a thick whack of wood that reverberates with a stiff metallic creak, evoking the manner of a dramatic grand entrance, albeit one quite literally unhinged. In the aftermath, there is a moment's quiet, then I hear Gavin stumble over the threshold, cursing it for having apparently moved just to spite him. Unnaturally heavy, his feet thud and thump in the discordant pattern of a rogue, off-rhythm drumbeat. One, Two, Two. Two, One, One. My pulse quickens in response. I have never heard, let alone seen, Gavin this far gone before, despite the sheer waterfalls of whisky I have known him to consume. My mind spins to think just how much he must have had. From the downstairs din, it seems his feet are moving faster than his befuddled brain can keep up with. Did he drive down from Scotland in such a state? My distress is momentarily suspended by relief he is alive at all.

'Kathleen!' Gavin shouts up the stairs, not bothering to ascend them or perhaps doubtful whether he could manage in his condition. He is not slurring, but nor is he far from it. That gentle voice I adore, airily spun from the ancient melodies of the north, sounds hoarse. Coarse. Strained. 'Kathleen, are you ready?'

Don't answer, my horrified reflection cautions me. *Let him think you gave up and left.* I know us well enough by now to understand that little good is likely to come from our being in each other's company like this. Me at my most melancholic and insecure; Gavin exhausted, drained and increasingly uninhibited. Even with total sobriety, it has been a long time since we brought out the best in one another. In the mirror, I see that my hand has shot up to grasp the necklace, clutching my pearls like an appalled elderly matron. Further bumps, followed by profanities, resound from below.

'Kath-leen!' This time Gavin calls with a coaxing, teasing tone, echoing his fruitless efforts to entice Kiko. It sounds singsong, a jokey yodel I would be tempted to call playful if we were both willing participants in the game. 'Where are you, Kath-leen?'

Don't answer. 'I'm coming.' *I can't let him down again*, I sheepishly remind my reflection. With one last, underwhelmed glance at the worried Kathleen in the mirror, I go downstairs.

'Finally.' The fog of alcohol lends my eventual emergence an element of genuine surprise for Gavin, having evidently forgotten the layout of his own house (technically, our house). From the landing we share, I understand why his clumsy feet are causing such an ungodly racket. Kilt shoes. To match his kilt, of course. Leaning lopsided against the bannister, he stands in the green-gold plaid that has so often mesmerised me, topped off with his thin white shirt. The cuffs are rolled more unevenly than usual; the fabric more creased and dishevelled. No sign of his jacket. It might be in the car or, for all I know, forgotten in Scotland. With every stumbling step Gavin takes, his leaden soles strike against our old, ill-used floorboards, intricate crisscrossed laces still miraculously woven over his shins. How in Heaven's name are they intact? An unsavoury image of Mary tying her son's laces before he left looms large in my imagination.

'Are you wearing that to the restaurant?' I ask unhappily, feeling dowdier than ever when faced with his handsome Highland dress. Infuriatingly, the roguish informality of Gavin's tipsy untidiness serves only to make him more dashing. How many times has he, brimming with boyish excitement, shown me an illustration like this in one of his ornithology books: a lavishly coloured male specimen accompanied by his smaller, duller female mate? Even the female blackbird is brown. If the roles were reversed, I suspect we would remark upon the fact that the female brownbird is black. Gavin gives no direct reply to my question, only raising a fair eyebrow as if in quid pro quo appraisal of my appearance. The scrutiny is blunted by the fact that his gaze remains slightly unsteady. Still, when his eyes coast over the pearls, my heart flips. Gavin shows no recognition.

'Ready when you are,' he asserts in a testing, adolescent tone of defiance. 'Unless you'd care to join me in one for the road?' Incredulous, I watch him produce a new drink as if by sleight of hand: a leather-bound hip flask emerging from his sporran. Was it pilfered from Monreith today? *Don't be common, Kathleen*, a vicious mental voice lambasts me, *it is not stealing from his own estate.* Although technically, as the eldest surviving male, the Maxwell lands and everything on them belong to Aymer, not Gavin.

The dukedom's youngest son, the heir without an inheritance, drinks deeply from his flask, free hand clenching the bannister to steady himself against the thirsty, swigging momentum. Resurfacing with a theatrical lip smack of satisfaction, he offers it to me. I decline. Gavin shrugs, pressing the flask to his lips for several long seconds more, then frowns as he gives the vessel a vigorous, searching shake to confirm it is now empty.

'Shall we?' With a grandiose gentlemanly flourish, he offers me his elbow. Stomach churning, I accept it. Thus linked together, we step outside, although not before I have surreptitiously swiped his car key into my pocket. Gavin has diced with death enough for one day and The Buttery is just near enough for us to walk. I must be careful for both of us tonight. Otherwise I fear someone will get hurt.

Chapter Thirty-Five

Improbably, that last drink combines with the fresh air to sharpen Gavin's senses, at least short-term. Focus newly intensified, he glances around us while we walk, appreciative and perhaps subconsciously soothed by the stillness of the Square's evening atmosphere. Yes, he is leaning heavily on me, my right shoulder giving tiny spasms of resistance as it struggles to withstand the sloping weight of his left. But I cannot pretend to hate the sensation. My heart aches to take care of him, a primal impulse that even the full force of my intellect cannot resist, and the vulnerability of overindulgence renders him briefly open to receiving what I have to give. If Gavin cannot want me, then him needing me must be my consolation. Dusk lies suspended over the city, London poised on the fragile cusp between sunset and nightfall as if the atmosphere is holding its breath. *If we could stay like this*, I think as we walk with our arms entwined, *I might almost believe I could be happy again.*

'How is …' I mean to ask after Mary. Yet even after years of tangential acquaintance, her title eludes any attempt at informality, smothering my efforts like the trailing ivy tendrils that leave Monreith House in perpetual shadow. 'How is your mother?'

Gavin stares down the road. 'She's been unwell recently.'

'Oh no,' I say, as sincerely as my conscience will allow. 'I hope it's nothing serious.'

Gavin goes to reply, then changes his mind, or else the encroaching mist of intoxication means that he can no longer find the right words. I search on his behalf, drawing not from any sparky psychic residue between us but from what I believe I can now understand of his behaviour this evening. His inebriated state suddenly makes sense. Whatever Mary said, it must have left him badly shaken. And without Mij, it is to drink, even more so than to writing, that Gavin now turns when he needs to absent himself from emotions too agonizing to endure. 'Shall we go back?' With bad news on his mind, he is surely in no real mood for celebration or company. 'If you'd rather stay home …'

292

'No.' That teenage tone returns, stubbornness tensing the lean muscles of his forearm linked with mine. 'I want to go out.' My own wants seem better left unspoken. And yet I do want to know more. After all, if Mary is seriously ill – with guilt, I spot the conditionality already creeping into my thinking – wouldn't Aymer have told Gavin? Or if not his eldest brother then surely their sister Christian? And as for Eustace … well, the middle Maxwell son is hardly the type to keep news, good or bad, to himself.

'We spoke about you,' Gavin says suddenly.

'That's nice.' The brief silence that follows suggests otherwise. Gavin shifts his weight when we turn another corner and my arm slides, elbow unlocking from his. Fingers numb, I wriggle and clench in an effort to restore sensation.

'We also talked about Mij.' Gavin is no longer looking at me, driven by the urgent impulse to pluck at a shrivelled, sunburnt leaf from a passing hedge. 'Mother hadn't heard about what happened to him.' Now I am glad we are no longer touching. I would rather bear this shame alone. The thought of the whole awful story travelling the length of the country, Monreith abuzz with gossip about my mistakes and the high price we have paid for them, makes my cheeks burn as I hang my head.

'I ought to see Mother more often.' Abruptly, Gavin reproaches himself. 'The blood is thicker than the water.' Not an idiom I have heard him use before. Biblical, of course – thank you, Father – in its full formal phrasing. His tone rueful and ruminative, the sentence hits my ear strangely, jarring like a jumped-over note or misplaced piano key. Originating from Gavin's lips, but I am willing to bet not from his heart. It seems Mary did more talking than listening today.

'Here.'

'Hear what?'

'No, we're here.' A little shakily, Gavin tilts his head in the direction of The Buttery's sleek glass doors.

'Good evening, sir. Table for … two, was it? Are you together?' An excellent question. Inside, Gavin proves astonishingly adroit at maintaining a show of sobriety for others. The drunken clumsiness of home becomes carefree charisma in company; loosened up and unleashed without inhibitions, his charm glows golden-bright for the multiple pairs of eyes that turn to watch the soft sway of his kilt as he strides across the room. Slow and unnoticed, I walk in his wake. A plain brown peahen pecking for crumbs behind her cock.

The white-clothed table to which we are brought is unexpectedly small; more glamorous than those of Sorbo's, if possibly even less spacious. The intimate size lends itself to romantic handholding, but of course nothing of that sort is on the menu for us tonight. Our legs, however, become inadvertently tangled; the cramped under-table space offering no room to accommodate Gavin's long limbs. I feel the coarse wool of his socks through my stockings and out of embarrassment – really, out of a fear that he will ask me to move – I shift until my own legs are tucked into a tight origami fold beneath my seat. It is an uncomfortable one, more akin to a stool. But Good Lord, I am surely not so aged as to complain about a restaurant chair? Planting my feet on the floor, I resolve to grin and bear it. To bear it, at least.

Our young waitress, a giddy, giggling creature no older than the Girton first years, actually blushes when Gavin thanks her *very much indeed* for bringing our menus.

'Anything to drink, sir?' she asks him keenly, ignoring me as she might a smudge in her peripheral vision.

'Now darling, how could any man refuse you? If you're twisting my arm, I'll have a whisky and water.' Some twist. Summoning up the strength to hold his gaze steady, Gavin makes a play at flirtatiously lingering eye contact that should mortify all three of us yet somehow succeeds in delighting two. The waitress titters, then flushes, which makes her titter even more. If I ever felt desperate for a drink myself, it is in this moment. But the young woman departs without a second glance at me and my camouflaged, middle-aged plumage. Several minutes pass before a young man with a sparse moustache and persona as cheerless as his facial hair arrives at our tiny table to take my order for a glass of wine.

Once sure both staff have left us, Gavin heaves a hefty sigh. 'I'm tired, Kathleen.' How odd that Tambi confessed the same thing last time he drank to excess. I wonder why men feel so exhausted when women seem to do most of the work? Certainly, I lack the energy to reply to Gavin. I can think of nothing to say, or rather, nothing he would care to hear. Instead, I scan the room, studying what counts as a fashionable eatery these days with dispassionate anthropological curiosity. We are the oldest here. The floor is crammed with young couples, most of whom are mercifully too busy enjoying their own small-table proximity to heed a mournful midlife duo like us. Yet I can imagine how we would appear in their shining youthful eyes. Two solitary souls, alone in each other's company, trying in vain to reconnect now their nest is empty. Rekindling. The word comes to me as I stare at the tall, tapered candle whose flame flutters between Gavin and me. These days, I feel my hands are wrapped around the charred black wick of what we once had, fingers cupped to protect an infinitesimal spark and praying Gavin will not decide on a whim to blow it out.

I endured a crisis dinner not dissimilar to this years ago, sitting opposite Charles to sift through the dying embers of our burned-out marriage. Our respective infidelities with Alastair and Inez, the latter five months into her pregnancy, sat like two smoking guns on the table. In a relationship riddled with bullet holes, it seemed redundant to quibble about who had pulled their trigger first.

'We could live like the Bloomsbury Group,' Charles had proposed, his tone tinged with a fear that I imagine common amongst men whose mistresses are expecting. Can one catch cold feet from swollen ankles? 'Not exclusively together, but …' Lacking the gumption to articulate whatever progressive sleeping arrangements he was envisaging, Charles resorted to breaking up breadsticks. 'Because we still love each other, don't we?' As I recall, I did not answer.

I still love Gavin though. One flimsy piece of flotsam to cling to throughout the storms. A quotation knocks for admittance at the door of my consciousness, the words of Cathy – Kathie, I want to call her – about her Heathcliff. 'Whatever our souls are made of, his and mine are the same.'

'Yours, sir.' His whisky and water. Service is strange here, too casual for the sleek surroundings, and weirdly we each seem to have been allocated one staff member who caters solely to their individual patron. Gavin's girl serves him with almost implausible pleasure, while the glum boy keeps his head down but is, I think, here for me. Is this how young people eat? The waitress deposits Gavin's glasses, giving another girlish giggle as her hand brushes his shoulder, but he resists the urge to drink while we wait for mine to arrive. Even in the hazy depths of that intoxicated brain, good manners are ingrained. And yet the struggle to abstain clearly torments him. Gavin's eyes are continually drawn to the dark amber double measure, darting back to it with a watchfulness that is half predator, half prey. Since the mention of Mij, it seems there are thoughts he needs whisky to wash away.

Restless, Gavin resorts to toying with the flame between us: pinched thumb and forefinger snatching at the flickering tip until it billows, twists and shrinks from him. The candlelight jolts in the displaced air each time he moves his hand; his face falls into shadow, cragged and haunted, before moments later being reborn into handsome, boyish brilliance. Even without alcohol, this game would be risky, and the imprecision of Gavin's drunken reach leaves me in constant fear that he will burn himself.

'Be ...' careful? The warning fades as I grasp its futility. Gavin is not my child. Not my husband either. Let him singe those fine fingers if he wishes. He'll learn his lesson, as they say back in Bavington. Attention recalled, Gavin stares across at me, a taunting silliness still in his face. Raising the candlestick off the table, he holds it up to me as one might an ancient artefact discovered in a darkened tomb. A relic from a lost world. Perhaps that is how he sees me now.

'Kathleen ... Kathleen ...' A sardonic snigger creeps into Gavin's tone, finding some obscure source of amusement in the phonetics of my name that is inaudible to sober ears. 'Kathleen ... Madge? Kathleen ...' He affects a pompous aristocratic accent, unaware that his own was more than halfway there. 'Kathleen *Sykes Davies.*'

'It's a long time since I heard that one.' How many names must a woman wear in a lifetime? I suspect none will ever feel like the real me. Not since I accepted that I will never be Kathleen Maxwell. 'Raine will do,' I tell Gavin. He nods stupidly as if receiving an order, giving me a wobbling ironic salute.

'And what did you do with yourself today, Kathleen Raine? While I was with Mother?' How childlike he sounds when he speaks of Mary. Like a little boy locked in a grown man. 'Did you write?'

'No.' I regret that my tone is so pathetically apologetic. 'Not poetry.' The candle's closeness is making me sweat, sticky beads rolling down my roasting cheeks and dampening the frizzy wisps around my hairline. 'But there is a lecture I'm working on ...' At a loss for any other subject I feel willing to discuss, I begin an abridged tale of William Blake's Arlington Court frieze. Uncovered less than a decade ago, squirrelled away since 1821 on top of a disused pantry cupboard, the newly found artwork I am researching is replete with the richly compelling symbolism that spellbinds all those who know Blake's work. *The Sea of Time and Space*, they call it, a phrase plucked from his letters and which for me feels unbearably bittersweet; evocative of an indefinable quality to which my poetry aspires and equally reminiscent of dear Mij's life and loss.

Academics have discussed the painting's formal properties, attempting to track its clandestine journey through the centuries. But no one, I believe, has recognised the classical allusions Blake so subtly anchored within his *Sea*. No one except me. I understand what is hidden in plain sight; I can hear the call for eternal connection that Blake wanted to share with the world. And if I commit to my research, one day I will be able to prove it.

Gavin absorbs little of the story, drifting off in disinterest from information too esoteric for his alcohol-addled brain to retain. His eyes fog, blue skies glazed with grey clouds. In impatience, he taps his index finger against the candlestick, in the same way that I suspect he wishes to tap his toes.

'Most people still think of Blake as an untaught savant,' I persist. If lecturers stopped every time their audiences looked bored, academia would grind to a halt. 'But I see the threads of antiquity woven into his work. It's fascinating really–' My fascination is cut short; the candle topples and Gavin's napkin goes up in flames.

'The water – get the water!' In unison, we reach for the glass, succeeding only in spilling it as our hands bump together. Smoke coils rise cobra-like from the flame-ravaged, blackening napkin; the acrid smell of burning cotton slithers into my nostrils, choking my throat. All eyes in the elegant Buttery are on us.

'Let me, sir.' My moustachioed waiter sprints over with a vigour I would not have guessed him capable of, decanting a water jug before giving the napkin a firm extinguishing thump for good measure. 'Our sincere apologies, sir,' he murmurs, obsequious enough towards male patrons, at any rate, to bear total blame for the inconvenience that Gavin has suffered in very nearly setting the premises alight. His waitress, laughter-free for once, soon appears to help the young man straighten out what can be salvaged from our table, working together to replace our sodden tablecloth with the brisk, practiced efficiency of nurses making hospital corners. Clean cutlery is required, as is a new candlestick – discreetly left unlit. When the waitress leaves us, chargrilled napkin clasped in her manicured hands, she shoots me a look of unmistakable recrimination. Where there is smoke, there is fire. Acquainted with us both for a solid fifteen minutes, she seems convinced that the real fault must lie with me.

'No harm done,' Gavin remarks dryly as they go off with our wet things, sinking back into his seat with his miraculously intact whisky. Perhaps miraculous is not quite the word: as the clean-up operation commenced, it was the first thing he leapt to save. Gavin takes a long drink. Chivalry be damned. I watch the apple in his thin throat bob, one droplet escaping to trickle down his fair-stubbled chin. I start to weep.

'Oh, don't cry, Kathleen. For God's sake, don't cry.'

Brought low by self-pity, I bury my face in my hands, watery vision straining past the prison bars of my fingertips to glimpse the creased navy smock whose folds slump as a dead weight across my lap. My hairpins have yet again broken free at the first sign of commotion and when I lower my head, my hair droops, tumbling to hang in heavy curtains on either side of my tear-stained face. At first, I appreciate how the dull weight muffles the outside world, but eventually I must surface from my self-made, smothering sanctuary to catch my breath. My weary eyes are swollen, barely blinking; my cheeks feel pallid and puffy.

'Poor old Kathleen,' Gavin says. 'You look like a fat squaw.'

Shock momentarily halts my tears. 'What did you call me?' I stare across the table at a man who suddenly feels like a stranger. Gavin shrugs, a show of nonchalance as if the slur were no more than an observation. He helps himself to another generous gulp. 'You're drunk,' I inform him. Tautological, that is what editors call such statements. Obvious enough to be rendered unnecessary. And yet it feels necessary to remind myself of just how heavily Gavin is intoxicated. He doesn't know what he's saying, this foolish, drunken lost soul before me, wading through the night with Heaven knows how much whisky swimming inside his veins. And if he doesn't know, he cannot mean it.

Gavin laughs mirthlessly, the sound harsh and hoarse. Eyes shut, I would hardly recognise it. 'Maybe, but you'll still be ugly in the morning.'

Struck so fast, the second blow as utterly unexpected as the first, I do not register the pain straight away. Churchill, my brain notes benignly, anesthetising itself with trivia: I'm sure it was Churchill who first made that 'joke'. I do not recall at which woman's expense. Several seconds tick by, numbly intellectualised, but then the wound Gavin has dealt me starts to throb. Blood drains from my head, dizzying and disorienting; my empty stomach drops in the struggle to digest his bitter insult.

'I don't need to stay and listen to this.' I say it as coldly as I can, feigning an iciness at odds with the hot humiliation coursing through me. And it is true. I should simply gather myself together and go, leaving Gavin to stew in the shame of his own inebriation. But I do not move. I cannot. I am shell-shocked.

'Oh, but Kathleen, you really should be thanking me ...' Gavin is rummaging through his sporran in search of his lighter and cigarette case. I hear the empty hip flask clink. 'I explained all about you to Mother today. As you know, she's a more ... traditional sort of woman.' His hands shake from the effort to light up, meagre flame flickering impotently in the vague vicinity of its target until dumb luck lets them collide. 'You remember?'

'I remember.' Why don't I go? Why stay here with tacky tears stuck to my cheeks and listen to his havering? I ought to let Gavin pickle and putrefy, left alone until tomorrow dawns with a punishing withdrawal headache that will feel – I hope – like it is cracking his skull in two. And as the physical pain subsides, the emotional equivalent will only have begun: the sober, sombre remorse that comes from having caused someone you care about great hurt. I am familiar with the feeling. I know what it is to wake with the taste of regret in my mouth, so strong and corrosive that it burns raw on every swallow. The first conscious breath I draw in the morning is always the worst, filled with the knowledge that it is my fault, my failure, why our beloved Mij will never breathe again. Maybe that is why I do not leave. Why I feel this strange, masochistic obligation to endure every last bit of Gavin's viciousness.

When it happened, his forgiveness had felt like too much to bear: an undeserved reprieve so generous I could barely bring myself to accept it. But in that rejection, as selfish of me as it was self-punishing, I see now that I sowed the seeds of my current suffering. Alcohol disinhibits, I have read. It exposes the repressed; it lets that which lurks within finally erupt. Gavin's poorly-thanked compassion has curdled over time into a much more natural resentment, his latent hatred of me growing silent and unchecked throughout these long, agonising months when we have lived together yet never more apart. I feel like one of the plaster-cast people of Pompeii who failed to heed the rumbled warnings, preserved in immortal ignorance because they left it too late to flee.

'Mother says women should always make an effort, not – what was it –' he feigns deep thought while taking another drag – 'let themselves go. But I told her, "No, Kathleen's too clever to worry about trivial things like looking old or unattractive. She has her poetry."' Gavin grins, the least kind smile I have ever seen. 'How is your poetry?'

'You already asked me that tonight.' I look down, away; I cannot bear to look at him. In the untouched cutlery, I catch sight of my ashen face and dull dark hair. The latter has blurred with the navy shadows of my smock, engulfing me like a shroud. 'I am not una ...' I abandon the protest unfinished. Choose instead the frank, unvarnished truth. 'I've given up dressing for you.'

Gavin raises an eyebrow in mockery. It wiggles and wobbles, unsteady as the rest of him. 'Is that what you were doing? Can't say I noticed.'

'Well, you don't, do you? Notice women.' His face falls. Neither of us is laughing now. In the sudden silence, Gavin's eyes dart around us warily, a fierce instinct for self-preservation alive even when his rational mind is doused in drink. Seconds later, his waitress reappears, a neat black-and-white shape emerging out of the blur that is my tear-glazed peripheral vision. In an instant, Gavin has knocked back the trickle of whisky left in his glass, bringing it down with a deliberate thud onto the outer edge of our table. He has no flirtatious gambit to greet the girl this time, the playful fun of false charm forgotten now my words have forced him to confront what is real. Quietly, permitting only a brief pause in puzzled hesitation, she removes Gavin's glass with the murmured promise to return with another. There is no mention of food. I have lost my appetite anyway.

'Do you know what your problem is?' Gavin challenges me once she is gone, pointing imprecisely across the table with the squat stub of his smouldering cigarette.

You, I think. *You are my problem*. 'Enlighten me. But do it quickly, before that next drink knocks you out.' Gavin's top lip twitches, curled almost into a snarl. He takes another drag before continuing. The cigarette butt is so burnt out, I feel sure he must be singeing his fingers. Perhaps he can't feel the pain anymore. I wish I couldn't.

'No matter how high you fly,' Gavin's trembling hand mimics a bird in flight, leaving a smoke trail hovering between us, 'wherever your poems or secret privy paintings take you –'

'Pantry, Gavin.' At least he did try to listen to my Blake story.

'– you'll never be more than a little girl from Ilford.'

'There is nothing wrong with Ilford.' If only I believed that. I almost did once, coming as close as I ever have to reconciling with my repressive, un-illustrious past and even feeling appreciative for how it had led me here to my present. Gavin was there. It was thanks to him, or so I had thought. I can see him standing in front of West View: tall and handsome beside my parents' diminutive privet hedge. That golden, encouraging

300

smile feels unrecognisable compared with the angry sneer facing me now. Was it all a sham? Nothing more than a voyeuristic vacation, feigning affection for a poor lower-class family before going back to a lochside mansion to mock us with his fellow aristocrats?

No. I don't believe it. Intoxicated or otherwise, those are not Gavin's true feelings. That he despises me personally, I am starting to understand; resentful and even vengeful for the suffering that my mistakes have caused him. I pray to God he never learns of my words at the rowan tree. But his hatred does not extend to others. Even and especially those far removed from the gilded cage into which he was born. Flawed though he may be, the man in front of me is not a snob. This drunken diatribe is being delivered in Gavin's voice, but I feel increasingly sure Lady Mary is now the one speaking.

'What was it you used to call the folk there?' As if reading my mind, a skill I cannot put past him, Gavin adopts an alternative tact. He does not need to condemn the people of my past. I have done it often enough myself. 'Soulless? Mundane? Menial?' I am to be convicted on my own testimony; hung from a scaffold that my misplaced arrogance has built. Gavin pauses his attack only long enough to mime a clumsy, faltering shape around his head. 'Narrow minds in bowler hats?' Words are weapons. I should have known better than to wield them so lightly. Was I trying to impress him or validate myself, I wonder too late: does this disgrace lie within the woman or the poet? My tears are falling again, tumbling from the corners of cracked, swollen eyes that weep in every sense of the word. I can taste them, droplets bouncing off my bottom lip to hit my parched throat and set my empty stomach growling on instinct. Through the shimmering film that coats my vision, I grow aware of an adjacent table having left what remains of a meat dish. Knives smeared in sauce that looks very much like blood; the off-white gristly bones stripped bare and defenceless.

'God, what a burden it must be to think you're so much smarter than everyone else.'

'Not everyone,' I mutter. 'Just you.' I bungle the retort through tears, but he hears it. Hears me. It is a truth that ordinarily neither of us wants to acknowledge. The fact that even when sober, Gavin's eyes glaze over when I discuss the subtler intricacies of Blake, his audible echoes in Yeats or the golden string woven through much of the world's greatest poetry. Certainly, he can memorise the taxonomies of the natural world with ease, his prose bearing the sophisticated hallmarks of a good education twinned with innate intellectual elegance. But knowledge, however polished, is not wisdom. For all my many, many faults, I seek to understand my life at a depth I am starting to suspect Gavin cannot or will not attain. The ephemeral, ill-informed opinions of strangers still hold too hefty a clout for him; even his passion for the natural world is often misdirected into winning the establishment's approval. I have never dared to admit it before, but perhaps a part of him will always be stuck in the shallows.

Across our small table, I watch Gavin's whisky-soaked ego try to rally from a blow that hit home. In the lull, his waitress returns, stony-faced as she delivers yet another double measure. Gavin's thin arm shoots out to pre-empt her. He swallows hard before continuing.

'Naturally, I'm no *poetess*.' I never called myself that. Only he did. I am about to remind Gavin of it when he looks down at his wrist, tapping it as if in consultation with a tricksy invisible watch. 'But isn't your masterpiece overdue? It had better be quite a poem after all this time.' He sniggers, struck by sudden idiotic inspiration. '*Kubla Khan*? "Kubla Kathleen Can't"?'

'You're ridiculous.'

'"The Rime of the Absent Mother"?' Wielded drunkenly for too long, his blade thrusts into my breast. Touching a nerve, they call it: an almost laughable minimisation. It feels more like he has severed an artery.

'I'd ... I'd rather be absent than cruel.'

'HA.' Gavin flings his head back, a fake laugh echoing off The Buttery's hard architectural edges. 'You think this is cruelty, Kathleen? Two old friends enjoying a frank chat?' The pretentious tone he used for Hugh's surname is resurrected. 'Two writers discussing character development?' Assassination would be more accurate.

'Harpoon,' I whisper, impaled and gasping for air myself. 'Harpoons are cruel.' In the latter days of Soay, Gavin designed his own weapons, meticulously crafted to pop out like arrowheads upon impact so the wounded creatures could not tear themselves free. Of course, that came only after he learned machine guns did not work. As I recall – in truth, the haunting image will never leave me – he fired three-hundred rounds into the first shark he ever saw yet still did not manage to lasso it. I turned my mind away at the time, so blinded by love I told myself I was misinterpreting his manuscript. But I refuse to diminish my intellect any longer. What brief semblance of a life did that poor animal endure, swimming away with such grievous, gratuitous wounds? Disfigured from bullet holes, pockmarked by a plague of lead embedded into the hulk of its flesh, I picture dark streams of blood rippling alongside that shark's noble, bulky body as it dived down to die in the depths. How can the man who loved Mij with such sincerity, who cries alone in the dark for the loss of one little otter, have wilfully killed so many? But then, I might ask how the man who once seemed so fragile and vulnerable that I could not help but give him my heart, can be the very one brutal enough to revel in its breaking.

'Sharks? Christ, they're just bloody fish, Kathleen.' Glass pressed to forehead in a theatrical tableau of despair, Gavin sighs a lofty 'no reasoning with women' exhale. It would be more persuasive if he had ever dealt with a woman besides his mother, his sister and me. 'They have brains the size of matchboxes.' For one furious hot-blooded rush, I believe he means my sex, and find myself readying to spear my fork prongs through his hand. But no. Yet again, Gavin is talking about sharks. 'They're tiny.' He tries to hold his unsteady thumb and index finger a minimal distance apart.

'Are they "cheat to scrape a third" tiny?' Caught off guard, Gavin's Oxford grad digits collide.

'Your degree didn't do much for you, Miss Twice-Divorced-by-twenty-five.' His calculations are out, needless to say, but it feels like a minor gripe when the major humiliation rings true. 'Doesn't Girton teach its girls anything, besides how to become whores?'

'Not all women are satisfied by their sons.'

Briefly speechless, Gavin looks ready to roar; inarticulate with rage or perhaps his system finally short-circuiting from drink. 'Don't you – don't you – don't you dare mention her.'

'I hope you mentioned to her that her darling boy's rent is late again.' Gavin slams down his second empty glass with a thick tablecloth clink.

'And what of your children, Kathleen? Anna, James ...' his hand is raised, ticking them off finger by finger. The third stays crooked, half-cocked as Gavin's eyes glint in drunken daring. 'Haven't forgotten one, have I?'

So this is love. The rotten, maggot-ridden fruit of my deep-rooted adoration. It is not bouquets and moonlight, only the thorny, Janus-faced intimacy of knowing someone so well that you understand better than any other person on earth what is the most powerful way to hurt them. It is luring them to trust, stockpiling their most shameful secrets as ammunition to keep dry underground, until the moment dawns when you step back to watch the fuse detonate, laughing to see their shock transfigure into horror as all they have believed in goes up in smoke. No Axis bomber or knife-wielding stranger in a shadowed alley could have inflicted more damage than Gavin has tonight. Yet he is a stranger to me now, or even worse, a counterpart turned antagonist, the face my eyes would instantly seek in a crowd of thousands made unfamiliar, foreign and monstrous. These hellish words have risen from the dark fiery depths of him, just as they did from me when I stood at the foot of his rowan.

'Crueller than you thought, am I, Kathie? A cursed soul who's bound for Hell? I'll see you there.' Even now, what we had irredeemably broken, there is some strange entwining magic at work between our minds. Both thinking of souls. Both thinking of curses. The psychic effect glitters worthlessly, a gossamer thread linking us a moment more before it snaps, fading to dust. Gavin leans and almost lurches over the table, his drunken breath hot as flames licking the stake at which I feel I have been burnt. 'Tell me, Kathleen, do you think Mij went to Heaven after you let that murderer cave his head in?'

Too late, I flee, clattering alone through The Buttery's glass doors to the consternation of the top-hatted doorman. Too late because Gavin's final words of what is surely our last supper echo behind me with shattering clarity, not just knives in my back but shards piercing my heart.

'If you kill yourself tonight, Kathleen, I will never forgive you.'

Chapter Thirty-Six

His apology arrives at Girton the next day. One of the youngest girls delivers it to my office after the mid-afternoon post: a luxurious ivory envelope, the penmanship shaky yet pressed heavily enough for ink to have bled into the grain. I stare down at a splodged blot billowing out over the squint 'i' in Raine.

'You'd understand if you had children,' I mutter as a scrawled version of Gavin's handwriting spills out onto my desk. 'They're the reason I'd never kill myself.' He will never know how close I came last time; Gavin has no inkling of those harrowing moments swept out to sea, the clawing storm-churned waves doing their damnedest to pull me under. It was the thought of Anna and James that saved me then, and if I could bear to speak to Gavin, I would tell him that they are why I would never do it now. Although to myself, sheltering within a sacred place of learning that my foremothers dedicated to the pursuit of truth, I must be honest: it is also because I believe him. Gavin would never forgive me if I took my life. He has already forgiven me for the unforgivable once.

I turned up at the college in what my mother would call the 'wee hours', so ashen and diminished I must have appeared more phantom than woman. Mercifully, the night porter admitted me with a disinterested nod. I went straight to my rooms. I have not left them since. But if I had, as I contemplated, gone skulking through the night in search of a beam and a length of rope; if I had run the bath in my meek little quarters with a stiff drink and a sharp knife waiting on the rim, it was the echo of Gavin's words that prevented me. And so, here I am. The ambivalent beneficiary of a new day's sunlight. A diffuse beam streams in, exposing the dust on my desk and making the thick, creamy page in my hands turn translucent. Every summer, or so it seems, Gavin finds a new way to break my heart.

'I was beastly and horrible, and I am deeply ashamed,' he writes. How much does he remember? His letter mentions no specifics, squaw or otherwise. The largest portion of it is spent in explanation, or rather excuse: Gavin elaborating on what he learned yesterday about his mother's apparent ill health. 'I fear losing anyone else.' I know the feeling. The next paragraph of today's epistle is weighed down with detailed references to Lady Mary's various doctors – all prestigious, all expensive – although to me, her prognosis seems clouded in confusion. Again, there is no mention of Aymer, Eustace or Christian being involved.

'Is she really ill?' At a loss for how to otherwise determine the truth, I quiz Elias later during a rare telephone call, deferring to his dubious yet undeniable authority as the fount of society gossip.

'I think she is more sick at the thought that her son might marry you.' Strange as it sounds, a part of me pities Mary then. How fearful yet far-removed from the man she claims to love. She must be, if she seriously believes there is a possibility Gavin wants to marry me.

'If it helps, Kathleen,' Elias adds after a moment, 'I suspect he dyes his hair.' Sudden laughter spills from me, hysterical unladylike snorts. I never expected to laugh again. But I have dwelt on that pale, spun-gold shade for what feels like years of my life, picturing the way those light-attracting strands shimmer as I close my eyes and drift off into thwarted, seldom satisfying dreams. And Gavin has been blond since babyhood. I have seen his childhood pictures on Kielder Bridge. Surely it is simply good fortune if the fairness has lasted well into his forties? He is a fortunate man. In most ways.

'I will never be the same person again if you do not forgive me,' my man of light's dark, trembling-hand missive concludes. An unusual sort of apology for me to find myself owing him.

'I am sorry that after all these years it should have ended like this,' I write back when I draft my reply, less a viable piece of correspondence and more a violent emotional emetic designed to purge the conflicted, contradictory mass of feelings that lies twisted within my centre. Re-reading after I have heaved up a little of my bitterness, I screw the sheet into a tight ball to toss away. Imagining myself to sound fearsome and finally strong, I have nonetheless still said sorry to him.

It has not ended, of course. I think now it will never end until we do. There can be no clean break from the intricate web I have woven throughout the years in an increasingly anguished attempt, I see only now, to bind our lives together. Shared home. Shared friends. Shared occupation. Even my beloved words are no longer solely my domain. Arrogant in my naivety, I never thought of myself as deigning to do conventional women's work. Too late, I recognise the subconscious spinning and threading through which I have laboured to interlock us, body and soul. Supporting Gavin, or so I thought. Ensnaring him, as I suspect Gavin himself would say. Psychically and physically, we are as tightly knotted together as a fishing net that would do the Mallaig men proud, and it makes real separation impossible. Within days, I have no choice but to return to Paultons, collecting further post and the rest of my belongings.

Again, Gavin is writing – again, I do not know what about – so he does not meet me straight away. I am left to wander my old house alone, reflecting sombrely how my former rooms look more and more like they have always belonged to him. Perhaps the better part of me left Paultons long ago. When Mij did. Bowled over by a resurging wave of grief, I recall his irresistibly sweet face here to greet me the last time I returned after a quarrel. Without Mij, we have no angelic apex to triangulate our two hard lines; no cherished cosmic child to play peacekeeper between perpetually warring parents.

'For you.' A bundle of mail in his hand, Gavin meets me on the landing. Mutual territory. More like no-man's-land. Two people cramped into one narrow space creates an embarrassing, claustrophobic effect. I take the letters from him but afterwards feel as if I have no room to manoeuvre. I seem to remember Gavin telling me, long ago, that staircases are a dangerous spot for animal bites.

'Boxed in,' he had said. 'The panic drives them to make poor decisions.' In the absence of further conversation, I start flicking through my clutch of envelopes. One letter catches my eye, stamped from the lawyer's office that deals with the Paultons lease. As if this year is not inauspicious enough, 1957 happens to mark one of the semi-periodic moments at which I must extend or sell Cooie's bequest.

'You won't renew, I assume,' Gavin remarks. Too flat for it to feel like a question. That he has already gone through, and given thought to, the bundle addressed to me is a prospective new battle I choose not to pick.

'You should take it over.' Am I joking? Neither of us laugh. Gavin's eyes meet mine. A rare occurrence these days.

'I couldn't afford it,' he eventually admits. His voice is wary, slow and low as if suspicious of walking into a trap.

'Call it a gift then.' My words echo in my ears from afar, corrupted and tinny as if conveyed down a poor-quality telephone line. What am I saying? The freewheeling sensation is unsettling, my tired mind ricocheting from one ill-advised sentence to another. My strained vision twitches and jolts as I imagine occurs before a fit. 'I can't afford to keep it on,' I tell Gavin. *I can.* 'And I have my Girton rooms.' *I don't have them. Not to own. The only place I own is Paultons.* 'You've already paid me enough in rent.' *He has not. Far from it. He himself has paid me nothing. Forget Lady Mary*, I think dizzily as the words spill from me like a bloodletting. *I must be the one who is ill.*

Gavin is torn. Childlike as he can be, I see the conflict clearly in his face. Keenness wrestling with distrust. Perhaps he fears that my implausibly generous offer must come with a catch. If it does, I am yet to think of it. He looks around us as if appraising the place with new eyes. Perhaps he is, now he knows he might possess it. Then his gaze returns to me. 'The lease ...'

'It's easily changed. Not even made out in my name yet.' *It is.* It sits inside this business envelope clasped in my sweat-saturated hands, all documentation complete except for the technicality that is – that was – my signature. Ear canals clenched tight from the sudden tension, I start registering urgent, disembodied sounds that quiver through me like the old air raid sirens. Cooie's ghost frantically ringing her phantom doorbell, ethereal fingertips poised over the press; the pear tree branches shaking their summer leaves with all their might, beseeching me not to abandon them. But I cannot stop. My words are gathering momentum beyond what I can control. They are the MacLeod twins hurtling down Ben Sgriol, small feet tripping inside big boots; they are Mij coursing sleek and strong over the waterfall's rock ledges, powering through the bright twisting burn and cresting the white-tipped waves faster than light.

'I want you to have it,' I tell Gavin. A lie, like all the rest. What do I really want? I will surrender anything – my home, my health, my happiness – to restore what we once had. Back at The Buttery, that ill-starred night of pitch-black insults I will never be able to forget, Gavin told me I was ugly, old, snobbish, solipsistic, a bad poet, a bad mother ... but by this penance, perhaps I will be cleansed. The spell will be broken; the bitter rowan curse appeased. If I freely and sincerely sacrifice Paultons to Gavin as the very last gift I have to give – beyond my heart, which belongs to him already, or the body that remains his for the taking even though I know he never will – then there is a chance he will see me like he used to. If not quite a goddess, then a force for good.

Gavin's resistance is weakening. I knew it would. 'How will I ever thank you?' *You'll love me again.*

'Don't mention it again.' I hand him the lawyer's letter, repulsed by the seedy moist spots that my sweating fingers have left. Politely, Gavin ignores them, or else he is too distracted by the windfall at hand to notice. We discuss what needs to be done, or rather I tell him.

'I've owned an island before, but never a house,' he laughs. I try to smile. With me dictating over his shoulder as he types, gently pointing out corrections when his excited haste gets the better of him, we enclose a vague explanatory note in the return correspondence to the lawyer. Gavin rushes to ready the envelope, head bent over his desk in eager concentration to complete the transaction, and the strange thought crosses my mind that this is how men must feel before a prostitute. This same sick, bloodless realisation of being poorer than when you started, understanding too late that what you truly wanted cannot be bought.

*

Only after I leave do I realise that I thought he would ask me to stay. Out of gratitude, or gladness, or simply inspired by the brief, beautiful renaissance of the connection that once came so easily to us. I had imagined Gavin would still want me in his home, sometimes, as I have always wanted him in mine. At Sandaig, was it not so? Gavin shared his Highland sanctuary with me, entrusting his Avilion. Say what you will about his 'other visitors', I was the only one permitted to take care of it and Mij in his stead. And yet this time, the door has shut with me on the wrong side. My own door, to make matters worse. Like Gavin's tempestuous Soay fishery work, I have given out my rope, piece by piece, until suddenly the end was swept through my grappling fingertips: last hopes lost to the unforgiving sea.

'You've gone far enough,' my soul aches to hear him say. 'No further. Please don't leave me altogether.' If the sentiment exists, it stays unspoken. I pack my books and other belongings. When the lease has been transferred and the appointed day arrives, I go.

Back at Girton, cloistered away with the youthful virgins and ageing spinsters, night falls slowly, draping the pretty eves in gradually growing darkness while I perch sleepless on the edge of my single bed. Around me is a ring of dull boxes that I was too despondent to unpack. My modest college bedroom already feels cramped by the new additions, an excess of possessions stuffed into a space that was never designed for a woman with a life beyond these walls. I suppose now I do not have one. Through the narrow, arch-tipped window, I watch the pale-grey moon shimmering meekly as if sunk underwater. Only a sliver of crescent is visible, her fragile scythe struggling to cut through the clouds before being smothered by rolling summer smog. Time and again, that symbol of female strength is sublimated, forced back by the dark, dense power that is blocking her sightline to earth. It cares nothing for her shine or potential luminosity, the vital gleam with which she wishes to illuminate the slumbering world below. All that matters to those clouds, relentless and impenetrable, is pursuing their course as they dominate the sky.

'It's not fair,' I announce childishly to my empty room. 'It's not right.' Shaking off the shackles of tiredness, I rise, creeping on the balls of my feet to negotiate the boxes without waking whichever professor resides below me. At my desk, fresh words stream forth in a way my poetry has failed to do for many months, resurgent eloquence spiked by my belated indignation as I compose a new letter to Gavin.

'I realise now that I should have kept a room back,' I inform him, much more matter of fact than I feel. 'A London base is surely never amiss, however seldom I end up using it. Why don't I keep on the attic floor?' The lease is signed, the house is his, yet too late, I am hit by the acute, riling injustice of me having continued to give while Gavin exclusively took. Less principled, too, a new fear is possessing me. I had hoped the offer of the house would cement our unstable foundations, assuaging my guilt and restoring my role as some sort of spiritual benefactress in Gavin's life. But without me retaining a link, however tangential, to the Paultons property, I have no guarantee I will even see him anymore. His gratitude is not the same as his affection. I am afraid Gavin will keep the gift, only to discard the giver.

'I could rent it from you,' I suggest in a desperate flourish of scribbled inspiration. 'No longer you as my tenant, but me as yours.' I scrawl that last line as might a genius or a madwoman, or maybe both, euphorically carving out the solution to a problematic equation that has plagued me for an age. 'K + G' proves an irreconcilable conundrum, yet 'K – G' feels like it will leave less than nothing. I work for most of the night on wording my shaky epiphany, crossing out and rewriting repeatedly until some semblance of balance seems restored. Having paid such a high price, I must have some certainty in return. I want reassurance that my sacrifice was worth it; I need proof that, on this occasion, my two wrongs might just make a right.

Gavin never replies. I am too humiliated to write again. Estranged, I suppose is the word. We are estranged. Or we would be, if I had ever been his wife.

Chapter Thirty-Seven

'Engaged? Anna, you're only a child.' But of course, she is not. Not anymore. I was younger than my daughter when I wed for the first time, although I pray her union will be a happier one. Yet can my little girl really be ready to be a bride? Time has moved on, the world has kept turning, while my eyes and my heart were too focused on Gavin to notice. 'What's his name?' I ask Anna, sick with shame that I should have to clarify such a detail.

Even so, a warm gold glow enrings her expression. 'John Hopewell.'

'So you'll be Anna Hopewell?' Stumbling through my surprise, I try the new name out for size.

My daughter shakes her head. 'Anna Madge Hopewell.' A noble name. I wish I were part of it.

'"Hope" is auspicious,' Helen tells me later on the telephone, her level tones working hard to soothe me from many miles away. As does, closer at hand, a stowaway cigarette of Gavin's from a pack that somehow became mixed up with my boxes. 'He's a responsible young man, Kathleen.'

'You've met him?' Bitter black smoke coils in my throat and I cough. Good Lord, his cigarettes are strong.

'No,' Helen admits. 'But she's mentioned him to me.' I keep on spluttering. 'He's a good Christian.' Irrespective of piety, I shall be having strong words with the Girton grounds team. Male marauders are apparently still breaching the barricades.

Soon, I have the chance to meet Anna's youthful knight errant in person. Her eyes shine in anticipation, those rich, dark pupils inherited from her father's side shimmering in the light as she proudly takes her new fiancé's arm. Tall yet slight, with the frail whisper of a moustache, John stands self-consciously in what is obviously his Sunday best. Anna herself is wearing a dress I have not seen before: crimson damask, simply cut, in the sharp dance-ready style that I realised at The Buttery is forever behind me. She is no longer pretty. Now, Anna is beautiful. I have not seen her looking so purely joyful in years, a rosy flush of happiness in full bloom across her cheeks. It has been absent, at least around me, for longer than I can bear to admit.

'Mrs Madge.' The young gentleman greets me solemnly, extending a bony hand. Anna nudges him gently. 'I mean, Mrs Raine,' he stammers. Another subtle prod. Maybe she is ready for marriage after all. 'Dr Raine?' John appears angst-ridden, almost comically wretched, and I decide I must put the poor lad out of his misery.

'Call me Kathleen. Please.' Relief washes over his pale face and he breaks into a smile with Anna also grinning widely. If it were possible, I think it makes the new couple look even younger than before.

Throughout our tea together in Cambridge, my college rooms being too small to comfortably accommodate a trio, I feel the embarrassing urge to offer life advice. Yet what can I possibly tell these two about how to have a successful marriage? Once, I thought I understood love better than the rest: selfless where others were indulgent, platonic while lesser mortals were consumed by the physical and coarse. But it seems that kind of love has eluded me too, a glistening cowrie shell dropped to the depths and carried off with the current, far out of my reach. I 'hope well', and indeed I pray, that the youngsters will be happy. To his credit, John seems earnest and dutiful beyond his tender years. But alone that night in my microcosmic Girton bedroom, I cannot dispel the haunting notion that he will not make Anna as happy as she deserves. Yet what value is my intuition to anyone now?

I still have my work, for what it is worth. To the naked eye, my academic career is flourishing, and only I know the stagnant, weed-ensnared swamp of procrastination and wasted potential that lurks beneath it. Belatedly, I am starting to realise that my studies were meant to be a holiday from my true purpose; a welcome respite from the trials of producing poetry but never my long-term intellectual home. Gavin used to joke – the memory of his light, silvery laughter cuts through me like a blade – that houseguests were like fish.

'After three days, they start to stink,' he'd say acidly, and I suspect neither me nor academia is still fresh. However much praise my papers garner in our closed, self-referential circles, however many piecemeal funding grants I am the surprised beneficiary of, I am starting to think I have outstayed my welcome. My escape turned into another prison. It has happened to me before.

Even if I did manage to compose new poems, garnering the courage

313

to listen again to my bruised, battered heart rather than my head, I would need to find a new publisher. To my and I think his own surprise, Tambi's vague notions of America have solidified into what can only be called a plan. The promise of Lady Liberty is calling: not dollar signs and glossy skyscrapers but an immeasurably more valuable freedom of style, ideas and creativity. Freedom, above all, of imagination.

'I've told them about you,' Tambi reminds me each time a new letter arrives from one of the transatlantic contacts he is already amassing, being nearly as gregarious on paper as he is in person. 'They're very interested in you.' Words every writer dreams of hearing. And yet however hard Tambi tries to persuade me, I refuse the offer to join him when he goes.

'My home is here,' I insist. What is left of it.

I try constantly to compose: ill-formed rough scribbles of half-ideas filling up my notebook pages well into each solitary night. But in the cold, cruel light of day, they are never the poems I hope for. These fragments are frail saplings, limp-leafed with stems easily snapped. Unworthy of a poet who once thought she would grow into something great. William Blake's work used to nurture me but now I sit small and alone in his shade, uninspired and afraid of who I will be if the words do not return. I hack away at stanzas and rogue phrases, watching words frozen in isolation collide across my page like ice blocks striking the stones of Kielder Bridge. If I could only recapture what I had then, back when the exquisite torture of unconsummated love seemed like the worst problem a woman could have. In those days I had poems to spare, a tumbling cascade of ideas flowing from me on a glittering stream of vision that I thought would never dry up. But now I am blocked. Stuck. Trapped. One night, my frustration turns to fury. Thwarted and enraged, I rip a pillow off my small single bed and scream into the depths of its feathery void.

'Everything all right in there?' A stranger calls from the hallway outside. Blinking back tears, I cast my eyes around the room for an excuse. My gaze lands on the mod con record player I cannot work, a gift that Anna and James sweetly clubbed together to buy me at Christmas.

'Sorry,' I answer. 'It's just a broken record.'

*

I am going mad. I must be. Having resolved not to think of Gavin, to erase his handsome, fair face from my mind or die trying, I believe I must be losing that mind entirely when I start seeing his name everywhere I go.

314

The awareness dawns gradually as the year turns, at first no more than a distant, indistinct rumbling like the growl of his approaching Bentley. And yet just as it used to be when that monstrous vehicle pulled up at Paultons, the sound and associated drama rapidly gather pace. Come springtime, I notice *The Sunday Times* alerting readers to the year's most exciting upcoming titles, highlighting one writer in particular of 'imagination, sharpness of eye and profound feeling for nature'. The *Daily Mail*, never knowingly out-sensationalised, announces its intention to serialise the same book over the summer. I spot a front-page advertisement on a copy left lying in the Girton common room and, ignoring the last inkling of wisdom left within me, I cannot resist peeking inside.

'Remember the name Gavin Maxwell,' the article commands. I stare down at the newspaper in my hands, horrified as if holding my own obituary.

By autumn, I know something ominous is building in the literary atmosphere: a cloying, choking pressure like the violent compulsion to retch that comes seconds before vomiting. Gasping for mental air, I resort to reading only my colleagues' international periodicals. But home or abroad, there is to be no escape.

'Buy this book if you have to hock your watch,' instructs the *Chicago Tribune*. The book's title? That, too, I can scarcely believe.

'We ought to sue,' Tambi broods darkly, turning the copy we have received over and over as if one last agitated rotation of its dust jacket will reveal the occult intricacies of copyright law, although I know as well as he does that he has no idea of how things work on the claimant's side of a suit. I do not say so. I do not say anything. I simply look at the book before me. My words in print above Gavin's name.

He has married me with a ring ...

'You're barely credited,' Canetti informs me a little too gleefully. He was the one who brought this copy. I deserved to see it, he said. 'Your entire poem is there on the opening page, but nothing of you as its author except a line buried amidst the rest of his acknowledgements. From *Year One*.' Which ought to be *The Year One*. 'See for yourself.' Book held out, he attempts to press it into my hands. Without touching it, I let it drop. Elias is only momentarily deterred. 'Bestseller of the year, that's what they're saying,' he drones. 'Just behind Churchill's memoirs and the Bible.' My God. 'He's overtaken D.H. Lawrence. Didn't you see the headline? "Otters mount *Lady Chatterley's Lover*."' Canetti chortles. I cannot crack a smile. Later, alone, I try to console myself with the thought that I must still exist within Gavin's consciousness, occupying a silent part of his heart despite his protestations. No author I ever knew would choose to title their book with the words of someone they did not love. Someone they had not loved, once upon a time.

Soon, the press attention reaches such a frenzied fever-pitch that I do not need to read his story to be familiar with its contents. And after all, I remember them. I was in them. Gavin's new book tells the tale of Sandaig, the sole spot on earth to which I feel my spirit truly belongs and yet where, to the rest of the world, Gavin now claims he retreated alone. Although 'I was not quite alone,' he qualifies in his opening chapter, according to Canetti, who reads several sentences aloud before I can beg him to stop. 'In front of me trotted my dog, Jonnie.'

'Jonnie.' I whisper the sweet old boy's name, imagining myself calling through the trees, beckoning the spaniel out from the shadowy forest of our past or perhaps pleading with time to let me return back with him the way I came. That night, my mind dwells on the memory of all those tense, lonely months at Paultons when I wondered what Gavin was writing, tormenting myself with the thought he did not wish to share his work with me. But I did share it. If I close my eyes, we are still sharing it. Gavin has written about our life without me in it, omitting me from the retelling as he exposes our Eden to a world full of strangers.

Sandaig's name is disguised. Its new identity is Camusfeàrna. 'It means "the Bay of Alders" in Gaelic,' yet another newspaper informs me breathlessly, promising to relay – 'exclusively', no less – every last vivid detail of the landscape that is forever mapped in my heart. Our paradise lost. Legs weak, I sink with that latest article into a Girton armchair, but I am no longer at the college. I am underneath those towering alders, their luminous pinecones twirling impishly through the windswept canopy like mischievous Highland sprites. Delicate fern fronds spring out in loose curls, feathered tips floating in the breeze and tickling my calves as I pass. The rush of blood in my ears fades in favour of the gushing waterfall beyond; the sweet scent of clover drifting by on the cool, moistened air. I hear the trickling percussion of breakaway streams, surging over smooth pebbles before settling in pools laced with ivory foam. I hurry on to where the torrent grows stronger. Mij might be just out of sight up ahead.

'Enough, Kathleen. That's enough.' Without Gavin to do it, I chastise myself as the tears swell, scrubbing with scrunched fists at my raw,

316

stinging eyes. Later in the mirror, I see the newspaper print has left them blackened. For now, I read on, as much as I can bear. Gavin makes no mention anywhere of the rowan.

'He's very handsome, isn't he?' I hear one Girton girl remark to another the next day, holding out Gavin's dashing dust jacket photograph for her companion and placing it inadvertently in my sightline.

'He dyes his hair,' I snipe as I pass. The girls spin, shocked and repulsed. More by me than by Gavin. Squirming with shame as I wriggle between them, I feel lower than a worm.

Minor acquaintances and those whom I have only ever known by sight start stopping me for conversation in the hallways, the courtyard and even once in the street. 'You know him, don't you, Gavin Maxwell?'

'No,' I invariably reply. I should say the same thing if they asked whether I know Kathleen Raine.

What I do know is that Gavin has new otters now. Being unable to bring myself to read the book is no impediment to discovering such details. The world is bursting to tell me more about the life of this intrepid, intriguing bachelor; all I need is to pick up a paper, any paper, and I can learn about his every move just like any other fan. There is Edal, a girl otter – a perverse maternal heartstring inside me is plucked by the thought of a female cub – and another little boy named Teko. 'Clownish and charismatic', one article informs me. He will be lovely, I am sure, but there can only ever be one Mij. Sandaig too seems to have undergone a transformation. Gavin's precious idyll has become a full-time operation that increasingly resembles a business. I suppose it really is a business, with all the money this bestseller must be earning him. An extension has been built and otter keepers have been hired. Jimmy Watt is the name of one such young chap and even newer, even younger, is a school leaver called Terry something or other. I wonder if Gavin's new employees understand him. If so, they do better than I.

I was his, my heart and soul given willingly into his keeping, but I understand now that none of it was ever truly mine. Not Sandaig with its cresting waves and the bright, twisting burn. Not Mij. Certainly not Gavin himself. Even my words have become his, the boy whose writing I nurtured choosing to wield the power I taught against me: Gavin's irresistible literary elegance eliminating me entirely from the official narrative of who he is. The new book's front cover haunts me as I toss and writhe sleepless: my poetry entwined with Gavin's prose as I used

317

to dream we ourselves would one day be. But this is no intellectualised intercourse, no transcendent spiritual congress. I am violated. Stripped. Invisible, irrelevant and ignored by the tens of thousands of people, perhaps soon reaching into the hundreds, who will pick up this book and see only Gavin's name.

'He mentions you once in the text,' Elias reports back unbidden. He is reading the whole thing, cover to cover, and seems to be enjoying himself immensely. 'You share a page with a neighbouring woman. The one whose family have that odd little house on the hill. Morag MacKinnon?'

'Mary MacLeod.' Her real name sounds plain in comparison. I can see why Gavin picked the pseudonym. How clever he is, how astonishingly skilful at crafting a gripping tale, to make the literary version more compelling than the truth. I wonder if the earthy realities of Sandaig will be strong enough to survive the dark glamour of fame. With the whole world believing in the fiction of Camusfeàrna, will my own recollections cave in and collapse? Yet however many bestsellers try to turn my memories inside out, I know that I can never doubt those moments on the shoreline searching for shells or watching Mij dive into the swirling waves, becoming one with the wild ocean tides.

Unprompted, Elias produces his copy for recitation.

'"With Kathleen Raine, Mij was rough and rumbustious … he took advantage of her whenever and however he could."' An honest statement, although I would have attributed the behaviour more to Gavin than to Mij. 'No explanation of who you are,' Canetti points out goadingly. But why should there be? I no longer know who I am myself.

'Is that it?' I ask. 'What does he write about Mij's …' I cannot bring myself to say 'death'. Canetti flicks forward casually.

'All he says is that the otter was in the care of a friend when it happened.' Clemency at last, after a fashion. I turn away before there is a risk of having to hear more.

Unwilling to face what feels like inevitable failure in trying to channel my emotions into poetry, I throw myself into research. The North Library of The British Museum beckons and I bury myself deep within its reading room, praying that the diligent librarians will one day lock me up with all the other dusty misattributions. They do not, needless to say. Closing time invariably comes and I must weave my way back home. My feet drag, scuffing the pavements like a child in ill-fitting shoes. As a girl, I would have playfully dodged every crack, but now I let my toes snag and sink.

318

Bad luck be damned. My fate was fixed years ago.

After a few minutes of pitiful pavement dwelling, I look up to find myself across the road from the bookshop. Slowly, inexorably, I draw near the window where a rowing boat once sat, filled to the brim with Gavin's *Harpoon*. A fast, high wave of bittersweet nostalgia hits: that launch party feels like another lifetime ago, yet in a heartbeat or two, I am back there. Catching his bright blue eyes across a crowded room. Now, Gavin's work again fills the display, his name printed below words written by me when I was overflowing with love for him. I fantasise briefly about hurling a brick through the bookshop window, producing some phantom suffragette toffee hammer to make all I can see crack and shatter. In reality, I simply stare, dull-eyed and empty. Strands of seaweed no longer adorn the window, only multiple press clippings devoted to the same man.

'Remember the name Gavin Maxwell.' Here, too, it is closing time, and I watch indistinct figures moving inside before they switch off the last of the lights. My pale reflection disappears as darkness falls over *Ring of Bright Water*.

Chapter Thirty-Eight

'Kathleen? It's me. Gavin.' As if I wouldn't know. Startled awake by the telephone, my drowsy, sleep-doused brain struggles to separate Gavin's real voice from the hazy residue of my dreams.

'What –' do you want with me? What entitles you to ring at this hour after excising me from your life, without even a reply to my last letter? What hubris, what incomprehensible arrogance makes you think that I will still care? 'What's wrong?' I ask him. In the darkness, I cast out in groggy approximation of the bedside table. My knuckles rap painfully against the cold metal base of an unlit lamp.

'It's Edal.' Gavin's voice is strained and close to breaking. 'She's ill and I ... I don't know what to do. Who else to call.' The line crackles, strangely faint and untested. In my other ear, the lightbulb hums, sending spasms of eerie yellow mushrooming across my Girton bedroom. Blinking sleep-encrusted grit from my eyes, I wince against the incipient brightness. 'She's so unwell,' Gavin groans. Somehow I can hear that his head is in his hands. 'It started out as an infected tooth, but soon the poison spread into her brain, and I ... oh Kathleen, I remember ...'

He remembers the bird at Monreith. That tiny scrap of fluff, now surely long grown if not gone altogether in a flutter of short-lived, forest-dwelling heartbeats, whom Gavin, childlike in his faith in me, was convinced that I had healed. 'I knew you were magic.' And I know that is what he is thinking. I only wish I knew for real how to manifest the miracle he needs.

'I'm coming.' Within the hour, I am on the Caledonian sleeper. Needed, if not quite wanted. I have no grand plan or bright idea. Only that Gavin cannot lose another otter.

Returning, however, I see that Sandaig itself is lost. Altered, at least. Transformed and not for the better. Lying low at literal sea level, the cottage is barricaded behind high wooden posts: a tall, imposing fence of timber spears running around its modest perimeter. The struts jut out incongruously from their swampy peat bog surrounds, tightly packed

320

pillars combining to create a defensive infrastructure that would suit a besieged city better than this isolated crofthouse. Rucksack weighing down one shoulder, stuffed with a random assortment of possessions I pulled together in the panicked early hours, I move to improve my view. Ocean waves used to air kiss Sandaig's timeworn white walls, but now their path is blocked. Barred. The burn's encircling trajectory is unchanged, yet an ugly box sits squat inside the ring.

The effect is discordant, out of tune with the bracing wilderness all around, but the main feeling I have is one of bizarre familiarity. 'Déjà vu,' Gay Taylor calls it. The indefinable, undeniable sense of having been somewhere before. In the formidable wood citadel below me, I see the uncanny materialisation of the fences that appeared in my dream – really, my nightmare – on that soul-chilling night at Kielder Bridge. In those days, I had yet to visit Sandaig in person, even if through Gavin's eyes I felt as if my spirit already knew it, and it had distressed me deeply to imagine myself on the wrong side of its rigid defences. Ten years later, the reality is no less disturbing.

Yet more fencing comes into view on my descent, struts interspersed with handmade signs.

Keep Out
Private Property
Private
KEEP OUT

The block letter urgency increases with every hundred yards until I arrive at the final sign, sinking in resignation. 'Otters. Keep dogs on leashes,' it pleads with whatever impervious passers-by have made it this far undeterred. Even in crudely painted lettering, I recognise Gavin's hand.

Something else has also shifted on the path bound for Sandaig. Is it the trees? Certainly, there were fewer planted last time on this hillside. Tapered trunks still narrow and juvenile, these neat new specimens seem to stand to attention as I pass, the earnest militaristic effect making me think of James and his passing-out parade. Moving closer, I spot several newly installed telegraph poles dotted along the forest's frontline. They feel phoney, like spies in my midst; dark interlopers working undercover to relay covert messages. This morning's faint, fragile telephone line suddenly makes sense and the convenience of the arrangement is obvious. Lifesaving, I hope, in the case of little Edal. And yet I cannot think Gavin is happy. To be in constant communication with the unforgiving outside world? Revisiting his sanctuary, it feels like enemy territory.

At the threshold, I look for my roses. Shorn-off stalks are all that remain, ragged twigs gaping where their bountiful blooms have been beheaded. I pinch my fingers at one neck as if to belatedly stem blood loss, feeling a coarse, grisly scratch under my fingers.

'A group of tourists cut them to take home. Souvenirs, they said. You wouldn't believe the bloody cheek of them.' The waves crash; my heart races.

'Hello, Gavin.' He is standing in the doorway, a dark shape ringed with light.

'Edal's in here, Kathleen.' His voice is gravelly, melodic notes buried beneath a rockslide of tiredness and tension. But the lilt I love can still be heard, if I listen hard.

'You know the way.'

'I know the way.' Gavin steps back and I follow him into the darkness.

He is wearing what I took to be sunglasses, but even indoors, Gavin seems disinclined to remove them. The frames are thick, wrapping around his fair temples, and when he next turns to face me, I see the blackened lenses are wholly opaque.

'What's wrong with your eyes?' I blurt out insensitively. Let the sub-wifely nagging recommence. Gavin is not offended though. After the horrors we have hurled at each other, one-off tactless remarks barely register.

'Conjunctiv-bloody-itis.' Eyes still hidden, his top lip twitches in an almost-smile. 'Picked it up last winter in Morocco. I was meant to be gathering material for my next book, but it all went haywire.' The country or him? Whatever the cause, someone who did not know Gavin like I do would be unable to read his expression. If the eyes are indeed the windows to the soul, a cliché I have always resented, believing as I do that poetry is the real route to things soulful, then Gavin's inner world is boarded shut, as fiercely guarded behind those shadowy lenses as the cottage inside its imposing wooden fortress. But I know this face, its subtleties and secrets, like the Ma'dan know every twist and ripple of their marshes; as William Blake knew the detailed, illustrative intricacies of his profound and personal visions. A single swallow, a second-long reflex, and I can sense when Gavin is holding back. A shallow breath or nervous twinge of a jawline muscle and I appreciate his anxiety as if the

322

angst came from my own heart. Whether we like it or not – and if he is aware, I am sure Gavin does not like it – I read him just as well with or without dark defences.

'Jimmy's gone to meet Bruce's boat,' he tells me. 'Fetching the vet back over from Broadford.'

'Skye?' Fifty miles distant, by both road and sea. My thoughts turn to the Cuillins outlined on the ocean horizon, fine ribbons of snow still garlanding their heavenward peaks. It is those hills from whence cometh our help now.

'Edal?' Gavin's inflamed voice sinks to a crackle when he reaches the chair by the fireplace. 'Edal, my girl? Kathleen's here to see you.' More to himself, a raw murmur I may not be meant to hear. 'She'll make you better, Edal.'

It takes me a heartbeat or two to get over the shock of seeing an otter that is not Mij. Edal's features are sweet, doll-like and feminine, perched prettily above a snow-white stomach and bib, yet she is bigger than he was, with a coat both lighter and sleeker. Or it would be, if not for her sickness. Regurgitation has soiled the poor creature's rich brown pelt, leaving it sullied with fetid stains. A swelling disfigures her dainty muzzle, bulbous and gruesome as it distorts her powerful jaws, and her head jerks at random intervals, juddering as if locked in fatal mechanical failure. Edal emits no cheerful squeaks of welcome, only a dull, constant hum that poignantly evokes her misery. When I approach, instinctive fear of a stranger wells up in her unfocused brown eyes. She tries to walk, but only her stubby front legs obey. Forced to drag the uncooperative back pair behind her, Edal manages only one step, beaten by the effort of manoeuvring a dead weight. Her long tail twists, paws jolting of their own accord. Short-circuiting. That is the cruel concept which comes to mind before I can resist it. This brave, beautiful animal is short-circuiting before our eyes.

'She doesn't know me anymore.' Standing behind me and presumably still wearing his spectacles, I cannot see the tears in Gavin's eyes. But I hear them.

'Yes, she does,' I insist, not breaking my gaze away from Edal's long body as it irrhythmically contorts. 'Say her name again.'

Gavin bends beside me. 'Edal,' he murmurs, gentle as a prayer. 'My Edal.' There is no obvious recognition. Edal's eyes stay glazed with vague, imprecise sadness. But her spasms briefly cease. Her tail stops

323

twitching. Her body remembers Gavin, even if her mind is too ill to do so consciously. Her love for him will never leave her, whatever agonies she endures. I should know.

'She's different from Mij, isn't she?'

Gavin nods. 'Separate sub-species. Mij's cousin, not his sister,' he simplifies for me in laypoet's terms.

'But still family?'

'Yes,' he agrees. 'She's still family.'

'Where's the other one?' I ask. 'Teki?'

'Teko,' Gavin corrects me, then sighs. A wispy cloud of cigarette smoke drifts past my left ear. 'He's in his quarters at the back of the cottage. I have to keep them apart for their own safety. They simply can't stand to live alongside each other. Too similar and yet too different, Jimmy says.' I can imagine.

'And he's bringing the vet from Broadford?'

Gavin nods numbly. 'Our last hope. Unless you can …'

I cut him off, the pressure of misplaced faith too much to endure. 'Then I'll keep a look out for the boat.'

'We will never doubt one another again,' Gavin murmurs as I rise. 'Never never.' *Neverland*, the phrase makes me think of. Home to the lost boy who never grew up and his loyal mortal woman.

I head upstairs to his bedroom. Our bedroom, as I used to believe. By the window, I wait, watching the churning sea whip up high crests of froth, gathering momentum as they travel before shattering glasslike over the sand. 'Mij, Mij,' their pulsing current seems to call, waves undulating in time to a dark, minor-key lullaby for the waterbaby who will never wake. Tortured by the thought yet compelled by the ceaseless motion of the tide, my head turns to the right of the shoreline. I see the rowan.

'If Edal lives, I will not seek out Gavin again.' Palms pressed to the pane, I make my promise. Cold sweat seeps across the glass from my fingertips. I keep my eyes affixed to those strong, sinewy branches. 'He can come to me if he wishes, but if not … if he doesn't want me, I'll let him go. I'll give him up.' The words threaten to choke me, but I continue. Gavin expects something of me, his desperate heart set upon spiritual intervention now it seems science has failed him, and from the ashes of all we glimpsed through together, this feels like the final lingering flame – in truth, the final forfeit – I have to offer. 'For him, please, *please*, let Edal live.' The gnarled silver trunk shivers in the wind. I fancy its fine emerald leaves are nodding.

'They're coming!' I cry to Gavin, stumbling downstairs in my haste to tell him that I can see the vet's boat coming in.

Chapter Thirty-Nine

'Mother?' It has been so long since I heard Anna say it, I almost forget that my daughter means me.

'Sorry, darling?'

Anna scowls, dark eyes deepening in intensity. 'You weren't listening.'

'Of course I was ...' I garble a poor-woman's defence, made more challenging by the fact that Anna is right. I was not listening intently while she reflected on the relative merits of Girton College Chapel and St Peter's in Martindale, Ullswater. Seated across from my daughter, spellbound by the anticipatory glow illuminating her complexion, I was thinking how strange it is that, two marriages down, I have never actually planned a wedding. Not like this at any rate. Not happily. And yet in an odd way, the contrast between our experiences gives me hope that Anna's marriage, too, will be different from mine. The delicate, poetic sensitivity that sometimes troubled her as a child seems to be metamorphosing into her greatest asset as a young woman: emerging from the chrysalis of shyness and self-doubt to embody a quiet intellectual poise few women twice her age could match. Certainly not her mother.

'You should ask Helen,' I suggest, deferring the decision to one historically far less flawed in making them.

'Or we could go abroad.' A provocative, adolescent energy flashes across Anna's expression, watching keenly for my reaction. 'What would you think if I married abroad?'

'If you're happy, I'm happy.' How that disappoints her, I do not know. Was I meant to protest? For a supposed wordsmith, I have an uncanny knack for saying the wrong thing to my child.

Change calls to us all, it seems, Tambi's plans likewise taking shape with a firmness that, to my shame, I hardly believed he was capable of. Although 'pragmatic' Tambi is still Tambi. Quintessentially whimsical.

'*Poetry London: New York,*' he announces dramatically when we meet the following day, hand sweeping through the air to mimic a newspaper headline. Front page, naturally. 'What do you think?'

326

'Might it be a tad confusing for readers?'

Alas, that effervescent mind has already bubbled up and over onto its next subject. Me. 'Have you sent your decision to the Bollingy yet?'

'Bollingen, Tambi. The Bollingen Foundation. And no, not yet ...' My own offer from The Land of the Free, leaving me in a paralysis of indecision. Powered in no small part by Tambi, news of my Blake studies has reached the shores of the States, and the Bollingen Grant offers funding for future study in exchange for a series of lectures on Blake, along with the other 'golden string' poets. A dream come true, one might say. Had I not recently learned to fear that very thing.

'My ship doesn't leave until the second of February,' Tambi tells me. 'And there's still room for you on board. Not in my cabin, of course, I could barely afford tourist class, never mind a stateroom, but ...' It is so rare to see him serious, it feels more meaningful than in less jovial folk. 'There's room on the boat for you, Kathie. What are you waiting for?'

What indeed? My children are settled. Achievements beckon me overseas. All I know is that Psyche also waited, enduring trial upon trial of separation and suffering, stoicism carrying her onwards even as the soles of her feet became bruised, bloodied and broken. What were stinging flesh and shrieking bones compared with her spiritual quest to be reunited with her love? Cupid could only bear to watch her struggle for so long before he sought her out again. And Gavin will do the same, I know it. I know him. He needed time to rebuild his defences, not least whilst facing fresh pressures from fame, seeking private sanctuary in the shade behind those protective dark glasses. But soon, once again, he will send for me: expensive ivory envelope, exquisite inked words. A letter beginning with thanks, perhaps, for being there for his Edal whose health, last I heard, is fully restored. I am the sole fellow spirit whose journey interweaves with Gavin's own. I am, for better and for worse, the only woman in his life. We rise and set, ebb and flow, short tempers sparking savage electrical storms that have always blown over in time. However painful it is to be parted, I am sticking patiently to my new rowan pledge. I will wait. I will be true. And the wild, oceanic universe will reward me for my fortitude.

Even as autumn creeps towards winter, I enjoy walking the long way back to my rooms through Girton's grounds, untroubled by the cold and feeling somehow stronger for surrendering control. Deliberately directionless, it takes a violent downpour one dusk to finally hasten me home, or at least indoors. I sense my hair frizzing, flyaway wisps

327

springing around my hairline while rogue raindrops slide off my nose and leave a cool, vacant taste on my lips. Confronting my sodden reflection once finally inside, I try and largely fail to untangle the strands that have plastered themselves to my moistened cheeks. The mess makes me laugh. I look like I have been crying.

Vigorously towel-patting my skin, the motion dislodges an envelope that must have been delivered whilst I was out. Thick ivory paper. Intense, ink-heavy script. I seize it instantly, damp fingertips smudging my own name in my euphoric, triumphant haste to hold it tight and never let go. Even blurred by rain, I recognise Gavin's writing. Pulse fluttering, heart singing, I tear it open.

My dear Kathleen,

Despite or because of all our storms and troubles, I would like you to be the first to know that I am going to be married. I pray that this will not distress you too much, and that sometime in the future we may meet with all recollections resolved, and the realisation that whatever we had was not for sharing in any conventional relationship, nor to be permanently destroyed by the separate courses of our lives. I will not expect you to meet or like my wife unless or until you feel like doing so – but hope that in time you may extend some of your love for me to Lavinia too, and realise that hatred or despair is the antithesis of all that either of us would want for anyone.

Love, Gavin.

Chapter Forty

The pool is stagnant. Swanless. I am struggling to breathe; I cannot swallow. Dead leaves fragment beneath my feet, blackened slivers of decay laid out along the park circuit we used to walk together. We? There is no we. Maybe there never was. Numb, I move to the water's edge and crouch, watching my sickly mirror image emerge from the weeds like an old, ghoulish Ophelia. My nose looks bulbous from below, cheeks puffy and pale from interminable weeping.

'You look like a fat squaw,' I tell my reflection.

Beautiful Lavinia must be divorced. I would surely have heard if Edward Renton had died, unless such society gossip plays out at too high a pitch for my dull peasant ears. Even if I had returned to spend more weekends at Monreith – not that Mary deigned to invite me back – I could never belong in the starry universe Gavin and his bride-to-be were born to inhabit. Her father was the King's Private Secretary. Mine is a bowler-hat Methodist. God-fearing. Love-petrified.

I wonder dully what Mary makes of this announcement, the cold-blooded memory of Gavin's mother cutting through me like this chilled late autumn air. It is hard to believe she is willing to accept any other woman for the beloved boy who shared her bed until he was eight, however elegant and well-bred she may be. Alone with Gavin, many miles from Monreith, it has been perilously easy for me to forget that he comes from a world in which pedigree reigns supreme, wives valued on much the same basis as championship spaniel stock like Jonnie.

Bred for breeding. The new idea strikes like ice water inside my veins. Lavinia may bear Gavin's child. The thought submerges me for one moment; in the next, I pray for my heart to stop. I wish my arteries would freeze over like corroded London pipes, cutting off my circulation and putting an end to this pain. I wish I was dead.

Why now? Why is Gavin choosing to be a first-time bridegroom at the age of forty-seven? Have Mary's health scares, embellished or otherwise, frightened them both into appointing her successor? But no, I cling to the cold iron struts of the bench – it is not our bench anymore – and compel my thoughts to find some semblance of order. For Gavin to make such a sudden, shocking decision, there must be a direct threat. Some perceived danger encircling, an ominous tightening of a noose or cinching in of a ring … fame. The notion of his newfound celebrity returns, my realisation slow and stupid. The relentless attention that comes with worldwide acclaim for a bestseller; the dark shadow side of what was once our beloved bright water.

The pressures of public life are encroaching upon Gavin's sanctuary, breaching his old defences faster than he can build new ones, and under such scrutiny, I can imagine him feeling the need for cover. A disguise. A decoy. Odd and unsettling, it gives me a brief rush of sympathy. Young Lavinia shines so brightly to be reduced to a pair of dark glasses. That she loves him, I do not doubt. What woman would not? None could resist succumbing to Gavin's charms if he chose to turn that dazzling, dizzying spotlight in her direction. Even this once-beautiful bluestocking was not immune. How I wish I had been. Futile and fatalistic, my mind scrolls through twisted memory reels from my time at Monreith, trying too late to recall what Lavinia was like with Gavin back then. I picture her seated at his right hand throughout supper, softening the blows of his brothers' mockery with gentle, encouraging questions about Sandaig. As a pair, they were the epitome of fair aristocratic elegance. I was simply too blinded by my own love to see it clearly at the time. 'Certain bachelors change around forty.' That comment alone cost me years of extra longing.

The fledgling hopes I harboured then in foolish innocence are flightless, wings broken. My beach-combed treasures, millennial shells that meant more to me than diamonds or rubies, are crushed into calcified shards. The flowers and fir trees of our shared childhood are wilted and rotten, their fallen leaves the worthless pages of a story no one but me cares enough to tell. To the rest of the world, another will be Mrs Maxwell. Another will take the name that my soul tells me I was born to bear.

'Mij.' Staring out at the mottled pond water, I moan our otter's name, my plaintive whimper carried off on the cold air as if I am still on the shoreline, crying out in vain for our cherished animal child to return. Mij represented the missing piece of both our broken souls; the waterbaby whose landbound parents loved him so dearly that they, in a way, continued to love each other. I know with the deep, unshakeable certainty that usually only comes to me through poetry that Gavin would not have

330

married another while Mij was still alive.

Splintered weed stalks protrude from the stagnant mire beside me. Congealed lumps of scum and sediment sully the edge of my path, faecal and grim. The world that once contained so much vivid, multidimensional beauty I felt compelled to turn it into poetry is now vacant. Void. Dead. Blindly following the sloping curve of the pond around the corner, I find that a little market is underway, a makeshift avenue of stalls causing a bottleneck of potential patrons. It seems everyone is selling out these days. Awaiting my chance to push through the crowd and start my mournful return journey back to Girton, I end up hovering beside a newspaper stand. The grainy front pages flicker, details washed away by my unfocused gaze. I blink. And again. Disbelief sends a wave of sickness through me, heartbeat thundering like a storm-wracked tide striking the shore.

'The Road to Romance in the Isles.' I grab the closest copy, fumbling in my purse to hand the startled seller ten times what the newspaper costs. 'The happy couple are not planning a long engagement, so excited to commence married life that they have already set the date. 1st February 1962.' My grip digs into the sheet; I feel the paper tear under my nails. '"It's been a whirlwind," the beautiful bride-to-be told our reporter when he visited her and Major Maxwell at his legendary idyll Camusfeàrna. "Our families have known one another for many years, but I never suspected that Gavin cared for me in that way." A healthy Highland blush bloomed over Miss Lascelles' English-rose complexion. "Then one day, he suddenly said, if I ever marry, it could only be you." The smitten fiancée giggled sweetly. "Such a surprise!" The newlyweds intend to honeymoon in Morocco after a wedding night spent in Northumberland and a luxurious reception at Claridge's.'

I seem to recall Gavin telling me years ago that he should rather die than spend another evening at Claridge's. It transpires Gavin has said a great many things he did not mean.

'For their special day itself,' the correspondent gushes, 'the service will take place at the Scottish Presbyterian Church in Covent Garden.' My imagination blooms with the picture of a vibrant, bustling flower market, the bridal party making their way along a street already strewn with petals. I see Lavinia as Eliza Doolittle, a born Duchess no matter how scruffy her surroundings. I feel more like the cold ivory tale of Pygmalion in reverse: a flesh and blood woman receding into lifelessness. 'Naturally,' the newspaper notes, 'this popular socialite has plenty of girlfriends eager to undertake bridesmaid duties, whilst the Major tells us he will be ably assisted by his two brothers and best man, Raef Payne.'

No longer can I fault the happy couple for their haste. It seems prudent to wed before the groom remembers that he would rather bed his best man than his bride.

Lavinia has two sons from her former marriage, the paper continues, who are delighted to have a new stepfather. The details are left discreetly opaque, but reading between the lines, I deduce the break came from divorce rather than widowhood. Ages fifteen and thirteen. Younger than James. Not quite as old as Raef was when he and Gavin met. Another mark on the list in Lavinia's favour?

'Are you alright, madam?'

I clench the newspaper, suppressing the retch rising up from the embittered depths of my stomach. 'Fine. Thank you.' Yet again, I am the disgusting one. Revolting. Perverse. Only a monster, exiled and cursed, could contemplate such a thought.

Locked in self-recrimination, I walk on, hands wrapped around the newspaper from which I cannot tear myself away. Within moments, my legs threaten to fail me again. I hurl out my palm, skin snagging against a nearby tree trunk as I reach out for its support. There is a photograph. Gavin and Lavinia together on Sandaig's shore. She is looking to him; he is looking out to sea. Gavin's long legs are encased in a pair of modern denim jeans that I have not seen before, the sleeves of his dark sweater rolled up over the forearms where, if he turned, I know those berry-toned birthmarks lie like lipstick kisses on his skin. Lavinia's white smile beams out from beneath a chic, neatly knotted headscarf, her cagoule cinched in by a piece of string at her waist. She seems happy. She is happy. If there is one look I ought to recognise, it is that of a woman in love.

Gavin glances out to the ocean with a dashing, mid-laugh smile, staring at the ceaseless waves that have so often mesmerised me. The wild, sweeping expanse of unconquered ocean opens before him, a shimmering glimpse of Skye just a hint on the pale horizon. Naturally, the newspaper print is plain black and white, but my heart adds the colours, recalling them with the same haunting, half-conscious intimacy of lullaby notes embedded into one's soul during the earliest days of childhood. I see the velvet moss of green lichen and rippling kelp strewn over the stones. The biscuit-crumb yellow of the sand, deepening to rich golden brown along the tapering strandline. The crisp, white-lined waves crashing forth from an ocean of coolly translucent blue that perfectly matches Gavin's eyes. The metallic twists of the rowan tree's trunk, just beyond the bounds of the photograph.

I thought he had married me with a ring, a ring of bright water whose ripples travelled from the heart of the sea. She will be married with a ring of gold that he gives her in sight of God.

I stumble on without seeing, my hipbone colliding with another stall. This one bears trinkets, magpie glints of coloured glass costume jewellery on sale for shillings rather than pounds. The glittering fakes remind me that I am wearing my pearl necklace, a relic from when the link to Gavin it represents still symbolised hope and not a millstone around my neck.

'I'll take this one,' I hear myself say hoarsely, lifting up a thin strand of faux-freshwater beads. The woman behind the stall nods, then turns her back to wrap the purchase in a creased square of tissue paper. I slip off my own necklace unseen, abandoning the genuine pearls to sink into a murky seabed of imposters. What is real and what is false makes little difference anymore.

*

The dream begins in a church. I am alone amongst the darkened pews, sliding clumsily through a labyrinth of slick hardwood benches in my inarticulate haste to reach an aisle of black flagstones beyond. A choir of disembodied voices repeats a sinister minor key scale, eerily absorbed by the cavernous, damp stone walls. From a cobwebbed corner more crypt than chapel, a meagre cluster of candles casts haunting, erratic illuminations. Looking closer, I realise with a weak cry of horror that the candlesticks hover upside-down, surreally suspended like flaming daggers pointing not to Heaven but Hell. Creepily compelled despite my terror, I reach out to touch one of those pulsing stalactite tapers. The unseen choir grows louder, a hypnotic descant luring me further down the shadowy aisle. My next step sends me falling, but not onto the church's cold flagstones. Instead, I am descending Monreith's spiral staircase, a frenzied swirl of crimson skirts engulfing me as I plummet, tumble and twist.

My screams are muffled by the stifling fabric; I bite down on a passing piece of red and taste blood, tart and metallic. Striking against the never-ending stairs, I feel like Alice down the rabbit hole, limbs flailing as I hurtle earthbound at a speed that renders size and space meaningless. Too large to believe I can survive without breaking my neck, yet simultaneously so shrunken I might be a powerless grain of sand, ricocheting down the cartilage turret of a fossilised shell. When at last I land with a muted thud, I scan either side of me to find whatever force broke my fall. Pulling back, my palms overflow with pale grey, plucked fledgling feathers. I hurry to stand, sickened by the sight, but ribbony tree roots are ensnaring my ankles, tight knots straining against my skin as I fight to free myself from their growing confines. The harder I tug, the firmer the ivy-like vice, my skirt billowing wide in the struggle until its top layer rises like a breaking wave, smothering my face as first a veil and then a shroud.

'Kathleen?' Through the gauzy mist of material, I hear Lavinia calling my name. Shoving the last of my dress layers aside, I gasp for air and see that she no longer wears navy blue but white. Pure white. Gavin's bride is ethereal, as transcendent as a Blake creation, and just like the very first time I saw her, the thought strikes me that this woman is too beautiful to be flesh and blood. Yet when she comes closer, her hands feel warmly human. With a gentle touch, Lavinia presses my palm to her breast. She is wearing a wedding ring. My fingers are bare.

'Thank you.' Lips light as air, Lavinia kisses me. Tenderly, thoughtfully, as if wishing to give me her blessing. But that's wrong, my mind insists with animalistic rage. Everything here is the wrong way round. It should be me. That single phrase rings in my ears and throbs in my chest, spilling from my lips with the acidic bitterness of a broken heart rupturing.

'It should be me.' As I speak, a blinding flash strikes the scene, electric energy engulfing Lavinia's train until her silhouette burns raw white with heat. When I can see again, it is Gavin himself standing before me, my trembling hand still held to his heart. With my other, I reach for him, frantic fingertips clamouring like those of one starved or near-drowned. In my chaotic peripheral vision, a stag's headless body wanders lost through Monreith's great halls; with a violent, whip-cracking wrench, a gold eagle breaks free from its marble plinth, shedding jagged splinters of metal as its wings beat with wild fury for the forest.

No sooner does Gavin's body yield to my touch than he is transfigured back into his wife-to-be. I am grappling for him while scratching at her, driven mad by vying, interwoven desires to have and, if not, to savage. 1st February. Every wedding day turns into a wedding night. I remember mine, although I have tried hard to forget offering up my youthful pound of flesh to Hugh. He took more than a pound, as I recall. My taut, lithe body back then was the only asset I had to pay the physical price of my liberation; escaping, or so it seemed, from Ilford and the fate that awaited me there. Will Lavinia feel similar reluctance? Similar fear? Or will she simply do all I have wished to: lips pressed to Gavin's ear as she begs him to enter her, crying out for him like a Highland wildcat in heat while she kisses each birthmark in turn, tongue flowing from his elbow to his wrist and everywhere else besides?

With a bitten lip, I wake to my own moan, tangled in the Soay fisherman's sweater of Gavin's that I still wear in bed for warmth. Its thick, salt-coarsened wool sits like an irritant hairshirt against my bare skin. The knitted checks have grown hazy with age, broken threads blurring lines until the once eye-catching pattern is left ugly and unintelligible. Scrunching the hem, I ram my dry, ink-stained fingers inside myself: nails scratching and scraping until, contracting from shock, the long-paused blood starts to flow. I thrust and writhe, body spasming, breathing ragged. When I scream, it is not from pleasure but pain, echoing the violent, storm-swept heart's cry with which I cursed Gavin at the foot of his rowan.

In the morning, I sail for America.

Part Three
1962

Chapter Forty-One

'Vision is not hallucination, it is imaginative insight, and compared with the visionary power of the imagination, the human eye is little more than a window. "I look through it, not with it," William Blake observed a hundred and fifty years ago.' Taking a breath, I step out from behind my lectern. For the first time in years, I believe that I am seeing clearly myself.

This talk had a bumpy start, I admit. I'd defy anyone to address Washington D.C.'s National Gallery of Art, especially as the first woman ever to do so, and not feel somewhat daunted. Limbs trembling, I had waited in the wings for them to announce my name. Dr Kathleen Raine, of Girton College, Cambridge, to deliver this May's annual A.W. Mellon Lectures. Who knew Americans cared so much for Blake? To polite applause, I strode stiffly across the stage, praying that slower movements would soothe my racing heart. Tight rows of unfamiliar faces stared back from floor and balcony, expressions alternately scrutinising and expectant. Hard to decide which was worse.

'William Blake has often been viewed as an uneducated visionary who owed nothing to tradition.' Too late, I felt the cloying pressure to clear my fear-constricted throat. Fingertips shaking, I left my first line in lonely, awkward suspension to reach for my glass, spluttering as soon as the tepid water hit my lips. 'Yet to the modern scholar,' I continued, lectern microphone crackling, 'many details of the great man's life have been subject to error and misunderstanding.' Twisted truths. Downright lies. God knows I am equipped to speak on that subject.

'Indeed, even Blake's ostensibly blissful marriage may well have been an exaggeration.' My notes lay neglected on the stand, diligent research swept away by poorly repressed rage. I knew, as must some in my audience, that I had described Catherine Blake in my first pamphlet as 'one of the exemplary wives of literary history'. But I arrived here in no mood to talk of happy unions. 'Intrigued by the idea of free love, it is just possible that Blake was drawn to his close friend, Mary Wollstonecraft:

339

an intellectual equal who, unlike his wife, had radical ideas of her own.' Were William and Mary lovers? There is little evidence to suggest it. Too little, in truth, to justify making the claim. And yet I felt suddenly unable, unwilling, to admit that someone as visionary as my poetic hero enjoyed the very peace in life that I lack.

'Unconnected and undereducated, perhaps Catherine came to bore him.' The unnecessary cruelty snagged in my dry mouth. I felt desperate for another drink but did not dare stop to take one. Instead, I dug my nails into the lectern, splinters breaking off to pinch my skin. If I am not good enough, why should Catherine Blake be? Why should I extend sisterhood to another when a whole decade of my faithfulness has been so brutally brushed aside? A man in the front row had started slinking down into his seat, preparing to doze through a disappointing, domestically-oriented lecture. What else does one expect from a woman? The scholar next to him – I clutched the lectern to stay standing whilst having to bear my shame – looked on with unmistakable, unendurable pity. Face flushed, tears threatening, I turned from her to glimpse myself in the half-empty water glass. Was it that obvious to these strangers? Heartbreak written so clearly across my face?

Frantic, I had scanned the room, eyes of every shade blinking back at me. Blue, grey, green … I sought out brown, rich dark brown that I might make stand-in for Tambi's. His real eyes were two-hundred miles away in New York, having been happily caught barely a day after disembarking by a beautiful young woman with whom he now cohabits. States apart as life and work called us in different directions, our plan was to catch up after my lecture. 'My triumph,' as Tambi had taken to calling it in his letters. He deserved better than this selfish, vengeful performance. So did William Blake. Even I did.

'Yet whatever the troubles of their early years together, William and Catherine always found time for levity.' Scrambling to recover, I was still ignoring my notes, but the improvisation no longer came from anger. I knew this material. More comprehensively than any other subject in my life. And I knew a story from Blake's colourful creative existence that could still turn the tide of feeling in my favour. 'Blake taught his wife to read, and a perennially popular legend reports they were once discovered reading *Paradise Lost* to each other in their garden entirely nake … well, shall we say, dressed as Adam and Eve? Although in some versions of the infamous tale, they are said to have been wearing helmets.'

340

Titters of laughter. Smiles interspersed with sighs of relief. Softened expressions supplanted frowns as my audience settled into trusting they would not need to witness my public humiliation after all. By sleight of hand, I recovered my notes and a little dignity with them. I would do what I came here for. Share the untold power of a poet who understood that our souls matter more than anything on earth. Express my deep, abiding gratitude for the knowledge there have been others like me, others determined to look through their mortal eyes with God-given imagination. That awareness has given me the strength to survive, since my hopes for the life that my heart told me I should have were ripped away without warning and offered to another. Blake remained. Poetry sustained. And now, at last, I am concluding my tribute to them.

'To Blake, nature represented "one continued vision of imagination",' I tell the hall, emerging from behind the podium's protection to deliver my final lines. My cheeks warm with enthusiasm under the intense auditorium lights; my pulse throbs, empowered to claim this continent as my own. 'His vision of the good life was pastoral, lived in imaginative harmony with nature ...' Don't think of him, I remind myself, averting my gaze from the few flashes of blond hair amidst the plentiful black and brown. Even Gavin does not have a monopoly on nature. I push aside the thought of us exchanging our poetry in the park; of watching waves crash within a hair's breadth of his home on the edge of the habitable world. Of rowan petals crushed in the palm of my hand. '"I see Every thing I paint In This World," Blake wrote, "to the Eyes of the Man of Imagination, Nature is Imagination itself. As a man is, So he Sees." To such a poet, or perhaps a prophet, nature always gives back. Thank you.'

Their applause fills the room, sound striking against polished wood panels in loud lashes that travel straight from my ears to my core. Retreating back behind the wings of the stage, I head down the small steps to where people are already gathering to shake my hand. My seldom-used smile muscles twinge as I make my slow way through the throng.

'Fascinating ...'

'Such an intriguing premise ...'

'So well delivered ...'

'An uncertain start, but by the end, *très important*.'

'*Excusez-moi?*' Annoyance shocks my schoolgirl French into automatic action. The man who spoke is last in line and, hand shaken, he refuses to let go. The crowd around us begins to disperse but he and

I remain awkwardly linked, fingers locked as if in readiness for either a dance or a duel.

'I mean no offence.' English again, but heavily accented. About my age, he is neat-framed and faintly dapper with an immaculate dark moustache. His eyes, too, are black, bright and beady. Fixed on me. '*Vraiment*, on the contrary. Not one of the many men I have heard speak from that stage could have achieved such a … how do you say?' The man keeps staring, as if retrieval of the words he cannot find is down to me.

'*Retour sur scène?*'

He is pleased. '*Exactement.*' I wriggle my wrist and the man finally remembers we are entwined. He lets go, without stepping back. 'Dr Raine –' he pronounces 'doctor' in the French manner, a growling stress on the second vowel that sounds more like '*or*' for gold – 'it's so clever what you have done. The way you've conducted your research, the message of Blake's work runs right through it. Reading what he read, if I have understood you correctly?'

'*Oui.*' I am starting to enjoy the French now.

'Uncovering symbols, revealing hidden traditions, and as you discover the history that influenced him –' this strange man waves his fingers, crisscrossing to capture the effect of multiple threads being woven together – 'you show us where he belongs in history. Blake saw connection in all things, and these things you connect to him. Quite brilliant.'

'Who *are* you?' If this man is a fellow writer, I do not recognise him. Another scholar? Rarer still to find a kindred spirit in competitive, cut-throat academia. But how can someone I have never met so intuitively grasp the nuances of my long research labours? How can he instantly comprehend the complexities I thought I had hidden in plain sight? Once upon a time, Gavin dutifully read my Blake work and made valiant attempts at analysis, yet at times even I had to wonder if some of it did not go over his beautiful blond head.

The man in front of me grins, sharp moustache ruffled by his top lip. 'Alexis Léger. *Enchanté.*'

'Kathleen Raine.'

Another moustache twitch. 'I know. May I take you to dinner, Dr Raine? *À deux?*'

'No.' The abruptness is knee-jerk, my manners unnerved by Alexis's bluntness. It has been over ten years since a man even appeared to court me. Surely such adventures are meant to stop after fifty. 'Thank you,

342

but no.' At sea with my surprise, I flounder, cheeks burning and palms sweating. One is already warm from his handshake. 'I have another engagement.' The excuse is true; I have the speaker's dinner tonight. As guest of honour, I can hardly fail to attend.

'I cannot tempt you to break it?' Black glitter illuminates Alexis's eyes.

'Perhaps another time.' Another me, I mean. A me who could appreciate an adventure; a woman who could bask in the glow of this gentleman's unanticipated attentions. A Kathleen who had not left her heart on the other side of the Atlantic.

Alexis accepts my rebuff with suave, casual confidence. One missed opportunity with a middle-aged bluestocking can be no great loss to a debonair Frenchman. He will have some young beauty on his smart-suited arm before the evening is out, I am certain. And yet even as I think it, Alexis reaches for my hand, raising it to his lips to offer the whisper of a kiss. 'I hope fate sees fit to permit us to meet again, Dr Raine.'

'Kathleen, please.' My skin prickles, tickled by his moustache.

Back in my room before the dinner, I study my reflection, pleasantly surprised with what I see. More silver strands than before ripple through my hair, yet my figure is streamlined: the misery of past months having inadvertently manifested in a trimmer, tightened physique. The effect is enhanced, if I dare to think it, by my dress. Red Italian silk, an impulse purchase egged on by Tambi to mark our arrival in New York and as shockingly flattering on my frame as it is far from my typical style. Curious, my fingers skim the freshly refined lines of my curves, flowing over hips and bust draped in glossy, vivid scarlet. How helpful to know that red is my colour. Thank you, Mrs Maxwell.

I move to the dressing table where, amidst the minimal beauty accoutrements of a woman terminally disinterested in such matters, Gavin's cowrie shell sits beside my notebook. Secreted shamefully in my pocket, I brought it with me on the boat; carried all the way across the ocean and perhaps even to the shore where it originated millennia ago. Why? I scarcely needed the reminder. And yet I wanted it even so, not of Gavin himself exactly, but of what we 'glimpsed through' together. He has forgotten, or so it seems, turning head and heart away from the humbling power of great ocean meeting expansive sky, where the quicksilver burn bound a ring about us both. But I never can. I owe too much poetry to it. Drawing deep, I turn to face north-east where I estimate Sandaig to be. No pull. No force inside me sparking alight. I suppose the connection tying me to that shoreline has been severed.

Downstairs in the hotel restaurant, I meet more applause, with further unfamiliar faces presented to me before we sit for dinner. Personally unfamiliar, I should say, because some come as close as poetry ever will to producing genuine household names. W.H. Auden, for instance, a man whose legendary inventiveness has shaped my discipline like few others.

'You must admit,' he drawls as if picking up the thread of an argument I do not remember starting, 'that Blake is one of the dotty poets?'

'Dotty?' Only the thought of Tambi's mortification if I insulted one of our 'great minds' persuades me to meekly bite my tongue. Beware heroes with feet of clay, as they say in Great Bavington.

More strangers are introduced and my mind swims through a watery blur of similar suits in varying greys. The true Blake devotees struggle not to express their obvious disdain for a woman doing what they think is a man's work. Specifically theirs, if they had only managed to publish it first. The others, mainly those who have already started drinking, look down on me with pseudo-avuncular leers. None are familiar. None are appealing. Until …

'Alexis?' In an instant, the gallery director is at my elbow, presumably inspired by my showing a pique of genuine interest in anyone.

'Dr Raine, may I introduce Saint-John Perse?'

'Who?'

Alexis laughs, his dark moustache dancing with mirth. '*Un petit nom de plume.* But you, madame –' once again, he reaches for my hand; once again, he kisses it '– you deserved my real name.' My fingers at his lips, I am speechless. Saint-John Perse is a celebrity. A famed French diplomat turned internationally acclaimed poet. And not just acclaimed, but award-winning. If I recall correctly, although my mind has seldom felt more muddled, did he not receive the 1960 Nobel Prize for Literature?

'You … you're you.' The stupid comment tumbles from me before I can stop it. I feel Alexis's smile spreading across my fingertips.

'Quite so. I am "the great I AM."' Another Blake quote. Even in my confusion, the recognition dawns.

'You … you would've had me miss being guest of honour.'

Alexis responds with a gentlemanly bow, lowering our linked hands. 'I'm sure you are that wherever you go, Kathleen.'

'But you tricked me.'

'*Et vous m'avez ensorcelée.*' And you have bewitched me.

344

Chapter Forty-Two

'Have I missed it?' Tambi stumbles across the state line a day too late for my lecture. 'I'm so – so – sorry, Kathie.' Only for him can kisses function perfectly as punctuation. In my peripheral vision, I sense Alexis observing us closely. 'There's been such a lot happening. Esta's expecting.' The exquisite *cohabitante*, evidently no longer just Tambi's lover but now his *femme* too. *Mon dieu*. Deep-rooted resentment of marriage notwithstanding, I suppress my shock to wish them well.

'I'd love to meet her one day,' I say, my mind marvelling at the unknown woman brave enough to become Mrs Tambimuttu. Tambi nods vigorously, his attention already transferring to Alexis at my side.

'And who exactly is this gentleman?' Perhaps because of the language barrier, Alexis seems to miss the friendly jocularity in Tambi's tone.

'Saint-John Perse, at your service, sir.' The modesty of his real name is shed in favour of the famous one. Strange as it is to me, Alexis appears to perceive Tambi as a threat; the competitive posturing of a hitherto muted masculinity striking me somewhere between comical and charming. Gavin never grew jealous of other men. Of course, that is not to say he wanted nothing from them.

Instantly comprehending Alexis's celebrity, Tambi laughs, loud belly convulsions of satisfaction.

'You're a prize, Kathie. You always did deserve a prize winner.'

Now, my friend is sleeping off the previous evening's liquid salutations while Alexis and I stroll through the gardens of Dumbarton Oaks. Washington D.C.'s prestigious research library has expansive, surprisingly secluded grounds that feel like a place to soothe the soul. Far removed from the frantic pace I have found more generally characterises the States, this beautiful landscape in microcosm is the only campus I have known to rival Girton for peace, stillness and serenity. As Alexis and I glide through the parkland, we pass several stone monuments to our literary ancestors, names framed by trailing garlands of ivy, but soon the formality of defined hedgerows and flowerbeds fades in favour of a reinvigorating return to wildness. Limb-like branches from the eponymous oaks sprawl balletically into leafy boughs above our heads; our path dips to reveal a hidden hill of cherry trees, their lilac petals ruffling like confetti caught on a breeze. Yet further, we find a pool, encircled by rows of little brick seats to create a unique watery amphitheatre.

'They call this Lovers' Lane Pool,' Alexis tells me. 'Shall we sit?' I watch the spring light glitter and dance over the watery ring.

'Not yet,' I say. 'Let's keep going.'

We arrive at an elegant glasshouse that Alexis names as Dumbarton Oaks Orangery. '*Voulez-vous entrer?*'

'*Oui, merci.*' Inside, the Orangery atmosphere – full of foliage, empty of humans save for us – makes me think bizarrely of a French bistro reclaimed by nature. Twisted wrought-iron furniture mimics the heart-shaped leaves of the thriving fig vines, spiralling over pillars and plinths to create an alternative sky full of foliage. Here, I consent to take a seat, surveying the sweep of parkland beyond as I look through the antique glass panels. Through, not with, as Blake would clarify.

'Tell me about your sadness, Kathleen.' I turn to face Alexis, his expression thoughtful and suddenly sombre. 'Tell me of the sadness that is weighing down your soul.' And I do. I unburden myself to Alexis, pouring out my miseries as if last night's good wine is still coursing through my veins, loosening my tongue and disinhibiting my emotions until I have imparted most, if not quite all, of my sorrowful Sandaig tale. The candour feels foreign yet cathartic as I speak of the coast, of the fierce crash of the waves and the dazzling twist of the bright burn; of the gush of the fern-framed, clover-dappled waterfall that I fear I will never see or hear again. Tears streaming, I tell Alexis of Mij. I tell him of my mistakes, that cursed harness and the curse itself. I even confess, although I had believed I could never bear the indignity of doing so, what happened on the boat over here.

I had promised myself as Tambi and I crossed the Atlantic that I was travelling towards a new life, at least temporarily; the desperate hope of future forgetfulness the only thing keeping me buoyant in the present.

'Then one day, I walked past First Class,' I tell Alexis. 'And I saw him.'

'Gavin Maxwell?' His idiosyncratic pronunciation submerges the 'a' sound. More like 'Give-in'.

I shake my head. 'Gavin Young.' That dashing, carefree young man

346

who has witnessed this woman at her worst: crippled with envy, maddened by heartbreak and vexed by the irrational desire for vengeance that I fear, in the darkest moments of all my solitary nights since, will never cease rebounding upon me and the ones I love. Young must be here, somewhere in the United States, but I never found out where or why. By unspoken agreement, we avoided each other's eyes.

'You have survived a great deal,' Alexis observes when I conclude, tear-stained and spent. 'You have courage, Kathleen.'

'Forgive me. I lack your courage'. That is what Gavin wrote to me years ago. But how can anybody think me brave?

'If I was truly courageous, my life would look nothing like it does,' I insist. I would not be alone, nor bereft. There would not be an ocean between me and my children. Yet Alexis will not permit self-pitying melancholy.

'A courageous life is not one free from mistakes or experiments.' He leans forward, that immaculate moustache mere inches from my face. 'The secret is being brave enough to put your head in the lion's mouth.'

'I ...' I don't know what I intend to say next. Alexis kisses me before I have the chance. His lips seek out mine, the tip of his tongue glancing my front teeth as my unformed words come and go without expression. His wiry moustache-bristles scratch my skin, his palm cupping my cheek to press me closer to him, and the sheer heat of proximity pulses through me as if this kiss were not just connection but conduit: the forgotten nearness of another body setting my heart racing in shock as much as lust. Is this desire? The feeling is so distant, at least, in reciprocation, and my surprise is so intense, I can scarcely define the sensation. There is a note akin to panic, my pulse rattling towards what feels like a frenzied medical emergency as if a succession of bullets is going off inside my brain. Genuine light-headedness, romantic in theory but in practice rather alarming. And absence. A strange, indefinable part of me feels absent. The poet, perhaps, as opposed to the woman. Unmoved by my body's odd, unpractised stirrings, she remains a dispassionate observer of proceedings, watching numbly from afar, like some vital part might as well be on the other side of the ocean.

We break apart. Both require a moment to catch our breath. French or not, kissing like that is a young person's game. Alexis's moustache is dishevelled, bunched over a top lip that shines with moisture gleaned from my own. His face is flushed. Clamping my hands to my cheeks, I feel mine close to beetroot. I start to laugh.

'*Qu'avez-vous?* What's the matter?' Neither irritation nor embarrassment helps to cool Alexis's complexion. '*Ce n'est pas* the response a man wants from a woman.'

'I'm sorry –' I stammer helplessly. 'It just feels so funny when I've … I've not been kissed for fifteen years.'

Again, Alexis fails to see the humour. '*C'est un scandale.*'

My laughter starts to subside. '*Oui.*'

Alexis shakes his head in incredulity. 'A woman like you …' Gavin once told me what sort of woman I was. That horrifying, haunted night at The Buttery. But this man thinks differently. '*Je te veux.*' I want you. The schoolgirl in me notes new familiarity in the pronoun. An appropriate shift for people who have French-kissed. The woman in me is occupied by other thoughts. 'I want you,' Alexis repeats reluctantly in English, as if afraid I may not otherwise understand. 'In body and in heart.'

'My heart isn't mine to give.' Alexis does not need to ask whom I mean. We have spoken enough about 'Give-in'.

'Such a man does not deserve it,' he tells me firmly.

'No,' I concede, wondering why it feels like a betrayal to say so. 'Perhaps not.'

'And I'm a marvellous lover.' Thirty-five years too old to be girlish, I force myself not to giggle again. God bless French directness. If Gavin and I were Parisians, or if Sandaig was in the South of France, might we have been better at expressing what we truly needed from one another?

'I don't doubt it,' I reassure Alexis. 'But I can't.'

'*Tu ne me veux pas?*' You don't want me?

'It's not that, it's …' As a supposed wordsmith, I lack the verbal dexterity to articulate what I mean. Loyalty. I guess that must be the concept. Mad, misplaced loyalty. It is not to Gavin, or not just to him, but to what we had. What we shared. The burn weaving its glittering way into my work; my poetry bringing forth the prose that has illuminated his brightness to half the English-speaking world. I cannot betray that power. Not again. Staring past the over-spilling fig vines of the most beautiful spot in Washington D.C., I visualise white rowan blossom under a high Highland summer sun. 'My heart is his,' I say simply.

The corners of Alexis's dark eyes droop in an ambivalent sort of sympathy. 'But Kathleen …' I look down. Our fingers are linked, although I cannot recall how it happened. 'Do you really think Monsieur Maxwell is spending his nights alone?'

'I ...' My vision of Gavin is swept away by new, tormented imaginings. Mrs Maxwell in her wedding dress. Mrs Maxwell in her bridal lingerie. Mrs Maxwell's slender, elegant limbs wrapped around Gavin's torso as they tumble into bed, her bright beauty drawing him away from the dark compulsions with which my own meagre charms could never compete.

'My apartment.' Alexis interrupts my tortured daydream, rising to remove from his pocket an ornately decorated calling card. With infinite gentleness, he slots it into my hand. Then he kisses it before taking his leave. '*Une femme peut changer d'avis.*' A woman may change her mind.

After a moment or two alone, I stand. The Orangery glows with warmth as the copper sun outside starts to set, glass panels projecting dazzling displays of bronzed light onto the slate tiles and casting rose-gold beams over the foliage until it gleams. I reach for the strand of a hanging vine, letting its diamond petals trail over the card in my hand. The motion recalls a girlish game still popular at Girton from what I overhear. *He loves me, he loves me not.* I need no rhyme to confirm Gavin does not love me anymore.

Lost in thought, I weave my way back along the route that I believe Alexis and I came by. I recognise Lover's Lane Pool, as much from the scent of petalled, perfume-infused water as by sight, then walk a slow, thoughtful circuit of its Roman brick seat surrounds. The world feels warm when I step into shimmering patches of this intense, climactic sunlight; chilled whenever my path draws me back into leafy shadows. Silencing my mind does not come naturally, but I try, listening to my senses and attempting to awaken a sensuality long repressed as I contemplate what it would be like to have a lover again. Spring air ruffles my hair, loose strands rippling in the breeze before returning to tickle my neck and whisper the wind's words in my ears. I tell myself it is Alexis. Kissing, glancing, grazing, caressing ...

Outside his door, I can see myself reflected. Black gloss silhouette standing tall, head held high with a self-respect I thought lost forever on the day I left England. I bend to push my note beneath the threshold.

'*Je ne peux pas. Je suis désolée. Je l'aime toujours.*' I can't. I'm sorry. I love him still. Withdrawing Gavin's cowrie shell from my pocket, I roll it one last time between my fingertips. Set it down on Alexis's doorstep. As I retreat, I whisper the last line of my note, hoping against all logic that the man on the other side can hear me. '*Merci.*'

Chapter Forty-Three

"Embrace me then, ye Hills, and close me in." I fold forward to scrub the clouded windscreen with my sleeve, clearing a compact crescent of visibility whilst trying my best not to swerve. Thoughts of Washington cede to Wordsworth as my little hire car bumps along another twisting Lake District lane, squeaking wipers roused reluctantly into action as a smirr of Scots haar descends over this English vale. I hate driving but forced myself to learn, on these very roads, in fact, when the children were small. A single mother cannot lack for fatherly skills. Now, dusting off the memory of my long-lost competence, I tell myself firmly that it is just like riding a bicycle. Except the other cars have horns, not bells, and a bicycle would not have windows that steam up most inconveniently with condensation. My speed is brisk, albeit some fifty miles per hour short of what Gavin would deem acceptable. But I must drive carefully and not just quickly. I cannot crash before getting the chance to meet my grandchild.

Anna and John eloped in the end. Abroad, as she had promised, or threatened, without sending word to me across the Atlantic. The new Mrs Hopewell did, however, write to share her next, even bigger piece of news.

'I'm going to have a baby.' Anna's neat, sweet handwriting still bears the schoolroom hallmarks of dotted 'i's and crossed 't's. Seeing them again had caused my heart to ache from a thousand miles away. Pushing personal shock aside, I knew instantly that no young woman should have to go through such a momentous life event without her mother. I knew, because I had to. The shame of my pregnancy with Anna, growing from the mess of my overlapping marital entanglements, proved too much for Jessie and George to bear back in 1934.

The Ullswater road ahead of me dips, nestled within a cool valley formed by silver hillsides on either flank, and I shiver, shaking off unhappy reminders of the past and determining to focus on the joy of the future. Anna's imminent new arrival is well worth recrossing the ocean for. Travelling east through the States before my return voyage, I was even able to pay a fleeting visit to Tambi, now happily ensconced in New York with his own expanding family.

'I suit a melting pot city,' he had observed with good cheer as we browsed the crowded shelves of Gotham Book Mart together, the titles offering a wide-ranging array of cultures, ideas and origins that very much matched the diverse city outside.

'It suits you too,' I told him honestly, happy to see the way in which Tambi truly did seem to fit a place where intellectual idiosyncrasies may roam without restraint. Even he and Esta appeared to be the perfect match. Guiltily, I set asunder my scepticism that any sane woman could tolerate Tambi's quirky inclinations for long. Their baby had arrived only a couple of weeks earlier: Shakuntala, her huge dark eyes dancing with the same spirited curiosity as her father's, and Tambi asked me to become her Godmother in an impromptu 'christening' that felt spiritually, if not quite officially, binding. The warm weight of Tambi's daughter in my arms, her tiny head beside my breast as she dozed through her worldly welcome, had sent a silent tear of unexpected, surely undeserved happiness cascading down my cheek and onto hers. Life goes on, her contented dream mews seemed to murmur. Nature always gives back. My thoughts had flowed to Anna's child-to-be, to Anna herself, and even to the undimmed memories of my own childhood: Aunty Peggy in Great Bavington and each winter's miraculous thaw into spring. There will be no end to snowdrops.

Arriving back in London, I spent as little time as possible in the city before beginning my sojourn to the Lakes. Amongst the familiar landmarks, fear took hold that to let my eyes linger on a street corner would be to risk catching sight of Lavinia coming in my direction. Beautiful as ever. Perhaps even pushing her own pram. The thought that a couple like the Maxwells would have a nanny to do it for them felt like a poor, ice-cold comfort. And so, I went straight to Ullswater – or more truthfully, I fled, seeking comfort in the cradle of Romantic poetry where these mist-wrapped mountains can shield me from the hard edges of modern-day life. My tiny car bumps along a track designed for horse and cart, the semi-circle of clear windscreen shrinking. Cockley Moor is little more than a soft slate blur as I pull up to Helen's house on the hill.

My friend sees me coming from the window, hurrying to greet me before I have time to knock. Helen looks older now – don't we all? – with her hair more white than grey. Yet as she stands on the threshold with her arms wide, it strikes me that those vivid emerald eyes have never looked more exhilarated.

'How is she?' I whisper urgently when we embrace. From the length of time it took Anna's US-bound letter to reach me, my best guess suggests that her baby is due soon.

Helen beams more broadly than I have ever seen her do before. 'They, Kathleen.' Her tight hold becomes necessary to keep me standing. 'Mother and son are both doing well.'

'Anna has a son?' My voice sounds suddenly hoarse, too weakened by shock to bear the full meaning of the words. My daughter. And my grandson. Helen nods, still grinning, and beckons me inside. As soon as I enter, I sense the house's centre of gravity has shifted. Recalibrated, rebalanced, revolving around a precious new apex. The force of it draws me into the living room. Curled up in an armchair overlooking the misted hillside, there she is. There they are.

'Anna.'

My daughter glances up at me, complexion pale but expression aglow with an inner light no level of exhaustion can extinguish. 'Hello, Mother.' Anna smiles, then almost immediately looks away, returning her attention to the blanketed bundle in her arms.

'He ...' In two steps, I have crossed the room to kneel by Anna's feet, reverential in awe at seeing, for the first time, my child holding her child. 'He's here?'

'He is.' The bundle squirms, a miniature pale pink arm emerging from the swaddles. On instinct, I reach out to meet that tiny waving palm. Elfin fingers, nails no bigger than forget-me-nots, brush my skin like butterfly wings.

'He's so small,' I remark foolishly, inarticulate with amazement.

'He is,' Anna agrees, looking down at her baby boy. 'But you'll grow big soon, won't you, Benjamin?'

'Benjamin.' I murmur my grandson's name, familiarising myself with the syllables that suddenly feel more significant than any others I have heard. I turn to Helen.

'Beloved,' she whispers. 'Benjamin means "beloved son".'

'Would you like to hold him?' Too keen to speak, I can only nod. Careful yet confident, Anna passes her baby to me.

Soon, little Benjamin and I are wandering together through Helen's

352

garden. Anna is taking the opportunity of some much-needed maternal rest, her heavy-lidded eyes closing as soon as she saw her precious charge secure in my arms.

'Can you see the lake, little one?' I ask, tilting Benjamin towards what is visible of the view. The mist lies draped across the pewter peaks of the nearby tarns like a fine lace veil over a bassinet, but the baby burbles his contentment even so.

'"These steep woods and lofty cliffs ... to me more dear, both for themselves and for thy sake."' Benjamin's lips part to blow a small, shining bubble in reply. Those deep brown eyes, so very like his mother's, make the baby mysterious and almost sage; the translucence of his tiny temples hinting at what already feels to me an otherworldly, possibly poetic intelligence.

'You're a bright boy, beloved Benjamin,' I compliment him. Benjamin wriggles, giving an airy sigh that I take to be his agreement.

Back indoors, Helen shepherds us into the kitchen, lest we disturb Anna's well-earned nap. Fully alert while his mother sleeps, every object in the room appears to pique Benjamin's intense newborn inquisitiveness. I pick up a teaspoon, twisting it in the light, and smile to see the serious fascination with which he watches the metal glint.

'Are you working on anything at the moment?' Helen asks me, stretching over to lightly tickle Benjamin's toes. The baby responds with another shimmering bubble.

'A memoir.' I set down the spoon. Benjamin squirms in disappointment. I shift his weight in my arms to let him see my face again, addressing to him the words that I want Helen to hear. 'I realised when I was abroad that I need ... to understand my life in a new way. Finally make sense of all that has gone wrong.' Benjamin gives a little gurgle, unintelligible yet melodic as burn water streaming over stones. *Songs of Innocence and of Experience*, Blake wrote. To make sense of the latter, writing is the sole skill I have. 'I want to understand better, so I can endure it better,' I tell Helen. Since America, my journal has at last been refilling. A long-repressed memory resurges of mine and Gavin's vicious quarrel beside Kielder Bridge and of my unfinished notebook lost forever, sinking into the cruel icy swirl. '*Some things don't feel wholly true until I see them written down.*'

Helen seems surprised. Cautiously pleased. Whatever the form, she knows I can only be at my best while writing. 'The Sherrards wrote to me recently,' she says. 'They sent their regards to you.' Helen hesitates. In the silent seconds that follow, we both focus on Benjamin: his fragile, poorly controlled limbs intent upon a hearty stretch. Managing to raise his diminutive clenched fists above his head, the baby yawns with a mouse squeak of satisfaction. 'Philip said that if you should ever wish peace and quiet to write, their house on Euboea is free for friends.'

'Go to Greece?' The thought of further travel makes my middle-aged bones weary. Becoming a young mother rewards one decades later with being a youngish grandmother, but I cannot deny that the physicality of my American adventure has left me pretty depleted. And besides, 'Won't Anna need me here?'

'For a while, yes,' Helen agrees. 'But later, a holiday? Perhaps this summer or the next?'

'Perhaps.' Through the window, I see the mist sinking deeper into the vale and instinctively press Benjamin close to my chest. The thought of sunlight glancing over turquoise waters, encircling a lush, undisturbed island coast is enticing. More conducive to creativity too. Maybe Anna could even bring the baby?

As my tepid ambivalence warms to optimism, I sense Helen is watching me closely. 'There's one other thing to mention before you decide … their neighbour.'

'Who?'

Uncharacteristically awkward, it is Helen's turn to face Benjamin rather than me when she speaks. 'Sir Aymer Maxwell. He's had a house on the island for several years, I hear.' Monreith. Glass-eyed stags and flailing tartan. Clinks from crystal whisky tumblers. Gavin's arm around my waist as we danced. Lavinia across the room.

'No.' My abruptness startles the baby. I look down in horror to see Benjamin's bottom lip protruding, rippling with miniature quivers as those huge, spellbinding eyes threaten to water. Panicked, I scoop his tiny frame into a tighter embrace, his downy-haired dark head cradled against my shoulder as, through constant 'shhs', I pray he will settle. 'Tell them no, Helen. Thank you, but no.' After a few disgruntled sniffles, Benjamin seems tentatively content to stay in his new position without protest. My arm aches from the weight, but I will not move him again. Our peaceful balance is precarious; I cannot take the risk of disturbing it.

In time, however, the baby's newfound proximity to my nostrils soon necessitates another, rather urgent development. Changing Benjamin's nappy is a lost skill that returns to me much more viscerally than driving, the old habit drilled during the thirties from relentless practice. Benjamin kicks out his chubby little thighs to evade my wet cloth, bare soles squirming mischievously while he lies on his back as if attempting to walk on air. Eventually clean and slotted snuggly inside a new doll-sized sleepsuit, I rock him gently back and forth as we wander back into the living room. Anna is just waking from her doze.

'Hello, my son,' she whispers, arms extending automatically for the baby. Their eyes meet; their bodies fit. I watch, amazed, to see Anna shine with a maternal grace that I know I never had, however often I had wished it. Helen has disappeared into another room, already intent on making arrangements for Benjamin's christening in two months' time. With those formidable organisational skills in her corner, I suspect that Anna's son will enjoy a more elaborate, formally binding service than Shakuntala's eccentric cribside celebration.

'I don't know what we'd do without Helen,' I remark, taking my seat beside Anna and the baby.

'I would've rather had you,' Anna says softly.

'Really?' The room grows still. Benjamin's delicate rippling fingers are the only source of movement. Soft swathes of pale grey fog are draped over the windowpane, obscuring our view so that we might be anywhere on Earth. Back in time even. Back on the day I walked away. To think of the woman I was … roaming and restless, crippled by constant emotional pain and a violent, illogical compulsion to write that she could neither harness nor deny. A lost soul who did not know what she was searching for. When I found him, it only made matters worse. 'But Helen's so ordered, compared with me. Competent and in control. Surely she was perfect …'

'Perfectionists don't raise happy children.'

'You weren't happy?'

Anna does not answer directly. She does not need to. My heart feels frozen, words submerged below a torrent of ice like my lost notebook. The regret and shame are such that I can scarcely breathe. 'Helen couldn't be perfect for us,' my daughter adds eventually. 'She wasn't you.'

A minute ticks by, punctuated only by Benjamin's blanket-bound stirrings. I bow my head, staring down at my skirt and its gathered bobbles where the tired navy threads have snagged after taking too many wrong turns.

'For an intelligent woman, Mother, you can be incredibly foolish.' From all the authors I know in this world, I have heard no more accurate description than Anna's of me. 'Why?' she asks.

'Why what?' But I know. Of course, I know.

'Why weren't we enough? Why did you love him more than us?'

'I …' my denial readies, a tidal wave about to crash, but I resist it. For once, I will give Anna all that she deserves. I will give her the truth. 'I loved the world he represented. The world where I believed our love belonged. There were moments when what I shared with him seemed to come from somewhere …' I gesture pathetically towards the window: there is nothing to see, but I hope Anna knows I mean the skies. Coincidentally, I am sure, Benjamin turns his tiny head to look.

'Like poetry?'

I blink in surprise. Benjamin snuffles. 'Precisely like poetry.'

'Motherhood isn't poetic,' Anna observes. 'It's … earthy, isn't it?'

'Yes. Earthy.' Once more, my daughter finds the right words where I have failed. Together, we watch the baby in her arms. Benjamin stretches again, his new extremities still learning to find their forms. From concentration, his lips purse and more bubbles appear, shimmering pearls of the sentences he is not yet able to say.

'I'm sorry.' The weakness of the words almost holds me back from speaking them, yet I persist. Trite and inadequate, they are all I have left. 'I was wrong. What I sought in the sky can be found on earth too.'

'Yes.' Anna's tone is compassionate – forgiving, I dare to hope – but unsurprised. I have the sense that I am not telling my daughter anything she does not already know. Benjamin issues a sweet, airy snort and Anna automatically starts rubbing his back. '"But why this here and now only when I loved I knew …"'

'I didn't know you'd read that poem.'

'I read everything you write, Mother.'

Helen returns to the room and I slip out shortly afterwards, seeking further fresh air to clear my head from the long journey, in every sense. The mist is dispersing, gossamer fragments of fog disintegrating into clusters of plump, shining raindrops. Out here, I am wearing my headscarf, a weak gesture at keeping my hair in some semblance of order, but as the patter of rain grows fiercer, I push it down to my shoulders and raise my face to embrace the full force of the deluge. Cool raindrops bounce on my skin, ricocheting off my eyelashes with every blink. I laugh, tasting

356

water, and spin with utter disregard for my soaked hair and spoiled clothes. This rain feels like forgiveness. The sublime natural world of Wordsworth and Coleridge sending me one last chance to wash away my sins. I raise my hands as if in gratitude, watching droplets course past my glistening fingertips and down my wrists to where my pulse is throbbing hard. Benjamin's is the soul to be christened, his little life soon to be celebrated inside a bright ring of love. Yet today, I feel like I am the one being cleansed.

Chapter Forty-Four

'He's divorced.'

'Who is?' A weak effort, but I am proud of trying. A new woman should start as she means to go on. Elias looks unconvinced, however, indulging in a cutting eye roll before sinking down in the centre of my small Girton sofa. Uninvited, I might add. Just like the visit itself.

'The marriage was a catastrophe,' he relays with unsavoury eagerness. 'Disastrous from day one. Lavinia came home early from their honeymoon. Alone. One can only imagine what must have happened ...'

'Mm.' I suspect I can very well imagine.

'There was a formal separation before the year was out,' Canetti continues. 'People say she spent the next month in a sanatorium.' He whispers the words, voice weighted with phoney concern. 'Lost almost two stone from the stress.'

'Poor thing.' Perhaps Gavin should market himself as a one-man weight loss solution. I myself feel unnervingly close to vomiting.

Canetti watches me closely, his excited expression akin to that of a front row theatregoer ready to relish an unfolding drama. 'Can you picture it?' he enquires keenly. I say nothing, although I can. How many times did I torture myself with visions of the newlyweds hand-in-hand on Sandaig shore, watching Edal and Teko frolic in the waves? How often did I imagine an elegant Silver Cross pram being wheeled around Paultons, every neighbour who used to be mine stopping to share their heartfelt congratulations? How many nights did I writhe in misery, picturing Gavin inspired by his wife's exquisite aristocratic beauty to give her all the love, in all the ways, that I could never entice him to give me? But now I know there is no baby. There was no love. Instead, I see whisky glasses hurled in temper, crystal shards striking the cottage walls; rich amber beads of liquid trickling down to seep into the flagstones. I hear screaming. Sobbing. Accusations and recriminations. Silence.

'The day she left him has become legendary,' Canetti gloats. 'It all started when ...'

'Elias …'

'When she drove up to his cottage from London …' I wonder, head and heart numb, how this Pandora's box of private humiliation has ended up opened and exposed to the world. What friend of a friend of a friend has betrayed them both? I should not listen. I will not listen. I turn away, facing the narrow arch window where young women are crossing the courtyard, arms laden with library books. But I can still hear Canetti's words.

'It was the last straw, you see. Lavinia had decided to give the marriage one final try. They say she's very kind-hearted.'

'She is.'

'Well, then, his kind-hearted wife drove all the way from London to Sandaig in one day. Seven-hundred miles!' Six-hundred and twenty-five, technically, but I lack the inclination to correct him. 'She arrives at the cottage, starving and exhausted, and finds Gavin already knee-deep in the day's whisky.' Canetti's acquired English makes the odd imagery resonate: the picture of Gavin's wool socks soaked in Scotch springs unbidden into my imagination. Good God, how much more poetry might I have written with the hours I wasted dwelling on that man in his kilt?

Elias presses on in the present tense as if narrating a radio play. 'They speak, and soon they quarrel, and then he informs her that he wants a divorce. "I can't write with you in the house," he complains.' One of the few criticisms never levelled at my door. Say what he will and no doubt does about me, Gavin cannot deny that I helped rather than hindered his literary career. 'So, Lavinia heads upstairs to her room –' Elias pauses, eager for me to note the sordid detail of separate bedrooms – 'and a minute later, she hears a gunshot.'

'What?' I spin to face him, flinching as if I had heard a bullet firing myself.

Canetti nods in faux solemnity. 'Mrs Maxwell charges downstairs in mortal terror that her husband has, what's the expression?' He mimics a gun cocked to one ear and a vile spattering from the other. 'Blown out his brains.' He halts again for dramatic effect. 'But there Gavin sits on the edge of his own bed. The epitome of health, except perhaps for reeling from drink. Oh,' Elias sniggers, 'and he was naked.' An invented detail, I tell myself. Designed to humiliate Gavin further. And yet somehow, I can believe it. He never liked to sleep wearing clothes.

'"There was a rat in the fireplace," he tells Lavinia, his shotgun still smoking. Total nonsense, naturally, although quite clever when you think about it. Don't you agree, Kathleen? Feigning death to make someone regret fighting with you while alive ... anyway, Mrs Maxwell takes herself back upstairs, and moments later she hears –' Elias stomps his feet on my floor, mimicking the thump of drunken soles ascending a staircase – 'her husband's heavy footsteps. He stands in the doorway, swaying rather than standing.

'"Go to sleep Gavin," she shouts and bless his intoxicated heart, that's what he does. Passes out onto the twin bed beside her. Makes a terrible mess of all the socks she'd been darning. At some point in the night, he rolls off and onto the floor, but enough drink has been taken for him to stay put until morning. Well, that was the end of it for Lavinia.'

Perspiring from effort, Canetti draws breath, basking in the triumph of his lurid retelling. Shakespeare and farce seem to mingle in the moment: a minor part messenger proudly anticipating applause. He will not have it from me.

'How on earth do you know all this, Elias?'

'Lavinia wrote it in a letter from the sanatorium.'

'A letter to you?'

'Well, not directly to me ...' Fleeting sheepishness passes over his face, the cloud of conscience soon clearing. 'But I have it on excellent authority.' I stay silent. Marital battlefield reports mean little to me now, having suffered my own grievous wound long ago. Elias, though, seems disappointed by my reserve. 'Guess what she said to him when they separated?'

'I'm sure I don't know ...'

'"You've treated me just as you treated Kathleen."' I turn back to the window. I cannot bear for Canetti to see my face. My thoughts drift through the pane towards Lavinia, wherever she may be now. Mistrustful of Elias as I am, I can imagine her saying those very words: cut-glass accent, soft heart shattered. Despite the insurmountable differences between us, in one aspect of our lives we share sisterhood. Love and suffering in the name of the same man, the man we each once believed would be our counterpart for life. A man of light whose long shadow cast us into cold, lonely darkness. Now it is Gavin who is alone.

'God is not merciful, but he is just.' I regret the words almost the second they leave my lips. Too late. Turning back to Elias, his eyes alight with malicious glee, I know that the message will snake straight to Gavin.

How many thoughtless comments has Canetti relayed from one to the other, twisting our words with his every self-serving step? Perhaps ever since our earliest days, there was a worm in our apple. A serpent in Eden, hiding in plain sight.

'I'd like you to go, please, Elias.'

His hurt at least seems genuine. 'But Kathleen, I ... aren't you happy?' A tone of bafflement, tempered by frustration. Did he really believe I would be glad to hear of Gavin's pain? Do those who know me think me so wicked, my moral compass so irreparably warped by thwarted love, that I would exult in Gavin's suffering?

'Goodbye, Elias.'

'You mean goodnight.'

'Goodbye.'

He rises from my sofa, oddly obedient, but then pauses. Within touching distance, without daring to touch. The stance reminds me of when strangers used to meet Mij, half-outstretched hands hovering between desire for proximity and wise wariness of being bitten.

'You matter very much to me, Kathleen. Perhaps more than you ever knew.'

'That's possible,' I concede curtly, holding open the door for him to go. 'It seems there's been a lot I haven't known.'

*

'Familiar with the area already, are you?'

'You could say that.'

The estate agent nods, flashing me an insincere smile of salesmanship. 'Then you understand just what a prize you've found in this place. It's so rare to discover a house around here that hasn't been divided into flats.'

'I know.'

'And at such an excellent price ...' Out of habit, perhaps, he relaunches part of his earlier pitch. 'Why, just think of the profit somebody could make if they had one to sell on the south-facing side of the square.'

'Just think of it.'

The man locks his briefcase with two brisk clicks and the thinly disguised disinterest of one for whom my significance begins and ends with completion of this transaction. If I buy, that is. The paperwork he has handed me rustles as I clench its edges.

'If you decide to make an offer, I certainly shouldn't wait around.'

361

Straightening his tie with one hand, the agent offers me one last, slightly sweaty handshake with the other. 'Our office number is on the sales schedule. Telephone by the end of the day, won't you?'

'I will. And thank you,' I manage to mutter. I watch him leave, slick suit creasing as he hurries towards the prospect of his next sale. Left alone, I sigh before staring down at the address printed before me. 47 Paultons Square. Home sweet home?

I have outgrown Girton. That much has been clear since I came back from the States. Although the hecticness of America became exhausting, on my return, I found the cloying claustrophobia of academia even harder to tolerate than before. The college might be a mental sanctuary but living full-time within its walls makes it feel like they are closing in on me.

'The beautiful bluestocking. Why, it's like seeing Achilles in Hades, finding you here,' remarked Stanley Spencer when he visited to paint the Mistress of Girton's portrait. How the elderly painter came to hear of my former nickname was beyond me, and I told myself not to worry about the words of a grizzled, if greatly gifted, old man wearing pyjamas under his suit. Yet the underworld analogy fitted. If no longer Psyche, I feel like Persephone, split between making the most of an ostensibly sunlit upper sphere and my unspoken, inconsolable mourning for all that I know to be lost. Since Canetti's visit, although I try to deny it, my only certainty has been unsettledness. Now circumstances are conspiring to compound the instability.

Following in his sister's footsteps, James has announced that he too intends to marry: Jennie, a young woman as accomplished as she is charming and who – my surprise was rapidly superseded by my joy – turns out to be a very distant descendant of Blake's great inspiration, Thomas Taylor. At the other end of the family, my parents' increasing fragility is inescapable. I hear it in my mother's voice, the frail trill of aged birdsong down the telephone. I see it in my father's handwriting, ink bleeds betraying the fearsome effort required not to let his letters shake. I know they will need more from me soon. Care to compensate for what my emotional restlessness once put them through. I resolved several months ago to find one house suitable for us all, although the search has often felt futile: frustration at the extortion racket that is London prices causing me to crumple numerous classified sections in distaste. Until this one became free. Miraculously affordable. I have had no time to ask Gay whether it is written in the stars.

'Can I bear to live here?' I wonder aloud, turning to study the house from outside. Number 47 unnerves me in its quasi-familiarity. It is the mirror image of 9, directly opposite my old home, although mercifully enough evergreen trees have been planted for the place not to be in my eyeline unless I look for it. Converted years ago by an owner of a more pragmatic turn of mind than me, there are no cosmic reverberations of Cooie's eccentric presence on this side of the Square. A neat garden; no pear tree. No wet paw prints giving an inkling that an otter has ever set foot here. What 47 does have is a comfortable guest space on its ground floor, although I confess that the prospect of living under the same roof as my parents again is an honour I have not dreamed of. Contemplating the tall terrace windows, their opposite numbers just visible in the top reflection, I realise that I have not lived with anyone for years. The last person was Gavin.

The idea of him out there, solitary and sorrowful, perhaps only feet from this front door, is one I resolve to close my heart against. Once, I turned my head in the direction I believed Gavin was; now, I avert my eyes assiduously from where Number 9 lies, stumbling down the street in my haste to pretend I am not tempted. My neck cricks, locked in an unnatural swivel of self-deception. Can I bear to live here? It appears not. And yet neither can I afford to pass up the chance to correct my folly in voluntarily relinquishing the first house I had.

Racked with indecision, I walk from Paultons with my head low, surrendering myself to a childish absorption with the intricacies of pavement cracks. Even without looking, I have a sense of my vague direction, some inner magnet pulling my feet by force to where I know the North Library awaits. I will find solace there, if nowhere else: the transcendent words of Blake, Yeats, Coleridge and the rest letting me relinquish the petty worries of ordinary life and remember what truly matters. Love. Little Benjamin. The profound power of poetry to sustain, restore and renew us; the greatest artistic endeavours of humankind being simply to glimpse what nature achieves with such effortless grace. It is towards the poets' illustrious company that I walk, imagining their verses in the air as if to create a numinous buffer between me and earthly troubles.

I barely see the other houses, the bus stop or the small chemist shop. A set of malfunctioning traffic lights up ahead captures my attention, but only because of the visual discord they create. Two men holding one ladder are in hapless attendance underneath, heatedly debating the diagnosis. The light itself is stuck at amber, a literal picture of paralysed ambivalence. I stop and stare into the glare of its defiant inner lightbulb. The electric ember seems seized by frazzled spasms of overuse, unable to give itself over to either a stop or a go.

'Kathleen?' *Don't turn,* I tell myself. *Keep walking until you reach the museum. Reach safety. Reach poetry.* But there is more poetry for me in that voice than in the many hundreds of pages I have read. It sounds hoarser than before, the cindery rawness such that I can almost hear his cigarettes, yet a lyricism drifts through each syllable even so. It calls to me. He calls to me. I will always answer.

'Gavin.' His fair hair is slicked back; his fine build swamped by a dark winter coat. As 47 Paultons Square distortedly mirrors Number 9, so do the changes in him since we last saw each other. Subtle to most. Notable to me. Gavin's hairline is altered, the wave that once swept over his right brow now brushed back into a sharp, eagle-like swoop. The shade, too, seems subtly tweaked in this orange-hued light. With a ferocious surge of forgotten loyalty, I shove from my mind Canetti's speculation about the chemical origins of Gavin's blond. Certainly, the tone is richer today: an almost raffish auburn fairness that makes for a more mature kind of debonair, also extending to Gavin's new roughly trimmed beard. A man of light who has walked through darkness. His heavy sunglasses are still in place.

I had not realised today was cloudy until suddenly the sun came out. I did not notice the monochrome nothingness until vibrant colour poured back in. To see Gavin standing before me is to feel blood rush back into what I thought was a cauterised wound. My cheeks flush from its strength; some crashing tide inside my chest aflow with vigorous fresh life. Less than a minute ago, I believed myself to be content: living on my own terms at last and reconciled with what had passed. But that was before I saw the better part of my own heart coming towards me around a nondescript city corner. Now a grave I did not know myself buried in is opening up, flooding me with light. Lost sensations stir, returning to me like the forgotten feelings of a long-amputated limb.

'Are you hurt?' Gavin seems to be limping, walking with a stick upon which he leans heavily, and yet he still succeeds in making it look oddly dashing. An acute pang of tenderness consumes my core before I can fight it.

'This cursed thing?' Planting his feet firm, Gavin raises the stick with a swing of disgust. 'A car accident just past Tormor. Stag leapt out into the road and the whole vehicle flipped.' He taps the stick against the toe of his left foot as if in reprimand. 'Now I'm forced to "hirple", as John Donald would say. Imagine having my only crash at ten bloody miles an hour.' Gavin laughs, a few crackling base notes laced with smoke giving way to a fluid, lilting melody of self-mockery. To hear it is like having my first drink of clean water in years.

He seems glad to see me. Like before, in the beginning, when I was a goddess who had turned her head and not just a woman whose irrepressible yearning repulsed him. For months, I have had so much stored up inside me to say to Gavin, anticipating the moment that I realise now had to come when I would have my chance to confront him. Yet now, the words fall away, wrong-footed as if I am standing here to deliver a lecture for which I have foolishly forgotten my notes. *You betrayed me*, I want to tell him. *Betrayed all we ever had and broke my heart into shards of worthless sea glass. I am your soul's wife, I've always known it and you did too, once, yet you chose another and left me to rot. Because of you, I cannot accept the love of anyone else, even that of a good, genuine man more passionate and poetic than you will ever be. My child hated me for years. A part of her may still hate me. I never saw it; I chose not to see it, so blinded was I by your light. Blinded still.*

'How are the two otters?' I ask instead. Gavin brightens. There was always one certain way to his heart.

'Four now. I have Mossy and Monday too.' Even the thought of them makes Gavin stand taller, lessening the intense pressure on his stick as his spine straightens and he smiles. 'Still cubs really, yet their temperaments are already chalk and cheese. Monday, the female, has such searing, unmistakable intelligence, but her companion Mossy is moronic.'

'That's men and women for you.' I blurt out the jibe without thinking, so thrilled to feel a little of our old familiarity return that I forget for how long it has been absent. Gavin pauses for a beat, top lip twitching; the joke seems to skim a nerve without touching it. He keeps on smiling at me.

'How is Teko? And Edal?' I hurry to drag our conversation back towards safer ground. Safer for Gavin, at any rate. Although he cannot know, it was for Edal's sake that I pledged not to seek him out again. I never thought to set a rule for what I would do if he sought out me.

'Oh, otters make life worth living. You remember?'

365

I nod. 'I remember.'

'Granted,' Gavin admits, 'things aren't as they were before. There have been challenges ...' The sentence fades without completion, whatever difficulties he alludes to going ultimately unspoken. I see Gavin contemplate sharing them with me: a momentary glimpse in what I can see of his face that reveals the fragile young man he was. Asleep in my arms, teardrops sinking into the exposed skin of my breast. But grievous wounds have been suffered on both sides since then. I have forfeited my right to know Gavin's every vulnerability.

'More importantly, how are you?' His interest appears genuine, the change of subject executed with typical elegance.

'Anna has a baby. Almost a year old now.'

'Ah.' Delight sparks in Gavin's expression, visible even behind his black glasses. 'My congratulations. Boy or girl?'

'Boy,' I say. 'Benjamin.' My last embittered comment against their sex echoes in my ears with regretful resonance. 'Beloved and bright.'

Gavin grins. 'Takes after his grandmother then.' Even shrouded by dark spectacles and thick winterish attire, there can be no dimming Gavin's charm when he wants it to dazzle. Yet almost instantly, his tone turns wistful, a sudden sadness seeping into the conversation. 'I wish Lavinia and I had been able to have ...'

'A cub?'

'Ha.' Laughter causes Gavin to cough, a charcoal-black hacking that hurts my throat in sympathy. 'Yes, a cub. But I suppose it was not meant to be.' In his narrative, the failure sounds cryptic and inexplicable. For a naturalist, Gavin has an uncommonly delicate grasp on the facts of life.

'I was sorry to hear about ...' My turn for the words to escape me. Pathetic as it is, I cannot bring myself to say 'your marriage'. The nebulous unformed apology hovers like breath in the crisp, cold air. How many 'I'm sorry's have hung between us over the years? How many more went unsaid? Gavin nods even so, intuiting what I intend and grateful for it.

'Thank you.' Thumbs and forefingers on his lapels, he hooks up his coat collar as if chilled by the memory of his ill-fated union. 'But how are you really, Kathleen? Not the children, *you*.'

'I'm ...' a French Nobel Prize winner's mistress and moving to America with him so I never *pense* about you again. 'I'm fine.'

'I read your Blake book,' Gavin tells me. 'The lecture that was published? *Nature always gives back.*' My words from his lips transport me to August 1949. We might be dining together at Sorbo's for the first time. Strangers who feel like soulmates; soulmates who are still strangers. If I could return with the benefit of hindsight, would I flee? Retreat into the blind anonymity of night where neither Gavin nor the many, varied agonies to come over the next decade could catch up with me? Mij might still be alive today if I had.

'What are you working on now?' Gavin asks, interrupting a reverie that cannot lead me to anywhere but sorrow.

'A memoir.'

'I'd like to read it someday.'

'Then you will.' My words sound weak. My breath seems to be deserting me. 'I should go,' I say suddenly. The urge to bolt is a raw, animalistic instinct. Whether from fear for Edal's life if I linger or a less worthy sense of self-preservation, I know that this time, I must be the one to leave first.

Gavin looks oddly regretful. 'Yes. Of course. Do take care, Kathleen. And please pass on my congratulations to Anna.'

'I will.'

'It really has been wonderful to see you.' Stick anchored between us, Gavin bends to kiss my cheek. His lips graze my skin, new stubble scratching. A pleasurable pain.

'Why did you never respond to my letter?' I blurt out. 'About keeping the top floor of Paultons.' Gavin does not look annoyed at my re-dredging the past. Not at all, in fact. But nor is he as surprised as I might have expected.

'Ah, the unposted letter.' The thought apparently amuses him, although I fail to see anything funny. 'Mary MacLeod found my reply to you in her son's jacket pocket. I'd asked Willie to post it at the time. Or maybe it was Jim? Either way, Mary berated him for the oversight, I can assure you. Imagine it sitting unsent for all that time.'

My words will barely form. I parrot Gavin's phrases back at him. 'Willie's jacket pocket?'

Gavin nods, seemingly unconcerned. 'As I say, it might have been Jim's.'

'What did you write? Would you – would you have let me keep the flat?' In times of trouble, literature always dominates my head. My troubled thoughts swirl with muddled memories of Hardy's *Tess* and the twists of fate that sealed her tragedy. Letters lost, never read; words in silence, staying unsaid. Stone circles of sorrow from which women are destined never to break free.

'Of course,' he confirms, casualness cutting through me. Tess's murder weapon, I remember, was a knife. 'What else could I have said? After all, I am a gentleman.'

'Goodbye, Gavin.' Determined despite my growing dizziness, I turn and force myself to walk away. Not permitting myself to look back, still I believe that I sense the moment when Gavin himself goes.

*

'Hyacinth,' I tell the baby, lightly bending the wand stem of a star-petalled bloom until it bows towards her sightline. Naomi's globe eyes widen further. 'And this one is an anemone.' The flower's large ocular centre stares back as if to equal her curiosity. Naomi is undaunted. Unafraid. Although still too young to even hold up her own head, her watchful gaze studies every specimen. A flimsy, frilled petal breaks off as we brush past and I hand it to the baby, who gurgles with pleasure at her gift. 'You'll go far, my girl,' I promise, feeling her body's sweet heat beside my heart as we wander the garden. 'You'll go far, Naomi Madge.'

James and Jennie's little one was born in and for spring, blooming with vigour and eternally seeking out the sun. Whereas Benjamin's elfin delicacy in his first days seemed to belong in the misted Lakes, his slim little limbs almost aglow with translucence, Naomi is already robust and rosy-cheeked. I plant my index finger at the heart of her plump pink palm and in an instant my diminutive granddaughter has seized me, the tight grip friendly yet fierce.

'Strength in gentleness,' I observe approvingly. According to Helen, that is the meaning of Naomi's name.

I have settled into Number 47, although Paultons Square feels very different from before, and the sensation of change is heightened by my family tree branching out at a rapid rate. My parents, at the roots, require ever more diligent nourishing, the gnarled veins and joints of my father's aged hands now almost too twisted for him to hold up the books he loves. Still self-sufficient, but only just, George and Jessie's visits extend from hours to several weeks at a stretch, and it is taking discipline not to dwell on what awaits me in years to come as an only daughter of elderly parents.

At the lighter, brighter end of the tree, new life is blossoming on both sides. Baby Naomi already admirably at one with nature. Young

368

Benjamin finding his feet before, unbeknownst to him, a new sibling arrives in late autumn. I never noticed the world turning so fast when I was a young woman myself. I suppose back then, my life turned along with it. Now, the sturdy centre of our specimen, my role is to support. And yet I feel hopeful again. As optimistic as the season suggests. My present is peaceful, and the future, well, who knows?

'Where go?' Benjamin toddles over the grass to my side, those perpetually sticky fingers seizing a pleat of my skirt. I bend down with Naomi still in my arms to stare into my grandson's deep, dark eyes. 'Where Gran'ma go?' he asks again, light voice laced with urgency. Strange as it seems, some quality in this little boy, still barely knee height, makes me feel as if he understands more of imagination than most adults.

'Grandma's only daydreaming,' I reassure him, my free hand stroking his rich black hair. 'She's not going anywhere.' Seemingly satisfied, Benjamin wobbles on less-than-sturdy legs to where the toys he keeps at 'Gran'ma's' are collected. 'Not yet anyway,' I say to myself.

'Hm?' Anna sighs as she follows her son across the garden, leaning her back against the wall and breathing pointedly through her nose. At last, the violent sickness of her second pregnancy is starting to pass, yet her pallid complexion still shows signs of strain.

'I think I'll take a holiday soon,' I announce, as casually as I can. 'Greece. Euboea, technically.' Anna says nothing. 'To write. But don't worry,' I insist, combating the criticism before she can make it, 'I'll be back before Baby arrives.'

'That's not what I'm worried about.' Benjamin glances up from his building blocks, those fine young senses attuned to minor key changes in tone. In my arms, Naomi burbles, squeezing her flower so tight that the petals fall.

Chapter Forty-Five

Cerulean. All I can see is cerulean blue. The technical name, gleaned long ago from Gavin's dust-gathering paint tubes, drifts into my thoughts as I bob on my back, staring up at a cloudless sky and letting the ocean lull me into relaxation. Legato waves stroke my starfish limbs while I float, enjoying the buoyancy. I let my sun-weary eyelids close but an aura of shimmering azure remains, lapping at the edge of my consciousness. It is not yet midday, but the air is already infused with warmth and the sweet scent of a nearby cypress tree. The sole idea in my mind, above the sensation of physical pleasure, is how long it has been since I felt any such thing.

Body coaxed by the soft current to glide gently closer to shore, I picture the way that the Sherrards' villa blends into the nearby hillside, its sun-bleached slates flecked with white like the tan-lines I know – although no one else is ever likely to see them – will be etched onto my skin when I finally remove this swimsuit. The thick heat builds by the minute, mercury rising to the apex at which only mad dogs and Englishwomen remain outdoors, so with reluctance, I let the tide carry me back in the direction of the deserted beach. My bare soles burn from hot sand rippling beneath me as I pad up to where the crooked stone path undulates towards the house. Trusting that none but the sun itself and that lone, noble cypress can see me in this shoreside enclave, I ignore the way my wet swimsuit skims and clings while I walk, sodden fabric hugging each inch of my bust, stomach and upper thighs. In this increasingly fierce heat, it will be dry by the time I am inside.

I cross the villa's tiled threshold with a hop, waylaid by the papery fluttering of something affixed to my sticky, sand-dusted foot. Contorting with the physical inflexibility I tell myself is only to be expected in a mature poetess, I reach down to remove whatever is stuck. A note. Shoved under the villa door while I swam. There is no stamp. Yet I can tell from the handwriting that it only came from the house next door.

Lunch? Scribble assent or dissent below. Gavin.

His casualness irritates me. After all that has passed, is this the best he thinks I deserve? A single line, throwaway words tossed in my direction like kitchen scraps hurled to dear old Jonnie. Not that he was ever fed sloppy seconds. Gavin has dashed off this invite as if our estrangement never took place; as if his marriage were merely a figment of my fantastical imagination. As if the book that brought him worldwide acclaim does not carry my words, silent and unacknowledged, on every front cover they will ever print for him.

My anger shocks me, rage burning strong as the Greek sun and with no light, bright 'shinkly' sea to ameliorate it. But why smoulder now when so much of this is my own making? I had always suspected that Gavin might arrive on Euboea this summer. More bluntly, I knew the risk I was taking in travelling here. To stand at a certain point of the Sherrards' terrace – not that I have tried, at least not deliberately – is to glimpse the terracotta pantile roof of Sir Aymer's island residence, a red emblem of warning or welcome that glows like the automatic lighthouse of Sandaig. I had believed that I understood the emotional danger I was dicing with; a game of Russian roulette played not with my brain but my heart. Except that I, may God forgive me, came out here hoping for a bullet to hit. The only salve for my conscience is my unbroken pledge to save Edal. I will not seek Gavin out. I have not, technically speaking. But yet again, here he is, seeking me out instead.

I reach for my pen. I am here to write, after all. The villa door remains open and I can see the mellow amethyst slope that denotes Mount Parnassus in the distance. 'The Temple,' Helen would tell me, a symbol of timeless knowledge and sound judgement. It is time I exercised mine.

'Too hot for lunch,' I write below Gavin's line. Scribbled dissent it is. With what feels like haste unsuitable for this cloyingly oppressive heat, I hurry into the bedroom to pull on a thin blouse and my lightest skirt. Slipping both pen and note into my pocket, I head back out the door.

Twisting cobblestones, unaltered for centuries, guide me along the coastline to Aymer's. Prickling sweat beads lie like pearls at the nape of my neck, my just-dried hairline dampening once more. An elderly couple passes, presumably shuffling towards the tiny market square that constitutes cosmopolitanism here. Their rough wicker baskets swing with the sea breeze, borne in the crooks of the arms that are not entwined.

'*Kalimera*,' the woman greets me. Her coppery lined face, framed by a sun-faded scarf, creases into a smile.

'*Kalli-mare-a*,' I attempt in return. *Good morning*. The old couple nod indulgently, silvery heads dipping in unison before they continue along the cobbles, twig-frail brown arm in arm. I wonder what 'soulmate' is in Greek? *Eros* is the closest I know.

I arrive at Aymer's door. Home or abroad, there is no mistaking a Maxwell residence. Opulence drips from each finial, luxury oozing from every hinge; white stone trellises with ornate scalloped edges garland the property just as ivy envelops Monreith.

'Typical,' I mutter, the olive trees alone witness to my bitterness. Glancing down, I review the note in my hands. Curt. Concise. A message Gavin cannot misinterpret. My hand hovers in front of Aymer's door but the moment passes, the tide of my courage ebbing away. The pen in my pocket feels impossibly heavy, pressing against me like an insistent child or otter determined to make its presence known. I should have realised it boded ill to bring it with me in the first place.

I score out what I have written. Add a new line underneath. Most unlike myself, I forgo proper punctuation, the words flowing in a single sweep like a stream rushing from waterfall to burn. Let Gavin decipher their meaning, should he wish.

Yes as always love Kathleen

*

Gavin waits for me at our taverna table. Even from behind, I would know his outline in an instant. Curled wisps of smoke escape to one side before his thin, nonchalant fingertips appear, clenching a cinder-tipped cigarette. The seats here are scattered, shuffled by staff and patrons throughout the day to achieve the perfect balance of sun and shade, but I manage to slip through the checked tablecloth maze. As soon as he sees me, Gavin rises, his left palm pushing down on the tabletop to prevent his weak foot from wobbling.

'Of all the taverns on all the islands in the world …' he teases, stretching over to kiss my cheek. His top shirt buttons are undone, the open collar exposing skin already starting to tan. Protruding collarbones, angular and lithe, cast rich shadows of burnished brown across the bronze that I can see of his upper torso. A glimmer draws my eye magpie-like to a dancing glint at Gavin's breast pocket. Tucked away, near his heart, is his grandfather's tie pin.

'How's your foot?' I home in on his injury to humble him in my mind. Reducing his power; conserving my strength. Hyper-vigilant from sudden anxiety at our proximity, my ears pick up the distant, dreamy lilt of what sounds like a Highland lament. I fear I am losing my mind, before realising that the street singing is not Gaelic but Greek.

Gavin raises his left foot in scorn. 'The heat helps. As much as anything can.' His sole lands back on the ground with a contemptuous, poorly controlled slam: whether accident or angry design, I cannot be sure, although knowing Gavin like I do, I suspect the latter. 'Are you managing to write here?'

'I am.' Since arriving, the words have indeed started to flow from me as they have not done for years, ideas intent upon expression simply streaming onto my page. I believe – I know – it is because this coast mirrors Sandaig. A sun-drenched Mediterranean echo of the last place where my imagination truly took root. A sanctuary only a few feet from the ocean; a deserted shore watched over only by a timeless tree of life. Perhaps the cypress will be merciful about my mistakes in a way the rowan never was. 'And you?' I venture in return. 'Are you writing too?'

Gavin snorts, the loud sound propelled by violent phlegmatic force. Despite his dark glasses – for once, our environment warrants them – I sense his eyes darting left and right in search of a taverna waiter. One drained glass already sits at his place. 'Well, the sequel is out, for whatever it's worth.' His voice is caustic and chilled. 'Didn't you hear?'

'I'm sorry. I've been busy.' God bless America.

'You haven't missed much. "A comedy of errors", one reviewer called it. Really, I'd had very little to write about, save for the succession of accidents that have befallen Sandaig since *Ring*.'

'Accidents? You mean, not just your …' I gesture to his left foot.

'Many more and many worse.' The rest of Gavin's reply must wait until he has taken a sip from the new drink just set down. 'Last winter was the most awful I've ever known up there. Can you imagine the waterfall freezing over?' I can, but in truth, what I picture above all else is sheer beauty. A swirling ice sculpture of frozen motion; glacial shards glittering in the translucent, elder tree-dappled midwinter light. Surreal as it is to visualise such a scene in this heat, I feel as if I can see the sparkling frost flashes and crystallised flakes of snow, a world I always suspected could transcend time preserved for one season in wondrous white. If only time had frozen when Mij was alive.

'At least ice melts,' I offer.

'Yes, and *The Rocks Remain*.' Sarcasm drips from Gavin's tone as more wine slips down his throat. 'That was the sequel's title. Chosen by Peter, I need hardly add.'

'But the otters … you told me in London they're doing well.' On our street corner, beneath the broken traffic light. The day he called out my name and beckoned me back into his life.

'Oh, Kathleen …' Elbows planted on the table, Gavin lets his proud head droop. 'You know more than anyone how wondrous a life with otters can be.'

'Yes.'

'But …' Gavin stares down at the bronzed back of his hand, wriggling his slender fingers as if unable to otherwise trust they are attached. 'There have been attacks.'

'Attacks on the otters?'

'By the otters.' Gavin lifts his head fleetingly, one strawberry blond fetlock tumbling forward. He meets my eyes with a wretched expression. 'Both Edal and Teko. With Edal, it seemed to be jealousy, savaging a guest who was wearing a sweater of Jimmy's. But soon it was Jimmy himself. And Terry …' The words catch in Gavin's throat. His hand is still squirming. 'Young Terry lost two fingers.'

'No.' My palm is on his before I can help it, sheltering Gavin as if to protect his own digits from assault. 'I can't believe it. Mij was so …' No word coined by callous, selfish humanity will suffice. Sweet? Childlike? Trusting of humans to his own tragic detriment? Yet even as I speak, a moment long repressed struggles to the surface. Mij and I momentarily at war in the Sandaig living room, the straps of his accursed harness snaking around us as we battled. *A near miss*, I said then, blaming myself for pushing a wild animal to the brink. And otters are wild animals. No matter how many words we dedicate to them.

Knocking back what remains in his glass and instantly requesting another, Gavin recounts the grim, gruesome tale in its entirety. Writer's block or not, he has lost none of his vivid descriptive powers. Soon, I am reeling in my seat to picture the brave teenage Terry's amputated fingers. Warped and blackened by the putrid spread of gangrene; severed and tossed with a flat thud into a hospital waste basin.

'Why?' I whisper the word, fearful to part my lips fully and risk retching. Why would the otters turn on the humans who care for them? Edal's illness springs to the troubled forefront of my mind: the secret reason why I only dare to let Gavin approach me and not the other way around. Perhaps her brain was never the same since. Sometimes I fear mine hasn't been.

'Oh, it's not their fault. It's mine.' Gavin mounts an instinctive, impassioned defence, subconsciously clenching my hand for emphasis. His grip hurts, but I do not pull away. Odd how love increases one's tolerance for pain. 'Those months when I was travelling in Morocco meant a devastating loss of routine for them. Mossy and Monday were less disrupted, being young and more or less wild anyway. But for Edal and Teko ... And then, of course, there was the press intrusion. Plus what must have seemed like a succession of strange humans infiltrating the cottage after my marri ...' Jealousy. That was the word he used to describe Edal's first attack. My heart swells in worthless sympathy for those two tormented creatures, because I know precisely the emotions they have suffered; the vile envy stoked by inexpressible heartbreak that makes you lash out. I understand, if Edal and Teko cannot, how it feels to be faced with the harm you have inflicted, long after the storm has subsided.

'Jimmy's leaving soon.' Gavin stares down at the dregs of his drink in the way that Willa is apt to interpret a tea-leaf swirl. 'Not bitter, which makes one of us. But he wants to start out on his own.' Gavin exhales, harsh and smoky. 'I don't see how the place will survive without him.'

'Can't the MacLeods help?'

Gavin stares back at me pityingly. 'Didn't I tell you? They're gone too.'

'Gone?' Disbelief convinces me I must have misheard, yet Gavin confirms it, his slight shoulders slumping in resignation.

'The boys are old enough now to go out into the world. And as for Mary and John Donald ... well, it appears life moves on for us all. Eventually.' The sand grain of truth in his words slips through my fingers, so implausible is the prospect of that family no longer sharing the shoreline with him. Gavin might as well be trying to convince me that Ben Sgriol has sold up and strolled away.

Our food arrives, appropriately Mediterranean fare, and Gavin attacks his plate with one hand, cigarette suspended from the other. Unburdening himself heightens his appetite. It was the same fifteen years ago, the first

375

time we dined together.

'There's no hope to continue as things stand,' he admits with his mouth full, a whisper-thin fragment of fish sticking to the new hirsute border between his lip and beard. If I were Lady Mary, I would reach over with my own napkin; if I were Lavinia, I would have permission from society, at least, to kiss it off. I do neither. Gavin takes another drink and the sliver disappears. 'What with maintaining the enclosures needed to keep Edal and Teko away from other humans, the place simply haemorrhages money. And it's not been helped by the Italian libel.'

'The what?' One shock after another is making it a struggle to swallow. In weary surrender, I push my poorly touched plate to one side.

Gavin shoots me a wry grin. 'You have been out of touch, Kathleen. I wrote my Sicilian books after all.' A bell trills in my memory, muffled and faint as if heard underwater. An aunt in Sicily, or so he said. Justification for a strange fascination with that other sun-saturated isle. 'It's an astonishing place,' Gavin tells me. 'Although the poverty is appalling. The conditions the peasants suffer are things one could scarcely imagine back in Britain, and yet their spirit remains indomitable ... *The Ten Pains of Death*, I titled that one. A tribute to them and all they endure. But it was the second book that sparked the trouble. Salvatore Giuliano. Have you heard of him?'

'No,' I confess, embarrassed by my ignorance. Contemporary figures seem less real to me these days than Blake and his devotees. But Gavin is happy to explain.

'He was a Sicilian Robin Hood or a bloodthirsty bandit, depending upon who you ask. The Mafia inclines to the latter view. Naturally, they have the government ministers in their pockets. Or in their crosshairs.' Gavin turns, not wholly joking, and surveys our surroundings as if suddenly watchful for spies. There are none, I believe, unless one counts the dozing waiter or a hungry gull patrolling the cobblestones.

'Isn't that a Mediterranean Gull?' I ask, keen to sound knowledgeable again.

'An Audouin's,' Gavin corrects me with one glance. 'You can tell by the bill.' I suppose he can. 'May I continue?'

'Yes. Sorry.'

'Well, one of those under-thumb ministers took me and my publisher to court for making his own Mafia link rather too explicit in the book.' Hidden behind his sunglasses, I am certain Gavin just rolled his eyes.

'Kathleen, you have no idea how galling it is when someone objects to you telling the truth.'

'Were you fined?' I keep my focus on the heated dramas of Sicily so as not to think of Kielder Bridge and snowstorms of hypocrisy.

'I most certainly was,' Gavin confirms, 'and that wasn't the worst of it. Try an outstanding eight-month prison sentence if I should set foot in Italy again.'

'Good God.' Further words fail me.

Gavin laughs. Even at this low ebb, he seems to get a kick out of notoriety. 'Oh, the Almighty had already made an appearance. That was the title of the cursed book in the first place. *God Protect me from my Friends.*' Quite.

'But how did it ... I mean, how did you ...' How *does* he get himself into such scrapes? If anyone else in the world had told me this story, I should have struggled to believe it. Yet Gavin has always been a magnet for the maddest eventualities. A veritable Michelangelo of chaos; apotheosis of all drama to be had within a hundred-mile vicinity. Near-death illness. Literary stardom. The otters themselves, for that matter. Is it the collision of aristocratic eccentricity with a dazzling, brilliant brain? Perhaps it is simply Gavin. Unchanged and yet never still.

Amused by my speechlessness, he shakes his head, sending a bright beam of sunlight bouncing off his lenses. 'I seem to recall a similar reaction from the Company.'

'The Company?'

'Gavin Maxwell Enterprises.'

'Oh.' How odd to think of the name that has dominated my mind and heart for over a decade set down in the unromantic records of Companies House.

'And so, I find myself writing to zoos.' Gavin lowers his tone, hoarse and confessional. 'Asking if they'd consider taking Edal and Teko from me.' Eyes shrouded behind heavy sunglasses, I hear the strain of tears suppressed.

'Gavin, I ...' My hand is still on his, skin tingling from my fervent wish to impart whatever nourishment he needs. Consolation? Compassion? Cash. Cold, hard and contemptible. A crazed, unravelling impulse tells me to offer some money myself. But truly, I have nothing but pennies to spare after purchasing the second Paultons.

'Will you sell Number 9?' I should feel indignant at so great a sacrifice from me coming to mean so little in the grand scheme of Gavin's life. And yet the only emotion I am aware of is my share of his grief. Precious as that house was and always will be to me, it fades into insignificance when I think of Gavin leaving Sandaig. His Avilion. His spiritual home. It is hard to imagine him surviving such a blow.

'I'll have to.' Feigning toughness, Gavin shoves his decimated dish to one side. Only fishbones and gristle are left, the luckless creature shredded without mercy as if it were the cause of all his misfortunes. 'I'll have no choice, unless another book idea comes to me.' Gavin permits himself a low moan, veering close to a drone of despair. I suppose anyone who knows him well – in fact, anyone who knows him at all – would appreciate that he is hardly built to be a worker bee. 'A miracle I very much doubt will occur.'

'Miracle is more reliable than calculation.' I used to tell myself that when money was tight in the forties. I used to believe it. Even with his eyes shielded, I see a glimmer of approval dart across Gavin's face. 'I'm sorry about you and Lavinia.' I can manage the full sentence now. A hollow victory. Gavin groans, stubbing out the last embers of his cigarette and instantly lighting another. To speak of their brief union evidently requires a new nicotine hit.

'That marriage was a misery for both parties,' he mutters. 'Each wishing the other to be everything they're not. I ought never to have … you have to understand, Kathleen.' Gavin leans forward in urgent intensity until I see my reflection, shadowy and oddly elongated, in his dark lenses. 'I had felt so alone in Morocco. Lost in every sense and unable to even speak the language properly. I … well, I don't mind telling you that for a while I went a bit haywire.' The word feels rustic and almost quaint. An understatement, I suspect. 'There had been a translator. Ahmed. A very fine young man. But then he …'

'Don't.' *You don't need to*, is what I should say. *Please don't*, is what I mean. Either way, Gavin seems to absorb my message.

'After it all,' he concludes, mercifully opaque, 'I couldn't bear to be alone.'

'You never needed to be alone.' A moment of stillness lingers between us, the sweet voices of unseen Greek singers still perfuming the air along with the cypress scent. Gavin stretches, leaning back in his seat and twisting his signet ring. It glints in the light, my vision blinking between it and his tie pin. Gold, silver; flash, shimmer. 'The divorce is proving a

378

trial too. Ostensibly a never-ending one. A spouse must prove adultery before it can be granted. But then, I suppose you know that.'

'I do.' To give him his due, Charles led with his own infidelity, my dalliance with Alastair being less concretely admissible than the incontrovertible fact of Inez's pregnancy. 'But how did you do it?' I press Gavin, genuinely intrigued. He wouldn't, would he? He could not possibly have told a court of law that he betrayed his wife, however much of a wife Lavinia ever was to him, with another m …

A smile at last, albeit a wry one. 'Old friends who run a hotel in Inverness helped me out.' Gavin sniggers. 'I visited their establishment with a young lady of the town, and they testified that we had been seen going upstairs together.' A lady of the town. Like a woman of the night. I feel foolishly naive not to have realised that stolid, reliable Inverness had any such industry. Embarrassment edges me close to laughter, struck by the hysterical absurdity of Gavin prowling dark northern streets in his sports car to pick up a companion. Inviting her in after taking her into his confidence, and then …

'What did you do upstairs?'

'Drank tea.'

We laugh together, the smoke clearing from Gavin's voice to let out that soft, silvery lilt I love. Our merriment is contagious: from the corner of my eye, I sense that even our waiter is chuckling as he gathers in the lunchtime glasses. Mostly Gavin's. We are sitting in the shade, strong midday heat balanced by a soothing sea breeze. I wish that time's waterfall would freeze once more.

'You know, there's another country I should very much like to visit,' I observe. 'Not that I can imagine how I'd ever get the chance.' The idea is fanciful, mere whimsy compared with Gavin's real-life explorations, yet I cannot resist sharing it. I want to help Gavin feel hopeful. As hopeful as I now feel.

'Where?' he asks, immediately intrigued. No run of bad luck will ever deter him from adventure.

'India.' A fair eyebrow shoots up from behind Gavin's sunglasses and I smile. It still gives me a thrill to surprise him.

'I've been reading about it –' A place left in the world where the soul is a subject of study. Where the everyman and everywoman give it thought as they go about their lives. Where William Blake, remarkably enough, is celebrated with greater enthusiasm and spiritual respect than back in

379

our own country. Where I believe that I could tell a stranger something of what Gavin and I have shared and maybe, just maybe, they would understand.

'Perhaps we should go together,' Gavin jokes. I am almost certain he is joking. 'Think of the book that'd come from it.'

Books, I think. The plural is important. Still, I say nothing aloud, simply enjoying the sense of renewed possibilities, however improbable, washing over us.

'Has Euboea been worth it for your writing?' Brief relaxation has softened the harsher lines of Gavin's face, making the years that have passed since we last enjoyed each other's company seem to fade and fall away. 'Your memoir?' He remembered.

'Well worth it,' I confirm. 'Not that I'll ever publish. Certainly not while my parents are alive. For the time being, I'm merely writing it for myself. To make sense of everything.' *To make it bearable*, I choose not to add.

'Am I in it?' The same question as at Kielder, sparking the first of many storms between us. Then, Gavin detested the fact that I had written about him, offended by the very revelations I believed too beautiful not to preserve on the page. But it is no longer 1950. Nothing I wrote would be incriminating now. This is 1967, a modern era with modern, more compassionate laws to protect people's private lives. Except in Scotland, I suppose. Gross indecency remains a crime for men in Scotland.

'Why don't you read it and see?' I offer playfully, indulging in a literary coquettishness that I am decades too old for. 'It's at the villa. If you have time, I could …'

'I have time.'

Girlish and gleeful, I hurry back over the cobblestones to the Sherrards' home, daring to break into an unpractised run once I feel confident that no one is watching. The manuscript lies at my bedside, tight-pressed pages of handwritten intimacy that I pick up as if preparing a gift or even an offering. Back at the tavern, Gavin receives them in silence, his delicate, reverential touch recalling that little injured bird we saved. He'll find it in there. Every word of what we have shared is there.

'Remember, it's really just for myself,' I caution, watching him cradle my pages with the same anxious attentiveness I would feel were he holding Benjamin or Naomi. And yet when I see my work in Gavin's grasp, I know my protestations fail to ring true. This memoir is not for me. Every word of it, written in my heart's blood, exists for him.

We kiss again when we part. It feels like old times, save for the coarse scratch of Gavin's beard on my sun-tender skin. Only when it stings do I realise that I must have been burnt.

Chapter Forty-Six

Moonlight skims the wavelets while I swim, a path of pale gold cutting through the midnight ocean. I fancy this thin shimmering band could transport me to Mount Parnassus, if I only wished it hard enough. Indulging in the fantasy, I beat a few gentle strokes towards it, then roll with the soft, supportive current until I am bobbing upright again. Warm water enrings my waist as I stare back at the shore. Straining through the shadows, I can make out the silhouette of the solitary cypress tree: a narrow cone whose tip arches subtly as if deep in contemplation. Beside it, a human figure. Tall. Slender. Limping his way to the ocean's edge.

'Gavin.' My waving arms windmill into an inelegant front crawl. Splashes land on my lips, salt trickling down my throat as my ageing limbs thrash in haste to reach the shore. Bare soles striking land, I grab a towel left in readiness and wrap it around my torso. Sand clings to my moist skin, swimsuit squelching beneath the cotton. Self-conscious and clumsy, I squirm to adjust its unflattering folds around my midriff.

'You haven't finished reading already? It's not too late to come in for a nightcap if you can bear to tell me what you think ...'

'You witch.'

'What?'

'You bloody WITCH!' Gavin lurches, his gait lopsided without his stick, and hurls my manuscript into the night air. The pages scatter, fragments soaring like the white-winged gulls that have long since disappeared into the darkness, sea winds whipping them in mid-air so that half ricochet across the strand and the rest plummet down onto the waiting water. Shock sends me to my knees and I grapple, clogged fistfuls of sand coming away with the few soiled sheets in reach. Moonlight glances over the pages and I catch glimpses of my own handwriting. Sodden. Sullied. Stripped of order or meaning.

'How could you?' Weak leg sickling, Gavin stoops to drag me back up to my feet, his fierce grip clamped around the damp flesh of my bare arm. The light shifts again and I see the raw fury in his face, cragged and contorted like a wounded animal. His stick is forgotten; his crumpled shirt presses against the pathetic little towel that covers me. His tie pin is gone. With a jolt of bile, the acrid acid flooding my throat, I realise that I have never feared Gavin physically before. The hurt he inflicted on me always lay in other realms, intangible if no less agonising. Now, for the first time in over fifteen years, I am afraid that he will hit me.

'"Let him suffer"?' With the free hand not clenched around my upper arm, Gavin plucks a scrunched single page from the breast pocket that earlier bore his tie pin. '"If we cannot be together in Heaven, then I want him here with me in Hell. My blood-soaked hand is on the rowan's bark when I speak. *Let Gavin suffer, in this place, as I am suffering now.*"' The inconstant ebb and flow of moonlight forces him to pause, scowling at my work before crushing it back into his pocket. From the awkward angle he holds me at, all I manage to make out is the eerie inverse imprint of my words, mirrored letters marking a confession for which I realise too late I will be hung. No, not hung. Burnt. 'You bloody witch,' Gavin repeats. Lip curling, tone curdling. 'How could you? Cursing me at my own rowan tree, beside the home I had welcomed you into ...' *I was not welcome that day,* I want to remind him. Gavin Young was the only guest he desired. But my protest goes unexpressed. The words will not come. Survival instinct or shameful cowardice? All I am sure of is my silence.

'I suppose I should say "well done", Kathleen.' Sneering, Gavin releases my arm to begin a sardonic, slow clap. My skin singes, throbbing where the dug-in imprints of his fingers are still pulsing hot. 'This sinister black magic of yours clearly knows no bounds. Tell me, did you secretly exult today, learning of all that I've suffered?'

'N-no.' One syllable is all I can manage, weak and worthless.

'Did it fill you with delight to discover how strong your powers must be? Bites. Bankruptcy. The court case. The car crash. Not to mention my humiliating excuse for a marriage ...' A new notion dawns on Gavin, fanning the flames of his rage. 'Lavinia has suffered too, you understand. The whole wretched business damn near broke her. But I suppose she was nothing but collateral damage to you and your vile incantation.'

'I did not cause Lavinia's suffering.' A perverse spark of self-preservation, or else an attempt to drag Gavin down with me. His behaviour towards his former wife lies in his hands, not mine. Doesn't it? And yet the shame will not stick. Gavin shirks from it, squirming out from beneath the burden that I would have us share, even if it is the last thing we ever do share.

'Then what about poor Terry?' Gavin jabs two fingers at me to make his point, a Churchillian victory sign as I lose yet more ground in our battle. 'Only a boy and crippled for life.' Whether at the memory of Terry's sepsis-ridden wounds or the thought of my betrayal, revulsion causes Gavin to twist away from me. A harsh line of moonlight severs his complexion in two: princely fair, villainous shadows. But I am cast as the villain in this drama.

'Didn't you read the rest?' I plead, appealing to his light side. 'How much I regretted that one moment of madness? It only happened at all because I had fallen so deeply, so desperately in love with yo-'

'1956.' Gavin's voice quietens. A flat, muted tone that haunts me as no volume of violent screams ever could. 'You cast this hex the summer before the Easter when … you killed Mij, Kathleen. Your curse killed my Mij.' I say nothing. I can say nothing. Whether rowan tree or missing harness, the root source spiritual or physical, it was my mistake that killed Mij.

Breathlessness engulfs me, light-headed dismay causing me to stumble a few steps away from Gavin. The tide is going out, only foam remnants left to wash over my bare feet. I watch each wave recede, backing up further with every beat as if the ocean itself is repulsed by my presence. The lost pages of my manuscript drift on its blackened surface, flimsy sheets face down and disintegrating as the sole copy of many months' work is swept away. Soon though, a commotion calls my attention back to shore. Gavin is pacing, lopsided steps kicking up microcosmic sandstorms as he roams in obvious agitation. His compulsive, painful rotations remind me of Edal as her brain buckled to infection. Was that poor creature's agony also my fault? Gavin's own pain is clear, unbalanced in every sense as he stalks across the shadowy beach. The sand shifts, unable to support his restless momentum, and I realise that my betrayal has also made the ground give way beneath his feet. Gavin never questioned my love. He trusted it. Trusted me. Childlike in outlook even at this advanced age, he believed that I would always be there, whatever I was asked to endure: a faithful spaniel bitch who could rival even Jonnie's devotion. *He took me for granted,* I tell myself, trying and failing to ameliorate my guilt. He presupposed a purity within me that I never claimed to possess. It seems debatable how much superstitious mythology of rowan curses Gavin really believes in, although, stomach spasming, I recall the Highland rumours of second sight and Sandaig's undeniable aura of numinosity. But either way, this blow was dealt by one of the few people – at times, the only person – he trusts. Yet again, it is I who has let Gavin down.

'I'm sorry,' I begin, uncertain where the sentence will end. Gavin spins shakily and I watch a heartrending vulnerability cross his features. Then clouds cover the moon. Fury scorches the hurt from his voice.

'That whole bloody manuscript is nothing more than raving madness.' One sand-sullied page blows near Gavin; he kicks out at it as if it were vermin. '"My white hawk"? "My Godsend"? "One consciousness in two minds"? I do not love you, Kathleen.'

'I know you're too upset to feel anything but anger right now ...'

'No.' For once, Gavin is not wearing his dark glasses. In a bright, resurgent beam of moonlight, his ocean eyes glint grey. 'I have never loved you.'

All I hear is my heartbeat. An inner tide swelling before a crash. 'You're lying,' I say, surreally composed. 'Do you think I can't tell when you're lying?' I call his bluff with baffling confidence, begging my inner self to believe it too. Ordinarily, it would be true; in normal circumstances, I can read Gavin like one of his books or even my own. But so much is in darkness now. 'Not romantically. I understand that. Not in the same way as your ...' I hesitate, not bold enough to say 'your golden youths'. 'But what we have is still ...'

'When did I tell you that I loved you?' Gavin hobbles back across the sand until we are only inches apart. On the stand, under the pressure of sudden prosecution, my mind blanks. It has felt so obvious throughout the years that he and I share something inimitable and irreplaceable. Nameless, perhaps, but what name fits other than love? To break it into pieces, plucking out examples as evidence to strengthen my case, is as reductive as the very worst of literary criticism: stripping poems down to their component parts as one might a faulty car engine, then expressing disappointment when the built-back-up version fails to move. Frantic, I rifle through pages of the book of lives into which I imagine mine and Gavin's story is written. Thousands upon thousands of his words must be recorded there, scribbled in ink or spoken by that melodic, mournful voice.

'At the end of your letters,' I offer meekly. 'You've always signed them "Love, Gavin".' The pallid moonlight above me shifts. Gavin's eyes soften back to blue with a fleeting show of pity.

'Well, I'm sorry you misunderstood me.'

'Perhaps you didn't say it, but you showed it.' I scramble to restate and reclaim the truth whose essence is escaping me. 'The birds, the shells and the waterfall ...'

'Birds, shells and waterfall.' Gavin echoes the words in the manner of a psychiatrist wishing me to hear my own folly. He should know, having visited several over the years. 'The birds were just birds, Kathleen. The shells were just shells.' A breath's pause, as if deciding whether or not to tread on the last of my dreams. 'The waterfall would be there whether you had been or not.'

'Sandaig ...' I have no point to make, even if Gavin would let me finish. Only a plaintive call for the place I once believed was my soul's true home.

'Sandaig is a house,' Gavin says, 'which I lent to one of my many friends.'

'*I look through it, not with it.*' William Blake understood the flaws of human perception. The foibles inherent within our imperfect, partial vision. We never say illuminated by love, only blinded by it. The garden of Eden that I had believed myself cast out from seems to evaporate in front of my eyes, a verdant picture receding into barrenness as if none of it had ever existed.

'We always said we shared one mind ...' Did we always say that? Or did I say it to myself? Regardless, I trusted that Gavin understood. But now he scoffs, throat coarse from cigarettes.

'You really believed I knew what you were thinking when we were apart?' An airborne page circles us before collapsing onto the sea. 'Kathleen, I never thought of you at all.'

I am sinking back into the nightmare of Mij's dark, watery grave. Submerged, I scrabble, wrestling with the cruel, choking weeds that seek to drown out what little is left of my sun. Horrified and close to hopeless, I alight on one final glint of gold.

'"We met at last in the heart of an otter."'

Gavin flinches. Sincerity flashes across his face; I think of lightning striking the sea at Sandaig. The boy inside the man is visible again for an instant.

'That otter's heart stopped long ago. Thanks to you.'

Neither of us can speak after that. We stand apart on the shore, enduring our shared grief in solitude. The waves billow. My manuscript sinks.

'You never loved me either,' Gavin mutters eventually, churlish as a child.

'I never loved you?' The oddness of that short sentence gives me a bizarre sense of hope. Perhaps he has gone mad. Haywire. For Gavin to claim that I never loved him seems no less perverse than to insist black is white. Earth is flat. The sun does not rise. I watch him stoop, left leg unsteady, to scoop up some sodden sheets of my work. Gavin fans them in front of me, tattered leaves buffeted by sea air. 'What was all this except infatuation? Obsession? Forcing me to fit the shape of some pathetic, delusional fixation that would mortify most women half your age?'

'You know nothing of women.'

'And you know nothing of real life, or real love. Except whatever you've read about it.' Gavin glares, the whites of his eyes gleaming wild in the shadows. 'Tell me one single person who has been close to you in your life whom you have not destroyed. Your parents. Your children. Your husbands.' That hiss again, emphasising the shame of the second 's'. 'Even myself, whom you say you love.' Gavin goes to take a step, left foot first, then grimaces to disguise the pain. 'You are a destroyer, Kathleen. Your love is a force more deadly than hate.'

Silence returns. The prosecution rests, assured of conviction. *James*, I want to whisper: the name of a loved one who has thrived, even if at times it was in spite of me. And yet I feel fearful to speak my son's name; terrified to tempt fate or whatever accursed forces my foolishness has unleashed. Spent, I sink to the sand. With a sigh, Gavin soon follows suit. We are too old for violent delights and violent ends. Damp grains discarded by the outgoing waves dapple and freckle my exposed thighs. Shuddering more from embarrassment than cold, I untie my towel to drape over me.

A few feet away, Gavin lifts a limp, water-stained page from the shoreline. He squints at it and laughs, humourless and hollow. 'You were right about one thing. I did go to bed with Clement.'

Do you think I can't tell when you're lying? 'You did not.'

'I did. It was before she was with Aymer.' Gavin crushes what little remains of my page inside his fist, letting the sodden ball roll down the coast on the breeze. 'The day she misplaced her gloves. For once, your instincts were correct.'

'You mean to tell me that at Monreith, we were your wife, your mistress and me?' Crimson taffeta. Appliqué blooms. A glass-eyed severed stag's head staring down in mute recrimination. Gavin offers me no answer, swirling patterns in the sand with his signet-ringed little finger. 'I'll ask her,' I threaten. 'I'll ask Clement myself when we're back in Britain.'

'You can't, remember? She found religion. Converted to Catholicism.' A snigger, for once not directed at me. 'Lives in a nunnery now.'

'Your performance didn't impress then.' His sniggers cease. The tide turns. When he next speaks, Gavin's voice is acidic as if his mouth is laced with a foul taste. Me, I suppose.

'Really, Clement was useful for introducing me to other men,' he tells me. 'A very open-minded woman in her day. There was one remarkably beautiful boy in particular. Tomas.' Gavin makes a show of stretching back, reclining as if to revel in the pleasure of recollection. 'He wasn't unlike her. Tall. Blonde.' Everything I am not. 'Born in Sicily, interestingly enough.' The Sicilian books. At last, a real reason for the interest. Gavin punishes me every time I write a word about him, yet some young man I will never know is allowed to inspire the journey behind two books?

'Our friendship ended in '54.' Legally, I suppose he must still call it that. Although I of all people know the vast, unbreachable gulf that lies between friendship and more. 'The break coincided with Jonnie's death. That's why I couldn't face being with the poor dog when it happened. The pain was just too much.' I know the feeling. I can scarcely see, hardly hear, for this deep swell of sorrow. All I recall, with humiliating clarity, is the sensation of Gavin's skin beside my own on the night that Jonnie died; lulling my love to sleep as his hot tears fell on my breast. I did not think Gavin could take more from me than he already has. My heart, my house, almost twenty years of my life. But even they were not enough. He is taking my memories too.

'Why didn't you tell me?' I beg, too depleted to rage anymore. 'If we were friends, why not tell me about Tomas? Or the rest?' I cannot be certain, the moonlight failing to shift in time, but I believe a look of guilt flits across Gavin's face. He knows as well as I do that 'whatever we had' was never so simple as friendship.

'I confess I found it easier back then to confide in someone like Clement,' he says. 'It felt good not to be judged.' A scream catches in my throat, scratching and shrill. Judged? Gavin dares to claim that I judged him? Too many protests rise up inside me at once. Yet before I can articulate any, the memory of my own words returns to haunt me. One word worse than the rest. 'Disgust.' Spat at his feet, bitterness dripping from my lips along with a tacky trail of vomit on that accursed summer's night at Sandaig. God forgive me, I did judge Gavin. I judged the way he is. It is no longer illegal in England. History is being made back home and my feelings will fall on the wrong side of it; so intent upon looking up at sky and stars, I failed to notice the earth turning beneath my feet. Another sentence I shrieked at Gavin after falling at his rowan's roots echoes in my mind, crueller than any curse. 'I've loved you in spite of everything you are.'

And yet the prejudice, or more honestly the hypocrisy, was never about the way he is. Not really. It is the way I am. The way I have wanted Gavin with such insane, insatiable desperation that it led me to hate what I believed was the force keeping us apart. That he should love me, and only me, has been my defining objective for nearly two decades: abandoning every lofty hope of attaining a Platonic ideal in favour of frenzied, obsessive possession. In the strangest way, perhaps Gavin is right. Perhaps I do not love him. Not as much as I want to be loved by him.

'It was all such a long time ago,' he muses, backhand sweeping the sand to brush away the squiggled marks he has carved. Yet again, my vision blurring from tears, I realise that our minds and hearts are many hundreds of miles apart. None of it feels like a long time to me. Blink, and I am back there. I fear the best part of me will always be back there.

'How I wish we'd never met,' I whisper. Burn the pages. Start a new book of life without the name Gavin Maxwell written in it. Meet the poet I could have become, if only my soul had remained my own. Surely Gavin feels the same?

He sounds hurt, even offended, by the suggestion. 'I only came to Paultons in the first place because Tambi told me you were lonely. He seemed like a helpful person to know when I was new to living in London, and he was utterly determined that we should meet. He said a charming man like me was just what his friend needed to cheer her up without her children ...'

'Please stop.'

'Of course, you proved to be a rather productive connection yourself.'

'STOP.' This time he does. Only the leaf-like rustle of retreating waves fills the quiet. The horizon seems paler, the whisper of dawn light flickering like a gold-edged page about to be turned. Or maybe I am hallucinating. With my most precious memories savaged, I feel unable to trust myself. Oddly, Young George, Hardy's infamous sheepdog, comes gambolling back through my battle-fatigued brain. I see Tambi herding Gavin and me together beneath my beloved Paultons pear tree, his mischievous, misguided attempt at matchmaking unwittingly driving his charges to their deaths.

'Are we even now?'

'Are we what?'

With a wince, Gavin rolls onto his left side to face me. 'When will my suffering satisfy you, Kathleen? Is there worse to come for me? More "toil and trouble"? Will this witchcraft of yours not end until I do?'

'Don't speak such nonsense.' I turn away, unable to endure what he is implying. Thick clutches of sand form ugly clumps inside my fists. Yet again, Gavin and I are locked at cross purposes: oppositional Saltire lines that cut across each other while doomed never to find peace side by side. Does he really believe that my heart's cry at the rowan came from strength and not pure, pathetic desperation? Does he truly think I would have wasted magical powers on a curse? 'If I had any control over your fate, Gavin, you would have known it long ago. You would have loved me as I love you.'

He gives no reply. Again, I am alone in my shame, if not in my sorrow. Across the ocean, the ethereal hint of impending sunrise enrings the dark water with brightness. What flotsam remains of my work is becoming more visible. Words blurred beyond all recognition; my manuscript sheets scattered in waterlogged disarray as they drift before sinking, lost to the depths.

'My writing will be remembered when yours is forgotten.' It seems the sole thing we have learned from almost twenty years entwined is the best way to hurt each other.

'That,' Gavin sighs, 'may very well be true.'

*

The sun is up by the time we part. Surreal blends of colour coast towards us, celestial bands of citrus yellow streaked with rich ruby and coral. To my tired, tear-ravaged eyes, the tones seem otherworldly: kaleidoscopic swirls raking across the sky as fingertip ridges might ripple through the sand. Without a wristwatch, I must trust in the elements to gauge time's passage. It feels to me like we have sat in silence for several hours. My body is drained, shivering as if post-fever, all my energy extinguished like Gavin and I spent the night making love. We never have. We never will. It has taken my stubborn, short-sighted heart far too long to accept that simple truth.

Stirring back into self-awareness and the memory of the night's many humiliations, I start to rise, fighting to subdue the pain that emanates from my stiffened joints and wrestle them into obedience. On my right, Gavin notices the struggle and extends his hand automatically. Some knee-jerk chivalric impulse is still buried in his aristocratic bones. Nobility in principle, however, makes for a comedic interlude in practice. Once I am standing, Gavin's temperamental left leg refuses to let him do likewise, and we find ourselves in the undignified position of me half-hauling him back to his feet. Two elderly writers, I think, wondering why I feel no wiser than on the first day we met.

'You didn't take it all so very seriously, did you?' Gavin asks.

Our hands are still linked. I make the break before I speak. 'No.' What is one more lie when everything else was false? Words do not matter. Even precious poetry cannot salvage me from this wreckage. Do I know Gavin Maxwell? Do I know Kathleen Raine? Do I know what is left for me, what broken fragments of the past I can cling to, now the last of my treasured memories have been trampled and crushed beneath his feet? No. No. No.

'If you publish …'

'I won't publish.'

'*If* you publish …'

'I won't.'

'Write something kind about me. Won't you?' Numbly, I nod. I never could say no to Gavin.

He kisses me before we part. *'Ae fond kiss and then we sever.'* He aims for my cheek, I think, but then his troublesome foot wobbles and our lips brush for a heartbeat. The moment is so fleeting, I scarcely feel it, save for the raw, irritant scratch of Gavin's new beard. A Judas kiss. That is what I feared I had given him in front of the rowan, after my mistake – whichever one of my many mistakes it was – caused our Mij to be lost forever. Has Gavin betrayed me as badly as I did him? Are we indeed 'even now', my suffering enough to cancel out what he has endured in some monstrous cosmic schema of hate? All I know is that he has broken me, just as he himself once appeared broken before my door.

Walking away, unsteady on my bare feet, a giddy fearlessness flows through me and I feel bizarrely emboldened by the thought that all is finally over. Gavin knows everything. He despises me. Our centre cannot hold; the worst has come to pass at last. And yet surely the sole silver lining of this savage, decades-long storm is that this accursed and all-consuming love can cause neither of us any more pain. In the night, Gavin called me his destroyer. Now I tell myself I have nothing left to lose, safe in the knowledge he has destroyed me too.

Chapter Forty-Seven

What is left of me returns to London, retreating behind the door of my house, if not my home, in Paultons Square. Red-rimmed eyes squeezed shut, I determine never again to look across at Number 9. When the grandchildren arrive, I hold them close to my heart, murmuring singsong silliness through my tears before handing over their gifts from Greece. An iridescent clam shell for Benjamin, the crinkled fan spanning almost as large as his little head, and an embroidered baby blanket for Naomi, whose chubby fists seize gleefully around the intricate pattern of vibrant colours.

'I have one for the new baby too,' I tell Anna, offering her a ribbon-tied version woven in softer, more delicate shades. Her pregnancy is visible now, the proud swell of her stomach matching the healthy rose glow in her cheeks that has, to my relief, replaced morning sickness pallor. Yet something still troubles her. My daughter's doe-like dark eyes carry a silent concern within their depths.

'Thank you,' Anna murmurs, without looking long at me. She lays the blanket over her bump, declining to say more.

I can watch over her now, I remind myself. I am home, and home for good. Alone at night, the shocks of Euboea still shudder through my ravaged nerves, but during daylight hours, I insist to anyone who asks – few do – that I feel liberated. At long last, I know the whole truth. 'Whatever we had' is at an end. Indeed, if Gavin spoke in earnest and not just to stab his dagger further into my bruised and battered heart, then whatever we had never existed at all. Regardless of whose recollections are right, I trust that the final storm between him and I has passed; our ocean will never again be rattled by violent bolts of rage and revenge. There is no reason I can see why our lives should collide again.

Not until *Raven Seek Thy Brother.*

'An ugly title, don't you think?' the Girton girl remarks to her companion, a copy of Gavin's new book clasped in her young hands. The second student opens her mouth to reply – to concur, I choose to think –

but catches sight of me and simply gapes, goldfish-wide and horrified. A sharp-elbowed prod at her friend nudges both young women into silence. Heads bent, they hurry away. I should run away from myself too, if I could.

'The title came from Wilfred Thesiger,' I want to call out after them, compelled to care about their education even at the expense of my emotions. Stolen from Thesiger, I should say. To see a single raven is an emblem of bad luck in the Middle East and so the Ma'dan – not an easily unsettled people, I would have thought – cry 'Raven, seek thy brother' if one flies past. Such trivia is of little use to me now, however. It is too late to ward off my fate.

'The curse of a poetess' gives Gavin's third Sandaig book its premise. An embittered, lovesick witch whose dark magic has blackmarked him, her wicked words giving shape to a narrative through which one pre-ordained catastrophe after another befalls his beloved idyll. The fleeting failed marriage to Lavinia, coyly described by Gavin as 'incompatible'. The car crash and subsequent injury, its debilitating consequences discussed at length. The decline of his paradise into a press-harassed liability. The imminent zoo incarceration of the otters whom fans all around the world adore. Every disaster is laid bare on the page, then laid out for all to see and read at my sinister sorceress's feet. For near twenty years, I have prayed to God, to the Buddha, even to the spirit of the Sandaig waterfall that I would be granted my rightful place at the centre of Gavin's life. Now at long last, here I am. The apex of his hatred.

With a gentlemanly flourish of faux discretion, Gavin declines to publish my name in his new book. Instead, he speaks only of a 'poetess', a once close friend who was there with him at Sandaig, so I may be assured that no one will guess who I am, except for anyone who knows either of us even tangentially. Given that the press is already obsessed with *Ring* and the quixotic adventurer at its heart – how agonisingly well I know the feeling – it seems inevitable that they should track me down within days.

'Why did you do it, Dr Raine?' The most tiresomely repeated query, to which I do not dare give an answer.

'Did you cast your curse on Gavin Maxwell before or after you met Saint-John Perse?' That from an earnest young broadsheet reporter, clearly better-than-average at background research.

'Care to share a spell with our readers?' A tabloid enquiry, yelled out at a distance lest I strike down the heckler with a hex. Would that I could.

Perhaps I must credit Gavin for a certain cleverness, having once and for all proved the point over which we have been warring since the Kielder snowstorm decades ago. He was right; I was wrong. Few things hurt more than being written about.

To my great shame, if this shame can grow greater, the barrage of coarse journalistic curiosity starts to assault the college's august walls: the great Elephant Ears doors groaning shut as, once again in Girton's history, male marauders must be barred at the gate. And yet even locked doors cannot stop letters. Within weeks, I find myself subject to a deluge like that which flowed through Gavin's letterbox before his *Harpoon* book launch. Envelopes pour in, fevered scribbles expressing not congratulations but furious and often downright mad condemnation.

'How could you?' The same angry sentence scrawled by different hands, sent on mismatched notelets whose enraged passage is paid by squint, unseasonable Christmas stamps. 'Witchcraft' proves the most common accusation against me, although plain 'evil' appears more than once. 'How dare you summon such wickedness against an innocent young man like Major Maxwell?' demands one indignant Miss. That Gavin is over fifty seems irrelevant to her point. Perhaps his Peter Pan energy will never dim for his legions of devoted fans. For me, the magic is long gone from Neverland.

'*Cailleach*,' hisses an anonymous note, the single word scratched in red across a strip of coarse brown paper. Even untranslated, the harsh vortex of foreign sounds communicates contempt, but I must look up their meaning to be sure. Gaelic. 'Old hag.'

If being barricaded inside the college while such correspondence arrives is bad, then London is worse. The city morphs into my Salem as I walk the streets shamefaced, weighed down and despoiled by an indelible witch's mark. The humiliation feels hot, yet oddly pure and almost puritan. I seem to be infected with a medieval psychic pestilence that causes acquaintances to avert their eyes or even cross the road to avoid contamination. I might as well wear a scarlet letter affixed to my chest, but which one for a hated old harpy? No 'A' for adulteress. Gavin never wanted me in that way.

I am the Wicked Witch of the West Highlands. A lovesick shrew or a jealous crone. 'Fat squaw,' Gavin's inventive drunken insult from years ago, is seldom far from my mind. Just like he did, some literary commentators question the veracity of my love for him, preferring to

395

present me as some sort of demented fortune hunter. What fortune? The fact that I gave Gavin his Paultons Square house seems to pass both press and public by. As does the knowledge, irrefutable to anyone who knows him, that Gavin never did anything or had anyone in his life other than because he wanted to. Still, the shame clings to me like smoke, the rotten tar stench staining everything I touch in a way that Gavin's cigarettes – up to eighty a day, he told me in Greece – should do but never seem to. The wild idea runs through my mind that I might write to Lavinia, seeking unlikely solidarity because we are survivors of the same disaster. Of course, I cannot. Lavinia occupies a social sphere far beyond my reach, our momentary collision merely a sign that I had overspun out of my own lowlier orbit. Besides, our two situations do not tally. Gavin wed Lavinia. And when her suffering grew too great to bear, Lavinia left Gavin. I have none of her validity. I had none of her good sense. Yet again, I am alone. Bookcases only gather to comfort me in my college rooms or the new, foreign-feeling Paultons. One night I reach for *Harpoon*, ignoring the inscription that I can no longer bear to read and rattling furiously past its opening pages until I find the sentence I seek.

> *He had moored the boat in such a way that when the tide went back it was lifted by a rock below the keel and capsized – but he was not likely to remember his inefficiencies when he had so desirable a scapegoat as the witch-woman to bear them into legend.*

'Why did I do it?' By telephone, in tears, I beg Helen for the wise counsel upon which I have so many times relied. 'What possessed me to show him my manuscript?' Unable to understand myself, I hope her sage silver-white head will help to explain.

'You wanted him to *see*,' Helen suggests. 'The two of you are not unalike in that regard.'

Surprise halts my tears. 'Whatever do you mean?'

'Well, you've tried all these years to show Gavin how you feel. Make him understand how much he means to you, despite everything that barred your way. Isn't that what you really hoped to achieve by having him read your memoir? To have him hold the evidence in his hands, asking him to see and acknowledge whatever it is that the two of you have shared.'

'If so, it failed.'

'Perhaps,' Helen admits. 'But hasn't he also been trying to confide in you? This shame of his …' Helen hesitates, ever discreet yet never judgemental. 'His nature. Gavin trusted you with it. Or he tried to.'

'But Clement Glock …'

'Confession isn't the same as true acceptance, Kathleen. Gavin only ever looked for the latter in you.' Looked, but did not find. Ashamed already, the thought makes me recoil from myself, my soul diminished by the realisation that I have fallen extraordinarily far from grace. I was so desperate to solicit from Gavin the type of love I could not have, I neglected to give him the one kind he actually asked me for. Compassion. Unconditionality. Faith in the goodness I had glimpsed within his playful, otter-like heart, however cruelly the small-minded, dried-out husk of our ordinary world wanted to condemn him for it. Platonic love, which I came to despise, never used to mean a shrunken version of romance. It could have been towering. Transcendent. Worth it all, if only I myself had been worthy of the power we once had within our shared grasp.

'Never was anything in this world loved too much,' Gavin used to tell me, 'but many things have been loved in a false way, and all in too short a measure.'

'It wasn't a curse, Helen.' Too late to plead my case, still I cannot help voicing a defence. 'It was my …'

'"Heart's cry".' Helen has heard all this before. 'I suspect his heart has cried too.'

One afternoon at Paultons, I run into Aymer in the street. On instinct, I brace, expecting either reproach or an ice-cold 'cut'. But he seems cordial. Older and wearier, as we all are. But also more approachable without a fashion plate blonde affixed to his arm.

'How is …?' Pathetically, I let Gavin's name slip away unspoken. With a half-hearted wave, I gesture towards the trees that block my sightline to Number 9. 'Is he …' Happy? Was Gavin ever happy, with or without me?

Aymer snorts. 'He's lucky to have you to blame for everything.' His pale grey eyes narrow. Never nearly as blue as Gavin's. 'My brother has spent his adult life looking for the broken mirror: a source of all the bad luck that isn't himself. Finally, he's found it. Thanks to you.' The irony stings. How many nights have I lain sleepless, praying only that I could be of some use to Gavin? More tears are shed over answered prayers than unanswered ones.

'Not that it can be said to have improved his mood.' Aymer inhales sharply, rolling those light eyes in chilly exasperation. 'If whisky's not going in, a complaint is coming out. Especially since Mother died.'

'Oh my goodness.' Lady Mary? 'I'm so …' sorry that my conscience will not permit me to complete the sentence.

Aymer simply shrugs. 'Stroke. Terrible shock for everyone at the time. She'd always been the picture of perfect health. Why, I don't recall her being ill a day in my life.'

*

Distraction comes with time, although the reason is an unwelcome one. The slow, sliding decline of my own parents' health gathers pace over a matter of months that feels like weeks and Number 47 is soon summoned into action to serve as their permanent home. That I knew this day must come does not make living through it any easier. Accompanying my mother and father as they leave Ilford for the last time, however much I detest the place myself; fighting to preserve the last flickering ember of my father's once blazing pride by letting him carry a single suitcase, after I have surreptitiously made sure it is the lightest. His painful physical frailty is at odds with a rigid, uncompromising determination to continue upholding his 'duty'. The formal tie that he refuses not to wear on weekdays swamps his brittle-thin neck bones, rattling inside a shirt collar that gapes several inches too big. My mother remains relatively robust in body, yet her tendency to untether from reality is hardly helped by a now-profound deafness. Both need someone to care for them. For both, that someone must be me.

What little energy I need not expend on their direct care is devoted to keeping news of Gavin's book away from them. My telephone calls to Helen, Winifred, Willa, Thetis and once even to Tambi across the Atlantic are kept private, door closed and mouthpiece muffled. Darting into the hall twice a day as soon as the letterbox clatters, I gather up our morning and afternoon post, squirrelling away any incriminating items before either parent has had time to rise. And yet despite my clandestine efforts, perhaps it is inevitable that one day I should be setting down their lunch only to find my father hunched over a newspaper clipping sent to him by a friend. A well-meaning, misguided friend.

'Gavin's written a new book,' he observes, spindling fingers struggling to bend the unyielding sheet so that our eyes meet. 'Why didn't you mention it, Kathie?' My mother, failing to hear him, stares contentedly out of the window.

'No reason,' I lie. 'We've been busy here, haven't we?' A nod and obliging, unfocused smile from Mother. No such dreamy acquiescence from him.

'"*Ring of Bright Water* broken by the dark power of a poetess."' Hearing the headline aloud is a stab to the gut. I fight not to flinch. 'They mean you, Kathie. Why would they say such a thing about you?' My father's tremor-prone fingertips rustle the clipping.

'It's not important,' I insist, bending over the elementary lunch I have prepared so that my threatening tears will not be visible. 'It's just that Gavin wrote something rather unkind about me in it.'

'Your Gavin?' The blotched, glassy film clouding my mother's eyes leaves her lucidity uncertain.

'He was never my Gavin, Mother.' This time, the confusion is clear in her face and, God forgive me, I do nothing to ease it. I simply wait for her to abandon the attempt at puzzling out what I myself have never been able to, retreating back into the ephemeral embrace of her eternally comforting dreams. How I wish that I could follow.

'I've been thinking, Kathie.' After lunch, my father appears at my study door. Inside baggy suit trousers, his sapling-slim legs shake from the strain of walking unaided. I jump up, hands outstretched as they used to be when helping Anna and James take their first, tentative steps. Lightly scolding him for the effort, I guide my father to the nearest chair. The exertion has rendered him breathless, but he presses on with his point. 'You should sue him. You can sue him.' A rare smile springs from the earthen lines of his elderly face. 'I've written to Longmans.'

'You've done what?' Alarmed, my mind turns to the bundle of letters I took with me to catch the afternoon collection. A slim, nondescript note that my father had quietly wedged in the middle of the pile. I told myself it would be rude to read the address, keen to preserve respect in defiance of the increasing indignities he suffers in being cared for by his own child. Evidently, I need not have worried. Not about that, at any rate.

'Don't fret, Kathie. It's a courteous letter.' My father wipes a handkerchief over his spectacles, leaving a still-larger condensation smear. 'I simply requested a retraction or apology if they wish to avoid Raine family legal action.'

'Father, I …' The comedy of his audacious, teenagerish scheme fades away as I appreciate the full pathos of this scene. George Raine in his late, late eighties, humbled by physical limitations yet taking it upon himself to defend the honour of the daughter who has surely disappointed him at every turn. My father knows nothing of the publishing industry. He has little sense of his vulnerability: an elderly, unsteady David squaring up to their moneyed and menacing Goliath. Plucky little Ilford taking on the might of the dukedom yet again. When will we learn? I used to complain my father never understood me. Now watching this twilight battle play out between bodily weakness and bloody mindedness, I wonder whether the passionate nature I failed to repress was in truth too close to home. 'You had no need to do that, Father.'

'I wanted to. It will teach them not to spread lies.' My father gives a chortle, throat croaking as if from disuse. 'Not too old to still surprise you, am I, Kathie?' I laugh, afraid that otherwise I will cry, because I cannot bring myself to tell my father that the accursed words Gavin quotes in his book are not lies. Even if they were, I could never sue him. It would be futile. The rest of Gavin's life would not be long enough for him to pay back all I have lost.

*

Anna's baby arrives, a healthy little sister for Benjamin, yet the birth coincides with sorrow almost as much as it brings about joy. The mystery I have sensed lingering behind Anna's mournful dark eyes is revealed when, slim fingers seizing my wrist as if to bind me to her hospital bedside, she confides just how low and frightened she feels.

'I'm scared, Mother,' she whispers in the quiet night hours after her delivery. 'Every breath I take, I feel afraid.' Anna stares up at me, her delicate features drained of all colour. Hair brushed back, only those mesmeric doe brown irises stand out against the pure white pillowcase.

'What are you scared of?' I stroke her forehead as I did when she was a little girl. Anna gives me no answer. Instead, she squeezes her eyelids shut to blot out the rest of the world, letting a solitary teardrop escape. But I know. I have felt the same fear myself. Only with her, strangely never with James, the quirks of post-natal suffering as illogical and inexplicable as Anna experiencing this torment with her new baby but not Benjamin. Whatever this monster is, the oppressive shadow that prowls maternity wards and looms to darken the cradles of shining bright, beloved newborns, its attacks follow no pattern. No rhythm. The only certainty is that mothers are its prey.

'The feeling passes. I promise.' It is what I wish someone had said to me. Having faith that the fear would not last forever, that this debilitating terror interspersed with paralysis could not continue indefinitely, might have given me the courage to stay back in the forties. Anna nods, trying hard to remain hopeful. Still, she tightens her grip on me. With or without it, this time I know that I must stay.

The feeling passes, yes. But it also takes time, and what are promises of weeks or months to a woman for whom every minute stretches out into a void of pitch black? Back at home, Anna's mood falls further, depression lowering her horizons and boxing her in from every side, until the doctors decide – plural, my own hopes sinking as the second and third opinions I have secured for her all concur – that she must be readmitted to hospital.

'Just a rest,' the last white-coated stranger tries and fails to reassure us both. John is downstairs with the baby, finding these consultations too much to stand. 'Doesn't a little rest sound nice, Mrs Hopewell?' Anna does not reply. She speaks only on occasion now. I travel with her in the ambulance, continuing to hold her hand even after her anxious grip gives way as the sedation takes effect. Sensing Anna's racing pulse steadying, my own throbs with fierce, violent regret. How I wish that I could retract each scribbled note I stuffed behind the Buddha's ceramic ear; reclaiming the energy that I sacrificed to a false God of my own sacrilegious invention and using it to make Anna better. The real curse, of course, is that I cannot. Whatever Gavin and the rest of the world think, life is not under my control.

'You will survive this.' My lips are at Anna's ear, a prayer coursing through me that her mother's voice – even a let-down mother like me – can bring her comfort.

'How?' The single word echoes like a groan, drifting from that eerie liminal land between sleep and wakefulness. 'How – do you – know?'

'Because I survived. And you will too.' Anna's eyes roll back, the next wave of artificial slumber submerging her. 'There can be no end to snowdrops,' I tell her even so.

In her absence, I care for her children, tending to them with the patient, attentive affection that my own offspring deserved but, to my shame, did not always receive. Under the strain, John and I lock horns over the most trivial domestic matters, minor gripes distracting us both from major fears.

'Don't interfere so much, Kathleen. It's not your marriage,' Helen cautions me after an especially ill-tempered clash. John fails to appreciate Anna, or so I had accused him. Temper cooling, I tell myself it is to the

401

young man's credit that he did not hurl the criticism right back at me. No, their marriage is not my own. I have no marriage, nor ever will again. After all that has occurred, I admit I struggle to believe happiness is a genuine possibility for men and women, save those lucky few able to give their love in ways that I, lofty though my spiritual aspirations were, resolutely failed to achieve. Edwin and Willa Muir. William and Catherine Blake. I hope such a peaceful and prosperous union is still possible for Anna, if certainly no longer for me.

'Welcome home, Mummy.' Growing bigger by the day, Benjamin hurls himself into Anna's embrace the moment she arrives home. Home to Paultons, I should say. Not wanting to question her, I simply accepted her wish that all three – John remains at their marital flat – should come here and stay with me. Anna bends to hold her son close, his plump little hand in hers as they cross the threshold together. A fragile stability emanates from her every step, precipice-poised like a tightrope walker. A moment's dizziness flickers before me and I realise I am holding my breath.

'I want her,' Anna says, nodding towards her daughter in my arms.

'Go to your mother now,' I whisper to the little one, passing the blanketed bundle back where she belongs. Baby mews at the movement – I suspend my breath again – yet soon she senses Anna's presence and grows calm. With a gurgle of clear contentment, the little one lies still beside her mother's heart.

In the weeks that follow, a new balance starts to settle over Number 47. My parents are downstairs; Anna and her infants above. Alone, I inhabit the centre and, for once, I believe it can hold. As a fortnight and then a month passes, my unexpressed but ever-present fear that my daughter will relapse is tentatively replaced by humble gratitude for our newfound, hard-won peace. My heart dares to swell when I watch my mother smile at the sight of her new great-granddaughter; my spirit sings to hear Benjamin's light, playful peals of laughter resounding from every corner of the house. James and Jennie often bring Naomi to visit, her robust and insatiable curiosity the ideal foil to her cousin's cautious sensitivities.

'Why it rain? Why trees grow in tubs? Why flowers have faces?' Naomi's growing fascination with nature encourages me to seek out an old story book that I wrote as a young mother. *The Story of Three Water Drops*. Unskilled in so many necessary areas of life, words were the best I had to offer my children back then. Perhaps they still are. Typically encouraging, Tambi helped me to secure a short run of the little tale and it is with profound, long-lost pleasure that I draw out its small cream cover. Our old friend Francis Rose's exquisite Blakean-inspired illustrations decorate my sweet, slight volume, imagining the liquid siblings' magical journeys under the sea, absorbed by the sky and, for the little girl droplet Violet, transforming into a snowflake just in time for Christmas morning. I never dreamed when I wrote it that I would one day share it with my grandchildren.

'"One, two, three water drops."' I tap one tiny nose after another, delighting in the giggles of the two toddlers and burbling baby. 'The way is clear,' I wrote almost as long ago, 'the end we shall not know. The sea will carry us where tides run and currents flow.' How could I have lost such wisdom along the way? Gavin, I guess. My 'infatuation', as he called it, swept away any sense I ever had. And yet the paradox remains. What might we have shared – not romance, no, but maybe more – if I had brought the humility I now feel to bear with him all those years earlier? Accepting the way he is, knowing that one cannot love wholeheartedly while raging against a part of the beloved.

His absence echoes in my life. My ears sometimes ring from the silence, unaccustomed to the vacant space where my mind and heart used to speak his name. Gavin's book is still out there. He is still at Sandaig, I assume. He exists, even though his insistence that my love is false and his own was never there causes me to doubt even that most obvious of facts. The notion makes me feel oddly memoryless, without foundation and divorced from all that once seemed to define me. A Keats quotation, known since childhood but under-appreciated until now, flows into my weary head.

I have clung to nothing, lov'd a nothing, nothing seen or felt but a great dream.

Chapter Forty-Eight

'I want to tell you something, Kathie.' My mother's eyes bloom huge behind her strong-lensed spectacles. 'I've never told anyone before, but I think you will understand.'

'Alright,' I equivocate, setting down my notebook and pen and pulling my chair closer to hers. Suspicion brews in me, which I try to suppress. How dreadful a secret can my mother be concealing at nearly ninety years of age? A former love affair perhaps, the visceral memories of passion returning as the tide of her rational mind recedes. More shocking yet, maybe a sibling I never knew about, lying in wait to stake a claim on my hypothetical inheritance. They are welcome; indeed, I could do with their help running this large household. Jesting aside, the anxious intensity in my mother's expression makes me pause. I lay my hand on hers, even the lightest pressure causing her crepe-thin, papery skin to crease. Dappled with age spots, I feel her elderly veins protrude, blue-green ridges of a relief map that tracks the twisting course of her long life.

'Tell me,' I say. 'Please.' Deafness and daydreams are barriers between us now, blanketing my mother in solitude just as a fall of snow muffles the world. Whatever the reason, I am glad when sunlight shines through.

'One day,' Jessie begins, as if I were a child in need of a bedtime story, 'at Kielder, I looked out across the heather moor.' My mother raises her hand and takes mine with it, a shaky gesture to reconjure that sweeping haze of purple and green. 'And do you know what I saw, Kathie? The moor was *alive*.'

Tears I have withheld since Anna's illness start to fall. My free hand swats at them, scrubbing my face, but my mother is not distressed. She is not looking at me. She is still in the memory. Still on that thriving, enlivening Northumbrian moorland of our childhoods. Teaming with a trillion spirits of nature, a shimmering mist of amethyst and emerald; more brilliant and precious than any jewel when seen through an eye of imagination. This is Jessie's secret. Never told to a soul before. The simplicity of a 'glimpse through', preserved in perfect silence until

404

old age allowed her to shed whatever reservations she had harboured. Perhaps she feared people would think her mad. Suspect white magic or worse, the fate I now know can still befall a woman judged to think or behave unconventionally. But what my mother saw was no witch's trick. No hypnotic effect or play of light. It was what I have tried, and too often failed, to make my life and work a tribute to.

'I do understand,' I tell my mother, keeping hold of her hand.

'Give this to Grandma,' Anna gently instructs Benjamin once I eventually return to the living room, my daughter holding out a slim cream envelope to her son while she shifts through that afternoon's post. The little boy conveys the letter across the room to me, plump palms held out in a proud picture of noble solemnity that would better suit a royal diadem. The instant she notices, Naomi drops her cloth flower bouquet to hurry after her big cousin, small flat soles slapping against the floorboards in her haste not to miss the excitement of an errand.

'What a clever boy – and girl,' I reward them both, two pairs of keen bright eyes anticipating my approval. I take the envelope from Benjamin. 'Thank you very much, young man.' Naomi babbles something in his ear, singsong syllables from the shared baby language they occasionally regress to and which only they can understand. Whatever she says, it makes Benjamin break into a sweet milk-tooth smile. The two scamper off into a corner of the room with the unmistakable intention of making mischief. *Mij-like*, I think happily, although the adjective could only ever make sense to one other person.

Still smiling, I flip over the envelope in my lap and see the handwriting. 'Mother?'

'I'm fine.' Shock trembles through my voice, but I fight not to show it in my face. 'It's nothing important.' Avoiding Anna's eye, I stuff Gavin's letter behind a cushion and rise to offer my services to the children's game.

Later, alone, I retrieve the envelope reluctantly. Stamped from Mallaig, I see. Better that than the excruciating awkwardness of it having been hand-delivered across the Square. Once, nothing could have made me happier than to see my name in this intense script, but now I stare down at Gavin's heavy-lent lettering and feel only apprehension. But why should I be afraid? Of 'whatever we had', there is surely nothing left to lose. Still, a queasy echo of emotion throbs in my chest as I open his letter: half-palpitation, half-muscle memory. Recalling the love without being able to feel it, as if observed from the wrong side of an ocean.

Inside, crisply courteous, Gavin asks for my early poems of Sandaig. Could I find it in my heart to send copies? He should like to have them. He does not explain why. I pause to consider what has become of the many volumes he already had from me. Every collection I ever wrote was gifted freely to the man who seemed to embody their imaginative spirit, my printed name crossed out on each title page so I could inscribe them to him by hand. 'Love Kathleen'. They are destroyed, no doubt. Were my words burned or drowned?

Either way, my depleted pride resurges to rage at this latest, unexpected insult. Gavin has the audacity to request new copies of my words without repenting those he hurled out into the world through *Raven* expressly to humiliate me. Perhaps he wants my work to inspire another book at my expense, or else to simply relieve a lost time before the gates of paradise were barred to us both. Yet hasn't he already taken enough? His actions picked me clean long ago, the raw bones of my potential ground down into dust or, at best, grimly preserved in the sinking peat that surrounds Sandaig. A waterfall of tears has flowed from me because of him; my soul no longer whole but shattered, sea glass shards crushed into sand and kicked along the shore beneath Gavin's carefree, careless feet. Even now, I sometimes fear that the best part of my heart, perhaps even of my poetry, resides wherever Mij lies on the midnight-black ocean floor.

Bled dry and bereft for so long, this letter acts as the transfusion I need. As I read it, something cracks: a fissure cleaving open all I had thought cauterised and sending a swell of enraged passion through my body. Its power makes me recall when Gavin and I met beneath the broken traffic light; a reopening of the grave, yet this time admitting not light but pure fire. I burn with it, leaping to my feet as if hot coals were shoved under my soles, and reach for my reborn-from-ashes notebook. On the way, I catch a flicker of my reflection. Cheeks flushed; eyes gleaming. He wants my poetry? Then he shall have it. I scrawl one fresh line after another, graphite pencil tip flashing from the furious speed. Even after all we have lost, this power has not deserted Gavin: his unfathomable ability to provoke me into action like no other, my creative spirit set alight again as if, in striking stone, he sparked a flame. One final glint of inner strength has not deserted me. As long as I breathe, I will remember, however much Gavin would prefer us both to forget.

If hate were love, if love were hate
It could not make our tale untold.

406

The grandchildren come with me to post my letter before their teatime. At the pillar box, Naomi stands on her tiptoes and Benjamin copies, their compact fingers wriggling to manoeuvre the envelope into a slot they cannot see. Both children giggle as they give it one last push. I watch it fall, my poem tumbling into the black. The last I will hear from Gavin, I expect.

*

'Excuse me, Dr Raine, but do you know Gavin Maxwell?'

'No,' I reply, as always. I am on my knees, palms coated in soot as I wrestle with my college room's temperamental fireplace grate in a futile effort to battle the chill. Of course, there are 'mod cons' these days, but to rely on them when my academic foremothers had no such recourse feels too close to admitting defeat. Heaving a hefty sigh, cold air frosting in front of my face, I turn to the student delivering today's newspapers as she shifts from foot to foot, screwing up the copy she holds for me into an anxious, ever-tightening roll. She may be eighteen but looks younger, most likely braving her first January freeze away from home.

'I'm sorry,' she stammers, rosy cheeks from the cold flushing deeper in embarrassment. 'I suppose it really is just as well ...'

'What is?'

'That you don't know him.' The girl unfurls the newspaper, gesturing to its headline as she drops it onto my desk. 'Such a dreadful thing. So sad about the poor otter.'

I do not notice her leaving. I forget the coal dust staining my fingers. All I am conscious of is that newspaper, its headline streaked across the page like thick smoke polluting a pale sky.

'Fire ravages writer's paradise: Camusfeàrna goes up in flames.' The strapline letters dart and flicker as my hands shake. 'Famed cottage destroyed. One otter dead.'

'Gavin ... Gavin ... Gavin ...' I chant his name incessantly, eyes jumping too fast for my stunned mind to process more than piecemeal fragments. It has been months since my poem reply to his letter; months since I spoke or even heard his name aloud. 'Say he's alive ... please God, say he's alive ...' Jumbled debris from a few rogue phrases starts to register.

'Lit cigarette.' 'Smouldering while asleep.' 'Alcohol mixed with medication.' What for? I wonder, still dazed. 'House stocked with

407

ammunition.' 'Uninsured.' 'A powder keg.'

'No fire engine could reach the spot,' one paragraph concludes. 'Onlookers were powerless to do more than stand and watch it burn.'

The men are safe, albeit suffering from shock. Gavin. Andrew, the new otter boy just brought in to replace the departing Jimmy Watt. And Teko. But Edal, 'Major Maxwell's beloved female otter, succumbed to the flames and perished inside her quarters. Maxwell's sole request before evacuating,' the paper adds, 'was for the unfortunate creature's remains to be buried at the foot of his rowan tree.'

I do not sleep that night. I am afraid to. My exhausted eyes sting, aggrieved by coal flecks mixed with tears, yet every time I try to close them, an image of flame-ravaged horror consumes me. I see Gavin stumbling barefoot as Sandaig burns behind him, fighting through some substance-fogged stupor to limp out into the unfeeling winter night. On every side, black-eyed beams smoulder and crackle, glowing devilish hot as they fall with a crash onto the flagstones; pitch-pine panels curl, sizzling viciously, the walls we loved engulfed by the violent fury of an inferno. My nostrils fill with imagined smoke as I watch the scene through Gavin's eyes, that intermittent psychic connection I long cherished but now wish I could switch off. Blazing hellfire bright against the blackened ocean, his idyll is left for ash. Wild flames are whirled by the brutal sea winds while the night sky, stars choked by smoke, looks on in silent mourning. And Gavin is mourning. For Edal, that charming if capricious animal reduced to a shrunken charred corpse, suffocated in a sleep from which she will never awaken. I pray to God she was asleep. Am I the cause of her suffering too? Did my fiery rage at the rowan ten years ago light the fuse of this searing tragedy? From six hundred and twenty-five miles away, I tremble in terror at the thought that I have killed another creature Gavin loved. Hell, if true, I have almost killed him.

Tormented, I fumble for the watch left at my bedside, squinting through the gloom to make out an hour hand hovering just after two. Sandaig may still be burning. Our *Paradise Lost* incinerated. Didn't the report mention ammunition? I visualise pyrotechnics, a macabre spectacle detonating against the primeval peace of the coastline, each lurid explosion offensively incongruous in a world where time itself seemed to stand still. Gone, the windowsill where I laid out our shells overlooking the ocean. Gone, the glinting gold fireplace whose inscribed message will always linger in me. Gone, Gavin's books and creel-stored sweaters, borrowed so that I could feel close to him. Gone too, the fish crate sofa and handcrafted desk at which we both wrote our finest work. Gone, the place Mij loved. Gone, the final place where he knew we loved him.

My mind reeling to picture the firestorm, towering pillars of flame rising before me, a Greek word comes, first encountered years ago when I began my Platonic pilgrimage to understand Blake. *Temenos*. A sacred precinct. A spiritual sanctuary. Wiser cultures than our own built whole cities around that apotheosis, an apex of imaginative unity at which to summon a life of worth into being. Sandaig was Gavin's. And being his, it became mine. Now it is lost, reduced to rubble, charcoal and dust.

But Gavin lives. He is still out there, surviving somewhere, although I cannot rush to his side and offer comfort as the woman I once was yearns to do. To be plagued by a picture of poor, troubled Edal's shrivelled little body is to imagine what could have befallen Gavin himself. Involuntarily emitting a cry, then biting down hard on my pillow lest I rouse the rest of the college, I watch in torment as a hallucinatory fire rises up to consume him, smoke coiling around Gavin's wrists and ankles to bind him as flaming debris falls from the rafters. Gavin chokes, smothered by smoke; his flesh smarts and begins to burn, those beautiful birthmarks warped by unbearable heat until they melt like blood pouring over his fair skin.

I abandon my bed and cross to my writing desk. Pen and paper are all I have left, the sole olive branch I can extend whilst stuck the length of the country away from him. To imagine Gavin suffering his last moments alone, us unreconciled for eternity, is a fate I refuse to countenance. Let him shame me, revile me, humiliate me in front of the whole world if he will: he must know that I love him. For better and for worse. The woman in his life, enduring after all this time.

A fantasy flits in of me setting off north, stuffing a train compartment or the boot of another unloved hire car with whatever cobbled assortment of clothing, food and well-earned whisky I could pull together for him in a matter of minutes. Then I could cradle Gavin like I did when Jonnie died, all secret shames from our shared and separate pasts forgotten as I murmur soothing lines of my old poetry in his ear. And yet I resist the urge to start packing, reminding myself to think of his needs, not my own. I know Gavin is safe, physically at least, with Andrew beside him and Jimmy still nearby. At his lowest ebb, after the savage tempests that have raged between us for so long, perhaps my presence in person would be too much for Gavin to bear. To truly love him, as I learned much too late, is to divorce myself – or maybe liberate myself – from the compulsive, half-mad desperation to know I am loved by him in return.

A telegram then. The quickest contact at my disposal, Sandaig's costly telephone installation having undoubtedly succumbed to the fire. I will write rather than speak my condolences; careful sentences crafted by trembling fingertips as I try to express the way in which I understand, better than any other, just what Gavin has lost in another otter's death. 'Love Kathleen,' I conclude my note, folding it as neatly as my erratic digits will permit and readying it to be sent at first light. But to what address? Gavin's Highland home is no more. He has no fixed abode, except Paultons. If he kept it. Either way, with so much chaotic, charcoaled wreckage to sift through, I do not see him returning to the city yet. Glenelg? Reluctance runs through me at the thought of committing that village's name to paper after the part its inhabitants played in Mij's death. Really, one inhabitant. I presume Big Angus is still in situ, his brutish cruelty and unconscionable deceit unchecked by a world ill-equipped to bring such callous actors to justice.

'In this life,' I qualify aloud, wishing I fully believed it.

At a loss, I retrace my mental steps, finding some sort of solace as I traverse again those sweet, halcyon days when our otter's heart beat strong and I knew, down to the ocean floor of my soul, that I belonged inside Gavin's ring.

'Major Gavin Maxwell, c/o Captain Bruce Watt, Mallaig.' Trust is rare these days, but I believe taciturn, compassionate Bruce will see me right if anyone can. Address decided, little is left to do except wait for sunrise. I creep back into bed, wincing as my iced toes brush each other under the covers, then berating myself for daring to complain of cold in the wake of the blistering hot horror that has just devastated Sandaig. Tearstained, I burrow into my blankets, rocking to fold the outer edges beneath myself and create a makeshift swaddle against the chill. Where does Gavin lie tonight? Restless on a foreign floor, perhaps zipped inside a borrowed sleeping bag that smells of strangers? Pathetic as it may be, I pretend he is with me. Beside me. Nestled in my arms, ready and willing to receive the comfort that my body and soul alike ache to give. I roll onto my side, spine curved to wrap my limbs around the man who is not there. Summoning the full strength of all I know imagination to be, I hope some essence passing from my spirit to his will keep Gavin warm tonight.

410

Weeks go by. They turn to months. No reply is forthcoming, yet I feel at peace with the fact. The wiser part of me, more poet than woman, had hardly expected it otherwise. The whitewashed walls of the place we loved have fallen, their cremated remains offered back to the earth and, it seems, the final remnants of what linked us along with them. But someday and somewhere, might not that energy be reborn? Not for us, perhaps, but back into the world where it belongs, springing forth from the soil that fed the rowan's roots and imbued the waterfall's path with alders, ferns, and wildflowers. I realise now the magic always felt borrowed, briefly lent to Gavin, me and Mij by some mysterious cosmic library of meaning. Knowing that Sandaig no longer stands, I am forced to relinquish my long, futile battle to reclaim or replicate what we shared there. In truth, it is a relief. One can only fight an unwinnable war for so long.

'Let's go see the flowers today, Grandma,' Naomi demands whenever she visits me, and I am powerless to resist obliging my small yet spirited granddaughter. From Paultons, we walk hand-in-hand to the park that Gavin and I used to stroll through, what feels like another lifetime ago. To Naomi and Benjamin, it is. If, as that younger woman, I had known what was ahead of me, those repeated heartbreaks shattering enough to crack ribs, I wonder – what I would have chosen to do? Slam the door shut in dear Tambi's face and abandon the dashing, enigmatic Major on my doorstep, heading off for my dinner alone? Perhaps I would have become the great poet I believed I was destined to be, bringing forth the work – perpetually on the horizon, in sight but never close enough to touch – whose presence has taunted me for near twenty years. Maybe a twist of fate would have led me to marry Alexis, settling down to a life of refined intellectual luxury with matching Nobel Prizes on our mantelpiece. Free from engravings, I am sure, Latin or otherwise.

'Look, Grandma, look.' A determined yank from waist height tugs my attention back to Naomi, gesturing with her free hand to where a stone just thrown into the pond is sinking. The genteel, meandering ripples of before are scattered, rhythm broken by impact: this sole, ostensibly small action rendering obsolete all that went before. Naomi is delighted. 'Will the ripples go on for forever?'

'Possibly,' I tell her.

Eternally in thrall to the flowers – their colours, shapes, centres or 'faces' as she continues to call them – my delectably headstrong granddaughter insists that we take our time as we wander the beds and borders. Naomi

411

drops to her knees without hesitation whenever an especially beautiful specimen catches her eye.

'Can we take her home?' she asks me, pointing to a fuchsia, five-petalled anemone. The pronoun tickles me. It is how I feel about flowers myself. Yet I shake my head.

'Better to treasure her here,' I advise, taking Naomi's diminutive hand in my own to cradle the flowerhead. 'Do you see her stem; can you picture her roots beneath the soil?' Naomi nods. We have chatted at length about how flowers grow. 'We don't need to possess her to love her. In fact, I think she'll feel our appreciation more if we simply let her live.'

Gavin will be setting down new roots, I remind myself, as an appeased Naomi skips on. He is beginning his life again and chooses, as is his right, not to have me in it. So accustomed am I to the habitual ache of yearning that my body barely registers it this time, a mere twinge compared with the agonies that cut through me in earlier years. My unrequited suffering can be perceived from a new perspective: a strandline demarking where a wild tidal wave once struck, longing for land. Yet in time, even the fiercest currents are absorbed back into the epic, primordial ocean. I want for Gavin now, not from him. His contentment and his peace, whether they coalesce with mine or not. Watching Naomi charge ahead, running around the pond that Gavin and I encircled so many years ago, I realise that I understand at last what made our 'here and now', our Paradise Lost, so transformative. Not him; not me. Something more. Something greater. My grandchildren unknowingly give it voice with their lyrical peals of laughter; it was there in every second we shared with Mij. I can see glimmers of it today in the anemones and the trees, in each fine-veined leaf and pale gold beam of spring sunlight. What Gavin truly gave me. What I hope, at my best, I gave him. We 'glimpsed through' together. That was all. That was everything.

I am alone in Paultons the next day when the post comes. Most unusually, all the others are abroad: three generations out of four setting off on an impromptu, late spring excursion. Waving from the window with my notebook in my hand, I watch James stride in front, carrying a well-stocked picnic basket. The primary physical strain comes not from the weight itself but the fast pace he must maintain to deter either Naomi or my father from injuring themselves in their zeal to 'help'. Behind them, my mother is sandwiched neatly between Anna and Benjamin as together they push the little one's pram.

'This will give you peace to write,' Anna had called to me as their exuberant cross-generational party headed for the door. Of course, I could have accompanied them, but my daughter is right, as so often. I will relish the rarefied quiet. Turning back at the threshold, Anna had shot me a conspiratorial grin. 'I understand why it matters now.' She, too, is writing; her own poetry collection soon to be published. It appears that not just pain but inspiration can be inherited. From ashes, phoenixes rise.

Content in solitude, the ink pours from my pen, raw ideas refined into shape as my hand skims rapidly over my page. Two hours or even three have ticked by when the letterbox clatter interrupts me.

'Blast,' I exclaim, smudging an ink-blot with my thumb for good measure. From the hall, the thin metal trills and chitters, like Mij's teeth in excitement or stress. A clouded thud hits my ears as an envelope falls to the floor.

'My dearest Kathleen,' Gavin begins inside it. I blink twice, shock vying with familiarity at holding his handwritten words again. 'Thank you for your telegram. Please forgive me for not writing earlier. I could not –' a word scored out; in the windowless hallway, I squint, suspecting it might be 'bear' – 'bring myself to reply right away. I had hoped to have more time, but as with so many hopes in this life, it was not to be.

'Since I last wrote, I have been in hospital. At my request, the doctors have been blunt. They tell me the lung cancer is inoperable; the prognosis a matter of months rather than years. There will be no more snowdrops.

'I am asking you to accompany me in spirit.'

He does love me. May God forgive me for that first thought, a final glint of sun on the shore before the breaking wave of grief submerges me. *He loves me.*

Chapter Forty-Nine

The island is singing. My ears ring with its music, what sounds like a thousand tiny bells aquiver in the bracing wind. Their high, haunting voices echo in my head as if I am dizzy, still reeling from a blow. I suppose I am. Standing on the sand as coarse sea grasses tickle my calves, I watch the boatman who brought me here beat his steady retreat to the mainland. Not Bruce but a stranger, stern and silent in his weighty overcoat despite the summer mildness to which even the Highlands are not wholly immune. Watching his black silhouette recede, the dark idea occurs that he would be better suited to bearing souls to the Underworld than the so-called 'White Island'.

Shaking off the ominous thought and unseasonal chill that accompanies it, I turn to begin a tentative exploration. Kyleakin. *Eilean Ban* in Gaelic. At least, that is what Gavin told me. A lighthouse island he purchased – yes, purchased – when his future briefly looked bright after *Raven*. Following the fire, he moved into the old keeper's cottage: a quintessentially Gavinish attempt at a practical solution to a problem. Not a simple solution, though. I should know by now that nothing with Gavin is simple.

The land lives up to its name as I cut across its pale sand dunes, powdered grains dusting the rocks whose ridges sink in increments towards the sea. The peaceful scene should feel pure and unsullied, the sandcastle turret of the adjacent lighthouse the only obvious mark of human handiwork. Serene. Silent. At least it would be, if not for the bells.

'What on earth …?' Some sweet metallic melody draws me around to the far side of the isle. I stop, astonished. Besides a succession of delicate little bells, trilling incessantly like fairy-tale folk whose silver skirts are set dancing by the sea air, many hundreds of miniature windmills are dotted over the granite rocks. Their child-sized blades whirl with a throaty drone, a buzzing base note to accompany the bell sopranos rejoicing an octave above. Planted at regular intervals, tall poles have also been wedged into gaps between the coast-lining stones. Bright strings of

414

bunting billow from them, multicoloured cloth triangles waving like a Lilliputian carnival.

'It's an eider duck colony. I told you I'd do it one day.' Gavin's quiet voice seems to silence the rest of the medley. At its first note, I spin. He stands on the brow of a small slope behind me. One hand on his stick, the other shielding his eyes against the light despite his ubiquitous dark glasses. 'Cottage is this way, Kathleen.'

I follow without hesitation, scrambling over the flourishing greenery and tripping on several camouflaged stones in my haste to catch up. We are upsides within seconds, so laboured and faltered is Gavin's own progress; his walking stick founders on the uneven terrain and I rush to offer my arm on his other side. With a scowl of reluctant resignation that even his heavy frames cannot disguise, Gavin accepts it. We walk forward as one. The cottage is yards away, yet every step seems an ordeal for him. His elbow feels frail linked with mine, the uncushioned bone prodding my ribs.

'Bloody – breathlessness,' he mutters, fresh beads of sweat laced over his brow. The cottage's white walls, so similar to Sandaig's from a distance, appear to me to emanate light, beckoning us onward with the promise of rest like a true sanctuary. *Temenos*, I think. All we have left without our Avilion.

'Why the –?' Only once we are safely indoors do I dare ask Gavin any questions. Ducking to hook his left arm around my right shoulder, the better for supporting his weight, I help him to sink into the nearest chair without even a glance at the room around us. Gavin groans, teeth gritted to limit the audible pain. To distract him, and myself, I mime a windmill motion with my index finger.

'It attracts the birds to the – nesting site. And the bun– bunting deters egg predators.' Gavin halts to cough, a prolonged hoarse hack that makes my throat contract in sympathy. Several seconds of spluttering pass before he is able to continue, his hollowed-out cheekbones concaving with every inhale. 'There have been – studies – to prove it in Iceland.' Muffling another groan, Gavin squirms in his seat to produce an item from his pocket. He wears trousers, not his kilt, despite the Highland setting: the fabric so flimsy and malleable that on any other man, I might suspect they were pyjamas. Who would blame Gavin if they were? For a moment or two, he rummages – my core spasms to notice how witheringly thin his hand is – before producing the object in question. Not a handkerchief, as

415

I had suspected, but his silver cigarette case, closely followed by a solid gold lighter.

'Gavin, should you really be ...' Already lighting up, he turns an exhale of smoke into a sigh.

'If not now, Kathleen, then when?' Shamed and sorrowful, with no answer to give him, I look away.

Considering his new cottage's interior with my proper attention for the first time, I am surprised to find it comprised of one long, remarkably modern room. Salacious press reports had relayed that all of Gavin's possessions were lost in the fire. 'Uninsured,' certain articles gloated, their tones as smug as is to be expected from those who will never taste success great enough for their failures to become public. Number 9 Paultons Square, it appears, was sold by Gavin back in '67. My ability to avert my eyes from 'his house' was evidently more thorough than I gave myself credit for. I had therefore expected his new home to be sparse in its furnishings. Now, I see the opposite is true. An opulent Moroccan rug runs nearly the length of the space, its sweep broken only by several plush, well-stuffed armchairs. Along one wall, towering windows frame the sea view; on the other, artwork in a wide array of styles brushes shoulders with an immense gilt-lined mirror. Hermetic luxury, one might call the genre. If not for the fact that the man who devised it is too much of an original to ever be replicated.

'This is quite a place,' I understate, leaning over the arm of my chair to study an ornate bronze sculpture beside me. *Icarus*, I realise with another chill. His metal mouth is fixed open in a scream, all the more harrowing for being eternally silenced. The melting remnants of elaborately fashioned wings slide down his back, toned body consumed by flames as he plummets to his demise.

Gavin clears his throat before replying, frowning at the effort and, I fear, the pain. Yet in this new, stripped-raw version of his beautiful voice, I detect pleasure at the compliment. 'Thank you. That chap felt – ironic.' This deep into illness, Gavin has clearly not lost his charcoal-black sense of humour. He moves as if to speak again, then thinks better of it. Through the erratic psychic vagaries of our intermittent telepathy, I understand that, for one reason or another, he lacks the breath to continue.

'Shall I open a window?' I offer, already at the sill by the time Gavin has given me a weak nod. I raise the sash to be met with a mild yet restorative wave of ocean air. The bells and windmills become audible again, a muted whirr underneath the dainty chrome tune being played out above. The sea winds add a soft, swirling accompaniment and – yes! – I believe I can hear the low, plummy calls of the eider ducks. Eardrums vibrating from the strange quartet they create, I breathe deeply. Gavin does too. Coughs. Repeats. Looking away lest I embarrass him further, I notice that by the window sits a tripoded telescope, its penetrating lens angled towards the mainland from where I just sailed.

'You saw me coming.'

'I did.' Mischief momentarily animates Gavin's jaundiced complexion. 'You should've seen your face when you stumbled upon the windmills ...' He laughs, the fluid lilting melody I have loved for twenty years trickling out between the cragged rock faces carved by his cough. 'It was good to see you, Kathleen. It – *is* – good to see you. You're looking well.'

'So are yo ...' My conscience cannot allow me to complete the sentence. Gavin nods even so, gracious as well as grateful for not being forced to listen to my lie. In agony at the thought, then in anger at myself for having the audacity to turn Gavin's suffering into my own, I move from him to wander down this long room's promenade. Gavin seems not to mind my curiosity; in fact, I sense he is flattered by it. We have never been precious about possessions. '*With all my worldly goods I thee endow.*'

'That desk was Wordsworth's, you know.'

I spring back from touching the smooth, sun-faded surface. 'Truly?' Gavin smiles. 'From the Lakes?' So many memories linger in me from those long-lost days in the mist-nestled vales. War and peace; my children and now their children. It touches my heart to think this handsome antique has made it here from the same part of the world.

'Grasmere,' Gavin confirms. 'Why, Wordsworth might have written –' another ragged attempt at a replenishing inhale, '*Tintern – Abbey* at that very spot.' I stare into the desk's time-glossed surface, a pair of wood whorls running along one edge as if the table itself has eyes. Closing my own like a pilgrim in prayer, I let my palm rest lightly on the wood.

'*In this moment there is love and food for future years.*' My soul will always belong with Coleridge, the *enfant terrible* of the great Lake poets, but it is a line by his sagacious, more sensible friend that echoes in my mind. Eyes still shut, I sense Gavin watching me. 'I don't know how you dare write here,' I remark to break the tension.

'And I don't know how you could resist.' When I reopen my eyes, I find Gavin grinning again. Seaweed in bookshop windows. He and I are entwined yet so seldom on the same page.

Whilst owning this famous furniture does appear to have inspired Gavin to become slightly tidier than was typical for either Sandaig or Paultons, loose papers have nonetheless accumulated on the illustrious tabletop. One small, scratchy-lettered note draws my eye.

'People were exceedingly kind after the fire,' Gavin comments as I lift it. 'Sent donations of all sorts. Clothes. Food. That five-year-old boy even posted up a tin of sardines.' I study the scrap, a disjointed juvenile script rambling across a diagonal.

Thes is for Teko case hees hungry.

Tears well. My eyes sting. The flood I have been fighting to restrain since I arrived prepares to breach the last of my defences. Hands beginning to tremble, I set down the short, sweet note, turning from it and Gavin as if in sudden urgency to see my reflection in the gilt-trimmed mirror. My face is drained, chalk white compared with Gavin's waxen sallowness. Tears blur my vision and my precise features fade, leaving only a pale ash void hovering above the grey smudge of my dress. I look bloodless. Gutless. I blink hard, clenching my fists to rouse courage as my face comes back into focus.

'Shall we have some music?' Ingrained good manners still in place, as well as his deep-set aversion to my weeping, Gavin offers a sleek change of subject and I do not hesitate to accept. Scanning around me as I stifle a sniff, I notice the record player sitting in the room's far corner, positioned beside a characteristically well-stocked bar. 'Maybe a dram too?' A faint note of desperation clings to Gavin's casualness, like the ephemeral aura they call the angel's share. '*If not now, then when?*'

'Certainly,' I say, pouring out two generous tumblers of whisky and water. I wish it would not be rude to take a sip before focusing my attention on the player. I never did learn how to work the one James and Anna gave me. Fortunately, Gavin's technical skills also lie within the narrow limits of our generation, his record player being a simple device that even I can operate without difficulty.

'No bells and whistles,' I joke, odd hypnotic orchestrations from outside still billowing in through the open window. 'What are you listening to?'

'See for yourself.' The excitement in Gavin's tone compels him to cough again. Something enigmatic in his words makes me turn to his record pile, intrigued.

'No.'

'Yes.' *Ring of Bright Water*. I pick up the sleeve, studying the record in dazed disbelief. A cheerful illustration of a tall, dashing man and a beautiful blonde – just like Lavinia, I think, stomach lurching – takes up most of what I have heard James call the 'album artwork'. And an otter. The glamorous couple are laughing as they watch a goofy, bug-eyed otter at play. 'A motion picture for every family, everywhere!' screams a line of text scrolling beneath their jolly family portrait. 'Palomar Pictures International Present' ... 'Rated G' ... 'Official theme song' ... 'From the pages of the bestseller'.

'Put it on. I think you'll like it.' I never could say no to Gavin. Numb and robotic, I remove the garish sleeve and drop the player's needle into a groove. After a crackle, strings swell. A childlike glockenspiel echoes down the long room, accompanied by a rich woody undercurrent not unlike the call of the eider ducks outside. A deep, resonant male soloist starts. Gavin and I are silent, and apart, as we listen to the saccharine love song. 'Quite pleasant, isn't it?' In the mirror, I see him smiling. My cheek muscles twinge from the tense effort to return it.

'I don't know much about "pop" ...' I know even less about this film. By choice. Buses pass Paultons regularly with its poster emblazoned across their red sides; the younger girls at Girton make arrangements to watch it at weekends whilst the older students seem mindful of not having such conversations within my earshot. Invariably, I turn my head or even change direction, at long last, putting my problematic mental blinkers to some sort of productive use. I had resolved to avoid this feted new cinema release long before I knew Gavin was ill, unwilling or perhaps unable to punish myself further despite my propensity for emotional self-flagellation. Personal humiliation matters little to me now. After *Raven*, how much worse could it get? But to watch thoughtless, avaricious film executives profit from playing out Mij's private little life on screen would be, I felt, even worse than selling my own soul. Whatever is left of it. I had chosen to ignore the picture, congratulating myself on my latent discovery of a modicum of self-control, but I realise now that all my efforts were for naught. I should have known I could never ignore this man.

'Imagine my words set to music,' Gavin muses.

'Our words.' I bite my tongue almost as soon as I speak, tasting bitterness. Is this who I am now? A woman prepared to pick a fight with a dying man? The last vestiges of my dignity tell me to stop, reminding me that I must surely be immune to mortification. And yet I cannot tear my eyes away from this jubilant scene of silver-screen perfection, my own dowdy reflection still a lone blur in my distant eyeline. I raise the record again, studying the woman's expression. Sweet. Mild. Maternal and near-beatific as her arms reach for their pet. Who is she meant to be? Me, Lavinia, or perhaps even Mary MacLeod: some Frankenstein's creature composite of all three, our best and most plot-appropriate attributes sewn together while the wasted, worthless parts of our ordinary womanhood were discarded on the cutting room floor. Mary's Celtic authenticity. Lavinia's regal beauty, the Grace Kelly of Sandaig, no matter how unhappily she and her prince lived ever after. And from me? What do I offer cinema history? Nothing. Neither looks nor a personality suited to stardom. It strikes me that there is a term for the role played by such people on film sets. Doubles. Stand-ins. I am nothing to this story except the one who was really there.

'Excuse me?' When my temper heats up, Gavin ices against me. Our natures irreconcilable, even as nature itself unites us. I cannot see his eyes behind those dark lenses, but I can picture their chilled, impenetrable blue. Gavin's voice lowers, illness lacing his coolly suppressed irritation with a few grumbling notes of gravel. Heart racing, I am hit with the image of myself on the ground outside Sandaig, sobbing as stone flecks embedded themselves into my palms while a bitter trail of vomit trickled from my lower lip.

'I don't want to fight. Not again. All I mean to say is that they –' I point to the record sleeve, Gavin's book title unfurling in bold print across its centre '– are my words.' '*With all my worldly goods, I thee endow.*' But since when was poetry an earthly possession?

Gavin sighs, making a show of a stretch with the pointed nonchalance he often deploys to buy time mid-disagreement. Now, though, his frail limbs are too stiff for theatrics. I watch him work to disguise a wince as his sapling-thin extremities extend. 'I can only suggest you speak to the Company if you so badly want recompense.'

'Recompense?' The song has stopped. My repetition is far too loud. Raising my voice at a dying man too? Even the eider ducks seem subdued in the frozen seconds that follow, the birds intelligent enough to take their mellow chatter off to a more peaceable part of the island. The bells linger, of course, ringing out shrill little judgements against me. The windmills mutter as if under their breath, blades buffering in the wind to create a dull hubbub of disapproval. 'You believe this is about money?'

Gavin's eyes are unreadable, hidden behind opaque black, but I cannot mistake his sneer. 'What else could it be about?'

'My ...' I stammer, left speechless in the futile defence of words I wrote a decade ago, never believing they would one day come to be known throughout the world. Amidst all our many, varied quarrels, we have never had this argument out. Gavin's prose. My poetry. His name published across continents underneath a line I wrote, perhaps the greatest I ever composed flowing freely as I lay in bliss beside his waterfall. On the page, we are forever tied together, but in person yet again he and I are diametrical factions, trapped on opposing banks of Kielder Bridge and unable to take the single step that might let us grasp the other's perspective. Gavin scorns me as rapacious, envy-wracked and hungry for my share of the financial spoils that success has delivered him, albeit at a terrible price. I stand here begging, yes, but not for anything material. It is my soul alone that pleads for Gavin to set aside his black-glass mask of disingenuousness: telling me, showing me, that he understands what my work was trying to say.

'This is not about compensation.' My eventual protest sounds weak, sullying me by implication even as I try to refute. 'I'm not interested in your ...' I reach for an appropriately venal word. 'Royalties.'

'Really? –' Gavin's hacking cough somehow communicates his scepticism. 'I thought finances might be tight these days. Living permanently with your parents.' How he knows that fact, I cannot imagine. All I am certain of is that he enjoys my embarrassment at it.

'I'm not bankrupt just yet.' A cruel retort, poking a tender, barely closed wound in him. A part of Gavin used to enjoy such a joust, our verbal sparring on the edge of decency and more than once, toppling over it. But he lacks the stamina for this fight. He sighs again, the heavy exhale clouded with phlegmatic crackles.

'Then what do you want from me, Kathleen?' Twenty years and I am no closer to an answer.

'Tell me who she is supposed to be.' Cowardice dissuades me from starting a deeper conversation that I know I lack the courage to finish. Instead, I hold up the *Ring* record sleeve, fingers pinching it like incriminating evidence on which I would prefer not to leave my fingerprints. 'This woman with "Mij". Pretending to be me, is she?'

'I think you mean "acting". They're Bill Travers and Virginia McKenna. A rather celebrated couple in film.' Drawing a blank, I stare back at the cover, although I suspect that Anna and James, and even Benjamin and Naomi, would know this attractive pair in an instant. 'They're both devoted to conservation.' Pride brightens what I can see of Gavin's expression. It is clear that he likes the term. And yet it had never occurred to me that caring for Mij could be classed as such work. Not work at all, in fact. At the time, I felt myself not his keeper so much as his mother.

'They're like you then, I suppose?' I ask Gavin.

'Well, yes.' The sunlight shifts, a sharp glint striking gilt to fall in elegiac elegance over Icarus's contorted torso.

'You've found a pretty luxurious hide.'

'I'm not staying.' Even the bells seem to stop at that.

'I …' I have no words left. They never did do us any good. Two sentences say it all: I love this man and I will lose him. Soon. 'I'm sorry, Gavin,' I whisper, my own throat closing.

'No. I'm sorry, Kathleen.' I cannot be sure what he means it for. The past minute or the past twenty years? I do not ask because, at heart, I have no wish to know. Now I just want Gavin to rest. I lay down the record sleeve, not upon Wordsworth's venerable writing desk but a less lofty adjacent chair. Similar fragments of intellectual ephemera have gathered in its wooden seat: loose papers, an empty cigarette carton and, at the very bottom, a book. I cock my head to read its spine. The one I never could bring myself to read. My poetry; Gavin's prose. Together in tribute to our otter, in whose heart we briefly met.

My movements cautious, wary as one approaching an animal whose feral temperament remains unpredictable, I cross the room to be with him. Gavin's chair is opposite mine and I shuffle my own until we are sitting side by side. Although this thinness is unromantic, the product of cruel physical corrosion more than Byronic psychological angst, his super-slim appearance feels like a visual echo of the state in which I first found him on my doorstep. August 1949. A soul's lifetime ago. Like his beard, Gavin's hair has taken on an auburn hue, flecked with silver streaks just like my own dull brown scalp. As I look, a rogue lock falls over his eyes. My hand gives a twitch. The thwarted ghost of the old instinct to brush it away from his face. Taking a drag, Gavin's dry lips purse tight around his cigarette, his wrist so narrow and frail that the wine-spill birthmark appears to be spreading. His loose watch swivels with the motion, coming to rest with its face on the inside. Wincing, Gavin crosses his legs and I glimpse the sharp ridge of his kneebone jutting through what are indeed pyjama bottoms. His gaunt limbs have no fat left, only slivers of wasted muscle. His body, if not his mind, is already leaving.

I reach for his hand. He allows me to take it. The touch of his chilled, clammy skin sparks a memory, vivid sensory ripples reaching me through time. We are lying in his bed; he is cradled in my arms.

'What would you do if you knew you were dying?'

'I'd send for you.' He has.

Accompany him in spirit. A rare direct request. Cupid and Psyche, I realise now, could never be together in this world of clay. In the next one, perhaps. The realer than real. Essential as breath; intangible as sea air. In this existence, our childish impulses have always weighed us down: bitter quarrels and petulant, self-indulgent passions leaving us helpless to harness a force we could neither forget when apart nor remember to respect when together. Since our first night, the first rowan tree that grew from one consciousness in two minds, Gavin and I have connected as souls rather than bodies. It was me who forgot that. Not him. Never him.

'I'm going into hospital soon. Ward 10, Royal Northern Infirmary.' Gavin removes his dark glasses to tell me. That true oceanic blue hits me just like it did on our first day.

'How long for?' I wish I needed to ask. But we already know. There will be no more snowdrops. My fingers entwine with Gavin's, his cool grip surprisingly strong like a newborn's survival reflex. The eider ducks have returned to sit outside his window and we both turn towards the sound of their mellow golden chatter. The soft, soothing coos match the waves lapping over the rocks.

Does he love me? Did he ever? As much as he could, I believe. And that is not what matters anymore. He is loved. He will be loved by me from the day we met until the moment death parts us. The joy and sorrow all blur, happiness and suffering alike insignificant in the presence of a power that was – is – as soul-transforming for me when it takes the form of engulfing darkness as that of blinding, brilliant light. For better and for worse, our lives have been interlocked. Two spirits sharing one earth. For a little longer still. Never before, I realise to my great shame, have

I come to Gavin without asking. Without begging. Without demanding or condemning. Debilitated by the humiliation of repeated physical rejection, I have frequently felt tormented by the idea that in earthly terms I was 'useful' to him. But didn't a part of me use Gavin too? I have sought all my life to transcend this menial, mundane existence, yet I lacked the courage required to take that leap alone. I made Gavin my symbol, transfiguring him into a precious apex or perhaps a false summit: the messenger I insisted was sent to accompany me on a journey that, all along, my soul needed to travel alone.

And yet he helped me as much as he could. We both did as much as we could for each other. If I had the strength left, I would regret all I never gave, being so focused on what I could not have. I would contemplate what might have been had I appreciated our 'glimpse through' with the radical, humble acceptance it deserved. The secrets I never let Gavin share. The love, not just tolerance, but real love I should have shown for the way he is; for the nature viewed as wrong only through the distorted, discompassionate prisms of our deeply unnatural world. Now, truly, I want nothing from Gavin that he cannot give me. Neither his promises nor his caresses, not even for him to stand still and receive a waterfall outpouring of affection. I love. I let it go. The fact feels as strong and fluid as the primordial ocean outside. '*The more I give to thee, the more I have, for both are infinite.*'

Thoughts of water make my mind and heart return to Mij. I see his wave-play on the cottage coast; his skilful show of glittering brilliance in the aquarium.

'Do you remember when we watched Mij swim?' Gavin asks me.

'Yes. I was just thinking about … yes.' Foolishly, I look down at our linked fingertips, wondering again how or why such mental transmission should occur at the oddest times.

'At the aquarium …' Weary as well as inclined to escape into the bright water of the memory, Gavin closes his eyes. Even those fair eyelashes look frail. 'We witnessed such beauty.'

'We did.' I cannot shut my own eyes. To do so would be to take them off Gavin. I will not, a second before I have to.

'You know, Kathleen, Mij must have been doing the same thing under the sea at Sandaig.' Gavin murmurs the observation, hoarse yet happy. 'The same magic. Same miracle. We couldn't see it. But it was there.' His hand in mine feels freezing. I wrap it within both of my own.

424

'It was.'

Borne on the silence between us, a different bird call drifts in. Distinct from the ducks' warm gold mews, these urgent cries scrape through the air, robust in volume yet raw in tone, almost as if the affliction in Gavin's lungs has become airborne. In the distance, I hear harsh avian dialogue peppered with rapid-fire, high-pitched squeaks, the birds apparently communicating directions to one another that are of the utmost importance.

'Eider ducks?'

Gavin shakes his head once, lacking the energy for more. 'Greylag geese.' No doubt, despite the frailty threaded through his voice. 'They'll be flying south for winter.' Gavin pauses, summoning up the strength to speak again. 'It's quite something to witness.' I rise with my hands on his arm, meaning to mirror our three-legged race feat from earlier and help him reach the window if not the door. But Gavin lets my touch drop.

'No, Kathleen,' he whispers. His blue eyes are the only colour left in his face. 'You see them for me.' I go to the doorway. From the threshold of Gavin's cottage, I watch the skein sweep by in fine, ribbony formation, the birds' skyborne backlit shapes following the loose 'V' of legend like an artist's impression of the letter. Cries cut through the clouds as they encircle the lighthouse: a bright, fluid flash of nature forming a ring above us before their beating silver wings carry them south. Not coming, but going.

Chapter Fifty

His ashes are buried beside the rowan tree. His wish, according to the will. The boy's head is resting on the roots.

> *Oh do not wake, oh do not wake*
> *The sleeper in the rowan's shade ...*
> *Storm without finds peace within,*
> *World is resting in his dream.*

The day of the service dawns crisp and clear. Eerily windless for what I know of the Highlands. Autumn wreaths the last of the late summer greenery with orange, bronze and berry red. *Our first season*, I remember. First and last. The cindered ruins of the cottage have been razed, leaving no manmade landmarks to identify the correct spot on the coastline. But I would know Sandaig in a heartbeat. Had I walked across the globe to find it, limping hundreds of thousands of miles on Psyche's bruised and bloodied feet, I would recognise this constellation of islands and their pearlescent shells glinting just below the crystalline surface. I would feel the throb of familiarity to re-encounter this silver-bright, twisting burn, enringing the rowan while a distant avenue of alders frames its gushing waterfall source. This landscape lies in the grooves and ridges of my fingerprints; it unfurls along the life and heart lines that spell out my fate across my palm. My soul's home. Not where we live, but where we love.

Bruce brought me here by boat. Thetis had offered to accompany me, but some journeys must be made alone. Almost alone.

'Miss Raine.' Pale and upright, Bruce had removed his cap and bowed his head, keeping it bare as we set off from Mallaig. Above us, white-winged gulls cried out in an angst-ridden chorus of squalls, expressing what felt like their shared mourning for all that this place has lost. The sea itself, though, seemed remarkably still as Bruce and I sailed, standing side-by-side at what I believe (Gavin would likely correct me) is called the boat's prow. I had gripped the metal rail, struggling for my next breath. Wordless, Bruce removed one hand from his wheel to wrap it lightly around my waist. A rare departure from reserve for a man so ordinarily undemonstrative. But I know better than anyone that not all can be expressed in words.

Afraid to be overcome before the service even began, I had stared down at my smeary reflection: a dark glimmer, distorted by chrome. Scarf swept over my head to combat the worst of the sea spray, I looked like the ashen-faced, black-shawled Highland widow I will never be.

'A'm sorry fae yer loss, Miss Raine.' Bruce had spoken his first full sentence to me only after we landed, shingles and sea wrack crunching beneath the boat's weight. 'I ken whit the Major meant tae ye.'

'Thank you.' This is not my loss, legally and maybe even morally. Yet my gratitude for Bruce believing it so was real.

Now, I stand alone, holding back from the small crowd gathered around the rowan's roots. A reverend is speaking. His face is unfamiliar, like several of those who make up the ring I am not part of.

'We commend to God our brother Gavin ...' My more-than-brother. My more-than-everything. 'Earth to earth, ashes to ashes, dust to dust ...' I avert my eyes as the pale wooden box is lowered, staring at my shoes where black flakes of crumbled charcoal still cling to the stubbled, split-stemmed grass. If I could, I would bend to reclaim them, these wind-scattered fragments that are all that remain of the place where Mij played and Gavin wrote; where I loved them both with every inch of my fallible, obstinate heart. The place where nothing now exists but my memories and our words.

'Amen.' I dare to raise my head. It is done. All feels still. Even the waves and weaving burn seem briefly at rest, as if a part of their life force has gone with him.

Soon, consoling murmurs start to ripple through the little crowd, flashes of movement catching my eye as hands are shaken and steps taken away from the graveside. I do not know most of these people. Certainly not most of the men. Raef must be one of these strangers. I never did discover what he looks like. I think of him as a boy, an overgrown child who broke a young man's heart, but he will have aged with the rest of us. Uncertain, I scan the men's faces as they swap their muted greetings, a pragmatic, business-like air taking over the condolences as they move further from the rowan. Their cool composure makes me want to wail, ripping asunder these pseudo-widow's weeds and hurling myself down onto the dirt as if this scorched soil were still burning; a raging funeral pyre that could rise up and consume me too. These men closing ranks have the power to publish his letters and profit from his enterprise. Quite literally, their Enterprise now. They will be the ones to tell his story. Our story. And in it, I will not be Gavin's goddess, nor his sister spirit, nor even simply the woman who loved him – who loves him still – with all her body and soul. I will not be the person with whom he shared two homes. I will not be Kathleen, whom he met at last in the heart of an otter. When they tell it, I will merely be a lovesick witch.

Outline slowly sharpening from the blur of unfamiliar faces, Mary MacLeod emerges. The relief of recognition calms my over-wrought nerves and I draw a deep breath, half-raising my hand in a solemn form of greeting. Mary takes a few steps towards me but then halts at an awkward distance. Embarrassed, I complete the rest of the gulf myself.

'Thank you for coming.' I feel mindful not only of the miles between here and the MacLeods' new home – Inverness, Gavin had told me – but, even more exhaustingly, the emotion that must be involved in returning to Tormor. Too late, though, I am conscious of having yet again presumed the position of hostess that I have no legal right to claim. Whatever my heart tells me, however core-consuming my abject sorrow, I am not Gavin's widow. Perhaps that is why Mary's expression remains stony.

'Kathleen.' Some unspoken implication shivers through the stiff syllables of my name, a creeping chill like the hard flakes of frost that will soon ice over the rowan's branches. Mary says nothing more and in the uncomfortable moments that follow, my mind turns to the memory of her boys when small, the twins' tiny fingers wriggling in the air to mimic the patter of Raine-drops. Breaking off from his conversation with an unknown man in a dark suit, her husband approaches.

'Well, it's yersel.' Wiry and stern, John Donald seems unchanged, yet Mary continues to stare as if she barely knows me. A few stilted sentences pass back and forth between her husband and I, hollow enquiries about work and our respective children, until even those trickling sand grains run out. 'I'll nae keep ye longer,' John Donald remarks, like he is guilty of monopolising my attention at a party. Glad of the excuse, I nod nonetheless. As we say our goodbyes and the pair walk away, John Donald makes a remark to his wife. His words are whispered. Hers not.

'I can't forget and forgive.' A sentence follows which I do not catch, save for Mary's resounding final word. 'Curse.'

I turn away. Turn again to avoid sight of the tree. The glint of red berries pursues me even so, hovering like ruptured blood vessels clustered in the corner of my eye. My scarlet letter. My worldwide shame. My witch's mark. And yet to me, the surest sign of a witch would be a woman who, against all odds, attained the one thing her heart desired.

I am alone. At least, my rational mind tells me I must be alone. Limbs weighted from within, feet dragging beneath me like Psyche's battered and broken stumps, I go to the graveside. Closer than I could get before. A whispered gust of sea wind ruffles the top layer of soil. A few grains are raised, and I follow their route: the drifting shimmer of airborne dust drawing my eyes towards a newly laid stone. Set into the rock, a slate-blue memorial has been engraved.

EDAL 1958 – 1968.
Whatever joy she gave to you, give back to Nature.

The wind returns, rediscovering its strength to set the rowan branches in rustling motion. I brush my fingers across an abundant cluster of garnet berries, natural riches hanging onto their tree of life by a fine, precarious thread. Ruby-bright, the bundle breaks with the breeze and falls into my palm. I lay it over Gavin's grave.

The clouds shift; memories flash in front of my eyes as if my own mortal life is at an end. A Greek island sunrise viewed through tears. The soft scrape of stubble against my cheek in a London street. Watching Mij in the water. Descending the stairs of Monreith to dance, crimson-petalled skirts shimmering beside golden-green kilt threads. Autumn leaves sent fluttering into the air by Jonnie; pages of poetry exchanged by strangers who felt – who knew – they had met before. Opening the door to Paultons, twenty years ago. I shut my eyes, wishing I could shut off the pace of my pulse and stop here. Abandon this life-weary body; shed my skin and surrender my spirit to the transcendent, numinous realm where a part of my heart feels he lingers, just out of sight. Visionless, my ears fill with the waves and waterfall. I listen for underfoot pebbles or the lilting melody of Gavin's laugh carried along with the current.

'Kathleen?' The calm, compassionate voice has a grounding effect. Spinning fast, feeling dizzy, I turn to face its source.

'I'm Jimmy.' Sorrow is etched across the young man's features, yet an inner resolve seems to be keeping his spine straight and shoulders square. His precise age, I cannot determine; clearly young but with an air of common sense aligning well with this wise, timeless landscape. He offers his hand. I take it. Our eyes meet and an odd, unexpected current of solidarity flows between us. Two for whom no depth of dark shadows can diminish an uncommonly bright light.

'Has anyone told you yet that a London memorial is planned?' Wearily, I shake my head. 'It'll be in the Church at Covent Garden,' Jimmy says. The thought of the city feels foreign. Far more than miles away. 'We're hoping Sir Aymer will be well enough to attend.'

'Aymer?' Only now do I realise that Gavin's eldest brother is missing. Is Eustace here? Christian? I did not notice them. They will have aged too, naturally. Compared with the lovestruck blushing rose they met at Monreith, I must be unrecognisable.

'Cerebral thrombosis, they said. He's almost as ill as Gavin. Was.' Jimmy flinches from the pain, familiar to me, of mistaken present tense. 'Certainly, he was too unwell to travel from Euboea to England in time.' The past is a foreign country. A country I try not to visit. Just in my eyeline, the rowan tree glints ruby and emerald.

'Tell me when and I will be there,' I pledge with what conviction I can muster. In truth, I am unsure if I can survive a second service. Time flows, generations come and go; summer beckons for Jimmy and peers while Aymer and I sink towards that winterish sleep from which no new mornings will spring. Yet Gavin was not elderly. Fifty-five. A life half-finished.

The thought torments me, my sense of personal suffering blooming fast as spilt arterial blood – I will never forget his Kiko – when I consider what the world has lost in his death. Words yet unwritten. Landscapes uncrowned by his dazzling prose. Rendered breathless by it all, I feel my focus slipping, my despondent gaze sinking to land on a glint of gold from Jimmy's little finger. Catching the light, as well as my eye. Gavin's signet ring. Intuitive as ever, Jimmy follows my line of sight and looks down.

'Gavin left it to me,' he explains, almost apologetically.

'Then he would be glad to see you wear it.' Would be. Not 'is'. Each sentence, every heartbeat I cannot stall inside my chest, is forcing me further away from him.

'He left you something too.' Jimmy gestures uphill. 'Come, Kathleen. I'll show you.'

I recall the last time I walked down the hill we now climb. Then, telegraph poles and paparazzi were intruders upon a paradise, but the press seems to have retreated: a latent sense of respect, or else the Company's collective might, persuading them to avoid the funeral service. The wood posts, too, are gone, ghostly hollows demarking where their willowy occupants were incinerated. A few rogue, singed splinters protrude from the peat wilderness, about to be reclaimed by resilient grasses already starting to regrow. '*Give back to nature.*' Soon this coastline will look like none of us were ever here.

'How's Teko?' I ask Jimmy, recalling too late that one creature does indeed remain living. Gavin's last, solitary otter. What will become of him without his devoted master? Jimmy's complexion pales underneath his healthy outdoors tan.

'He ... he died two days ago. We found him drowned at the bottom of his pool. He was old, of course. The vet suspects a stroke or seizure. But that's not what I think.'

'No.' Nor I.

'Here.' A minute or so more and we have reached Gavin's Land Rover. Perhaps it is Jimmy's Land Rover now. The vehicle is parked askew, angled from experience at what must be the last accessible spot for Sandaig. Jimmy dives into the driver's side, rifling past an assortment of papers and unsteady piles of coastal life paraphernalia. Wellingtons, nets, a few rogue windmills that never made it to the Kyleakin colony. Order was never foremost in Gavin's eccentric, inventive mind. 'Apologies for the mess,' Jimmy calls out to me, rummaging with his hands wedged beneath the front passenger seat. 'I haven't had time to ... I'm sorry.'

'Don't be,' I say. If I breathe deeply, holding still, I believe I can detect the faint, lingering scent of cigarette smoke.

'Aha.' Jimmy reverse clambers out of the car, clasping Gavin's old rucksack. I recognise this battered, strained-seam bag from Mij's day and even earlier. One glance at that wind-beaten canvas fabric and I can picture its straps slung across Gavin's slender, strong shoulders, smiling as he strides with faithful Jonnie at his side towards a humble whitewashed cottage awaiting him at the ocean's edge. 'Yours.' Jimmy reaches into a zip compartment to produce a red leather-bound book. 'He was keeping it at his bedside. Your last letter to him was tucked inside.'

In silence, I take the small volume from him. The rich gilt-tooled jacket feels tactile and limber beneath my fingertips. In colour, it is closer to crimson than rowan. I open it to the first page and blink, shocked to be met with my own words. I turn leaf upon leaf, uncovering more poems – my poems – that were written in heart's blood long ago as my spirit overflowed with love for this place. Love for this man. Sorrow and transcendence; elegiac lines alongside verses of pure, profound gratitude. The poems he asked me for, without saying why at the time. All are here. All were there. Accompanying Gavin in spirit.

'And he left this for you.' Reluctant as I am to draw my eyes away from the book, I look up in time to glimpse a fleeting glitter as Jimmy opens his fist. Gavin's tie pin. The Order of the Garter. Belonging to the Duke of Northumberland back when he and I were children. Alone, together, in our very first Eden. As Jimmy places the pin inside my palm, I raise its fragile gold stem to what is left of the autumn light. Prick my finger on the tip. Welcome the pain as worth it.

When next I glance up, Jimmy has withdrawn to the far side of the car, showing an animal lover's instinct for knowing what any creature needs at a given moment. Standing separate, I look down at the deserted shore. My eyes track the bright silver ring of the burn and the solitary rowan bound inside it; my ears attune to the soft rhythmic breath of the tides and the whispered song of the far-off waterfall. Gavin's book of my poems is pressed to my heart, my last letter to him secreted within its lining, but I have no need to open the volume to re-read my words. While I live, I will remember.

For me, this earth is simply the place where you are. Without you, it will be the place where you are not.

Epilogue

Gavin Maxwell died on 7th September 1969 at the age of fifty-five. Kathleen Raine lived almost thirty-four years in the place where he was not, before she died at the age of ninety-five on 6th July 2003. Her later years saw her become a world authority on Blake, Yeats, Coleridge and other great poets, receiving The Queen's Gold Medal for Poetry and founding the journal *Temenos* (later The Temenos Academy) as an intellectual and spiritual home for 'the Arts of the Imagination'. In 1983, at the age of seventy-four, she travelled with her botanist granddaughter and her friend Thetis Blacker on the first of two journeys to India, where Kathleen was welcomed by the country's creative community as one of poetry's most brilliant and visionary minds.

Gavin was the love of her life. And 'for better and for worse', Kathleen wrote, she was 'the woman in his life'.

> *Suddenly the trees looked strangely beautiful:*
> *'It has taken the form of trees,' I said,*
> *'And I of a woman standing by a burn.'*
> *So near I stood to your new state*
> *I saw for a moment as you might*
> *These sheltering boughs of spirit in its flight.*
> *Shall you and I, in all the journeyings of soul,*
> *Remember the rowan tree, the waterfall?*

On a Deserted Shore, 1973

433

Author's Note

To learn more about Dr Kathleen Raine's life, a fascinating and unforgettable – if sometimes shattering – starting point is her series of autobiographies. From earliest childhood to becoming a great-grandmother, these four volumes chart her evolution as a woman and as a poet with raw, radical honesty. Kathleen explores the extraordinary range of ideas that she encountered throughout her ninety-five years with characteristic intellectual rigour, as well as scrutinizing the consequences of her own life choices with uncompromising, even merciless clarity. For readers of *Remember the Rowan*, I would especially recommend her third autobiography *The Lion's Mouth*: a candid, heartfelt reflection on her relationship with Gavin Maxwell that served as the inspiration and emotional 'Compass Hill' of this novel. I also have a soft spot for her fourth and final volume, *India Seen Afar*, dedicated to her cherished friend Tambi. Halfway across the world, it appears that Kathleen discovered the end of what she had experienced with and through Gavin was in fact only a beginning …

Her oeuvre as a writer and scholar crossed continents and centuries, and those interested in the academic achievements referenced in *Remember the Rowan* will uncover a treasure trove of thought-provoking publications. They include *Blake and Tradition* and its abridged version *Blake and Antiquity*, the text of Kathleen's prestigious A.W. Mellon lectures, which is quoted from in this novel in combination with her *William Blake* (the shaky start I give her first, eventually triumphant lecture can be attributed to dramatic licence). Her wider work on her fellow great poets – although Kathleen would have been too modest to count herself amongst their number – ranged from Blake to Coleridge and Wordsworth, from Yeats and Vernon Watkins to her dear friend Edwin Muir and beyond. Excellent foundations here are *Defending Ancient Springs* from 1967 and *That Wondrous Pattern*, Kathleen's 'Essays on Poetry and Poets', which was published posthumously in 2017 (edited by her literary executor and one of her *Temenos* / Temenos Academy co-founders Brian Keeble).

The timeless magic of Kathleen's writing – the "Wisdom of Words", to use the title of a poem from her 1987 collection *The Presence* – even extended to two enchanting children's books: *The Story of Three Water Drops*, 1946 (described briefly in *Remember the Rowan*) and *The World of Living Green*, 1947. Sadly for today's youngsters, neither book is still in print, but I shared video presentations on them at the Homage to Kathleen Raine International Conference, which took place in March 2022 at the Sorbonne in Paris. The films with accompanying texts can now be accessed via my website.

All of Kathleen's poetry collections referred to in *Remember the Rowan* are real, and those featuring work composed during her twenty years with Gavin include *The Year One* from 1952 (the definite article remains absent from *Ring of Bright Water*'s acknowledgements to this day), *The Hollow Hill* from 1965, *The Lost Country* from 1971 and, perhaps most poignantly, *On a Deserted Shore* from 1973. Kathleen published this profoundly moving epic sequence of love and loss after Gavin's death and it is quoted from at the very end of *Remember the Rowan*, in addition to giving the novel its title. 'To my sorrow,' Kathleen later confessed with typical humility, it 'is the only poem I've written which I'm absolutely sure has a life of its own, which will endure'. While I must agree to disagree with our heroine, what is sure is that to read anything from her extraordinary body of work is to be richly rewarded: offering a unique opportunity to deepen one's understanding of the world and our place within it. The more she gives to us, the more we have. Both are infinite.

For secondary reading, Philippa Bernard's posthumous biography of Kathleen, *No End to Snowdrops*, is an indispensable source of well-researched information. I am also eagerly awaiting the publication of Dr Jenny Messenger's *Kathleen Raine: Classics and Consciousness* from Bloomsbury's 'Classical Receptions in Twentieth-Century Writing' series and Dr Claire Tardieu's *Kathleen Raine: A Voice for the Twenty-First Century*, arising from the Sorbonne Conference. In addition, I can offer my own, much humbler non-fiction contributions to writing about Kathleen's life. *"But why this here and now only when I loved I knew": Remembering Kathleen Raine* was published by the Women's History Network on 14th June 2022. It would have been Kathleen's 114th birthday. To mark her 115th, I chaired an online 'Happy Birthday Kathleen Raine' event hosted by the Scottish Poetry Library, and later in 2023 I published

'As woman is, so she sees: winding the golden string of Dr Kathleen Raine's William Blake scholarship' with Bluestocking Oxford.

From Gavin Maxwell's literary career, all the books cited in *Remember the Rowan* exist, including *Harpoon at a Venture, Raven Seek Thy Brother* and, of course, the iconic *Ring of Bright Water*. For determined readers who enjoy doing research of their own, I also suggest seeking out *The House of Elrig*, Gavin's childhood memoir. Now out of print, it is perhaps his most underrated work, with its vivid tales and eccentric cast of family characters having helped to infuse *Remember the Rowan* with what I hope is a quintessentially 'Gavinish' colour and charm. Douglas Botting's authorized *Gavin Maxwell: A Life* also provides a substantive, thoughtful study of this complex and contradictory character, albeit at times parting company from Kathleen's own recollections (to which, in cases of conflict, *Remember the Rowan* has always stayed faithful). At least Botting does Kathleen the courtesy of giving her a name, unlike several other works published on or produced about Gavin. Most shamefully, a 1979 BBC film of his life, *Ring of Bright Water and Beyond,* identified Kathleen and credited the actress who played her only as 'the rowan tree woman'.

Within such a context, it may seem intriguing that, as an intellectual and spiritual pioneer who railed against convention, Kathleen felt herself to be 'no feminist'. To her, perhaps no political creed could be compatible with the rejection of materialism that lay at the foundations of her work, and she also observed perceptively in *India Seen Afar* that the goal of simply achieving parity as 'honorary men' risks devaluing the feminine, the intuitive and by implication Imagination itself. Yet from a twenty-first century vantage point, I believe we can identify earthly conditions that exacerbated Kathleen's suffering and to which, ironically, her great vision may have blinded her. From girlhood, her social and economic survival (just like that of her peers) was conditional on male approval, whether in the form of a father, a husband or both. As a mother, her admittedly imperfect choices concerning her children have been judged harshly by history, condemned for decisions often identical to those made by their father without any such comment or criticism. Kathleen was silenced in and stripped from the *Ring of Bright Water* story by men with their own tales to tell and prosper from. Her loyalty to Gavin has been mocked as mere delusion, despite obvious evidence of her intellectual brilliance; he was and still is lauded for an emotional sensitivity that he shared with Kathleen, yet hers has been reduced to volatility and even hysteria. As late as 1968, she was shamed as a witch, that smokescreen accusation all too often deployed in Scotland and beyond as a weapon against women who have resisted every other effort to suppress their innate power.

In writing *Remember the Rowan*, I hope to play my part in restoring Kathleen Raine to her rightful place as one of the greatest poets of the twentieth century, encouraging new minds and hearts alike to keep faith with what she witnessed. Above all, I hope this book shines a light on the woman whose poetry and passion have been hidden for too long behind *Ring of Bright Water*.

Kirsten MacQuarrie, April 2024

Acknowledgements

My heartfelt thanks go to the whole team at Ringwood Publishing, whose indefatigable determination to produce writing not just of value but of worth does Tambi proud. I am especially grateful to Sandy Jamieson, Isobel Freeman and their fellow Directors, to my assistant editors Júlia Pujals Antolin and Ella Wolfle, and to my publicity lead Felicity Deacon for their energy, enthusiasm and insights. I also want to express particular appreciation for my multi-talented lead editor Matilda Eker, a blossoming new publishing professional who understood from the start not just what *Remember the Rowan* aims to achieve but why. Thanks to you, I could trust that my work was always in safe hands, and I am honoured that in readers' hands it is now framed by your own (art)work. As this beautiful cover design reflects, the sky really is the limit!

Thank you to Faber & Faber for granting me permission to enrich the novel with Kathleen's poetry, and to the Gavin Maxwell Estate for allowing me to include the text of his real-life, life-changing letter to Kathleen at the end of chapter 39.

Thank you to the people of Ullswater, especially Hilary Rock, Jane Brimmer and beautiful Beattie. I will forever appreciate your generosity of time and spirit on my first of many visits, walking in Kathleen's footsteps from 'a rock, high on Place Fell' in Martindale to the very spot where *The Marriage of Psyche* was completed. Thank you also to the truly Great Bavingtonians of today who welcomed me warmly to wee Kathie's 'happy fields', particularly Muriel Ramsden and not forgetting gorgeous donkey Dorabella. Closer to home, thank you to Heather Ryce for introducing me to otters Orla and Harry!

This novel has more broadly been one of physical and spiritual journeys, and as such I wish to express my sincere thanks to a range of archival sources including the Temenos Academy, Girton College, Dumbarton Oaks, the Charles Deering McCormick Library, the Gavin Maxwell Museum, the British Library and the National Library of Scotland. I am particularly grateful to Scotland's National Librarian

Amina Shah – a true Winspiration – and to Dr Colin McIlroy for patiently enduring the enquiries of 'the otter girl'. With apologies to my fellow reading room researchers, I have shed tears, laughed out loud and felt my characters closer than ever thanks to all our libraries offer. To preserve these essential resources and keep them free for every citizen to access is, as Kathleen might say, a great battle forever worth fighting.

Speaking of libraries, as I so often do, I want to thank my fantastic feminist friends at Glasgow Women's Library including Wendy, Naomi, Gabrielle, Sue and Adele. Courageous champions of our sisters past, present and future, I cannot wait for Kathleen to be honoured as one of your Women on the Wall. Like her, you turned to life and to hope after the long haul … I would also like to thank the incredible CILIP Scotland community, especially Sean McNamara and Leah Higgins: amazing advocates who gamely accepted the presence of two invisible yet high-maintenance colleagues.

Mille mercis to Professor Clare Willsdon and Elizabeth Moles. Thanks also to Jenny Messenger, Rebecca Rowe and Caroline Watson, my fellow modern-day Rainedrops! To Elaine Wallace and Jennie Grady, and now the babe who inherits the world we have loved, thank you both for welcoming a fledgling writer into the Soutar Festival family and introducing me to the most enchanting fairy godmother I could wish for. Sara, I promise to pay forward the good fortune I've found thanks to you coming into my life – should you ever need me to shimmy up a ladder after midnight to snag a rare plant, I'm your girl.

To all at Kathleen's cherished Temenos Academy and especially Professor Grevel Lindop, whose wise, calm counsel has been a source of support throughout *Remember the Rowan*'s journey to publication. Miracle is more reliable than calculation, indeed, and thank you for continuing to keep that particularly precious flame alight.

To Grandma, my own Jessie and Scotswoman of Imagination, who was the very first reader of *Remember the Rowan*. To Mum, who taught me to see that the moor is alive. Never was anything in this world loved too much, I understand thanks to you, and that includes our animal angels.

To Gavin Maxwell who, for better and for worse, became the man in my life. Scotland shall not know your like again. A century on, the compelling charm of your bright lights and dark shadows is undiminished. Like so many before me, both human and lutrine, I have struggled to resist.

Above all, this book is dedicated to one woman, one poet, one soul and one spirit, Kathleen Raine. Hearing you as my daimon has been the privilege of my life. I pray that the wisdom of your words will be an eternal part of my here and now. May this chord tremble into the harmony of the spheres. May the world that you inhabit one day be created.

Timeline of Poetry and Prose

Part One – August 1949

- *The Pythoness*, Kathleen Raine, 1949
- *William Blake*, Kathleen Raine, 1951
- *The Year One*, Kathleen Raine, 1952
- *Harpoon at a Venture*, Gavin Maxwell, 1952

Part Two – July 1956

- *The Collected Poems of Kathleen Raine*, 1956
- *Ring of Bright Water*, Gavin Maxwell, 1960

Part Three – April 1962

- *The Rocks Remain*, Gavin Maxwell, 1963
- *The Hollow Hill*, Kathleen Raine, 1965
- *Defending Ancient Springs*, Kathleen Raine, 1967
- *Blake and Tradition*, Kathleen Raine, 1968
- *Raven Seek Thy Brother*, Gavin Maxwell, 1968

Epilogue – September 1969

- *On a Deserted Shore*, Kathleen Raine, 1973

Further Reading

By Kathleen Raine

Autobiography

- *A Question of Poetry* (Richard Gilbertson, written 1946; published 1969)
- *Faces of Day and Night* (Enitharmon Press, written 1946; published 1972)
- *Farewell Happy Fields* (Hamish Hamilton Ltd, 1973)
- *The Land Unknown* (Hamish Hamilton Ltd, 1975)
- *The Lion's Mouth* (Hamish Hamilton Ltd, 1977)
- *India Seen Afar* (Green Books, 1990)
- *Visiting Ezra Pound* (limited to 90 copies; Enitharmon Press, 1999)

Selected Poetry

- *Stone and Flower* (Editions Poetry London/Nicholson and Watson, 1943)
- *Living in Time* (Editions Poetry London/Nicholson and Watson, 1946)
- *The Pythoness* (Hamish Hamilton, 1949)
- *The Year One* (Hamish Hamilton, 1952)
- *The Collected Poems of Kathleen Raine* (Hamish Hamilton, 1956)
- *The Hollow Hill* (Hamish Hamilton, 1965)
- *The Written Word* (Enitharmon Press, 1967)
- *Six Dreams and Other Poems* (Enitharmon Press, 1968)
- *The Lost Country* (Hamish Hamilton, 1971)
- *On a Deserted Shore* (Dolmen Press, Hamish Hamilton, 1973)
- *The Oval Portrait* (Enitharmon Press, Hamish Hamilton, 1977)
- *Fifteen Short Poems* (Enitharmon Press, 1978)
- *The Oracle in the Heart* (Dolmen Press, Allen & Unwin, 1980)
- *The Presence* (Golgonooza Press, 1987)
- *Living with Mystery* (Golgonooza Press, 1992)
- *Collected Poems* (Golgonooza Press, 2000)

For Children

- *The Story of Three Water Drops* (Nicholson and Watson, 1946)
- *The World of Living Green* (published as Kathleen Madge; Lutterworth Press, 1947)

Selected Scholarship and Other Non-Fiction

- *William Blake* (The British Council, 1951)
- *Coleridge* (The British Council, 1953)
- *Defending Ancient Springs* (Oxford University Press, 1967)
- *Blake and Tradition* (Princeton University Press, 1968)
- *William Blake* (Thames & Hudson Ltd, 1970)
- *Yeats, the Tarot and the Golden Dawn* (Dolmen Press, 1972)
- *David Jones: Solitary Perfectionist* (Golgonooza Press, 1974)
- *Blake and Antiquity* (Routledge & Kegan Paul, 1979)
- *'What is Man?'* (Golgonooza Press, 1980)
- *That Wondrous Pattern: Essays on Poetry and Poets* (Counterpoint, 2017)
- 'Introduction' in Thetis Blacker, *A Pilgrimage of Dreams* (Turnstone Books Ltd, 1973)

Secondary Reading

- Anna Madge Hopewell, *Communications* (Enitharmon Press, 1967)
- Jane Williams (editor), *Tambimuttu: Bridge Between Two Worlds* (Peter Owen Publishers, 1989), with Kathleen Raine as consultant editor
- Val Corbett, *A Rhythm, a Rite and a Ceremony: Helen Sutherland at Cockley Moor, 1939 – 1965* (exhibition catalogue, 1996)
- *Lighting a Candle: Kathleen Raine and Temenos* (The Temenos Academy, 2008)
- Philippa Bernard, *No End to Snowdrops: A Biography of Kathleen Raine* (Shepheard-Walwyn Publishers Ltd, 2009)
- Brian Keeble, *These Bright Shadows: The Poetry of Kathleen Raine* (Angelico Press, 2020)
- Dr Jenny Messenger, *Kathleen Raine: Classics and Consciousness* (forthcoming)
- Dr Claire Tardieu (co-editor), *Kathleen Raine: A Voice for the Twenty-First Century* (forthcoming)

By and about Gavin Maxwell

- *Harpoon at a Venture* (Rupert Hart-Davis, 1952)
- *God Protect me from my Friends* (Longmans Green & Co. Ltd, 1956)
- *A Reed Shaken by the Wind* (Longmans Green & Co. Ltd, 1957)
- *The Ten Pains of Death* (Longman Ltd, 1959)
- *Ring of Bright Water* (Longmans Green & Co. Ltd, 1960)
- *The Otters' Tale* (abridged version of *Ring* for child readers; Longmans Green & Co. Ltd, 1962)
- *The Rocks Remain* (Longmans Green & Co. Ltd, 1963)
- *The House of Elrig* (Longmans Green & Co. Ltd, 1965)
- *Lords of the Atlas* (Longmans Green & Co. Ltd, 1966)
- *Seals of the World* (Constable & Company Ltd, 1967)
- *Raven Seek Thy Brother* (Longmans Green & Co. Ltd, 1968)
- John Lister-Kaye, *The White Island* (Longmans, 1972)
- Douglas Botting, *Gavin Maxwell: A Life* (HarperCollins Publishers, 1993)
- Richard Frere, *Maxwell's Ghost* (Birlinn Limited, 1999)

Founded by Dr Kathleen Raine and her fellow *Temenos* editors in 1991, under the patronage of His Majesty King Charles III, the Temenos Academy is a charity which offers education in philosophy and the arts in the light of the sacred traditions of East and West. In addition to its educational programme, the Temenos Academy funds the Thetis Blacker Temenos Batik Scholarship, a biennial award for artists in batik.

To learn more about the Temenos Academy and support its work, please visit www.temenosacademy.org.

More to read:

If you enjoyed *Remember the Rowan*, you will most certainly like these other Ringwood books:

Song of the Stag
R. M. Brown

Cait and her childhood sweetheart, Kenzie, are from Storran's borders: idyllic, traditional, and completely opposed to separatism.

When Kenzie is called up to the ranks of the Queen's Watch to hunt down Storrian Separatists, they move together to the city of Thorterknock, where Cait quickly realises that her charming countryside life is not the reality for every citizen of Storran. Struggle abounds on the cobbled streets, as does the battle for Storran's liberation from the Five Realms.

Drawn to the enigmatic Separatist firebrand, the Fox of Thorterknock, and her tales of a secret heir to Storran's long-empty throne, Cait finds herself swept into a struggle for freedom, with Kenzie and the Queen's Watch on one side, and the Fox and the Separatists on the other.

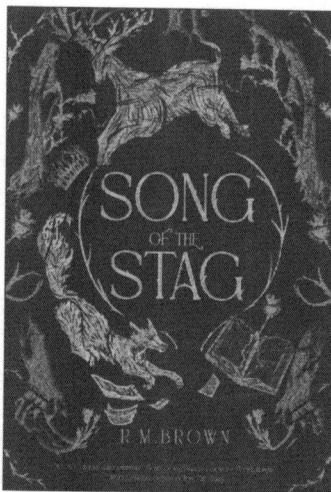

ISBN: 978-1-917011-02-0

£12.99

Kitten Heels
Maureen Cullen

"It was a man's world, that was for sure. It certainly wasnae a thirteen-year-old girl's."Kathleen Haggerty is resourceful, brave and tireless — but fated to work in the bra factory like her mother. It's 1962, and Kathleen resents her situation. She has to look after her three younger siblings whilst her mother works part-time, collect the wages from her absentee father, and sacrifice her social life for responsibilities she never asked for. When Kathleen's grandmother dies, the entire family dynamic changes - leaving the relationship with her mother to suffer.

Written by Maureen Cullen, a retired social worker and the winner of the 2022 Ringwood short story competition, *Kitten Heels* is a humorous, character-driven novel, dealing with issues of poverty, mental health, and the role of women in 1960's working class Clydeside.

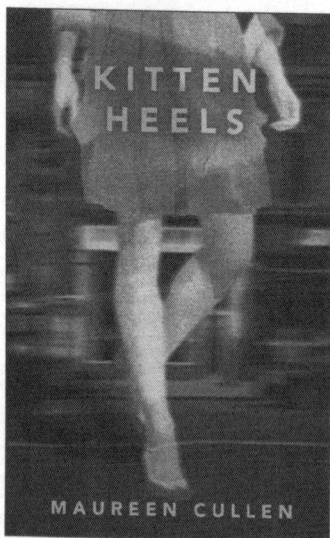

ISBN: 978-1-917011-01-3

£9.99

What You Call Free
Flora Johnston

A historical tale of two courageous women who challenge our grasp of what it really means to be free.

Scotland, 1687. An unforgiving place for women who won't conform. Pregnant and betrayed, eighteen-year-old Jonet believes nothing could be worse than her weekly public humiliation in sackcloth. But soon she discovers that a far darker fate awaits her. Desperate to escape, she takes refuge among an outlawed group of religious dissidents. Here, Widow Helen offers friendship and understanding, but Helen's own beliefs have already seen her imprisoned once. Can she escape the authorities a second time?

This extraordinary tale of love and loss, struggle and sacrifice, autonomy and entrapment, urges us to consider what it means to be free and who can be free – if freedom exists at all.

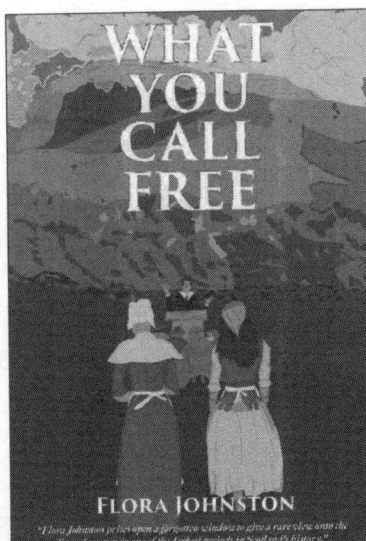

ISBN: 978-1-901514-96-4
£9.99

Bodysnatcher
Carol Margaret Davison

In the late 1820s, two Irish Immigrants, William Burke and William Hare, murdered 16 individuals and sold their corpses for use in anatomical dissections at the University of Edinburgh. Their killings ended when Hare turned King's Evidence, and Burke was hanged.

However, the question of whether their female accomplices, Nelly McDougal and Margaret Hare, were involved, has never been determined. Told by way of alternating confessions, Bodysnatcher is both a graphic depiction of one of Edinburgh's most notorious crimes, and a domestic story of a relationship unravelled by secrecy and violence. The novel dives deep into the twisted psychology of William Burke, giving the reader an inside look at a mind descending into madness.

A blend of true crime and gothic horror, Bodysnatcher is a powerful portrayal of desperation, poverty, and the disempowerment of women and may leave the reader in doubt as to whether all the criminals were actually caught.

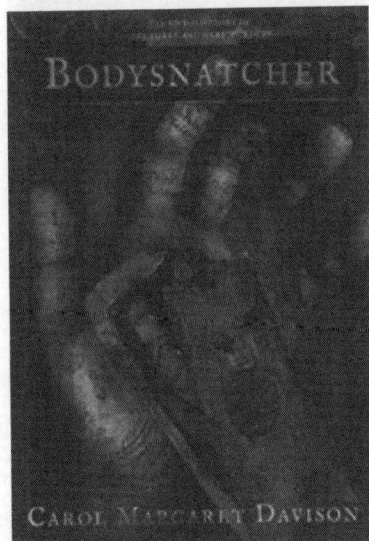

ISBN: 978-1-901514-83-4
£12.99

The Carnelian Tree
Anne Pettigrew

A dead body, a disappearance, and an epic lost in time. Unrelated incidents on the surface. Judith Fraser's Oxford sabbatical quickly takes a sharp turn when she gets tangled in the mysterious murder of a colleague. With threads leading nowhere, conflicting impressions about people around her, and concern for increasing risk to her loved ones, whom can she trust? Her eccentric housemates? The CIA? Or, herself?

A uniquely amusing and page-turning mystery novel set in 2003 on the eve of the Iraqi War, The Carnelian Tree follows the journey of Judith Fraser as she probes into people, power, politics, and sex, only to discover that some things remain unchanged.

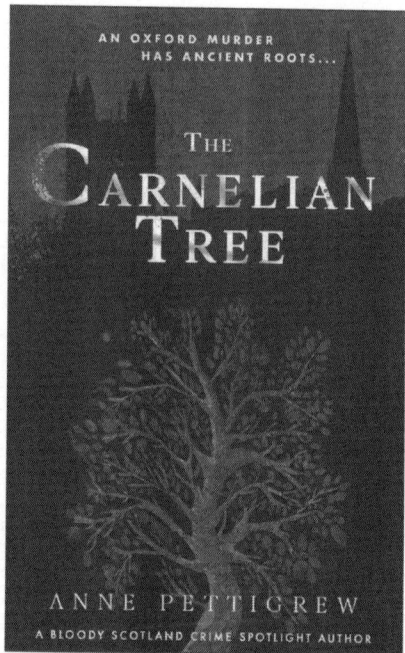

ISBN: 978-1-901514-81-0

£9.99

Inference
Stephanie McDonald

Natalie Byron had a happy life in Glasgow. She had a steady job, supportive friends and a loving family. Or at least, she thought she did. The morning after a date, Natalie wakes up inside a strange house, in a strange bed, sleeping next to a man named Jamie who claims he is her boyfriend. Outside the window are rugged cliffs surrounded by an endless sea. Fearing she's been kidnapped, Natalie flees, but when everyone around her insists that her life back in Glasgow is nothing but a delusion, Natalie begins to doubt her own sanity. There is one thing Natalie is sure of. She needs to get off this island.

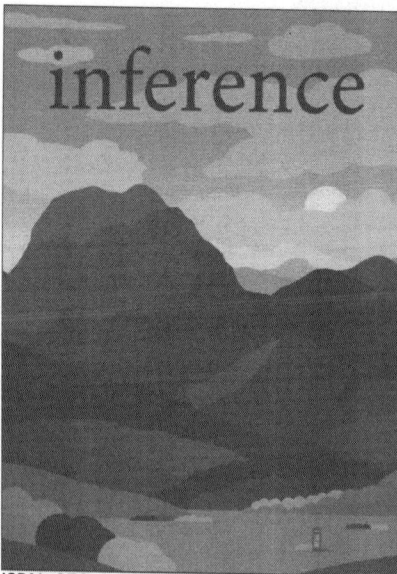

ISBN: 978-1-901514-68-1

£9.99

Raise Dragon
L.A. Kristiansen

In the year of 1306, Scotland is in turmoil. Robert the Bruce and the fighting Bishop Wishart's plans for rebellion put the Scottish kingdom at risk, whilst the hostile kingdom of England seems more invincible than ever. But Bishop Wishart has got a final card left to play: four brave Scottish knights set off in search of a mysterious ancient treasure that will bring Scotland to the centre of an international plot, changing the course of history forever.

ISBN: 978-1-901514-76-6
£9.99

Revenge of the Tyrants
L.A. Kristiansen

The fight for the nation's soul has begun, and nothing will ever be the same. While the King of Scots wages a desperate, bloody war for Scotland's independence, four intrepid Scottish knights embark on a treasure barge. What follows is a journey directly to the heart of the conflict, and a vivid depiction of the scheming, treachery and violence it entailed. Meanwhile, Kings Edward the first of England, Philip the fourth of France, and Haakon the fifth of Norway have their own reasons to thwart the Scots, and each will stop at nothing to gain their victory.

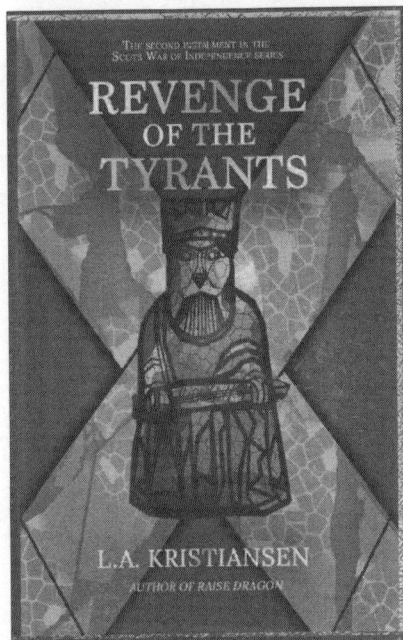

ISBN:978-1-901514-89-6

£12.99